Praise for *Guardian of the Freedom*:

"Radford's 'Merlin's Descendants' saga, of which this is the fifth volume, is an impressive example of the new sub-genre in which the Matter of Britain is projected forward in time. This volume, set early in the reign of George III, finds him not taking the advice of the current Pendragon, Drake Kirkwood. Kirkwood has the excuse of ill health for not being more forcible, but the situation allows for the increasing influence of Dr. Milton Marlowe, a member of the Pendragon Society with fewer than the requisite scruples. Drake is also handicapped by his sister Georgina's soldiering abroad, coming home to recover from wounds, and then being sent on a secret mission to the restive American colonies. There the deadly question is squarely thrown up to her: Is the Americans' quest for freedom likely to destroy the Pendragon line and unleash chaos on the world? Or does it represent the next stage in the cause for which Merlin's descendants have fought for centuries? Saga stalwarts will keep reading until they find out." —*Booklist*

"As with the previous volumes, Radford colorfully evokes an historical period and superimposes a magical overlay with a complicated story of interpersonal conflicts. Another fine novel from one of our better fantasy writers." —*Chronicle*

"The latest entry in Radford's historical fantasy epic following Merlin's heirs through the ages presents a resilient heroine and an intriguing period in both English and American history. Readers who like their historical fantasy with a tinge of feminist philosophy should enjoy this well-told adventure." —*Library Journal*

"Radford's impressive historical fantasy series has taken readers from Aurthur's court to the Boston Tea Party with ease. Now, merging impeccable period detail and true-life heroes and villains with magical influences, this dark fantasy spins a web that will entangle series fans and new-comers alike." —*Romantic Times*

Also by
Irene Radford

Merlin's Descendants
GUARDIAN OF THE BALANCE
GUARDIAN OF THE TRUST
GUARDIAN OF THE VISION
GUARDIAN OF THE PROMISE
GUARDIAN OF THE FREEDOM

The Dragon Nimbus
THE GLASS DRAGON
THE PERFECT PRINCESS
THE LONELIEST MAGICIAN
THE WIZARD'S TREASURE

The Dragon's Nimbus History
THE DRAGON'S TOUCHSTONE
THE LAST BATTLEMAGE
THE RENEGADE DRAGON

The Star Gods
THE HIDDEN DRAGON
THE DRAGON CIRCLE
THE DRAGON'S REVENGE

IRENE RADFORD

GUARDIAN OF THE FREEDOM

Merlin's Descendants:
Volume Five

DAW BOOKS, INC.
DONALD A. WOLLHEIM, FOUNDER
375 Hudson Street, New York, NY 10014

ELIZABETH R. WOLLHEIM
SHEILA E. GILBERT
PUBLISHERS
http://www.dawbooks.com

First paperback printing, April 2005
1 2 3 4 5 6 7 8 9 10

DAW TRADEMARK REGISTERED
U.S. PAT. OFF. AND FOREIGN COUNTRIES
—MARCA REGISTRADA
HECHO EN U.S.A.

PRINTED IN THE U.S.A.

Author Notes:

Most of us learned the important names of the American Revolution in grade school. George Washington, Thomas Jefferson, John Adams, Benjamin Franklin, and others. Granted, these men led the revolt that changed modern concepts of government completely and irrevocably. For there to be a revolt, there had to be many thousands of average people like you and me behind those leaders. In this book I tried to put the focus on the people whose names were barely recorded in history or not recorded at all. I tried to show the ripple effect of one small change on politics and economics.

The idea of a Masonic conspiracy to "throw" the American Revolution in favor of the American colonists has been documented in many sources; some of them are speculative, others more reliable. Of that other Lodge, the secret one with global perspectives and reach . . . Conspiracy theorists abound who claim that such an organization is responsible for much more than can be documented. I like to think that some league of well-educated and honorable people work behind the scenes to maintain a balance in this world. Several of my research books suggested that Great Britain never followed through with advantages, or completely overlooked opportunities to win the war. Why this happened is open to debate.

One of the purposes of science fiction and fantasy is to trigger new ideas in the readers. I invite you to explore further in any history book, whether scholarly or speculative and form your own opinions. I hope by the time this book is released to have a bibliography on my Web site for each novel in the *Merlin's Descendants* series to show you the sources that helped me form my opinions.

Books are only as good a resource as the people who read them. I am indebted to a number of people who loaned me books and those who actually did research for me and then synthesized the information into doses I could tolerate and understand. Lea Day has been very generous with her extensive library, her time, and her military expertise. Buzz Nelson as well is a wealth of knowledge on military history and weaponry. Coach Don Peterson has aided me in learning to fence and to stage sword battles. Mike Moscoe, Beth Gilligan, Deborah Dixon, big brother Jim Radford, and Bob Brown have all given me critiques, brainstorming, and support in creating this work of fiction. I thank them all.

As I write this, we are gearing up for a major and important election. Please remember some of the rights that my characters and our ancestors fought and died for. Please remember that our government was created by the people and for the people and that only we can affect change. Every vote counts. Every voice counts. Without our participation we open ourselves, our freedoms, and our place in history to the agents of chaos. You never know when Tryblith, the Demon of Chaos, will strike again.

Irene Radford
Welches, Oregon
October, 2004
www.ireneradford.com

GUARDIAN OF THE FREEDOM

Prologue

The Danube River Valley, Northwest of Belgrade, late October, 1763.

"YOU can't do it," Captain Roderick Whythe scoffed.

"Will you lay money on that?" I asked. I wanted more from him than just money. Hard to tell if he would be more horrified that I, a mercenary soldier, lusted after him, or that I, a mercenary soldier, was truly a woman.

Behind me, twenty mercenaries roared with laughter.

"Time limit!" one of them yelled over the top of the noise.

"A full minute by my timepiece," another answered, drawing out his gold pocket piece, loot from some battle.

"Will you stake me with that gold bauble?" I asked my comrade.

He pulled the timepiece close to his chest and shook his head.

Whythe eyed me with skepticism. Almost reluctantly, he drew his wallet out of his scarlet uniform coat. He laid a single golden guinea on the table between us.

I reached to possess the coin.

His hand landed atop mine. "When you have won the bet." His deep brown eyes twinkled with surety that I could not perform the feat he commanded.

"Very well," I sighed as I stood and unsheathed my saber. My breast band was too tight and itched. I dared not adjust it in this company.

Three men stood up and exited toward the privy. I cursed inwardly. My bladder was as full of ale as theirs. But

I couldn't seek privacy while others were out there pissing against the wall.

I shrugged my shoulders and eased some of the tension in my back. Once more I had to prove to an Englishman that rules, even the rules of nature, meant little to me.

I would defy gravity as I defied life and death on a daily basis.

Whythe's eyes grew wide at sight of my finely balanced Polish saber, a straight blade with a sweet spot well down the forte for more strength in the steel and better balance in my hand. Or on my fingertip.

I took three deep breaths, centering myself. Then I placed the tip of the saber on the index finger of my right hand. The weapon stood straight in the air, balanced as if stuck in stone.

"Geor-gie! Geor-gie! Geor-gie!" my mercenary companions chanted while pounding the crude tables in the smoky tavern.

I breathed in time to their chant, using the rhythm to maintain my center. The tip of my saber had yet to draw my blood. The blade fought me, wanting to return to Mother Earth. I tricked it, shifting and sidling to keep it in place.

"Geor-gie! Geor-gie! Geor-gie!"

"Where'd you learn to do that, Major George Kirkwood?" the Englishman, Captain Roderick Whythe, asked. He, alone of the troops, wore a clean uniform. A red coat over white breeches, waistcoat, and shirt. Shining black boots and powdered hair. At least he did not drip lace like so many of his foppish comrades.

My company showed the wear and tear of a mercenary camp on the border of the Austro-Hungarian Empire, in this troubled year of 1763. Mud splotched our green coats and brown breeches. None of us powdered our hair or bothered to maintain a wig. Shining boots was a task for batmen, but we had few enough of those left and employed them better. Otherwise we occupied snowy winter nights, when even the Turks would not mount a raid, with the mundane chores of mending and polishing.

The Englishman was an outsider in more than dress. He had come to recruit light cavalry for some political favor between the English king and a German princeling. I'd been in Saxony a month ago acting as courier to my colonel's banker, and just returned to the front. I needed to stay away from the Germanies for a while. Just as I needed to stay away from England.

A summons to return home to Kirkenwood in the north of England weighed heavily in my pocket. I could replenish myself at Kirkenwood. My family could imprison me there as well.

I needed to win this bet to remind Whythe that he was not one of us; had not lived cheek by jowl with us, fought side by side with us, buried friends with us.

I also needed that guinea. Travel to and escape from Dresden had proved expensive. Travel home would cost me more than the guineas I did not have.

"I learned balance and concentration from my sword master, Captain Whythe," I replied to his question. The saber wiggled a fraction, I corrected with a slight shift of my hand and arm.

"I heard that Giovanni Giacomo Casanova only passed on his art to his mistresses," one of the Portuguese shouted above the noise of the rest of our company.

"Would you care to accuse me to my face of being Casanova's 'mistress'?" I asked. I snaked out my dagger with my left hand and held it level with the scrawny Portuguese's nose.

He gulped but kept his countenance even.

A loud guffaw from the younger son of a Venetian doge masked any reply the Portuguese cared to make to my riposte. A round of laughter and backslapping followed.

The Earth thrummed through the soft soles of my boots. The vibrations set the hair on my arms and my nape atingle and hummed in my teeth disharmoniously

"Turks!" I called. I went cold. Everything I had worked for these last three years depended upon keeping the Turks away from Vienna. As long as they kept Belgrade as their frontier, I had no problem with them. The moment they crept into Austrian territory, they threatened all of Europe. All of England.

With a flick of my finger the saber spun upward. I caught the grip and sheathed the weapon before the men had a chance to react.

My comrades scrambled to their feet.

I snatched the guinea coin out from under Whythe's

nose and pelted out of the crude tavern ahead of them into noon sunshine. No time to relish the warmth on my back or blink away dazzle blindness. No time to think.

"Colonel, sir." I burst into Heinrich der Reusse's cabin with only the most cursory of knocks. The sight of Mathilde, the village barmaid and whore, naked and kneeling between my colonel's equally naked knees with her face buried in his crotch brought me to a skidding halt. I turned my back on the intimate scene, jealous of the whore.

"Sir, the Turks are coming," I blurted out my message before the man could curse me, or the woman could finish with her ministrations.

"How many? Where from? When? By land, or up the river?" the colonel barked. The rustle of righted clothing and untangled limbs came after his questions.

"Five hundred cavalry, sir." I sneaked a peek beneath my arm, admiring the colonel's lusty proportions.

"Get yourself atop that hill, Major. I do not know how you do what you do, but you have never failed me yet. I need to know every detail of their raid to the fourth intention before they even think it."

"Yes, sir!" I turned on my heel to face him and snap a salute.

The barmaid postured to emphasize her ample bosom. I spared her only the slightest glace. My gaze lingered a little too long and a little too low on the colonel.

"Out, brat," he admonished me on a laugh.

I fled, blushing to my ears. Prince Heinrich from the Sovereign States of Reusse knew more of my history than any man. Only from him would I tolerate the semiaffectionate abuse.

Estovan, my batman, and as female (if not feminine) as I beneath her uniform, met me atop the knoll southeast of camp with my horse fully saddled and ready to ride. The big dun stallion pawed the ground and snorted, eager for battle. I paused long enough to check pistol and musket, though I knew Estovan would have primed and loaded them. I also checked the extra powder and shot in my kit.

Then I double-checked my French dagger-pistol, a custom-made blade with a tiny gun hidden in the hilt. This little treasure had come to me from my sword master, Casanova. It shot truer than most firearms and doubled as a blade. It rested comfortably in its scabbard, as much a part of me as my saber and rapier.

Then I donned my light armor: cuirass belted across my chest, gorget slung around my neck, greaves along my shins, gauntlets on my forearms, and a helmet.

With no more reason to delay, I took a deep breath and faced the approach the Turks must take. With feet planted firmly upon Mother Earth, I took a deep breath. On the exhale, I emptied myself of worry, of stray thoughts, of everything but the vibrations in my feet. My hands came up, palms out, fingers slightly curled, letting the wind off the Danube whisper information to my exposed skin.

Colonel der Reusse hovered behind my left shoulder, waiting for me to learn what I could. I breathed in the scent of his skin, still perfumed with male musk, his warmth, and his reassuring authority.

"One hundred *toprakli*—the irregulars—with muskets held in reserve on our left flank. Two hundred fifty *miri-askerus*—short-term levies—with pistols and scimitars for the main charge down the center. One hundred *kapikulu*—the salaried regulars—on our right flank, between us and the Danube, to come in a second wave behind the primary charge. They will come around that hill, hidden from our view until they are directly upon us. Those are the ones we need fear most. They will not surrender and they take no prisoners."

"We only have two hundred men left!" Heinrich followed up with several colorful curses. Our trip to Saxony had been cut short before we could recruit new men.

"Sir, the cavalry is a ruse. To keep us from watching the river. Another five hundred on barges. They aim to push through all the way to Vienna!"

"Not while I guard this sector." The colonel turned and shouted to his messengers. Post riders vaulted into their saddles and galloped away. Time to alert the Austrian regulars. They needed to get off their lazy arses and man the big guns on the bluffs above the Danube. Heinrich followed up with orders deploying his few men and resources.

"We've faced worse odds, sir," I reminded him.

"I've got a bad feeling about this one, Georgie. Tell me, can you see far enough into the future to know if I survive this day?" We all knew that if he survived, at least some of us would as well. Heinrich was a true prince. He would die defending his men.

"My gift for seeing the future is imperfect at best. I know for certain only what the Earth Mother tells me. I know troop movement and placement. What we do with that information determines our future."

"That's what I needed to know, Georgie." He squeezed my shoulder with affection. "Get to your horse. Take thirty men and keep the reserves on our right from coming to the aid of our enemies."

Thirty men to hold off one hundred.

"Yes, sir." I knew and trusted every one of my men. I considered the odds about even. The Turks fought with formidable courage and skill. We were better. We had to be. "Good luck, sir. I'll join you for a drink one hour after sunset." The stability of Europe, and therefore of England, depended upon keeping the Turks out of Austria.

"Thank you, Georgie. Oh, and take the pesky Englishman with you. Time he earned his keep."

"He's not one of us, sir," I reminded him.

"Then let him see you and your men in action. If any of us survive this battle, Whythe is welcome to take us back to some safe uprising in the Germanies, or whatever. Closer to home anyway. From the Germanies I could check in on the wife and her herd of offspring." He marched back down the hill to his own waiting horse. Orders streamed from his mouth with brisk efficiency.

"Major?" Estovan asked, always careful to observe protocol though we were, in truth, best of friends.

"I'll not see the colonel after this. One of us will die this day." A tear crept into my eye.

The clash of swords, gunfire reports, and screams of dying men off to my left made me clench my teeth and bite my lip. I dared no more reaction than that in front of my men. From the copse that hid us, I could not see how our comrades fared against the Turkish charge. I needed to be there with them, fighting to save them.

"Sir." Estovan nudged my horse, making him sidle.

Automatically, I corrected for the slight movement and brought my attention back to my task.

A slight shift in the breeze brought me the scent of our quarry. The Turks' sweat became more acrid than their horses'.

I unsheathed my saber and raised it. My men, plus the Englishman, duplicated my action. As one, we kissed our blades, murmuring private salutes and prayers. A deep breath steadied me. Then I whipped the blade down and away. I heard a satisfying snap of the air singing against the saber. All around me I heard similar cracks.

We charged out of the copse, downhill into a dell. The Turkish Aga hesitated a fraction of a heartbeat in mounting his horse.

I fired my musket, telling the ball where to go, willing it to find a target. The ball caught the commander in the throat. He dropped dead halfway into the saddle.

A volley of musket fire burst upon my ears. Ten or twelve more Turks fell.

The remainder of the enemy hesitated no longer. They vaulted into their saddles, spurring their mounts forward in a single motion. Scimitars swept out of their sashes. Eyes flashed and combatants yelled.

The curious ululation of their battle cry set the hairs on my nape to tingling.

I fired my French dagger-pistol. The ball lodged deep in the sword arm of an enemy. Then I drew my regulation firearm with the bigger and more deadly ball. The shot went wild, as they did so often.

Gunfire from my men and the Turks near deafened me. Swords clashed. Horses screamed and reared. Hooves beat the air.

Men fell.

The smell of blood burned in my nose. Dust choked me and set my eyes to watering.

I blinked away the impediment and selected my target. A big man with dark skin and a big jewel in the center of his turban, a *corbaci* or colonel, thundered toward me.

I caught the curve of his blade with my blade's forte and pressed it away from my chest. A quick *doublé* and I came upward with a classic riposte. He countered with a neat parry and attack. I evaded by ducking low, trusting my horse to obey the command of my knees and remain in place.

The corbaci continued the lunge. His blade slashed my side as I dropped level with my saddle. My saber found his throat on a backhanded riposte while he and his horse corrected their balance.

He slumped and slid to the ground.

I moved on before he hit the dirt.

Two more Turks met death from my blade.

My arm grew weak. I shifted the weapon to my left hand and felt no stronger. I wanted to press my right hand against my side. My arm wouldn't move. I looked down at the growing red stain that dripped onto my thigh.

The first Turk had sliced more than my coat.

Another was on me. He wove his scimitar with alarming speed. I was hard-pressed just to keep him at bay. My blade faltered.

My dun stallion reared, flashing his iron-shod hooves close to the enemy's face.

As the horse came down, the beast circled, taking me farther from my opponent. Our two horses nipped at each others' flanks. I hauled the dun back under control, putting another two yards between me and the Turk.

I risked a quick look around. My men acquitted themselves well. More of them remained ahorse and fighting than the Turks. An alarming number of both lay upon the ground bleeding. The Englishman was still up. His blade dripped red. He fired his pistol. Only a flash in the pan that exploded backward and did not ignite the powder in the barrel.

He threw his arm across his eyes, dazzle blinded. Whythe could not see a Turk galloping toward him. I pressed my horse between the two. The dun back-kicked in the face of the oncoming steed. That horse reared. The two beasts bit at each other.

The Englishman recovered and saluted with his blade. Then he dispatched his Turk, leaving me faced with one of my own.

Sweat poured into my eyes. I was flushed and cold at the same time. Too much blood was pouring from my side.

My opponent pressed his horse toward me, blade steady, eyes murderous.

Frantic, I slashed wildly, without pattern. I caught his shoulder with an uppercut. I pressed closer, driving home the point. Then I yanked the cutting edge sideways into his neck.

A red line appeared across his throat. His eyes opened in surprise. His mouth formed an "Oh." Then his head lolled to the left, half severed.

My saber lodged against his spine. I no longer had the strength to pull it free.

His body fell from his horse.

Numbly, I tumbled after him.

The blackness receded a little from my vision. Rough hands pressed against my neck. I fought my right hand free. It clutched my dagger-pistol. "Filthy scavengers!" I screamed in the local trade patois. Then I slashed at the hands that pressed against my wound.

"Wheest, little 'un," a man whispered in a rough Scottish brogue. The Englishman's batman. Ian. Civilian, old family retainer. I knew no other name for him. "We'll nay hurt ye."

"I guess he's alive if he can curse and fight in his condition," I heard Roderick Whythe say. A chuckle of relief seemed to well up from his belly.

"Estovan?" I asked after my own batman. My voice croaked. Weakness threatened to rob me of any volume or authority.

"We have not seen him," Captain Roderick Whythe replied.

"How many?"

"Of your thirty, ten still live."

"Turks?" I asked before I dared breathe in relief.

"Nearly all dead. Ten or fifteen may have fled."

"Heinrich . . . der Reusse?"

"That I do not know. Ian tells me that the main charge and the reserves have been repulsed. Dead and wounded still need to be assessed."

Several long moments passed. I may have lost consciousness.

"Best we get him to the surgeon, Ian," Whythe said.

Panic churned in my belly. My breathing became ragged and painful.

With an eye half open, I realized Whythe had pressed a wad of cloth torn from his shirt against my wound. Ian gently bound the cloth in place with strips from his own garments. Then he rolled me over and gently shoved one arm beneath my shoulders and the other beneath my knees. Without apparent effort, he rose to a full stand without hesitation.

"Not the surgeon," I wheezed, barely able to breathe above the pain of being moved.

Both men looked at me strangely. "You are sorely hurt, Major Kirkwood."

"The surgeon is a butcher. All he knows is lopping off limbs. Will chopping off my legs cure a punctured lung?"

"There is no other option . . . sir," Ian said gently. He looked deeply into my eyes with understanding.

"A woods witch. Half a league to the east. Away from the river. A copse surrounded by stands of wheat gone wild. Round hut. Smells terrible."

"The woods witch it is, then," Ian said and began marching away.

"I do not know . . ." Whythe protested.

"Captain, swear to me by the Widow's Son that you will not betray me to the surgeon." That one sentence took nearly all my breath.

"I swear it," Ian whispered.

I had not thought him a Freemason. Servants did not usually dare join. The hierarchy within Masonic Lodges paid no attention to nobility and social rank. A footman could become a Grand Master, holding authority over the baron who employed him. Private soldiers often rose above their officers in the secret society. The Lodge demanded secrecy upon terrible penalty. Equally terrible punishment came to the man who betrayed an oath to a brother Mason.

Whythe remained silent.

"Ye'd best take the oath, sir," Ian muttered. "Major Kirkwood will not rest easy and heal unless you do."

I almost heard him think a more dire consequence.

"Very well. By the Angle and the Compass, I swear to keep your hiding place secret."

"By the Widow's Son," I insisted.

"By the Widow's Son, I so swear," he replied reluctantly. Ian heaved a sigh and kept walking.

Safe now. I relinquished my secret to the big Scot. He'd keep it safe. He had to, he had sworn.

A secret that began back . . . when had it begun?

Chapter 1

*Kirkenwood Manor, Northern England near Hadrian's Wall,
June 21, 1753.*

I STOOD on the ramparts of the ancient castle of my clan,
spyglass pressed firmly to my eye. The hills and curves of
the land blocked my view of the road. The glass was just for
show. Vibrations through the soles of my feet told me who
approached our land and how far away they were.

My da had died seven months ago. Now the family gathered to confirm my older brother as successor to a heritage
as old as the land, and more sacred than either the village
priest or the king acknowledged.

At fourteen, I stood on the edge of the festivities, aware
of them, affected by them, but not truly a part of them.

"It's just the Marlowes," I sighed in disgust.

"Lemme see, Aunt Georgie, lemme see," my niece Emily
jumped up and down beside me. Her blonde curls and
clear blue eyes danced with excitement. Only three, she
tagged behind me everywhere and wanted to do everything I did.

I was certain she did not understand what had set the
household into total upset, but she had absorbed the excitement. Nearly twenty relatives thronged Kirkenwood Manor.
Many of them had pets—cats, dogs, birds, snakes, even a
hedgehog. Familiars really. The relatives insisted their animals must remain with them at all times. The house could
not contain them all. We'd had to put many of them in the
care of tenant farmers and the more wealthy in the village.

Gently, I knelt beside Emily and positioned the glass so

13

that she could see through it. I did not care that dust stained my summer frock and rough rocks tore the lace on my petticoat. If Lady Emma, Emily's mother and my sister-in-law, had allowed me to wear a coat and breeches, she would have no complaint about the cost of replacing my wardrobe.

"Fuzzy." Emily stuck out her lower lip in a deep pout. I knew that look. She'd cry in a minute.

"Let's focus it, then," I said and twisted the eyepiece a little to the left.

"Ugh."

That must mean the focus was worse. So I corrected to the right until a smile brightened her delicate features. "I can see the old chapel!" she crowed. "Raven's perched above the door."

There was always a raven perched there, if he wasn't guarding the well head up here on the heights.

"Let's look a little higher and farther along the road." I lifted the end of the glass so that it pointed in the proper direction. "What do you see now, Emily?"

"Road, and a lot of dust." She pouted again and returned the spyglass to me.

"Did you look with magic?" I asked quietly. At the age of three she wasn't ready for formal training, so her father Drake had not bothered to test or question her. But I had.

Emily grinned from ear to ear. "Can we play the magic game?"

"Just a little of it. Now think about Mother Earth."

"Earth isn't my mama," Emily giggled as she always did on this formulized reply.

"The Earth is mother to us all, even your mama. The Earth gives life to all. She feeds us with knowledge and power as well as food and water." I recited the familiar litany.

Emily closed her eyes and scrunched her fair eyebrows together as she concentrated.

"Draw the power and knowledge from Mother Earth. Bring it to your feet." I waited a moment until her expression cleared slightly. "Do you feel it, Emily? Can you feel the horses and carriages pound along the road?"

"Yes!" She opened her eyes in wonderment. "Aunt Budgie is riding behind the carriage. A long way behind."

"Aunt Budgie!" I stood up and faced south by southeast

and concentrated upon the road where it curved around and between a series of moors. One by one, I sorted through the various vibrations that tickled my feet. Three carriages, four horses for each. Three outriders ahead and three more behind the entourage. And then . . .

Yes! Aunt Budgie defied convention and rode a mile back with a footman. She mounted a fine Arabian steed that flowed along the road. Despite the fatigue of a long journey of over three hundred miles and creeping old age, the horse showed a fine spirit and alertness. Just like his mistress, Great-Aunt the Honorable Bridget Kirkwood. She carried a new title since her latest husband had died— I think he was her third. I didn't bother keeping track. Budgie was a Kirkwood, as was I, and made her own rules.

Her presence and blessing on tonight's proceedings made them special and validated them for me.

"They're still five miles out. We have time to wash and change before they get here." I grabbed Emily's hand and hastened her across the rubble of the ancient castle toward the twisted path to the base of the tor and thence to the family manor by the lake.

Emily held up her arms for me to carry her.

"You are getting too big for this," I complained as I lifted her into my arms.

She rested her head against my shoulder.

"Tired," she murmured.

Of course. She'd used magic. I took for granted the simple tricks of watching and listening with senses beyond normal. I'd been practicing and building up stamina for nine of my fourteen years. Emily was just beginning. Magic drained her more readily than it did me.

I cursed every building stone, twig, and stray rock that made the path more treacherous than usual. If only I had defied Lady Emma and worn the coat, breeches, and stout boots I used for sword practice, this trip would be easier. But then, by denying me clothing suitable for running wild across the moors and engaging in sword play with my brother, my sister-in-law hoped to keep me within the manor learning to behave like a lady.

I'd never be a lady, even if I was the sister, daughter, and granddaughter to the Earls of Kirkenwood.

"Let me take her," my brother Drake said the moment

we mounted the steps to Kirkenwood Manor. He lifted his sleepy daughter from my arms and let her snuggle against his broad chest. He'd put on weight these last two years. His wine-colored suit and stock strained across his middle. His yellow waistcoat no longer buttoned closed. Shouldering the responsibilities of an earldom while Da lay dying of a weak heart had increased his appetite for rich food and decreased the time he spent actively moving about the estates. Drake didn't have the time anymore to train with sword and rapier, or take his fine-blooded horses and wolfhound familiar on wild rides. Mostly he sat in his office shuffling papers about. He peered at everything squint-eyed and hunched his shoulders.

"Georgina!" Lady Emma protested as I trooped into the entry hall with my brother and niece. She carried her squalling second daughter, Belinda, on her shoulder, patting her back and murmuring soothing sounds to her.

"That frock was new not two months gone. You need to learn more respect for your clothing and your manners. You will not leave your room for the next three days. Not even to join the family in tonight's celebration."

"Now, Em," Drake cajoled his wife. They made a charming picture standing there together, his dark auburn hair, straight and thick, matched the one-year-old on Em's shoulder; Emma's fair hair and porcelain delicate skin a twin to Emily's. His dark suit with only a little lace contrasted nicely with her pink gown that dripped ornamentation. They gazed at each other lovingly.

"You know, Em, that tonight's ritual is a duty, a responsibility for every Kirkwood with talent. 'Tis not a game. Georgie must come. My installation as the Pendragon of Britain will not be complete without her." Drake stood a little straighter, a little taller as he spoke of the family tradition with pride.

"Oh, very well. I will need her help in dealing with all of the relatives coming out of the woodwork. But after they leave, Georgina, you will be confined to the manor for two weeks. You will learn to behave properly."

"Yes, m'lady," I said meekly, dropping a deep curtsy. I glanced up at Drake through my lowered lashes. We exchanged a merry twinkle. By the time all our relatives departed, Emma would have forgotten my punishment and the reasons for it.

Half an hour later we made a typical family portrait seated before the fire in the family parlor overlooking the lake when Simpson, the family butler, announced the arrival of our cousins.

"Dr. Milton Marlowe," Simpson intoned.

Cousin Milton appeared behind the family retainer. Travel dust creased his sober brown clothing without a single thread of lace. Fatigue lines creased his long face. He only graced our home with his dour presence for major holidays and special occasions, like the installation of a new Pendragon as head of the family and guardian of Britain's magical integrity.

His mother had been sister to my grandfather.

Drake stood and took Milton's hand in his own. Belle, Drake's wolfhound familiar, and the only dog allowed in the house, rose with him. She wove a herding path around Drake's legs. He neatly avoided tripping over her. He'd had a lot of practice in the past three years since her birth.

Belle's teats hung heavily beneath her. She waddled stiffly with each movement. She looked as if she'd give birth any moment, right here on the Persian carpet.

Emma would be horrified, of course. But the timing was perfect. The dogs chose the next Pendragon. Fitting that Belle give birth to her first litter on the night of Drake's confirmation—hopefully just after. She needed to attend the ceremony, as her ancestors had for so many human and dog generations that we'd given up counting them.

"You must be weary, Milton. Come let's get you settled. We've given you the gold room." Drake eased our guest toward the staircase.

"My sons," Milton said quietly. Two young men entered the room. Neville, the elder, wore a new scarlet uniform, also devoid of lace at cuff and neck, with lieutenant's bars on his shoulders. His lean face and form with medium coloring might be handsome if he ever smiled. I'd certainly never seen anything but a perpetual sneer of distrust and dislike.

I allowed my eyes to cross slightly as I looked into the empty space near his left ear. His aura, a reflection of his life energy, seemed to jump outward in tight layers of yellow and orange with a small black smudge at the center.

Black on the left shoulder! Death sat there.

Oh, if only I had Drake's healing talent I might see what disease ate at him. Or was it a personality flaw that drew him into death's hungry maw?

His brother fairly danced into the room, interrupting my survey of Neville Marlowe. He wore a bright plum suit with a deep-purple waistcoat that demanded gobs of lace to accent the excellent cut of the cloth. But since his father had paid to outfit the boy, there was no ornamentation for Barclay, not even gold buttons, only plain bone ones.

"Barclay," I held out my hand for him to kiss, as a proper lady with a courtesy title of Honorable should greet a relative with no title but some familiarity.

"Lady Georgina," Barclay greeted me with a nod and a slight bow. He then turned his full attention upon Emma, the ranking lady in the room. He knew his manners and protocol better than I did.

Eventually, Barclay flashed a grin at me. Two years older than I, and already he stood as tall as his father and brother. We'd shared more than a few childhood adventures whenever the families met. His eyes lingered on my slight bosom—not enhanced or pushed up by a corset—and my green frock. He lifted one eyebrow in question. We'd not likely ride barely broken horses bareback, or explore the castle ruins while I dressed this way.

He looked disappointed. Then his eyes twinkled with mischief.

"So sorry you'll have to share a room with your sons," Drake said quietly to Milton. "We're simply bursting at the seams with relatives."

Milton closed his eyes wearily and nodded. When he opened them again, he glared at Barclay as if he were a smudge upon his pristine life.

Simpson cleared his throat to gain our attention. "Lady Bridget Kirkwood," he said quietly when all eyes looked his direction.

"Aunt Budgie," both Drake and I cried and rushed to be the first to embrace her short, round figure.

"Now, now, there is plenty of me for both of you," Aunt Budgie giggled and swatted us away. "But only if you give me room to breathe." She fluttered a black lace fan set against a layer of bright pink silk. Her riding habit was black as well, brightened by accents of pink, including the long feather in her hat. She wore her widow's weeds with a flare of defiance.

"Come, Georgie, show me to my room. I must wash away this travel dust." Aunt Budgie draped her arm around my waist—I was too tall for her to comfortably reach my shoulders.

"We have to share," I said meekly, a little embarrassed that my brother's wealth and grand position did not extend to more private rooms.

"All the better."

"I'll sleep on the floor if you need the bed to yourself," I whispered. I'd sleep out on the moors if I thought I could get away with it.

"Not necessary. You are not so tall, yet, and I not so fat that we can't both fit." She guided me upstairs with more strength and haste than I thought she possessed. My grandfather's youngest sister, she was more of an age with my father than her siblings. She still seemed old to me. I'd lost a lot of relatives to old age and disease lately.

Once comfortably ensconced in our room with hot wash water and a tea tray, Aunt Budgie patted the bed beside her for me to sit. "We have to talk, Georgie."

"Is it bad?" She sounded very serious and adult.

"No. 'Tis a good thing. But you must be prepared for tonight."

My eyes opened wide. We did not discuss the ceremonies of the Pendragon Society outside of formal meetings. I was only an Apprentice and I already knew the penalties for divulging secrets.

"Drake has written to me that he intends to make you a Knight tonight."

I didn't think my eyes could grow any wider. "Don't I have to be sixteen? Doesn't the entire Inner Circle have to vote me in?" I sank beside my great-aunt, letting the soft, down mattress support me. My legs wouldn't hold me up much longer.

"Not tonight. We . . . the Inner Circle recognizes that your brother must now begin to build his own network of supporting magicians. One of the Knights will take his place within the Inner Circle, councillors to the Pendragon. Drake must replace that Knight with an Apprentice. You my dear. You must be trained to stand beside your brother, to help him with magic as well as the politics of guarding Britain against magical incursions from outside this land and this world."

I gulped rather than speak. Aunt Budgie had all but admitted that she was one of the Inner Circle. No one but those eleven councillors and the Pendragon knew the identity of the others. No one.

She had entrusted me with her greatest secret. And her life.

Inwardly, I vowed to never do anything to endanger that trust, or confidence.

"Now, you must be ready to prove yourself worthy of knighthood. You will be asked to perform a magical feat, one that will show your talent, your strength, and your willingness to serve."

"What? What will they ask of me?" My mind spun with possibilities, with ideas, and with dread.

What if I failed?

"You will not fail, Georgie. And no, I did not read your mind," Aunt Budgie laughed. "I read your face. You will not fail, because I will not allow you to."

I swallowed heavily and nodded. "What will I have to do?"

"I don't know. It is something only Drake knows. You have to be prepared for anything. You have to be prepared to risk your life. So, until midnight, this night of the Summer Solstice, you must rest, eat lightly, and meditate."

I grimaced. I was rarely tired, had a prodigious appetite, and hated to sit still long enough to meditate.

"Do it, Georgie. Believe me, you will be glad you did at midnight."

Chapter 2

The Lake at the base of Kirkenwood Tor.

"DO you trust me?" Aunt Budgie asked me solemnly. We stood at the French doors in the family parlor overlooking the lake. I wore a simple white woolen robe with the hood thrown back. She wore a similar robe in deep midnight blue, the same color as her eyes, and Drake's eyes, and Barclay's eyes. Mine were a pale amber brown, totally different from anyone in the family, except possibly my mother. But I had no memory of her, only a small and vague portrait in my room.

Barclay used to taunt me, claiming that, because I had not the Kirkwood eyes, my magic was just as vague and undefined as that portrait.

I felt strange without constricting undergarments. A good kind of strange, freer and lighter. Almost nude, almost naughty.

"Yes, Aunt Budgie, I trust you." I tried very hard to keep the excitement out of my voice and my feet still.

"Good." She lifted a blindfold and affixed it around my head. A few strands of my hair caught uncomfortably in the knot. I tugged at them. She slapped my hands away.

Blackness disoriented me. Not even the weak candle-light from Aunt Budgie's lantern leaked through the thick, dark cloth. I dared not adjust it. Right now, I wasn't certain I could find my own face with my hands.

"The trick to working blindfolded is to forget thinking with your eyes," Aunt Budgie said quietly. Her voice seemed to come from everywhere and nowhere. Maybe she circled me as she turned me around and around.

Just thinking about it made me dizzy.

I lost my balance standing still.

"Close your eyes, silly girl, and think with that other sense, the magic that makes you special."

I took a deep breath and let it go. Then another. The sounds of night birds came from in front of me. Behind me the house creaked as it settled. Above me, Emily sighed and rolled in her sleep.

"Good. Now we can meet the others for the ceremony."

"Shouldn't I know how to get there if I am to be made a Knight?"

"*After* we make you a Knight, you will learn the way. Not before."

I sighed. "This would all be easier if I had a familiar."

Aunt Budgie took my hand and walked me forward. I counted the steps on the flagged terrace; the stones felt cold and damp beneath my bare feet. I curled my toes, anticipating the three steps down to the grassy sward.

"If you need a familiar, the dogs will find a way to get you one. Now don't think about your steps, just feel the textures and sense the open and closed spaces around you."

"You mean, I might get a puppy from Belle's litter?" I was suddenly too excited to care that I stepped down and down again. The startling change from cold stone to soft grass nearly upset my balance again. I clung more tightly to Aunt Budgie's hand.

"Don't wish for that!" she reprimanded me. "For the dogs to give you one of their own means that your brother will not live long enough for Belle to whelp again."

"Oh." A bit of fear tasted rancid in the back of my throat. "I'd never wish for Drake to die."

"You wouldn't want to be Pendragon anyway. Not at your age." Budgie guided me across the grass.

Again a change in texture alerted me that we moved beyond the kept grounds. I cast out my senses as Da and Drake had taught me. Twin oak trees should be just ahead of us, marking a faint game trail into the woods and the marshy ground where the lake drained into a stream.

"The Pendragon carries awesome responsibilities, Georgie," Aunt Budgie continued, her quiet voice leading me as much as her hand. "Since German George became

our king, we must act in secret, more than we ever have before, to maintain the balance of good and evil in Britain."

"But isn't it good that we have a Protestant king? And
His Majesty is descended from Charles I."

"The Hanoverian kings are sometimes a blessing for
England, sometimes not. Both George I and his son
George II are more German than English. They have no
tradition of listening to a Pendragon, seeking advice or
council. They don't know enough to look beyond the normal world for sources of trouble and evil. Being Pendragon
in such an era of disbelief means walking a very narrow
and jagged political edge as well as losing a great deal of
one's sense of self in the magic."

I had to think about that for a while. No wonder Drake
had become more quiet and withdrawn of late.

We walked a little farther, I forgot to keep track of my
steps and the twists and turns on the path while I considered what it meant to be Pendragon and just how much
Drake must rely on his Inner Circle and his Knights to do
his job. I had to become the best of his Knights to help him.

"We're here," Aunt Budgie whispered. Then she abandoned my hand.

I sensed that she moved away, that others awaited her.
They stood very still. I could not hear rustling robes or shifting feet. Was that someone taking a deep breath beside me,
or just the rising wind before the next summer storm?

Frantically I reached out with my magic, trying to find
who awaited me. Had they called a demon to challenge
me? My family had faced demons before. They didn't always win the battle.

My senses backlashed into my mind. Stabbing pains
pierced my eyes and temples. I bit my lip until I tasted
blood. I would not cry out in fear.

My dinner twisted in my stomach and threatened to
come up. My bladder suddenly filled. Now I wished I'd
obeyed Aunt Budgie's advice and not eaten a full meal of
soup, fish, meat, sweet, and savory, along with several large
cups of tea.

Concentrate, I scolded myself. *Concentrate and open
your mind. Don't reach out, just be open and receptive,* I
told myself. Immediately, my heart rate slowed and my

breathing calmed. Part of me shivered, knowing how vulnerable I was with my magical shields down and so little clothing between me and . . .

Listen carefully, an anonymous voice came into my mind. It might have been Drake, but I couldn't be certain. We had not communicated much mind to mind. This voice felt a little alien, more self-assured than my brother and a little bit cruel.

Listen to my instructions.

I stilled my mind and my body, waiting, keeping only a small part of me aware of the possibility of magical attack and ready to defend myself.

Good. You follow orders. A mental chuckle came through with the voice. But it did not sound mirthful. It sounded . . . controlling.

Drake would never sound like that. This must be someone else. Someone from the Inner Circle who had more on his mind than just testing me.

Who?

A shaft of searing light pierced my eyes. My knees wobbled. I had to lock them to remain upright. The pain shot through me again. I almost cried out.

But this time my magical defenses reacted before I could think. Shields slammed into place and flung the pain back toward the sender. Weakly.

A mental grunt told me the magic attack found a target. I'd done little or no damage.

I put my hands to my face, rubbing my temples and my eyes to ease the lingering soreness of mind and body. Surreptitiously, I shifted the blindfold a mote. A little of the forest clearing, lit by witchlight sitting atop twelve magicians' staffs, came into view. The Otherworldly flames did not hiss or waver in the light drizzle that dampened the land. We all smelled of wet wool and sweat. Wood lay ready for the touch of flame ten paces in front of me. Twelve magicians stood in a circle around me with hands folded into their deep sleeves and their hoods drawn. Height and breadth gave me my only clues to identity.

Drake, tall and straight, must be the magician directly across the circle from me. Short and round Aunt Budgie stood to his right. Tall but stooped without his walking staff, Sir Mathew Garbeleton, a distant cousin we called Uncle Matt, stood to Drake's left.

My attention lingered on Uncle Matt. He often shook his staff at his children and me when we set off his quick temper with noise or childish games. Could he attack me?

A quick look around the circle gave me no other candidates.

I had to survive this test. 'Twas only a test. Drake would not let anyone kill me. If he knew about it.

That touch of cruelty in the commanding voice made me suspicious.

Approach the fire at the center of the circle. This time I recognized Drake's mental voice.

I took eight of the ten paces that separated me from the fire pit.

Light the fire.

Drake knew that calling the element of Fire, brother and opposite to my primary element of Earth, eluded me. Wet wood from the night's drizzle made the task all the harder.

"May I take off the blindfold?" I asked.

No! came a resounding chorus from twelve different voices.

If I had asked telepathically, would they have consented? No way of knowing now.

I had to find a dry spot within the wood for the fire to ignite. Not an easy task without eyes and without touching the wood.

Think without eyes, Aunt Budgie whispered. It came so faintly, I almost did not catch the advice.

She'd said that before and it helped me follow her blind. So I opened my senses once again, still keeping a wary part of me alert to another magical attack. This time, I spun a tiny tendril of magic outward, like a thread and let it tickle the wood, routing out the moisture.

Wood was akin to Earth, my element. It responded to my touch, pushing and guiding my magic toward its center, the deep core of the stack.

"She's taking too long," someone whispered. I could not tell if he spoke with mind or voice. The words *felt* like the one who had ordered me to drop my shields and then attacked me.

Part of me panicked and pushed the magic deeper into the wood. Maybe if I set up enough friction within one of the kindling pieces it would set fire to itself.

"Hush. She may have as much time as she needs to do it right," Drake whispered back to the unknown speaker.

Do it right. I had to call the element of Fire, not just force the wood to burn.

> *"Earth in the wood,*
> *Air in the rustling wind,*
> *Water from the rain,*
> *Fire complete the good*
> *Spell I cast*
> *Among the kindling lain."*

I ran the spell through my mind several times and decided it should work if I concentrated hard enough.

The task should not have been this easy. Something was wrong with the setup.

One deep breath to clear my head. A second to center my thoughts. And a third to call the magic.

Line by line I spoke the words out loud, thinking hard about elemental fire and the fuel I promised it to feed upon.

Cease thinking with your eyes.

I stopped in mid-word on the fifth line. Something was wrong.

A whiff of something out of place crossed my nose. Naphtha. Naphtha laced with sulfur. A very volatile amount of the clear liquid soaked the ground right around the wood and spread . . . spread directly toward Drake's feet. Any fire at all threatened to make a living torch of my brother, the Pendragon of Britain.

Chapter 3

DRAKE breathed a sigh of relief. His baby sister had stopped in time. He did not have to negate the elemental Fire, his primary element, with its sister Earth. Water would do nothing to keep him from burning alive—the usual and most dreaded death for those convicted of witchcraft.

Good thing he did not have to draw upon even more magic than he already had worked tonight. His fasting and meditation had left him dizzy and disoriented. He wasn't certain how much more he could do.

The signet ring of the Pendragon, a red enamel dragon rampant on a black field, weighed heavily upon his hand right now.

"She failed. We'll have to find another Apprentice to elevate," Dr. Milton Marlowe said out loud. He raised his hand as if to throw off his concealing hood.

Give her time! Drake reinforced his mental command with a sharp stab into his cousin's mind.

Milton reeled back a step, breaking the symmetry of the circle.

I can do this. Please, give me a chance, Georgie pleaded. Her communication came on a tight and private line to Drake.

Proceed, he replied quietly. Even as he gave the order, he prepared a spell to force Earth to shift and break the line of naphtha as well as to cover with dirt the volatile liquid from Persia.

Georgie flashed him a big grin. Had she eavesdropped on his mind and found the dousing spell? He didn't think she had the power to do that.

But she had the wits to figure it out. Georgie was the one

person he wanted around in a crisis because of her quick thinking.

She has had time, Milton snarled. *You did not give Neville extra time with his first attempt and he is twice the magician this chit will ever be.*

Belle pressed against Drake's leg, reminding him that she, too, was running out of time. Her labor had begun. The pups needed to be born. Soon.

"Now, boys," Aunt Budgie intervened. "I have kept track of the time. Georgina is well within the limits. Proceed, Georgie."

Silently, Drake thanked his aunt. He needed her wise and sensible counsel. Milton, however, had lost his famous patience. Why?

Georgie picked up Drake's dousing spell. She recited the arcane words as she circled the fire, drawing a physical and a magical line between the wood and the naphtha. He watched her steps grow slower and slower as she tired. She wasn't used to controlling her magic with spells. She usually just did what needed doing without fine control.

"She needs better training," Aunt Budgie whispered to him.

"And practice," Drake mumbled.

Belle whined her urgency. If Georgie didn't hurry, the first pup would come forth right here. Right now. She wanted her bed in the inglenook of the kitchen, not this open and unprotected place.

Georgie finished her circle and then recited her first spell to call Fire to the wood.

Fire burst from Georgie's pointing finger into the wood. It gobbled up the kindling and set to devouring the larger pieces of dry elm. The flames reached upward and outward, it found a tendril of naphtha and shot along it directly toward Drake.

The air reeked with sulfurous smoke straight from hell.

Drake felt a shout of malicious glee somewhere off to his left. Who? What?

"Damme," he cursed as he set the Earth to trembling and heaving at his feet. Georgie had not completed her circle. She'd left a hair's breadth unclosed. Enough of a pathway for the fire to find and reach the flammable liquid.

"Oh!" Georgie gasped, her mouth wide with horror.

Tears streaked her face below the blindfold. She choked on the demonic smoke.

Drake waved his hand and the running fire slowed, but kept coming. Smoke billowed all around him, obscuring his vision and clouding his mind. He stepped back and out of the puddle of naphtha. But his feet and the hem of his robe were soaked with it.

Belle bugled in distress, pushing him back and back, putting her life and those of her precious pups at risk.

"Georgie, complete the task. Fire will answer only to you tonight," Drake said sternly. She couldn't fail. But he also saw how drained she had become.

> *"Mother Earth*
> *Guide and Friend*
> *Honor your servant*
> *Bring Fire's trail*
> *To an end."*

She leaped and landed between Drake and the creeping flames. Her heels dug deeply into the ground, disrupting the flow of naphtha.

Fire stopped coming.

Georgie sank to her knees in exhaustion. Deep coughs racked her lithe body.

Belle lay down beneath a flowering shrub, panting, no longer able to hold back the birth.

"I say she failed. Elevation to Knighthood denied," Milton crowed. Georgie just cried.

"Your first action as Pendragon was a disaster. Is this how you intended to guard all of Britain?" Milton asked. Seven of the eleven members of the Inner Circle, including Uncle Matt, shifted and sidled until they stood closer to Milton than to Drake.

Dr. Milton Marlowe paced Drake's study restlessly, waiting for his cousin to return with Belle and her puppies. Getting the massive dog and her offspring from the sacred clearing to the manor required the strong backs of a number of retainers, a door to carry the dog on, and plenty of warm blankets and hot possets. The possets were for a worried Drake.

Drake's concern for the animal worried Milton as much as the younger man's disgrace tonight. He behaved as if the *dog* were as important as his wife about to give birth to a son and heir.

Tonight did not portend well for the future of the Pendragon Society. Good thing his great-great-grandfather had seen fit to bring all of the talented relatives together and form the secret society rather than depend solely upon one person. The fate of Britain during these unbelieving times was too precarious for just one person to shoulder the burden.

But the Society still needed a strong leader. Drake would never be that.

For the first time in his life, Milton questioned the wisdom of relying upon the *dogs,* mere *animals,* to choose the leader.

Something must be done. Milton appeared to be the only one capable of doing it.

"Ah, Milton. You waited up." Drake appeared in the doorway, slightly disheveled in breeches and shirt, without a stock or coat or waistcoat. The man had lost all sense of decency to meet with a valued colleague of the Inner Circle in such a state of dishabille.

"I am happy to report that Belle and her twelve puppies are all safely ensconced in the kitchen. The runt appears a little unhealthy, but he is nursing. Both Belle and I have hopes that he will survive." Drake poured a large measure of brandy for himself. He looked pale and shaken as well as disheveled.

Milton shook his head to indicate he did not need the restorative or the tray of sweets sent in earlier.

Drake settled into his favorite armchair beside the fire with the tray and a second snifter of brandy. He ate greedily. A little color returned to his face. His hands took a little longer to stop trembling.

"We need to discuss what happened tonight, milord." Milton decided to put the conversation on a more formal note.

"A minor disagreement. Georgie lit the fire and stopped it from reaching me." Drake dismissed the incident with a wave of a sticky pastry that dripped honey.

Milton shuddered at the cloying sweetness that would clog his throat.

"The fire should never have escaped the circle. She did not complete the task," Milton argued. "We cannot allow such carelessness to invade the Pendragon Society."

"I have a few questions about that as well." Drake wiped his mouth with a serviette while he decided which treat to consume next. "I think we should ask Georgie herself what happened." He picked up a date stuffed with a walnut and dipped in honey.

"I'll ring for Simpson to fetch her." Milton rose and walked to the bell pull.

"It's two in the morning. Can't this wait until a more decent hour?"

A true leader would not have asked. He would have commanded.

"This must be settled tonight!" Milton insisted and yanked upon the tapestried pull.

A few moments later, Georgina stood hesitantly in the doorway to the study. She had donned warm woolen breeches, shirt, and coat in defiance of her sex. More evidence of her unsuitability for the Pendragon Society. Proper decorum must define the Society now that so many refused to believe in the necessity of magic to defend Britain. Milton refused to give the unbelievers, especially King George II, who had more interest in his German holdings than in England, any excuse to undermine the rights and responsibilities of the Pendragons.

"I'm sorry, Drake. I apologize for failing," Georgina said simply.

"Thank you, Georgie," Drake replied quietly between mouthfuls of the last stuffed date. "Please come closer. Do you need something to eat or drink?"

"No, thank you. Barclay and I had bread and cheese and ale. Aunt Budgie insisted."

"Great Aunt Bridget," Milton corrected the girl. No wonder Drake lacked leadership if he allowed such informality from a *child*.

Georgina just glared at him.

"I need to know why you put up your shields, Georgie. You entered the sacred circle with your shields down and your senses open. If you had remained that way, you would have sensed the naphtha sooner and had the stamina to deal with it early on." Drake leaned forward to look the girl directly in the eye.

Milton wondered if she would tell all or have the courage to own up to her mistake.

Georgina remained silent for a long time.

Milton began to hope that she would maintain her silence.

"I was attacked," she said so quietly that Milton had to strain to hear.

"What?" Drake bolted upright, upsetting the tray of food. It clattered to the floor. Crumbs flew everywhere. "That is not possible."

"Someone I did not recognize ordered me to drop my shields and then sent bolts of pain through my eyes." Georgina firmed her chin and faced her brother squarely. "I had no choice but to protect myself. This appears to me as a surreptitious and cowardly attack on you, Brother."

Drake sank back into his chair.

Milton tapped his foot nervously. "Obviously, an outsider followed and spied upon us. We must find the intruder."

"Who would dare? The Pendragon Society is secret and sacred," Drake mumbled.

Georgina turned around slowly and faced Milton with as much determination as she had faced her brother. "Are you certain the loyalty of every member is impeccable?"

What did she know?

"We are all related by strong ties of blood, education, and long tradition," Milton replied. "I know of no better test for loyalty."

Georgina quirked her eyebrows up in question. But she kept her mouth shut.

"We have rivals." Milton addressed Drake.

"The Freemasons?" Drake asked.

Georgina's head swiveled rapidly between them, following the conversation.

"Not the Masons, they have too many of the same ideals as we," Milton dismissed the notion.

"Scottish Rite Freemasons borrowed many of our rituals and ideals. Grand Lodge, however, is too conservative for my liking. Of the unbelievers, they speak loudest against magic and Otherworldly menaces. They would gladly see an end to both Scottish Rite and us."

"I will begin seeking the intruder among them," Milton said flatly.

"Do that." Drake sat up straighter. Defeat no longer dragged him down. "I will begin asking my own questions."

"And the girl? She knows too much to be thrust out of the Society. Yet she failed in her task. We cannot administer oaths."

"Georgina did not fail. She was manipulated by outsiders into not completing her circle to contain Fire."

"She is not worthy of Knighthood if she can be manipulated."

"*We* did not set the wards properly if an outsider could break through to manipulate her. I shall administer the oath in the presence of the Society after tea, at our general meeting."

"And my . . . the new member of the Inner Circle?" Milton asked.

Georgina looked at him strangely, as if he had let slip some vital piece of information. He hadn't. Had he?

"The Inner Circle will meet after luncheon. As we always do on the Solstice. Now we must all rest. I have set up a cot in the kitchen for myself, next to Belle. I will see you both when we break our fast." Drake dismissed them by leaving the room.

"You will keep this discussion private, Georgina." Milton made certain he stood between the girl and the door.

"Of course. We do not wish to alert our enemies that we are on to them." She had a disconcerting way of appearing logical and . . . damnit, *correct.*

"And you will leave the investigation to your betters."

"My *betters?*" Her eyes flared with dangerous anger. Her fingers curled as if she held a weapon. She shifted her feet apart *en garde.*

Milton dared not back away from her, show any weakness. Like a malevolent cat, she would pounce, attack from the rear.

"Those who know the world and magic better than you. You overstep your abilities and your authority, Georgina. Watch yourself. Membership in the Pendragon Society does not make you immune to reprimand and punishment for errors in behavior."

"The same for you as well?" She assumed a less threatening posture and a milder expression.

"You are cheeky and seek above your station, child. I will be watching you." He turned on his heel and marched out of the study.

"And I'll be watching you as well."

Her words crawled up his spine like ice.

Chapter 4

Kirkwood House, Chelsea, England, near London, December 24, 1755, Yuletide festival.

"BE quiet now, Emily, and we can peek into the parlor," I whispered to my five-year-old niece. We both wore forest-green gowns trimmed with narrow needle lace. Emily's red petticoat and the red bows trimming the stomacher matched the bunches of holly festooning the hall. My white petticoat and trim evoked the ivy that twined the banisters. We'd been singing "The Holly and the Ivy" hymn all afternoon.

Since my sixteenth birthday, I had started wearing my hair up and taking more pride in my femininity. I almost looked forward to my first season, either this coming spring or the next one.

I was as anxious as Emily to inspect the presents gathered in a neat display beside the hearth. I really wanted to get my hands on the new Italian rapier I had asked Drake for.

Emily crept to the double doors of the formal parlor. She pulled down the latch. It remained locked. She pouted in concentration.

"No, Emily. You must not unlock the door with magic. Your mama will detect the spell and refuse to let you light the candles if she thinks we peeked."

Lady Emma had little magic of her own, but she could sniff out the workings of others with the surety of a bloodhound.

I fished a hairpin from beneath my lace cap. "This, Emily, is a skill every lady needs to know." I pressed my ear to the door as I inserted the pin in the lock. The murmur of voices stayed my hand.

"Sixteen is too young for a season," Drake said most insistently.

"We need to find the girl a husband before she becomes even more headstrong and wild," Lady Emma replied, equally insistent. "I blame your father for not providing the girl with a gentlewoman's influence after your mother died. Georgina grew up in a household of men, with a man's expectations."

"Lemme see," Emily whispered, trying to press her eye to the keyhole.

"Whist." I pressed a finger to her lips.

She obeyed but still tried to peer inside.

I had to hear every word. They discussed my future, without giving me a choice or a chance to voice my opinion.

"Georgina has a most generous dowry. Sufficient to attract the most reluctant groom. When the time comes. The proper time," Drake said.

I extended my senses, the better to listen to this horrific conversation. I no longer cared if Emma detected me.

"If Georgina grows any bolder, no man who can control her will have her," Emma riposted.

"Georgie needs more time at home to train. I need her magical strength, and her skill with a sword at my side. We have never discovered who attacked her on the night of my installation. Please, Emma, think on this before you commit to Georgie's debut this April."

I sensed Drake reaching out to his wife. But not to me.

"My dear, I have considered this, long and hard. Georgie is a terrible influence upon Emily. Do you truly wish your daughter growing up more concerned with horses and swords than with a woman's natural ability to nurture a household and family? What good is Georgie to you, the Pendragon, if she is so headstrong she refuses to listen to you?"

"What if we arrange a betrothal between my sister and our cousin Neville?" Drake asked. A bit of humor crept into Drake's voice.

Anger began to boil in my stomach. Not stuffy and pompous Neville. I'd sooner marry the recently widowed steward of the home farm. Or Cousin Barclay. Now that idea presented possibilities.

"Neville. An excellent idea." Emma's tone melted with delight. "He's a strong, intelligent young man, an excellent officer. He's already proved himself in battle in Germany. She respects that."

I snorted. I'd read the battle reports from German George's newest campaign to expand and secure his continental territories from the French and Spanish. Neville survived a skirmish. That did not mean he distinguished himself.

"And Neville is a strong magician. He will curb Georgie's wilder impulses. And keep her close to home," Drake added.

A long moment of silence ensued.

I had to hold my breath and count to ten, three times, to keep from shouting and throwing the Persian vase filled with holly and ivy on the stand at my elbow.

Unable to contain myself any longer, I heaved on the latch with all of my strength as well as enough magic to open the stoutest lock, then flung the door open. It banged against the wall and bounced back into Emily's face. I marched the length of the formal parlor to catch my brother and his wife in a clinging embrace.

Nothing unusual about that. They never grew tired of touching each other. In fact, Emma was breeding again. And so was Belle, Drake's familiar. They took this as an omen that perhaps this time Emma carried a boy.

I refused to be turned into a brood mare producing a new baby every other year. I had talents and uses suited for better things.

"I will not marry Lieutenant Neville Marlowe," I announced. "He thinks altogether too much of himself and he has no sense of humor." I didn't add that his idea of a joke involved some form of cruel punishment—usually directed at his younger brother Barclay.

"Georgie, don't take this the wrong way." Drake reached a placating hand to me.

I slapped it away as if batting aside a poorly aimed rapier thrust.

"You either want me to marry a pompous ass or auction me off to the lowest bidder—someone who will *settle* for me," I snarled at him.

A smile crept over Emma's face. "Neville is a bit full of himself," she admitted.

"I will have none of your choices. I'd sooner die a spinster than marry someone you choose who can 'control' me."

"That is enough, Georgie," Drake said firmly. "I am your guardian. I have been for over three years. I know what is best for you."

"Do you?" Tears of rage burned my eyes. I turned to flee. "Do you know anything but what you choose to believe? When was the last time you looked at the world beyond your books and ledgers? When was the last time *you* truly searched for your enemies and carried the battle to them?"

"What do you mean by that?" Drake grabbed my elbow roughly. He crushed three layers of expensive lace. His face filled with too much color and his breathing became short and shallow.

"I mean that you questioned a few Freemasons to see if they knew who your enemy might be. But you never looked farther, or closer." I yanked my arm free, knowing I'd have bruises there in the morning. For all of his portliness and myopic view of life, Drake still fenced with me regularly. He still had the strength and wits to defeat me more often than I scored upon him.

"That is not . . . not . . ." Drake clenched his left fist. The high color drained from his face, leaving his cheeks and jowls waxy white and flaccid. He clutched his chest with his right hand. His head hung down, too heavy for his neck to support.

"My dear." Emma touched his shoulder tentatively. Her other hand cupped her swelling belly. She, too, grew pale. Her chin trembled and she bit her lip to control it.

Drake opened his mouth to draw breath.

"Emily, summon the servants," I called loudly. I knew she could reach the bell pull on the wall just to the left of the double doors.

With firm hands I guided Drake to the settee and forced him to recline with his feet up. Belle raced in from her favorite nook in the kitchen. She plunked herself down beside Drake and placed her heavy head upon him, keeping him in place. Then I pushed Emma into the nearest chair. She panted deeply, like the dogs did in labor.

"Milady?" Simpson asked from the doorway.

"Summon Dr. Marlowe, instantly. And the midwife. Have Lady Emma's maid help her upstairs. *Now*."

He barked orders to the rank of footmen behind him.

"Forgive me, milady, for the presumption." He bent to lift Lady Emma into his arms.

"No. I will stay with my husband," she gasped between too rapid breaths.

"You need to be abed yourself, Emma. Go. I will stay with my brother." I drew Emily out of the way of our butler.

"What can you do, Georgina? You don't have the healing talent. My lord Earl is the only one in the family with that ability and he can't heal himself." Emma gasped as if in deep pain.

"Dr. Marlowe will be here shortly. Until then, I can keep my brother's heart beating. Belle and I can do it. Now go. Save your baby if you can."

My sister-in-law succumbed to logic and allowed Simpson to carry her out.

"Sometimes a woman has to have a man's expectations and order the world to do her bidding," I mused.

"Emily, go to Nanny and stay with her." I pushed the trembling child toward the door as I knelt beside Drake and centered myself and my magic with deep and even breaths.

I had to keep the panic at bay. I could do this. No one else could keep my brother, the Pendragon of England, alive.

"I want to help," Emily lisped.

"Of course you do, sweeting," Barclay said as he dashed into the room.

A long look of understanding passed between us.

"Father is already on his way in the carriage. I came ahead on horseback for the family dinner before church services." He knelt beside me and took my hand.

Warmth and reassurance flooded through me.

Then he took Emily's hand as well. Emily draped her arm around Belle's neck.

"Do it, Georgie," Barclay commanded gently. "Count the beats and keep his heart going. Emily, Belle, and I will give you strength."

And so they did. With my next breath I felt strength and courage flood my heart and mind. My misgivings faded to a niggle of doubt.

I placed my left hand directly above Drake's heart. It

stuttered and fluttered in its struggle to stay alive. His breath came in uneven gasps. Too shallow. Too wet.

One by one, I closed down all my senses, listening to my own heart until the strong and steady pulse dominated my awareness. Then I pushed the rhythm down my arm into my hand. My fingers tingled in time with my heartbeat.

With my eyes closed, I visualized four cords of life extending from my fingers deep into Drake's chest until they wrapped around his heart.

Kathump thump. The cords squeezed and released, squeezed and released Drake's life force into a natural heartbeat. *Kathump thump.* Again and again I made his heart match mine. *Kathump thump.*

It hesitated, tried a counterpoint. I pushed harder, bolstered by Barclay and Belle. I couldn't sense Emily. A moment of near panic. Had I harmed the child, demanding too much magical strength?

"Easy, Georgie. Concentrate. Breathe. Keep his heart beating," Barclay whispered.

Kathump thump.

Drake's body rebelled with disharmony. *Thump, thump, thripppppp, thump.*

I saw a blockage in his veins with my mind's eye. But I could not find a way to break it up or force his blood to flow down new pathways. All I could do was keep him alive until his heart got so used to beating in union with mine it forgot how to quit.

Harmony. I had to get his body back in harmony with itself.

I hummed "The Holly and the Ivy," the only tune I could think of. *Kathump thump.* Slowly, very slowly, Drake's heart complied with my demands.

My strength faltered.

A few more moments. Just a few more moments. Father is nearly here, Barclay whispered into my mind.

My will faltered. He took command of my thoughts and pushed the heartbeat into Drake once more. For ten more beats my mind was his, his was mine. We understood each other, loved one another, became one another.

I took a deep breath and found another ounce of strength. He gave me a little more. We both tired. Emily had already fallen asleep and dropped out of the spell.

Belle whimpered, uncertain how to proceed.

Kathump thump. Drake's heart beat on its own, still weak, but in a proper rhythm.

Ground the spell, Georgie. Withdraw slowly, Barclay guided me. *Tendril by tendril, bring the magic back into yourself. Pull it back, gather it up, and send it back into the Earth where it came from.*

I followed his orders, too tired to think on my own.

"What have you done, Barclay?" Dr. Milton Marlowe shouted as he dashed to my brother's side. "Mucked it up again? You can't do anything right."

My rapport with Barclay severed immediately. I don't think I could have read his mind, or his aura even if I had my full strength and magic.

Milton took charge of the scene, dosing my brother with tinctures and tonics.

Barclay said nothing as he half carried Emily and me up to my room and to bed.

I remembered his gentle kiss upon my brow and my lips for many months afterward.

Chapter 5

Marlowe House, Bayswater District, London, England, early March, 1756.

"GET out of my way, you clumsy oaf." Dr. Milton Marlowe elbowed his younger son Barclay out of the way in his hurry to reach the carriage first. He reached the conveyance just as the footman lowered the step.

"Neville, how fare you?" he asked his older son inside the carriage. He braced his foot on the step and leaned in to inspect him.

"A damned uncomfortable ride from Dover, Pater," Neville drawled weakly. "Methinks the coachman drove deliberately through every pothole and rut he could find. Dismiss him immediately." The young man's face looked pale and drawn. He wore his scarlet uniform coat draped over his left shoulder, misshapen by a wad of crude bandages.

Military surgeons were worthless, judging by the way they had treated Neville. Milton doubted they'd done anything other than stop the bleeding. Bayonet wounds were notoriously dirty. Neville needed bleeding and purging to cleanse his body from battlefield poisons.

"Father, 'tisn't Jenkins' fault the Crown does nothing to repair the Dover road," Barclay interrupted.

"You know nothing, boy. Keep your opinions to yourself until you have something worthwhile to say," Milton snapped at him.

Neville heaved himself forward, preparing to debark the carriage.

"No, Neville. Wait there. I'll have the servants bring a

42

chair. They'll carry you to your room. Cook has prepared a nice clear broth for you."

"I've drunk an ocean of broths. I need some real food to rebuild my strength. I have to be ready to return to my regiment in two months. We've been posted to the American colonies," Neville said. "And I can walk. If I couldn't walk, I'd still be stuck in the stinking surgeon's tent dying of gangrene or starvation or some such."

"I'd not have left you languishing under their bungling care, Neville." Milton backed out of the carriage, keeping a firm and supportive grip upon Neville's undamaged arm.

Barclay moved to Neville's other side, eager to assist.

"Out of the way, Brother." Neville batted at Barclay with surprising strength in his wounded arm. "Why is he always in my way, Pater?"

"Barclay, go find something to do," Milton ordered. "Gambling with your friends, or racing horses on the heath."

For once the boy obeyed. He turned on his heel and ran across the square to the main road. Milton turned his attention back to Neville, the good son, the talented son, the important son.

Kirkwood House, Chelsea, England, late April, 1757.

Drake gauged Georgie's attack. He parried to his quarte and followed through with a neat riposte to her high sixte. She was always vulnerable high and inside.

But she surprised him with a counter to his exposed septime.

"Touché!" she proclaimed, triumphant at winning this bout.

Fifteen points to his twelve left Drake breathless and sweating. He hated to admit that since his heart attack two and half years ago, he had lost a lot of his agility and a lot of his zeal for this kind of activity. Now his little sister bested him more often than not.

"Another round, Drake?" she asked. Perspiration glistened on her upper lip and brow. She positively glowed with health and high spirits. "We haven't practiced enough of late."

The time had come to curb her high spirits before she

wound up a childless spinster. Two seasons she'd had and not a single offer for her hand.

Emma had warned him that he should have acted sooner, more decisively.

"Not today, Georgie. We must talk." Drake removed the foil from the tip of his rapier and sheathed the blade.

"Have you found our enemy?" she asked, sheathing her own weapon.

"Not specifically. My last scrying spell showed a center of black magic in Kent, though."

"Kent? So close?" Georgie looked ready to brandish her blade again and go charging off through the streets of London in search of a demonic coven.

"I found only residue. Possibly quite old." Drake stayed her weapon hand. "Calm down, Georgie. 'Tis not your battle. I will handle this in my own time and my own way."

"If this is not the battle for one of your Knights, then whose?" she demanded, hands on slim hips. In shirt and breeches with her breasts bound and her hair tied back in a queue, she looked like a beardless boy anxious to join the army.

As magnificent as his sister had become, Drake had to end her fascination with weapons and battles here and now. Emma wouldn't let him sit down to dinner with her again if he didn't.

" 'Tis a battle for other of my Knights, Georgina."

Her nostrils flared and her eyes widened at his use of her proper name.

"And why not mine? I am as skilled in magic as you will allow me. More skilled in swordplay than any of your Knights, including Cousin Barclay and his sniveling elder brother."

Major Neville Marlowe had been posted to New York with his regiment last year. Barclay had given up his dissolute friends and wastrel nights to purchase an Army commission on the day Neville returned from Europe. He'd finished his preliminary training and awaited his first posting.

"The time has come for you to take on a different task for the Pendragon Society, Georgina. You have more than enough magic for this."

"Oh?" She raised both eyebrows, intrigued, but also wary.

"Our numbers decrease. We need our magicians to intermarry and breed more magicians." That ought to appeal to her sense of loyalty and her oath of obedience to him.

"Who?" She stiffened and glared at him sidelong. Her fingers curled around her sword's grip, ready to battle everyone.

"Sir Mathew Garbeleton."

"Uncle Matt?" she cried in dismay. "He's older than the hills and crankier than a ram in shearing season."

"He is a distant cousin, and an adequate magician, one of my most loyal supporters."

"With two sons older than me, two daughters near my age, and three dead wives." She turned as if to stalk into the house.

"Mathew's last wife died of a fall from her horse." Drake stepped in front of her, blocking her path with his bulk.

"His third wife to die in such a manner. Isn't that a little suspicious, Brother? Perhaps a convenient explanation to cover the fact that he hit her so hard he broke her neck. Don't you fear for my life with such a man?"

"No. You have just shown me how well you can defend yourself. You have not shown me how well you can obey. You took oaths when I made you a Knight of the Pendragon Society."

"Not in this, Brother. I will not marry this man, no matter how much you need me to breed. Look to your wife and daughters for that."

Drake's wife, Emma, had just birthed a third daughter, Patricia. This might be her last pregnancy. The miscarriage of a baby boy that Christmas Eve two and a half years ago had left her bedridden and weak of blood for months at the time Drake needed her most while he recovered from his heart attack. This last confinement had cost her much in strength. Of the two older girls, Emily and Belinda, only Emily showed any signs of magic, and hers was as wild and uncontrolled as Georgie's.

Both of them needed discipline. Drake fully intended to rectify that.

"This is for your own good, Georgina. You need to follow the rules of society as well as the rules of fencing and magic."

"Meaning?"

"Meaning, no more dressing as a man. No more sword-play, no more riding astride. And no more arguing politics with every man you meet. You must learn to behave as a lady. If the government is ever to acknowledge and accept the Pendragons as valid defenders, then we must all present a respectable image. We must avoid any taint of scandal. You, Georgina, are a scandal waiting to happen."

"This is Lady Emma's idea."

"I am your guardian."

"You haven't made a decision on your own in years. Emma is your strength and your chief adviser in life and in the Pendragon Society. Though if she had Kirkwood blood in her so she could join the Pendragon Society, she doesn't have enough talent to qualify for membership."

"You would do well to emulate Emma in behavior and attitude."

"If that means submitting to the abuse of a man like Sir Mathew Garbeleton, never." Her voice rose to a near shout. "He beats his dogs and his grown children with that gnarled walking staff he always carries."

"The betrothal papers are signed and witnessed. Your dowry is placed in trust. The announcement will be made tonight at the Earl of Hastings' ball. You will marry Sir Mathew at the end of the season."

"No."

"Go to your room, Georgie. And stay there until you can obey me. Your maid has orders to remove all of your male clothing and your weapons, including the suit you have hidden beneath the false floor of your wardrobe. Nanny will see that you are fed bread and water twice a day. But until you can dress properly, and behave decently, I will keep you confined." The words tasted bitter in Drake's mouth. He hated to break Georgie's spirit this way.

"If I consent, may I keep my blades and breeches?"

"That is up to your betrothed."

"You blighter, he's a Puritan. He won't allow me to leave the bedroom, nor say a word except in acquiescence!"

"Don't be ridiculous. Sir Mathew is a reasonable man and loyal to the Pendragons."

"Are you certain? You investigated him with the same lack of thoroughness you investigated the attack upon us the night of your installation as the Pendragon. Do you truly know your friends or your enemies? Perhaps they are one and the same." Head up, back straight, she marched back toward the house. At the kitchen door she paused and turned. "Cousin Milton was right, you aren't suited to be the Pendragon. 'Tis a sign of inbreeding in the dogs that they chose you."

"Psst, Aunt Georgie," Emily whispered at my locked door. "I brought you a chicken leg and some cake."

"Thank you, Emily, but how can you get it to me?"

Drake had put his own seal upon my locked door so that I could not open it with magic.

"Silly," Emily giggled. "I can break any of Papa's spells. He puts them together too fast and doesn't ground them properly."

"Bless you, child."

My stomach growled noisily as I watched the latch shift. Within seconds, my ten-year-old niece had broken through a spell that had defeated me all afternoon and evening.

Drake had reasons for not allowing me to learn more magic. He said it was because I was undisciplined. Now I suspected he needed to hide his own incompetence and feared having stronger magicians close to him.

I wolfed down the food Emily brought me while I continued pacing. Still agitated and not thinking clearly.

"Sit and drink the ale," Emily said. She looked over her shoulder frequently, checking the corridor for signs of eavesdroppers.

I grabbed the mug and quaffed half the soothing liquid in two gulps. Then I finished the meal.

"You can't marry that man, Aunt Georgie," Emily whispered.

I raised my eyebrows at her. "I know that. But how do you . . . ?"

"Cook told me that he beats his servants and his dogs. They are so afraid of him, they dare not leave his employ."

"I have to run away. If I stay anywhere in England, your papa will find me."

"Where will you go?" Her chin trembled and the crockery on the tray she still held rattled.

"Paris first. Then Germany." A plan began forming in my head. My pacing took on a pattern as I gathered essentials for a journey. "As long as King George II concentrates his money and his might on Germany, England is vulnerable to attack from France or Spain."

"Why is that important?" Emily sank heavily into the chair at my dressing table. She set the tray down and began fidgeting with my hairbrush and pins. "The Pendragons are responsible for guarding England, in England."

"But the danger lies in Europe. Your papa refuses to look beyond the end of his nose for enemies to England and enemies to himself. I have to do something. I have to work clandestinely at the source of the problem." I knelt beside her and looked deeply into her blue eyes, trying to make her understand my view of the political puzzle.

"What can you do alone?"

"Maybe I won't be alone. There are other secret societies. Some acknowledge magic. Some are not afraid to tackle dangerous situations."

"The Freemasons don't . . ."

"Grand Lodge Freemasons are as blind as your papa, and more conservative. But there are others, possibly the Knights Templar, possibly someone else. I will contact you when I know more." I jumped up and started packing my things into a carpet bag.

"You will need money. Weapons," Emily said flatly. She stared at the pots of makeup and vials of perfume that I never used.

"Now that you have opened the door, I can get them. Thank you, Emily."

"What will I do with you gone?"

"Watch everyone. Be careful."

"And if Papa tries to marry me to someone as nasty as Sir Mathew?"

"Go to Cousin Barclay. He'll protect you. I will write to you, Emily. And you can always find me in the scrying bowl."

Her face brightened a little. "Papa keeps a bag of coins in the bottom drawer of his desk. You can get them if you remember that he never grounds his spells." She smiled. A fat tear quivered on the edge of her lashes.

"Be good, Emily. And careful. And remember that Barclay will protect you if I cannot."

I slipped away from everything I had known and cherished to face the grandest and most dangerous adventures of my life.

Chapter 6

Paris, sunset, late May, 1757.

MY carpet bag weighed heavily in my hands as I walked deeper into the Latin Quarter of Paris. I needed new lodgings. The inn near the cathedral had grown too dear for my waning funds. My bag of coins had emptied rapidly in my escape from Drake and travel through France. Now I wandered the streets in search of a respectable place that would take me, an unaccompanied woman with few funds.

I'd found a dagger in Drake's desk along with the coins, but didn't have time to find my masculine clothing and rapier the night I left. Determined to conserve my funds, I hadn't wasted any on clothing or weapons.

Now I realized I might have spent less in travel and lodging as a man than as a woman alone.

Uncertainty and the long hours I had searched exhausted me. The heavy woolen traveling gown was too warm for the soft Parisian summer. Now the sun came near to setting. I had not eaten since I broke my fast.

So far I had accomplished little in seeking to contact the Lodge that I knew must work in secret to maintain a balance of power in Europe. I had written to one man I knew only as a Knight Templar. He had not answered my request. So I presented myself at his door and was promptly rebuffed by stout servants with the deep auras of magic workers and the muscles of professional assassins.

Now I strode down increasingly narrow and dark streets. I edged closer to the buildings, protecting my back, making myself more vulnerable to those who hid in the shadows between buildings and in stairwells.

Three men swaggered around the corner before me. They moved with the exaggerated care of men who had partaken too liberally of their wine. I stopped and tried to melt into the shadows. My hand eased through a slit in my skirt to the dagger strapped to my thigh. Three big men. I might have defended myself with a rapier.

I breathed deeply, centering myself, wondering how to come out of this alive and unscathed. No physical weapons. Did I have enough magic? Did I know how to use it? The land here was foreign to me and did not respond to my magic in the same manner as England did.

They didn't waste time on words and taunts. The biggest of the three grabbed my carpetbag and ripped it open.

"Nothing but lace fripperies!" he snorted in disgust and flung the bag behind him. "Where's your money, *putain,* whore?" He leaned over me, smelling of garlic, rancid sweat, and stale wine.

I scrunched my nose against the stench of him.

"Think you're too good for the likes of me, *putain?*" He grabbed my sturdy traveling gown at the throat and pulled me closer. I had to stand on tiptoe to keep from choking.

I whipped out the dagger and pressed the tip against his throat apple. "Take your hands off of me," I replied in the same gutter French he used.

Anger made me prick his skin until it dripped blood down my blade.

He screamed.

His companions yelled. Then they descended upon me, tugging at my hand where I gripped the dagger, dragging at my clothing.

No time to think. Just react. Cut, stab, stomp. Elbow to the gut. Knee to the groin.

I kept my back as close to the wall as I could. My vision narrowed to whichever man came closest to me. I saw nothing else, smelled nothing else, fought nothing else.

And still they kept coming at me. With fists and knives of their own.

Hard hands twisted me away from my current attacker. Dizzy, I slipped to my knees and dropped my dagger.

A moment of gibbering panic. And then the battle fury took me once more.

Before my head cleared, I scrabbled until my fingers closed upon the grip on the long knife. Then I twirled upward, slashing as I rose.

"*Arrêter!*" a cultured voice commanded as a man clasped my wrist. His fingers pressed upon the nerves so that my hand opened of its own accord.

The dagger clattered to the cobbles at my feet.

Blindly, I struck out with fists and feet.

"Did you not hear me, *ma petite?*" the man asked. His voice was cultured, yet strangely accented.

Finally, my senses cleared. I looked up into his clean-shaven face. A handsome face with even features and clear skin. Dark hair curled around his ears beneath his powdered queue.

"Look around, *petit oiseau,* little bird. We have defeated your assailants and sent them scuttling into the gutter."

Shocked into stillness, I did look around. Only we two remained in the gathering shadows.

The man's grip on me gentled, but he did not release me. Strangely, I was content to let him hold me.

"Who are you?"

"Your rescuer. But I might not have needed to rescue you if you had wielded your dagger properly."

"I would have a name, so that I might thank you properly. And I do know how to wield a dagger, a rapier, and a saber properly."

"Giovanni Giacomo Casanova, Chevalier de Seingalt, at your service." He stepped away and made a sweeping bow worthy of a courtier. "Now, come with me, *petit oiseau.* I will teach you how to wield a saber, a rapier, and a dagger properly."

Kirkwood House, Chelsea, England, August, 1759.

Milton Marlowe muttered the words to sever his rapport with the water in the scrying bowl. He leaned back and rubbed his temples with his eyes closed.

"Your sister still eludes us, milord," he said quietly to Lord Drake, the Earl of Kirkenwood.

Satisfaction that Georgina no longer interfered with his plans and his magic warred with disquiet that he had not found the power or the right spell to break through her shields.

"I do not understand it. We are of the same blood. Yet she hides from me physically and magically. Two years she's been gone!" Drake rested his head upon his crossed arms on the table.

"She cannot keep up this cloud forever, milord." Milton reached across the table to squeeze the earl's arm. "Even all of the Scottish Rite Freemasons combined cannot keep me out for more than a few moments at a time. I will find her."

Georgina's continued eluding of his spells gnawed at him. How did she manage it? She was not a powerful magician. She must have joined forces with the wielders of darkness on the Continent. Rumor had placed her on the doorstep of a man with connections to the outlawed Knights of the Temple of Jerusalem. In the past two years, since her disappearance, Milton had heard reports of a woman of her description in Vienna, Florence, Madrid, Prague, Berlin, and Marseilles. Always she was accompanied by Casanova, the greatest wizard, or the greatest charlatan of the age.

"I thank you for trying again. I know your schedule is busy since your court appointment." Drake lifted his head wearily. The puffiness around his eyes matched the swelling in his hands.

"I had need to check on Lady Emma's confinement. My time in this household is always a pleasure, milord." Milton did not want to talk about his Masonic connections that had gained him entry to the king's privy chamber as assistant to the underphysician of His Majesty.

George II ailed, but he was determined to remain alive until his grandson and heir reached his majority. His Majesty wanted to avoid a regency that might leave England weak and vulnerable in the constantly changing balance of power in Europe and the colonies in America.

Milton agreed with the king and poured as much magical strength into him as he did tonics and potions.

"You look as if you are in need of bleeding again to

balance your humors, milord," Milton observed. "Your skin is pale and you sweat too easily."

"I'll feel better once I've eaten. I believe Lady Emma has requested liver for luncheon. She says that liver makes her feel stronger and quiets the baby. Will you join us?"

"Of course." Milton nodded. He needed to observe Drake closely to make certain his ill appearance was only a need for food.

" 'Tis chill today for August," Drake said. He shuddered once and looked to the empty hearth. "I'll have Simpson lay a fire."

"The room has gone suddenly chill," Milton replied.

Drake left in search of his servant and a wrap. Sure evidence of his not thinking clearly. He should have used the bellpull to send for Simpson.

A cold wind circled around Milton.

Milton's mouth felt suddenly dry. This was no normal draft caused by a sudden summer storm. He took a deep breath to center his powers and look more closely at the wind.

Something nagged at the back of his mind. A worry, a doubt, a fear. He wasn't certain which.

Threads of sparkling red swirled about the room. They darted from corner to hearth to ceiling to window, coalescing and separating.

"What evil is this?" he asked the air. He felt as if an icy hand enclosed his heart.

The scintillating threads convulsed with laughter.

Don't you recognize me, Pater? Neville asked.

"Neville? What is this? Some new scrying spell?" His heart stuttered and his anxiety welled to the surface. Despite the frigid room, he broke out in a sweat.

Hardly, Pater.

The threads gathered and turned misty. Within their depths, Milton could almost make out the outline of a human form. A badly misshapen form that dripped red . . . dripped blood.

He gulped. His stomach roiled.

"Neville why are you missing an arm and a leg?" He wanted to run away, make this . . . this *thing* go away. It wasn't Neville. It couldn't be Neville.

The form became clearer. A face appeared. Neville's face. His eyes looked like burning coals set deep in a bottomless brazier. He cradled his severed arm and leg in his good arm. Blood and gore covered him.

Milton's gut twisted and turned against him. He had to close his eyes, but the horrible vision remained etched into his mind with burning acid.

"Neville?" *Oh, God, make it not so. Make this some hideous demon and not my son.*

I think I'm dead, Father. I'm dead? He looked askance at the arm and leg he cradled. *You've got to bring me back. You have to reconnect me to my arm and leg. You called me through time and space. You can't leave me like this!*

"I called you? My God, the scrying spell. I summoned you instead of Georgina! What do I do, Neville?" The smell of burning sulfur grew strong in Milton's nose. He nearly gagged.

His mind gibbered in fear at the ghostly presence. He grew colder yet.

You must find a way to make me live again so that you can heal me. Don't leave me like this. Neville reached forward. He dropped the missing leg, his severed arm still in his hand.

"Back from the dead? That's impossible." Milton shuddered with new cold and dread. "My son, dead? It can't be!"

No, it isn't impossible. There is a spell. I saw it once in an ancient grimoire. You have to find that grimoire.

"What grimoire? Where?" A morsel of hope. Perhaps he could undo the gory demise of Neville. But it would take work. It would take power. A great deal of power that could only be raised by black magic. Blood magic.

Evil magic.

To save his son he would do it. He had to do it to bring Neville back.

Look in the family archives at Kirkenwood Manor. But the grimoire is protected by magic. You'll need to make Cousin Drake let you in.

"He'll never do it if he knows why I want the spell book. 'Twill take black magic. I'll have to go to the continent to learn the substance and form of it. Drake has scruples against using blood magic. Even to restore the dead to their loved ones."

Then trick him. You have to do it. You can't leave me like this!

Chapter 7

Marlowe Hunting Box, County Kent, England, just after midnight, March 5, 1764.

"I EXPECT you to be on time, Barclay," Dr. Milton Marlowe ordered his younger son. Without looking at the miscreant, he fingered a sachet of catnip, cumin, thistle, and lavender that rested in his left coat pocket. The unique combination comforted him. They helped him keep the dead close within his heart.

Barclay lounged in the deep, wing chair by the hearth, one long leg draped over the arm, his beaver tricorn hat dangling from his fingers. The boy had obviously chosen that particular chair because the deep rust-and-gold upholstery matched his breeches and brocaded waistcoat. The golden color of his breeches, and the gold braid and buttons on his coat were only a shade darker than his hair. His brilliant blue coat matched his hooded eyes.

Milton refrained from looking at this peacock of a second son. His colorful clothing mocked the sober black of mourning that Milton wore. Barclay had not the decency to wear an armband in remembrance of his slain older brother.

" 'Tis absolutely essential, Barclay, that we press our cousin until he is utterly dependent upon me for his every decision," Milton reiterated his arguments. No telling if his indolent son had heard or comprehended him the first time.

"Easier to befriend him than scare him to death. He already trusts you with his precarious health," Barclay muttered in his cultivated drawl. "I have to return to my regiment by dawn tomorrow." He flowed into a more upright position and straightened the real lace at his cuff and neckcloth. He could not settle for mere Belgian lace, or even Nottingham work but had to have the best from Alençon.

Milton cringed at the expense exhibited in his son's clothing, his fine horseflesh, his gambling debts.

"Our cousin's scandalous sister returns from the Continent today. We cannot afford for the Earl of Kirkenwood to entrust too many family secrets to Georgina."

"Right-o. And a woman can't be trusted," Barclay finished for him. "Especially a woman tainted by rumor and gossip." He yawned.

"You know what you have to do."

"Yes, I do. I will be on time." Barclay ambled out of the snug room.

"Follow him, Samuel," Milton ordered the silent bodyguard who watched from the enclosed inglenook.

The quiet snick of a latch was the only indication that Samuel had even been there.

Milton breathed more easily. He wanted to trust Barclay as he had trusted Neville.

You cannot, a new voice spoke directly to his thoughts. *You cannot trust anyone but yourself, now that I am gone.*

Milton looked across the dim room. There in the half-light by the window a misty form coalesced. The shade wore the tattered red uniform of his regiment and clutched his dismembered left leg and right arm against his chest. His face and body were covered in blood that threatened to drip onto the worn carpet.

"Neville," Milton said on a deep sigh of regret. More of his eldest son's ghost took form. The odor of burning sulfur and old blood filled the room, replacing the lighter scents in the sachet that kept the ghost close. Milton breathed deeply of it, cherishing these remnants of Neville's too-short life.

My sib will bungle this chore as he has bungled everything else in his wasted life.

"I shall watch him closely. I have alternate plans."

You have to gain access to the family archives. We need the book.

"By this time tomorrow I shall have the key." Milton had scoured England for other old spell books and texts on wizardry to no avail. Many of them contained spells promising to bring the dead back to life. None of them had worked.

His only chance to restore his son to his bosom rested in a nearly forgotten book deep in the family archives. Only Drake knew how to break the multiple layers of magic that protected them.

You had better have the key by midnight. Neville faded from view leaving behind the unique perfume of his half existence.

Dover Port, late morning, March 5, 1764.

"Could you not have worn a decent garment, Georgie?" Drake Kirkwood, seventh Earl of Kirkenwood, asked me as he nearly shoved me into his traveling coach.

"My pardon, Brother," I grunted, settling into the seat facing the boot of the closed conveyance with my saber nestled along the seat beside me. "I have no other clothing." My threadbare mercenary uniform hung loosely on me. I'd had to add braces to the breeches to keep them from falling off. Six months of fever and recovery will waste a body something terrible.

Behind us, three servants loaded my trunk atop the coach. It contained more weapons than clothes. The fancy French dagger-pistol Casanova had given me I kept on my belt, and the Polish saber's scabbard I'd slung over my shoulder. Those two blades I trusted in no one's hands but mine. I'd have belted on the rapier I'd stolen from Casanova, too, but had no wish to bristle any more weapons in public.

I wondered briefly at the absence of my brother's wolfhound. She would have taken up an entire seat in the coach by herself. Drake would explain later if he felt I needed to know.

"You could at least have powdered your hair," he continued his litany of grief against me. "You are barely fit to be seen in polite society. If anyone here recognizes me, they will think I import an assassin from Italy. For the amount of money I paid for your passage home, they should have provided you with a bath and laundry." He wrinkled his nose.

Drake had never approved of the life I chose. Now that I had returned, still weak from my wounds and the long overland journey from Belgrade to Vienna and thence to Rome and a ship to England, he found reason to vent his contempt with every word and gesture.

I retreated into silence rather than give him excuse to find fault with something else. At least he had paid for my return home.

I should have returned last autumn when Drake's daughter Emily first summoned me. As I lay in the hut of the woods witch, raving with fever, I dreamed of home. I screamed with the nightmare of Drake's betrayal of me seven years before. I had not been back home since.

Home. The sodden chill of southern England felt as alien as Belgrade. I needed to go north, to Kirkenwood, feel the harsh wind in my face and listen to the silence of life on the moors of the border country, smell wet sheep, and taste the simple but hearty fare of Mrs. Simpson's roast lamb and pudding. Then I could heal properly. Then I'd make sense of myself and know what to do next with my life.

Then I could find the threat against my family that Emily had written of, and eliminate it. As my mercenary comrades guarded a physical border against the chaos of the Ottoman Empire invading Europe, my family guarded a metaphysical border against darker forces of Chaos.

My brother settled his considerable bulk into the forward-facing seat. His creased waistcoat and superfine coat took several moments of patting to settle across his round belly. Delicate Honiton lace edged his cuffs and neckcloth. Of course every one of his buttons was ornate and fashioned of gold. They matched the buckles on his shoes and the head of his walking stick. A gaudy ring topped with a large cabochon ruby, its fitting hinged, constricted the flesh of his pudgy fingers. What kind of potion or poison did he hide beneath the stone? I saw no trace of the dragon rampant signet on the smallest finger of his left hand. I shuddered with a new chill.

A few pats to his perfect white wig righted it. Beneath the three rolled curls on each side I caught a glimpse of his own short, dark auburn hair, much more gray than I remembered. Too gray for a man of two and forty.

"You have put on more weight since last I was home," I said, with only the slightest sneer.

"Expected in a prosperous man of my age." He looked down his long nose at me. His Kirkwood blue eyes looked rheumy and half glazed. Drake rapped the roof of the coach with the gold knob of his walking stick. The coach jolted forward. "Father of a goat!" I cursed in Italian. I grabbed with both hands the still tender scars on my side.

"Georgie?" Drake leaned forward solicitously. He placed a gentle hand atop my own. "How bad is it?"

"Bad eno'." I winced as the carriage turned off the cobbled road onto a rutted path. Where had Drake directed his driver? We should stay on the main road for the fastest route to London. From there I would continue north to home. To Kirkenwood. Drake's care of me helped ease the sharpness of the ache in my womb and my ribs and subdue my questions.

"I had believed you invincible until I received your letter at Yuletide." He kept his hand upon mine. I wondered if he tried to ease my pain with a healing talent.

"None of us, even the ones called the Pendragon of Britain, are invincible, elder Brother. Soon or late, we all die." I had faced death many times on a field of battle and broken free of his thrall.

I had learned a more intimate acquaintance with death during three bleak months secreted in the hut of the woods witch. Heinrich der Reusse and his men had searched for me. I made certain they never found me, not even to ease their minds that the Turks had not captured and tortured me. In my weakened state, from blood loss and fever, the secret of my sex was too vulnerable to exposure.

The two batmen, Estovan, with a minor thigh wound, and Ian, smuggled my few belongings to me before Estovan returned to Spain. I trusted no one else. Whythe never showed his face at the hut. But he had given his word as an Englishman and an officer in His Majesty's Army, to forget my hiding place. I trusted his oath as a Freemason more. "You will heal well eno' once I get you home, Georgie," Drake said with a trace of his youthful forcefulness. "London's gentle climate will soothe you."

"I thought to go home to Kirkenwood. No one stays in London during the summer." I needed to stand among the castle ruins atop the soaring tor and survey the ancient demesne. I wanted to walk the circle of standing stones that ringed the village, to caress the patterns in the granite that might be the faces of my ancestors.

"Emma is too near confinement to risk traveling north this year. Belle, my latest wolfhound, also nears her time. 'Tis her first litter."

This tiny mending of the breach between us needed nurturing, not further rending. The safety of the family, of all England might depend upon our cooperation.

"And Emily, your eldest daughter?"

"She entertains her sisters quite admirably while Emma is confined. Indeed, Emily has nearly become their governess."

"She is, what, eighteen now?"

"Fifteen."

So young. And yet she had summoned me home with great authority, as if she knew many more of the family secrets than I had at that age.

"Once we get you home, we'll outfit you properly, introduce you to society once more. Emily is nearing an age when she should begin attending the occasional musicale or intimate gathering. I trust you to chaperone her while Em and I are occupied with the baby. We hope for a boy this time."

Lady Emma must hope for the longed-for male heir so she could quit having more babies. She faced the dangers of childbed for the fifth time. Or was it the seventh? I did not envy her.

"A suitable marriage for you will help," Drake continued without pause. "No one need know of your . . . er . . . checkered past."

I almost chuckled at that. "If polite society ever got wind of my . . . er . . . checkered past, I would never receive a single invitation, respectably married or no," I told him. I expected no man, respectable or no, would marry me now, for many reasons and not just my scandalous behavior with Casanova, my sword master and lover.

We traveled along another half hour in almost companionable silence. Once my body adjusted to the sway and jolt of the coach, I found myself dozing off.

An unusually harsh lurch brought me awake and reaching for my saber.

Drake stayed my hand. "We have stopped at a coaching inn. Our cousin, Milton Marlowe, will join us here. He travels south from York on His Majesty's business," he said quietly. I looked into the corners to see if something lurked there that should not be disturbed. I could think of no other reason for his near whispers.

I was the most dangerous person inside the coach.

"I am surprised that Cousin Milton graces our presence. 'Tis no major celebration or holiday."

"He stood as godfather to my youngest two, Martha and Hannah."

"I barely remember Emily's christening, though I stood as her godmother. She is nigh on fifteen now. I was twelve at the time and more interested in horses and swords than a bawling infant." Though I'd taken the child under my wing once she showed signs of intelligence and personality.

"You were always more interested in horses and swords than duty and ritual. I had hoped you would marry someone older, to give you a stabilizing influence."

I snorted at the memory of the man he had contracted for me to marry, Sir Mathew Garbeleton, safely dead now from apoplexy, Emily had reported. No doubt he'd become enraged at some imagined indiscretion of his grown children, servants, or horses and fallen dead in the middle of beating them with his gnarled magician's staff.

You, dear Brother, were more interested in proper behavior and clothing than embracing life as it should be lived. Would that our roles and ages were reversed.

Before I could voice my thoughts and cause a further rift between us, I left the coach. With my feet planted firmly upon Mother Earth, I stretched upward and arched my back. My ribs and the tight scars across my belly protested the movement. The pleasure of moving my limbs again outweighed the discomfort. Before I'd finished my casual movements, I had assessed the inn and courtyard for likely ambush. The open door to the hayloft above the stable made me nervous. So did the tiny window tucked up beneath the shadowy eaves of the half-timbered inn.

Turks could hide an ambush there.

I shook myself, physically and mentally, to remind myself that I had left that enemy far behind. Even the deep forest we traversed now was reasonably civilized these days.

Then an eager-eyed boy of about twelve came running from behind the stable, offering to water our horses. "Do they need a measure of grain?" he asked as he dropped the step below the coach door.

Drake barked an assent at him as he lumbered out of the coach. He moved so awkwardly with his great girth that I offered him a supporting arm as he stepped down. He took it gratefully, forgetting for the moment that I was the one with grievous hurt to my body. He breathed heavily, almost wheezing.

I began to understand why Emily wanted me home. My brother's ill health portended dire consequences for England.

We found our cousin ensconced in a private dining room above the taproom. Stark but good furniture in a dark, polished wood gave the simple room an air of elegance. The whitewashed walls above the dark wainscoting and broad floorboards lightened it considerably. The landlord had closed the shutters but lit nearly a dozen oil lamps about the room. The cozy light made the room inviting and warm. The welcoming aura in the room did not include the heavily muscled man standing in the inglenook where he watched everything. From his stance and the peculiar bulges in his pockets, I gathered he was heavily armed. From his silence, I guessed him to be a professional soldier, possibly hired as a bodyguard. For whom? Cousin Milton or Brother Drake?

My next glance took in the sumptuous dinner spread upon the table: meat pasties, puddings dripping in fat, breads spread with sweet cream butter, soups, fish in a rich brown sauce, and sweets. Five different kinds if I counted correctly. Three bottles of wine and three more of port graced the sideboard with an assortment of glasses. Not a bit of ale or beer in sight.

No wonder my brother near waddled when he walked if he consumed such fare daily.

I sighed in resignation. Perhaps I could manage some of the soup and bread with a little watered red wine, though I would prefer a mug of beer. Cousin Milton stood to greet us, as was proper for a country gentleman in the presence of an earl. He nodded his bewigged head slightly; he only rated two rolled curls above his ears. Milton Marlowe stepped forward and embraced Drake in hearty welcome.

Worry lines now crinkled around Milton's eyes and brow. His sober black clothing made his fair skin look pale and ghostly. Deep creases shot down from his mouth, as if in perpetual frown. The smile he flashed briefly at Drake seemed forced. I wondered what had befallen Milton's younger son, Barclay, since he purchased a commission. Had the army cured him of being pigheaded. Life among soldiers had certainly changed my attitude toward authority.

I didn't care that Milton's older son, sourpuss Neville had died in the colonies some time ago.

Drake's nose worked like a dog's, twitching at the heavy scents wafting up from the table. Mine found something stronger and stranger to worry at. His stomach growled. Mine rebelled. He seemed not at all embarrassed by the impolite noise. His attention remained focused upon the table as he broke the embrace with his cousin and he sat before the feast.

Drake was intent upon his food and paid me no mind. Milton gave me one sneer, then worked at ignoring me, as if I did not share the same air as he.

"There is no liver!" Drake whined.

"Now, remember, my dear cousin, I have advised you time and again that if you are to overcome your bouts of melancholia, you must forgo liver." Milton seated himself next to my brother, dishing lavish portions of everything upon both their plates.

I wondered that Milton had not the same girth as my brother.

I sat opposite them, still forgotten, and ladled out a small amount of soup for myself.

"You know how I crave liver, Milton," Drake said. He reached for the bell. "Em serves me liver."

"Liver causes your melancholia. You may not have it. As your doctor, I insist." Milton grabbed my brother's hand before he could tug the embroidered pull. His hand stretching forth from his black cuff took on the look of talons on a bird of prey. On the middle finger of his left hand he wore the dragon rampant ring that should have been on my brother's hand. Alarums ran up and down my spine. I rose from my chair, hand on my dagger-pistol. "Since when does the Pendragon of England pass on the symbol of his office before his death?"

I focused intently upon Milton's hand.

"This has nothing to do with you, woman," Milton sneered.

I slid the dagger out of its sheath in one easy glide.

"Have the dogs chosen him? I see no wolfhound pup at his heels."

"Georgie, put away the weapon," Drake pleaded. More like whined.

"You have not been in England in seven years, Georgina," Milton said coldly, logically. He stilled his body and removed his hand from my brother's arm. Every inch of his posture screamed wariness. He kept his eyes on my dagger. "You have not helped your brother defend England throughout this long war with France and Spain. I have. You forsook all claim to your heritage. I did not."

"I have been defending England in other ways." The British army would not have me as an officer because I did not have the funds to purchase a commission. My work could not have been carried out from the position of a private soldier. I had accomplished much as a mercenary and freelance agent of a society almost as ancient as the Pendragons and much more aware of the world beyond England.

But these two hidebound men would not understand what I had done, or why I had done it.

"The Pendragon must remain in England, Georgie," Drake said quietly. "You deserted us."

"You planned to exile me with a marriage to a monster."

"He would have tamed you." Drake looked up at me with bewildered eyes.

"Since when does a Pendragon need taming?" I snarled.

My spine prickled with unease. A new chill entered the room that had nothing to do with the March wind that blew outside. I looked around warily, still keeping the dagger-pistol aimed upon my cousin.

Mist began to coalesce in a dark corner, well away from Samuel's watchful position near the window. I'd nearly forgotten Milton's silent bodyguard. Now I wanted him closer, watching my back against this new menace.

Samuel edged closer to his master, farther away from the misty form.

Milton fingered something in his pocket. A genuine smile crept across his face.

Drake opened his ruby cabochon ring and dumped a dark powder into his wine. Liver? He seemed more concerned with his food than by the eerie presence that had joined us.

You will not threaten my father. A tenor voice pierced the back of my neck. I whirled around to face the thing.

I barely made out the form of a man within the cloud. Red sparkles obscured my vision.

"Neville." Every hair on my body stood on end. "The ghost of Neville, killed in the colonies."

"Tortured by Red Indians, abandoned by his colonial troops," Milton said sadly.

I am the obedient son. I protect my father. You will sheathe your weapon.

"Or what? What harm can you do me?" Calmly, I sheathed my dagger and turned to take my seat again. I reached up and placed my hand flat against my chest, feeling the talisman that rested under my shirt. The small gold circle with an enamel eye had seemed only a pretty trinket when I bought it in Venice. Later I learned it was a powerful charm against the evil eye. As I fingered the jewelry, I muttered a phrase in Arabic.

Milton gasped and reached a hand to his throat. His face went white and his eyes bulged. He finally drew in a large gulp of air when he loosed whatever he had in his pocket.

Behind me, Neville screamed.

The chill in the room vanished.

Drake just kept on eating.

Chapter 8

On the road to London in the Kentish Woods, near sunset.

THE coach rumbled along the road at an agonizing pace. I
wanted to be up and doing. Milton kept grinning at me as
if he knew something I would not like. My instincts told me
I should watch him closely. But Drake kept the shades
drawn. The air in the closed conveyance became stuffy and
overly warm. My nose itched from the smell of garlic that
permeated my brother.

I let my eyes drift closed while Drake and Milton droned
on about politics.

"At least that bungler, the Earl of Bute, no longer holds
the power of prime minister, despite his personal interest
in the king." Drake referred to King George III's tutor
who reputedly spent too many nights in the bed of the
king's mother. I did not know the particulars of Bute's year
as prime minister, and suspected his influence over the
king had waned but not evaporated.

Despite Milton's appointment to the court, I suspected
that George III had no more interest in listening to the
Pendragon than his grandfather and great-grandfather had.

"Now that the peace treaty with France has been signed,
Parliament must turn its attention to recouping its finan-
cial losses from seven years of warfare," Milton continued.
"And now the Indian rebellion has broken out anew along
the colonial frontier near Detroit. Time the colonies assumed part of the expense for their defense."

As a mercenary, I had fought on the fringes of the Seven
Years War that had engulfed France, England, the Germanies,

and Spain as well as their possessions in the New World. I'd helped Heinrich der Reusse choose assignments for our battalion that would maintain stability in Europe. If the Ottoman Empire had broken through Austria's defenses, they could have swept over the war-torn countries and won all the way through to Paris. From that position they would have presented an even worse menace to England than the French and Spanish combined. Obsessed with my mission, I had paid little or no attention to who had doled out money to me and my troops, as long as they paid promptly what was promised. Few of us on the battlefront stopped to consider where that money had come from.

"His Majesty thinks that we should rewrite the old Sugar Tax of 1733 and this time enforce it. Lord Sackville agrees," Milton said firmly.

Sackville's name sounded familiar. I wondered why it left me with a sour taste in the back of my throat.

"Smuggling runs rampant through the colonies," Milton preached on. "The ingrates delight in circumventing the law. The customs officials make more money from bribes than from their salary. That's what comes from appointing men with no property or income. They have to look elsewhere to support themselves. We must make the colonists law-abiding subjects of His Majesty George III once more."

Silently, I applauded the enterprising customs officials and the men who bribed them. Property did not make a man competent.

Perhaps I should decamp to the New World and join the smugglers. Now that was a profession that might appeal to me since I'd severed ties with my mercenary battalion, the Pendragon Society, but not that other secret Lodge, a Lodge more ancient and broader in its membership than the Pendragons could ever be.

"Milton, I do not think this a good idea," Drake said slowly. He played with his rings to cover the snap of the cabochon ruby closing. "Since the days of George I and his Prime Minister Walpole, royal policy has been one of Salutary Neglect. This has worked quite well to the benefit of both England and the colonies. The colonies have prospered. We have prospered from their trade. Lady Emma says . . ."

I opened my eyes a slit. Drake's face went soft and gentle as he spoke of his wife.

"Times have changed," Milton stated. He pounded his fist against his thigh. The dragon ring flashed, fueled by his emotions.

"Still, I do believe I shall travel on from London with you, Milton. My place is at His Majesty's side. You should come too, Georgie."

"The travel . . ." I objected. Just thinking about the extra days in a coach bouncing along rutted roads made me slightly ill. I had taken nearly three months to travel from Belgrade to Rome because of that. I could tolerate horseback better than a coach, presuming I trusted the horse.

Right now, I needed out of this coach.

"Nonsense. You will mend quicker now that you are back on home soil."

"Home soil or foreign does not matter. I need air." Clumsily, I jerked open the door and climbed upward.

"Georgie," Drake tried to call his sister back. "You'll take chill. It's starting to rain."

" 'Twill make more room for you and Cousin Milton inside."

The moment I settled upon the box, next to Josiah, the driver who had served the family for decades, my stomach settled. The wind in my hair felt like heaven, almost as good as standing upon the tor at Kirkenwood and letting home nourish my soul.

"Georgie!" Drake raised the window shade and leaned out the coach window. He worried about this black sheep of a proud family. Worried too much, some said. " 'Tis unseemly for you to ride with a servant. Besides, you are not well. You hardly ate anything, and your color is not good," he pleaded. Em would berate him soundly if any harm came to Georgie while under his protection. The care of the far-flung family was his responsibility. He could no longer allow Georgie to thwart his authority at every turn.

"Thank you for your concern, dear brother, but I do believe the fresh air will revive me better than the closeness of the coach."

"Nonsense," Milton said. He thrust aside the shade on the opposite side and leaned out the coach window. "The moisture in the sea air will clog your lungs. When we arrive at our coaching stop, I shall bleed you. That will inhibit inflammation better than anything."

"No, thank you." Georgie turned away from them and faced forward, seemingly quite comfortable.

"Stubborn Kirkwood!" Drake muttered. Georgie would never change. "When we stop for the night, I shall attempt a healing spell," he said to Milton. "I must keep my skills in practice as well as give Georgie strength enough to mend."

"Is that wise, dear cousin?" Milton asked. He had resettled in the seat with his back to the driver. He stretched out his long legs with a sigh of relief. "Magic drains you so, you might open yourself to sickness again. The melancholia . . ."

"Is well under control. I look forward to helping Georgie regain strength with drills and mock duels. I believe a foiled rapier the more suitable weapon for that. A long time since I sparred with a partner worthy of my youthful skill." Drake plunked himself into his own seat. Just the thought of the exercise with Georgie made him feel better. If only he had not eaten that third piece of gateau with double cream. Some more liver would help his digestion. Too bad he'd used the dose hidden in his ring.

He smiled then, remembering the extra packet of dried liver his wife, Lady Emma, had packed in his luggage. A little in his wine and Milton would never know.

Too bad Em could not accompany him on this journey. She had a way of soothing and diverting Milton. She also found logical reasons to obstruct Milton's frequent requests to do research in the family archives. He was not yet the Pendragon and had no need to rummage about among the dusty records.

Drake puzzled over that a moment. As his heir, Milton should have full access to all of the family secrets. Was Em using her limited magic on them to make them agree with her?

Nonsense. She had sworn off magic during her pregnancy to avoid damaging the babe. She just had more logic at her command than Drake did.

"I hope you will be able to return to London in time for Emma's confinement," Drake said. He wanted the best physician in the realm to tend his beloved wife. Milton was the best. With his magic augmenting his learned skills he never lost a patient.

"Your wife is old to bear another child—four and forty." Milton shook his head. "She should not have conceived again. She has borne five daughters. Too many pregnancies for a woman of her constitution." Milton frowned deeper than usual.

"We hope that this time she carries a boy."

"We all do, Drake. If you have no male heir, the title and estate revert to your uncle's son, a man with no belief in the Pendragon. The heritage of the Pendragon will pass away from Kirkenwood. The archives might disappear. You really should move it to some place more accessible to the members of the Pendragon Society."

"Georgie can . . ."

"George Kirkwood is a woman—a tainted and unnatural woman. She will never be suited. Everyone in the family knows that." Milton snapped his mouth shut and closed his eyes. Clearly the conversation was over.

Drake sat back in the specially padded cushions. He studied his cousin closely. He had trusted Milton implicitly for years. Why did the man's words bother him now? Georgie was strong-willed and rebellious, certainly. But she also commanded a great deal of magic if she only controlled it. Perhaps as Milton's consort . . .

Silence prevailed except for the creak and groan of the coach springs. Drake occupied his mind by reviewing classic fencing moves. His hand curved into a natural grip. He rotated his hand as if he held a rapier with the pommel positioned properly between the wrist bones, elbow in, thumb and first finger controlling the angle.

In his reverie, he made a studied effort to ignore the half smile playing across Milton's face. His eyeteeth showed between his lips in an almost feral grin. Or was that a grimace?"

"Have you reconsidered initiating my son Barclay into the Inner Circle of the Pendragon Society?" Milton asked. He kept his eyes closed, but spoke as if he knew Drake watched every nuance of expression.

"Barclay is still too young, he has not demonstrated a mastery of talent required for such elevation."

"Two years older than Georgie. He has studied hard

since his brother's death. I believe him ready to pass any test you might put him to."

"Barclay still thinks with his prick or his sword and not his head."

The coach lurched to a stop, then swayed uncertainly as if the horses still pawed the ground.

Before Drake could open his senses and discover the source of the interruption, a strange voice, hoarse, male, edged with desperation, rang out. "Stand and deliver!"

Drake's stomach ran cold. He would have to exercise his dormant dueling skills now.

Chapter 9

I CURSED the highwayman who sat his horse directly in front of the coach. He leveled a pistol at Josiah's head. His hand remained steady with his middle finger resting lightly against the trigger. An unusual grip; not usually the strongest finger. But then he might have a hair trigger on his weapon and not want to fire prematurely with his more dominant digit. A black kerchief covered the lower half of his face and a black tricorn hat—almost green with age and dulled in spots by frequent rubbing—shadowed his eyes. Broad shoulders. He controlled his horse with balance and knees.

A vague familiarity brushed my mind. Something about the way he sat the horse . . . All this ran through my head in two heartbeats. My eyes never left his face. His gaze never met mine.

Obviously, he had decided that with my patched and faded clothing, too big now on my slight frame, I was only a coach boy, unworthy of his concern.

I dipped my head so that my own tricorn slid forward and shadowed my face.

Two more men circled the coach on prancing and nervous horses. They had not the same fine control as their leader. They, too, carried pistols. But their hands trembled—with excitement or fear? I could not disarm all three of them before one of those pistols fired and killed or injured someone. I had not loaded and primed my dagger-pistol—too dangerous to do so in a jostling coach.

Where was the second coach loaded with servants and baggage and the hulking silent form of the man I judged to be Milton's bodyguard?

Josiah nudged my knee with his own. I chanced a glance at him. His eyes dropped and his foot moved a fraction.

Then I saw it. The belled muzzle of an old blunderbuss lay beneath the seat. I had set my saber beside it without noticing when I climbed aboard. The brass gleamed with recent polishing. I had no doubt Josiah kept it primed and loaded. I slid several inches to my left. The highwayman remained focused on the driver.

The two accomplices began banging on the door, demanding that Drake exit and relinquish his valuables.

Drake called out some kind of excuse, his exact words muffled.

"If you even think of drawing a weapon against us, we will shoot you through your fat gut!" the leader shouted in a rough accent that hailed from the wharves of London. His eyes flicked to his left, farther away from me.

I dropped one foot over the side of the seat, seeking the handhold I knew was there.

The coach door creaked open. The leader's attention returned to Josiah who remained as rigidly still as possible while keeping the horses under control. Some of his nervousness must be conveyed to the animals through the reins. The offside leader lifted both front hooves two feet off the ground.

The highwayman backed his horse. I thought I knew him then. I could take him in a fair fight.

This Wharf Rat knew nothing of fairness.

I grabbed the blunderbuss and my saber as I dropped to the ground. Ignoring the aching wound in my gut, I fired into the chest of the nearest thief.

Bright red blood blossomed. The spray caught me in the face. The sweet coppery smell clogged my senses.

Quickly, I wiped my eyes free with my left sleeve and drew my saber with my right. It came free of the scabbard, nearly singing as I swept it through the air.

Suddenly the world righted. My focus narrowed. Control flowed through me from the Earth Mother.

Two more pistol shots. Wharf Rat's shot whizzed over my head. A scream. Who?

No time to wonder. I leaped for the leader still ahorse, before he could reload. Our bodies crashed just as he reached for his blade. Together we tumbled to the ground. Rolled. We engaged blades before fully standing.

Yelling like a mad Turk, I parried his first thrust with a vicious swipe. Too strong. I left myself open while recovering my balance.

He wielded an antique broadsword, thick and clumsy. Still, he held it lightly, expertly. Some kind of etching ran the length of the blade.

Cold fear swept through me. The sweat on my face chilled. My mind sobered. My body stilled.

Wharf Rat lunged wildly, aiming for my exposed heart. I leaned back with a slight twist. The blade whistled by me.

I parried and countered. He caught my saber, hilt to hilt. His blade was longer, heavier. I disengaged and backed off. I watched the familiar way he held his weapon, carried his shoulders. Watching, waiting for the telltale . . .

"I would know the face of my opponent," I whispered. A feint took my blade higher. A flick and his hat spun into the wind. He barely blinked.

Fair hair ruffled in the breeze and swept into his eyes. I attacked with a vicious slash from his seconde, his right shoulder to his quarte, near his left hip. He countered by a quick envelope, pushed me aside, and backed away. The wind swept his long hair free of restraint and into his eyes. He did not let it distract him. "You are well trained," I taunted.

"So are you." Wharf Rat lost the roughness of his accent. His words hinted at the moldy halls of Oxford and a hint of northern moors. His blue eyes twinkled. Thrust, parry, riposte, pres, disengage. I wiped all expression from my face and let my eyelids droop. If he shouted his intentions with his gaze, I'd not allow him to read mine.

More blade work. Test. Withdraw. Reconsider.

He feinted. I caught his mask with the tip of my blade. Both of his hands flew to his face. Before I could catch a glimpse of his visage, he turned and ran. Vaulting into the saddle, he galloped away without looking back.

"Damn!"

"Georgie!" Milton called me. Panic made his voice choke.

Dread froze me in place.

"Drake?" I whispered. Milton would only call me to his side if Drake ailed.

Swallowing deeply, I turned and ran to the other side of the coach. If Drake died today . . .

"Not yet!" Milton grabbed hold of Drake's collar and shook him, like a terrier with a rat. Desperation turned his knuckles white and narrowed his focus to Drake's blank eyes. "I'm not ready for you to die yet."

He pulled Drake away from the fallen outlaw. Drake kept his hands outstretched. Blue magic dribbled from his fingers. His eyes rolled up and his head lolled in unconsciousness.

"That won't help," Georgie said, kneeling on the other side of the fallen outlaw. She reached for her brother's hand.

Milton dropped his grasp of Drake rather than risk touching Georgie's tainted hands.

Get the key, Neville's voice reminded him. *Don't let him die until you get the key.*

"Drake," Georgie whispered. "Brother, come back to the living. Do not follow this outlaw into death." She cradled his hand in both of hers. Then she lifted it to kiss his palm, like a lover.

Milton shuddered in revulsion.

Drake blinked.

Milton sighed his relief. He hadn't had to attempt a healing spell to save the Pendragon of England.

"He's a thief, Drake," Georgie said a little louder. "He's not worth your life. Too many of the living need you. Think of Em and her confinement. She needs you at her side. The entire family relies upon you. You cannot follow that man into the light just yet."

Drake's chest heaved, and he blinked his eyes rapidly.

"Thank God you came back," Milton said on a long exhale. The heavy pressure of dread left his chest. He could not allow Drake to die until he had the key to the archives. Everything depended upon that.

"Georgie, brandy, my bag," Milton snapped. Now that Drake had decided to live, Milton could help him. This, he

knew how to do. For once, Georgie obeyed and did not
question every word. Perhaps the life of a mercenary had
cured the brat of that disgusting habit.

Georgie thrust a flask into Milton's hands and then knelt
beside Drake. "Breathe slowly, Brother. Count it out, just
as you taught me, lo, those many years ago."

"In, one, two, three." A weak smile flickered across
Drake's face, then vanished.

Milton set the flask to his cousin's lips. "Drink, Drake.
Just a little. Tiny sips."

The Pendragon obeyed. A little color flushed his cheeks
and his eyes focused.

"Thank you. Both of you." Drake grasped hands with
both of them. Then he sat back on his heels and took another long shuddering breath. "Breaking free of the trance
gets harder every time. Following a soul into death, guiding
him into the light is very compelling."

"Have you done this often?" Georgie asked.

"Any time is too often." Drake closed his eyes again evad-
ing the issue.

What had he been up to?

Curiosity almost made Milton probe deeper. Prudence
kept his mouth shut. If he were ever to gain the secret of the
archives, he needed to prove his discretion to Drake, as well
as gain his cousin's complete trust. He'd never do that as
long as Georgie stood between them.

Why had Georgie returned now?

Milton thrust the flask at his cousin once more, fearing
he would drift off. Drake refused the restorative with a
passive hand.

Milton insisted. "We have to get moving before that man
comes back. You need another drink." This was not the
time for Drake to develop a sense of independence.

" 'E'll no return this night," Josiah said in his hideous
northern accent. "Won't take a chance on us recognizing
'im." He kept stern hands on the bridles of the lead horses.
All four animals pawed the ground and bobbed their heads
nervously. They did not like the smell of blood coming
from the two dead highwaymen.

"If he fears recognition, then he is well known to one or
all of us," Georgie said, rising and picking up the mask and
hat. "Leave them here for him," Drake ordered as he

crawled to his feet. He took Georgie's elbow. "How can I thank you, dear sister, for your expertise with pistol and blade? They might have murdered us where we stood." He bent slightly to kiss Georgie's cheek.

"Sister," Milton spat.

Next time, Milton would be the one to revive Drake. Next time, Milton would pry the secret of the archives from Drake, then let him die.

Chapter 10

White Hall Forecourt, London, March, 1764.

"CONGRATULATIONS, Major." Major General William Howe shook Major Roderick Whythe's hand with vigor. His small, beady eyes twinkled with true enjoyment.

"Thank you, sir." Roderick withdrew his hand as soon as politeness allowed and snapped his superior officer a smart salute. Pride and satisfaction puffed his chest just a little. Father would not recognize Roderick's achievement, but His Majesty's Army certainly appreciated his efforts. He'd earned this promotion with his blood, his sweat, and the total loyalty of his troops. Not to mention recruiting Prince Heinrich der Reusse and his crack light cavalry regiment into the service of His Majesty George III. Roderick did wish, though, that the young Major Kirkwood had recovered from his wounds soon enough to accompany them. Not much more than a boy, Georgie handled blades, pistols, and horses better than any other man in the mercenary company. He'd be missed.

"If you'd had a noble patron or a bit of land, I could have promoted you two years ago," General Howe muttered. "You deserve this, Roderick."

"Thank you, sir." An acorn of anger burned in his gut. Anger at his father for throwing away the family heritage and wealth. Anger at himself for turning down an offer of patronage three years ago out of stubborn pride.

Putting aside his emotions, as a gentleman should, Roderick turned to the red-coated troops lined up behind him. He wanted to include his men in this moment of personal triumph. Part of him wished that young Georgie could also witness this moment, acknowledge his achievement.

As one, his men raised their hands to their brows as if a puppet master yanked the appropriate strings.

Niceties of the promotion ceremony complete, General Howe beckoned Roderick to accompany him into the state building. "Put aside your stubborn pride, Steady Roddie. Seek out a patron or you'll go no further in His Majesty's Army," Howe warned. "Is it possible your family could come up with something to help you purchase another step? 'Twould go a long way toward improving your status with the prime minister."

Not bloody likely, Roderick thought. His family had only a small estate left that they barely held together for his eldest brother. A second brother had found a patron and entered the church. His sister had become a governess without prospect because of a lack of dowry. Even if Roderick put together the purchase price of the next promotion from battlefield booty—as he had on the Austro-Turkish border—many superior officers would create ways to keep from promoting him because he had no land or title.

"We've had disturbing reports from the colonies," the general said without preamble.

"I hear disturbing reports on the street and in every tavern," Roderick replied.

"This Indian war on the upper Ohio. Pontiac's War, the colonials call it. Chief Pontiac is running rampant, taking scalps, making deep inroads into our frontier." Howe led Roderick to a small office. He paused with his hand poised for knocking. "We replaced Major General Jeffrey Amherst with Major General Thomas Gage. Tom is having a hard time cleaning up Amherst's mistakes. I'll be transferring you to be aide-de-camp for Virginia. We've got to do something to protect the frontier there. The colonials insist upon moving ever westward despite royal policy restricting them east of the mountains."

"Yes, sir." Excitement ran up and down Roderick's spine. He'd wanted to return to the colonies for some time now. Six brief months three years ago had only whetted his appetite for the land and the people.

"I trust you to report accurately, directly to me."

Roderick's excitement collapsed into a heavy knot in the

back of his neck. Howe wanted him to spy upon another general. Was there no loyalty left within the ranks of His Majesty's Armies?

"By the Compass and the Square, I'll know what truly happens in the colonies," Howe snapped. "We'll set up a number of special couriers for your reports. Gage's letters have to go through scribes and aides, couriers and ship's captains. All have the opportunity to alter, filter, and lie. Then the reports reach the War Office and go through any number of petty officials and members of Parliament before I hear them. One wonders if the king and prime minister even see the original."

Roderick hesitated to make a Mason's oath to General Howe for something outside Masonic business. The last time he'd made such a vow he had to keep Major Kirkwood's location secret from the lad's closest comrades and Prince Heinrich der Reusse. Der Reusse had become a good friend. The secret gnawed at Roderick like a festering sore.

"Tampering with His Majesty's dispatches is illegal," Roderick said instead.

Howe looked at Roderick skeptically. "Surely we both know that even the Royal Mail is no longer sacred when it comes to colonial matters. Why should military couriers be any less inviolate?" He pushed open the door and entered the small chamber.

A chill slid up Roderick's spine. Surely the mails must remain inviolate. Keeping them safe was a sacred trust placed upon the postmasters.

Prime Minister Grenville and another man sat silent and uneasy around a tea table near the window of the small office. Roderick did not know the gaunt man with the haunted eyes on the left who stared fixedly out the window. Grenville tapped a rolled up report upon his knee. Two dishes of tea cooled before them. Grenville acknowledged Howe's entrance with a nod. The other man remained silently brooding.

"Milords." Howe tucked his hat beneath his arm and executed a neat bow to the room in general. "My aide-de-camp, Major Roderick Whythe."

The lords barely nodded in acknowledgment. No one made a move to introduce the lords to Roderick.

"Lord George Sackville," Howe whispered out of the

side of his mouth. "Treasurer for Ireland. The post has made him very rich."

Roderick gulped. He'd heard of the Irish lord. He'd commanded a crack regiment during the war, bungled battle orders, and been court-martialed. But he'd resumed his seat in Parliament and won new awards on the political front.

"Amherst has truly bungled it, William," Lord Grenville blurted out. "Gage is having the devil of a time cleaning up after him. The bloody savages have won nearly to New York." He waved the rolled report about as if it were responsible for the mess.

"General Howe, you will be responsible for recruiting an additional three thousand five hundred troops to augment Gage's current complement," the prime minister continued. "They must assemble at Portsmouth and be ready to sail by early June."

"I want you to sail earlier," Howe muttered for Roderick's ears only.

Roderick's heart beat a little faster. A campaign of this magnitude could earn him land grants in the colonies. He thirsted at the prospect of owning something other than his horse, weapons, and uniforms.

He would earn back the respect his father had gambled away.

"And how are the men to be paid, milord?" Howe asked.

Grenville consulted a sheaf of papers on the tea table. "Parliament has agreed that the army shall recruit, arm, and feed the troops out of their new funds from the Exchequer. The colonials will see that they are paid. They will also provide uniforms for their own troops added to ours."

"We expect to hear that the savages have been beaten and the colonists acquiescent by autumn," Sackville finally added his opinion. "Those churlish colonials are little better than the Irish. We'll have to leave the troops in America to keep them from falling back into the barbarism of the Red Indians."

Howe cocked an eyebrow at Sackville's words. Roderick stifled his own unease. If all went well, he would become one of the colonists. At least a landowner among them.

"Parliament is drawing up a number of measures to raise revenue to pay for this little expedition. As well as to help reduce the debt incurred on behalf of the colonies during the last war." Prime Minister Grenville rubbed his hands together eagerly. "We'll have the treasury balanced and the colonies showing a profit within two years."

Profit sounded good to Roderick. He could use a little of it before he sailed. He wondered if he could presume on his new promotion and get enough of an advance from the paymaster to settle his debts with his landlady. His bonus for recruiting Prince Heinrich der Reusse had all gone to repaying old debts on behalf of his brother, to the tailor for new uniforms suitable to his promotion, and a small donation to his chapter of the Grand Lodge of Freemasons for charitable works. Surely, once he landed in the Americas, his pay would stretch farther than it did at home. It had to. He had no more reserves and no patrons.

"Major Whythe," Lord Sackville said. He kept his back to the room, looking out the window at the parade grounds below. "Before you depart with the troops for the colonies, I have a little assignment for you."

Roderick quirked an eyebrow at Howe. The general shrugged his shoulders.

"The Earl of Kirkenwood has brought his sister home from Europe. I would have you make their acquaintance and report to me the woman's plans."

"An earl's sister, milord?" Roderick shifted his feet uneasily.

"She was last seen in Dresden on the arm of your good friend Prince Heinrich der Reusse the night the King of Poland was assassinated. The Ministry of Foreign Affairs would know her role in that plot."

The Dragon and St. George Tavern, Maidstone, England, that same evening.

> "Maiden, I give to you Watkins ale."
> "Watkins ale, sir," quoth she.
> "What is that, I pray you tell me?"
> " 'Tis sweeter far than sugar fine
> And pleasanter than Muscadine."

I sang the familiar words to the drinking song, as loudly and raucously as the men inhabiting The Dragon and St. George Tavern this night. Laborers and craftsmen one and all, not a gently-born face among them. Except possibly mine and that was obscured by a brown powder mimicking evening stubble. At the end of the next verse I downed a goodly portion of the beer in my mug. So did each of the fifteen men gathered around the long table. From the cover of my wooden tankard I watched them for a gesture, a cock of the head, or a shrug of the shoulders that echoed the arrogant highwayman. His mask bulged slightly in my coat pocket. I held his hat upon my knee. It was far too large for my head, but I wanted it nearby, to confront the man with it if he dared show his face in Maidstone this night.

Drake and Milton presumed I rested comfortably at the manor of a friend where they boarded for the night. I had threatened Milton with the sharp edge of my dagger when he tried to bleed me. He left my private room on the third floor among the servants' cubicles in a huff. Drake went off to procure me a "decent" gown. I doubted he'd find any woman in town near eno' my height willing to sell such a garment. Even if he found one, I doubted I'd wear it.

My drinking companions and new best friends started in on the next verse of the bawdy song. I mouthed the words, preferring to concentrate on the men mingling around the edges of the room rather than deepening my voice and keeping in tune with them. I watched carefully through many long verses of the song. If my quarry frequented a tavern near his place of ambush, it was not this one.

Time to move on. I rose from my place, tucking the worn hat beneath my arm. The closeness of quarters forced me to sidle along behind the benches and watch my feet. When I looked up again, I saw him.

My heart skipped a beat. I'd never forget his face, nor his body and the way it had once fit snugly against mine. Our minds had blended once in perfect rapport. Not tonight. Not ever again.

His fair skin and hair and the brilliant blue of his eyes had not changed. He had discarded the roughly woven and poorly cut brown suit of the road in favor of a finer gray coat with big brass buttons, a green waistcoat, and brown breeches. Hints of lace at throat and cuff, nothing flamboyant. His fair hair was neatly combed and tied back in a queue with a green velvet ribbon. The buckles on his shoes matched the buttons. This was no impoverished gentleman. To further the image of respect and prosperity, despite the man's relative youth, the tavern keeper handed him a pewter tankard frothing with pale beer rather than the rough wooden cups and dark brews he served to the rest of us.

Then I realized my quarry had been standing in a corner near the door for a long time, engaged in deep discussion with three other men. I approached him, intent upon throwing the worn beaver tricorn in his face.

"If the colonists are honest Englishmen, same as you and me, as they claim," the highwayman said. He spoke in a more refined accent now. "They need to pay taxes same as you and me."

"But Grenville means to punish them, not just tax them," the tavern keeper said, leaning over the end of his bar to join in the conversation. "They did not provoke war with the bloody French, nor with the savages. They lost scalps and lives in that war."

"But we're paying for the war against the French and Spanish on the Continent. We should not be expected to pay double taxes for the bloody colonists." The highwayman abandoned his three companions to press himself against the bar. He and the tavern keeper stood nose to nose, alike in height, build, and stubbornness.

I had heard part of this conversation before today. Was the entire country obsessed with the colonies and the proper means to pay for a war?

How did one pay for troops, provisions, transportation, horses, uniforms, and weapons? I had always presumed the government had the money in hand. No merchant would embark upon a costly and risky enterprise without knowing beforehand how to pay for it.

"Colonies have always paid their way through trade!" one of the three abandoned by the highwayman said loudly.

"They ain't truly Englishmen born and bred. Not like us," another man from the crowd interjected. "Seems like they owe us more than just taxes for lettin' them live on England's land."

"Ain't no cause for Parliament to suddenly demand taxes where no direct taxes have been paid before," the tavern keeper proclaimed. "We wouldn'a let Parliament suddenly tax us on the air we breathe, just 'cause they need money."

"They tax everything else, why not the air, too?" someone from the depth of the room shouted.

This earned a loud guffaw.

"If taxes weren't so high, honest men would not be thrown off their land when the rents come due, forcing them to take to the road," I said softly. "Do we want the colonies full of highwaymen, same as here?" I kept my gaze leveled on the man who had crossed swords with me earlier and when I was fifteen. He wore his blade now. As did I. My hand itched to draw it.

He turned his deeply blue eyes toward me. If my words had struck home, he did not reveal it by so much as a lifted eyebrow. My right hand rested uneasily upon the pommel of my saber.

We stared at each other for several long moments in mute challenge. The room stilled around us, sensing a duel brewing.

"Ah, you, boy, we need to get back to our master," Josiah, Drake's coachman, shouted to me from the doorway.

The highwayman looked into his beer, then took a long swallow. Over the rim of his elegant tankard his eyes shifted from the doorway to me, to the crowd, and back to me.

Josiah placed his big, callused hand atop mine on the pommel of my sword. "You do not want to tangle with him in here, where he has friends," he whispered.

I bowed slightly to the highwayman, promising to meet him again. Next time on my terms.

"Captain Marlowe," Josiah bowed to my opponent. "Your father wishes you to pay your respects this evening at the home of Baron Whitford, two miles north of town, if you would."

"Very well, Josiah." The highwayman nodded. He set his tankard down upon the bar with a solid thunk. "Shall we seek my honorable father now?" He marched out of The Dragon and St. George without further ado. Not once did he acknowledge me.

"So, my cousin Barclay Marlowe is a captain in His Majesty's Army. Which regiment? Who is his colonel?"

Why had he taken to the road? I did not believe he needed the money. But then he hated rules as much as I did. And I had taught him how to break most of them.

Chapter 11

Whitford Manor, two miles north of Maidstone, England.

DRAKE must have heard me creep past his room toward the garret reserved for me—as if I were but another servant instead of a close relative. Actually, a little better than a servant, Josiah would sleep on the floor of the kitchen. The coach full of servants and luggage that had followed several hours behind us might end up sleeping in the stables. I did not want to guess where the hulking and silent Samuel, Milton's bodyguard, slept as long as he kept his knowing eyes and his brooding presence away from me.

I had barely removed my clothing and slipped into bed wearing the beribboned and lace-trimmed night rail laid out for me when my brother knocked on my door. Should I blow out the candle and pretend to sleep?

My brother knew me too well. He also had talents I had never dreamed of tapping. He probably read my mind even as I debated.

"Georgie?" Drake whispered. The latch lifted quietly and he poked his nose into the room. "Oh, good, you are still awake." He moved into the tiny chamber without further invitation. My temper boiled. Even my mercenary comrades had enough consideration for each other to wait for a summons. Hadn't Drake's wife and five daughters taught him to respect a woman's privacy? Maybe they did not need to. Maybe he read their minds as easily as he read mine and knew when to enter and when to wait.

I opened my mouth to shout at him. But he forestalled me with an open palm held up.

"Please, Georgie, I need to talk to you."

I glared at him. "Make it fast, Drake. I am tired, I hurt, and no one has so much as thanked me for saving your selfish, parasitic lives. Nor do either of you care that . . ."

"Georgie, I have come to talk to you about your condition." He raised his hand again. "And to thank you for rescuing both Dr. Marlowe and myself."

I raised my eyebrows at the formality of our cousin's name. Earlier they had used the familiar form of first names, very intimate terms between a belted earl and commoner. An intimacy that had developed since I had left home seven years ago. Prior to that, the Marlowes had visited Kirkenwood or the London house only upon important occasions, like the ceremony inducting Drake as the Pendragon of England, or Yuletide dinners.

"What about my condition?"

"I think I can help you. I am the only member of the family since our grandfather to have the healing talent."

Tonight he had retrieved and wore the signet ring of a dragon rampant rouge on his right hand. The ring he should never have taken off since he became the Pendragon at the Summer Solstice in his thirty-first year.

"My wounds have healed. I need only regain my strength." I crossed my arms across my middle and tried to sink deeper into the bolster pillows.

"Have they, Georgie?" He made no move to come closer to the bed or to sit in the room's only chair—a rickety cane bottomed one that would never support his bulk.

"Perhaps we should discuss your health, dear brother. You seem more fragile than I. Pity you can't use the family magic upon yourself."

"I wish I could roust the bouts of melancholia that strike me low. I wish I could regain my youth and vigor. But, alas, the talent does not work that way. I can only be of service to others. I wish, Georgie, to be of service to you."

A vision of Drake's face wasted from pain and disease flashed across my mind. Fleeting. Gone so quickly I might have imagined it. Or glimpsed the future. I'd never done that before. I began to shake. My talent for reading troop placement and the enemy's strategy had nothing to do with this terrible premonition.

"Breathe, Georgie. The only way to move through the vision is to breathe. On my count."

Together we drew long breaths and released them. My focus narrowed to the sound of his voice, that fine tenor that cut through the fog of a vision. Many long moments later I opened my eyes. Drake's face remained pudgy and pink. "You always said that a vision of the future is only a warning. 'Tis not writ in stone."

"Aye." Drake lifted my wrist, fingers positioned to count my pulse. I heaved a sigh and knew what I had to do. I had to bring my brother back to health. The thought of the family titles and honors going to a cadet line frightened me. The thought of Dr. Milton Marlowe becoming the next Pendragon frightened me more. I did not know the man well. The presence of his ghostly son boded ill.

To stay close to my brother and protect him, I'd have to dress as a lady, daughter and sister to belted earls. Damnation, I hated the thought of donning a corset.

"Now tell me the source of your biggest hurt, Georgie." Drake seemed to move on from the vision as if they were an everyday occurrence. Perhaps, for him, they were.

If I wanted to stay close to him, win his trust, I had to let him try his magic on me. I had to trust him. I'd fled London seven years ago partly because I had lost my trust in him.

"My ribs." I touched the sore spot beneath a ridge of scar tissue on my right side. "They feel as if they broke and then did not align when they knit." I could not bring myself to mention the damage to my womb. A female was always valued more for ability to bear children than to think or wield a sword.

"Hmm." Drake pulled up the chair and sat close by the bed. The contraption groaned and sagged. The legs looked as if they might bow outward. Fortunately, he leaned forward rather than stressing the back. My brother began another round of deep breathing before he placed his hands, one atop the other, on the place where I pointed.

Through the coarse linen of the night rail, and the tight bandages I wore to support the wound I felt his heat. His hands nearly burned their imprint upon my skin. I gasped and drew several long breaths, exhaling completely, to keep from jerking away from him.

On the third breath I shifted my gaze from a cobweb on

the ceiling beam to Drake's face. He glowed. A look of transcendent peace came over his visage. Blue-white energy enveloped him.

Fascinated, I placed my own hand atop his. I met a tingling resistance and had to push through the light. The moment my hand touched his, the power within the light leaped to my heart. Then it spread through me. My heart stuttered. My lungs burned.

I forced myself to breathe again. The startling stab of energy became pinpricks all through my body. And still Drake radiated heat from his hands into my body.

The room dimmed around me. I almost cried out my alarm. My eyes scanned the situation, seeking a vulnerability in Drake or an opening for retreat. I found that the light had spread to include me. My own hand added to the heat and light of Drake's talent.

Awed, I stared openmouthed at the merging of our hands to my body.

A grinding pain in my side nearly yanked me out of rapport with Drake. A sound of bones rubbing against each other that hurt my ears almost as much as the rebreaking and resetting of my ribs hurt my body.

Then nothing. No sound. No pain. No heat.

I panted in relief.

Gradually, the light dimmed and collapsed back within Drake. He grounded the spell, leaving no stray magic loose to work unguided mischief.

Except for one small shaft of too-white light that shot back into my hand.

Drake sat back in his flimsy chair, head flung upward. In the flickering candlelight his skin looked gray. I lay panting against the bolsters, too thunderstruck to ask what had happened.

"You will need support upon those ribs for a few days," Drake whispered, as if he had not the strength to speak louder. "Bind them tightly."

Much as I hated to admit it, a corset would do that. "What did you do to me, Drake?" My own voice came out hoarse, barely above a whisper. A sign of weakness I hated. Enemies took advantage of any sign of weakness.

"You did it, Georgie."

"What?"

Surprise sent me upright. The ribs protested, but only slightly. Nothing like the pain that had stabbed me when the carriage lurched.

"You added your own talent to mine. Together, we performed an impossible feat."

"I thought . . ."

"My talent is moderate. I can reduce fevers, set newly broken bones, boost a body's ability to heal. On someone I know well, I can find the root cause of illness and force it to flee. But this . . ." He shook his head and stared at me in wonderment.

"I thought a person could not heal herself."

"I have never heard of one doing such. I must think on this. Perhaps you did not perform the actual magic, merely added your strength to mine to make it powerful enough to do the impossible. This could be your true talent. A catalyst for magic."

If he spoke truly, then perhaps I could use other than the discipline of diet and exercise to heal my brother.

But not tonight.

"Sleep well, Georgie. Sleep free of pain and worry. You are safe here." Gently he kissed my forehead and departed. I barely heard the snick of the latch as sleep claimed me.

Never trust a civilian to secure a perimeter. Drake Kirkwood, seventh Earl of Kirkenwood trusted his servants to protect his noble personage against thieves, brigands, and unwanted intruders. Baron Whitford trusted his servants to keep his home inviolate.

No one bothered to guard my door against those already within the household.

I awoke to darkness with a start. Sleep left me reluctantly. I felt as if I had to swim through its heavy veils. Had I lain unconscious for hours, minutes, or days?

At first I felt guilty that I had slept through my watch. I sat bolt upright and threw off the covers. My feet tangled in the night rail. I never wore such a cumbersome, and feminine, garment in the field.

Then I remembered. I had put my mercenary life behind me. My current campaign lay with my brother's health.

How long had I slept after his healing spell left me free of pain for the first time in months? Pain had become such a constant companion I almost missed it now. The candle had guttered. Shutters blocked out the cloudy night sky. I saw only a vague outline of the door where a little light leaked from the night lamp at the head of the stair.

Cautiously, I stilled my mind and my body and listened to the night. The manor creaked and settled as buildings will. A cricket chirupped outside in the forecourt. Neither sound alarmed me.

Something had awakened me.

A faint sound of shuffling feet and quick breathing came from the other side of the door.

Without thinking, I grabbed the dagger-pistol from beneath my pillow and slid noiselessly across the floor to the back side of the door. I held my breath.

The latch lifted. The door opened a fraction. A silent shadow wiggled into the room. It advanced one step.

I grabbed one of his seeking hands and twisted his arm up behind his back. In the same movement, I rose on tiptoe and held my blade across his throat.

"Who are you and why do you invade a lady's bedchamber?" I asked boldly. My heart leaped to my throat in excitement with the thrill of outwitting the brigand. My fingers and toes tingled with the urge to engage in swordplay.

The night rail was too long and voluminous for such dramatics.

"Cousin Georgina, is that you? Why do you sleep up here with the servants? Such a room fits the station of a . . . a family outcast, not the beloved sister of an earl."

I scraped the stubble upon his throat with my blade.

" 'Tis I, Barclay Marlowe," my captive said on a deep gulp. "I need to talk to you, Georgie."

"Such consult would not wait 'til morn?" I pushed his left arm higher against his back. I had to lift my heels even farther off the cold floor. Few men topped me by more than an inch or two. My cousin had grown a handspan or more since our last . . . encounter.

"I must depart before dawn," he explained, trying to shrug, or twist off my hold on him.

"More like you need to make excuses for your behavior this afternoon before I speak to my brother." I pressed my thumb upon the pressure point on the inside of his wrist. Something metallic clattered to the floor and bounced.

Instinctively, I hopped back to avoid losing toes to whatever he had held.

Barclay reared back, pushing me into the wall.

My grip on his wrist loosened. He swung free.

We both dropped to the floor, feeling for the lost weapon. I knew it had to be a weapon.

My foot brushed something cold and sharp. I felt a sharp slice across my toes. The blade skittered across the floor. I bit back a curse as warm blood oozed over my foot.

His hand grabbed at my waist.

I kicked back.

He rolled.

I leaped and landed atop him. Once more I found his throat with my dagger. I cocked the pistol portion even though I had not loaded the weapon. But he did not know that.

"Now tell me why you violated my privacy past midnight carrying a weapon?"

He let forth a low chuckle.

" 'Tis no laughing matter." I pushed the edge of my knife just below his throat apple.

He heaved. We rolled. I found myself on the bottom with my hands pinned near my ears. But I kept hold of my dagger.

"I find it strange that the mistress of Giovanni Giacomo Casanova should protest the presence of a man so vehemently." He wiggled his torso atop me suggestively. I raised my knee sharply and connected.

He grunted, but did not let go of me. I had not the leverage to hurt him, merely to remind him of his vulnerability. "I was told that the coach boy, who defended my father and the earl against a highwayman, slept here." He lost the mirth in his voice. "Or could it be that my delightful Georgina and the coach boy are one?" He spoke as if he knew the truth of that statement.

I did not need to see his face to know he cocked one eyebrow at me.

"You guess wrong. I am no coach boy. Why do you seek him with stealth and a blade? Surely a coach boy is no threat to the likes of you." I avoided discussing my sword master and mentor, Signor Casanova.

"The boy's impertinence offends me."

"Surely a man as important as you is above offense from a servant. You have no need to play the assassin. A simple word to my brother will see the boy punished."

"But you will reward the boy on the side, mitigate his punishment. Perhaps I should punish you myself." He captured my mouth with his own in a savage kiss.

I bit his lip. He persisted, coaxing my lips to part with his impertinent tongue.

For a few brief seconds I welcomed the warm intimacy of our last meeting. Then I bit his tongue.

He jerked his face away, muttering curses I cared not to hear.

"Know this, Cousin Georgina, if you speak out of turn about me to your brother, your brother will die. I swear it by the Griffin and the crystal-topped staff."

I had no answer to that oath. We of the Pendragon Society did not so swear lightly.

"We of the Pendragon Society know how to keep secrets, when it benefits the family," I hedged.

"Drake Kirkwood, the Earl of Kirkenwood, is in serious danger. Unwise words will be his death warrant. Keep the secret of the family archives as secret as your activities these past five years," Barclay said. His entire body stilled. His words penetrated my mind with quiet urgency.

"Get you gone from here, Cousin Barclay." I raised my knee again. He released me and sank back on his heels. Then he rose gracefully to his feet. In a single heartbeat he was gone, leaving me alone with my thoughts. And my unquenched desires.

Even as inexperienced teenagers we had managed to take each other to unimaginable heights of ecstasy. Only Casanova had been a more imaginative lover.

Chills of premonition ran up and down my body. Barclay had an inventive mind in other ways as well. I had few doubts that he was the potential assassin of my brother that Emily feared. I had to know more before I decided if he worked alone or acted as part of a larger conspiracy.

Chapter 12

WHY did I allow that bastard Barclay to live? I stabbed an imaginary target on the byre wall with my rapier in my left hand. If I had killed Barclay in my room, no one would have questioned my pleas of self-defense. I could have flung my dagger into his back as he retreated. But would that have ended the threat to my brother?

I slashed wildly with my saber in my right hand at the dead Turk who lived only in my dreams. I danced around my imaginary enemies behind the stable and repeated a series of exercises from a different angle, with a different play of light upon my target. As my anger at myself and at Barclay dissipated, I concentrated on my drills. Slowly, methodically, I worked through a series of drills my beloved sword master had used to teach me the finer art of swordplay. I honed precision in my aim and balance in my stance.

An hour ago, before I had left my room, I had watched Cousin Barclay Marlowe ride out in full military uniform and equipage for an unknown destination. I'd not have the opportunity to press him for more details.

Now dawn glistened on the horizon. Despite the fine cool drizzle, I soaked my shirt from the inside with sweat. Too long, during my recovery, I had neglected these drills.

Barclay Marlowe was good with a blade. I had to be better, and maintain my edge. I had few doubts that eventually he and I would meet on the field of honor and duel to the death. Whether his or mine, or both of ours, I could not foresee.

Now I moved through the progression of skills and positions grateful that Drake had healed my wounds more completely and properly. No longer did every movement catch on the misaligned ribs. Even the ridged scars had burned down to smooth skin, a different texture but no longer unsightly.

Would that my womb had healed as well. My normally easy cycle had become erratic and painful.

"May I drill with you, Georgie?" Drake asked. He stood to one side dressed informally for travel with an ornate rapier slung at his side. Without his powdered peruke and his walking stick, wearing a plain coat with pewter buttons, he looked less bloated and vulnerable than he had the day before. Less pompous and disapproving as well.

My eyes crossed of their own volition. A death's-head rode over my brother's visage. I shivered with a new awareness of his mortality. Unless I performed some kind of miracle, Drake had not long upon this earth. I could no longer look upon him as the indestructible patriarch of the family, inheritor of strong talents, and protector of our ancient heritage.

I rested my blade tips, blunted or foiled with clay for practice, atop my boots while I surveyed him, and thought.

"I see you used your allowance to invest in some fine weaponry," Drake said. He approached me cautiously.

"Damascus steel. Polish design. Perfectly balanced. Made specifically to my height and reach." I flipped the rapier up, swung it through two figure eights, one in each direction. The flexible blade whipped through the air with a satisfactory ripping sound.

"Devoid of ornamentation," he said with a slight frown.

"Working blades. I do not wear them for show." I brought the saber up and began a complicated drill, working the two blades in opposite spirals, bringing them closer and closer with each pass, making certain the two never touched.

"How many men have you killed with those weapons?" Drake gulped.

I remembered how his talent had reacted to death yesterday—he'd tried to follow into death a man he had not killed himself, and a stranger at that. If he killed a person himself, in battle or in a duel, would the death-link take him as well?

My blades stilled almost of their own accord.

"I do not remember how many have died at my hand.

For the last two years I fought dozens of skirmishes against Turkish regulars, Janissaries, and Mussulmen on the border of the Ottoman Empire. In that time, I recall at least seven full battles. A soldier loses track of the casualty lists after a while."

Yet, if I concentrated hard upon my reflection in the saber blade in bright sunlight, I could relive every kill with that weapon. I tried not to do that very often.

"Your talent does not force you to follow your victims into death, then." Drake's eyes closed and his lips moved in some silent prayer. "A blessing and a curse."

Did he refer to my talent or his?"

"I could not be what I am if it did."

"Your talent has grown since you left home."

I shrugged and turned back to attack imperfections in the byre wall. "I have practiced my arcane arts as well as swordplay. Casanova saw to that. He allowed me to grow in any direction I chose."

This time I alternately slashed and stabbed. Then I tossed the blades and switched hands. Slash and stab, stab and slash. I counted the rhythm and kept the weapons moving always on the same count. No faltering. No break in my concentration.

"Do you use your talents in battle?"

"Rarely. I have not the need when I have my skills."

"Is it skill alone that allows you to feel through your feet where your enemy stands? Is it skill alone that allows you to determine friend from foe in the heat of battle when dust and blood obscures uniform and visage."

I halted my drill, lost my count, and nearly dropped the saber. "I followed your career, Georgie. I maintained correspondence with your colonel, Prince Heinrich der Reusse."

This time I grounded the tip of each blade atop a boot while I thought of a reply. "Heinrich never told me . . ."

"He had no reason to tell you."

"Yes, he did."

"I requested he not." Honorable to the last, my Heinrich would never betray a confidence. In two years on the battlefront he had never once revealed my secret by so much as an awkward glance or slip of the tongue. I trusted that my colonel had not betrayed another secret to my brother, that we had been lovers one night. Only one night, before I joined his regiment. After that, he treated me as just another soldier.

But then, my joining the regiment had been his idea, after I disarmed him three times in a row, while wearing only my petticoat. Each time he lost his blade, I'd taken a strip from his nether garment so that by the last bout he stood stark naked and I nearly so.

"I think the time has come to initiate you into the Inner Circle of the Pendragon Society, Georgina," Drake said.

He jolted me away from a very pleasant memory.

"I am no Master Magician." I returned to my drills, studiously avoiding looking into my brother's eyes.

"You were initiated into our Order as an Apprentice when you were twelve, studied hard, and advanced to Knight when only fourteen."

"Since I turned eighteen, I have not studied magic, nor have I attended a single Pendragon Society meeting or communicated with any of the magicians except an occasional letter to you." I did not tell him about my regular correspondence with Emily.

My aim was off by the width of a finger. Damnation. Drake destroyed my concentration.

"Among our ancestors is a long tradition of solitary study and separation from the family."

"I know the family history." I spoke a little too loudly and vehemently. Why did I protest so much? Too much? Being allowed into the Inner Circle of the secret society would keep me close by Drake's side where I could defend him.

"Our numbers dwindle, Georgina. I sense a need to bring you into the Inner Circle. I shall sponsor you. I shall train you, as I hope you will train me in the fine art of swordplay."

"What about our cousin, Barclay Marlowe?" I suspected Barclay's father, Milton Marlowe, had already achieved entrance into the small circle and might one day succeed Drake as the Pendragon. That membership remained secret from the lower ranks as well as the general public. Not even His Majesty knew who comprised that membership.

"Milton is pressuring me to admit Barclay. I have not

seen the young man in a year and more; his military duties keep him elsewhere."

I raised an eyebrow at that announcement but said nothing.

"I shall have to interview the young man before I can decide."

"You can decide that I am eligible so quickly, Drake?"

"I have witnessed your magical power, Georgie. I know you can become as great, or a greater magician than I."

"You refused to see that seven years ago. You refused to allow me to learn enough magic to advance in the Society. You pushed me to marry an ancient martinet with Puritan leanings. He'd have killed me before he let me work magic!"

"He'd have tamed you so that I could teach you properly." Drake's face grew red. He clenched his rapier so tightly his knuckles turned white and the blade quivered.

"I question your judgment," I said mildly, holding onto my temper. "I challenge your right to dictate my life."

With a visible effort, Drake mastered his temper. "We shall have the induction ceremony in London before Dr. Marlowe and I depart to join His Majesty. You must exhibit your talent to the brethren. What can you do?"

"This." I stuck the rapier into a nearby hayrick and balanced the tip of my saber upon my finger. "No magic. Just balance and skill."

"Then why, pray tell, is your aura glowing bright amber, the same color as your hair and eyes?"

I dropped the sword.

Milton hugged the corner of the stable. From here he could observe Kirkwood and his whore of a sister without being seen. He listened carefully and cursed Kirkwood's plans to induct Georgie into the Inner Circle. The opening among that august gathering belonged to his son, Barclay. A male untainted by scandal.

Georgie must be reminded of her true place in society. As a follower and a dependent, never a leader. And if she did not comply?

Well, then, Milton was skilled in medicine. He knew what

could cure a body and what could kill. A little too much of the most benign draught could cripple Georgie's health. Or even kill her. No one would suspect Milton's interference. Her wounds from her ill-advised sojourn on the Continent might flare up and fester at any moment. A fitting end to a woman who presumed herself as good as a man.

Whistling a jaunty tune, Dr. Milton Marlowe strolled back to his bed within the manor. His place in the Pendragon Society was secure. On the morrow he would journey to King George III's side and secure his place in the cabinet, and Barclay's place in the army. Perhaps he could find another chore for Barclay, one less dangerous than provoking illness and heart failure in Drake by that staged encounter with a highwayman.

Chapter 13

The Green Mermaid Tavern, Westminster, London, noon.

"YOUR regiment will go with mine to the colonies," Roderick Whythe told Colonel Prince Heinrich der Reusse.

The mercenary took a long gulp of his beer before replying. He looked around the dark tavern, assessing the crowd, constantly vigilant.

"When?" der Reusse asked. His eyes drooped and his mouth turned down. Roderick did not know if the man had smiled since leaving the Austro-Turkish border. He'd lost a lot of men on the last campaign, including Major Kirkwood.

"Early June we set sail from Portsmouth."

"I've lost my heart for campaigning, Steady Roddie. Mayhap the time has come to resign."

"You miss Georgie."

"Aye."

"Georgie was the brightest and best of them," Roderick said. "I'm certain he survived." They'd had this conversation many times in the last six months.

"You don't know the bloody Turks." A spark of anger lit der Reusse's eyes. "They torture prisoners." He swallowed deeply. Then he swallowed again. "If Georgie survived . . . he . . . would not be the same major who led so boldly, or the same youth we all loved."

Roderick bit back the obvious heartening statement he wanted to make. He looked at the floor, at the table, at the bottom of his tankard, anywhere but into der Reusse's eyes. He'd given a Masonic oath, as well as his word as an officer and a gentleman, not to reveal the young man's condition or location.

"You know something!" der Reusse grabbed Roderick's wrist and squeezed with amazing strength. Roderick had to release his grip on his tankard or risk broken bones. "I gave my oath by the Widow's Son." He clamped his jaw shut and looked away.

"Georgie lives." Der Reusse let out a long, hissing breath.

"I did not say so."

"I should have known that cat has more lives than—than a cat." Der Reusse leaned back on his settle and loosed a laugh that echoed around the rafters. A smile lit the big man's face. Years of care and worry flaked off his countenance.

A number of heads turned to stare at Roderick and his now-jovial companion.

"I said nothing." A knot of guilt twisted in Roderick's gut. How would he explain this to his Grand Master?

"You did not need to say anything, Major Whythe." Der Reusse sobered, but his mouth still twitched with enjoyment. "I have learned to read you well these past six months. Your oath is not violate."

"You do not know . . ."

"I know Georgie Kirkwood. I should not have wasted so much effort in grief. That one will turn up to plague us sooner or later."

"We leave for the colonies within two months. If Kirkwood returns to England—supposing he lives—he will not find us."

"Trust me, Roderick. Georgie Kirkwood will find us if for no other reason than to make my life miserable. I'd almost rather go back to my wife, the castle, and a crumbling principality that constantly bankrupts me rather than face Georgie's wrath. But, oh, it will be good to see . . . him . . . again."

"He promised to show me how to do that trick."

"Balancing a saber on a fingertip?" der Reusse asked.

"Aye. I've tried numerous times and failed, or nearly lost my finger."

"Don't even try. Georgie has specially balanced swords and talents that are not natural to men. Come, my friend, let us drink to Georgie's health. But . . . I'm a bit short of coin tonight."

Roderick signaled the barmaid to refresh their tankards. "Er . . . Is Georgie related to the Earl of Kirkenwood?" He remembered his other assignment.

"Brother, I believe," der Reusse said absently, more concerned with the froth atop his ale.

"May I use my acquaintance with Georgie to call upon the earl?"

"Um . . . I suppose. Do you have reason to make yourself known to the holder of one of the oldest titles in the land?"

"A whim of my superior officer." Roderick took a long drink from his own tankard rather than meet his friend's probing gaze. How secret was this inquest into the death of the King of Poland? Should he drag der Reusse into it?

But then Prince Heinrich der Reusse had been in Dresden with the earl's sister on that night.

Roderick decided he did not like this spy business at all.

Kirkwood House, Chelsea, England, late afternoon.

"This dress does not fit," I hissed at Drake as we approached Kirkwood House outside of London. "I'm embarrassed to be seen wearing it." He'd procured a sober gown from somewhere that had enough length in the skirt to properly cover my ankles, but in consequence had four times the girth I needed. It sagged hopelessly around my inadequate bosom.

My wounds had much improved, but still ached. I had chosen to wear a corset, laced lightly, under the gown. The restrictions of posture and demeanor came back to me as nearly forgotten skills. Familiar as an old dagger I had put aside for a newer, finer weapon, then retrieved. I could still look and act a woman, but it was no longer my choice.

The blasted garment had no place to hide a sword. That was a comfort I had been forced to relinquish along with my coat and breeches. I had to content myself with the dagger-pistol secreted in a pocket. This time I kept it loaded and my hand upon it to keep it from discharging accidentally.

"You must take your place in society, dear sister," Drake said mildly, offering me his arm.

"Cousin Milton will sneer at me in disgust."

Cousin Milton had gone ahead with the servants and his bodyguard. I guessed that he preferred their lowly company rather than taint himself by sharing the coach with me. He planned to meet us at Kirkwood House after attending to business in Whitehall.

"But the family must endure the scandal of my presence," I muttered. "Let me proceed north to Kirkenwood on my own."

"Ah, but you have redeemed yourself by a fortuitous marriage to Italian nobility," Drake said affably as he led me up the steps to his town house.

"I did?"

"That is the tale we will put about. You are now a widow, evicted from your dower by an ungrateful stepson. He cast you out with only the clothes upon your back, no jewels, no horse, no maid."

"How lucky for me that you came to my rescue, dear brother."

"There is to be no mention of your life as a mercenary. I have kept that secret from my wife and daughters. You have lived a most unseemly life, Georgie."

"So unseemly that Cousin Milton does not approve of your decision to initiate me into the Pendragon Society." I did not know if I approved either. I suspected the Society had become hidebound and inactive, more interested in pursuing magic for magic's sake than protecting England from her enemies.

"Milton will not approve of any initiation except for his son's. I shall deal with him later. I am the Pendragon. 'Tis my decision."

"Remind him of that next time he leads you down the garden path," I muttered. I itched to ask if Drake had recognized Barclay as the highwayman. He probably would not have listened to me if I mentioned it.

My brother seemed to have forsaken his spine for dependence upon Dr. Milton Marlowe. When I had left England, the Marlowes were but distant relatives seen once or twice a year. Now Drake could barely move without consulting Milton. I wondered if the doctor had some hold over my brother.

The usual line of liveried servants greeted us in the front

entryway. Countess Emma did not show her face. Society deemed a woman in advanced pregnancy an embarrassment; she could not politely greet me publicly. Cousin Milton awaited us as well, standing rigidly in the entrance to the salon, his bodyguard nowhere in sight. As we entered the stately foyer, a bevy of giggling girls, ranging from five to fifteen, flew down the staircase to envelope Drake in hugs and kisses. My brother lifted the youngest, Hannah I think she was named, into his arms and properly bestowed a welcoming greeting upon her doll as well as the girl's cheek.

Milton's frown deepened.

I could not help twitching a smile at him. Women made him uncomfortable! He'd find it hard to spend much time in this household.

Then from behind the green baize door that led below to the kitchens and servants' domain, a wolfhound lumbered forward. Drake immediately deposited his daughter on her own two feet, to take his familiar into his arms with the same affection he bestowed upon his offspring. "Ah, Belle, you've whelped!" he patted the dog's heavy teats and slack belly. "How many?"

The dog bestowed a sloppy tongue across his face. He snuggled into her neck ruff.

Milton winced. Then he dropped to one knee and gave Belle a grudging pat upon the head.

Belle ignored him. Smart dog. She knew he did not truly like or trust her. But if he wanted to be the next Pendragon, he had to accept a wolfhound as a familiar. The dogs always had final choice of the one who would lead the family and guard Britain against the unseen forces that sought a chink in our spells to keep them out.

"Yes, Belle, I know you have eight wonderful puppies. I will come view them in a few moments. First I must greet my lady wife," Drake said.

The dog leaned into him, allowing him to scratch her ears. I could tell by the way she drooped her long neck that she did not totally understand Lady Em's priority over the puppies. She accepted it, nonetheless.

Suddenly I felt the deep ache of loneliness in my midregion, the place where a child would never grow. This time I longed not for human companionship, but for that very intimate blending with a familiar.

Belle looked at me. Her gaze fastened upon mine far longer than a normal dog could hold a stare. Then she opened her mouth and drooled. Having grown up with dogs all over the house and kennels, I knew she laughed in pure delight.

Drake disengaged from caressing his familiar and started for the stairs. "Coming, Belle?" He paused on the third stair and looked at the wolfhound.

Belle had other ideas. She pranced over to me and grabbed my wrist in her massive jaws. Gently she tugged. I had no choice but to follow. She could crush my arm in an eye blink if she chose.

Convinced that I followed, Belle led me through the green baize door to the lower reaches of the house.

"Since you will not come view the puppies, it seems that I must," I quipped over my shoulder toward my brother.

His face lost a great deal of the joy of homecoming. His five daughters grew preternaturally still.

"Yes, Georgina, it seems you must." Slowly Drake trudged up the stairs.

Emily, the eldest hurried to catch his hand.

Milton scowled deeply. Then he turned his eyes upon mine. They seemed to shoot lances of flame at me. I recoiled.

Then he smiled and joined me. "We shall both honor Belle's babes," he said.

But his smile did not reach his eyes.

•

Chapter 14

"IT'S all right, Papa," Emily Martha Georgina Kirkwood consoled her father. "Belle knows best. If she chooses Aunt Georgie, then Aunt Georgie is the best candidate to follow in your footsteps." She patted his hand, trying to disguise her deep disappointment.

Belle should have chosen her! She, Emily, was the one who had sent for her aunt to return home and help Papa. She, Emily, was the one who had done her best to keep Papa strong and alive while Aunt Georgie lingered on the Continent.

"Belle is young yet. She may whelp again," her father sighed.

"Certainly she will. And you will live to see it." Emily was determined that he would.

Drake Kirkwood looked at her sharply then. "Will I?"

"Of course," Emily snapped back with more assuredness than she truly felt. "I have seen it in the quizzing glass."

"Your magic is not noted for its consistency, Emily. You are young yet. I dare not trust your visions of the future. Tonight I must initiate Georgie into the Inner Circle."

Emily bit her lip, holding back her dismay. Her father must truly feel death's cold hand upon his shoulder if he moved with such haste. And if he told her the identity of one of the Inner Circle.

"And you, dear child, shall move up to the rank of Knight."

"But . . . but I have not yet reached the age . . ." Hope soared in her breast. As a Knight of the Pendragon, she had the right to assist in all spells cast by the Inner Circle.

"No matter. 'Tis my decision. Georgie will need you by her side. I trust you, Emily, to keep her on course through the troubled times ahead. You can help her navigate the morass of histories and grimoires in the family archives. The key to all political dilemmas lies in the archives."

"Yes, Papa." Emily cast down her eyes rather than allow her father to see the resentment in her eyes. Aunt Georgie knew nothing of the factions that threatened to tear Britain apart. She had hardly practiced magic at all these last five years. Her morals were questionable at best. Her fashion sense nonexistent. She had no bosom and barely any hips—hard to tell for certain in that horrible gown that did not fit her properly. What man would want her? She had not the king's ear. She had deserted England when Papa needed her most, during the war that dragged on so long.

Emily knew in her heart that if Aunt Georgie had remained at Papa's side, the Inner Circle would have cast spells to end the war and keep England safe and prosperous. Instead, the hidebound elders had withdrawn from active participation in politics, in land management, in life!

Georgina Marie Deirdre Henrietta Kirkwood would make a terrible Pendragon when the time came.

"The dogs know best, Emily," Papa said. He took her hand in both of his. "The dogs always choose the best person to become the Pendragon, even though we do not always agree with them at first."

Before Emily could counter her father's pronouncement, her mother appeared at the top of the stairs. Her pleated robe barely disguised the bulk of her pregnancy. The soft ivory color appeared creamier than her skin. Blue veins showed through on her hands and neck. Dark shadows encircled her eyes.

Emily gulped in despair, as she did every time she was permitted to see her mother. She needed no magic, no preternatural visions to tell her that Mama would not survive birthing this babe. The family desperately needed Mama to produce a son. Without a male heir, the earldom and Kirkenwood estate must pass to a second cousin. Belle, and all of the other wolfhounds, had already turned their noses up at that sniveling teenager with pockmarked skin, limited education, and a severe stutter as a potential heir to the Pendragon. The boy had no magic and less sense to run the estates.

However, Mama and Papa had not turned their backs on the possible match between Emily and the heir presumptive. What was his name again? Emily could only remember his runny nose and pimpled skin, and that she stood at least half a hand taller than the young man.

She'd rather marry Cousin Barclay Marlowe. Now there was a dashingly handsome man to make a maid's heart flutter.

"Did I hear Georgie?" Lady Emma's hazel eyes searched the foyer.

"Aye, Em. Belle took her off to the kitchen to see the puppies," Papa replied. "I've missed you, Em." He climbed the last step and wrapped his arms around Emily's mother, laying his head upon her shoulder. "I needed your counsel on this journey. I needed your calm. And I needed your love." He breathed heavily with each word.

Emily closed her eyes in despair. All her efforts to improve Papa's health had failed. Belle's favoring of Aunt Georgie suddenly seemed ominous. The wolfhound had to choose a successor to Papa now, because he would not live to see another litter born. Such had always been the way of the Kirkwood wolfhounds, through many generations, all the way back to the time of King Arthur Pendragon and his Merlin.

Myth and legend suddenly merged with reality. Emily had to grasp the banister for support. Her head spun and blackness threatened her vision. She could not give in to it. Not now. Not until she was alone and would not upset either of her parents with the dark portent that shoved itself in front of her eyes.

I watched Belle settle into her padded box in the inglenook beside the massive cooking hearth. Seven squirming balls of fuzz wiggled closer, each finding a teat to suckle. The eighth pup, a female, bleated helplessly, lost and alone in a corner. She could smell her mother but had gotten turned around. Barely two days old, she had not yet the sense to figure out how to point herself in the right direction.

I knew she would figure it out eventually, but my heart went out to the little thing. Gently, I lifted her in one hand. "You are an ugly little thing," I chuckled. She had a white patch over one eye and one white foot. The rest of her brindled fur was a muddied mix of brown and gray. A quick check beneath her tail revealed that I had correctly identified the littlest puppy as female. Then I placed her in front of a vacant teat up near Belle's foreleg. She latched on and eagerly drank of her mother's milk.

Belle lifted her head and licked my hand before I could retreat. Her caress extended to include the baby I had rescued. She nudged my hand, willing me to linger and cherish the pup.

I obeyed the silent communication. The pup's heart beat loudly in my ears, her need for food, warmth, love became my own.

"Her name is Newynog, 'hungry' in Welsh," I whispered. Then I laughed. She was indeed hungry and touching her made my own stomach rumble.

Did this mean that I would inherit the runtish female?

I gulped at the implication.

Cousin Milton knelt beside me so close that he knocked me off-balance with his shoulder. Instinctively, I reached for the floor to balance myself. At the same time I lashed out with my left hand. Milton grabbed my swinging hand, a deep scowl on his face.

"Watch where you strike, whore," he hissed at me.

Belle growled and bared her teeth.

Milton reared back and lost his own balance. I rose, needing to face my enemy prepared to attack or defend.

Instead of meeting my unspoken challenge, Milton placed his hand upon the largest and most aggressive of the new pups. He stroked the brindled gray and black fur with a gentleness that surprised me.

Belle looked up at me. She opened her mouth and let her tongue loll in a doggy laugh.

I bit back my own reaction. Milton had selected a male pup. A male could never act as familiar to the Pendragon. Belle might let him have the pup as a pet, but not as a sign of favor. Rather as an acknowledgment of his stupidity and mystical blindness.

"All of your babies are beautiful, Belle. I appreciate the

honor of you showing them to me." I bowed to Drake's familiar and swept out of the kitchen, head high, spine straight, steps graceful, as only a confident woman can.

Milton hastened after me, nearly treading upon my heels. I whirled and stared down my nose at his presumption. He stood only half a hand taller than me. Our eyes met. Within the depths of his pupils I saw flashes of anger . . . and . . . power. He centered his magic in preparation for something.

I knew it. I saw it, a latent beast waiting to spring at me.

I knew how to fight Milton the man with sword and dagger. I did not know how to engage in magical combat.

Frightened at my own inadequacy, I broke eye contact and retreated with as much dignity as I could muster. I fled to the protection of my brother's side.

"Belle chose me to take a pup," Milton lied.

"Did she now?" Drake looked up from the stack of mail that had accumulated during his absence. "Come show me." The earl lumbered to his feet. Milton hastened to clasp his elbow and guide him upward.

Drake leaned heavily upon him and breathed heavily.

"Milord?" Milton checked his cousin's pallor and pulse.

"You know what this means, Milton?"

"That the dogs have confirmed me your heir."

"It also means that I shall not live to see Belle whelp another litter. She is a young dog and should seek a mate within the next year," Drake said sadly. "I should have liked to see my daughters grow a bit before I . . . before I die."

Suddenly Drake straightened his shoulders and firmed his chin. He marched toward the green baize door with new resolution.

"Milord, as your heir, I need to know how to access the archives. We must remove it to a new place of safety before the estate is entailed away from the Pendragon Society." Milton hastened after him. He tried to keep the breathless eagerness out of his voice and failed.

"We shall see. Show me the pup Belle has given you." He pushed open the servant's door and descended the narrow stair keeping his head up and his gaze straight ahead.

Belle eased out of her box to greet Drake. She nudged his hand, begging for pets. Her tail beat a tattoo against the wall. Milton wondered that she did not dent the plaster.

"I've come to see your babies, Belle," Drake cooed at the dog, continuing to ruffle her ears.

Eagerly the dog bounced back to her box.

Milton followed her cautiously. All eight wads of fur slept tangled with each other in an indistinguishable heap.

Belle climbed back into her box and nudged each one with her nose as if counting to make certain all were present and accounted for after her brief absence.

The big aggressive pup that Milton had singled out lifted his head and yawned. Then he bleated an inquiry to his dam.

Belle settled and made her teats available. The pup put his head back down and returned to his slumber. Belle lowered her massive head to her own paws and closed one eye. The other she trained upon her babes, ever watchful.

"May I, Belle?" Drake asked. Then he reached in and pulled out the ugly runt. Belle reared her head up.

After checking under the tail for the sex of the pup, Drake held it out to Milton.

"Belle would never give me, your heir, such a tiny and unhealthy runt. She presented me with this one." Milton reached into the pile of puppies and retrieved his chosen animal. He held it gingerly in his two hands, not at all comfortable with the squirming creature.

Drake raised an eyebrow. "This one? Are you certain?"

Belle reared up her head and opened her mouth in a doggy grin. Disgusting drool dripped from her teeth in slimy ropes.

"Of course, I am certain."

"Then you are not to be my heir. That pup is a male. The Pendragon's familiar is always a female." Drake breathed a sigh of relief. "But I understand that Georgie has been honored with this one." He held up the runt. "It is imperative now that we initiate Georgie into the Inner Circle. Tonight."

"You have agitated for change and modernization for the Society for years. Why rely upon this archaic tradition now? The choice of your heir is more important than the whim of a mere dog. You cannot allow that woman, that whore, to take control of the Society and the Inner Circle."

Milton's chest constricted in indignation. He had a moment of panic as his breath came in sharp and short.

"I must. The dogs always know best." Drake retreated up the stairs.

"We shall see about that, Cousin. We shall see," Milton ground out between clenched teeth. He glared at Belle and her disgusting puppies.

Chapter 15

Kirkwood House, Chelsea, England.

AS I expected, Lady Em and her daughter Emily began ordering my life to fit their mold before we took tea. I had barely kissed my sister-in-law in greeting before she sent footmen running to fetch her dressmaker and to invite select friends with eligible bachelors in their families to join her for luncheon on the morrow.

"Drake tells me that you are now a widow," Lady Em said, tapping her teeth with her fingernail. "I am happy to see that you gave up your hoydenish ways long enough to attract a respectable man."

I bit my cheeks to keep from retorting that, if anything, I had lived even more *hoyden* than before I left England.

"You married some Italian prince, an older man, tragically killed in a hunting accident," Em continued her musings. "His ungrateful son threw you out without a penny or a gown."

"And he confiscated her dowry. You had to borrow your maid's gown to cover your shift and make your escape," Emily added on a wistful sigh. "You loved your prince, despite the differences in your ages. Such a romantic tragedy." My niece actually wiped a tear from her eye.

What kind of gothic nonsense had she been reading?

I rolled my eyes and counted backward from one hundred, in Italian, to keep from fleeing. My brother needed my protection. I could not desert him just because his wife and daughter annoyed me.

While they fussed and prepared to present me to polite

society anew, Drake made plans of his own for my introduction to an entirely different Society.

At the chime of ten of the clock, when the family had retired, the servants had finished their day's work and doused the sconces, I slipped out of my room, clad only in a simple robe of thin wool in a deep midnight blue. I crept down the stairs to Drake's private solar. As a teen I had actively participated in the Pendragon Society. The ritual of bathing, meditating, and fasting came back to me with ease. The robe whispered against my naked skin, rasping just enough to bring my senses to tingling awareness. Thus I prepared to meet the Society in magical forum.

From my years as a debutante living in this house, I remembered which floorboards might creak and betray me. I did not need magic to make a secret rendezvous, only memory.

A breath of damp night air slinked through the unlatched windows in the solar. I followed their invitation and stepped onto a flagstone terrace.

Something in the scent of that draft enticed me, lured me farther into the gardens. Drake had said that I would know how to find the meeting place of the Pendragon Society. Knowing the nature of this secret enclave—not so different from the Freemasons in structure and that other secret Lodge I belonged to—I knew that I must use magic in some form or the layers of protective wards surrounding them would never open to me.

I began tracking as I would a band of raiding Turks. The breeze smelled alien, in its own way as exotic as the spices wafting from a foreign cooking fire.

"You had to pick a night with no moon to guide me, Drake," I whispered into the darkness. "Not so much as a glimmer of starlight to reveal obstacles as a deeper black among the shadows."

Then I realized that preternatural forces obscured any light that might leak from the heavens, or the house, or any of the outbuildings. I was on my own with only a haunting whiff of magic to lead me onward.

Shadows found me. They wrapped themselves around me, cushioning my footsteps on the wet grass and moss. Keeping my breathing shallow, I became the shadows, used them mercilessly as a cloak. I stepped and sniffed, moved sideways, then forward, turned right, then left and left again.

I sensed the tall solidness of the garden wall that separated the back of the house from the lane. Reaching out a hand, my palm connected with dressed stones, mortared together. My fingertips explored the wall where the scent lay heaviest. Nothing unusual. But then, my hands were covered with calluses and had lost much of their sensitivity for this kind of work.

My only option seemed to be magic. As Drake planned. I did not like the uncertainty of magic. My skills were rusty.

Back to the beginning, as I had gone back to the most basic drills of swordplay after my long recovery from battle wounds. Three deep breaths and exhalations cleared my mind, made me feel lighter, less troubled. I took three more breaths, releasing as much air as I took into my lungs. More light filtered into my vision. The wall became almost visible, a deeper blackness against the dark garden. Behind me, the mass of the house appeared darker yet.

A faint thrumming came through my feet. Similar to the sense of Turks racing toward me, but enough different that I knew no danger threatened. I needed to approach this new presence rather than flee or confront it with weapons.

My mentor and lover Cassanova had frequently blindfolded me during practice so that I would use all of my senses to counter his attacks. With a partner such as he, I fought better blind, for his blade moved faster than my eye could follow. I needed to trust my hearing, my sense of smell, and that other sense of knowing where he stood or crouched, loomed or retreated.

Loving him with the blindfold in place proved an equal challenge and more gratifying than I'd imagined possible.

With my eyes closed, I quested forward once more with my fingertips and the latent power within me. Unhindered by my mundane senses that found stability in what they wanted to find—like a solid wall—my hand met a cool nothingness indicating a doorway. Gulping back my fears, I stepped forward. I had never run from a fight and I did not intend to do so now.

A long tunnel led me onward and downward like a birth canal back into the womb of the Earth Mother.

Or a grave.

Face your enemies with courage and no one can think ill of you, Casanova's advice whispered into the back of my mind.

"Courage, you say?" I whispered back. Even that small sound echoed along the tunnel.

My mentor, or rather my memory of him, did not reply.

Mindful of the way sound traveled along this corridor I concentrated on keeping my footsteps silent. Years ago, Drake had taught me to imagine a cushion of air beneath my feet. I held the image firmly in my mind as I followed where the exotic scent of magic led me, head up, spine straight, and clutching my dagger-pistol hidden within a secret pocket of my robe.

Soon enough, I sensed the air around me spreading out. A room or a cavern. I listened to the area with my ears as well as my mind. Here a shuffled footstep, there an intake of breath across aged lungs. Slowly, secretly, I opened my mind, the way I had been taught and let them tell me how to bring forth light to reveal their presence.

Gauging an opponent in battle, or a duel, or a drill was not so different. Casanova claimed that the way I anticipated his moves smacked of magic. Perhaps it did. I hated the thought that I might mistakenly cheat on the field of honor by unfairly using the family talent.

This was a different kind of battle. Here I had to use magic against other mages more practiced than I.

Drake's mind remained closed to me, but I knew he was there. Something about the density of the darkness seemed familiar. Milton, too, awaited me. There was an acrid taint to the shadows about him. Instinctively, I sidled away from him.

This brought me closer to a sense of laughter, feminine, light, and gay. A woman who approached life with humor. I knew her then for Great-Aunt Bridget—Budgie we'd called her as children. The merest brush of my mind against hers showed me a gesture and a few words to release the spell set by my brother as a test for me.

In the back of my mind I felt the unformed dreams of a new puppy. She wanted to give me something, strength, knowledge she could not yet tap.

I took her courage, added it to my own store of strength. I raised both arms high, palms out.

At the same time I concentrated on the shielded flame I knew must be hanging in the center of the chamber. I invited the elemental Fire to shoot forth and seek new homes in the torches that ringed the room.

> *"Bring light to the world*
> *With the light, rebirth*
> *Rebirth invites enlightenment*
> *Tanio, Fire, join with*
> *Earth, Pridd,*
> *Air, Awyr,*
> *And Water, Dwfr.*
> *Join and grow, complete the circle,*
> *light and darkness*
> *Birth and Death.*
> *As it is written, so shall it be!"*

Then I added one last prayer. "Blessed Be."

Light flared. A dozen torches rested in brackets affixed to the wall. They blazed with only the feeble light of mundane fire.

Ten magicians, each clad in midnight-blue robes identical to my own, stood blinking and gaping in a circle to my right and left, I filled the empty eleventh spot. Each of the magicians held a staff. Cold mage flame, too white, too bright, shot upward from the top of each staff.

I do not know how I did that.

I do not believe I was supposed to be able to do that.

Murmurs of discontent rose around Drake in a tide of . . . of malevolence. He had to blink several times before he could separate the sources of all those ill feelings. Across the circle from where he stood, a clump of great-uncles and second cousins contemporary with Drake's father bent their heads together. Scowls marred their faces. These were the men who had never quite forgiven Drake for succeeding his father as Pendragon, instead of one of them.

Georgie stood immediately to their left, looking as amazed as Drake felt. The traps he had set were fierce enough to repulse an Apprentice, delay a Knight, and puzzle a Master Mage. Georgie had walked straight to the inner sanctum without hesitation. She was only supposed to entice the mundane flames onto the torches. She had done that and more. Ever so much more. She had drawn forth elemental Fire on her first try and attached it to the staffs of the masters. Those staffs were supposed to be protected, inviolate. Drake almost laughed at the consternation among his fellow mages.

"Darfod, Cease," he commanded with a slice of his hand atop his staff. The cold, white light shrank to a tiny ember, tried to flare, failed, and finally succumbed to his magic.

It should have vanished at his first thought.

A bit of sweat trickled down his back.

Just how powerful was this sister of his?

All around him, he watched his comrades-in-magic struggle to regain control of their most personal tools of power. With their frustration rose an equal amount of resentment and a sense of violation.

Suddenly Drake knew something akin to what a woman must feel with the threat of rape.

He shriveled.

And there stood Georgie grinning like a cat who had just stolen a lick of cream out from under Cook's nose. She'd get herself killed with these tricks. "She has not passed the test," Milton proclaimed. "She did not draw forth mundane fire to light the lamp."

A wave of noise grew around the members. Some agreed with Milton. Some did not. Drake grew chilled.

"The lamps burn with mundane fire. We are blinded by the brighter mage light," he countered. Then he turned to face the assembly. "Belle has chosen this applicant as my successor!" he said loud and clear.

"The wolfhound has chosen!" Great-Aunt Budgie answered him. "So it is written, so shall it be."

"Blessed be," Georgie finished for her.

"Time to change the rules," Milton said. "We have debated this change for decades. The time has come to act upon it."

No one seemed to hear him. One and all, the Inner Circle turned to Georgie and bowed to her. Except for Milton. He turned abruptly and left the chamber.

Safely ensconced in his carriage, Milton faced Samuel de Vere, his bodyguard. "Give me your arm," he commanded.

"Why?" The young man kept both his hands upon the carriage seat, knuckles white with his grip.

"You know why," Milton snarled as he fished among his clothing for his athame, his ritual knife. His hands tangled in the loose folds of his ceremonial robe. Damn, he should have dressed before entering the carriage.

"What kind of spell do you need to cast? You just left the Inner Circle and the sacred chamber. Your magic should be depleted," Sam said.

"If you had been listening as I commanded, rather than flirting with the kitchen maids, you'd know that nothing progressed as planned. Milord named that whore Georgina his heir in magic." Milton's hands shook with anger.

"You plan some mischief against milord earl?" Sam pulled his hands behind his back.

"You knew when I hired you that I work magic. I need your blood. Now give me your arm." Milton held out his hand, expecting the man to place his arm and his trust there.

"I hired on to learn how to control my magic. You've taught me well enough, sir. But this . . . this is evil."

" 'Tis not evil. 'Tis necessary. Lord Drake has bungled everything badly. England is in danger as long as he controls the Pendragons. We'll certainly fall victim to invasion of some sort if he allows his sister to follow him. Now. Give. Me. Your. Arm."

Sam gulped. Then slowly, reluctantly, he drew forth his left arm and placed it in Milton's grasp. He closed his eyes and gritted his teeth. The big muscles along his jaw and neck bunched in anticipation of pain.

"For England," he said quietly. "I do this for England."

"And me. You do it for me, your mentor and guide," Milton insisted.

Sam took another deep breath and swallowed. Then he scrunched up his face. "For you, sir. I'll follow you anywhere, obey any order after what you have given me in knowledge and opportunity."

Milton smiled grimly. 'Twould do.

He slashed Sam's palm with one swift, sure flick of the blade. He murmured a few arcane words in an ancient language he knew Sam had no knowledge of. Then he fell into a light trance as he wove a compulsion around his bodyguard.

If the man weren't so naive and innocent, he'd be useless. As it was, his questions and doubts grew stronger every day. His usefulness was waning. Soon, Milton would find a way to dispose of Sam and replace him.

In the meantime, he had chores for him. Chores that required his muscles and blind loyalty and not his intelligence.

Chapter 16

AN eerie wail awakened me near dawn. I froze, assessing the danger. My body did not want to move, more from fatigue than wariness. I had forgotten how draining magic could be. Although the oath ceremony following my initiation more resembled a drunken party than a serious rite, I'd had to keep my magical wards active all night to avoid the mind probing, friendly and malicious, from my relatives. We had not retired until a bare hour before the uncanny cry awoke me.

The wail came again and I knew it for Belle, Drake's familiar. My blades came to my hands without a thought before I managed to get my feet to the floor.

Outside my room I nearly ran into Drake. His nightcap sat askew atop his head and his nightshirt was rucked up revealing doughy calves. His eyes searched every corner with panic and magic.

Since my initiation earlier that night, I seemed more sensitive to the presence of power. He flung his wildly, seeking Belle.

But he just stood there, trusting his magic. He needed skill and action.

I hurtled down the stairs, saber at the ready, cocking the dagger-pistol. For the first time I allowed my instincts to release my magic in a quest. I found Belle in my mind with no trouble. Something—someone—else thrust against my thoughts and retreated, leaving my senses reeling and my eyes nearly blind with pain.

Not so different from fighting a battle with a head wound. I plunged on, feeling my way toward Belle's inglenook with my feet, my hands, and my mind.

The floor beneath my bare toes thrummed in warning. Someone had invaded the house.

Cursing the long folds of my proper night rail, I approached the kitchen with as much speed as possible. The magic hummed within me. I knew only one enemy awaited me. Only one man had ever bested me with sword or dagger or wits. Cassanova, my lover and mentor. My sword master. The man who menaced my brother's house and distressed his wolfhound familiar was not Casanova.

What could distress a wolfhound? Belle stood over forty-eight inches at the shoulder. She'd been bred to run all day at the heels of a horse and then take down a marauding wolf. Her massive jaws could crush the arm of a man or the leg of a horse.

"En garde," I shouted as I burst into the kitchen.

Belle stood frozen in place on the far side of the primary hearth. Only her voice worked though she strained every muscle to break free of a magical paralysis. In the cavernous room, lined with brick, her wails reverberated, piercing my ears, driving my thoughts in circles.

I forced my concentration away from the dog, though my heart ached with her. Only one thing would cause this grief. Her babies.

A moving shadow drew me out of sharing Belle's agony. I followed it out the back door and up the steps into the yard, blade at the ready. The man slipped away from every attempt I made to close the distance. I knew him as male because of his height and the breadth of his shoulders. Something about his stance and posture seemed familiar. The predawn darkness added confusion to the shadows.

Somehow, he managed to always keep the same distance ahead of me. When I put on a burst of speed, so did he. When I slowed, conserving my breath, so did he.

We passed the garden wall, using the gate. The magically hidden portal tingled slightly against my skin as I passed. I ignored it, intent upon my quarry.

The lane behind the garden stretched straight for about one hundred yards. Then it twisted in a long series of curves around a hill. I should have been able to see any figure fleeing down the lane, or hear him scramble through the thick brambles and underbrush of the copse across the lane.

Nothing. I opened my magical senses that had not truly closed after last night's ritual.

Nothing.

The man must be a master of dark magic to disappear so completely. He had to have access to powers beyond my ken to get past Belle's guard.

Belle.

The wails continued. My gut twisted in grief. Whatever ailed her, ailed me, must ail Drake even more.

Given my earlier vision of Drake's imminent death, I dashed back to the kitchen.

My brother hunched before Belle's box. The great wolfhound remained frozen in her pose of warning by the hearth. With a gesture I released her. She turned immediately to her box and nudged the inert forms in the nest with her nose. Seven puppies dead. An eighth lump of fur rested upon Drake's knee. I recognized the white splotch on the foot and over one eye of the little female. My puppy. Newynog.

My gut twisted in grief. Tears streaked my face. A blue glow engulfed my brother, the puppy, and Belle. It pulsed—pounded—against the tiny dog.

A narrow layer of white light shrouded the puppy, keeping out the healing blue magic Drake wielded.

My heart twisted. My magic wanted to rush forth. I reined it in, knowing anything I tried was useless compared to what Drake could do.

He could do nothing more. The puppy, my puppy, had died. As had her brothers and sisters.

Murdered.

Murdered with magic.

"You will live!" Drake demanded of the fragile lump of fuzz. "You must live," he pleaded.

Magic poured from his body in a river of power. He had none to spare after last night's ritual and the copious amounts of hard spirits he'd drunk.

A tunnel of light opened before him. It beckoned and enticed. The misty forms of eight puppies lifted from their inert bodies, too weak of will to resist the siren song of death. The little female, promised to Georgie as a familiar waited until last, nudged aside by her older, larger siblings. 'Twas fitting that the runt should wait in death as she had in life.

Drake grasped her spirit's tail, pulling her back.

She fought him, wriggling and twisting. She let forth a mournful bleat. *Do not leave me behind. Alone,* she seemed to call to her brothers.

"You will not be alone," Drake said quietly. "Your mama awaits, as do your mistress, and I. We will cherish you."

"Drake, let go!" Georgie shook his shoulder. "Go no farther."

Drake blinked. The pup almost twisted out of his grip.

" 'Tis not your time, Drake. Do not go into the light. I need you. Britain needs you."

None of that mattered. Georgie would succeed him so long as he could save her familiar. The puppy stopped struggling away from him. She turned and looked at him in indecision through her closed eyes. He could save her.

"Drake, Em needs you. 'Tis too close to her time. She'll die without you. She'll die because you valued the life of a dog over hers. A dog who hasn't even opened her eyes yet." Georgie gulped back a tear.

Georgie never cried, even as a child with skinned knees and bruises.

"Think of Em!" she nearly shouted.

Drake let go of the puppy's tail. She slipped away into the light, leaving him behind.

"Em," he whispered. "Em will know what I should do."

Chapter 17

THE wave of grief-laden magic hit Milton in the belly and in the forehead like a pugilist's fist. He rocked backward, jarring his neck and spine against the hard backrest of his closed carriage.

This close to Kirkwood House, only one person could unleash such anguish. Drake.

Milton pounded the roof of the carriage to signal the driver. "Where to?" came the garrulous reply.

"The front door, you idiot!" Milton shouted. "Where else would I go at a time like this?"

"Home?"

"I will pretend I did not hear that," Milton mumbled to himself. Across from him, the ever-present Samuel, released from his trance now, retrieved a small pistol from his pocket. He busied himself silently with priming and cocking the weapon.

Neville's ghost sneered at him from beside Samuel. The bodyguard seemed oblivious to the shade's presence. His magic probably wasn't strong enough to sense it.

After Georgina's rather ostentatious display at the initiation at midnight, Milton had not traveled far. The implications of the wanton's power troubled him. He needed to think, hard, about the consequences of her elevation to the Inner Circle of mages. And the temporary exclusion of his son, Barclay, from those ranks.

After Georgina's demonstration of power, none of your comrades, even your closest allies, will hear of creating a new post for another new mage, Neville said.

"If we had the key to the archives, Georgina would be no

threat to us," Milton replied silently with his mind. "I could make you whole and alive."

He shook his head, dismissing his temporary failure. The horses surged forward, pushing Milton deeper into the unyielding cushions. He would arrive at Kirkwood House in just a few moments. A little time to compose himself. But not too much. Drake had to know how far his magic would reach. At the same time, Milton needed to be calm enough to aid Drake through the tragedy that had unleashed such ominous vibrations. Half of London would rouse feeling restless and depressed if Milton did not sedate Drake quickly.

Before the sedation took effect, Milton must coerce the secret of the archives from the Pendragon's closed lips.

He bounded out of the carriage before it came to a full halt. He did not wait for a servant to open the door. He did not wait to summon the butler. He barged into the foyer of the house turning his head right and left, seeking the source of magic.

Drake's anguish nearly repelled him from the house. It flooded the ground floor, leaving no distinct trail to its source.

Milton paused a moment, gulping air and concentrating his own power. "Like to like, seek and find," he whispered to himself.

An image of Drake kneeling beside his dog's box flashed before his eyes and was gone. Enough. He pushed through the green baize door and hastened down the steps to the sunken kitchen. The sight that met his eyes nearly turned his stomach. Eight puppies lay dead, seven in the box, one on Drake's lap. Drake wept openly. So did Georgina. A sword lay beside her as she stroked the tiny head of the puppy resting on Drake's knee. Belle sat on her haunches and lifted her head in an ear-piercing howl. One of Drake's pudgy arms draped around the dog's neck. His sobs sounded nearly as loud. A dozen servants and Emily, the oldest daughter, hovered on the other end of the kitchen, not knowing how to approach the Earl of Kirkenwood during this very intimate moment between himself and his familiar.

Milton had to hold his ears to protect them from the noise, psychic and mundane.

A miasma of blood and sulfur invaded his senses and he

knew that Neville had also been drawn to the scene. Death sought death. But the pups would pass on to whatever fate awaited soulless animals. Neville must continue halfway between until Milton gained control of the archives and accessed a particular grimoire. If Drake divulged the key, then the death of eight pups was worth this agony.

Milton fought forward, like wading through deep water until he too knelt beside the charnel box.

"Drake, you must calm yourself," he said, shaking his cousin's shoulders.

Neither Drake nor Georgina seemed to hear him. Belle snarled and snapped at him.

"Drake!" Milton pushed some magic into his voice, compelling the earl to listen.

Drake turned bleak eyes upward. Tears streamed from his eyes and his nose.

"Someone killed them. Killed them all," Drake sobbed.

"It is the end of the line," Georgina gulped. "Without another familiar . . ."

Her words trailed off at the unspeakable horror of her thoughts.

"I had no idea the bonds between the Pendragon and his familiar could be so strong," Milton whispered in amazement. "No idea at all. None."

After a few moments of fighting back the grief that threatened to engulf him as well, he snapped his fingers at Emily, Drake's daughter, who continued to hover behind him. "Brandy. Now," he shouted at her. She did not respond immediately. He glared at her. "Samuel, guide her."

His bodyguard nodded, then took the chit's elbow to guide her up the stairs.

Then Emily blinked her eyes rapidly, as if coming out of a trance. A brief nod of compliance and she dashed upstairs without assistance, presumably to the liquor cabinet. She left a trail of ungrounded magic in her wake. Samuel absorbed it and guided it back into the earth as he followed at her heels.

Milton had to steel himself against a few stray wisps of power seeking a spell. If he allowed it to invade him now, he'd not be able to think clearly to deal with the crisis.

Emily returned in moments with a decanter half full of potent liquor. Samuel remained at her heels.

Milton stared at the clear amber liquid.

"Uisquebagh," she said succinctly. "Better than brandy." She waved the single malt beneath her father's nose. The heady fumes made Milton dizzier than her ungrounded magic did.

Drake blinked and looked about. His head moved in short jerky spasms.

"Drink it, milord," Milton ordered his cousin. Blindly, Drake fumbled to grasp the decanter. Emily held it to his lips and tilted it a little. A small sip of the whiskey trickled into Drake's mouth. He coughed and his eyes went wide. Moisture gathered at the corners of his eyes and threatened to spill over.

"Dead," Drake mumbled. "All of them are dead. 'Tis the end of the line. 'Tis the end of us."

"Don't let the despair take you, Brother!" Georgina shook his shoulders and screamed in his ear. " 'Tis only the end if you give in to the blackhearted fiend who did this. 'Tis only the end if you allow it to be."

Drake jerked his head up and stared at his sister a moment. Milton could almost see the silent communication between the two. Jealousy gnawed at his heart. He should be the one Drake confided in, not this tainted whore of a sister.

Drake seemed to rouse a little as he hugged Belle closer.

"You need to be abed, milord," Milton said gently. He needed to wrest control of the situation away from Georgina. All his hopes and plans for the future, for his son's future were for naught if she usurped his authority. "Help him back to his bed," Milton ordered the servants who still clung to each other on the opposite side of the kitchen. "I shall prepare a draft to help him sleep."

Four stout men, including the family butler and Samuel, came forward. Expertly, they hoisted the Earl of Kirkenwood to his feet and guided his steps toward the upper stories. Georgina made to follow. At her first step she cringed and sank back to the floor, the voluminous folds of her night rail pooling about her.

"Your feet, Aunt Georgina!" Emily exclaimed as she knelt beside the wanton and examined the soles of Georgina's feet. Only then did Milton notice the dried blood mixed with mud that covered both soles.

"Emily, can you clean and bind her wounds? I must tend

your father." Milton left the kitchen abruptly, unnerved and aroused by the sight of the blood on the woman's skin. He could never forgive himself if he succumbed to his need to lick the blood from Georgina's toes. That way lay madness. He needed a clear head tonight and tomorrow. Blood magic—Black Magic—always left him drained with a headache worse than a hangover.

And a need for more.

But, oh, the power he unleashed when fueled by blood and death!

Belle gave each one of her dead pups one last caress with her tongue. Then she wedged herself between one of the servants and Drake's hand. She nudged him until he responded with a vague scratch of her ears. Her strong neck and shoulders helped support him on his long trek back to bed. The family butler shouldered Drake's weight on the other side. None of them had to grieve alone.

Milton trailed behind, left out of the intimate circle of master and dog and servant. Even Samuel was closer to the earl at this moment than Milton.

As the green baize door swung shut behind him, he heard Emily speak, her voice tinged with awe. "I can't believe you ran out after the intruder in your bare feet. That was so incredibly brave of you. And so romantic. You could have been killed."

Milton bit back a rebuke to a woman who would step so far out of her place to do such a foolish thing. Unseemly. Immodest. Wrong.

Freemason's Hall, Grand Lodge, London, the next afternoon.

"The pater is negotiating the chit's dowry as we speak."

Roderick Whythe heard a lascivious chuckle follow the drawling statement. Something about the lack of respect for the intended bride made his skin crawl. Such comments had no place in the hallowed halls of the Freemason's Lodge. "She's only fifteen, but I like 'em young. Easier to train them correctly," the drawling voice continued.

"Why the rush, Marlowe? Surely you aren't ready to give up your bachelor ways for an untried girl who hasn't even put up her hair yet," an older, more sedate voice said. It was slightly muffled, probably by a pipe.

Roderick's nose drew in the fragrant aroma of burning tobacco. He longed for a slow draw of hot smoke down his throat. His purse would not allow him the luxury. Unless someone else was buying. A good enough reason to join the conversation. He lowered himself into a wing chair adjacent to the ones occupied by the two conversationalists.

Then he looked at his companions. Lord Sackville and Captain Barclay Marlowe. Two unlikely mates. But then Marlowe was known to be ambitious, and Sackville manipulative. Look at the way he had ordered Roderick to become a spy.

"Seems as though there is a messy bit about an entail to the earldom and the estate," Sackville said before nodding acknowledgment of Roderick's presence. He made no indication that he had called Roderick here for a discussion of the Honorable Georgina Kirkwood, sister to the Earl of Kirkenwood and erstwhile companion of Prince Heinrich der Reusse.

Roderick knew Captain Barclay Marlowe slightly. A likable enough chap when he wasn't drunk. Until now. The man's attitude toward his intended seemed so . . . callow. A man was supposed to respect his intended. A man who followed the rules of society kept such crass opinions to himself.

Marlowe tended to sprawl, physically and mentally, overwhelming any space he occupied. The comfortable chair by the fire seemed far too small for the man, yet he only topped Roderick by two inches. Something about his posture, dangling one long leg over the arm of the chair and flinging his arms about to emphasize each statement made him look bigger. Or was it just more flamboyant? Another trait a true gentleman did not exhibit.

Marlowe's uniform certainly exhibited the latest cut and froths of lace usually associated with court dandies rather than the military.

"If the Honorable Emily Kirkwood can push out a son before her pater dies, then the child becomes earl and I have twenty-one years of guardianship over one of the biggest estates and oldest titles in the land." Marlowe scratched most indelicately, indicating another reason why he was so anxious to get on with the marriage to a child.

At mention of the intended bride's name, Roderick's attention focused more closely upon Marlowe.

"Kirkenwood is hardly the most profitable earldom in England. Nothing but moors and peat bogs up along the border," Sackville commented, sucking noisily on his pipe.

"Ah, but the sheep!" Marlowe chortled. "That dastardly climate makes the beasties grow wool a foot deep and more. I'll enclose the whole place and run sheep. Kirkenwood will be turning a tidy profit in no time. Meanwhile I can ensconce me and the wife in Mayfair. The Chelsea house will have to go. Too old and unfashionable."

Roderick shuddered. He'd seen too many hollow-eyed refugees from enclosed estates. Some had found safe haven in the New World on the other side of the of the ocean. Too many had died of starvation on the road. His own father had tried to enclose their few remaining acres and failed miserably. The cost of fences, livestock, and skilled shepherds had plunged the family further into debt and removed rental income from the tenant farmers.

None of that would have happened if his father had behaved as a gentleman and not squandered his inheritance on drink, cards, and loose women.

Roderick decided to change the subject.

"I met a Major Kirkwood on the Continent last year."

"Could be any one of hundreds of cousins or bastard byblows." Marlowe dismissed the acquaintance with a wave of his hands. But his eyes narrowed in speculation. Sackville leaned forward, his casual attention suddenly rapt.

"The family goes back to Adam and Eve. They've got the records to prove it," Marlowe said.

All three men laughed. This past decade London society had become obsessed with tracing their families back beyond written records, trying to find mystical connections that would qualify them for a number of "secret societies" that were far from secret. To Roderick's mind the only one of those societies with a truly ancient tradition was his own Freemason Lodge, and he dismissed much of the more mystical claims of the rival Scottish Rite. He liked the sober consistency of Grand Lodge. His Lodge. This Lodge. Why was Marlowe here when he'd never attended before?

"Even I am a distant cousin. My grandmum was sister to a grandfather of the current earl," Marlowe continued, obviously more interested in speaking than listening. "Which makes me the perfect candidate for the Honorable Emily's hand. Have to keep the bloodlines pure. There are too many bastards running around boasting Kirkwood blood. That is probably who your major is. A filthy bastard tainting the family." Marlowe's foot, the one that dangled over the arm of the chair, twitched rhythmically, belying an unstated unease.

"Possibly," Roderick admitted. Georgie Kirkwood's blithe attitude and jolly humor in the face of overwhelming odds suggested a lack of close family ties.

He accepted a pipe from Sackville. The hot aromatic smoke burned his throat. Then it expanded into his lungs in an exciting blast. He released it upon a satisfied sigh. He took his next draw slowly, savoring the taste and the sense of euphoria induced by the tobacco. This might be the last he could enjoy before actually reaching the Colonies.

"As much as I look forward to bedding the virginal Honorable Emily, it's her young aunt who truly excites me," Marlowe droned on. "Georgina Kirkwood has spent the last seven years on the Continent living openly as the mistress of Giovanni Giacomo Casanova, and others, before marrying some creaking old Italian prince who died and left her without a farthing. But I was her first lover, before she eloped with Casanova. I prepared her for the master!"

No. Georgina Kirkwood could not be Major Georgie. Roderick jerked awake from his contemplation of the pipe. Just a coincidence of names. No woman could masquerade as a man in a company of mercenaries. Not for any length of time. Could she?

That would make the blithe young man of his acquaintance a likely suspect in the assassination of the King of Poland, as well as der Reusse's mistress.

Chapter 18

Chelsea, Kirkwood House.

"WHAT happened to your sneering disapproval of me, Emily?" I asked as she bathed my feet for the third time the next day. Dr. Milton Marlowe devoted himself exclusively to my brother, the earl, completely ignoring me. The ointment Emily applied to the cuts burned my skin and smelled terribly. But it seemed to be working. Of course it did; Aunt Budgie had supervised the mixing of it.

I could stand and walk in light slippers for almost an hour before I needed to sit again. That is, if the servants and my niece allowed me out of bed long enough to stand on my own.

I had thought myself tougher than this. But I had always worn boots on military campaigns. I had not built layers of callus on my feet as I had as a child running wild across the moors of Kirkenwood.

Inactivity chafed upon my mind. I should be up and doing, investigating last night's nefarious attack. I should be organizing a guard to watch over my brother. I should be ordering his meals with an eye to countering the disease that ate away at him.

"You took grave injury in defense of my father and our home," Emily said. She kept her eyes lowered so that I could not read her. "You are braver than I could ever be." This last came out on the barest whisper.

Then she looked up at me and gave a wistfully romantic sigh. I could see stories spinning in the back of her head.

I sighed, too, in resignation. Teenage girls did tend to

dream. But I had envisioned captaining a pirate ship, sailing free across the seven seas. Emily, however restricted her imaginings to the same gothic stuff of books available from every pushcart in London.

"Courage is often foolish pride in disguise," I replied gently.

"I'd be so afraid . . ."

"A good soldier is always afraid. 'Tis fear that keeps us alive."

"Are we soldiers?" Emily's eyes opened wide. Did she know my history? Drake had suggested that she did not. But then he probably did not know how much women overheard and how rapidly they spread gossip.

Last night's initiation ceremony flashed across my mind. The stated purpose of the Pendragon Society: to guard Britain against the forces of darkness with magic. The oaths I had taken had bestowed upon me a sense of purpose.

"Yes, Emily. All of us within the Kirkwood family who are members of the Society, and therefore the ones who possess magical talent, are soldiers against the darkness of evil. That is why the middle ranks are referred to as Knights. You are the ones who must be out in the field, rooting out black magics and enemies of Britain and therefore enemies of us. Our magic comes from the land. We are woven into the very fiber of Britain. I taught you that when you were three. And if we are ever brought down, then Britain will fall, too." I began to shake all over.

"The puppies!" we exclaimed together.

"The wolfhounds are as much a part of the Pendragon as . . . as magic," Emily breathed. "We have to get Belle back to Kirkenwood immediately so she can breed." She began gathering up the soiled bandages and pots of ointment.

"Wait, Emily. Belle will not come into estrus again for six months. She cannot breed again until then."

Emily sank onto the stool beside my bed, clutching her tools of healing like a talisman. "Oh?" Her mouth remained agape.

" 'Tis the natural cycle of dogs. Cats will breed again immediately. But not dogs."

"I did not know." She hung her head.

" 'Tis not your fault that your parents protected your

delicate sensibilities. Time now to broaden your education. Women are capable of breeding every month. Dogs twice a year. Cats come into heat and stay there until they become pregnant."

She blushed a fierce red and averted her eyes from mine.

"Six months. We have time then to find out who did this and keep him from doing it again," she said with more firmness. She began to resemble the vivacious child who had helped me escape from this very house seven years ago.

"We have to keep your father alive until Belle whelps as well."

Emily's mouth fell open and she met my gaze again. "We can't let him die. He's my da," she breathed.

"Whoever did this knows how deeply your father ails and how closely tied he is to the dogs. Your father tried to follow the puppies into death. I think his heart nearly stopped last night. Only his concern for Belle and your mama kept him alive."

"What can we do?"

"We can do many things." I outlined a light diet with lots of fresh water, no liquor, and plenty of liver for my brother. "And when he is on his feet again, we force him to walk, to take any exercise with him that we can."

"But Cousin Milton . . ."

"Knows nothing of your father's disease. He knows only how to bleed his patients or lop off limbs. There are other ways to heal. I have studied many of them, read many learned treatises from other cultures. I know how to help your father, and now you know the best treatment. We have to keep your father alive another six to eight months, at least, until Belle breeds and whelps again."

Chelsea, England, Kirkwood House, the next morning.

The next morning, I eased myself onto a straight-backed chair in the morning room. Lady Emma had insisted I finish taking my breakfast in bed. I was too restless to stay there. Both my mind and my body cried for action.

The walk down a flight of stairs and across the width of

the house had hurt the deep cuts in my feet. Getting out of the confines of my room and breathing fresher air had been worth the pain. The weak sunshine streaming through the windows helped my spirits more.

A maid appeared long enough to slip a stool under my feet and disappeared again in the silent glide expected of well-trained retainers. I reached for the dish of tea that had appeared on a low table next to my elbow with the same silent anticipation of my needs. The cooling liquid bit on the back of my tongue, strong and sweet, though I'd have preferred the rich and frothy chocolate Casanova drank. As a restorative, chocolate surpassed even tea and brandy. The English had a lot to learn.

"Have you heard?" Emily burst into the room, her eyes agog and her breathing rapid. The flush on her cheeks spoke of excitement rather than alarm.

"Tell me," I ordered. "Is your father recovered from his ordeal?"

"Partially." Emily bounced to my side.

"Then tell me what has put a rose in your cheek and a spring in your step."

"Father and Cousin Milton have signed a marriage contract for me. I am to marry Captain Barclay Marlowe within the month."

My heart chilled. "You know so little of the man." The only excuse I could offer without telling all. My instincts screamed that he was mine. I remembered how we had fallen into a tangle of limbs after I bested him at broadswords when I was sixteen; how we had kissed and explored and loved with tender excitement . . .

My instincts also suspected that he was the enemy. Instincts I could not ignore since my initiation into the Inner Circle of the Pendragon Society.

"He is a Knight of the Pendragon. As am I now. As you are." Emily was not supposed know who held rank beside my brother in the Inner Circle. "Our fathers would know if Captain Marlowe lacked in character. When you left seven years ago, you told me that he would protect me when you could not."

"He is so much older than you." My arguments looked bleaker and bleaker. I had no say in the matter. Neither did Emily for that matter. I had run away to the Continent to avoid just such a situation—marriage to a much older man who would be a stabilizing influence on my wild and wanton ways.

I did not think that Cousin Barclay would prove a steady influence on anyone. He had as many secrets as I. Like why was he pretending to be a highwayman? Was he the one who had murdered the puppies?

Both incidents could have severely compromised Drake's health, even his life.

Emily did not have the choice of escape as I had. At fifteen, she had not yet come out, had met no other men, had not the experience of life or the determination to be her own person. Her only option was to go with me when I left my brother's household.

I could not leave yet. Drake, the entire line of Pendragons, depended upon my ability to protect my brother.

Before I could think of another argument, Simpson, the family butler, appeared in the doorway and cleared his throat. He proffered a silver salver with a single card upon it.

"The gentlemen requests an interview, madam," he intoned with just the slightest hint of disapproval.

Of me or the gentleman?

I took the card and read the name. A dozen curses in as many languages came to mind. I would have loved to deepen the scowl of disapproval upon Simpson's face, but refrained. If I were to survive in this household, I needed allies at every level. Simpson and his opinions controlled the entire servant population.

"Major Roderick Whythe," Emily read.

"Don't even think what you are thinking," I growled.

"A gentleman caller, already. Wherever did you meet him?"

None of your frigging business. "In Europe. Vienna I think." Near enough the truth. "Simpson, inform Major Whythe that I am indisposed. The entire household is indisposed." I limped back up to my room, never daring to peer out of a window to look upon the face of the man who had saved my life. He could betray too many of my secrets and thus hamper my efforts to keep Drake alive and functioning.

Kirkwood House, Chelsea, England, later that day.

"Now what?" I stared down at Belle. The big wolfhound pranced about my feet with a daintiness that belied her bulk.

"She clearly has something to tell you." Drake sat forward from his wing chair by the fire in his study. Emily kept her nose buried in a novel within the depths of the matching chair opposite her father.

"You have to be more specific, Belle. I speak five languages and read two more, but I don't speak dog," I told her.

Belle increased her circle to include Drake. She nipped at my skirt and tugged on his wrist as she passed us in her growing excitement.

"I believe we must follow her." Drake heaved himself up.

Belle dashed for the door.

"Why do I have the feeling we have done this before?"

Slowly I picked my way in the dog's wake. My feet ached and each step sent lances of fire up my limbs. Some of Belle's excitement leaked into me and I ignored the pain the better to share some of her joy after the tragedy of her puppies' murder.

Just as Drake and I reached the door, Belle dashed back to retrieve Emily. The girl looked over the top of her book at the dog. "Must I?" Her eyes strayed back to the novel.

"It appears you must," Drake said. He creased his brows in puzzlement as Belle gently took Emily's wrist into her mouth and tugged.

Emily closed her book with her finger stuck inside to mark her page, then slid out of her chair rather than lose her arm to the dog's jaws.

When we were all gathered in the doorway, Belle danced ahead of us to the green baize door. We followed until we reached the kitchen landing. Belle stood proudly in her birthing box, nudging several furry objects.

I crept forward and peered inside. Six kittens, their eyes just open, squirmed and mewed until Belle settled and they could nurse.

"Cats?" I asked the dog.

Babies. No mama. The answer came into the back of my mind more as an image than actual words.

"Orphaned kittens?" Drake asked as he, too, came to

view the new members of Belle's family. "I have read of such things, dogs adopting orphaned cats, cats adopting orphaned pups. But I never thought to see such a thing."

"Nor I." I bent down to stroke the top of one kitten's head, then another. One little calico seemed to press her head against my fingers, wanting more. I obliged her.

"Kittens!" Emily squealed. She joined us at the edge of the box. "May I have one, Belle?"

Belle didn't answer. The big dog captured my gaze. The calico abandoned her meal at Belle's teat to find my hand. She butted my fingers, begging for more caresses.

"It seems you have a replacement for Newynog." Drake sat back on his heels. "Belle believes you have a task to complete as Pendragon. But you are not to be the next Pendragon. How strange."

"I think we need to keep this a secret," I warned both Drake and Emily.

Emily just kept playing with all of the kittens, no one in particular.

So why had Belle included her in this little ceremony?

Chapter 19

Kirkwood House, Chelsea, England, two weeks later.

DRAKE wiped sweat off of his brow. He stared numbly at the foiled rapier in his hand.

"You leave yourself open and vulnerable," Georgie taunted him.

"We've been at this nigh on an hour, Georgie," Drake protested. He hated the whine in his voice, hated the weakness that beset his limbs.

For the last two weeks, neither Georgie nor Emily had given him a moment's peace. Every waking moment they badgered him to walk the country lanes, to spar with dagger or rapier, and to drink gallons of water. They denied him extra servings at table and whisked him away before the sweet was served. Already his clothing looked baggy. At least they allowed him to satisfy his craving for liver.

Beside him, Belle sat and opened her mouth in a toothy grin, her version of a laugh.

"Do not look so superior, Belle," he warned. "You look mighty silly yourself, nursing a litter of kittens!" Today, her adopted children frolicked around her feet, exploring the world of the house garden. The big calico female kitten strayed under a rosebush. Belle stuck her nose in among the thorns and grabbed the erring child in her mouth. Only a bit of black tail with a white band and an orange tip showed. Deftly the monstrous wolfhound deposited the kitten back among her brothers at Belle's feet. Dog-slobber matted the multicolored fur. Otherwise it seemed undamaged from its sojourn in Belle's mouth.

The mother dog proceeded to lick the kitten clean, against loud protests and another attempt to escape.

Belle's gentleness with her fragile charges never ceased to amaze Drake.

"Stop staring at the kitties, and defend yourself!" Georgie ordered. She took up an en garde position, ominously close to Drake.

"I'm tired."

"You will be more tired when I'm done with you."

The chit breathed easily and looked as fresh and vigorous as she had when she dragged Drake out of his private study for a spot of exercise.

The errant calico dashed to escape Belle's vigilance once more. In a single bound it landed upon Georgie's booted foot, then scampered up her breeches, across her back, and onto her shoulder.

Before Georgie could bat the intruder away, the kitten settled in for a bath, nuzzling her chosen one's ear with every other lick.

Belle heaved a sigh of relief and turned her attention to the other five kittens, none quite so daring as the calico.

"What?" Georgie looked askance at the encumbrance on her shoulder. "Are you ready to leave the litter?"

If the cat answered, Drake did not hear it.

Drake shifted his gaze from Belle to the kitten and back again. His familiar seemed to have lost interest in the bold female. "Does the kitten speak to you yet?" Drake asked, still puzzled at Belle's insistence that Georgie have a familiar. He lowered his sword and approached one long step toward his sister.

"Don't be ridiculous. This is a cat. An infant cat." Georgie tapped her blade nervously against her boot.

"Hush, Georgina. Open your mind and listen," he snapped at her. This was too important to put up with protests and mind-blind attitudes.

The dogs always knew when a member of the family needed a familiar.

For once, Georgie obeyed him. She closed her mouth with a snap, and stilled her body. Her grip on her sword loosened. "All I hear is a rumble of contentment," she whispered. "No, there is more. Much more. I'm feeling a great deal of satisfaction and . . . and awe at how big the world is. So much bigger than Mama's box or this garden. So much bigger than the people. Than me!" The last came out on a squeak.

Drake shook his head in amazement. "Then it is settled. You are fully bonded with your familiar. She will spend less and less time dependent upon Belle. You must care for her." A strange calm came over Drake. Whatever was coming, his sister was now ready to tackle the task.

He wondered briefly if this meant that henceforth, the Pendragons would be accompanied by mere cats instead of the majestic wolfhounds of Kirkenwood.

Regardless, Drake had a protocol to follow. He dropped stiffly to one knee. He tugged at the signet ring on the littlest finger of his left hand, with its red enameled dragon rampant on a black field, symbol of the Pendragon. The gold band jammed and he could not get it over the folds of skin around his knuckle.

It had come off last month when he shared it with Milton. He'd lost weight since then. The ring should slide off easily. Why not now?

"Stay, Brother." Georgie placed her hand atop his. The kitten balanced easily on her shoulder, digging in her claws just enough to grasp waistcoat fabric.

Drake was amazed at the instinctive balance and blending of his sister and her new familiar.

"I must acknowledge you my heir," Drake protested, still struggling with the ring.

"Not today. When the time comes, the ring will come off. You gave it to Milton when you thought he might succeed you. Then you retrieved it to work your healing magic on me and never returned it to him." She stopped to take a deep breath and look deeply into the eyes of her kitten.

"Do you not see, Drake, this is an omen. You are not to relinquish your hold on life yet. I am but a temporary substitute. Something comes. I will be needed where you cannot be or have not the skills to succeed. But you are still the Pendragon of Britain."

Her words rang in Drake's ears with preternatural truth. He looked to Belle for confirmation. She ignored him, settling in to nurse the five kittens. Georgie's calico tumbled from her perch in her hurry to get to Belle and share in the meal.

"Perhaps . . ."

"Ahem," Simpson cleared his throat from a respectful

ten paces away. "Excuse me, milord. A courier from the palace."

Drake pushed himself to his feet, surprised that he did not need Georgie's help. Perhaps his sister's regimen was aiding his health after all—for all the pain and hunger.

A courier in red royal livery stood stoutly beside Simpson, not giving him the respectful space as senior servant in the situation. Drake scowled at the man. His face remained impassive.

When Drake had his full balance, he tapped his foot with his own rapier, much as Georgie had done earlier.

Finally, the courier proffered a folded parchment bearing the gaudy red personal seal of the king.

No wonder the man considered himself above all those present, including an earl.

Drake grabbed the packet and broke the seal. The outer page was nothing more than a blank envelope. Inside he found a missive written in His Majesty's precise hand, noting the date and time of day of his penning.

"I am summoned to Windsor this very afternoon. Excuse me, Georgie, I must hasten." He nodded to his sister and began stalking toward the house. Drake's mind spun with possibilities. His Majesty, George III, had never before summoned him as the Pendragon. Like his grandfather and great-grandfather before him, he had been raised with German sensibilities and no tradition of the ancient heritage. This letter was clearly addressed to Drake Kirkwood, Seventh Earl of Kirkenwood, and Pendragon of Britain. Something dire must transpire.

Belle lumbered to her feet and followed. The six kittens struggled out of their drowsiness from nursing and scampered at the dog's feet.

The courier remained unmoved at the sight of the massive wolfhound nursing six kittens.

"Is there a reply, milord?" the courier asked.

"Yes. I shall pen a few words. You may wait in the kitchen." The courier sniffed but said nothing.

"Georgina." Drake half turned to face his sister. "You will come with me, though I wish Lady Emma could come, too. She perceives so much more than I do." He paused a moment looking at an upper window of the house. He thought he saw his beloved wife observing everything, but the glare on the glass obscured the interior. "You may be my heir only temporarily, but while you are, you will accompany me in my official duties. Make yourself presentable to meet the king and prime minister. We leave within the hour."

Marlowe House, Bayswater District, London.

Dr. Milton Marlowe bent over his scrying bowl. A secret smile played across his face. He watched the Honorable Emily Kirkwood as she penned a love letter to Barclay, her newly affianced suitor.

"She appears totally engrossed in her task," Samuel de Vere said tightly. He rested a heavy hand upon Milton's shoulder, lending him strength and clarity. Samuel's one strong talent lay in seeing things in the far distance.

Milton waved his hand over the water. The vision of Emily, looking very attractive and grown up with her hair twisted into a pile atop her head, and the heavy Marlowe signet ring on her left hand, vanished.

Samuel wilted slightly, but kept his hand on Milton's shoulder.

"The girl is completely enthralled with Barclay and the idea of marriage. I have no need to cast a spell upon her to ensure the wedding takes place next month." Milton brushed Samuel's hand aside.

The big bodyguard sank into a nearby chair without asking leave. He looked pale. Strain lines radiated out from his eyes and curved downward from his mouth.

"What ails you, young man?" Milton snapped. Samuel had no business tiring so easily from such a minor spell.

"I do not like this, sir."

"Like what?"

"Spying upon an innocent young woman with magic." Samuel averted his eyes and hung his head.

"I doubt that the Honorable Emily is so innocent," Milton sneered.

Samuel's lips thinned as he pressed them together.

"She is essential to our plans, Samuel. For the good of all England we need the Honorable Emily. She is our only hope for keeping the Kirkenwood estate and the Pendragon Society from falling into the hands of incompetent mundanes."

"Yes, sir." Samuel didn't sound convinced.

"My son is our best choice for husband to her. I'd marry her myself if I thought her father would agree. But he wouldn't agree to that." Milton had no desire to wed again either. His union to Neville's and Barclay's mother had been a cold and emotionless affair. The woman had done her duty in providing him two sons and a significant dowry, then had obliged the world by dying in childbed. Yet Neville had died—most horribly—and Barclay was a wastrel. But he could justify his existence by gaining Milton access to the archives. Then he could restore Neville to life and set the world on its proper course again.

"Forgive my impertinence, sir, but your son Barclay does not love Miss Kirkwood. He might hurt her," Samuel protested.

"As long as he does her no damage so that she can provide an heir to the earldom, how he treats her is not my concern." Milton shoved his chair away from the table and the scrying bowl.

"Sir." Samuel's lips thinned again and he narrowed his eyes. "If he hurts her . . ."

"You will do nothing. Your impertinence grates on me, Samuel. You could show a little gratitude after I removed you from obscurity in a clerk's position that did not pay you enough to live in the most modest circumstances." Milton paced around the room. He picked up his athame from the altar in the corner. He ran his thumb along the razor-sharp blade.

"You are in danger of having your employment terminated, Samuel. I have need of a great deal of blood for the ritual to remove you from our coven. So much blood you probably will not survive."

"Yes, sir. I will not interfere."

His expression implied he had more to say, but Milton could not read his intentions in his face or his aura. He slunk out of the dark room.

He thinks too much, Pater. Thinkers are dangerous. They cannot be controlled, Neville reminded him. His ghost clung to the altar and the herbs and rituals Milton kept there for that purpose.

"I can control Samuel de Vere."

Can you?

Chapter 20

"WITHIN the hour, he said," I grumbled to Emily as I traipsed down to the ground floor in high heeled slippers, clocked stockings, powdered wig, face paint, complete with beauty spot, and a gown of brocaded blue taffeta with a yellow underskirt. The panniers bumped against the railings as I made my clumsy way. Bits of things seemed to be flying off me as tatters in the wind. I could have bought a vineyard in Italy with the amount of lace on the sleeves of my underbodice, fichu, and cap.

Thankfully, the gown belonged to my sister-in-law and fit me loosely enough I need not wear a corset.

Drake stood in the porte cochere with his timepiece in his hand. "Seven minutes late, Georgina. Lady Emma is always precisely on time, even if she has to wait a few moments above stairs." He snapped the miniature clock closed.

I thought he wore a corset to confine his belly in his bottle-green coat with scarlet frontings to match his waistcoat. Beneath his elegant wig, his face appeared a mite thinner than it had a week ago.

"Do you know how long it takes to dress for court?" I screeched at him. My vision suddenly doubled. I saw myself from below, a long way below, as well as my own view of the entryway. I stumbled blindly but caught my balance with a hand on the banister. Almost.

Then to compound my scattered thoughts and dress, I tripped over my kitten on the last stair. I stumbled and flailed. After bouncing off the wall and a bench, I landed in Drake's ample arms.

"I thought the cats were confined to the kitchen!"

A wash of satisfied mischief upset my balance further. How was I to manage with a familiar doubling my senses and skewing my perspective?

Drake steadied me with a disapproving cluck. "How can you appear so graceful, elegant, and feminine in men's clothing with a sword in your hand and so much the opposite when attired appropriately to your sex?"

When I had my balance, he set me away from him as if I were tainted.

By his standards I was tainted.

"Perhaps the rules for feminine behavior and clothing need changing," I snarled. "I cannot protect you from assassins, magical and mundane, dressed thus!" I held up a bit of my overskirt, revealing more of the costly lace trim. I did not show him my favorite dagger-pistol in the secret pocket designed for a mirror and comb.

"I do not need protection. I am the Pendragon. I have defenses." He pivoted on his well-shod heel and strode toward the waiting carriage. "I will not argue on this, Georgina. Come, we will be late."

I snorted, then thought better of the retort that seemed merited. "We would make better time on horseback. I could wear Lady Emma's habit," I grunted as I squeezed acres of gown, pannier hoops, and petticoats into the seat facing the rear. A true gentleman would allow the lady to face front. Drake saw me as an unmanageable hoyden rather than a lady. I did not protest as that might lessen my argument for riding horseback.

"One does not arrive at court atop a horse, Georgina. Now hush and allow me to ride in peace."

I held my tongue, barely, for the two-hour journey to Windsor, the king's favorite residence.

Drake shifted and fidgeted the entire way. I wondered if he was nervous about meeting His Majesty and Lord Grenville, or if his body rebelled against the rocking carriage. "Say it!" he finally hissed at me.

"Say what?" I opened my eyes wide and stared at him, all feminine innocence.

"What you have been longing to say. I would be more comfortable ahorse. As would you."

"I do not need to say it. You just did."

Our arrival up the long drive to Windsor ended the

discussion. We were led through an elaborate protocol from room to room until we finally bowed before His Majesty, George III, in a private solar. The young king busily potted a miniature rose while his prime minister sorted through an endless sheaf of folios and dispatches. King George wiped his hands on a damp towel and gestured us toward the hearth. He sat straight and proper upon a wing chair, legs neatly crossed at the ankle. He did not offer my brother and me a seat. We were not favored enough for that familiarity. Instead, he stared at me askance.

"You brought a woman with you?" Grenville asked from his own chair at the writing table by the long windows that led to the famous rose gardens.

"My sister, the Honorable Georgina Kirkwood, Your Majesty. And my heir."

"Your estate is entailed to the next male legitimate blood relative," Grenville snapped. "As all titles and estates should be."

I bristled at the insult to me and my kind, but kept my mouth closed. Arguing with this man would gain nothing and only prolong the time I must stand in shoes that upset my balance and pinched my toes. I'd rather lop off the prime minister's ears with a rusty dagger. That would gain me less and cost me more.

"Do I have to remind Your Majesty that I have inherited more than an earldom?" Drake asked, raising one eyebrow. Its thin and graying fairness nearly got lost in the folds of extra skin, diminishing the superior effect of his expression.

"I do not see how one spinster, a rather long-in-the-tooth spinster at that, can aid you, Milord of Kirkenwood." King George fished a quizzing glass out of the pocket of his plain wool waistcoat. He proceeded to inspect me, and presumably found me wanting.

"My sister is a widow," Drake hastened to add before I could say something to remind these men that I was in the room and heard every word they said about me. "She was married some five years to a minor prince in Italy."

"And reverted to her maiden name?" George put away the glass, but still continued to address my brother.

"My family is more ancient and honorable than nearly

every noble house in Europe," I said. "My stepson rules his principality with a heavy hand. He cast me out with little more than the clothes on my back. He also confiscated my dowry. I am well shut of the place and will speak of it no more!" I lifted my chin and stared at the king in high indignation.

Close enough to the truth. I had lived with an Italian nobleman for some two years in Paris. And I had left his home with little more than the clothes on my back. He had left more hastily with every possession of value he could carry in the dead of night, including several pounds of chocolate. I was better off never speaking his name in public.

King George inspected me again, without the glass and with more respect. As a dowager princess, he deemed me more worthy than a mere spinster. I inspected him with equal scrutiny, looking down upon him as if he were a mere frog in my path.

"She may stay," he said at last. "Now, we have business to discuss, Kirkenwood. I have use for your peculiar talents in the colonies."

"How may I assist, Majesty?" Drake bowed slightly.

I kept my knees locked, not dropping into a curtsy.

"Show them." George gestured to Grenville.

The prime minster handed Drake a stack of pamphlets from the larger sheaf of papers. "These circulate through the colonies faster than the royal mail," he grunted.

I peered over Drake's shoulder at some of the titles. "In Defense of Our Rights as Englishmen." "Royal Violations of Our Charter." "Land Ownership Is Worth Less than an Honest Man's Toil: A Craftsman's Right to Vote."

I needed to read no further to know that all of the publications were inflammatory at the least, bordering on rebellion and treason more likely.

The titles echoed many of my own sentiments. I had, perhaps, less respect for authority than had the colonists. But I had taken actions to live my life as I saw fit, I had not wasted time writing pamphlets.

The earth tilted beneath my feet. My senses reeled for a moment. I needed to clutch Drake's arm to remain upright. More than the heat from the fire and the pinching of my toes fueled this dizziness. A new path for the future appeared before me. I had never questioned the natural order of monarch and nobility at the top of the government. With land ownership came responsibility to one's people, and therefore more privilege—as in the right to vote.

But if I deplored the worldview that women were weak and inconsequential, why should I not question the form of government and the rights of a landed few?

Just like I had never questioned where and how an army received its pay, I had never questioned the rights of Englishmen. Only the rights of English *women*.

Now, seemingly I must.

"Breathe, Georgie," Drake whispered. "Keep your eyes open and breathe deeply. Lock your knees."

"They are locked," I whispered back.

"Keep the semblance of awareness," he ordered.

"Is there a single instigator?" Drake held up the pamphlets. "The authors all seem to be pseudonyms. Josiah Truthteller, A gentleman in His Majesty's service, Verity Goodbody." He held up each pamphlet in turn as he read the author's name.

"There is no consistency in the style of the pamphlets," Grenville said. "These are but a few of hundreds of pamphlets that circulate the colonies every day. Some more literate than others."

"I see references to Cicero, Locke, and Titus. Few are accurate." Drake handed them to me. The first two were folded and stitched into a single quarto. The third a full octavo. All closely printed, filling the pages.

"For all their lack of sophistication, I find the logic clear and . . . coherent." I wanted to say the arguments were compelling, but dared not.

"Insidious treason," Grenville spat. "Satan himself speaks logically."

"If Satan, or merely a few rebellious traitors have found an audience among Our loyal colonists, We have need of the truth," George said. He steepled his fingers and peered through them. His thumbs waggled behind the walls made by his fingers. In agitation? Or contemplation? "You, Milord of Kirkenwood, with your . . . er . . . preternatural talents, are uniquely qualified to provide it."

If you have these talents, indeed.

I heard the king's doubts as if he had spoken.

Drake and I exchanged knowing glances. He had heard them, too.

"You must sail to the Americas, Kirkenwood, and gather as much information as you can." Grenville handed Drake several unfolded pages. The heavy seals and dangling ribbons indicated letters patent and passport. "Your reports will aid His Majesty in formulating plans to suppress this . . . cancer that infests his loyal colonists."

"Majesty, you put me in a most awkward position." Drake bowed as low as his corset allowed. "I recognize my duty to you and to Britain in this matter. However, my countess awaits her confinement. We pray for a male heir after many years and five daughters. My own health is not the best. You need a different agent. One younger and healthier."

"He cannot go," I insisted. " 'Tis not fitting for the Pendragon to leave Britain. You, Milord Earl, are tied to the land. Leave and England becomes more vulnerable to the agents of Chaos."

The Earth pulsed against my feet seconding my warning. Danger awaited us all.

"Then you must go in my stead, Georgie," Drake turned toward me, his face lit with excitement.

"No." I could not leave him. He needed my protection. Even now, I fingered my hidden weapon. I also sharpened my senses to take in the aura of menace I felt coming in waves from Lord Grenville.

"Of course she cannot go." King George looked at me aghast. "A woman is most unsuited to this task."

I firmed my chin and stiffened my spine. I was suited to the job. Admirably suited. I had done it before for that other secret Lodge.

But I had to keep my mouth shut. I could not put Drake in danger by leaving. Nor could I betray my allegiance to that other Lodge that had directed Heinrich der Reusse and me through so many political . . . adventures.

Chapter 21

Kirkwood House, Chelsea, England.

"LORD George Sackville," Simpson intoned from the doorway of Drake's private study.

I looked up from the folio of protection spells I studied.

"My brother and I will receive Lord Sackville in the parlor, Simpson." Where had Drake gotten to? Probably in Emma's solar, where he spent nearly every waking moment.

"You will receive me here, Mistress Kirkwood." A slender man with hooded brown eyes and a receding chin pushed past Simpson. The scent of pipe tobacco clung to him like damp stockings. And something else.

Did I smell burned sulfur around him?

The butler looked sharply over his shoulder at the intruder. I'd never seen him lose his aplomb before. Then he masked his startlement. Every good servant knew how to do that. He looked to me for confirmation that I would receive the Irish lord in this intimate surrounding without benefit of chaperone.

What more damage to my reputation could the man do than I had already done myself?

But then the taint of scandal still clung to this slender man with the beetling eyes. He might be accepted, even courted, in Parliament, but his name rarely appeared on invitation lists for polite society.

I had never been court-martialed. He had, after badly bungling his orders and losing a battle during the war.

"Have we been introduced?" I looked down my nose at

the man. Though his barony outranked my honorable status, I did not rise to greet him or curtsy.

He stared back at me. "Introductions are unnecessary. I know who you are and you know me." He turned a harsh glare at Simpson. "Leave us."

"Mistress Georgina?" The good butler remained firmly rooted in place.

"Escort Milord Sackville to the parlor. My brother the earl may receive him there. If not, then show him the door." I returned to my book.

"Where were you October last? The fifth of that month," Sackville demanded.

I stilled. Where had I been? Days, months, even years blended together when living on the battlefront.

"That is of no import." I shrugged away the man's impertinence. But there was something about that date. Where had I been?

"You may serve tea here, Simpson." My scandals might outweigh his at that.

"M'lady?"

I stared at the butler, imploring him to go away, but not too far.

"Tea, m'lady. For two."

He closed the door behind him. I did not hear the latch click.

"Where was I on the fifth day of October last, Lord Sackville?" I finally asked. Cold dread washed over me.

"A woman of your description was seen in Dresden." Lord Sackville looked about him for a place to sit.

I did not offer to clear one of the chairs of its litter of books and parchment rolls, maps and charts.

"There are many tall women of fair coloring in the Germanies."

"How many women in the company of Prince Heinrich der Reusse who are expert with a rapier?" Failing to find a clear seat, Sackville perched atop a precarious pile of tomes on a straight-backed chair beside the desk, facing my wing chair beside the cold hearth.

I remembered the night. I'd lost a bet to several junior officers, a single draw of cards that I had not been able to predict. But then, I had been as drunk as they. The penalty was to dress as a woman and attend a soiree upon the colonel's arm.

Heinrich and I had laughed long about the irony of my losing the bet. We'd planned all along for me to attend the soiree as a woman, with multiple weapons hidden within my petticoats and my towering hairpiece. I had fulfilled my end of the bargain with calm if not grace.

"I have the prince's acquaintance. I have attended many functions with him in the last five years."

"Have you used these other occasions to cover your activities as a hired assassin?"

"You have the wrong of it, m'lord. I am no assassin!" I half rose, betraying my anger. "If I had a sword to hand, I'd run you through for the insult."

The Lodge that directed my activities did not call strategic removal of obstacles to peace and stable governments assassinations.

"But you cannot deny that King Augustus III of Poland met an untimely death that night. At the same soiree that you and Prince Heinrich attended."

"That was an accident!"

"A planned accident perhaps?" He smirked.

Silence. He had the right of it after all.

"Can you deny, Mistress Kirkwood, that Augustus' death has upset the balance of power in Poland? Catherine of Russia seeks to insert one of her lovers onto the throne. A puppet under her control." Sackville grimaced as if saying the Russian queen's name left a bitter taste in his mouth.

"Augustus was no more than a puppet of the German Electors and the English king." With Russia in control of Poland, they were in a better position to stem the tide of Ottoman incursions into Europe.

King George's policies tended to be as shortsighted as those of his grandfather and great-grandfather. Austria stood between the Ottoman Empire and Europe, between order and chaos; therefore, the Ottoman Empire need not be considered while developing foreign policy.

"English alliances in the Germanies are essential to very profitable trade agreements. If, because Russia controls Poland, our German allies must go to war to protect their borders, those trade agreements are in jeopardy. And we must send yet more troops to support our allies. We could see another Seven Years War—a more expensive war than the last. You have done England a great disservice, Mistress Kirkwood."

The scene flashed before my memory. The scent of burning candle wax in an overheated room, overlaid by the heavy perfumes of the crowd in too small confines, nearly made me dizzy. Laughter, champagne, and heady chocolate had filled the minds and hearts of everyone there, including Heinrich, Prince of the Sovereign States of Reusse. He'd said something out of turn. A man took offense and drew his sword.

Heinrich had answered the challenge with his own blade. A brawl ensued.

King Augustus III of Poland was an obese man whose girth did not allow him to move out of the way. I did not see whose blade pierced the puppet king's heart.

Chaos erupted. To defend myself and Heinrich, I'd stolen a sword from a nearby courtier and literally cut a path for Heinrich and me to exit. No need to use my own blade or my dagger pistol. Someone else had done my job for me that night.

We'd left Dresden within the hour and returned to the safer environs of the Austro-Ottoman border.

None of this did I relay to Sackville.

"If you are convinced that I was present on the night of King Augustus III's death and that I have done a disservice to England, why have you not brought this information before Prime Minister Lord Grenville, or the king himself?" If he spoke, I could well end up in the Tower, or worse. I had a sudden craving for the spicy bitterness of chocolate. Tea would have to do. I poured myself a cup without offering any to Sackville.

"You are in a unique position to atone for your ... er ... mistake."

I glared at him, not liking the turn of the conversation. He had atoned for failing to obey orders at a crucial moment during the Battle of Minden in 1759 by maintaining a brilliant career in the House of Commons and serving the government at every turn.

"If trade with the Germanies is disrupted, or we are drawn into another war, His Majesty will need alternate sources of revenue," Sackville said blandly.

I had heard this argument before. Very recently.

"The American colonies are rich, yet pay very little into the Exchequer."

"The Stamp Act," I said quietly.

"Is in danger of being repealed."

"Enforcement of the Sugar Act?"

"Smuggling is a way of life in the colonies, almost an honorable profession."

"The pamphleteers . . ." Suddenly I knew what Sackville would demand in return for his silence.

"Your brother refused His Majesty's request to journey to the colonies as his spy. I charge you with fulfilling the duties of the Pendragon in the New World."

"In exchange for . . ." Where had he learned of the role of the Pendragon? The office was supposed to be secret from all but the Pendragon Society and His Majesty.

"I offer you my silence and, therefore, your freedom."

Whitehall, London, mid-April, 1764.

"We need to consult an expert on colonial affairs," I said firmly.

Drake paced the small office in Whitehall while we waited for my letters patent and passport to be drawn up, signed, and sealed.

Having accepted the necessity of traveling to the colonies, I found myself almost excited about the adventure.

"Best if you begin your quest for information in ignorance and therefore free of prejudice," Drake replied. He paused his restless movements long enough to stare out the window at the regiment drilling their horses in close formation.

Normally I, too, would occupy my time with the same distraction. Since my interview with the king, nothing was normal. I had gone from unwanted spinster sister to valued royal spy in a matter of moments. But I still had the threat of traitor to the king hanging over me.

I expected to be gone from England for six months, perhaps a year. Then I could return and aid Drake in shoring up England's defenses against whoever had murdered the puppies, and sought to end the line of Pendragons.

In the meantime, I had placed a number of protection spells upon my brother, upon his house, his family, and the secret meeting chamber. I'd also given Emily the keys to the spells so that she could renew them if necessary.

If I had to lose my freedom, living the life I chose as a mercenary, then I would take an active role in the leadership of the Pendragon Society. That offered me a measure of freedom, and a sense of purpose.

"All of the pamphlets I read came from a city called Boston," I mused. "So why does His Majesty send me to the colony of Virginia, several hundred miles south of Boston?" In the past weeks, I had improved my knowledge of colonial geography three hundredfold. I still had alarming gaps in my intelligence gathering about this assignment. I did not like entering any campaign with less than full information.

"The citizens of Boston tend to be craftsmen and merchants," Drake replied. He came to sit beside me, speaking eagerly. The animation in his face banished much of the bloating of disease. "The men of Virginia are mostly large landowners. The Virginians will provide the leadership of any rebellion that foments over the proposed new taxes. These landowners are the intelligentsia of the New World, educated in England and Europe. World travelers, sophisticated men. The northerners are mostly home-educated Puritans, incapable of organizing anything more than a small mob of sailors and vagabonds."

The ground thrummed into my feet. A buzzing sound, like dozens of angry bees beat against my ears in rhythm with the Earth.

"You truly believe that any threat to His Majesty's sovereignty over the American colonies will come from the plantation owners."

In that instant I knew that he believed it to the bottom of his soul. But the Earth told me that another truth existed.

This talent for truth telling was new to me. Yet it came through a familiar path. The Earth Mother had never failed me.

"Tell me, Brother, does a gentleman by the name of Benjamin Franklin still reside in London?" Even in Paris and Vienna I had heard of the learned gentleman from the city of Philadelphia. I needed more information. I could think of no more illustrious man than the good Dr. Franklin to give me the information I craved.

"Alas, Georgie, Franklin quitted London more than a year ago."

"Then I shall find another with firsthand knowledge of the personalities and leadership among the prominent colonists." I rose from my chair. Doing it gracefully, in a gown and heeled slippers, came easier today than last month.

Just then a deputy minister bustled into the room with my papers.

I leafed through the passport and letters patent as we made our way through the maze of rooms toward an exit.

"Drake?" I stopped my brother who had stridden ahead of me. "They have given me a new name."

"A necessity considering the work you will be doing." He shrugged off my misgivings.

I tasted the words written before me, Georgina Mondo, widow. The name tripped off my tongue pleasingly enough. Could I become this woman? I had hoped His Majesty would listen to my pleas to allow me to travel and work as a man. He had overruled me, not knowing my true history and accomplishments.

"I am to be governess to three children!" I squeaked. My heart beat in my throat. Children! I could no more teach three strange children than I managed to keep the names of my brother's daughters straight. Only Emily, with hints of strawberry in her hair, stood out in my mind as a separate personality. The others became a blonde blur in my mind, ranging in size from miniature to petite.

"The only natural position for you to take, Georgina," Drake reminded me.

"The only natural position for a lady of education and good reputation," I muttered in reply, not truly caring if he heard me or not.

Drake kept on walking. At least he had a spring in his step these days. His walking stick had become more of an accessory than an aide.

A familiar masculine outline appeared before us, backlit by the sunshine in the forecourt. I could see none of his features. I did not need to. Looking frantically for another exit, I pressed myself against the wall. Hopefully the shadows would hide me.

"Milord of Kirkenwood," Roderick Whythe greeted my brother. He doffed his uniform hat and bowed deeply, as befitting a wellborn gentleman to an earl.

"Have we been introduced?" Drake asked. He looked down his nose at the top of Whythe's head.

"Not formally, sir. I do have acquaintance of a relative of yours. One Major George Kirkwood, late of Heinrich der Reusse's mercenary company."

"Georgie?"

Drake did not betray me by a glance over his shoulder. But I detected a shift in his position, so that his body angled more toward mine, five paces behind his left shoulder.

"Aye, milord. We called the major Georgie. I lost track of him outside Belgrade and wondered if you know his whereabouts." Whythe kept his eyes upon my brother.

I shrank farther into the shadows, praying that he did not look past Drake's shoulder.

"I fear we've lost Georgie," Drake said. Almost the truth. If I were to become Georgina Mondo, widow, and governess to three brats, then Major Georgie Kirkwood was no more.

"My condolences, milord. May I call upon Lady Emma with an offering of sympathy?"

"Lady Emma is indisposed. She is not receiving."

"Then I shall trouble you no further, milord." Whythe bowed again and retreated one step before turning.

Did his shoulders slump in sadness? I wished I could read his aura as Drake could. I needed to know why he had sought me out. I needed to ease the pain from his posture.

"You can't hide from him forever, milady," a man with a deep Scottish brogue whispered into my ear. "He's tried to see you a number of times. Upon orders."

I jumped and started. Ian, Whythe's batman stood next to me. His gaze remained fixed upon his superior officer and not on me.

"Where did you come from?" I whispered back to him. I could only guess that Sackville had sent Whythe to spy upon me. I truly detested that man.

"I came from the same place he did." He indicated Whythe with a nod of his head. "We been reviewing the troops for inclusion in our next venture."

"And what would that be?"

"I am not at liberty to say, milady."

"Will you betray me to your master?" I did not dare ask how he knew me, clad and bewigged as suitable to my rank, when he'd seen me previously as a skinny young mercenary soldier of light cavalry.

"Not unless you wish me to, milady."

"Did you tell him that the Georgie Kirkwood he seeks is female?" Ian must have guessed as much when he carried me to the woods witch after the battle.

"Nay, milady. 'Tis your secret to tell. Not mine." He bowed and moved off. After two long strides he paused. "Ye'll meet him again, milady. You won't be able to hide then. Best you form a story he'll believe."

"Good thing I sail for Virginia thirty days hence."

"Interesting. So do we." Then he, too, disappeared into the sunlight.

Chapter 22

Kirkwood House, Chelsea, England, late May, 1764.

"I WISH you did not have to go, Aunt Georgie," Emily said as she selected three petticoats. She tossed them onto the bed. Daisy, their maid, picked them up, rolled them neatly, and tucked them into the trunk at the foot of Georgie's bed.

"I wish I could stay as well. I am needed here. But the sooner I go, the quicker I can return. Though I would have liked to stay for your wedding," Georgie replied. She looked at the servant as if she willed Daisy away.

"Daisy, will you see if the laundered garments are dry yet?" Emily said. She shooed the girl away with her hands.

"Yes, milady." Daisy bobbed a curtsy and backed out of the doorway. She craned her neck back around the doorjamb as she turned toward the servants' stairs.

Emily kept her mouth closed until she heard the woman's steps retreat.

"She will gossip to the others," Georgie said quietly.

"Aye. The servants know more about us than we know about ourselves."

"I know I cannot counsel you to abandon this marriage, so I must advise you to be cautious with your heart, and with your life." Deep furrows creased Georgie's brow and from her nose to her chin. For half a moment she looked much older than her twenty-five years.

"Is it true that you are widowed?" Emily asked shyly. She dared not ask if her aunt had . . . done the unthinkable, lived with a man not her husband. "When I wrote to you, the addresses you gave me . . . were never in Italy, and certainly not to a palazzo."

Georgie reared back her head and roared with laughter in a very inelegant and unfeminine manner. A wealth of experience lay buried in her eyes.

"Your father wishes the lie we tell were the truth," Georgie said, wiping her eyes clear of mirthful tears with her sleeve. "If the truth be publicly known, he could not allow me to reside in the same household as his respectable wife and five innocent daughters."

"You have never married," Emily gasped. Her heart fluttered with forbidden excitement.

"No, I have never married."

Emily did not know how to phrase her next question.

"Yes, I have known the love of a man as if we had married," Georgie continued. She leveled her gaze upon Emily.

Emily squirmed under that penetrating gaze.

"I have the experience to advise you in many things your mother would not think of."

"As . . . ?" Emily asked hopefully. She had a vague idea of what to expect in the marriage bed. One could not live in the country long and not know *something*.

"As in relax and take your pleasure as it comes. There is no shame in enjoying your husband when he comes to your bed. 'Tis natural, beautiful even. You need not fear him or conceiving until you are ready."

"But . . ."

Georgie smiled and sat upon the narrow bed. She patted it in invitation. Emily sat, wide-eyed and eager. Her aunt whispered many things to her in the next few minutes. Of ways to delay a man until she had her own pleasure, of herbs and schedules to avoid conception, of ways to pleasure a man so that he never sought another's bed.

A step in the corridor reminded them that Daisy returned with an armful of freshly laundered underthings.

"Remember to listen to what he says in the quiet afterward. A man has no bridle upon his tongue once his lust is satiated. As long as your father lives, Barclay will dare not hurt you physically. You can guard yourself against hurts to your heart if you listen to him," Georgie finished. She rose and began rolling one of her blades in another petticoat.

"Captain Marlowe loves me. He would never hurt me,"

Emily replied in hushed tones. Her head whirled with confusion. So much of what Georgie had said sounded logical, the product of much experience. No one had dared speak of such things to Emily, how to manipulate a man to quicker—was arousal the word she had used? Or to prolong his attentions. How to ready herself when his ministrations seemed inadequate. The entire conversation seemed as much a violation of her modesty as what she must endure in the marriage bed.

"The words come easily to a man's tongue when the promise of a rich dowry impels him. His actions in bed will tell you more than any of his words."

Several moments of silence ensued while Daisy clattered into the room.

"Let us stroll in the garden, Emily." Georgie grabbed her elbow and propelled her out of the room. "We must speak of plans to keep your father alive and well as long as possible."

As they steered toward the long windows leading to the terrace from the morning room, the calico kitten pounced upon Georgie's foot.

"Ah, I see your mama has taught you to stalk and hunt," Georgie laughed. She picked up the tiny bundle of fur and cradled it in her arms. Immediately, a soothing rumble erupted from the kitten's throat.

"I envy you the familiar," Emily sighed. She stroked the cat's ears with one finger. It leaned into her caress and lifted its chin for more scratches. "Have you named her yet?"

"I have tried to query her for a preference. She does not care. When I tried to ask Belle why she gave me this one, all I perceived was a sensation akin to the word 'Because.' "

"Because," Emily mused. "Because. *Oblegid* in the old tongue."

"Oblegid," Georgie rolled the word around her mouth as if tasting it.

"Yeow!" the kitten agreed and nuzzled into Georgie's palm.

"Then Oblegid she is," Emily chuckled. A sense of warmth invaded her chest to replace an emptiness she had not realized she possessed. "Do you think Belle will allow me to have one of her adopted children?"

Georgie paused a long moment. "Ask her."

They moved out-of-doors, winding a path through the budding rosebushes.

"I found a spell for protection against magical attack in one of Papa's books. I think I can duplicate it. Then I must convince Papa to wear at all times the talisman imbued with magic by the spell," Emily confided on their third circuit.

"You will manage, Emily. I have confidence in you," Georgie said. She seemed distracted by the kitten's purr.

Belle bounded up from the kitchen. She nosed Georgie's skirt and prodded her arms with a wet nose. Georgie showed Belle the kitten. Belle licked Oblegid once. Her tongue covered her like a blanket.

"Do you need to take her back now?" Georgie asked the dog.

Belle settled into a lazy stroll to match their own.

"I guess the mama is happy to allow you custody for now," Emily said. Her hand rested naturally upon Belle's ears.

"Ask her," Georgie prodded. "She understands more than most dogs. She is a familiar after all."

"Belle," Emily stopped walking and looked into the dog's eyes, as she had seen her father do time and again. "Belle, may I have one of your kittens?"

The dog did not reply by so much as a flick of her tail.

Georgie gasped.

Emily looked sharply at her aunt.

"I think you had best attend your father when he takes Belle back to Kirkenwood for breeding six months hence." Georgie's words came out strangled as if each one hurt her to speak. She kept her eyes closed and her hands trembled. Oblegid tried to climb to her mistress' shoulder, but Georgie held her too tightly, almost fiercely. "Be there when Belle whelps. No matter what Captain Marlowe or his father dictates. Be there!"

"Why?" Emily breathed. The air around Georgie's head grew yellow, then darkened to amber, shimmering and scintillating at the same time. The entire world hushed.

The hairs on Emily's nape rose in fear. She bit her lip to keep from running from this awesome—fearsome— woman. Suddenly she no longer wished Georgie to remain in England.

"Belle will grant your heart's desire. No one will dare question her judgment."

"At what cost this gift?" Emily choked out. Goose bumps raised on her arms. Her spells were not enough. Calling Georgie home was not enough. Everything she did was not enough.

"At the cost of your father's life and great risk to your own."

"You have upset my daughter," Drake said quietly as we went in to dinner.

Lady Em, of course, kept to her rooms. Her legs had swollen badly today and the babe weighed heavily on her spirits as well as her body.

Our cousins, the Marlowes, followed us into the dining room. They seemed always to be in attendance on the family. Only fitting, I supposed, now that Barclay and Emily planned a wedding within weeks.

Barclay carefully avoided any direct conversation with me, or being left alone in my company for more than a single heartbeat.

I had to smile at the signs of his embarrassment. The intimacy of our teenage indiscretion lay between us like a sleeping beast, ready to snarl into life at the slightest provocation.

Emily clung readily to Barclay's arm, smiling up at him with an eagerness that did not soothe me. Every time she looked at him, unease skittered through my limbs, demanding I draw a blade.

"Emily does not appear upset," I returned sotto voce.

"Her betrothed eases her fears."

I sniffed at that notion. Barclay courted her with a purpose that had nothing to do with his heart and everything to do with his pocketbook.

"There is something you and I must do. Tonight. At midnight. In the chamber," Drake finished on a whisper. Then he looked up at the guests with a bright smile and false chatter about the excellence of the wine.

The conversation bored me. Discussions of foxes and crops and the proliferation of licenses to public houses. Dr. Marlowe viewed this as the beginning of a revolution meant to topple the natural order of classes.

I jumped in with an argument drawn from my own experience. "To deny the working classes a pint after a hard day's work shows a distinct lack of responsibility. The public house is necessary to the well-being . . ."

"Taverns provide gathering places for malcontents to stir up trouble!" Milton roared. "A good wife makes her own beer and serves it to her husband. Any man without a wife to make his beer needs to go out and find one."

"In my experience . . ."

Drake shot me a warning glance. A mental probe stabbed me behind the eyes at the same time. Discussion of my military career was out of bounds at table.

I bit back my retort but not my anger.

Barclay winked at me, laughter just below the surface.

Drake merely made polite noises that might have agreed with either of us.

"Have you heard, my dear," Barclay interrupted the conversation. He directed all of his attention toward Emily. "I have purchased my next set of colors. I shall come to our wedding as a brevetted major!"

He had my attention as well as Emily's. What had he done to deserve promotion?

"Pater arranged it," he lowered his voice conspiratorially. But his eyes strayed to mine. He looked as if he needed my approval more than Emily's.

"Too many officers are given promotion on merit alone," Dr. Milton grumbled. "They have no breeding or blood. No money or land. How can they have a stake in the welfare of our beloved nation if they own nothing but their boots? True leadership can only come from the landed classes. The responsibility of higher rank sits more easily upon their shoulders."

I opened my mouth to protest. I had earned every one of my military promotions by exhibiting leadership, intelligence, and responsibility. During my years as a mercenary I had owned little more than my uniforms, my horse, and my blades, with no expectation of earning or inheriting more, other than through loot.

As a female, I had been raised to believe that men alone could lead, fight, and take responsibility for the world outside the home.

I had defied the rules and made my own. I longed for the freedom to do so again. When I came back from the colonies, I promised myself.

The rest of the evening passed in idle chitchat that meant nothing to anyone. The conversation did not cover the tension rising between Milton and myself. I sensed that both of us longed to lash out verbally and physically at each other. More was at stake than the issue of public house licenses and the question of merit promotions.

In a flash I understood how desperately Milton longed to become the next Pendragon. How far would he go to inherit the position? Would he kill innocent puppies to end the ritual of the dogs choosing the heir?

I looked at his soft hands and shuddered. More likely Barclay would carry out the dirty deed at his father's behest. A military man who had seen combat during the war, the younger Marlowe might well have enjoyed the act that nearly sent Drake into death as he tried to follow the spirit of the beloved pups.

When the highwayman had died in Drake's arms, Milton had said . . . what had the doctor said? "I am not ready for you to die yet!"

Had something changed since then, or was there another magical assassin I must look for? I could not remain long enough to discover who. I had pledged myself to spy for the king in Virginia—or go to the Tower for treason.

At last I looked up. We had passed from sweet to savory. The servants cleared the remains. Emily nodded to me. 'Twas time to withdraw and leave the men to their tobacco and port.

I rose from my place opposite Drake. As senior lady present, I had the responsibility for ending the meal. Some perverse imp in my mind wanted to stay and share the wine and a pipe. I'd done it often enough as a mercenary.

Drake leveled his gaze upon me with sternness.

Not tonight, he whispered into my mind. *Do not defy convention tonight.*

I wished I could thrust the thoughts back at him, as I would a weapon. *The rules of convention have no purpose!* None that I could see. I chose to withdraw with Emily. But I would not wait patiently in the drawing room for the men to join us for cards, or music, or whatever mild amusement these "respectable" people allowed themselves.

My kitten and I would patrol the house and gardens, adding our own wards to Drake's against intruders magical and mundane before my midnight rendezvous with my brother. They could not protect Drake against enemies he willingly allowed into the house. I prayed that Emily's protection spell and talisman combined with mine would work.

As I wandered the grounds, I devised a new spell. A spell of inaction and indecision. This one I would put on Cousin Milton.

Chapter 23

POWER pulsed around Drake, waiting for his command to unleash it. Impatient beast that it was, it tried time and again to escape his mental control.

"Not yet," he whispered into the semidarkness of the cavern beneath his home. All four elements shifted restlessly. His body, through the elements, told him that the stars had wheeled around to midnight. He needed sleep.

He sat uncomfortably upon the ground inside a pentagram inside a circle.

He wished Belle had abandoned her kittens for a few hours to aid him in this spell.

"Not much longer," he reassured himself. "Georgie is usually prompt, provided she does not need to dress formally." He chuckled silently at the memory of his usually graceful sister tripping over her skirts and stumbling over her heeled shoes.

In the back of his mind, he sensed Belle's mutual enjoyment of the memory. She was never far from his thoughts. She gave him mental strength and stability even when absent.

Before him lay kindling and sticks ready for a flame. He had drawn the sigils himself at great cost of his energy. If he'd brought Emma to assist, he would face this spell with more strength and assurance. He could not risk her. She'd used none of her slight talent since discovering her pregnancy. Magic took too much energy and nourishment away from the baby.

He heard the slightest chink of a pebble rolling along the passageway from the garden.

"Right on time," he said. He kept his back to the entrance and his sister, knowing instinctively that she stood waiting for his command. No one else could have penetrated to this depth tonight. He'd made certain of that when he laid the magical traps to guard his privacy.

"I come at the command of the Pendragon," Georgie said. Awe tinged her voice. She had not yet grown accustomed to this place, or to the powers that simmered beneath the surface of her personality.

"Enter the pentagram," he said.

She hesitated a moment, then circled around, deasil, along the path of the sun. She paused at the point facing him where he'd left two inches of the circle and pentagram open. He nodded to her to enter there. But she continued around behind him once more, completing her circle. Then back to the opening.

Good, she had remembered her training. He had not the strength or will to close the sigils on his own. Not and be able to do what he must.

One cautious step brought Georgie into the circle. She stooped and closed the drawing with her right index finger in the sand. Then she repeated the procedure inside the pentagram.

"You would be more comfortable standing, Brother," she said softly, offering him a hand to assist him up.

He took it gratefully.

"Will you light the fire, please, Drake?" She stood nearly eye to eye with him, the stacked kindling between them.

" 'Tis something you must learn to do on your own. But in the interest of time and preservation of your energy, I will do it tonight." This Drake could do almost without thought. He snapped his fingers and pointed at the fuel. Tanio, elemental Fire jumped from his index finger into the dry wood. The flame sputtered, disappointed that it must remain small and symbolic. It wanted to rage and burn. Awyr, Air, rushed to aid her brother Fire. Drake ordered her back, a separate entity for now.

"Why did you call me here, Drake?" Georgie whispered. She kept looking around, as if she expected the shadows to take on form, substance, and life.

"I must awaken your mind so that you may link to me. Written reports may serve the king. But they are always incomplete and delayed by months. I, as Pendragon, must know what you know, when you know it. For the defense of the realm and her people, I must be able to see through your eyes and give you news and information that relates to your mission."

"Will it work over such a great distance?"

"It must."

I did not like the paleness of my brother's skin, nor the clamminess on his palms. He overtaxed himself. He fasted too long and then gorged after working magic. He needed more balance in his life and his diet.

Drake began chanting in Old Welsh. I had studied this language once and never fully understood it. Then I had forgotten most of it during my years on the Continent.

A wall of power rose up around us, defined by the circle. It arced and sealed us. I knew better than to try to touch the translucent walls. Everything outside it appeared distorted, tilted a few degrees to the left of normal.

My senses tried to compensate for the shift. I lost focus and balance.

Then Drake's right hand snaked out and clamped onto my face. One fingertip pressed against my left temple. The others fanned across my brow and face. At each point of contact, my skin burned clear through to the bone.

I wanted to jerk away from him, knew I could not.

My own hand stretched forward and clasped Drake's face in the same configuration. Somehow, my much smaller hand stretched to cover his broad face. As each fingertip made contact, a surge of fire raced through me, back and forth between us until we both glowed from the flames within.

Lightning flashed across my vision. Inside and out, I saw/felt/heard/tasted/smelled the acidic tingle on the back of my tongue. New ideas, strange knowledge, arcane thoughts opened to my mind. Faint dreams became possibilities.

Drake sagged against me.

We had not finished. I knew not how to ground the magic he had unleashed. Leaving it half complete would backlash threefold.

Ruthlessly, I gave him whatever strength I had in my body and my mind. My knees grew weak and my hands trembled. Not enough. His eyes rolled up and his tongue lolled. Somewhere around my feet I heard Belle whimper and Oblegid mew.

I needed more strength, more power. Frantically I searched the cavern for whatever latent magic might have embedded in the rocks or soil.

There! A faint scintillating light called to me.

I latched onto the glimmer with my mind and fed it to the blending between my brother and myself. Another light appeared and I grabbed it, too, along with three more.

Drake sagged less. His eyes focused on mine.

"Almost complete, Georgina," he whispered.

The pathways between his mind and mine blossomed. I suddenly knew him as intimately as I knew myself, all of his hopes and fears for the future, his intense love for his wife, the way he cherished his daughters, and every magic spell he had ever cast.

The flood of knowledge rocked me to my core. I could not withdraw from the intense intimacy of our sharing even if I truly wanted to.

Somewhere in the distance a heavy door slammed. A gust of wind raced down the corridor from the outside. Thudding footsteps intruded on my concentration.

A veil slid between Drake and me. His mind withdrew until I smelled only echoes of his thoughts and tasted only hints of his emotions.

The dome of power surrounding Drake and myself flickered, faded, dissolved. The bonding shattered, incomplete, ungrounded, lethal. Loose magic bounced and ricocheted. It became spears of dark green light. The power needed an anchor.

I reached out and grabbed one spear with my hand before it could pierce my heart. My hand burned and blackened. My bones seemed to crumble to ash, and still I held the backlashing magic.

Drake snatched another spear out of the air. He grimaced and closed his eyes.

In a moment it was over, the magic grounded safely. I slumped, cradling my aching hand. Strangely, the skin was still pink and whole. The joints worked. I could touch it without sending waves of pain through my entire body. But it ached terribly.

"What happened?" I asked, finally having enough sense to look around.

My cousin, Barclay Marlowe, stood in the arching entrance to the cavern.

"I say, old man, what's going on? I thought the temple was empty."

"How did you get in here?" Drake whirled upon the man. His face turned a livid red.

I shared the heat of his anger, the whirling confusion of a spell interrupted.

Outside, Belle woofed her concern. Drake reached with his mind to call her. I knew this, became a part of the summons.

"The gate was open. I sensed no barriers. The temple was supposed to be empty," Barclay protested.

Then the guilt flashed through me. The scintillating lights I had used to add fuel to the spell were the traps that Drake had laid to keep intruders out. I had sabotaged the spell and weakened my bond with Drake out of my own ignorance.

Chapter 24

The home of Richard Jackson, Private Secretary to Prime Minister Lord Grenville, London, England.

"OMNISCIENT Jackson!" Roderick greeted his old school chum in a warm embrace with an enthusiastic slap upon the back.

"Steady Roddie Whythe, as I live and breathe!" Lord Grenville's private secretary returned Roderick's greeting in the foyer of his fashionable London home, forgoing the formalities of receiving him in the parlor. "What brings you to London? Last I heard you were on the godforsaken Austro-Ottoman border."

The two men retired to Jackson's private study at the back of the house. As he accepted a glass of sherry and a comfortable chair before the fire, Roderick chatted about his adventures at the edge of civilization.

Jackson related some of his own adventures in the political arena; his election to Parliament and his stimulating friendship with Dr. Benjamin Franklin, which led to his eager study of colonial affairs. That knowledge had led Lord Grenville, the new prime minister, to tap him as personal secretary.

"When Dr. Franklin returned home, Pennsylvania retained me as their agent," Jackson concluded.

Roderick contemplated briefly requesting his friend's patronage for his own career. Jackson was certainly in a position to sponsor promotions and annuities for him.

Then he dismissed the idea. A gentleman exhibited his leadership and earned his promotions. Roderick had a better chance of doing that in the colonies. But first he had a job to do for General Howe and the prime minister. He had intelligence to gather and reports to write.

"I've come on business, Robert," Roderick admitted. "Within the hour I'm off to Portsmouth and thence to Virginia."

"Massachusetts, Connecticut, and Pennsylvania pay me to represent their interests in Parliament. I have little contact with Virginia." Jackson leaned back in his chair and surveyed Roderick with narrowed eyes and a furrowed brow.

"But you correspond with Dr. Franklin," Roderick prompted.

"Yes . . ." Jackson drew out the word into three syllables, clearly hesitating to commit to more.

"Dr. Franklin informs you of the mood of the colonials." Roderick did not yet know if he approved of the noted scientist, sage, and diplomat. A man who had earned his fortune through hard work and intelligence. Many in London dreaded and eagerly anticipated his return.

"In my capacity as Parliamentary representative I correspond with a number of colonials," Jackson hedged.

"Before I embark to oversee the Virginia battalion, and march them to reinforce General Gage's troops on the frontier, I need to know what opposition I will run into. Will these people house and support the troops as required by Parliament?"

Jackson spent several long moments staring at the fire. At length he heaved a heavy sigh. "The colonials object mightily to housing and feeding fourteen additional regiments among them. The colonials were promised land, the freedom to expand indefinitely to the west. Now the frontier settlements are overrun by Chief Pontiac's alliance. His Majesty has ordered all settlers to return east of the mountains. The colonials feel as if their rights have been revoked. They argue that troops are sent merely to enforce the tighter restrictions upon smuggling and aid in the collection of the new taxes, not to restore the frontier to them."

"Everyone pays taxes . . ." Roderick protested. Even his wastrel father managed to pay his taxes, most years.

"The colonies in America are unique. Revenues have been gathered from them solely as excises, import and export fees. English factories prosper from the sale of manufactured goods to the colonies. Merchants and shipping companies prosper from transporting the goods. The government prospers from taxing that trade."

"Do you tell me that the colonies have never paid taxes?" Astonishment dried up the spate of protests Roderick brewed in his mind.

"Never a direct tax."

"And supporting our troops?"

"They have always paid their own militia, fed, clothed, and housed them. But regular British Army troops have been supported from home. Even during the war."

"And now Lord Grenville insists upon a change."

"His Majesty insists upon a change," Jackson said quietly. "Lord Grenville is merely the instrument of that change. The crown is in debt millions of pounds sterling from the war. The money has to come from somewhere. The colonies owe their fair share of the debt."

"Certainly they do. We defended them against the French, and from the Indians incited to war by our enemies," Roderick agreed.

"They do not believe so," Jackson jumped in. "The colonials feel as if they fought their own war with only minimal assistance from England." Jackson leaned forward and speared Roderick with his gaze. "Tread carefully, Steady Roddie Whythe. Tread carefully and keep your eyes and ears open." Jackson's brown eyes blazed with fervor.

Roderick sat back, putting physical and emotional distance between himself and his friend. He could think of no words to counter Jackson.

"We enter dangerous times, my friend," Jackson continued. "Chaos reigns too often. Our troops have more and more trouble suppressing it, here, on the Continent, and in the New World. I do not want to hear that you have been hung in effigy or tarred and feathered by a mob. The colonials are intelligent, opinionated, stubborn, and volatile. Be very careful."

"I shall," Roderick said with more confidence than he felt. Did he truly wish to throw in his lot with these disrespectful and uncivilized people for the sake of owning his own land?

"I have survived numerous military campaigns because I am careful," he reassured Jackson as well as himself.

The memory of a Turkish saber slicing toward his neck flashed vividly before his mind's eye. He relived the blinding dust, the stench of blood, the broiling sun upon his back, the nervous steed between his knees. The cold fear that he saw death in the eyes of his attacker.

And then a slim lad charged between him and Death, on a horse too big for him, but which he managed to control as if they were one creature. Major Georgie Kirkwood had slashed and jabbed with his own saber, dispatching the enemy.

"In your dealings with the Privy Council and House of Lords, have you encountered the Earl of Kirkenwood?" Roderick asked.

"Upon occasion." Richard Jackson absorbed the rapid change of topic effortlessly.

"Have you ever met a younger brother or cousin of his, a Major George Kirkwood?"

"Can't say that I have. I did meet his sister just yesterday. She, too, is sailing for Virginia, perhaps upon the same ship as you. Georgina Mondo is her name, widow of some petty Italian prince. Her brother called her 'Georgie.'" She asked many of the same questions you did."

"Was she tall, about five feet six inches? Slim, amber-haired and -eyed? Moves with a fencer's grace?"

"Yes. Fetching woman. A bit long in the tooth for my taste, but experience does add spice to the encounter."

"I wonder . . ." Roderick beat a tattoo upon his sherry glass with his fingertips. "I wonder, indeed."

Warping out of Portsmouth, England aboard the good ship Hyacinth, *early June, 1764.*

Fresh air at last! I scooted out of my snug cabin aboard the packet *Hyacinth*, headed for the bow. I breathed deeply, bracing myself against the wind. A hooded oilskin cloak protected me from the inevitable drizzle. In another time and place I would have embraced the elements without heed to my clothing or coiffure.

Henceforth, I must be a woman who cared about such things. I must put aside the last seven years of my life as if they had not happened.

I shuddered in memory of the girl I had been seven years ago when I fled my family and the life planned for me in polite society.

For all the feminine fripperies my new mission required of me, I'd not become a spineless puppet.

"You'll take chill standing out here in the wind," a familiar male voice growled.

I stiffened my spine and turned slowly to face the man. Not by a flicker of an eyelash must I let him know that I recognized him.

"Have we been introduced?" I asked in my iciest tone. Turks in the souk had been known to flee from me when I spoke so.

"My pardon," Roderick Whythe bowed, doffing his tricorn. Moisture gathered in his dark hair. His sober civilian clothes made him seem younger, less careworn than the military man I had fought beside on the frontier of Christendom.

Instantly, I longed for those more carefree days. Death had stalked us every day and night, but we knew his name and accepted his presence as part of life. I had few thoughts of tomorrow back then, only of today and how to live it to the fullest. Now I must walk and speak carefully, ever mindful of who I was and the mission assigned to me.

I'd done this before for the secret Lodge that I must never name. They approved this mission as a move against the growing chaos in the New World. Therefore, I must embrace it, with all of its restrictions and dangers.

Drake's mind brushed against mine. Familiar and cherished, yet removed. I needed to complete my tasks and get back to him as soon as possible. Oblegid mewed from the inside pocket of my cloak. For half a heartbeat Drake came closer, reminding me that if Major Roderick Whythe recognized me, he could betray me to the enemies of England without knowing what he had done. He could betray me to my enemies and land me in the Tower.

I could not afford to end up in the Tower. Drake could not afford for me to end up in the Tower. Neither could my Lodge—though they'd engineer my escape if they found it useful.

My protection spells had to keep my brother safe until I returned.

"Principessa Georgina Mondo del Porto Ricinum." I extended my hand, palm down, for him to kiss.

To my utter astonishment, he brushed his lips across my knuckles.

"I did not realize the *Hyacinth* transported royalty to the New World," he said as he straightened. He tried to catch my eye with his own.

I refused to look at him directly. Who knew what familiarity he might find there. I had to keep him from making any connection to the mercenary soldier fighting for Heinrich der Reusse.

Major Roderick Whythe was an honorable man who believed in the rules of society. I had broken every one that he probably held dear.

He would betray me. I jeopardized my life and my freedom every moment I spent in his company.

The Isle of Wight.

"A pity I could not cross blades with her again," Barclay Marlowe said wistfully. He sighed.

Dr. Milton Marlowe stared at his son. The fine hairs on his nape stood up.

"Do I detect a bit of regret?" he asked. He narrowed his focus from the retreating sails of *Hyacinth* to the droplets of moisture that collected on Barclay's face. An annoying one hung from the tip of his nose, not yet heavy enough to drop. The boy ignored it, as well as the thickening mist that must surely have penetrated his fine uniform coat.

Neville stood behind his brother, always clutching his severed limbs. The rain passed directly through him, mute reminder of his half-life, half-death.

Now that the bitch has removed her influence upon Drake Kirkwood, we must obtain the grimoire, Neville reminded Milton.

"Georgie is most skilled with a dagger. Another bout would test both our skills," Barclay said. He refused to meet his father's gaze, a sure sign that he lied.

"You have fallen in love with the bitch!" Milton roared. He clenched his fists rather than slam them into Barclay's handsome face. Too like his mother in his fairness. Those deep blue eyes with their long dark lashes and his fondness for flamboyant clothing were a certain telltale that Major Barclay Marlowe had inherited feminine weaknesses.

Neville, even mutilated and covered in gore, appeared more masculine, more handsome, more suitable as Milton's heir—as heir to the Pendragon.

"Not love, *Pater*," Barclay laughed. "One does not love Georgie Kirkwood. One enters her orbit temporarily and hopes she allows you exit when she's done with you. I do not have the courage to love her. More like curiosity. I wonder what bedding a wildcat like Cousin Georgina would be like."

"Concentrate on getting a son on your virgin," Milton spat. "Concentrate on becoming the Earl of Kirkenwood with control of the estate and the archives."

"Cousin Georgie is our only rival of any substance. She is gone, hopefully for good. We have nothing more to fear," Barclay said. He placed his hand on Milton's shoulder and squeezed hard.

"We have everything to fear if Drake's wife bears a son. Or if you do not get a son upon Emily." Milton refused to show the hurt from his son's bruising fingers.

"Do not worry, Pater. If the Countess of Kirkenwood bears a son, neither she nor the babe will live long. As for my own bride, I will get a son on her on our wedding night. I have found an ancient 'Gyptian spell that will guarantee it." Finally, Barclay removed his punishing grip from his father's shoulder.

Behind him, Neville nodded his agreement with the Gypsy spell. The idea for the marriage had been his.

Milton resisted the urge to rub his offended anatomy.

"Just make sure you do it. Seduce the girl before the wedding if you can, bring her into our circle of magic any way you can. Leave Drake and his wife and the babe to me. I choose the time of their living and their dying." Dr. Marlowe retreated to the shelter of his closed carriage. He mused over a list of poisons at his disposal, discarding each in turn. "What I truly need is a dose of datura. I wonder if the local woods witch has any ghostweed growing in her herb patch."

Barclay caught up with Milton. He used both strong

hands to forcibly swing his father around to face him. "Pater, be careful. The weed will suck you into whatever spell you use it for. It will enter your body and soul as surely as it does your victim's." He spoke as if he honestly cared.

Samuel approached, ready to separate Barclay from Milton if need be.

Milton waved off his bodyguard.

Ghostweed will bind me to you through eternity, Father, Neville said, licking his lips in anticipation. *If you do not acquire the grimoire and bespell me back to life, I can share yours!*

Milton almost shuddered. The intimacy of such an existence repelled and enticed him. Neville was the only human being he dared to share so much with.

"Never fear, my boy," Milton said. He picked up Barclay's hands one by one and removed them from his shoulders. "I know how to use ghostweed safely. I control it as I control my magic. It does not control me," Milton reassured himself as well as Barclay.

Neville smiled knowingly, as if he planned to control the weed and the spell and his father.

Samuel shuddered and turned away. His mouth worked as if he forced bile back down into his stomach.

"Are you certain you have that much power, Pater?" Barclay asked. He raised one eyebrow sarcastically.

Milton snorted and ducked into the closed conveyance he had hired. "Do not fear for me, Barclay. Fear for yourself if you fail me and our Order. I will be the Pendragon by the end of the month with or without you."

You both need to fear if you fail to get the grimoire.

Chapter 25

Aboard Hyacinth *in the North Atlantic, June, 1764.*

"YOUR Highness," Major Whythe tipped his tricorn to me as I passed him on my way up to the deck.

Maddening man, he insisted upon using my made-up title. I cringed inwardly at the lie.

Lies to protect my disguise had never bothered me before. Why now? I wanted to shout at him to call me "Georgie," and dared not. We'd almost been friends back in that dirty mercenary camp on the edge of nowhere.

Instead, I nodded with whatever regal poise I could muster and reached for the gangway railing.

"May I hold the kitten for you?" he asked. " 'Tis a bit rough today. You'll need both hands on the railing to keep your balance." Then he had the audacity to actually hold out his hand for Oblegid.

The traitorous cat mewed and scrambled from my arms into his. She butted her head into his chin and purred. I could hear the musical rumble as well as feel the satisfaction in her tiny mind. A sense of satisfaction and . . . and safety washed over me. I grabbed the handrail for balance.

Then Oblegid turned her face and looked at me with her slitted eyes. I made eye contact with her as Drake had taught me when seeking rapport or information with a familiar. A set of double images of Major Whythe beside me, me beside him, my face on his body, his face on mine flashed before my inner vision.

"Your Highness!" Major Whythe grabbed my elbow,

keeping Oblegid cradled against his chest with his other hand. "Are you faint?"

I jerked my arm away from his touch. The intimacy implied by Oblegid's contact with my mind frightened me. I had no regrets about giving my body to certain men. I had kept my soul and my heart intact every time. Roderick Whythe threatened that.

"*Si*," I whispered. I allowed a tinge of Italian into my accent, reminding him of the difference in our stations.

"May I escort you back to your cabin?" He gestured back toward the cabins, keeping his hands away from me.

"A breath of fresh air. Such close quarters." This time I placed my right foot upon the step and hauled myself upward.

"Are you certain that is wise, Highness?" The blasted man continued to retain custody of my kitten.

"Very certain, Major Whythe." I made it up another step. And then another.

I concentrated so hard upon putting one foot in front of the other without looking at Major Whythe that I did not notice Oblegid jump from his arms and dash ahead of me until she sat on the top step and mewed. Her concentration remained upon the man behind me. Mine upon my path.

Oblegid yowled and dug in her claws.

The ship lurched.

I lost my grip on the handrail.

The ship rolled back in the other direction.

I fell into Major Whythe's arms.

Oblegid launched herself onto my chest. She butted her head into my chin and purred in triumph.

Whythe tightened his hold on me. A peculiar tingling warmth rippled outward from every point of contact with his body. I closed my eyes and feigned a swoon.

Aboard Hyacinth, *in the North Atlantic.*

"You will have to become a better actress if you wish to convince me of this swoon, Your Highness. There are better ways to avoid me." Roderick dropped the Principessa del Porto Rincinum's legs.

She scrambled to get her legs under her and clutched her kitten before he withdrew his arm from her shoulders.

He felt strangely cold when she put the great distance of six inches between them. With effort, he kept his hands at his sides. Without her slight weight pressed against his chest, he felt empty.

"If you must use a title when addressing me, I prefer to be the Honorable Georgina Kirkwood," she replied haughtily.

Roderick raised his eyebrows at that. No one ever accepted a reduced title. With the title came prestige, honor, money, advancement.

"The title I was born with," her ladyship replied. "A much older, prestigious, and wealthy title than my late husband's." She busied her hands with petting the cat that nestled between the crook of her elbow and her breast.

Roderick suddenly envied the cat its position.

"Your father was an earl." He had to prattle inanities rather than grab the woman's hand and hold her close once more. Even presume to kiss her.

"My brother, my father, my grandfather. All earls going back six or seven generations." For the first time she looked at him directly, challenging him to guess the rest of the tale.

There was something about those amber eyes that grew deeper in color when she concentrated . . .

"And your husband?"

She shrugged. "Insignificant, with a greedy little toad of a son. I hate the man who gave me that title. I want nothing more to do with it."

He understood. Women of quality had no choice but to marry where their families decreed. But somehow he knew that if the late Prince del Porto Ricinum was a cruel husband, he probably could not intimidate Georgina Kirkwood.

"As you wish, milady." He executed a slight bow, all the while maintaining eye contact. "We have met before, milady, have we not?"

She turned her face away before she spoke. "No, Major, you have never met *me* before."

Again he had the feeling she did not complete the statement.

The ship tilted again. He steadied himself against the bulkhead. She grasped the handrail of the gangway and swung herself around to sit on the third step, bracing her feet. A shorter woman would have sat lower. He knew from holding her that her legs were long and muscular.

The cat continued to snuggle against her breast.

"The storm increases," he said tightly. "We should return to our cabins."

"Perhaps." She looked over her shoulder at the closed hatch to the upper deck with longing.

Another tilt of the deck below her feet and she sighed. "Yes, the cabin will be safest."

"May I escort you?" He offered her an arm while still bracing himself against the bulkhead.

She looked at his arm, then looked at the deck as if debating.

"Very well, Major Whythe." She placed the now sleepy kitten upon her shoulder, grabbed the rail with both hands and drew herself upward with practiced ease. When she had established her balance, she placed her right hand in the crook of his elbow.

The deck shifted again. She braced with her feet rather than cling to him as most women would.

"You have sailed before," he said.

"Often enough to know a few tricks to keep my feet under me."

In almost companionable silence he guided her down the narrow passageway to her cabin—the best on the small packet. Their shoulders brushed the bulkheads as well as each other. Less chance for the heaving ship to toss them about in such cramped quarters.

She paused with her hand on the latch. "Thank you for your concern, Major." She seemed reluctant to part from him.

"My pleasure, milady." He wanted to linger. "I met a young man on the Continent who might be a relative of yours."

She turned wide and frightened eyes upon him. A name almost formed on her lips.

"Georgie Kirkwood. A major in a mercenary company on the border between Austria and the Ottoman Empire." He watched her carefully. Georgie Kirkwood had the same eyes. They had to be the same person. Or closely related.

"So that is what happened to my half brother. Our elder brother disowned him at the same time he married me off to the highest bidder."

Roderick relaxed. He did not like the path his thoughts had turned in lately. Imagine the absurdity of believing a woman could handle weapons and horses and battles with the same competence as Georgie Kirkwood.

"You have not heard from your half brother in the past eight months?"

"I have not heard from him directly for close to seven years."

"And now your older brother ships you off to another continent. Are you to manage family property there?"

"Hardly. I am to be governess to a passel of brats."

"Surely, a woman of your station . . ."

"Cannot be allowed to open her mouth too often in polite society. I might express an opinion of His Majesty in particular, or men in general that brings scandal to an old and mostly honorable family." She snorted indelicately.

Roderick grew chill. Here was a woman who broke society's rules regardless of the punishment meted out by her family. He did not want to like her forthright and experienced attitude toward life.

"Oh, my God!" Georgina Kirkwood covered her suddenly pale face with both trembling hands. Her eyes rolled upward.

The kitten jumped away from her and scuttled off to crouch several paces away.

"She's dying."

This time she truly fainted into his arms.

Chapter 26

Kirkwood House, Chelsea, England.

DRAKE heard his wife's mental call before the maid hastened into his study. He passed the girl in the doorway as she raised her hand to knock.

"Milord," the maid bobbed a hasty curtsy. "Her ladyship sent me . . ."

"I know, the labor pains have begun. Send for Dr. Marlowe. This minute!" The stairs presented a formidable barrier. His pulse thundered in his ears and his breathing came in short, painful gasps. He clutched the handrail and dragged himself the rest of the way.

He repeated three ancient words over and over in a litany meant to strengthen his will over the weakness of his body. Somehow he reached the upper level. Darkness crowded his vision and stars burst before his eyes.

Em's soft moan from the master suite drew him onward, and he ran his hand along the wall for balance and direction. As he neared the closed door, Em let loose a scream.

Instantly his vision cleared and his head anchored more securely to his neck. He knew what he had to do.

"Emily," he whispered with his mind and his lips.

His oldest daughter poked her head out of her bedroom, farther down the hallway. Her wide eyes looked frightened, her face pale.

"Come, stand with me," he commanded.

Emily shuffled toward him, her eyes darting toward the closed master suite at frequent intervals. At last she clasped his palm. He could not tell if hers was clammier than his.

"Your mama has survived labor before, Emily," he tried reassuring her.

"But with my sisters she was younger, healthier. She does not carry this babe easily." ·

"Aye. And I could not ease her burden with magic. 'Twould have damaged the child. We must give her as much mundane strength as we can."

"How?"

"You need only rest quietly at my side. Open your mind to me, as you do in training."

He watched the girl take a deep breath, settle her shoulders, and close her eyes.

"Breathe deeply. In and out." She did so. Once, twice. Then she faltered and gasped. Her next breath came on a sharp inhalation.

"Emily," he reprimanded her.

"There is blood! So much blood!" The girl covered her face with her hands and ran back toward her room.

He heard the door slam and the latch click. Belle bounded up the stairs to replace her.

Drake yanked open the door that separated him from his wife.

"Milord!" the midwife protested. The portly woman whirled around and spread her skirts so that Drake could catch no glimpse of his wife in an indelicate pose.

Belle nosed her way into the room and sat beside the bed, convenient to Em's hand.

Mrs. Simpson, the housekeeper and his butler's wife, rose from her place at Em's head. "You must leave," the midwife said. She clucked her tongue and gestured as if shooing chickens. She included the dog in her gesture and look of disgust.

"I cannot help her from out there."

"You cannot help her in here," the midwife protested.

"You might be surprised," Mrs. Simpson said quietly. She avoided Drake's direct gaze. She always did.

"I have been present at the birth of each of my five daughters." Drake drew himself up to his full, imposing height. "I shall witness this birth as well."

"I never . . ." the midwife humfphed.

"There is always a first time." Drake shrugged and positioned himself at Em's head. Belle shifted to sit upon one of his feet. He took a wet rag from the basin on a side table, wrung it out, and bathed his wife's face and neck. "Breathe, my love," he coaxed. "No matter how much it hurts; you must breathe. Deep and long, or fast and short. It matters not so long as you keep air flowing through your body."

She gave him a weak smile. Then she scrunched her face and let loose a scream. The pain lasted longer than her scream.

Drake bit his lip. Em's pain seemed to rip through his own innards as surely as it did through hers. Belle licked his hand. The pain eased.

"Breathe," he advised himself as well as Em. "Just keep breathing."

Hour after hour he counted the breaths with his beloved. Time after time he bathed her brow. When asked, he helped her shift to a new position. All the while he gave her every bit of strength in his body and in Belle's.

And all through that long afternoon and evening the smell of blood and death frightened him and made Belle restless. He tried to close his mind to it. He visualized the three of them, himself and Em and Belle, holding their new son at his christening. He imagined the boy growing tall and strong with the Kirkwood blue eyes and Em's blonde hair and a wolfhound of his own.

Each time his vision shattered when Em screamed with new pain.

All the while he recited spell after spell to give his own waning strength to Em. He drew mercilessly upon Belle's unconditional love and support to keep him upright.

Em weakened visibly with each pain. Her screams became whimpers.

Each contraction depleted his reserves of strength. He came close to losing consciousness. Belle sagged in exhaustion.

In a harsh whisper, he pleaded with Em to live; to find the strength within to live. "I don't care if the babe lives or dies, Em. I need you. You have to live."

Darkness fell.

The midwife shook her head and stared at Drake helplessly.

Mrs. Simpson set her chin and pursed her lips. "Give your place to me," she ordered the midwife. "I've birthed three of my own and helped three of the lady's daughters into the world when they came more quickly than you." She shoved the exhausted woman off of her stool. Her hand disappeared beneath the draperies covering Em's legs.

"Just as I thought. He's turned bottom round. Ah, there, I've got a foot. And another. Now hold her, milord. Hold her tight."

"You'll kill her!" the midwife protested.

Mrs. Simpson glared at the woman. "She'll die anyway, the babe, too, if I do not do something."

"I will not be a party to this." The midwife huffed and darted out the door.

"Stupid woman, knows less than your dog about birthing," Mrs. Simpson said, and bent her head to her task.

The blast of fresher air from the hallway relieved some of Drake's fatigue. Emily and two of her sisters, Simpson the butler, and Daisy, his daughter, all peered around the doorjamb. Belle moved to the doorway and stood diligently in front of all of them, barring entrance to the birthing room.

Em shivered, so weak, even that small change in temperature chilled her.

"Close the door," Drake ordered. He did not care who obeyed, so long as the cooler air vanished.

Belle nudged it shut. It latched with a tiny snick.

"Now, milady, let us try one more time," Mrs. Simpson said. Her tone and her face radiated confidence. Her eyes betrayed her. They looked bleak.

Drake's heart sank.

"Now push, milady. Push with all the strength you have left. Press on her belly, milord. Press hard." Without further warning, she yanked and twisted her arm. Then she held up a pink and wrinkled boy by his heels. The long, pulsing snake of the umbilical stretched out from his navel, still connecting him to his mother.

Drake held his breath. He counted slowly to ten. How long could the babe live without taking air into his lungs?

As Mrs. Simpson snapped a finger on the infant's heels his head swung around and his eyes opened. He seemed to stare at his father with strange sentience.

One more snap of the fingers and the babe opened his mouth and bawled his displeasure with the world.

"He lives," Em whispered. "Our boy lives."

But she gave up on life for herself with the last word.

White light engulfed Drake. Emma seemed to stand just beyond his reach beckoning him forward. He could join her. They could be together forever, without the concerns of the world pressing against his consciousness day and night.

Belle wailed her grief.

A whip of dark amber light, the color of Georgie's aura when she worked magic, snaked around his neck and tugged him away from Em and the engulfing white light.

Drake jerked back to the sickroom, aware of a baby crying lustily. His baby. A son to inherit his honors, his wealth, and responsibilities.

He should feel great joy at having sired a male at last.

He wanted to follow Em, the love of his life, his helpmate, confidante, and friend. How could he continue without her?

Chapter 27

Aboard the Hyacinth.

I CAME to my senses to find a man's hand fumbling with the front laces of my gown. I captured his wrist in a grip made strong and callused by years of wielding saber, rapier, and pistol.

Then I opened my eyes, almost surprised to find myself still aboard the *Hyacinth*. I should be back in London, beside my brother, consoling him in his grief, protecting him and the vulnerable infant boy.

Name him Griffin, as our ancestors always named the eldest and the heir, I whispered to my brother. *I sense that strong magic will grow in him.*

I do not know if Drake heard me through the sound of his own breaking heart.

Major Whythe bent over me, concern and bewilderment drawing his mouth into a frown. He had his eyes closed and had turned his face away.

I nearly melted with affection for his care of me.

Sharing the moment of my sister-in-law's death made me ache with grief—my own and Drake's. I thanked God, Mother Earth, and whoever else might have been listening that, through my link with Drake, I had helped drag him away from following his wife into death.

Without those emotions weighing me down, I might have laughed at the major's embarrassment. And kissed him to ease his distress.

"Surely there is a better time and place for such intimacies," I said. On the field of battle I had laughed at death any number of times. I still fell into sarcasm and irony to mask my fear and pain.

With a minor grimace, I reluctantly lifted his hand from contact with my garments. A lady would have slapped him. I was no lady.

"Milady." He blushed. Actually blushed.

I could not remember the last time I had seen a man color so deeply, so quickly. I liked him the better for it.

But I had to keep my distance from him. No good would come from me giving my heart to any man until I had finished my mission and returned to England.

When Roderick Whythe learned the truth about me, he would not want me. I could never give him children. I was useless as a wife to any man.

"If you sought to loosen my laces so that I might breathe easier, 'twas not necessary." With regret, I struggled to sit up and discovered my erstwhile rescuer had managed to deposit me upon my own bunk.

"I could not find your maid, milady."

"I have none." Further survey revealed the door to my cabin propped open with my letter casket, despite the pitching of the ship. Major Whythe had taken pains to ensure propriety, even while hauling my weight and gangling frame through the narrow portal with the deck heaving beneath his feet. I suppressed a smile.

"What kind of gentlewoman travels without a companion?" He reared back, horror replacing the concern on his face.

"A lady with too sharp a tongue and too many opinions, who is bundled off to a subservient position to keep her from disgracing her family," I snapped back. What good were society's rules about proper chaperones when I could defend myself and my honor better than most men could?

But I could not tell him that. Not ever. Too much depended upon keeping my secrets secret.

"You said, 'She's dying,' just before you fainted." He changed the subject rather than explore my impolite past.

"I thank you for rescuing me, and now you must leave to observe propriety." I dropped back onto the bolster and turned my face away from him.

"You have too many secrets, Georgina Kirkwood. Be

warned. I will discover what you are truly about before I allow you to endanger anyone, including yourself."

I rolled my eyes rather than answer him. But I did not relax until I heard the door close and the latch fall.

Then I wrapped my arms around myself feeling suddenly very cold and alone. Hesitantly, I reached out with my mind, desperately seeking my brother.

I encountered only a fuzzy mist surrounding a wall of grief. Somewhere in the distance a baby cried, as alone as I and more frightened.

No one could ease the emptiness within me. At least my brother's son had a father and sisters and servants to care for him. I had no one.

The one man who intrigued me enough to allow into my confidence and my body saw too much, guessed too accurately. I had to keep my distance from Major Roderick Whythe, no matter how much I wanted him.

Kirkwood House, Chelsea, England, late June.

"You have but to name the day, sweet Emily, and we can be married," Barclay Marlowe pleaded.

Emily Kirkwood bit her lip, sorely tempted to give in to her betrothed's pleas. He knelt before her chair in the drawing room. Her father had not seen fit to insist upon Daisy, nor any other female, chaperoning this visit. Only the two of them would know if she bent forward ever so slightly to steal a kiss.

Surely no harm would come to her reputation if she kissed her betrothed.

"Major Marlowe . . ."

"You must call me Barclay. We are family. We are betrothed and soon to be married. Surely Christian names are appropriate now." He grabbed her left hand, the one that bore his ring, and kissed the stone of his family crest, a merlin falcon on the wing.

"Barclay, you tempt me sorely. I want nothing more than to be your wife." She wanted more to give over to him the burden of running the house, taking care of her sisters, cajoling her father into eating and exercising, protecting herself and her family from whatever magical menace threatened them all.

For the past two weeks she had spent more time in tears than fulfilling her duties as the new mistress of the house. She spent hours sitting in her darkened room, with her arms wrapped about her knees, rocking and moaning in fear.

Barclay could take away the nightmares, ease her responsibilities, care for her father.

But she could not marry him yet. She had to conform to society's conventions. "We are a house of mourning, dear Barclay. My mother but a few weeks in her grave. Father is ill with grief. The heavy responsibilities of caring for my young sisters, this household, and my infant brother have fallen on my shoulders. I cannot desert my family now, throw caution to the wind, risk dire damage to my reputation, merely to satisfy my desires."

"We need not celebrate our marriage with grand ceremony. A quiet affair with just the family. I would not ask you to leave this household in such a dire time. We could live here," he implored. He turned her hand over and kissed the inside of her wrist.

Delicious chills ran up Emily's back.

"You could continue to care for your family, but with the authority and respectability of a matron, rather than a young girl." Now his lips rested upon the black lace edging her sleeve.

Her belly grew warm and heavy, her knees and will weak.

"Darling Barclay, our pressing need to wed no longer exists." The ache of disappointment felt almost as heavy as her grief over the loss of her mother. "My father has a male heir. The title, estates, and honors are secure." She closed her eyes, drinking in the wonderfully warm sensations of his mouth upon her pulse point while his fingers stroked her palm. His other hand rested upon her knee. Even through the weight of her heavy black moiré gown, his touch burned her skin with improper familiarity.

"Children are fragile, sweet, sweet Emily. One infant son is no guarantee that the heritage is safe. We both know there is more to inherit than just the physical estate." Barclay looked up and held her gaze steadily with his own. He seemed to be trying to communicate with her through his eyes.

Emily nearly panicked. Her mental shields grew stronger in instinctive reaction. Only her father had penetrated her mind during training. Only her father had the privilege of delving into her most private thoughts. Papa was a formidable magician. She had had to work hard to learn to keep him out.

"Let down your shields, Emily," Barclay whispered. "Let me see what fears you hide." He caressed her cheek gently.

"I cannot." She jumped up and hurried to the door. "Three months from today, when our period of deep mourning ends, I will wed you, if you still want me."

"Emily."

The sharpness of his tone brought her to a halt at the doorway.

"Emily, I sail for Virginia in less than a month. My regiment has been assigned to guard the colonists against depredations by the Red Indians. I would marry you before I leave. Before another man has a chance to snatch you away from me."

She turned back to face him. Her heart beat too quickly and too loudly in her ears for her to think clearly. Her own fears of having this man invade her mind as well as her body on their wedding night closed her throat.

"For God's sake, Emily, say something." He rose from his kneeling position and stalked over to her. Gently, he cupped her face with both hands as he bent his face to hers. "Yea, or nay, say something. Anything. Please. I would know how I have offended you."

"Barclay, please, do not ask me to drop my shields."

"If that is what you wish, my sweet." He kissed the tip of her nose. "Though I had hoped to share the most complete intimacy possible with you on our wedding night." His mouth moved to her lips. "I look forward to teaching you more about magic. I want to be the one to initiate you into the Inner Circle."

He took three short kisses, almost nips, before she melted into his arms. Her mouth moved beneath his, as he deepened the next kiss. Only his big, strong hands upon her neck and waist kept her knees from turning to pudding.

"Let us marry within the fortnight. Please."

"If Papa agrees." She leaned against him, trembling against his heart. Barclay must be one of the Inner Circle

of the Pendragon Society. He had as much as admitted it—
though that was a serious breach of sacred oaths. Surely
she could trust him with the key to the protection spells
around her father.

No, she could trust no one. Her mind had to remain inviolate even from her one true love, Barclay Marlowe.

"My father and I will make certain your papa sees reason." He kissed her again, long and deep.

Reason or madness, she could not tell. She knew only
that, without him, she felt empty.

But what if he found out that she had violated her oaths
to the Pendragon Society and had broken into the archives
on her own?

Aboard Hyacinth, *in the Atlantic.*

The next few weeks passed with agonizing slowness. I
spent most of my time avoiding Major Whythe or trying to
make contact with Drake. I timed my jaunts above deck
for when Roderick returned to the tiny lounge or his own
quarters. His batman, Ian, avoided me as well. I wasn't
even certain the servant had sailed with Roderick, except
that I caught an occasional glimpse of him.

I spent too much time locked behind my door. Without
enough room to drill, I occupied the long hours by reading
the magical texts Drake had placed into the secret compartment of my trunk. I read the political tracts Lord
Grenville and Omniscient Jackson had given me. I wrote in
a journal.

I wrote to Emily, giving her advice, expressing my concern that our wards around Drake might not suffice under
direct attack. Twice we met ships headed back to England.
I entrusted my letters to the captains, praying that my niece
received them in good time.

When boredom overtook me, I practiced quiet meditation and reaching out to Drake, trying to strengthen our
link. He shut me out.

I knew he grieved and worried that he would do something stupid to ease his heartache.

In the fourth week I found a ritual for distant communication in one of the magical texts. I had all the paraphernalia I needed in my trunks. I had nothing else to do, so I began.

Drawing a pentagram within a circle was familiar. I made sure that I dumped Oblegid into the center before I closed the lines.

Finding true North took a few moments. Without landmarks and with the constant motion of the ship, I had lost my inner sense of orientation. But after a few moments of thinking about it, I felt a gentle tug at my back. When I turned to face in that direction, the world seemed to relax with a sigh. Even the choppy seas seemed quieter. I set my first candlestick there in a puddle of melted wax. I made a quarter turn to the right and set the next to the East. It settled comfortably where I placed it, refusing to slide off with the constant shifting of the decks. Then I moved on to South and West.

With my field in place I sat at the center with my kitten in my lap and set a tiny brazier in front of me. A bit of moss for kindling and a shard of mace, a sprig of dried marigold, and crumbled deer's-tongue to symbolically invoke the powers I wanted, completed the preparations.

Now for the hard part. I had to bring all four elements into my spell.

I knew how to do this. I had to think symbolically. My mind kept insisting that Earth was dirt. Oblegid mewed in that plaintive way of hers when she needed her sand box. Of course, I had dirt of a sort. But it was in the closed cabinet so it would not slide around the cabin and dump its contents.

"I usually plan ahead better than this," I grumbled. But thoughts and daydreams of making love with Major Roderick Whythe, of waking up beside him, sharing my world with him, distracted me too often.

Impatiently, I smudged the lines of the Pentagram, murmuring a prayer of forgiveness to whatever spirits governed such things. Oblegid dashed off my lap and stood at the base of the cupboard. Not exactly stood, she fidgeted her hindquarters. While she used her box, I dipped a thimbleful of clean sand from the fire bucket onto my palm.

I had Earth. Air came from my lungs. Water . . . ah, a little wine left in the bottle beside my bed. It helped me sleep. Sometimes. Fire?

The tinderbox would not do. Fire had to be elemental and not mundane. I'd learned that much about magic before I turned ten.

Resigned that I would have to generate Fire myself, I scooped up Oblegid along with my other supplies and plunked her back down in the middle of the pentagram. I closed the lines once more with a bit of chalk.

I began my incantation, dropping my herbs into the brazier with an invocation to the spirit of each to perform its miracle. Words I did not know flowed from my mouth as I dribbled sand over the herbs. I added the few drops of wine. Then I blew Air across the whole.

Lastly, I concentrated on Fire. The elements of the spell became impatient. They wanted to return to their separate existences. I could not allow that to happen. Finally, in desperation, I breathed again, thinking about flames crackling on the hearth on a chilly, rainy evening.

Fire erupted from my mouth in a long steady stream. The kindling moss burned bright for a moment, ignited the herbs, turned the sand to glass nodules, and the wine boiled and threatened to spill over the brazier.

A tendril of smoke arose from the blaze. It invaded my nose. The aromatic scent disconnected my head from reality. I was in the cabin. I sat upon the deck. I viewed the world from the crow's nest. I saw all the way to England. My vision honed in upon the house on the Thames in Chelsea.

A like mind reached up and latched onto mine. I blinked and saw the dark cavern of the Temple. Someone sat within a pentagram within a circle, as did I. A cone of power around the other magician blurred my vision.

It must be my brother working a spell.

The deck beneath me tilted. The earth beneath the other magician seemed to tilt as well. My eyes crossed and refused to find a proper horizon. My senses skittered around me chaotically.

"Are you drunk, Drake?" I whispered.

The scent of sulfur and wine drifted across my nose.

He did not reply to my question. His connection to me remained weak and elusive. I reached deep into myself for a sense of order, direction, stability.

The connection took on an almost tangible firmness, like a spiritual umbilical.

He stood within his pentagram within a circle—no, I saw more clearly now. He stood within the circle, outside the pentagram.

I began to breathe short and shallow. I knew of no spell that required the worker to remain half removed from the core of magic.

The scent of sulfur grew stronger.

The magician began to chant. I heard the individual words, could not discern their meaning. This was one of the few languages I had never heard before, nor read.

The deep bass voice continued, sending reverberations throughout the hidden chamber akin to a huge Chinese bronze gong. It resounded across the miles and echoed about the subterranean chamber.

Not Drake's voice. My brother spoke and sang in a fine tenor.

Chills ran up my spine. The hairs on my arms and nape bristled. Oblegid hissed in warning.

The center of the pentagram glowed red. A black morass thickened at the core. Red lightning shot outward.

The inky cloud coalesced into a domed head, a dragon maw and two red eyes.

I trembled in fear. The magician, who had access to the temple of the Pendragon Society, had raised a demon. Not just any demon. He had raised Tryblith, the Demon of Chaos, bane to many generations of my family.

Who? The demon mind asked my mind. His eyes seemed to bore deep into my soul. *Welcome.*

Chapter 28

RODERICK leaned on the taffrail of the *Hyacinth* watching the stars and the luminescent wake of the ship. He spent a lot of time here of late, wondering, thinking, waiting. Waiting for Georgina Kirkwood to make an appearance above deck. The bosun had told him that the lady crept out of her cabin at night sometimes, after the bulk of the crew and the few passengers had retired, as if she feared the sun. Or someone who stood in the sunshine.

He guessed she avoided him. Had he offended her so deeply when he tried to rouse her from her swoon?

She had not acted offended, or frightened. Merely . . . distracted, anxious for her privacy.

"I should avoid her as well," he murmured to himself. Women like Georgina Kirkwood Mondo, Principessa or Honorable, who had no respect for rules, brought trouble to society. He'd run across one or two in his career, courtesans mostly, who used their bodies to wield political power in the courts of Europe. Roderick was glad that His Majesty George III had banished such women and their chaos from his court. The young king seemed devoted to his bride and their children. The only women allowed near the queen had to pass rigorous moral standards set by the royal couple.

Women like Georgina had to seek other venues for their manipulations. He shuddered at the thought of tender young lives entrusted to Georgina as their governess. She would corrupt them, give them ideas that would likely rock the stability of their world. In the wrong hands ideas were dangerous weapons.

He had no doubt that Georgina, like his father, was the wrong person for raising children.

Still he waited and stared at the sea and the sky and wondered what it would be like to hold Georgina Kirkwood in his arms.

He smelled her perfume before he heard her light step. Something astringent and musky. More enticing than the delicate florals currently in vogue. He turned to face her, keeping a casual pose against the railing.

"Good evening," he called to her.

She ignored his greeting as she hurried to his side, clutching the rail with both hands. In the moonlight he watched her knuckles whiten from the intensity of her grip. She dragged in several deep gulps of air with her eyes closed.

"Has something frightened you?" He moved a handspan closer to her, automatically reaching for the sword he should carry, but did not while in civilian clothing.

"I frighten myself." Her rich, alto voice sounded huskier than usual.

When he looked at her face more closely, he sensed that something had shattered her defenses. The mask of refined superiority had dissolved. She looked almost vulnerable.

"May I assist you in any way, madam?" He leaned closer, needing to reach out and draw her into his embrace, soothe her qualms and comfort her trembling shoulders.

"Talk to me, Major. Talk to me of everyday things, of chess, and politics, and economics. Talk about the damned weather if you must. Just remind me that we are both human and that everyday matters . . . matter, that there is order in this world and Chaos does not reign." She turned her face to him then. The dim light from a shielded lantern showed her blue eyes wide and imploring.

" 'Tis a fine warm night," he said. He returned to his indolent pose looking out over the sea, making certain that his shoulder was within a few inches of hers. She could lean against him if she chose. Keep three inches of separation if she preferred. "We make good time. The captain tells me we should sight land within a few days."

"Summer comes earlier to the southern latitudes than it does back home. I wonder what flowers are in bloom in Virginia." She picked up the thread of conversation with a kind of forced deliberation, keeping her tone light.

"The camellias will have faded along with the daffodils and tulips. But the dogwood and hawthorn are usually quite showy. I do not know the names of all of the plants. A tree they call magnolia, perhaps."

"You have been to Virginia before?"

"During the closing months of the war."

"Did you meet any Red Indians?"

"A few."

"What are they like?"

"They are men, the same as we."

"Tell me about their languages, their culture, their legends. Please." The note of desperation was back in her voice.

"Each tribe is different, yet similarities persist among them. I do not speak any of their languages."

"I am told they run naked through the woods."

"They wear a minimum of clothing. Only what is necessary to protect them from the elements. As you said, the climate is warmer than in England. In summer, clothing can be a sticky encumbrance. I am not certain this is a conversation suitable to a lady." He half straightened, wondering if he should retreat.

"Have you not yet learned that I am no lady? Tell me what you know, please." She placed a restraining hand on his arm. The strength of her grip surprised him. As had the callouses on her palm. She had a man's hands, the hands of a man used to wielding a sword, for all of their long-fingered grace and well-groomed nails.

A thrill of excitement coursed up his arm from her touch.

"Milady . . ."

"Call me 'Georgie.' Please, just for tonight, talk to me as you would a friend. I need you to be my friend for one night."

"I should like to be more than just a friend." Gently he lifted her hand to his lips and kissed her palm. What had come over him? He should run away from this woman.

But the moonlight, the stars, the warm southern breeze, and the scent of her set his blood to boiling and made coherent thought impossible.

"Can you drive away my demons?"

He pulled her close, wrapping one arm about her waist while still holding her hand captive to his lips. He suckled her little finger. "You give me the strength to slay dragons and capture demons."

"Dragons I can live with. But I need you to banish the demons of my mind. Reaffirm life for me." She rose on tiptoe and kissed him with desperate passion.

"Lady, tonight I can deny you nothing."

As Roderick's lips met mine, I let his warmth wash through my mind. My memories of the demon Tryblith probing my mind eased away with the gentle emotions of the man who held me.

I breathed a sigh of relief and allowed my body to melt into his.

Tryblith poked and prodded at my magical shields. I could not let him in. I dared not think of him anymore.

Roderick's hands upon my back began to wander upward and around toward my breast.

I banished the demon from my thoughts, as I should have done when first I touched him. He clawed his way back to me.

Nothing would satisfy either of us but a full blending of our minds.

I could not allow that. I needed to know who in the family was foolish enough to try to control a demon. And why.

Drake was in danger. But he shut me out.

Ruthlessly, I put all of my being into responding to Roderick's increasingly insistent kisses. My open and receptive mind shifted to anticipating the man's wants. I leaned into him, felt the hardness of his response to me. A smile crept through me, I moved his hand up to cup my aching and heavy breasts, grateful that I had left off my corset.

He squeezed gently. A thrill of excitement leaped from his hand to the heart of my femininity. His touch pushed away the demon that battered at my mental shields.

"Georgina?" Roderick asked gently between tiny nipping kisses against my neck.

"Yes. Please."

We retired to my cabin, kissing the entire way, loosening clothing as we went.

My gown hit the deck before he could close the door. His coat and shirt followed a heartbeat later.

The wonder in Roderick's expression as he watched me shed the first petticoat brought new heat to my face and loins.

"I have dreamed of your beauty," he said quietly. "You surpass my dreams." With that he kissed me once again, worshiping my mouth with his, caressing my face with gentle fingertips.

The last vestige of the demon's presence in my mind fled. Tonight I belonged only to Roderick.

I stepped out of my petticoats, standing before him in only my fine lawn shift. The light from a single shielded lantern must backlight me, revealing all of the shapes and shadows of my body to him.

He reached for the neckties of my shift with one hand while the other clutched my side. His thumb caressed my waist in widening circles. Beneath his touch, a tingle along old scar tissue, burned smooth by magic, ran back and forth along the thin white line left by a Turkish scimitar. Suddenly shy, I extinguished the flame, plunging us into anonymous darkness.

Our fumbling and caressing became frantic. I heard my shift tear before I felt the cool whiff of sea air against my skin. His hot lips followed his hands from my breast to my ribs. Gently I twisted and shifted his path away from scars to my navel and lower. I moaned. He groaned.

We found the narrow bunk by falling upon it crosswise. As I lay sprawled, he knelt between my thighs. His tongue proved more mobile than his hands. And more satisfying. Delicious chills coursed upward from his ministrations. Fevers of excitement chased downward.

I convulsed. He lay atop me, kissing my puckered breasts. I flipped him over and returned the favor with mouth and hands working in spirals up and down and up and down.

As he began to tremble, he lifted me upward by the shoulders and centered me upon him. He entered me with haste and little delicacy. My body started at the intimate invasion and then opened to receive him in convulsive contractions.

He gathered my breasts in his fists and squeezed. I tightened around his member.

Up and down. We found our rhythm. We found delight. We found union of heartbeat and purpose. We twined together for one momentous explosion of the celebration of life and then collapsed together, wrapped in each other's arms. Safe from the world, safe from ourselves. Free of boundaries and constraints.

"I love you," he whispered.

I snuggled closer against his chest and murmured a reply that might have said the same.

Chapter 29

MORNING sunlight streamed through the tiny porthole of my cabin, giving reddish lights to Roderick Whythe's hair. His head lay pressed against my naked breast, his lips achingly close to a puckered nipple. I sighed in deep satisfaction. He opened his eyes and smiled. I smoothed a lock of dark hair off his brow. He reached up and traced my cheek with the delicacy worthy of a painter applying the last glow to the Madonna's halo.

He stretched to kiss me. I drank greedily from his caress. Not once during my five years as a mercenary with Heinrich der Reusse had I indulged my passions. Not once in all that time had I found a man I could give myself to freely. Now Roderick had opened the floodgates of my emotions.

"Oh, Roddie, what are we going to do?" I sighed.

"I had not thought to marry until I possessed land of my own in Virginia. Now I think on it, I see no reason to wait. You need not take on the onerous occupation of governess to another woman's children." He did not look convinced.

Perhaps memory of the wild and wanton night we had spent together dampened his enthusiasm for marriage to such as I. One thing to bed me, quite another to shackle himself to me till death do us part.

I could not commit to him and a life in Virginia. I had a mission to complete. Then I had to return to England. Before the day grew any later, I had to contact Drake, even if I had to batter at his shields with every weapon at my disposal. He had to be warned. Someone close to him had loosed a demon.

Not just any demon. Tryblith, the Demon of Chaos, now stalked the family.

"I have no intention of marrying again." I sat up, keeping the blanket close against my chest. I left his naked body exposed.

In the narrowness of my bunk, I could not help but notice how he reacted to brazen nudity. Any man would react. Why did I taunt him so?

"What demons did you wish me to slay last night?" he asked. He did not move away from me. The coldness of his tone put enough barriers between us.

"Demons in my mind only." The horror of Tryblith probing my mind returned to me like a fist slammed between my eyes. Tryblith now knew every secret I possessed. How would he use that information? How would the magician who had called him use it?

For good or for evil? For the Pendragon Society or against us?

I had to contact my secret Lodge as well. How? They employed magic and magicians when necessary. Few among them possessed even a hint of talent.

"What kind of monster was your husband?" He reached for me.

I bolted out of bed, suddenly afraid and confused by the anger that crossed his face.

Casanova was no monster! I wanted to scream. Neither had he been my husband. His enemies and rivals had considered him a blackhearted minion of the devil, or a warlock of darkest magic. I knew better. I had worked what little magic he needed for his nefarious schemes to earn money.

Then I remembered the fictitious husband Drake had invented for me. The Prince del Porto Ricinum—the Prince of the Port of Bugs. Probably ugly bugs.

Such an awful and unlikely name. Drake must have laughed long and loud at the choice.

"What do you mean?" I asked, grabbing my chemise. I held up the thin cloth, willing it to become a formidable barrier between us. My first instincts had been right. I should stay away from this man. I needed to get rid of him now.

Oblegid chose that moment to crawl out of her basket. She stretched her back, pushing her hind end into the air. Then she rocked forward and extended each rear leg in turn. A big yawn and an inquisitive mew. Fully awake, she stropped my bare ankles. The tickle of her fur against my sensitized skin made me want Roderick's touch more than ever.

Then the little minx hopped onto the bed and began stalking the strange scents surrounding the man in my bed. Bad enough that she intruded into our privacy, my familiar had the audacity to curl up beside my lover and purr.

"What kind of husband could teach you to service a man so well in bed and yet leave you trembling and terrified when alone? Did he beat you? Flaunt his mistresses before you?" Roderick sat up, draping the blankets across his middle. Another good barrier.

But one hand stroked my kitten.

I almost laughed at his questions. No man would dare beat me. Even before Casanova had taught me to use my blades so effectively, I knew how to defend myself. As for flaunting mistresses, Casanova had never made secret his affinity for multiple partners. I remembered one night with two other couples . . . I blushed and turned my back on Roderick Whythe.

"Did you know that you have nightmares; that you talk when you dream?"

I gasped and felt my face grow cold and clammy. What had I said?

"You moan and scream in remembered pain. In the middle of the dream you refused my touch. But when the dream passed, you welcomed me into your body. What did he do to you?"

"Major Whythe, perhaps you should return to your own cabin and forget this night. Forget me. I have no place in your life, nor you in mine.

"Georgie . . ."

Oblegid mewed a protest at his sudden movement as he reached to grab my hand.

With effort I evaded his grasp—hard to do in the cramped confines of the cabin—keeping my spine rigid and turned toward him. I wanted nothing more than to throw myself into his arms and fall onto the small bed once more, with or without the troublesome cat.

A baby's wails intruded upon my efforts at composure. I heard them in the distance, diffused as if hearing them through another's ears.

"Did you hear that?" I asked, whirling to search every corner of my cabin.

"Hear what?" He'd managed to pull up his breeches.

Only a few passengers sailed on this ship. None of them had small children. I was the only woman and I had not given birth in the last few minutes.

The baby screamed louder. I felt myself lifting the child roughly with alien hands.

Drake's baby. Little Griffin. My nephew.

Scream! I commanded him, suddenly very afraid for the child's life. I tried to force my hands open to put him back. I refused to be a part of a demon kidnapping the babe.

"Georgie?" Roderick grabbed my shoulders. "Georgie, what ails you?"

Scream, kick. Do not give in!

"Georgie!" Roderick lifted me back onto the bunk. He caressed my face in concern.

"Go," I pleaded through gritted teeth. "You must leave me now, and forget this past night."

Little Griffin tired. But the alien hands, big hands, with long talons, held him awkwardly. I pushed my strength into Griffin, willing him to defend himself.

"I can never forget last night."

I looked at Roderick with tears in my eyes. "Neither can I, but we can never be together again. I can never be wife to you." Then I gave him the strongest argument in my arsenal. "I can never give you children."

Then I returned all my focus into protecting my nephew with all the magical power I had.

Emily looked up from her contemplation of fabric swatches for her wedding gown. Because of the family's deep mourning, her choices were limited to dark purple or possibly midnight blue.

"Why is the baby crying?" she asked Daisy, her maid. "He should be sleeping now."

Daisy kept her gaze focused upon embroidering new monograms upon Emily's undergarments. "Babies cry. Sometimes for no reason."

The shrieks took on a sense of desperation and fear.

"Not like this." Emily let the fabric swatches fall from her lap as she dashed for the door.

Belle pelted along the corridor from her father's suite toward the stairs to the nursery. The wolfhound wasted no breath on bugling her approach.

Emily increased her pace, heedless of her long skirts and very tight corset. She began to understand why Aunt Georgie fought wearing one.

The steps to the nursery seemed steeper than usual.

"Nanny!" Emily called. "Where are you, Nanny?" She heard only the baby's continued cries. An unseemly oath escaped her lips.

She increased her pace.

Heavy steps sounded behind her. She spared a brief glance over her shoulder. Her father lumbered up the stairs. He clung heavily to the banister, breathing heavily. Pain filled his eyes.

And grief.

And guilt.

"Damme, I'll not allow anything to hurt you more, Papa," she muttered as she mounted the last stair. The door to the nursery yawned open before her as the mouth of a cave. All beyond it lay black, impenetrable.

"Magic," she breathed.

"God, protect us all," her father echoed her trepidation. He made a sign against the evil eye and fingered the Byzantine talisman Emily and Georgie had bespelled to protect him. It glowed an ugly red warning.

Baby Griffin screamed once more. Emily sensed his tiredness. He began to succumb to his attacker.

Putting aside all her fears, Emily dredged into the core of her for a ball of mage light. Slowly, like peeling a layer of skin off, the power shifted from inside her onto her palm. The effort left her raw, tired, and strangely light and free of the restrictive barrier that kept it within her.

With a mighty heave, she thrust the mage light toward the nursery. It hit the wall of blackness with a thunderous explosion. A thousand points of light mixed with an equal number of shards of blackness. She held her arms over her head and ducked.

The cascade of splintered magics fell around her like the sparks from a blacksmith's hammer striking white-hot metal. An ember burned through the thick grosgrain of her gown. She swatted it with fingers and mind, beating it into coolness.

When she looked up again, the veils of blackness hung in tattered streamers. She thrust them aside as she dashed into the nursery.

A black shadow slipped away from her, through Nanny's room to the back stair. Belle ignored the shadow as she took up a protective stance beside the still whimpering baby in his cot.

Emily drew a deep, fortifying breath and replaced the wolfhound beside Griffin.

Griffin whimpered pitifully. Belle licked his face. He screamed once more in fear.

"Nanny?" Emily called as she lifted her tiny brother to her shoulder. Belle, her job of protection surrendered to a human she trusted, leaped to follow the intruder.

"Nanny!"

No answer.

"Nanny, where the hell are you?"

"She's here," Papa panted.

Emily whirled around, still cradling the baby. The plump, middle-aged woman who had tended Emily and each of her sisters in turn lay slumped in the corner behind the door. Blood trickled from a gash at her temple. Her mouth lolled open. A bit of drool moistened her chin. Her skin looked waxy, the color of new tallow. The Earl of Kirkenwood knelt beside her and tested Nanny's neck pulse.

"Is she . . . ?" Emily could not speak her worst fears.

"Aye," her father confirmed. "Already cooling. Some ten minutes, my guess."

Emily gulped. Her belly clenched.

"Who would do such a dastardly thing?" Her gaze slid to the back staircase where the shadow had disappeared.

"A mortal enemy who does not wish me and mine to prosper," Drake Kirkwood said sadly.

"A mortal enemy who does not wish the Kirkwood heritage to continue from your line." Emily shuddered. "He tried to kill or kidnap your infant son, Papa!" Her fears turned to outrage. Aunt Georgie had been right. An evil power was at work here.

How could she, Emily, an untried girl of fifteen, fight this monster?

"I fear you speak the truth," Drake said. Gently, he closed the blankly staring eyes of the nursemaid. He bowed his head in prayer.

"You have to seek out this enemy, Papa. You have to destroy him before he destroys us." The words sounded as if they came from Aunt Georgie. Emily bit off the last one. She did not know how to fight a black sorcerer.

Her chin trembled and tears started anew in her eyes.

"I fear I have not the strength to engage in such a formidable battle, Emily." Drake Kirkwood, seventh Earl of Kirkenwood stared up at her from his crouched position. His eyes looked bleak. Hopeless.

Belle slunk in and plunked herself down at Drake's feet. Her head hung low in defeat. She had obviously lost track of her quarry.

Drake automatically drew her close and rested his face in the dog's fur.

Go to Cousin Barclay. He will protect you if I cannot, Aunt Georgie had said just before she left Emily alone seven years ago.

"I know someone who will take on this fight on our behalf." Emily tried to break through her father's preoccupation with both her words and a touch of magic. Relief shed a heavy weight from her mind and body. She did not have to take on this task alone. She could share it with someone else.

Her father looked up at her without comprehension, needing to be led through the thought process.

Emily could not tell if her magic had managed to touch his mind or not.

"My betrothed, Major Barclay Marlowe, will aid us in this quest. He has a stake in the continued prosperity and well-being of the family. He has the strength, physical, moral, and magical to be your successor in more ways than one, Papa."

"His father is more suited." Drake whispered.

"Cousin Milton is older than you by ten years or more. We need someone younger, more vigorous. We need Barclay. Father, you must apply to the ministry. Barclay cannot be sent to Virginia. He must stay here, in England, to protect us all."

Her father did not answer. He continued to bow his head over the fallen family retainer. "We shall miss Nanny sorely," he mumbled.

"Father? Did you hear anything I said?"

"Go in peace. We mourn you as one of our family."

"Milord!" Emily shouted.

Tears streamed down Drake's face.

"Very well, Milord Earl. I shall seek audience with the ministry in your stead. As I shall run your household and raise your children." *And quake in fear when I am alone.*

The baby gurgled in new contentment. Emily looked at him where he rested his tiny head upon her shoulder. He stared back at her, a strange awareness in his gaze, as if he knew her thoughts.

"What can you tell me, little one?" she whispered. "What do you know about the man who wishes us so ill?"

Chapter 30

The docks on the James River near Jamestown, Virginia.

FOR the next day and a half I tried every spell I could think of to contact my family. I tried the ones written in the texts I had brought. I tried variations of those spells. I tried new spells of my own devising.

Every time I thought I had reached my brother or Emily, a formidable barrier arose to stop my spell. Or the spell drifted away into the ether.

Someone—hopefully Emily and not the demon—had layered barriers upon protections upon walls upon shields about the Pendragon and his household.

I exhausted my supplies of herbs. I exhausted myself and my cat.

Anxiously, I awaited landfall so that I could find new ingredients and new strength from the land.

The heat hit me like a smothering wet blanket. The stench of rotting fish and seaweed rose up like a malevolent miasma. Insects buzzed around my head, setting up a dissonance within my ears at war with the tingle of my magic. I think I swayed as I negotiated the gangplank to the docks.

Oblegid slept in a small basket I carried on my arm. I sensed that she did not like the heat either and chose to snooze through the worst of it.

"Milady?" Major Whythe cupped my elbow with a steadying hand. "Are you well?"

So great was my distraction that I had not realized he approached so close. I thought I would sense his presence, were he a mile away.

"The heat only," I replied. As much as my heart ached at his gesture of solicitude, I steadied myself and shifted away from his touch.

"Georgie," he whispered.

"Good-bye, Major. Forget me, please." Frantically I searched the docks for signs of the carriage promised to escort me to my first assignment as a spy for King George III. Best I get on with it so I could return home. I considered boarding the next ship but still hoped to break through the barriers to warn my family.

I had never been so alone or lonely in my life. How could I fight a demon from a distance of three thousand miles?

Unless . . . a new idea struck me. Suddenly I was anxious to get settled at my new home to try a different approach to the problem.

Three carriages waited nearby. Two gentlemen, fellow passengers, each entered one, greeted by stately Negro slaves.

A lone coachman, as dark of face as his counterparts, waited beside the third conveyance. I did not recognize the gaudy crest adorning the doors. The closed coach was newer than my brother's. More gilt adorned it than Drake's entire fleet. The matched black horses sported white-and-green feathered headpieces and bells on their gilded traces.

I shuddered at the ostentatious display of new wealth. I had an idea that only the antiquity of my brother's title would impress the owner of this equipage.

A Negro coach boy of about twelve, skinny and tall for his age, dressed in green-and-white livery with too much gold braid—cut to the latest London style—approached me. He whistled a jaunty tune. His eyes met mine boldly. I had expected submission from the slaves of the colonials.

All of the blackamoors I had seen in Europe carried their pride in stubborn silence. Still they would not meet the gaze of a white person, and never of a lady.

"Miz Kirkwood?" the coach boy asked. He drawled his words, imparting at least two extra syllables to each.

"You must address her as 'milady,' " Roderick corrected the boy.

"Massar say she jus' d' governess now," the boy returned. He saucily put his hands on his hips and challenged the major with twinkling eyes.

Recognizing a kindred sprit, I stepped between the

major and the cheeky child. We were both slaves of a kind, he in legal bondage, I chained by the accepted behavior of society.

"Mistress Kirkwood is the proper form of address now," I said.

Major Whythe seethed. I sensed the waves of resentment flowing out of his mind before I noticed his posture.

"And what would your name be?" I asked my welcome committee.

"Zebadiah," he announced, sticking out his skinny chest like a proud peacock. "And Malachi, he be d' driver."

"Milady," Roderick interrupted. "This is an insult, sending two slaves to escort you. No chaperone, not even a member of the family to welcome you."

"Major Whythe." I rounded upon him. "This is not your concern. Nor are you to ever use my title, should we have the misfortune to meet again." I kept as much indignation in my tone as I could while inside I cried with loneliness. For my own emotional safety I needed to insult him so that he could never forgive me.

Roderick's face paled. Then he pursed his lips and clenched his jaw. "Very well, Mistress Kirkwood. I leave you to your fate." He stalked over to where Negro dockhands unloaded the ship's hold of luggage, mail, and light cargo.

I reached into the basket to pet Oblegid, to rouse her. Since I could not allow myself to touch Major Whythe, I desperately wanted the soothing comfort of her soft fur.

My familiar squeaked a protest and settled back into sleep.

I flounced toward the coach, praying for the safety of a dark interior before my tears spilled down my cheeks.

Greenwich Palace, London, England, July, 1764.

"I still do not believe this a wise move, Emily," Milton hissed at the girl. Only fifteen and she carried herself with the mature poise of a princess.

Milton scanned her aura. She kept it tightly guarded. But traces of panic and fear echoed in a slight tremor of her hands when she fidgeted with the black brocade of her skirts and her skin was pale. He had to keep her anxious and uncertain of her abilities. Else, she'd not be the malleable brood mare his son needed to further Milton's goals.

"The Honorable Emily Kirkwood and Dr. Milton Marlowe," the liveried servant announced to His Majesty, George III, King of England, Scotland, Wales, and Ireland.

Emily swept ahead of Milton into a private audience chamber. The liveried servant bowed as she passed. He straightened before Milton.

Milton fought to keep from grinding his teeth at this strict observance of protocol. Why should this untried slip of a girl receive respectful bows while he, a renowned physician, Master Mason in the king's own Lodge, and frequent adviser to the king was treated the same as the merest beggar in the street?

Why? Because of a title. "Soon the king must knight me, and grant me land and honors. He has to. I am too valuable to him," Milton muttered to himself.

Not before you have found the grimoire and restored me, Neville hissed in his ear. *I must be your heir, not Barclay. He is too impulsive, too unrestrained.* The ghost remained invisible. Only his words and his scent of burned sulfur and old blood lingered to remind Milton of his constant presence.

Emily looked at Milton sharply, as if she had overheard Neville's words. He knew she could not. Milton kept his son's ghost hidden behind magical shields.

Emily sank into a deep curtsy before the king, her skirts pooling about her as a dark stain upon the patterned carpet.

George posed regally with one arm upon the mantel and the opposite leg turned neatly to display his shapely and unpadded calf. He offered her a hand to ease her rising, openly appraising her youthful figure and face.

"So young to come on such an important mission," George III said almost idly.

"Majesty." Milton offered his own bow of respect.

George flipped his hand at Milton in a casual acceptance of his presence and permission to stand. All of the king's attention focused on Emily. Barely ten years older than the girl, George seemed totally devoted to his wife, but he was still young enough to appreciate beauty when he encountered it. Why else would he keep the girl's hand trapped within his own for so long?

Emily blushed and lowered her eyes a moment. Then she met his gaze boldly, with her spine so straight and stiff she might not need her corset.

"Majesty, I come to you a humble supplicant on behalf of my father, your Pendragon."

Milton started at her presumption. 'Twas his place as her male relative to speak. 'Twas his place as a member of the Inner Circle of the Pendragon Society, as Drake's heir apparent, now that Georgina had been dispatched half a world away, to act as agent in this or any other matter.

The king dropped Emily's hand.

Milton breathed a little easier.

"We respect the antiquity of the honors of the Earls of Kirkenwood. Any other title your father might presume is of little value to me. We live in a scientific age and no longer depend upon the superstition of times past." George faced Milton more directly. "What is the nature of this petition?"

"As a man of science," Milton began. He had to clear his throat at the rapid change of direction. "I, too, view the honor of the title of Pendragon to be one of respect for the antiquity of the family. Presumption of the title has little to do with the dire consequences we face as a family."

Emily shot him a look that was meant to wither him to a babbling idiot. Had she been older, more certain of her strengths and beauty, she might have succeeded. Milton ignored her. A small smile crept across his face. Once more, he controlled the interview. As he should have from the beginning. By the end of the week, he'd have Barclay married to Emily, the chit pregnant, and Barclay neatly dispatched to the New World to control Georgie. That would leave him agent and steward of the Kirkwood estates, fortune, and archives!

Remember the archives, the grimoire that will restore me to my body and life. We have to have that above all else, Neville reminded him. *Get custody of the archives.*

"The Honorable Emily is betrothed to my son," Milton said hastily, to keep the conversation under his control. "We, as a family, agreed to an early engagement and marriage between the two because my cousin, Emily's father, is not well. If she bears a son prior to her father's death, then that grandchild will be a viable heir. We have recently lost Lady Kirkenwood in childbed. An infant son survives, the only heir, a vulnerable heir, to the entailed estates."

Milton paused for breath.

"Already we have thwarted a kidnap plot against my tiny brother—possibly a murder plot—Your Majesty," Emily interrupted. "You yourself have a small son and heir. Think of the tragedy if he should fall ill or be murdered by your enemies."

George frowned. He reportedly spent many hours with his children, playing with them, teaching them, singing them to sleep.

Before Milton could inject his own comments and wrest control of the interview away from her, Emily plunged on. "If something should happen to this tiny child, Majesty, it will truly break my father's health and his will to live. The title and estates will pass to a cadet branch of the family, who have had Jacobite leanings in the past. I fear they do not love Your Majesty as we do."

"Emily, that is history. You have no evidence of your cousin's sympathies," Milton protested. Such evidence must exist, though. Milton had searched for it as diligently as he did the book of spells that would restore his true son to him. Should the worst happen and Kirkenwood revert to the distant cousin before Drake revealed the secret of the archives, Milton could use that evidence to control the next Earl of Kirkenwood.

Emily ignored him. "We need the protection my fiancé, Major Barclay Marlowe, can provide. But he is scheduled to sail for the colonies in only a few weeks. Please, Majesty, I beg of you to reassign him to the Horse Guards here in London." She sank into her curtsy once more.

"What think you, Dr. Marlowe, of this plan? Do you wish your son to remain in England, or to serve Us in the colonies which need protection from the Red Indians and from malcontents? You know that the colonies are on the brink of falling into chaos."

"Majesty, my son is dear to me. England is dear to me. I cannot choose." Milton crossed his right hand over his heart and dropped his gaze to his boots. He had to bite his cheeks to keep from smiling as broadly as he wanted to. He knew George had to believe the decision his alone. Emily was too bold and forthright.

Emily scrunched her eyes in an expression he could not read. But a bolt of red flared from her tightly controlled aura.

Traitor! Her voice came into his mind as clearly as if she had spoken. How had she penetrated his shields?

"We know your young heart aches at the thought of separation from your betrothed, Emily," George returned his attention to the now fuming girl. "However, We have need of experienced officers in the colonies. You would not deny Us Major Marlowe's service?"

"I am your obedient servant, Majesty." Emily dipped another curtsy, not nearly so low or respectful as her first. "May I remind you of the services rendered to your predecessors by my ancestors? We have served you in more than mundane ways as advisers and protectors."

Milton nodded and bent a leg. When he arose, he caught the young king's eye. George looked quite smug in his triumph over Emily.

"You speak of magic, Lady Emily." George's face became stern and forbidding.

Emily seemed undaunted and unafraid.

"We will have no talk of magic at Our Court," George insisted. He began to sweat. Did superstitious fear drive his refusal? Or did he sense Neville's presence and fear harm from the shade?

"As you wish, Majesty." Emily continued to stare defiantly at her king, despite her deferential words.

"With your permission, Majesty, perhaps I should escort my cousin to her home. These past few weeks have been trying for the entire family." Milton secretly gloated at thwarting Emily. Barclay could be put to good use in the colonies. He could remove Georgina Kirkwood from the Inner Circle . . . permanently.

"Majesty, we have not addressed how we are to protect my brother and the rest of the family. Young Griffin is heir to one of the oldest families in all of Britain." Emily stood firm.

"We suggest you retire to the isolation of your estates to care for your father as a proper daughter should until the period of mourning has passed." King George narrowed his eyes as he inspected the young woman. "We have decided you are too young and immature for marriage. Dr. Marlowe, We know that you have the best interests of your family at heart, but We believe your son is more valuable in the New World. The wedding is postponed until his return. 'Tis the law that all those of noble birth must have royal or parliamentary permission to marry. Disobedience will send all of you to the Tower."

"Majesty . . ." Milton protested. "Perhaps a quiet wedding in the next few days, before my son departs with his regiment . . ."

"When he returns and not before." The king waved his hand in dismissal. "You will stay in London, Dr. Marlowe. We have need of you," George added as an afterthought. He flashed a Masonic hand signal that Milton dared not ignore.

Milton had no choice but to bow once more and retreat, both he and Emily thwarted. What good all of his plots without the marriage and access to the family archives at Kirkenwood?

We must go to Kirkenwood and break through the barriers guarding the archives.

"Soon," Milton promised his son. And himself.

Chapter 31

On the road to Five Oaks, Virginia.

"HOW much longer?" I called to the Negro driver out the window of the closed carriage. We plodded along at a speed a crawling infant could outdistance in a matter of moments. I supposed the slow pace kept the dust from flying too freely. But it did not stir a breeze to ease the oppressive heat.

My clothing clung to my skin, chafing every time I shifted position. Sweat ran beneath my arms, down my back, between my breasts, and the inside of my thighs.

I had taken off my little straw bonnet an hour ago and now used it to fan myself. It did little good. The perky brim of my hat had proved less than adequate to shield my eyes.

How did women survive in this climate?

I wished I could shed my petticoats. My mercenary uniform wools would be more comfortable than the multiple layers of proper clothing.

"Soon, missus. We be there soon," Malachi, the grizzled coachman, replied.

Zebadiah leaned down from the box, his white teeth grinning in sharp contrast to his black face. "Mammy promised me corn bread and chitlin's for supper, but you gets to eat at d' big house with da massa. Fine Smithfield smoked ham and greens," he explained with the enthusiasm of a youth for any meal.

"Almost there, missus," Malachi said as slowly as he drove the carriage.

"I will believe that when I see it," I muttered.

The heat was so intense, I actually lifted my skirts to my knees, hoping to fan some air to my sweating nether parts. It did not help. The moist air aggravated the chafing, moving or still.

"Lookee! Missus, lookee da big house," Zebadiah called.

I stuck my head out the left-hand window of the carriage. I saw nothing but broad-leafed trees lining the road.

"T' other side, missus," Malachi said. He managed to insert at least three extra syllables in each word.

The carriage rocked a bit as the road began to climb. At the top, Malachi reined in the horses. I dutifully stretched and peered out the right-hand side of the coach. Through the thick trunks of the trees I caught glimpses of a white building and sunlight glinting on water.

The carriage jolted forward. As we rounded a curve in the road, I got a better look at the "big house." Whitewashed clapboard siding covered the neoclassical architecture. Graceful columns across the front supported an extended upper story that offered a shaded veranda. A few long windows opened to whatever stray breeze might happen by. Green shutters flanked the windows as protection against storms—or marauding Red Indians. Large trees, five by my count, provided shade. In winter, their bare limbs would allow more light into the interior. In front of the house, a broad lawn, littered with sheep and goats, swept down to a small lake. Numerous waterfowl dotted the water's surface. We were too far away to determine if they were ducks, geese, or royal swans.

Briefly I wondered if King George owned all of the swans in the colonies as he did in England.

Malachi drove the carriage around to the back of the big house. No grand entrance at the front for me. I was the new governess and, therefore, not much better than a servant. A tall black man, again in the green house livery, opened the door for me and offered his hand in assistance.

"Welcome to Five Oaks, madam," he intoned in a voice that rumbled from the depth of his body. His eyes remained carefully averted, as any good English servant's would. I wondered if this man's reserve had been beaten into him, as clearly Zebadiah's forthright cheerfulness had not yet been tempered.

I ignored his proffered hand and alit on my own. He

looked down his broad nose at me as if I were the inferior being. I smiled at him as I surveyed the rear courtyard. A kitchen building faced the back entrance. A long stable and carriage house ran off at an oblique angle. Both had the same whitewashed clapboard siding as the house, but lacked the decorative green trim and shutters.

Normal stable odors became an overwhelming miasma in the heat. I touched my nose with my handkerchief. Would I have the privilege of riding the master's horses? I longed for the freedom of a wild gallop after two months confined to a small ship and several hours within the coach. In the distance, behind the stable I caught glimpses of other buildings, grayed, unfinished wooden siding, not nearly as grand as the parts visible to polite society.

"Dulcie will show you to your quarters, madam," the liveried servant said. The deepness of his voice set up a resonance in the back of my throat. Did he sing? I hoped to hear him if he did. Perhaps in church on Sunday.

"Dulcie?" I saw no sign of anyone who might answer to that name. Half a dozen children romped and wrestled in the packed dirt of the yard. They wore scraps of clothing and had bright ribands tied into their tight curls. None of them had skin as dark as the two men. Now that I thought about it, Zebadiah was several shades lighter than either Malachi or the steward before me.

Chickens bobbed and pecked at bits of seeds and insects. Three dogs nosed about the foundation of the kitchen. More cats slept in the shade. But no Dulcie.

Oblegid poked her head above the basket. She wiggled and squirmed until I lifted her free and set her on the ground. I had the growing sense that she sought a patch of sand or loose dirt. Suddenly, I began to wish for the necessary and some privacy. I had been cooped up in the rocking carriage for too long.

A young mulatto woman hurried from the house. She hiked her skirts indelicately above her ankles as the chickens rushed to her, cackling loudly.

"Massa want to speak to you afore you settle in, missus," Dulcie said on one long exhale. Her deep brown eyes sparkled with some inner excitement. "James, you see that dem trunks is sent up to missus' rooms beside d' nursery. Zebadiah, you go see if Mammy needs you in d' kitchen."

Malachi apparently did not need orders. He led the horses and carriage off to the stable area, shuffling at the same speed we had driven here.

"You come with me, missus," Dulcie directed. She kicked at a too-bold rooster as she turned back toward the house. "I ain't one of your hens, Mista Obnoxious."

The bird flapped his wings, rose up and crowed in challenge to her authority. Then it darted down to peck at the girl's soft slippers. But Dulcie had moved on.

I followed, stepping delicately around a number of animal droppings. The smell only added to the sour taste of thirst in the back of my throat from the dizzying heat.

By contrast, the interior seemed cool and blessedly dim. I sighed in relief and paused just inside the doorway.

Oblegid caught up with me and slipped beneath my skirts, free to walk with me but hidden from confrontation with my employer.

"Best you come, now, missus. Massa don' like to be kept waiting," Dulcie threw over her shoulder. Only then did I note that her hurried pace equaled a casual stroll in London. No one moved very fast in this climate. I wondered at how much worse it would get before the end of summer.

Deep inside the maze of rooms and wings, Dulcie paused before a double door of dark wood. Intricate carvings adorned each of the four panels around a traditional cross in each plank. I'd never known a "witch" door to keep me out and I had more talents than most supposed witches. Especially since being initiated into the Inner Circle of the Pendragon Society.

Sir Thomas Mercat rose politely from behind his desk when I entered his study. Walls of books captured my attention before he did. Floor to ceiling, bookshelves filled two sides of the room, fifteen feet long each, at least, and equally high. A rolling ladder would help me reach the more obscure titles at the top.

I gravitated to the books, gently caressing leather spines with gold embossed titles. I found classics in the original Latin and Greek, Aristotle, Cicero, and Sophocles. I found French philosophers in translation, three Bibles each in a different language, and many volumes of sermons. Philosophical texts and scientific treatises sat side by side.

"A library to rival my brother's," I breathed with reverence.

"Ahem," my employer cleared his throat. "Mistress Kirkwood, while I appreciate your love of learning, my daughters' education will be restricted to more gentle arts."

I gulped. "Daughters." I had hoped for sons. Boys I could teach military tactics and marksmanship. Boys I could ride and hunt with. Young men would learn to appreciate the art of swordplay and how to care for a fine blade. What did I know of girls?

"Yes, daughters. Three of them."

My heart sank as I surveyed Sir Thomas. Not much taller than me, he had begun to go to fat around his middle, leaving his bandy legs and skinny arms out of proportion. He peered at me through square spectacles that sat low on his nose. I was tall enough that I could see how his dark hair thinned on top. His age escaped me, perhaps ten years older than me, perhaps more.

"Your accomplishments are quite impressive, Mistress Kirkwood, but my daughters have little need of ancient philosophers. They are more in need of refinement. They spend far too much time in the company of rowdy slave children. Recently I heard Maria, the eldest, singing one of their hymns." He visibly shuddered. "Where she learned it, I do not know. The darkies have their own church quite separate from ours."

Beneath my skirts, I felt Oblegid arch her back. I could not tell if she protested the man's attitude or his daughter's association with slaves.

"How . . . how old are your daughters, Sir Thomas?" We had not introduced ourselves. There seemed no need for that politeness. Neither of us could be other than who we expected.

"Maria, the eldest, is ten, Rebecca and Penelope eight and six."

I smiled rather than reply. I had hoped for at least one of my charges to be nearing her debut, an older girl would have suitors from town, possibly students who associated with the free thinkers and the writers of the questionable pamphlets.

I had to report something to Lord George Sackville and Whitehall or face arrest.

"I expect you to begin lessons with the girls at eight of

the clock on the morrow. Music, deportment, fine needle-work." Sir Thomas sat back down again, clearly having exhausted his chosen topic of conversation.

"And what of reading, and sums, sir? Surely the girls must practice those skills as well in order to one day assume their duties as wives and mistresses of their own homes." Any topic to keep me separated from a needle and thread. I knew how to cobble a rough seam or sew on a button, minor repairs to my uniforms. Every soldier knew that much. But fine embroidery? Needlepoint? Tambour work? Would he expect me to teach them to make lace?

Panic nearly made my knees knock together.

"You may have an hour a day to keep them in practice by reading the Bible and counting their fripperies," he sighed and returned to the sheaf of documents he had been studying when Dulcie and I interrupted him.

"And exercise, riding lessons? Surely you cannot object to them taking the air." I did not suggest dancing. My skills there were long out of practice.

"I know what is best for my daughters, Mistress Kirkwood. I will brook no interference!"

I glared at him for several long moments. He did not back down. I'd known Turkish warriors who avoided me when I stared thus. This man did not flinch.

"What about shopping excursions? How far are we from town?" I asked more meekly.

"The village of Five Oaks is close enough for the occasional shopping trip for ribands and such."

"The village," I said flatly. "What about the city, Williamsburg?" A flutter in my belly told me my mission for the king would not prove easily accomplished. My freedom was in jeopardy and I had hardly begun.

"The children have no need for venturing into the city." Now Sir Thomas frowned, as if I had trespassed onto a forbidden subject. "You may accompany Lady Mercat into town once a month for your own shopping. But not until autumn. The summer heat precludes associating with crowds."

"Autumn." I'd hear no political debates, encounter none of the pamphlet writers until autumn. I must make do with the company of three small girls for two months at least.

My heart sank. Emily would be more suited to this job

than I. She, at least, had experience with her younger sisters. I must write to her for advice.

Perhaps I should have stayed with Roderick Whythe. He, at least, met with officers and town officials. My mission had failed before it began. I could not foresee when I could return home.

"Mistress Kirkwood," Sir Thomas broke into my whirling thoughts. "You have a reputation as something of a bluestocking. I will have none of your outlandish ideas around my children. My girls know their place. I intend for them to keep it. You are here as a favor to Lady Mercat's cousin, Lord George Sackville, and for no other reason."

Chapter 32

Kirkenwood Castle, near Hadrian's Wall, England, late July.

DRAKE stood alone atop the castle ruins of Kirkenwood. Four generations ago, his family had forsaken their ancestral home for the more comfortable manor beside the lake. Today, he did not want comfort. He needed to feel the cold wind pouring out of Scotland onto his face, to smell the storm brewing at sea to the west, to remind himself that he lived, that he had a thriving son to inherit his honors and talents, and that he had responsibilities to both his family and to England.

He wanted life to be normal again, with Em at his side, guiding him, giving him strength, helping him think clearly.

Em had died. She would never climb the tor with him again. Never hold his hand again. Never whisper the day's events to him as they lay side by side in bed.

But, perhaps, here in the lonely reaches of England where the wind was a constant companion, where spirits dwelled within the wind, she would return to him.

Belle sat patiently at his feet, alert but not wary. He scratched her ears and cherished the warmth of her big body as she leaned her considerable weight against him.

A fine drizzle leaked from the sky. He closed his eyes and allowed the elemental Water to lave his face as well as his spirit. "Even the gods weep at your loss, Em," he whispered to his dead wife.

He'd half hoped for an answer. Only the wind whistled through the broken piles of stone that had once been a strong keep.

"Why do you not haunt me, Em?" he asked the sky. "My family has reported ghosts and specters for centuries. Can you not grant me this one small comfort?"

The rain came down harder.

Belle whined, reminding him that he had not been well for many months. He needed to get out of the chill wind.

Oblivious to the large drops pounding against his face, Drake turned his steps toward the village. The place had outgrown the original confines within a stone circle. Neat cottages and shops sprawled across the moors now. The giant stones that defined the life of Kirkenwood still stood. Most of them anyway. Drake had taken great pains to secure two of them that had weakened their contact with the Earth. About fifty of the original one hundred formed the circle, another twenty or so lay upon the ground, becoming a wall for a cottage here and there, some had been broken up to restore broken sections of the castle walls. Outside the stones, a dip in the ground marked the original protective ditch.

Drake descended the castle tor carefully. He lumbered down the hill, though the last two months since Em's death, he'd lost a good deal of the bulk around his middle. No appetite for food. No appetite for life without her.

Belle scouted the path before him, pausing frequently to make sure he followed safely. Since the family had abandoned the original castle, the route to the village had become overgrown with thistle and gorse. At the first upright stone, he paused, placing his hands upon the whorls in the granite. Out of long habit he traced the outline of a face.

This stone was said to contain the face and spirit of King Arthur of legend. He faced east, the direction of the sunrise, new beginnings, and change. As a youth, Drake had spent a great deal of time memorizing every grain of this stone. "I wanted to be like you, Arthur," he said to his long-dead ancestor. "I wanted to be strong, a warrior and a wise leader."

Regretfully, he dropped his hands. "Alas, time and fate made me other than strong, other than a warrior." Though he still knew the proper end of a sword to hold and how to hold it.

Belle rubbed her face against the next stone in the arc. Wren, Arthur's mistress and ancestress of the Kirkwood clan, was supposed to reside there, along with her beloved wolfhound familiar, ancestress to Belle and her entire line.

Drake turned his back on Arthur's stone and marched across the village to the upright that faced west, the direction of . . . of death, he thought. The direction he longed to go, to be with Em. But not yet. His duties to life were not yet done.

Perhaps west was the place of new beginnings as Irish lore told. The colonies lay to the west. He sensed tremendous creative energy building that way. Georgie had gone there in his place. She belonged there. Her free spirit would attune to that land.

He returned to his homage of the stones.

"Hello, Merlin," he whispered. Rain dripped down the stone, darkening certain facets more than others. "Are you pleased with the clan that your daughter, Wren, begat? Do I please you?"

This stone's face was fainter than Arthur's, harder to discern, often a mystery. Drake almost saw the face of a smiling old man. He'd never seen any of the stones smile before.

A song began in the back of his head, something lilting and haunting.

"Em?" he whispered, hopeful at last that his wife's ghost had joined him.

Look further, a deep voice that could have been many voices sounded in his head, like a gong between his ears.

Drake shook his head to clear it of the noise.

Go, you must wait upon the Lady.

"What Lady?" In the speaking he knew.

"The Lady," he breathed. No one in living memory had encountered the legendary Lady of the Lake. The three or four accounts he had read in the journals of his ancestors seemed so fantastic Drake had dismissed them as dreams, or metaphors.

Surely in these modern times, when science had stripped away mysticism and replaced it with stark reality, the Lady had been relegated to myth.

Go. The wind whirled around Merlin's stone and literally pushed Drake back toward the manor and the lake stretching beyond it into the few tracts of timber left on the estate.

He gave up fighting the wind after only a few steps. Supernatural forces seemed to have plans for him. The moment he relented and followed the path dictated, the song in his head became less strident, more compelling. Belle danced at his side to the rhythm of the song.

"Can you hear it, too?"

Belle yipped and leaped in the air, snatching at mayflies. In July? Or were they faeries?

On a day like today, anything could happen.

"I hear it, too," Emily said, emerging from the library windows that looked out over the lake. Awe tinged her voice and brought a glow to her face. Almost, the care lines that had matured her prematurely faded. "What is it, Papa?"

"Something wonderful." Drake grabbed his daughter's hand and pulled her toward the lake with renewed vigor. He imagined that the wind that pushed him was the loving hand of his wife's spirit, returned from the dead to guide him.

"I'm surprised no one else has come to investigate," Emily said, looking around in wonder.

"I believe that you and I are the only ones who can hear this." Drake directed them toward the south end of the lake, away from the manor and the cliff face. Before they had gone more than one hundred yards, the ground became uneven and soft, the trimmed and rolled lawn gave way to scrubby bushes and sedge grasses. Saplings sprang up and masked the stream that exited from the lake.

"We are shielded from view here," Drake whispered. He tested the marshy ground with the toe of his boot, gauging the advisability of advancing further.

"Look, Papa." Emily dropped his hand in order to point toward a rippling disturbance in the water. She clung to a tree branch and leaned forward.

Drake resisted the urge to haul her back. This adventure required that they both test their willingness to step beyond safety.

Drake did not like adventure. He hated abrupt changes. All of his life, all of his years as the Pendragon of Britain and leader of the Pendragon Society, he had worked hard at maintaining tradition, propriety, and life in a balance, smooth running on an even keel.

A chuckle sounded in the back of his head. The laughter could have come from Em's spirit, or Merlin's, or any one of several hundred of his ancestors. Perhaps all of them together.

Life defies balance when left on its own.

"Oh! Papa, it's her," Emily breathed.

The mayflies that might be faeries concentrated their swooping flight over the center of the ripple.

Drake peered at the disturbance. Was that a human figure lying just beneath the surface?

He kicked off his shoes, preparing to dive in and rescue whoever had stumbled into the lake. Village children often swam beyond their strength and foundered here.

Adventure had found him whether he wanted it or not.

Before he could take the first step into the water, Emily waded in, heedless of her shoes, her simple gown, her modesty. His daughter threw propriety and the rules of society into the wind.

Just as Georgie did. He did not like that idea at all.

"Emily." He reached to pull her back, to allow him the proper place of acting the hero.

Then he realized his daughter was oblivious to anything but the Otherwordly song and her own mission.

Emily reached the outermost ripples. The water came to her knees. Her black skirt billowed out in the lake like a malevolent dark cloud, or a poisonous mushroom.

The submerged figure drifted closer to Emily. Now Drake could see a feminine form, ethereally pale, silvery hair floating in the mild currents. Her gown looked old-fashioned, formfitting. It clung to her body in a most immodest display. Gemstones seemed to encrust the fine fabric. Perhaps only the summer sunlight sparkling on the water.

Emily took another step closer, almost within reach of the drowned woman.

She had to be dead. No one of this world could survive so long underwater without breathing.

Is she of this world? The voice came into his head once more.

Finally, Drake took a step into the water, shuddering against the slight chill. Then another step and a third.

Suddenly, the drowned woman opened her eyes. Their

deep penetrating blue seemed to pierce him to his soul and find him wanting. Her focus shifted to Emily. Then she thrust her right hand upward, clutching the grip of a mighty sword. Light reflected off the silvery blade, nearly blinding him. He thought he saw writing on the broad blade meant for cutting rather than poking.

Not a modern weapon. Something out of antiquity.

Something out of legend.

I gift to both of you Excalibur. Learn to use it well, the woman called in a loud voice without moving her lips.

"Thank you," Emily said reverently. "Oh, thank you, kind Lady." She clasped the grip just above the Lady's hand. At no point did they touch each other, only their joint possession of the sword Excalibur.

I am not kind. You will curse this weapon and what you must do to secure England from the forces of darkness. The lady began to sink back into the untold depths of the lake.

Both of you must take this sword. Both of you must know how and when to use it, the Lady said. She sank no farther.

Gritting his teeth against the cold water and the soft bottom of the lake, Drake plunged forward. He stumbled and flailed. But his hand came to rest atop Emily's.

The Lady released her hold on the sword and sank slowly away. She uttered no more words of wisdom or of warning.

A coldness enclosed Drake's heart.

What had he done? What had he promised the Lady and his ancestors by taking hold of the legendary sword of mystical origin?

He had a feeling that his life would never be normal again. Or as normal as the life of a Pendragon could be.

Chapter 33

Kirkenwood Manor.

EMILY sat on the floor before the fire in her father's private study with Excalibur across her knees. Not the room behind the parlor that everyone knew about, where any of the servants could listen at the door. This private room lay behind the wine cellar, deep within a natural cave system that honeycombed the tor. Three magical traps lay between the secret entrance and the main room. Today, Papa had shown her the secret to the third of them. She had already penetrated it, but she did not tell him that.

Tonight, while Papa slept, she would replace them all with stronger wards and puzzles.

She must write to Aunt Georgie for advice on wielding the sword. Maybe she shouldn't name the sword, just ask for tricks on handling a big, heavy weapon. Why hadn't she heard from Aunt Georgie? Surely enough time had passed for a letter to reach home.

With one delicate finger she traced the runes etched into the blade of the magnificent sword. She almost understood the prophecy enshrouded in the arcane markings. Almost. The truth of the sigils evaded her. When she concentrated hard, they meant nothing. When she allowed her thoughts to drift, she could almost grasp a sense of them—more a picture of what they represented than actual words.

Honor, truth, and promises. Justice, peace, and law.

Despite the centuries since its last appearance she found not a trace of rust or neglect. "Excalibur held its edge well," she said.

"There is a text somewhere over there," Papa gestured toward the far wall, "that says time runs differently in the Otherworlds." He looked at her over the rim of his square spectacles. He had a great tome open before him on the tall worktable at the center of the stone room. Dozens of scrolls, dull quills, dried-up bottles of ink, and strange rocks anchoring loose pages littered the surface. More books, scrolls, and loose pages filled the floor-to-ceiling bookshelves on three sides of the twenty-foot-square room.

The hearth offered the only heat and light other than an oil lamp on the table, when Papa remembered to light it. Sometimes he seemed to be able to see in the dark better than with light. Perhaps this was a reflection of his affinity with death.

"If time runs differently in the Otherworlds, then the Lady might believe she offered this sword to one of our ancestors just a few days ago."

"Possibly," he murmured, still rummaging among the texts and folios on the shelf.

"Papa!" she shouted.

He looked up at her, startled by her vehemence.

"What distracts you so from this . . . this miracle." If she had been standing, she would have stamped her foot.

"Research, Emily. Before we can hope to know why we have been gifted with this mystical artifact, we must know how it has been used in the past." Papa returned his gaze and his attention to the book in front of him. He used a glass to make the words large enough and clear enough to read. "Now hush while I decipher this text cloaked in a spell."

"The Lady said we would need to use it. We've done nothing with it for four whole days!" Fear rose up in her. She had no right, no status, no training for the tasks to come. Yet she had to face them, head on, as her ancestress Ana Griffin had when King John tried to murder her.

Another ancestor, Griffin Kirkwood, had refused the sword and sought peaceful means to end the religious wars in France. He had won temporary truces, but never a full peace during his short lifetime. He had died defeating the Demon of Chaos, as had his lover.

Emily and her father might die, too. Since the death of Mama, she had dreamed too often of such a fate. *I have to survive. My family needs me alive. There is no one else to mother my sisters and baby Griffin.*

Shivers ran up and down her spine. Gooseflesh broke out on her arms and back.

She climbed awkwardly to her feet. Difficult enough to do in long skirts with many petticoats without assistance, but while keeping the sword from banging against the floor, nigh on impossible. When at last she had her balance, she held Excalibur cradled across her arms, much as she did baby Griffin while he slept; the only way she could manage the weight of the weapon.

"To use the sword means to wield it. You were an accomplished swordsman, but not for many years. I have never been allowed to hold a weapon before. We need to practice!"

"That is not a practice weapon." Papa finally looked up from his study to stare at her aghast.

"And how would I know that without some training?"

"You . . . you sound just like your aunt."

"I think we need Aunt Georgie. What I do not understand, is why the sword came to us and not to her." Emily gulped. Dozens of possibilities came to mind. Aunt Georgie might not live. Papa would train her, Emily, and then die before their duty was complete. Emily would succeed her father. . . . She banished those last thoughts. She would not contemplate her father's demise, by natural or supernatural means, by illness or murder most foul.

"Georgie is not suited to . . . to do what must be done. She does not believe in rules. There are rules for dealing with Otherworldly artifacts. They are dangerous without rules. The world is dangerous without rules."

"Aunt Georgie's attitude toward rules has nothing to do with this. She is not here! Clearly the danger is here and we must prepare. Now. Before it is too late." Emily approached her father with caution. For all of his slow moving bulk, Papa had height and massive strength. He could be a formidable foe if pressed.

Anger flashed across Papa's face at her challenge. He rose and clenched his fists.

Briefly she caught a glimpse of the powerful and dynamic man he had been in his youth. Before his heart attack, before this strange disease of the blood.

"Sometimes having the freedom to break the rules is the only way to defeat the enemies of Britain," she said more quietly. Holding the sword helped her keep the nervous tremors in her knees and her hands from showing.

"Cousin Milton should arrive tomorrow. We will consult him about this." Papa turned back to his study.

"No, Papa. We will consult no one about this. If the Lady had wanted an audience, she would have chosen a different time, a different part of the lake to present this magical sword to us. Excalibur must remain a secret between us until the time comes to vanquish the forces of darkness." Emily planted her feet in a broad stance and firmed her chin. "I have read the journals of our ancestors as thoroughly as you. Excalibur is not a weapon to be brandished openly."

"You have the Kirkwood stubbornness, I'll give you that," Papa chuckled. He retreated one step and relaxed his stance. "Very well, we begin your training now. Go up to Georgie's old room and see if she left any of the breeches and shirts she traipsed around in when she was your age. Boots, too. Those delicate house slippers will be ruined by the exercises I put you through."

"They are ruined already." Emily laughed out loud. "I waded in the lake in them."

"Then why are you wearing them? They are not fit to be seen." He peered more closely at the black grosgrain that showed patches of gray where the dye had run.

"Because they are more comfortable ruined than any of the others more suitable to be seen in," she chuckled.

"More like your Aunt Georgie every day. Be careful, Emily."

She laid Excalibur upon the mantel, kissed her father's cheek, and dashed from the room before he had a chance to change her mind.

Five Oaks, Virginia, near sunset.

The sun near blinded me as it set behind the rolling hills around Five Oaks. I rode directly toward the blaze. Sir Thomas allowed me one hour each evening to ride his

lands on the horse of my choice. He blustered when I chose
the finest gelding in his stable. That horse was supposed to
be reserved for him, but he never rode it, finding the work
of managing such a spirited animal too fatiguing. I gloried
in the challenge. The horse gloried in fighting my control.

I watched a thunderstorm build to the northwest. Great
piles of roiling clouds piled one upon another, promising
rain and wind. I welcomed the relief in the heat it would
bring.

Off to my left, I heard the field hands singing a slow
melody to the rhythm of their work. This was a sound that
permeated life at Five Oaks. I paused a moment to listen.
They must be working late to get in the early grain before
the storm beat the stalks into the ground.

Dogs bayed in the distance.

Abruptly the song stopped in mid-phrase.

The disharmony jarred my senses. I turned the horse toward the field, just over the next rise.

Men shouted and women wailed. The noise seemed muffled in the heavy air.

I dug my heels into the horse's flanks and urged him to
hurry. He shied and rolled his eyes. We took a few moments to sort ourselves out, but I mastered the beast. We
plunged forward.

At the top of the slight hill I hauled the horse to a halt.
He reared and pawed the air, turning himself to dash back
the way we had come. Ruthlessly, I plunged my mind into
his, seeking control.

Reluctantly, he obeyed.

I focused on the scene below me. The field hands stood
frozen in place scattered about the acres of barley. The
overseer, James Banks, held three braces of dogs on long
leads. He had a whip looped around his shoulder. The dogs
strained forward. Sir Thomas sat his horse at the edge of
the field. He balanced a fowling piece across his pommel.

"Loose the dogs," Sir Thomas called.

Banks unclipped the leads. Six dogs leaped forward,
bugling that they had the scent of their prey.

I looked to my left, west. At the edge of the crops someone thrashed through the tall grain stalks. From this distance I could not distinguish features. I did not need to. The
ragged shirt and glistening dark skin told all.

A slave tried to escape. Sir Thomas intended to get him back.

Before I could think to intervene, the dogs reached their quarry. In a ravening mass they brought the man down.

He screamed.

My horse scented blood and shied.

I mastered the horse, drove my heels into his flanks, and pelted down the hill.

Sir Thomas raced ahead of me to the fallen man.

The overseer reached the dogs and called them off.

The slave whimpered and huddled into a fetal ball.

A shiver of movement to the side behind Sir Thomas caught my attention. Three more field hands slipped into the tree line beyond the planted field. A quick look at the faces of the remaining slaves confirmed my suspicions. The first man was a decoy, a martyr to freedom.

I gulped.

Sir Thomas dismounted with an almost casual air. He strode over to Banks and uncoiled the whip on the overseer's shoulder.

"Stop!" I screamed at my employer. "He's hurt enough." I slid off my horse ungracefully before he came to a full halt. With all of my weight, I clung to Sir Thomas' right arm. With any luck I could keep him from whipping his slave.

I could see the man now, smooth of face and lean of body, barely more than a boy. He looked up at me with a glimmer of hope in his wide eyes.

"He knows the penalty." Sir Thomas glared at me with steely determination.

"Give off, miss." Banks pulled at me from behind. " 'Tis got to be done."

"This is none of your affair, Miss Kirkwood," Sir Thomas said. "Return to your charges now and I will forget your misguided sympathies."

"He's just a boy," I protested.

"Old enough to work. Old enough to know the law." Sir Thomas yanked his arm out of my grip. Slowly, with a wicked smile upon his face, he readied the whip.

"You enjoy this," I gasped.

"Enough. Remove yourself from my presence." Sir Thomas' smile vanished.

"No. I will see this through. I will know the sort of man I work for. The sort of man Lord Sackville trusts and calls family." I stiffened my spine and shook myself free of Banks' grasp.

I had witnessed floggings before, as standard discipline in the military. Never had I witnessed so prolonged and vicious a punishment.

With a snap more cruel than the sound of a sword whipping through the air, the whip bit into the slave's back. He screamed and blanched.

A woman behind us wailed in anguish.

Blood welled up along the slave's back. The sharp coppery smell of fresh blood, the acrid scent of fear, and the sour taste of pain nearly choked me. I'd smelled this before, in the midst of battle. But these scents were tainted by cruelty. I wondered that they did not hold the odor of a demon-burning sulfur.

Sir Thomas was as evil as any demon loosed upon England. He did not bring order to his world, he opened the doors to Chaos.

Chapter 34

Five Oaks Plantation, Virginia.

I WAITED two days before acting. Sir Thomas and I walked warily around each other, neither acknowledging the scene in the fields. The whipped slave, Billy, lived. A surprise considering the viciousness of Sir Thomas' flogging.

Had he prolonged Billy's punishment because I watched without flinching? I thought my employer wanted me to flinch, to gag, and to retch. But I did not.

I donned an old pair of breeches, shirt, and dark coat. I used a tricorn tipped low and a mask made from a dark kerchief to hide my features. My rapier and dagger came to hand easily. I held them fondly, as I might a long lost lover.

These blades were more true to me than any man had been.

At the dark of the moon, with only a little starlight and my instincts to guide me, I crept out of the house. Hugging the shadows, I slunk across to the lines of slave cabins. Row upon row of long clapboard buildings divided into single rooms for each family looked indistinguishable in the gloom.

I had scouted the way, though. Easy to pick out the cabin Billy shared with his mother and half a dozen younger brothers and sisters. Several times a day, the Negro women made excuses to slip into that cabin with basins of fresh water, bandages, and ointment to treat the man's wounds.

Three rows over, five cabins down, I counted. In about every third cabin a candle shone through the open windows. They emitted just enough light to keep me from tripping over the dry ruts in the ground.

I heard the chunk of a bootheel on stone. Someone else wandered these deserted passageways. I froze between two houses, each six rooms long.

The man moved smartly along, rattling the door of each cabin as he passed. The silhouette of a whip coiled upon his shoulder identified him as James Banks, the overseer.

" 'Scuse me, Massa Banks, I needs to use the privy," a small voice said quietly.

"Too late. No darkies outside after lock down."

"But, Massa Banks . . ."

"Sorry, kid. Can't take a chance on anyone else trying to escape. We lost three the other day. Likely to lose Billy, too. His fever ain't going down."

"But, Massa Banks, I can't hold it till morning."

"Too bad. Go piss in the corner. Can't make the place smell any worse." The overseer moved on to the next door and rattled the fresh new padlock there.

When he had passed over to the next row, a small figure wiggled out of the tiny window well above ground. No adult could fit through the opening. I hastened over to catch the child before she fell and broke a leg.

As I grasped her about the waist, she turned big, frightened eyes upon me. "Who you?" she whispered, too terrified to scream.

"Just someone who wants to help. Now run to the privy quick. I'll boost you up to get you back in," I replied in equally hushed tones.

The little girl ran around the corner and returned right smartly. I lifted her up until she grasped the window frame and scrambled back to the safety of her home.

Sometimes you have to break the rules because it is the right thing to do.

Then I proceeded down three more doors to Billy's home. Inside, I heard soft moaning and quiet words meant to soothe.

Before I lost my courage, I tested the lock. All went silent inside. I sensed several persons holding their breath.

The padlock was strong. "I am a Kirkwood. No lock can keep me out," I said under my breath. I had not done this since I was sixteen. It was one of the first spells I mastered. Push a lever here, jiggle a piece there. I used a hairpin and no magic. The thing opened in my hand with barely a sound to alert Banks.

The door opened with a squeak. I willed it quiet. With a finger to my lips to signal silence, I crept inside.

The smell of sweat, fever, and infection assailed my nose, even through the mask. I swallowed deeply and took shallow breaths through my mouth.

Five people lay sprawled on the floor along the far wall. They wore few clothes, trying to stay a little cooler in the heat that was trapped inside the house.

I doubted they slept, but they made no move to evict me.

"Quickly, we have to move now," I whispered.

"Who you?" a young woman with her hair bound up in a white kerchief asked. She huddled over the prone figure of Billy.

His back was a mess of festering sores.

"A friend. I've come to take him to the West. To freedom."

"Massa kill us all if you do."

"He can't afford to do that. Just tell Banks that Billy died and you had to bury him quick in case of contagion." I moved farther into the room, assessing how I was going to get Billy on his feet. He might be skinny and wasted by fever, but he would stand a full hand taller than I and at least equal my weight.

"He'll die out there." A tear escaped her. She ducked her head and dabbed at her face with the back of her hand.

"Where was he planning to go before?" I took the basin of water from her and began washing the wounds clean of the ugly green ointment someone had slathered on his back. I figured the goo made the infection worse.

"West. To the Red Indians," the girl said softly.

I looked at her sharply.

"We heard the tribes need strong men to help fight their war along the frontier. They gives us freedom if we help fight."

"Are you his sister?" I asked.

"His wife."

I looked at her more closely. No more than fifteen, she showed signs of pregnancy. was maybe four or five months along.

"Then you are coming, too. I'll help you get him off the

plantation and into the wilderness. You'll be on your own then. I have to get back so I am not missed."

"Yassah." Hope lit her eyes. Before I could say more, she bundled a few things into a red shawl; flatbread and a hunk of cheese, two shirts, the pot of green ointment.

I took the pot from her, sniffed it, and put it back on the floor by the fire. "Keep the wounds clean and put strips of willow bark on them," I told her. Back home, I would have had access to dozens of healing roots and herbs. Here, I had not yet had time to learn the flora.

"You there, in the corner, help me get him up," I called into the tangle of people.

"Don' hear nothing, don' see nothing. Ize asleep," a man replied.

"Then walk in your sleep and help lift him."

"Yassah. Ize asleep. Ize walks in my sleep. Talks in my sleep, too." The man shuffled over to us. He too was tall, more muscular than Billy. A man in his prime. He placed his hands beneath Billy's armpits and hoisted him upright in one smooth movement.

Billy groaned. The girl rushed to his side with a flask of water. He sipped at the precious liquid. Then he opened his eyes.

"We'ze goin' west, Billy," the girl whispered.

"I heerd."

"Can you walk, Billy?" I asked as I shoved my shoulder beneath his arm. The girl moved beneath his other arm. He leaned more heavily upon me.

"Oncet I get a going, ain't no stoppin' me." He flashed me a big grin and began walking.

I had no choice but to keep up with him.

As we passed through the door I reached back and closed the padlock once more. From inside I heard the man say on a chuckle, "I don' see nothing, I don' hear nothing. Ize asleep."

Sometimes you have to break the rules because it is the right thing to do.

"Sir Thomas, Ah have need of words with you." Lady Mercat glided into her husband's study late one sultry afternoon.

I quickly gathered the papers on Sir Thomas' desk where he had outlined a rigorous schedule of music, dancing, and needlework for his daughters. Since the day I witnessed his punishment of Billy, he had loaded me and his daughters with more and more assignments. I no longer had time to ride each evening. His daughters rarely left the house at all.

With a brief nod to the mistress of the house I exited the room. I did not bother leaving behind a telltale of magic to listen further. Lady Mercat rarely had anything of import to say.

But she spoke before I had fully closed the door.

"Ah have decided that Rachel shall be your next companion," the lady said as if pronouncing the posting of a royal diplomat.

Her tone made me pause with my hand still on the latch and a sliver of air between the door and the jamb.

"I do not believe I know this Rachel," Sir Thomas said with caution in his voice.

"She was a field hand injured last harvest. Since then, we have put her to use dusting the nursery and lesser bedrooms."

"Is she . . . ?"

"Comely enough to satisfy you, and intelligent enough not to get uppity. You know I cannot abide uppity coloreds. Ah truly regret losing a valuable house slave, but the last one had to go, insisting her child was as good as mine just because you had fathered it."

I heard the shudder of distaste in the lady's words. At the same time I could not believe what I heard. Lady Mercat had actually selected a mistress for Sir Thomas.

"If you would return to my bed . . ."

"Ah shall bear you no more children, Sir Thomas," the lady insisted. " 'Twould kill me. Ah am too frail." Her voice trailed off as if she were about to faint.

I'd seen her do that too many times to rush to her side. Her "vapors" came upon her too conveniently.

Sir Thomas murmured some soothing words. I did not pause to listen further. Disgust drove me to the stables.

And anger. No man had the right to compel a woman to his bed, be she his wife or his slave. Was there any difference?

I doubted it. Thank God and the Earth Mother I had never committed myself to the dominance of a man. Thank Casanova for teaching me skills to maintain my independence, to know which rules of society were worth keeping and which must be broken.

The rule that a woman must marry, or must have the protection of a man, was one I intended to keep breaking.

The moment I appeared the grooms began saddling my favorite gelding. He pawed the ground restlessly, as much in need of a wild gallop as I.

Angrily, I drove my heels into his side. The horse turned his head to nip at me and swished his tail, as he would a pesky fly upon his back. I controlled him with the reins and gave him my heel once more. He bounded out of the stable yard and over the first fence with little more encouragement.

The slight breeze of our passage cooled the gloss of perspiration on my face. My hair tumbled out of its coil. I let it fly free.

A quarter of an hour later I reached a copse hidden from the house by two hills and a ridgeline of trees. Here I reined in and jumped free of the sidesaddle. The horse cropped eagerly at the lush grasses sheltered from the parching sun.

I strode immediately to the gnarled roots of an oak tree near the center of the copse. Something resembling a clearing spread before the tree. I reached deep into a cavity in the tree until my fingers touched oilskin. Carefully, I pulled the bundles free and unwrapped my blades. The saber and a dagger rested in one, my rapier and the dagger-pistol in another.

I grasped them eagerly, hefted them, savored their weight and balance. Imagining Sir Thomas and his vaporous lady within a tall fern, I slashed at the greenery until a pile of crumbled fragments littered the ground.

Then I turned my attention to downed and rotting limbs, struggling saplings, and more hapless ferns. Lord Sackville, Lord Grenville, King George, and Cousin Milton earned my full fury. Barclay's image I saved for a clump of laurel. By this time I'd burned off most of my anger and treated him with only mild annoyance.

Major Roderick Whythe never became part of my

evening ritual of symbolic death and mutilation. But somehow I associated him with the protective oilcloth that protected and cradled my saber and rapier. The weapons were an extension of me. Deep in my heart I wanted the major to care for me as the cloth did my blades.

Chapter 35

Marlowe Family Hunting Box, Kent, England.

MILTON paced the ebon circle drawn around a pentagram in the cellar of his Hunting Box. This work was too dangerous to conduct in his modest home in London. His twelve disciples followed in his wake. In unison they chanted memorized Latin phrases in response to his own recited spell.

As he reached the beginning point of the circle, he stepped onto the point of the pentagram and began walking that pattern. His men followed until they were strung out along the lines of the sigil of power. Making certain he had the undivided attention of each and every one of his followers, he pointed toward the piled logs at the center. Elemental Fire leaped to his command and ignited the kindling and ritual herbs laid out for it. Then the first five men retrieved burning brands from the fire and lit similar fires at the five points of the sigil.

As flames sprang to life at the fifth point, power flooded Milton's body. It drowned his senses and pulsed in his joints.

He savored the taste of the magic, the heaviness in his blood, the scent of burned sulfur. The comforting presence of Neville at his shoulder added to his sense of well-being. Together they could accomplish so much.

But Neville's life had been cut short by barbaric Red Indians in a most grisly manner. The colonial regiment he'd been assigned to had done nothing to help him. They had not even given him decent burial.

The need to restore Neville to life had led Milton to study black magic and form this coven.

"Through time and distance, through the mists of Other-worlds, we summon you," Milton chanted.

His men echoed his words.

A sluggish morass of darkness rose from the central fire. Red eyes with a vertically slit pupil opened slowly within the amorphous black.

Silence lay heavily upon the ritual. Several of the acolytes shifted uncomfortably, shrugging shoulders and easing their necks from the weight of magic. Samuel de Vere was foremost among them.

Milton felt a question in the back of his mind from the being in the darkness of the Otherworld.

"In return for a favor, name your deepest desire and I shall find a way to grant it," Milton told the being. His chorus echoed the promise.

You will grant my freedom.

"If I am to grant you freedom, I must know your name." Milton knew enough demonology to realize he had to name the creature to maintain control of it. Else, it would run free and never answer his call again.

We have no bargain.

"For a connection to my son, who does not answer my call, nor does he appear in my scrying bowl, I will give you form next time I call you."

A beginning.

"I need to know if my son, Major Barclay Marlowe, has learned anything from our cousin the Honorable Georgina Kirkwood. She could tell him the secret we must know if he seduces her."

Kirkwood! The demon screamed and sank back into the depths of the unknown from whence it came.

Five Oaks, Virginia.

"Not tonight," Sir Thomas said jovially.

He was in his den with an unannounced visitor and I did my best to listen through the closed door.

"The others will miss you at the cock fight, Sir Thomas," the unknown man replied.

I wished I'd seen more of him than just the top of his

head from my observation post at the head of the stair-case.

Sir Thomas kept me above stairs whenever he had visitors now. I was not even allowed to take tea with milady and listen to the gossip of her friends.

"Your purse was much heavier when you left last week than when you arrived," the visitor said seriously. "I and some friends have need of winning back some of those guineas."

"Ah, but tonight one of my colored gals is ripe for breeding. I need to plant my seed in her before the young bucks get wind of her."

I gasped in horror. Who? Probably Rachel. He spent a portion of most every night in her room in the attic. To take the woman for pleasure was one thing, to deliberately impregnate her quite another. Nearly half the house slaves under the age of fifteen had the lighter skin and straighter hair marking them as his get.

"May I announce you?" James, the butler of Five Oaks, asked. His deep voice carried through the hallways of the big house.

I knew that if Sir Thomas Mercat did not know I eavesdropped at his study door before, he certainly did now.

"No need to disturb Sir Thomas, James." I straightened from trying to peer through the keyhole and gathered what was left of my dignity around me. The little coil of magic I had sent through that keyhole to enhance the quiet conversation within snapped back at me. The recoil flashed before my eyes and sent stabs of pain deep within my head.

"Sir Thomas has a guest. I shall speak to him later, when he is alone." I had to say something to allay the snoopy butler's suspicions of me. Difficult when I had to also mask the blinding headache from the improperly grounded magic.

I needed to leave here. I had learned nothing to report to Lord Sackville or Lord Grenville. And Sir Thomas disgusted me. I could free only so many slaves before he traced their disappearances back to me.

At least he never turned lustful eyes toward me. Lady Mercat would never allow him a white mistress. I might get uppity ideas and supplant her.

Out of the corner of my eye I caught a glimpse of

Oblegid stalking the butler. Mentally I instructed her not to pounce. Never to pounce upon James, who might use his butlery authority to have her banned from the house, or worse, possibly thrown into the lake.

Oblegid froze in place and flattened her ears, not at all happy at how I had spoiled her game. I promised her more action tonight. She might be a tool in my rapidly forming plans.

Plans that did not include a suspicious butler.

I stepped away from James, angling toward the back of the house. The servants would not gossip with me about where and when the master would perform his foul deed tonight. But they gossiped among themselves when they did not know I listened.

I needed a drink, preferably something strong and fortifying. Or rich and spicy chocolate.

No one drank chocolate here. That beverage was dismissed as "Frenchy decadence."

If I were still a mercenary, I'd have no trouble walking into a tavern and ordering any local brew. James and the master alone had control over the whiskey cabinet where they stored the local potable they called bourbon. They mixed it into a kind of julep with mint. The visitors all proclaimed the concoction excellent and unique.

Lady Mercat drank copious amounts of it to ease her "vapors."

I had yet to be offered a sip of the sweet drink. Besides, I liked my whiskey neat.

"If you are hungry, missus, Rose will bring you a tray," James said sharply. He moved quickly to stand between me and the back door which led to the kitchen building, and the hotbed of gossip.

"I can fend for myself in the kitchen, James," I said equally sharply. I tried looking down my nose at James, but his superior height made that very awkward.

Then I wondered why Rose, a child of no more than ten and still clumsy, took Dulcie's place in delivering food.

"Mammy does not like strangers in her kitchen," James insisted.

"I am hardly a stranger. I live here. I have lived here for three months." I refused to back down.

So did he. I was beginning to mistrust and seriously dislike the men in this household.

Major Whythe did not back down easily from me and I trusted him with my life on the battlefield.

But not with my secrets, even in bed.

"Missus, you don' belong in d' kitchen." For the first time since I had arrived, the butler dropped into the dialect common to all of the other servants. Slaves, I reminded myself. African slaves.

I might be a servant to the master and mistress of the household, but I was English, white-skinned, and free to leave. If I dared.

If I chose.

"Have Dulcie bring me something cool to drink. And some bread and cheese. I shall skip supper. I have the headache." I turned on my heel and headed for the sweeping staircase at the front of the house.

"Dulcie has duties elsewhere today. I will send one of the other girls."

Dulcie? Dulcie had no other duties than to wait upon the whims of me and the family.

I stopped myself from flying back down the stairs and into Sir Thomas' study. Three deep breaths and I had control over myself. I could stop this. But not dressed as a proper governess. I needed a masculine guise.

"Not good for you to ride alone at night, missus. Best you go in the morning, when it's cool," James called after me. The man knew me too well.

He did not offer to send any of the men with me tonight to help. He suggested rather that I abandon my plans and leave Dulcie to her fate.

He did not know me as well as he thought he did.

Twilight did not linger in these southern climes as it did at home. In high summer, I had hours of daylight before the sun crept toward the horizon. Not as many hours of light as I would have at Kirkenwood, but enough.

As soon as the girls had had their supper and I had supervised Annie tucking them in for the night—Rebecca and Penelope gave the slave big hugs and sloppy kisses upon her cheek, a show of affection I had never received, nor had I witnessed them giving to their parents—I crept down the back stairs and out a side door. This house exit was used very little, but led more directly to the stables than the back door that faced the kitchen building. My elegant riding habit in a whisper weight, midnight-blue gabardine blended nicely with the shadows. The gray gelding greeted me with a welcoming whicker. He'd not been ridden in days and was eager for a good run.

The slaves were either eating their own dinners or serving the Master and Mistress of the house and their mysterious guest. I wondered if the man had been invited to "view" Sir Thomas' activities tonight.

My anger grew at the thought. I had made love with Casanova in the presence of others who indulged in similar pastimes, without much hesitation. Quite another matter to have an audience cheering on a rapist.

I took a few moments to run my hands over the fine lines of the stranger's mount. Good bloodstock, Thoroughbred and Andalusian cross, I guessed. He had room in his big barrel chest for a strong heart and lungs. He'd run forever before tiring. Someone had bred him specially or paid dearly for him. His equipage of finely tooled leather had the stirrups set quite short. A crest I could not identify was stamped into the saddle, embroidered into the saddle blanket, and etched into the stirrups. Not enough light penetrated the dark recesses of the stable for me to see the details of the heraldry and my fingertips were too callused to discern the lines.

Taking a deep breath I narrowed my focus and let the magic flow through me into my eyes.

A second deep breath brought the crest into sharp focus. I saw the royal crown, the seal of the colony, and the personal touches of the governor. Colonel Francis Fauquier.

Why had His Majesty's appointed governor for the royal colony of Virginia come to meet with Sir Thomas Mercat alone and without being presented to the family, without the household even being given his name?

I'd have to find out by other means. This was the first interesting thing that had happened here.

Right now I needed my weapons. I picked up Oblegid from the shadows, placed her before the saddle of my favorite mount and climbed aboard myself, disdaining a proper sidesaddle for the comfort of riding astride.

Sir Thomas would feel the sharp edge of my saber before I allowed him to rape his own daughter.

But first I had to retrieve my weapons.

Chapter 36

The forest, west of Williamsburg, late evening.

"WHAT have you found?" Major Roderick Whythe returned Ian McTavis' smart salute. Good to have his batman at his side and a horse between his knees; to be doing something. He should have left this patrol to his lieutenant. But for a few moments, while directing his men to their search patterns, he'd almost forgotten Georgina Kirkwood.

"Sir," Ian curbed his restive horse a proper three paces from his master. "We think we have found a cache of weapons. Possibly put there by Indians."

"Show me," Roderick ordered, biting back the expletives that rode on his tongue. No need to worry the men with his own fear that Chief Pontiac's allies had penetrated this deep into the colony. Until now, the Indians had contented themselves with burning isolated farms and murdering the inhabitants on the frontier; raids against people who had not the means or the numbers to mount a serious defense.

Penetrating this deep into civilization could only mean that the confederated tribes had achieved an unprecedented degree of cooperation.

Despite King George's order banning settlement west of the mountain crest, stubborn Virginians refused to retreat. Even those who had resettled near the new boundary remained vulnerable to Indian raids.

Roderick spurred his horse a little too sharply and the beast jolted forward more abruptly than he liked. Another betrayal of his anxiety. Ian raised an eyebrow at his lack of finesse but said nothing.

Together they trotted along a barely discernible path. About one hundred yards farther along, two of his men stood in a clearing around a massive oak tree. Private Jones fingered a fine saber. Its scabbard and protective oil-skin lay at his feet. As Roderick watched, the private balanced the flat blade upon one finger several inches down from the hilt. The distinctive straight blade and grip looked far too small for the private's beefy fist.

Roderick's heart skipped a beat. He had seen that blade before, along with the dagger Private Martins toyed with across the way. "That is no Indian weapon," he said, trying to steady his breathing. The last time he'd seen a straight Polish saber with a deep sweet spot designed for perfect balance, young Major Georgie Kirkwood killed a Turk with it. That Turk had been bearing down on Roderick with bloodlust in his eyes.

"Not these, sir," Ian explained. He pointed across the clearing toward a series of smaller trees, each with freshly disturbed earth around the roots.

Roderick dismounted. "Put the saber away before you hurt yourself, Jones," he ordered. He did not think he could keep silent if he watched the man try to balance the tip on his finger as Geordie had done.

How did that sword get here, in the wilds of Virginia?

A tiny voice in the back of his head reminded him that Georgina Kirkwood lived in Virginia. Surely the woman he had made love to did not have custody of these blades, identical to the mercenary major's.

Or the same blades.

She had claimed not to know her bastard brother's fate. But she had acted too casually at the news of his probable capture and death.

He refused to contemplate the implications of his thoughts.

"We saw the disturbance in the dirt, sir, and dug down a few inches. We found this." Ian knelt and pushed aside some more soil revealing part of a wooden box. With a few flicks of his fingers, the corporal outlined a long, narrow container. "Six muskets per box. Six boxes. All new, and English made. Stolen from the garrison, if I read this right," he said.

"Powder and shot?" Roderick asked.

"We was looking for that when we found the sword and

dagger," Jones said, then added a hasty "sir." The man, little more than a boy, had a lot to learn about respect, for his
officers as well as the saber.

"Call in the rest of the men," Roderick ordered. "I want
all of these weapons confiscated and returned to our stores."

"And the blades, sir?" Ian asked quietly. He, too, must
have recognized the weapons. He'd carried Major Kirkwood, bleeding and probably dying, from the field of battle. The wounded man had refused to relinquish his weapons
despite his weakness and loss of blood.

"I shall take possession of the saber and dagger until we
discover the owner." If these were truly the weapons of
Major Georgie Kirkwood, then where was the rapier and
the dagger-pistol he prized so much?

"Most likely the owner stole the muskets," Jones muttered.

Roderick knew whom he had to seek out to determine
ownership. The one woman he had vowed to forget, but
could not. Had she stolen the muskets?

If so, he was duty bound to arrest her.

Curse the man! I knew Major Roderick Whythe recognized my saber and dagger. Why else would he take personal custody of them? Had he found the rapier as well?

Silently, I dismounted and tied my horse to a leafy shrub.
Then I inched my way to a large tree near the edge of the
clearing. I watched by torchlight as twenty men of His
Majesty's Army dug up six boxes of muskets, from the secret shadows of the forest. I wished I could know what
Roderick Whythe thought as he tested my weapons. Most
of my mental energy went into keeping my gelding quiet.
More important that I avoid discovery than to eavesdrop
on the mind of the man I might have loved under different
circumstances.

Roderick moved out of my line of vision. He slapped the
flat of my saber's blade against his palm as he walked. I sidled around the tree trunk that hid me. With every step I
cursed the heavy skirts of my riding habit. They continually
caught on the low shrubbery, rustling loudly. I paused three
times in my circuit, holding my breath. Each time I was cer-

tain one of the men, or worse Roderick, would come to investigate the noise.

Luck was on my side that night, a bit of wind ruffled the leaves in the upper canopy of the forest. The soldiers must have thought the sounds of my passage were nothing more than a stray breeze.

Why were they taking so long in leaving? I needed to get back to Five Oaks and take Dulcie to safety before Sir Thomas raped her.

I peeked around my protective tree at the men loading a box of muskets behind the saddle of a sturdy and placid mount. Roderick watched in silence, still playing with my saber. Then as the men moved off to assist with the next box, Roderick had the audacity to take my sword and balance the tip on his outstretched finger!

I gasped in anger and dismay.

I bit my tongue to keep angry words from flooding out. I stepped on my right foot with my left to keep from charging forth and demanding possession of my weapons. My fists knotted and I pressed them hard against the bark of the tree.

Oblegid patrolled the opposite side of the clearing. Her messages were distorted by distance, overlaid by the enticing smells of mice and other small night creatures.

The gelding whickered a greeting to the other horses. In my anger, I had lost control of my magic!

Quickly I clamped down on the horse's instincts to amble forward and investigate the others of his kind.

Before I could do anything else, a hard hand covered my mouth. "Hush," an almost familiar voice whispered.

Roderick? No. I would know the feel of his body pressed against my own, the scent of him. I would sense his aura before he came close enough to touch me. Our one night as lovers had bound our spirits together more firmly than a marriage ceremony.

I stilled my entire body and my mind, waiting assessing, preparing.

"Good girl," the stranger said. This time, the words came into my mind, more as an image of an older brother or cousin patting a pigtailed bully on the head. He used magic more than speech to communicate.

Barclay! I almost screamed the words. Military discipline kept me quiet. I shifted my balance and broadened my stance. I was ready to flee or fight, whichever seemingly had the advantage.

"We have to wait. I have to follow them, to see who among my men is smuggling arms to the Indians," he continued in the same hushed tones as before. He seemed unaware that I tensed my back.

I have no intention of betraying my presence to these men, I sent back to him.

He eased his hand away from my mouth, but kept his body pressed against my back.

I have need of your help, I added, thinking of my plans to free Dulcie. *But I need my weapons first.* I did not have time to waste diverting Barclay.

Barclay and I stood there in silence for many more long moments, pressed into the bark of a massive oak tree. At times I almost believed we merged with the trunk, much as our ancestor, the Merlin of legend and myth, did as his final punishment for betraying the gods.

The warmth of a big male body, taller and broader than Roderick yet not so massive as barrel-chested Heinrich der Reusse, penetrated my back and arms. A languid peace settled on me. I think I leaned back, relishing the physical comfort of a man. He wrapped his arms around me. Perhaps he nuzzled my neck.

Liquid fire shot up from my loins to my breasts making my heart beat faster. His heart sped, stuttered, found the same rhythm as mine. I turned slowly within his embrace. Our lips met in unspoken agreement. As they had nigh on eight years ago . . .

The Moors west of Kirkenwood.

"Surrender!" I demanded of my cousin as I stood with my blunted rapier at his throat and my foot upon his chest where he lay spread-eagled upon the ground, breathless and sweating. I was sixteen, he almost eighteen. Our dueling ground was a patch of moorland two miles from Kirkenwood village and the standing stones.

I forgot why his father had traveled north that hot sum-

mer. We usually saw him at the house in Chelsea at Yuletide or Easter, if at all. It did not matter why they had
come. I gloried now in the triumph of defeating my taller
and older and very male cousin at his own sport.

"I'll never surrender to a girl." His right shoulder shifted
and I knew he was about to try some dirty trick.

I hopped away from him. Damn, my foot caught in my
petticoat. The fine linen and lace tore beneath my heel. I
cared not for the frippery. But Emma, my sister-in-law, did
and she'd take a stripe off my hide with her tongue when
she found out that I had challenged my cousin to a duel.

Emma barely tolerated my insistence upon practicing
with weapons. As long as I did it in private, she held her
tongue.

Barclay was a much more satisfying adversary than
scarecrows and hayricks. My cousin grabbed my ankle and
yanked.

I flailed and landed on my bum. My skirts flew up.

He tackled me with gusto. We both went down.

"You surrender," he demanded. His eyes blazed with
fury and triumph and . . . something else.

I licked my lips, suddenly dry with nervousness.

He mimicked my action.

Our gazes locked. His deep blue irises drew me in, invited me to explore the maze of his mind.

Ever reckless with magic as well as propriety, I arched
my neck ever so slightly, bringing my mouth a fraction
closer to his.

He closed the distance, locking his mouth upon mine.

At the same instant I dove into his mind. The intensity of
his explicit desire nearly rocked me out of our mental
unity.

He grabbed my shoulders hard enough to leave bruises.
I held his face more gently. Somehow I forced my own
need past his urgency. He released my mouth and stared at
me, eyes, mouth, and mind open to mine.

Heat rose in us both. Moisture dampened my thighs. His
hardness pressed through too many layers of clothing.

Without another word we fumbled and pressed and
kissed and fondled. Too quickly, he found a way into me. I
was wet and ready; still the size of him and the fierceness
of his thrust shocked a strangled cry from my throat and

mind. My pain only excited him more. With my mind as open as my legs I shared his thrill of pleasure. Then we shot upward with the glory of a shared climax.

We lay back panting, blushing, and utterly satisfied.

The next day he and his father left Kirkenwood, their business finished. I saw him only once more before I ran away from home, the night of Drake's heart attack the next Yuletide.

Chapter 37

Woodland west of Williamsburg, Virginia.

"I'VE waited eight years to do that, Georgie," Barclay whispered.

I did not have time to indulge this flare of passion. Sir Thomas Mercat's plans must be moving apace by now. I reared back, straining at Barclay's suddenly fierce embrace.

"You'll wait another eight years or more to repeat it," I replied. I did not even like my flamboyant cousin, a bully, betrothed to my niece. Nor did I trust him. His mind remained closed to me. I doubted he trusted me either.

"Easy, you have no fear of me," he whispered. Then he tucked me beneath his chin and soothed me with gentle strokes along my spine, as he would a restless wolfhound. I turned again, putting my back to him. He kept me enfolded. I felt his body react with interest at the proximity of my bottom.

I did not stand so comfortably. My mind raced, forgetting for a moment that my other lover, Major Roderick Whythe, directed his men in recovery of stolen weapons not ten yards away. How could I rescue Dulcie? The dark forest, full of the night noises of breeze and bird and animal, gave me no answers.

Eventually, the sounds of twenty or more men mounting and moving east toward Williamsburg penetrated my fevered brain.

"What do you truly want, Barclay?" I asked the moment I judged it safe to speak.

"To thwart my father by fair means or foul."

"And that includes seducing me?"

"If necessary." He nuzzled my neck again. I stood rigid and unresponsive.

"I need your help to rescue someone in dire need," I stated bluntly. Once more I widened my stance and found my balance. The Earth responded comfortably to my feet.

"Later, my love. Why talk? Why think? We have only to do." He rubbed his chin upon my hair—somewhere, somewhen I'd lost my hat. His hands began to roam up and down my arms, pausing beside my breasts. He spread his fingers wide so that his fingertips brushed against me in intimate little circles.

You will become just like him if you give in to your body now, I thought. His temptations left a bitter taste in my mouth.

"There is much to consider," I hedged. "I have duties tonight."

"There is nothing to consider. We are unique, you and I. We have but to take what pleasure we want when we find it." This time he bent to kiss my neck. "We need have no secrets between us."

I felt his tiny probe of magic seeking entrance to my mind, as another part of him sought entrance to my body.

His mind remained closed to my own probe.

"Part of being unique, being a part of the Kirkwood family and the Pendragon Society is to take responsibility for . . ."

He cut off my words with another searing kiss. I kept my lips placid and my mind blank.

He reached with both of his big hands to lift my skirt. The movement threw his balance forward. He leaned a little too heavily against me.

I had to stop this.

With another shift of balance I found the leverage I sought. I grasped one of his arms with both hands and yanked. His long body landed in front of me with a satisfying thud. I still held onto his arm, which I twisted.

Oblegid pounced upon his chest and growled. But she purred and drooled at the same time, completely destroying her image of menace. She still viewed life as a game.

"Georgie," Barclay pleaded through gritted teeth. "Georgie, you will dislocate my shoulder." His breathing seemed a little ragged.

"Not unless you have dislocated this shoulder before." I twisted a little more.

He gasped.

"I have."

"When, Cousin Barclay?"

"When I was thirteen, wrestling with your brother. He sought to teach me a lesson."

"What did you do to invite that kind of punishment?"

"I . . . Gods, that hurts."

I did not ease off the pressure. "What did you do?"

"I gave a stable lad a black eye for not saddling my horse fast enough."

"Small boy, about nine, gap-toothed, extra finger on his left hand, walked with a limp?"

"Yes," he moaned

"You deserved the punishment. Ezra couldn't move any faster. And you had no right to strike any servant, especially one not of your own household."

"So Drake taught me." His eyes threatened to roll up in faint. Or feint?

I eased up on the twist, but kept pressure on his arm. He stayed where he was.

"Now tell me about those muskets."

"Tell me what secrets are hid in Resmiranda Griffin's grimoire that my father seeks it quite diligently." He grinned up at me seductively.

I applied new pressure to his arm.

He gasped in pain, dragged in two long gulps of air and then spoke. "I was sent clandestinely to investigate the disappearance of supplies, the buildup of arms among the Indians. An officer's loyalty is suspect." His breathing came a little easier as he got used to the pain.

I increased the pressure. "Which officer?"

"Damnme, woman, where did you learn to do that?"

"I was taught by the best."

"Your lover, Casanova."

"His successor." I was not about to name Heinrich der Reusse and thus bring his regiment of mercenaries into association with me.

If someone remembered that Major Georgie Kirkwood had achieved Master Mason status, Barclay could turn the entire brotherhood against me. The next step required of all practitioners of Freemasonry would be to murder me by means most foul.

"What of my niece, your bride?"

"King George postponed the marriage, sent Drake and the entire family packing back to Kirkenwood until the mourning period has passed. Then His Majesty dispatched me here, free of the encumbrance of a wife. Free to be his spy in the army."

Had the king dispatched another because he did not know I reported to Whitehall? Had Lord George Sackville and Prime Minister Lord Grenville even told the king that I had replaced my brother in the role of spy? Or did they not trust me?

I eased the pressure on Barclay's arm a little. "Freemasonry has made deep inroads into all ranks of the army," he said quietly. "They identify with their colonial brethren. Such alliances outside the military could undermine any campaign."

"Or to deal with the disruptive pamphleteers." Curses! I had just diverted the conversation down a road I did not want to travel. Not at all.

"That still does not make things right between us." I shoved his arm forward.

It dropped limply to the ground. He moaned and rolled, clutching his shoulder with his left hand.

"For the moment, it appears you and I work toward the same purpose. I'll let you return to your mission and me to mine." He would be of no help to me now. Not with his sword arm aching and near to dislocating.

Then I went in search of the rapier. Luck was with me. Ian had looked no farther than the first packet wrapped in oilskin. The second packet, containing my rapier and my French dagger-pistol, remained where I'd hidden them in a hollow among the roots.

My cousin still rocked back and forth on the ground where I'd left him. I watched him a moment as he struggled to sit without jarring his right shoulder. He managed it. Just. He'd have a time climbing aboard a horse.

His aches and pains gave me time to mount and ride back to Five Oaks.

A single lantern burned low inside one of the slave cabins. The open door showed more shadows than detail. All the other quarters remained dark. At the big house, a single candle burned inside Sir Thomas' study.

Dashing back into the house and changing to my breeches would take too long. I dismounted and lashed the gelding to a post outside the stable. Then I cut and ripped off the clumsy skirt of my habit, leaving me clad in the trousers held in place by braces. The dark fabric should obscure the feminine cut of the garment. The jacket I threw across the saddle for later. Wearing only a loose-sleeved shirt and the breeches, I should be just another anonymous male.

But my face was distinctive and known to all on the plantation. A broad strip cut from the skirt with eye holes and tied across my face made an effective mask.

Holding my rapier loosely in my right hand and the dagger-pistol in my left, I made my way to the windowless cabin with light glowing from the open doorway. I did not believe Sir Thomas would sully his home by bringing the girl to the servant cubicles in the attic.

Movement inside the cabin made me freeze in place. I wrapped the darkness around me. Willing the Earth to cushion the sound of my steps as if I scouted an enemy campsite, I tiptoed slowly to the side of the door. One peek inside confirmed my worst fears. Dulcie lay naked upon the cot against the far wall. Her dusky skin made a sharp contrast to the bleached white sheet beneath her. Her huge dark aureoles lay flat against her small breasts, the nipples flaccid. The nest of dark curls at the juncture of her thighs remained dry. She kept her legs clamped together. Good girl. She wasn't going to give in easily.

Two men stood with their backs to me, the overseer holding his discipline whip, and the stranger. Official observers to this ritual rape.

Sir Thomas loomed over the cot.

As I assessed the situation, he fumbled with his trouser buttons. Dulcie's eyes went wide with fear at sight of the man's engorged member.

I knew her fear. In Paris I'd been set upon by a a band of thugs intent on robbery, rape, and murder. Cassanova rescued me before the men completely overpowered me. Just.

I knew the violence men did to women. And I had sworn never to be a victim again. Nor would I allow another to become one. If I could save her.

I burst in, weapons aimed at my employer's now naked butt.

"One move and I cut it off," I shouted, making certain to roughen and deepen my voice.

"How dare you trespass on my private property, you rogue!" Sir Thomas screamed, whirling to face me. He seemed oblivious to the fact his breeches dangled around his knees and his drawers hung open.

My eyes focused upon the drop of liquid dangling from the tip of his cock.

"How dare you violate every moral law in the Bible! In any culture," I snarled back at him.

His face took on the blank look of puzzlement.

I blinked and focused on his aura. He honestly did not believe he sinned in any way.

"Get up, Dulcie," I said.

She slid to her knees beside the cot, for the first time attempting to cover herself with her hands. "Please, Mister Rogue, don't hurt me," she pleaded, visibly trembling.

"I have no intention of allowing any man to hurt you ever again. Put on some clothing. We are leaving."

"Stealing my slave is a crime of the worst magnitude," Sir Thomas growled. "We will hunt you to the ends of this earth."

"Try?" I smiled at him, lowering my extended rapier to point directly at his balls.

He blanched.

Out of the corner of my eye, I caught movement. I lunged left with the dagger and hooked the overseer's whip. The length of leather tangled with the blade. The razor-sharp edge severed through two loops, considerably shortening his weapon.

Another movement to my right.

The stranger brought a pistol to bear. Cocked. Ready to kill me. At this range he could not miss.

Chapter 38

BLOODY hell!

I shifted my rapier's aim to the stranger and launched myself sideways into him.

A pistol fired. Mine?

The stranger and I rolled, wrestling for possession of the pistol.

Someone moaned.

I came up, fists flying. I kicked at the man's wrist. The pistol flew out of his hand and skidded under the cot.

Oblegid yowled and threw herself into the fray.

Sir Thomas yelled. My cat clung to his face, claws buried in his skin.

The overseer landed a fist in my gut.

Air exploded from my lungs. I doubled over, lashing out with my feet.

Oblegid retracted her claws from Sir Thomas' face and flipped onto the overseer's back.

The man dodged me but not my cat. He roared in pain as Oblegid sank her teeth into his neck.

Sir Thomas yelled something else.

The stench of blood filled the room.

Whose?

Three men alive and kicking—literally. That left only Dulcie. My dagger-pistol had been fired.

"Bloody hell!" I screamed with mind and voice. A quick glance over my shoulder showed Dulcie still kneeling, hands held in an attitude of prayer.

Sir Thomas moaned and slumped. I finally noticed blood staining the side of his shirt. Not a mortal wound.

The stranger grabbed my ankle from his position on the floor. I had no room to dodge him, unless I stepped upon Sir Thomas.

"You shall pay for this, rogue," James Banks, the overseer, snarled. He picked up the remnants of the whip and flicked it. The two feet of thin leather coiled around my wrist.

I bent my palm and sliced the whip with my dagger. Banks stumbled off-balance from the sudden change of tension.

With a neat side step, I pushed him into the stranger. The two of them tripped over Sir Thomas.

I tossed the sheet over Dulcie, shoved her to her feet and literally dragged her out of the cabin. She sobbed continually. I don't know if she was grateful or too afraid to do aught else.

With frantic shoves I managed to get Dulcie atop the gelding at an odd angle. I vaulted up behind her, slapping the horse's rump with the flat of my dagger. He took off at a wild gallop.

I clung to the saddle cinch for dear life.

After half a mile the shouts of my potential pursuers faded in the distance. They would have to gather their wits and their horses. Would they take the time to saddle their mounts?

Oblegid clawed her way onto the saddle blanket before me. She crouched there, hissing at the passing wind as if it, too, was her enemy.

Dulcie continued to shudder with her sobs. I ignored her as I turned the horse west.

"You'll be safe," I promised her.

"Massah said 'twas a honor to bear his get," she choked.

"The master is your father. 'Tis no honor, but an abomination."

"What will I do?" she asked, finally gulping back her tears.

"Join others of your kind who have fled the master. In the west. You'll be free."

"With the Red Indians?"

"Yes."

"They ain't civilized." She clutched the sheet more tightly across her breasts.

"But you will be free."

"Don't know how to be free."

"Then you'll learn."

"Massah say we ain't bright enough to learn to be on our own."

"The master is sorely mistaken."

"And who be you to question Massah?"

"A masked rogue who seeks to right a few wrongs and break a few rules."

"Break a few heads, too."

"That, too." I grinned. I had found a new career. I'd fare better within the greater population of Williamsburg. I ran too much risk of being recognized at Five Oaks. As soon as I saw Dulcie to safety, I'd hie myself to the city.

Hours later I thought to remove my mask and stuff it behind the saddle. Later I would dispose of the thing where Sir Thomas could not find it and use it as evidence of my crimes against him.

What of his crimes against Dulcie? By the rules of society he had committed no crime. Dulcie was his property to do with as he pleased.

I was the criminal for disrupting his lawful attempts to breed a slave.

Society cared not that the girl was his daughter, a human being. I cared not for a society that allowed such atrocities.

Returning to Five Oaks for my trunks and my journal made my stomach turn. Later I would sneak back and retrieve my books, but not the cumbersome clothes of a governess. I left that life behind as my familiar and I rode east, toward the city where I would recover my other blades from the man I thought I could love. Tonight I hated all men. Especially those who thought with their cocks rather than their brains.

Faint rose-colored light awakened the fields. Heavy dew glistened upon the corn and the Indian maize. Field after field rolled away along the gentle hills in every direction. Crooked fences, made of split rails laid atop each other in zigzags marked the divisions of crops and ownerships. Behind the fences often lay neat farmhouses, usually made of white clapboard, some, more prosperous farmers, built with brick.

The dirt road seemed well graded and dry. Few deep ruts or potholes threatened the horse's steady gait. We ate up the miles quickly. As we neared the city, traffic increased. Farmers brought their wagons onto the road, laden with cabbages and carrots and fresh vegetables. Other farmers drove sheep and pigs and a few milch cows ahead of them.

Afraid that someone might recognize Sir Thomas' horse, I abandoned the road for the fields and copses that lined the way. Half a mile outside the city I dismounted and turned the horse so that he headed back toward his clean stable and fresh grain. A smart whack upon his ample rump made him turn his head to look at me. His wide eyes questioned my intentions.

"Go home, Rex." I whacked him again, a little bit harder.

He dipped his head and munched on a tuft of grass.

"All right, stay here." I headed toward the city at a brisk walk. Within a few steps I heard heavy hoofbeats upon the ground. I peeked over my shoulder to make certain Rex had indeed decided to go home. "What are you doing?"

The horse bobbed his head and bumped against my shoulder. His entire attitude suggested that if he misinterpreted my orders, 'twas my fault.

"You need to go home," I informed him, trying once more to turn him in the proper direction.

He resisted and draped his huge head over my shoulder. Then he relaxed his knees as if he expected me to hold him up.

"Get up, you great oaf!" Reluctantly, he assumed responsibility for remaining upright. "If you weren't already gelded, I'd do it to you now."

Then I heard what drove him. Oblegid mewed plaintively from her nest beneath the saddle blanket.

"Silly kitten." I scooped up the sleepy cat. "You were so quiet I forgot about you. I'm not used to a companion in a fight." My familiar answered by snuggling into my arms and purring. She was more than willing to accept responsibility for my neglect. I rubbed my face against her fur, apologizing profusely.

My anger at the loss of my weapons evaporated. Cool logic came to mind. I knew precisely where, when, and how to retrieve them.

I walked the horse to a spot beside the road, where he would be found, and tied the reins to a low branch. He neighed in a plaintive tone when I abandoned him. "I will not add the capital crime of horse theft to the long list I have committed this night," I whispered to him.

He kept up a discordant racket as Oblegid and I continued into the city.

Chapter 39

Williamsburg, the stables behind the print shop.

RODERICK rubbed down his horse in the stable behind the home and shop of the local printer, Joseph Royle. The place smelled of hot lead, ink, pulp, and glue as much as of straw and horse.

He leaned his head against the beast's withers, tired but not sleepy. He'd sent Ian to his bed an hour ago rather than seek his own and leave caring for the horse to the batman.

He had to think. Surely he could find a logical explanation for Major Georgie Kirkwood's weapons to be in the secret possession of his sister, Georgina Kirkwood Mondo, la Principessa del Porto Ricinum. If there truly was such a place with the unlikely name of the Port of Bugs.

And if there was not such a place, Georgina's title was bogus. Perhaps everything she had told him began with a lie.

The lie that Major Georgie Kirkwood was her bastard half brother. What if . . . ? But she had not had any scars where he knew the mercenary Georgie had been viciously slashed by a Turk. Not a raised scar that his hands could discover as they explored her body. He'd not seen her flesh by light of day . . .

His thoughts circled and circled. They always came back to the issue of who had hidden the blades and why. Had the same person stolen six crates of muskets and one hundred rounds of powder and shot? If so, he dealt with a traitor to the crown who was in league with the Indians and, possibly, the French.

A slight shuffle in the straw stilled him. Who disturbed the stable so late?

Slowly, so as not to betray his presence by any abrupt movement or shift in shadow, he peered around the stall opening.

"You might as well show yourself. I know where you lurk, Major Whythe," the now all-too-familiar husky voice of Georgina Kirkwood said. No trace of emotion colored her tone. Or was it truly a young man's tenor voice?

Roderick strolled out of his hiding place. By the feeble light of a single lantern near the door and a sliver of moonlight, he discerned a masculine outline. Georgina's voice. Georgie's figure. Which? Or both?

Both in the same person.

Suddenly a dozen images ricocheted around his head. He almost lost his balance trying to make sense of it all. Just as abruptly as they had assailed him, his memories settled into a cohesive pattern. He smiled, then realized she could not see him in the gloom.

"I am here, at your disposal, Major Kirkwood. Perhaps your rank is as big a lie as your military career, Georgie."

"My military career was never a lie! I earned every promotion. I led my men with honor and distinction." Her voice trembled, just a little.

"It was all a lie. If your men had known you for a thief and a smuggler of arms to the enemy, they would never have followed you into battle. They would have feared, resented, and hated you," he baited her, knowing that for whatever reason she had sought him, his only advantage lay in disrupting her concentration through her emotions.

"I'll show you why my men followed me." She lifted a naked blade and held it steadily en garde. Then she took two steps closer. The rapier tip rested a scant two inches from his heart.

"May I defend myself?" Roderick kept his hands at his sides.

Georgie nodded.

Roderick ducked back into the stall and retrieved her perfectly balanced saber from his tack. He prayed that the extra length and weight of the blade, along with his longer reach and stride would give him an advantage over her slender and deadly rapier. He'd never be a match for her skill.

He adjusted his hold on the grip meant for a much smaller hand.

How had he ignored all the clues before this? Now that he looked at Georgie and her weapons, he would never again mistake them for masculine counterparts.

He took a deep breath and assumed a tense en garde. At least she gave him the chance to physically prepare. Half a heartbeat later she launched herself forward and past him. A slight tug on his uniform coat told him she'd scored a touch. Not daring to look down, he whirled to face his opponent. His gaze focused on her hand and the tip of her rapier.

His uniform felt baggy, loose fitting where moments before it had fit him snugly.

Georgie smiled. Something feral brightened her countenance. He spotted the tip of one eyetooth piercing her lip.

His blood heated with lust at the sight.

He swallowed the emotion. She counted on distracting him. He had to concentrate in order to stay alive.

She flicked her wrist.

He parried, remembering to keep his movements tight. The broader moves of saber against scimitar in battle would leave him open and vulnerable. More vulnerable than he already was. A nod of approval from her told him he'd done something correctly. With her next movement, he blocked her high and slid his blade down hers.

She coupéd and disengaged before he could pres. This time she slashed low and to her right. Something dropped into the straw at their feet. Again that grin and he dared not check to see what damage she had wrought.

"You could kill me quickly," he said. This time he lunged into the attack.

She didn't even bother to counter. She ducked and her blade slid beneath his attack and flicked. Something else fell to the ground.

This time he felt a decided loosening of his breeches. He backed up three long strides and glanced down. Two buttons gone, upper right and lower left.

A little of his dignity remained.

"If I wanted to kill you, you would not be breathing right now," she said.

"What do you want from me, Georgie?" He was careful

to refer to her more masculine sobriquet, give her the illusion of maintaining her secret.

"Something worse than death for an Englishman."

"Have you resorted to Red Indian torture?" The question of who had smuggled muskets, powder, and shot to the natives remained high on his priorities. Had Georgie done it? Why? What did she have to gain?

"You would endure torture." Another twist of her wrist.

He parried and sought a riposte. She blocked him and struck again. Another button plummeted to the ground.

"No, I want your complete humiliation, Major Whythe." A fourth button followed its brethren. Barely a full minute had passed in their duel.

Roderick gulped. He had forgotten that this woman had little respect for rules. She had little respect for anything other than her own perverted sense of right and wrong.

Even the love they had shared for one brief night meant nothing to her.

Georgie chuckled again and cut away the top left button exposing his drawers.

He blushed. She laughed and lowered her blade.

"I'd take the seat, too, but will accept my blades in return for the ragged ends of your . . . dignity."

"Granted." He lowered the saber, placed it across his arm and offered it to her in surrender, all the while keeping a grip on his breeches. His gaze locked on hers.

"The dagger, too," she said breathily. Her eyes did not drop away from his penetrating stare.

"With my tack." He did not offer to fetch it.

She hesitated one long moment, licked her lips, and finally looked away.

"That trick of yours, Georgie, balancing the saber on your finger, it's the blade more than your skill," he called out.

She poked her head out of the horse stall. "I trust that piece of information will remain our little secret," she said raising the saber until the tip was only two finger lengths from his Adam's apple.

"My word of honor." Roderick gulped.

"Good."

"One more bit of information before you depart," he said quietly, though he knew himself vulnerable to her unpredictable whims.

"Yes?" she sheathed both swords, stuck one dagger behind her braces, and hefted the remaining one, flipping it into the air and catching it time and again, first by the tip then by the grip.

"Why are you selling weapons to the Indians?"

"Me? You think I stole those muskets?"

Roderick nodded, keeping his eyes upon her hands and how they handled the dagger. He did not want that weapon embedded in his heart.

"Why would I wish to arm the natives?"

"That is what I asked you."

"No, you did not. You asked . . . I will not argue semantics with you. I have not the time." As if in response to her observation a bird chirped outside. "You must look elsewhere for your culprit, Major Whythe. Perhaps closer to home."

"How close?"

"Under your nose." With that, she saluted him jauntily with the dagger and disappeared into the predawn shadows.

"Damnation!" Roderick made to follow and tripped over his breeches.

Chapter 40

Kirkenwood, mid-October, 1764.

EMILY flicked her new rapier against a straw man target, testing its flexibility. Bits of hay scattered in the wind.

An excellent weapon that fit her hand and strength. But it was not a broadsword like Excalibur and handled differently. Still, she needed to learn the basics. She swiped at the scarecrow again from a different angle. Straw exploded upward. A bit of chaff caught in her eye, making it water.

She rubbed it roughly with her left hand, keeping the sword in her right.

"How dare you treat such a fine blade so callously!" René du Pec screamed. The French sword master tugged at his scraggly hair in exasperation. The tie about his queue had disappeared half an hour ago in the middle of demonstrating a new drill for Emily.

"How am I to get used to the weight and feel of it if I do not practice with it?" she asked. In the brisk wind off the North Sea, her own hair tended to fly out of any restraint she attempted.

The wind always blew at Kirkenwood, especially up here in the bailey of the ruined castle. She almost wished for the additional layers of clothing dictated for women rather than the breeches and coat she wore today. A couple of extra petticoats and a nice woolen shawl would help ward off the damp bite in the air. They also restricted her movements. Perhaps she should keep moving to stay warm.

Without warning, she lifted her blade in salute, whipped

it down to the side with a murmur of a prayer, then lunged
at du Pec.

He parried her easily and replied with a neat riposte. She
batted his blade aside and countered the attack. He backed
up just enough to make her touch so insubstantial it did
not even dent the fabric of his coat.

"You must be faster than that, mademoiselle." Du Pec
stepped aside and swatted her backside with the flat of his
blade as her next attack took her past where he had just
been standing.

"How . . . ?" Before Emily could finish her sentence, du
Pec flicked his blade against her now exposed chest in the
same movement she had tried against the straw man.

Emily backed up, acknowledging the touch with a nod of
her head. A large hand covered hers. She jumped sideways,
startled. Her blade came up automatically in defensive mode.

"Good instincts, Emily," Papa said on a chuckle. He'd
lost weight these last months, gained some muscle, too. He
began to look like the father she remembered from her
childhood. "Shift your grip to here." Gently he moved her
fingers to a looser, more flexible grip.

Du Pec scowled. "Perhaps you would care to spar with
me, Monsieur Earl?" His accent thickened and his eyes
narrowed.

Papa took the rapier out of Emily's hand, tested it for
weight and balance, then nodded. "En garde," he said with
enthusiasm. More enthusiasm than Emily had heard in his
voice in many a long year.

Almost before du Pec had time to assume his own en
garde, Papa attacked fiercely. He slashed and lunged, withdrew and parried the sword master's inadequate counter.

Du Pec found his balance and slashed mercilessly at Papa.
If his rapier had not been foiled with a clay button he'd have
torn Papa to ribbons. Papa gave nearly as good as he got.

Emily had trouble following the action, giving names to
only about half the moves. The men danced quickly, back
and forth, around, hopping over the debris of a ruined castle. Their blades moved more quickly.

Papa's breath came in quick, shallow pants. Du Pec
seemed hardly winded.

Emily stepped closer to the action, concerned.

"Stay back, Emily," her father ordered. "I will not have you hurt." Each word came out more labored than the last.

Du Pec pressed Papa closer, engaging the blade, pressing it hard. Then a quick coupé, disengage, and killing touché.

Papa dropped the fine rapier and stepped back, clutching his chest with his right hand.

"Papa!" Emily screamed. She caught his big body as he slumped to the ground. "You've killed him," she accused du Pec, tears streaming.

"Hardly," du Pec said. He rested the point of his weapon upon the top of his boot and struck a casual pose. He looked down his nose upon his employer, the Earl of Kirkenwood, with disdain. "He does not bleed."

True enough. Emily ran her hands quickly across her father's chest and down his arms seeking an external source for the anguish that twisted his face and contorted his limbs. All the while each breath seemed an ordeal in itself. She remembered that look all too well.

"Get help," Emily cried. She found her father's heartbeat with her fingertips. It stuttered and faltered.

" 'Tis not my place . . ." du Pec began.

"Damn your eyes, man. He's dying. Get help now." She grabbed the dropped rapier with her right hand, keeping her left atop Papa's heart.

Du Pec backed up from the rock-steady point of the rapier within inches of his throat apple. "Oui, mademoiselle." He backed farther away from her, then turned and ran down the path to the village.

Emily dropped the blade once more, gulped back her tears, and returned her attention to her father, seventh Earl of Kirkenwood, Pendragon of England.

His heart faltered again. She pushed upon it through his chest, pushed with her magic as well as her hand. "Beat damn it. Beat!"

Her arm came alive with power. Tingles became fire. Became agony. And still she poured everything she knew about herself and her talent through her hand into his chest.

Georgie and Barclay had done this for Papa once before. If only she could remember what they had done, how they had done it.

"Enough," Papa gasped. "You will kill yourself. Not for

me." Feebly he tried to grasp her arm and pull it away from him.

"I will not allow you to die," she told him. "You will live a while yet."

"A while yet. Not well, but a while." His breathing eased a tiny bit. "You have to grab hold of the spell. Keep the spell going. Curb the Chaos. Tryblith is close to freeing himself," he gasped. Then he closed his eyes.

"What spell, Papa? What do I grab hold of? Who or what is Tryblith?"

He did not answer.

Frantically, Emily ran her hands up and down her father's body seeking a trace of magic, any tendril of power that might give her a clue. By his left hand, his dominant hand, a tiny tingle brushed against her fingertips. She paused, concentrated.

A sense of calm, rationale, and logic invaded her. The opposites of Chaos, disorder, and rampant violence. She had a dim sense of Parliament and the king at the other end of the magic thread.

Neither King George III, nor his father George II, had sought Papa's advice as the Pendragon. The spell Papa grasped at had sought to keep the king and Parliament balanced and rational.

Then the mere trace of magic vanished. The fibers of the spell unraveled and slipped away. She grabbed at it, with her physical hand and her magic, but it was gone.

Rural Virginia, west of Williamsburg.

I waited. The moon had set, dawn not yet arrived. Faint starlight showed me the thin sliver of track that passed for a road in these rolling hills. Scattered trees seemed to droop in the humid night air, little cooler than the day before.

I sweated beneath my coat and waistcoat. I longed to shed the dark garments, but my white shirt—grimy though it was with sweat and dust—would reveal my presence. The strong gelding beneath me dozed, hipshot. But I knew he would awaken in an instant. He always did.

Lord Grenville's gold had purchased the finest mount I could find, and rented good stabling for him.

If the prime minister knew how I spent his money, he might withdraw his support, despite the detailed reports I sent him each week now.

A quick flash of light to the west. Then I heard the solid clop of horses making their weary way along the road. A soft murmur of voices and the tramp of feet. Three mounted men and a patrol of perhaps twenty marching behind.

My quarry approached. I gathered the reins. The horse brought up his head alertly, ears flicking and mouth playing with the bit. I curbed his natural urge to plunge forward with my knees and my mind.

We centered ourselves across the road.

"Hold," Major Barclay Marlowe said as he caught sight of me by the light of the pole lantern carried by a corporal. "What business brings you out so late?"

"Mayhap I am up early," I quipped, adjusting my grip on my rapier.

"What business?" Barclay growled. Obviously, the fatigue of a long patrol shortened his temper.

"My business is with your sergeant, Rodger Axely."

Men shifted away from the man who rode directly behind the lieutenant and my cousin. Even the corporal at the fore eased to the side of the road.

Barclay must value this sergeant if he rode like an officer rather than marching with the men.

"The masked rogue," the lieutenant muttered.

I grinned behind my mask, a somewhat more comfortable and efficient affair than the strip of cloth I'd used to hide my features from Sir Thomas Mercat.

"Have we met?" I asked. I loosed the dagger-pistol from its sheath at my belt. This escapade could prove dangerous.

"Not officially. I carry a warrant for your arrest," Barclay snarled. He kneed his horse forward.

I felt his magic probing for my identity. I sent it back to him, fragmented and scattered. He reared his head with the backlash. He'd have a headache and worse temper for the next day or two.

"Oh, dear. I cannot allow you to apprehend me just yet. I have justice to mete out to your sergeant." I kept Barclay at the center of my attention, but the lieutenant in my periphery.

Again the shifting away from my quarry. A slight man of middle years slumped in his saddle. I did not need to see his face to know he was the man I sought. I had memorized his form, his posture, and his misdeeds.

The recruits seemed more interested in watching than in protecting their sergeant.

"I will not allow you to molest any of my men," the lieutenant insisted.

Barclay sat silently, with a bemused smile upon his face. Even without magic I knew how he planned to trap me.

"But you allow and condone his molestation of innocent women?" Anger began to heat my face. I longed to discard the mask and plunge forward, brandishing all of my weapons. Twenty to one. Not safe odds even with my advantages.

"Stand aside, Lieutenant Richards, or add your name to my list of those requiring justice."

"I will not stand by . . .".

I charged, circling my rapier above my head like a broadsword. The lieutenant and Barclay ducked. My horse took me past the three mounted men. As I passed Barclay, I pricked his horse's rump with the tip of my dagger. The steed took off across the field. His men followed on foot, eagerly. The lieutenant debated with himself, then followed his superior.

Major Marlowe hauled hard on the reins. The horse came to a reluctant halt. The men milled aimlessly.

Sergeant Axely kept on going in the direction of Williamsburg. But not toward safety.

I cut him off half a league down the road. Behind us, I heard the arguments of the soldiers with their officers. They'd all heard reports of the Masked Rogue and how he only went after men who deserved the punishments he meted out.

Oblegid leaped from her hiding place on my saddle. She tangled herself around Axely's horse's legs. The big beast pranced and sidled, doing his best to avoid stepping upon the little cat. Then Oblegid snagged the horse's foreleg with her claws.

The horse reared.

Axely slid to the ground.

I dismounted and lunged for the man with my rapier. I'd not do him much damage with that weapon; unless he did something stupid and forced me to run him through.

"Get up, you cowardly pox upon the face of the earth," I snarled at him.

"I ain't poxed, you . . ."

Before he could curse me, I pressed the tip of my rapier upon his belly, just above his crotch.

He gulped and swallowed his words.

"I could geld you right here."

He nodded.

"I will settle for a formal apology to Mistress Johnson."

"She ain't nothin' but a barmaid," he sneered.

"She is a woman and deserving of your respect."

"She was willing enough . . ."

"I heard her say no."

"Don't mean nothing."

"Do you want me to geld you here and now?"

"No."

"But that really means yes."

" 'Taint the same."

Barclay had his men together and approached at a rapid trot. I had not much time.

I flicked off three buttons on Axely's breeches. He tried to roll away from me. I caught his backside with the rapier and slit the breeches neatly down the center.

For good measure I lunged and pricked his left butt cheek. A trickle of blood stained his white breeches. He'd not sit comfortably for several days.

"An apology to Mistress Johnson. And I will be watching to make certain you do it."

"Or?" Axely gained his feet, seemingly gaining courage from his approaching comrades."

"Or I'll catch you in a dark alley when you are alone and slit your throat." I whipped around and fired the dagger-pistol. The pole lantern shattered. Hot lamp oil spilled across the roadway.

Horses shied. Men crashed into the rear ends of the officers' horses. Barclay cursed.

I vaulted back into my saddle, happy to find my cat already nested there, between the pommel and the saddle blanket. With a quick jab of my spurs, my well-trained gelding gathered his legs beneath him and leaped off the road into the copse.

In moments the darkness hid us. With the silence that

only my magic could impose, we made our way back to our rented stable. Barclay and his patrol straggled in an hour later as the sun crested the horizon.

Sergeant Axely lagged behind, limping, leading his horse. The recruits jabbed elbows and snickered among themselves.

Betsy Johnson would have her apology tonight. Lieutenant Richards would make certain it happened or he'd lose the unity of his men.

Barclay, though . . .

He'd come looking for the Masked Rogue. But he'd not find the man he looked for. Even if he did find me.

I whistled my way back to my lodgings, content with the progress of my mission. More and more military men treated the people of Williamsburg with respect and acknowledged their rights as English citizens, rather than face the Masked Rogue and his blade.

Chapter 41

Kirkenwood, England, mid-October, 1764.

"DR. Milton Marlowe, miss," Simpson intoned.

Milton pushed past the officious butler. "Emily, my dear, I just heard. How is your father?" He stopped short just inside Drake's capacious library. Emily stood at the reading podium, a very large tome open before her. It was not the family Bible, but equally thick.

Could it be the very grimoire he sought? His heart beat a furious tattoo in anticipation.

He breathed deeply to calm himself. No sense in giving the girl the advantage of seeing him agitated.

Neville's ghost reached an insubstantial hand for the book. He passed right through it, unable to grasp anything in the real world.

Emily turned the pages of the book by waving her finger above the text. Milton had never seen his young cousin display magic so openly. Come to think of it, he'd never witnessed her use of magic at all, not even in the assembly of the Pendragon Society.

Magnificent that she could waste so much energy on such a simple trick! Even in her homely gown of blue muslin with a lace fichu and mob cap she looked every inch the accomplished witch.

He suppressed a moment of deep longing. Barclay would yet return from the colonies to claim her as his bride. And the training of their doubly magical children would be left to himself. He would see to that.

"Papa is . . . is stable," Emily stammered. Tears formed in

her eyes. "The local surgeon has bled him and given him a draught to make his heart beat steadily. I believe it contains minute amounts of foxglove."

"And your sisters? The baby? How do they fare?"

"All thrive. Their governesses and tutors keep them occupied. But they miss their papa . . . and mama." She choked on the last words.

"My dear, dear child. This is all too much for one of your tender years." Milton hastened to her side and draped his arm about her shoulders. He took the liberty of kissing her temple.

But his eyes strayed to the text of the book. His eyes crossed trying to read the arcane symbols.

"I will survive this crisis. I must." Emily gulped back her tears and stiffened her spine. A tiny barrier of space came between them.

Milton felt the rebuff as an almost physical blow. Had she used her magic to push him away?

"I have written to Aunt Georgie for advice."

"Allow me to prepare a draught for you, Emily. 'Twill ease your mind and allow you to sleep. I will help you through this. You do not need your," he shuddered, "aunt."

"I have many things to do in Papa's stead. I need advice—not help. I cannot sleep just yet." She resumed her reading of the massive text.

Milton peered over her shoulder at the handwritten lines that scrawled across the page. He could make no sense of them. They must be cloaked in magic.

"Should you not be tending my father rather than making courtesies to me?" Emily asked. She barely looked up from her perusal of the book. The barrier of space between them intensified. The shadow of her body across the pages made them more unreadable.

Milton found himself on the other side of the podium, facing her, two steps closer to the door. What did she study so earnestly that required secrecy?

Emily leaned forward. Her lean figure covered the pages. "What do you want, Cousin?" she asked sharply.

"Remember your manners, Emily," Milton scolded. He took another step forward. If she would just stand straight again, he might catch a better glimpse of the text, or the title of the book. He might be able to penetrate whatever cloaking spell made the words appear as gibberish.

"I do not have time for manners!" she snapped. "Do you not understand? Papa has left the realm in shambles. He has no organization, no secondary plans, no trained successor!"

"My dear, the Pendragon Society . . ."

"Knows nothing. Papa kept all of us in ignorance of too many things. I am just now puzzling out the complexities of what he tried to do."

"Perhaps I can assist. If I had access to the archives . . ."

Once more Emily stiffened. "The archives. What do you know of it?" Her eyes narrowed. A shimmering aura snapped into place around her entire body, protecting her from magical assault.

"I know what any member of the Pendragon Society knows. The records and grimoires of all of our ancestors back to King Arthur's Merlin, all contained in one protected room, somewhere in this barony. No one but the Pendragon has ever had access to the archives. If you know where it is . . ." He jerked his head at the book in front of her, obviously belonging to the archives. "If you know anything, share that knowledge with me. Share your burdens with me. I can help you. I was your father's closest associate."

Cold calm settled on Emily's shoulders, almost as a visible mantle. "The archives are closed to all but the Pendragon. Only the one chosen by Papa and the wolfhounds to succeed him will know how to open them."

"You lie, Emily. You have already been in the archives." Milton laid a hand upon the book. Magic burned his fingers where they touched the dried ink of the text.

"Have I?" Emily opened her eyes wide in feigned innocence.

"Yes, Emily. You have. I can smell the lie on you. I am the only member of the family powerful enough to protect you, your infant brother, and your sisters. I am the only logical one to succeed your papa." He tried to make his voice gentle, to keep from alarming her with his urgency. Success was within his grasp. He could almost taste it. With the archives he could achieve all of his goals, overnight. No more need to dance attendance on Drake. No more need to listen to the ditherings of the Inner Circle. No more need to nurture Barclay or tie himself to Emily and her potential children.

Neville would return to him, whole and hale. Alive! Together they could rule this world and several of the Underworlds. But he needed the spell from Resmiranda Griffin's grimoire.

"This book comes from the archives, does it not?" Milton placed his hand possessively upon the tome. He let the magic in the writing tantalize his fingertips. The magic, slight as it was, wound its way up his arm. At the large shoulder muscle, it balked. He pushed it toward his eyes. If it would only reach his eyes, he could read the arcane text.

"Papa left this book here, in the library. He gave me instructions to read it," Emily said as smooth as silk. No trace of a lie colored her aura.

"I . . . we must open the archives. If your papa dies before giving me the secret, it is lost forever," he ground out through clenched teeth.

"Only the Pendragon is allowed access to the archives. And his successor. The dogs will decide who that is to be when Belle whelps." Emily closed the book smartly.

Milton had to jerk his hand free lest it be crushed between the massive leaves.

"Has your father's familiar come into heat again?" he asked, nursing his stinging fingertips. The unfulfilled magic he had let into his system backlashed down his arm and over to the top of his spine. He ached all over. He hadn't allowed a spell to go ungrounded in thirty years. He'd forgotten how much it hurt.

"Belle mated two weeks ago with the dominant male wolfhound in our kennel. But if Papa dies before she whelps, then she will die, too. The line of the Pendragons will die with them. We cannot allow that to happen, Cousin Milton. I have sent for Aunt Georgina to return. Belle favored her with a pup once. She will do so again."

"For the love of God, Emily, you can't bring Georgie back now!" Milton began to tremble in agitation. That blasted woman would destroy everything, especially if she took a familiar from the wolfhound.

"Why not, Cousin Milton? Do you fear my aunt?"

"No, no, never that, Emily." Milton breathed deeply to cover his rampant emotions. "Just before I left London, I heard that Lord Sackville has ordered a warrant for Georgina's arrest. Something about an assassination in Poland last year. If she sets foot in England, she will go to the Tower. A trial could take years to come before the bench. She will be of no use to anyone in the Tower."

"Then I will call back my letter." Emily ducked her head and stared at the book for many long moments.

Milton tried to push a probe into her mind. He needed to know what she was thinking at this moment, know the source of her hostility.

With his mind he imagined a blood-red arrow piercing the girl's eye, penetrating to the center of her brain, breaking apart, spreading its questing magic through her system.

The arrow failed to penetrate her aura. She protected secrets. The secret of the archives. What else? He had other ways of finding out, and then . . . Quickly Milton grounded the arrow before it could backlash.

Emily continued to stare at him, daring him to try again.

"Of course. I will tend to your father now." Defeat weighed heavily upon his shoulders, especially since he had been so close, so very close, to achieving all he longed for, all he needed to complete his tasks.

"Be sure that Papa lives yet a while, Cousin Milton. If he dies, so does our magical protection of England. England is most vulnerable right now."

"What do you know?"

"Too much and not enough. I know that the colonists organize an embargo of imported British goods. I know that many merchants and shipping magnates already tighten their belts and grumble to Parliament. A single match to such volatile tinder will explode in a fire that cannot be extinguished. Chaos will be loosed upon us." She opened the book again and peered closely at the words.

Clearly, Milton had been dismissed. He'd kill her right now, but she knew how to open the archives. He knew it. She knew that he knew it. He had to keep both Emily and Drake alive until he broke through their protections.

"What to do?" Emily asked herself. She gathered up the huge book of spells—written by any number of her ancestors and compiled into one reference by her great-grandfather. How to get it back to the hidden room without Cousin Milton spying her trail? How to keep Excalibur a secret?

He would follow her. She had no doubt of that.

Would it be so bad to unburden herself to this cousin whom Papa had trusted so implicitly?

Aunt Georgie had warned her to trust no one. If only Emily could break through the layers of protection around her aunt and speak to her directly through a scrying bowl.

She stopped in her tracks with a new thought. Dr. Milton Marlowe wanted to be the Pendragon and control all of Britain. He already had the ear of the king. How much more influence and power would he have as the Pendragon?

After reading the spells and journals of her ancestors Emily realized that betrayal was inherent in her family. Quite possibly, Milton had made up the story of the arrest warrant. Or possibly made up the assassination story to force Sackville to order the warrant.

King George had dismissed Papa as ineffectual, his powers unnecessary. Cousin Milton seemed more persistent. And more ruthless. As the Pendragon he could force himself into the inner circles of power at court and in Parliament and control . . . control everything from the economy, to the colonies, to the weather.

He could not afford to have Aunt Georgie challenge his authority.

Emily shuddered in apprehension. The book weighed heavily in her arms. There had to be another route into the archives; one where Dr. Milton Marlowe would not think to look.

A small smile played across her mind. She knew the way. She'd read of it years ago in the journals of her ancestors.

With a lighter step she returned to her room and donned her fencing clothes. Time to think like her Aunt Georgie as well as act like her. Time to banish her fears with positive action.

Cousin Milton did not know how resourceful the Kirkwood women could be. Or how secretive. He'd have a hard time learning anything at Kirkenwood. Emily would see to that.

Chapter 42

Williamsburg, Virginia, mid-October, 1764.

"MAJOR Marlowe," Roderick hailed the tall, blond officer across the square.

A bright smile creased the younger man's face as he doffed his tricorn hat and bowed politely. Every move Marlowe made looked graceful and easy. No wonder he'd cut a swath across Virginia society. The young lady on his arm twittered behind her fan. The third such simpering miss Roderick had seen with Marlowe this week.

Roderick hastened across the square, dodging a rapidly moving gig driven by a different officer who escorted yet another twittering daughter of some wealthy planter. How long before the merchants and landowners who had opened their homes to His Majesty's troops began demanding marriage to their vulnerable offspring?

How long before the local swains began challenging those officers to duels for corrupting their sweethearts?

"Good day, Major," Marlowe said, making the first greeting as was proper to a more senior officer—if only by a few weeks.

"Major." Roderick nodded, then swept off his hat and bowed to the lady. Unfortunately, his bow was not nearly so graceful as Marlowe's had been.

"Miss Jane Cummings." Marlowe presented the lady on his arm.

Proper introductions required some polite chitchat about the fine autumn day, the brightness of the sunshine, and the crisp smell of apples and fallen leaves. The color of the leaves led to a discussion of the lack of a shipment of silk from London, (the embargo was such an inconvenience) before Roderick could broach the subject uppermost on his mind.

"Major Marlowe, I have need of your services," he finally stated a bit too abruptly for the rules of polite society.

"Oh? How so?" Marlowe lifted one eyebrow in an intrigued expression.

"I need to expand my knowledge of fencing beyond the English style and rudimentary skills."

"Certainly you have not achieved the elevated rank of major without a working knowledge of swordplay."

"A working knowledge only. I would learn finer technique. Barracks gossip makes you the best in the colonies. I would learn from you."

Marlowe smiled and lifted his chin.

Preening before the lady, Roderick thought. Smug bastard.

"Oh, are you seeking to engage the Masked Rogue?" Miss Cummings gushed. She disengaged her hand from Marlowe's arm and clapped her hands together in childish delight. She pouted prettily. Roderick noted that she had scrubbed her face clean and wore none of the artificial color or beauty patches so common in London.

"If the occasion arises, I shall engage any of His Majesty's enemies," Roderick made a small bow acknowledging his purpose.

"Ye'll not defeat the Masked Rogue!" Marlowe exploded. His hand went to his sheathed saber. His face turned red and he clenched his jaw.

"Have you engaged the man who seeks to defend women's honor, be they insulted barmaids or jilted ladies?" Roderick asked. He had a good idea of who had initiated the raids against His Majesty's soldiers and officers, but he dared not voice that opinion. No one would believe him.

Except possibly Major Barclay Marlowe.

"The Rogue has also freed common criminals," Barclay snarled.

"Are they common criminals or uncommon patriots?" Miss Cummings asked.

Both majors stared at her in disbelief.

"If a man writes a pamphlet questioning His Majesty's

right to rule, then he commits treason and must be transported home for trial and execution," Marlowe explained to Miss Cummings as if speaking to a child.

Roderick raised his assessment of the girl's intelligence, but wondered at her father's politics.

"And if the man did not write the pamphlet, but was falsely accused?" she defended her position.

"Then the truth will come out in a trial," Roderick jumped into the conversation.

"But the trial will be in England, the jury selected there. He will not be judged by his peers. Such is the right of all Englishmen."

Roderick could not bring himself to state the accepted counter argument, that colonials were not true English citizens. He wondered for half a moment if the colonials had the right of it.

Such thinking would get him court-martialed. He veered back to the origins of the conversation. "No matter the guilt or innocence of the prisoner. The Masked Rogue had no right to free a lawfully arrested man from gaol."

"A swordsman riding a fine chestnut gelding cut my patrol to ribbons last week." Marlowe continued to scowl. His words came out barely above a whisper.

Roderick had heard a slightly different version from his batman.

"Cut their uniforms to ribbons more like." Roderick swallowed his own mirth. What had that patrol been doing to earn the wrath of the Masked Rogue? He'd never heard of Georgie being so reckless as to attack an entire patrol of twenty men by herself. But then, she'd ridden into the teeth of battle against one hundred Turks with only thirty men to back her up.

"I am certain that if any man can bring the Rogue to justice, 'tis you, Major Marlowe," Miss Cummings exclaimed, taking Marlowe's arm once more. She looked as if she swallowed a smile.

Marlowe patted her hand solicitously. "I shall teach you fencing, Major Whythe, what I can. Meet me tonight at sunset behind the Raleigh." Barclay jerked his head toward the tavern near the governmental buildings, where all the locals met to read the latest inflammatory pamphlet and discuss politics most vehemently. Then he turned smartly

and nearly dragged Miss Cummings off toward the west
end of Duke of Gloucester Street. "But I shall be the one to
bring the Masked Rogue to justice. My justice," he muttered.

"We'll see about that," Roderick returned. "I hope
merely to keep my uniform intact next time I meet . . . him."

Drake struggled to keep his eyes open while his pen fair
flew across the page of his journal. Pouring his magic into
the writing, to obscure the true meaning of the words from
the casual reader, took more strength than he had to spare.
He paused long enough to breathe deeply, or as deeply as
he could around the congestion in his heart. Then he
dipped his quill and scratched more formulae upon the
page.

"Milord!" Milton exclaimed from the doorway. "You
must rest, husband your strength." The good doctor
marched to Drake's bedside and firmly removed both quill
and lapdesk from his hands.

"I must . . ."

"You must get well. Parliament means to go ahead with
the Stamp Tax. They have directed Lord Halifax to gather
data on public transactions for the colonies so they can
predict the number of stamps to print and the expected
revenue. Militants prowl the streets of Boston in protest.
Chief Justice Thomas Hutchinson of the Massachusetts
Colony reports violence. He fears for the lives and property of loyal colonists. My Lord Earl, Master Pendragon,
Drake, you have to get stronger, Parliament will listen only
to you."

"No, they will not. Modern men have no respect for
magic or magicians. They have no respect for my office, for
me." Drake sank back against his bolsters, more tired than
he wanted to admit. He had to finish his records for
Georgie. His sister was the only one strong enough to master the spell.

"I must inform Georgie . . ."

"No!" Was that an edge of tension in Milton's voice?

"Georgie must come home and handle this." Drake narrowed his focus, trying to keep from falling asleep again.
His cousin had gone pale and ground his teeth.

Suddenly Milton brightened. "Georgie is on a most important assignment for His Majesty, Drake. You and I can handle Parliament. Now tell me what must be done. You shall be the brains, and I your brawn. Together, we will keep the ship of state on an even keel."

Drake relaxed. Of course. Milton could handle the spell. Milton had the ear of His Majesty. He could counsel prudence, caution, and patience.

Shakily, Drake pushed the accumulated leaves of his journal toward his cousin. "Read," he said with effort. The breathiness of his voice frightened him.

"The words . . . your writing is unclear. You are not well, milord."

"My mind still works, Milton. 'Tis my heart that does not function properly. Use your God-given magic to read what I have written." Drake lay back, exhausted by just those few short sentences.

Had he overestimated Milton's abilities? How had the man been admitted into the Inner Circle if he did not have the magic to decipher this simple spell?

"I thought perhaps that was the case, milord. But I needed your permission to read the family treasures."

"Yes, always easier. Read. Read what you must to keep this family together and the Pendragon Society operating on an even keel. We will need the talents of all of the Inner Circle and the support of all of our Knights to weather the coming crisis."

"Have you seen the future, milord?" Milton reached for the loose pages eagerly. His eyes opened wide and he read eagerly, as if he were a starving man presented with a meal. Only now he starved for information.

"My dreams are vivid, if puzzling."

"But are they true dreams?"

"They carry the weight of prescience. I see a narrow and twisted path through the violent chaos of the next decade. This spell is the only way to keep that path open." Drake paused to take a deep breath. *Use the spell. Share it with those who support you best. Georgie. Emily. Barclay,* he said with his mind. Easier than forcing out words while breathing. Then he gasped and lay back, fighting to keep air moving in and out of his lungs.

"Yes. I shall use this and share it with my best supporter.

Barclay." A long pause while Drake concentrated on taking his next breath.

"Cousin," Milton intruded upon Drake's efforts. "Milord.
I need my son among the Inner Circle. I work best with
him. We missed inducting him last meeting. Your sister
usurped the attention of our other members and we had no
time for a second ceremony."

*When I am well enough to conduct another ritual. We . . .
I will create a new position within the Circle for him.*

"I shall hold you to that, milord. How do I find the
archives? I need other texts to maintain this spell. It is very
complex."

You need nothing more than what I have written. Clouds
of troubled sleep enfolded Drake's mind, shutting out any
further comments by his cousin.

Chapter 43

Kirkenwood.

EMILY glared at the tumble of stone blocks, as if they were to blame for everything that had gone wrong with her life in the past . . . how long? . . . six months.

Why couldn't her great-grandfather have left the opening to the tunnels that cut through the tor to the crypt and the secret archives a little more obvious and easily entered?

Because others might find it.

The voice, voices, in the back of her head came from everywhere and nowhere at the same time.

"But how do I find it? I am of the blood, I need to gain access to the archives in secret."

So does he.

Emily ground her teeth in frustration. She dared not follow the path through the wine cellar. The magical traps had to be sprung in proper order with precisely worded spells. Cousin Milton would follow and mimic her every step and word.

"Who are you?" she asked when she had regained control of her emotions.

You know.

"No I don't. Are you my father?"

In part.

What did that mean? She tasted the concept of many voices combined. In part her father.

"In part my Aunt Georgie?"

Silence.

Who else did she know with enough power to speak with wisdom across a distance? Across a great distance.

That idea sounded more likely.

Across the greatest distance? Between life and death.

"Mama?"

Perhaps in time.

Mama had not been born into the Kirkwood family. She did not have much magic. But she had wisdom and knowledge. She had guided Papa through many troubling times.

A comforting weight rested upon her shoulders. Mama had only a slight magical power in life, but her ghost might in death.

"I've got to figure this out. Mama, help me."

You know. Deep in your heart you know who speaks and why. This time a single voice, a feminine voice, drifted across the wind, like whisper soft silk.

"Are you my ancestors?"

Silence again. Yet this time she felt as if that other presence in her mind lightened with acknowledgment of her answer.

"My ancestors," she mused. "My ancestors!" She turned away from her study of the jumble of huge building stones.

There was a place at Kirkenwood where members of the family were said to reside in death other than the cemetery and crypt. A place where they could watch over the current generations. She aimed her steps downhill, to the village and the circle of standing stones that defined it.

At this time of day, most of the villagers were about their work in shop or field or workshop. A few children tussled in the dirt before the houses. Their mothers kept watch while they knitted or mended in their doorways. Occasionally, one would call out to a neighbor, similarly occupied. Another spoke a reprimand to a child who became a bit too aggressive in the wrestling match.

Then quiet prevailed for a few moments. The women ignored Emily, deliberately excluding someone from the big house in their gossip.

Emily made her way to the center of the village, marked by the largest standing stone. Well over fifteen feet high and bigger around than the largest oak tree she had ever seen, she could not guess the weight of the monster. Ancient tradition had left an open space around the stone. Houses and shops crowded the lesser stones—each one at least ten feet high with a girth three men would need to link hands to span. Life in the village centered on the stone circle, taking it for granted and respecting it at the same time.

She had grown up with these stones a looming presence. Everyone in the family knew the stories, how the whorls of granite became the faces of the Pendragons when they passed on; how the most revered of her ancestors inhabited the stones to guide the current generation.

How a single raven haunted the castle well or the chapel lintel and portended great change when it spoke to a member of the family. But the raven came and went at random after the family abandoned the castle.

Emily looked for it now, hoping it might fly to the top of one of the stones and speak to her, approve of her quest. Perhaps it could link her to Barclay, her estranged fiancé.

She longed to share the stones with Barclay. A deep ache opened in her middle at the thought of the distance in miles and minds that separated them. Would they ever marry now? Would he survive the tumultuous tour of duty in the colonies?

Do you truly wish to know the future? a voice asked in the back of her mind.

"Papa says the future is not ours to know. Those with prescience can only catch glimpses, fragments of possibilities."

But what do you want?

"I want to find another entrance to the family archives."

You must journey far for such a thing.

"How far can it be? Half a mile?"

A journey through time and Otherworlds. A dangerous journey.

"More dangerous than allowing Cousin Milton to find the archives? More dangerous than allowing my father's spell to remain ungrounded and undefined?"

More dangerous than leaving Britain unguarded.

Emily's skin turned cold and clammy. The fine hairs on her nape stood on end. She gulped back her fear. A little thing like a trip through the Otherworld would not deter Aunt Georgie.

She faced the Turks in battle and risked her life. You risk losing your soul.

"I've got to do it. I've got to find the precise spell Papa left ungrounded."

You have chosen.

Thunder boomed upon the wind. Lightning exploded in the skies. Rain poured down upon her. The earth tilted.

Blackness yawned before Emily. She closed her eyes and took one step toward the standing stone.

And fell . . .

Williamsburg, Raleigh Tavern, late October.

Roderick raised his saber in salute to Major Barclay Marlowe, kissed the blade, and swept it downward. He longed for the smooth balance of Georgie Kirkwood's weapon. His own was adequate, but just an ordinary blade. He wondered how much better he might have performed in this lesson with a master's saber.

Marlowe returned the salute. Then they both wiped sweat from their eyes. "You learn quickly," Marlowe said with a nod of approval. "You are well grounded in the basics."

"I have much more to learn."

"Then practice. Drill that parry/riposte until you can do it in your sleep. Then we will have another lesson, Major."

"I shall. May I host you to a mug of ale?" Together, they donned waistcoats and jackets. Now that they had ceased their bout, Roderick noticed a bite in the wind that had not been there yesterday. He welcomed the layers of wool over his rapidly chilling skin as the sweat dried.

"Allow me to buy this round. My funds are less limited than yours and I owe you thanks for offering me a challenge to my skills." Barclay clapped him soundly on the back.

"Hardly a challenge . . ."

"You have more skill than you think. But compared to my cousin, we are both amateurs."

"I understand that Georgie Kirkwood studied with the legendary Casanova in Italy." Somehow, Roderick could not bring himself to refer to Georgie as a he, now that he knew the truth behind her masquerade.

Marlowe's gaze slid up to the sky rather than meet Roderick's.

A wall of noise greeted them as they entered the common taproom.

"Here or a private room upstairs?" Marlowe asked.

"Here is fine," Roderick replied, surveying the crowd and spying two other officers in attendance, as well as a number of the local dignitaries. The few military men who frequented this tavern were usually paid to listen closely to the local politics. Many of the local patrons held seats in the House of Burgesses, the local version of Parliament. Government House squatted just across the way, a large brick pile with little grace in design.

Marlowe raised his hand, two fingers lifted in signal of their preference, to the innkeeper, James Southall, behind the bar. The man nodded acknowledgment. The two majors slid onto opposite settles at a table to the left of the door. Marlowe took the side facing the room. Roderick was forced to put his back to the crowd. His skin crawled with unease.

Ever since he'd found the cache of smuggled weapons, he had distrusted leaving his back unguarded and his line of sight impaired. One of his fellow officers had betrayed His Majesty and the army by selling weapons to the enemy. An enlisted man had not the access to the stores. It had to be an officer.

Who?

Marlowe dropped his head and retreated to the shadowy depths of the settle. "Do not look up," he whispered as he sank lower.

"Why?" Roderick asked. He thought his voice sounded normal, but against the hush of Marlowe's tones his question rang out and filled a sudden hush in the room.

"Why?" asked a coarse feminine voice that had its origins on the docks of London. "Why, 'cause, he's 'fraid o' me." The barmaid laughed loudly as she plunked two frothy mugs on the table between them.

"I fear no woman. Nor man either," Marlowe said defensively. But he did not rise up from the shadows.

"Drink eno', or do ye want food, too?" the woman asked. "I ain't supplyin' nothing else. Food an' drink. Thas all."

Something in the curve of her cheek and the arch of her brow where dark curls peeked out from beneath her mob cap struck a chord of familiarity in Roderick. He started to open his mouth . . . The woman fixed a fierce expression and looked in his eyes.

He closed his mouth with a snap. For a moment he drifted off in sudden weariness. His eyes closed of their own volition.

When he opened them again, the barmaid had gone. He caught a glimpse of her swishing petticoat as she disappeared into the depths of the kitchen.

"Who was that?" Roderick asked, not at all certain he should ask. Or wanted to. Something about her . . . The weariness grabbed him again.

"She calls herself Cat. Short for Catherine, I'd guess," Marlowe said around a yawn. "Has a cute little cat that follows her around like a puppy dog. A calico." His eyes drooped as heavily as Roderick's.

A moment later Roderick snapped awake as suddenly as if someone had lit a candle in his mind.

"We must have worked harder than I thought on our lesson," Roderick said, wiping his face with his hand as if he could scrub away the tiredness.

"Work hard," Marlowe mumbled, still half asleep.

Roderick took a long draught of ale and forgot about his fatigue. His lingering thoughts about the barmaid with the lovely bosom and refined cheekbones, despite her rough accent, drifted away as mist in sunshine.

Chapter 44

IN the inglenook, out of sight of Marlowe and Whythe, I took a deep breath and tried to calm the pounding of my heart. What now? I could not keep up this masquerade as a simple barmaid for long with those two frequenting the Raleigh Tavern.

Neither of them had come into the establishment where I worked during the last month. Few military men did. The local politicians, students, and elite did not welcome them into their discussions.

And their discussions became benign at the first sight of a scarlet uniform.

But I could not pack up and leave now. I learned more about the locals and their politics in a single day in this tavern than I had in my entire time with Sir Thomas. My reports to Whitehall grew fatter each week with details of the local economy, the culture, and the loyalties of Virginians. They truly did not wish separation from their king. They sought only to preserve their rights and freedoms as Englishmen.

I continued to write to Emily often, with no idea if she ever received my letters. I'd had no replies since arriving in Virginia.

Despite the constant pain in my lower back from lifting heavy tankards and heavier trays, and the blisters and pains in my feet and calves, I needed to remain an invisible barmaid at the Raleigh Tavern. Men spoke freely in front of me. They confided their woes and their secrets to me. They revealed their true feelings in the way they moved their bodies and gestured. I did not need magic or extra skills to do my job here. I need only tolerate the hard work.

Why had I always disdained the women who followed armies? They did so much of the cooking and cleaning that kept the men marching and fighting. Men might consider women's work demeaning, but I defied any one of them to perform that work for a solid week and then get up and do it all over again the next week and the week after that.

Knowing this about men, I had not told Prime Minister Grenville that I had changed my name and my life, only that I had changed situations to be nearer town. Had he taken as truth my report that the Stamps required for every legal transaction in the colonies would have to be paid for in tobacco and sugar? Few in the colonies had coins jingling in their purses. Tobacco was the most stable currency in Virginia.

I wished my rapport with my brother was as complete as my reports to the government. I knew only that he ailed and the baby had cut his first tooth and tried eagerly to sit on his own. Nothing more.

Emily remained strangely silent other than one terse letter warning me not to come home, that treachery awaited me.

But now my position was threatened by the arrival of my cousin and the man I wished could be my lover. I had warded off their undue notice with a simple sleep spell. I dared not repeat the magic too often. They would soon learn to shrug it off.

Oblegid bounded toward me from the direction of the kitchen. Her mind was filled with the taste of fish Cook had given her. Fresh fish from the river. She grew fat and lazy from the attentions of the staff.

"What good are you as a familiar if you sleep all day?" I whispered to her as I scooped her into my arms.

"I knew another woman who owned a kitten with almost identical markings," Major Roderick Whythe said, coming up behind me.

Instinctively, I threw out a mist of magic between us. Roderick blinked hazily. He should no longer feel a glimmer of recognition.

But he did not go away. He stood there with his hand extended for Oblegid to sniff. Then he stroked my cat's head with one finger. The traitorous beast purred and butted her head deeper into his palm.

I hissed in my mind at the cat. She ignored me as I gnashed my teeth.

And Roderick did not go away. His eyes cleared.

"Nice disguise, Georgina," he whispered. He looked up and met my gaze. A smile flickered across his mouth before he returned his attention to Oblegid.

I blinked at him in amazement. How had he cast off my spell so quickly? So completely?

"Cat, get your arse back in here, you lazy slut!" James Southall, the innkeeper, hollered for me to deliver drinks.

"Watch yer loaf, you big oaf," I called back at him in the cant of my adopted accent. "Or ye'll feel the back of me hand on your pate!"

Wild laughter accompanied the exchange. As I peeked around the corner of my nook, I saw my employer wink at a patron. They baited me deliberately.

"Why, Georgina? Why the disguise, the degrading job, the total denial of who you are and your position in society?"

"You would not understand." I made to move back into the taproom.

He restrained me with a hard hand upon my arm.

"I have work to do."

"Why would I not understand why you are here?"

I glared at him in anger.

"Tell me, Georgina, or I announce your true identity to every man in Williamsburg, including your cousin, the expert swordsman."

"Barclay Marlowe is a fraud. He is nowhere near the expert..." I caught myself before I betrayed my own expertise.

"Not as expert as whom?" Roderick met my gaze again.

An overwhelming compulsion to honesty washed over me. Did he have magic of his own?

I did not care. I need only tell him why I, the daughter and sister of earls, with titles and an income of my own, worked as a barmaid wearing a dark wig and speaking with a coarse accent. If I did that, then I could keep the rest of my secrets.

I hoped.

"His Majesty needs to know what transpires in the colony. I spy for Whitehall," I whispered, as much with my mind as my words, letting the image of my reports to Prime Minister Grenville cover my other activities.

"I suspected as much," he replied. "Good luck." He

kissed my cheek and returned to the settle where my cousin proceeded to drink himself silly.

I breathed a deep sigh of relief and returned to my work of delivering drinks and listening to one and all.

Thomas Jefferson discoursed with Peyton Randolph and newcomer Patrick Henry. They always had something interesting to say or a pamphlet to compose, or a law to draft. Just five minutes before they had begun outlining an address to the king and Parliament about the Stamp Act. I needed to know the contents of that address before they presented it to the House of Burgesses. I also needed to know which petitions they discarded as too extreme or controversial.

I could count on the handsome redhead, Thomas Jefferson, to put forth the most romantic notions of a perfect world in beautifully eloquent language. His prose tripped off his tongue in a compelling lilt. I wanted to believe every word he said. The practical, military-trained part of my mind rebelled at his notions. They would never work in an imperfect world, populated by greedy and self-serving people.

Randolph and the others curbed the young man's enthusiasm, but I could see them leaning toward his views.

If I were to stay here, I had to divert Major Roderick Whythe and Major Barclay Marlowe.

How had Roderick broken through my spells? I needed to work harder at maintaining my anonymity. None of the local leaders paid attention to a lowly serving maid. They spoke freely in front of me. They would not if they believed me in collusion with two British officers.

Perhaps I needed to find a way for General Gage to send Barclay Marlowe and Roderick Whythe elsewhere for several months.

But General Thomas Gage was in New York, several hundred miles away.

An argument erupted between Jefferson and Randolph. I swept up several full tankards and went back to work.

Place unknown, time unknown.

Blackness engulfed Emily. Blackness tinged with red around the edges of her eyes. Every bone and muscle in her body ached. Yet she could not feel her form with her hands to ease the pains. She couldn't even find her eyes to feel if they were open or closed.

Where was she? How long had she drifted here in pain and darkness?

"Oh, Papa, what have I done?"

A new level of pain washed through her and around her. Her mind closed down.

When she roused again, the pain had receded. For a while. She did not know how long the relief would last. She had no way to measure the passage of time or distance.

Concentrate. She had to concentrate. She had a mind. She knew pain; therefore she had a body.

What would her father have her do in the archives, for training?

Breathe.

She blanked her mind of all but the need to breathe. In on three counts, hold three, out three. Again and again.

Gradually, the sensation of air moving in and out of her body returned. Each inhalation brought new stabs of pain, in her legs, her arms, up and down her back.

She did her best to ignore the pain. Breathe in. Breathe out.

Fire straight through her back broke her rhythm, robbed her of what little control she had gained. She screamed. The strident sound echoed and resounded as if she stood in a well.

Malicious giggles chased her screams around and around.

She grabbed her temples and sank to her knees.

"Stop. Oh, please stop," she moaned, over and over again.

At last the sound receded and faded away.

Emily forced herself to open her eyes. Dozens of pairs of blinking red eyes stared back at her.

She screamed again, and knew nothing more but the paralyzing noise.

Chapter 45

Williamsburg.

"BROTHERS, let us assemble," the Grand Master of the Freemason Grand Lodge of Virginia called from the stoop of his farmhouse on the outskirts of Williamsburg.

As if controlled by one mind, a dozen men fell into ranks and filed into the parlor. I took my place toward the rear, the proper place for a newcomer, despite the Master Mason insignia upon my white apron. Reluctantly, I doffed my tricorn as I entered the building. I might feel out of place in this gathering; no sense in looking the part as well.

My last communication with Lord Grenville had been a letter of credit. Cat the barmaid could not collect funds on the letter. I had to establish a new identity to make use of the funds. Once acknowledged within the community of Masons, the Lodge would accept the letter. But they had to get to know George Kirkwood first.

Inside the parlor of the simple farmhouse dozens of candles blazed as brightly as a tavern's common room. Here I could seek out familiar faces and figures. Scarlet uniforms nearly outnumbered civilian clothing tonight. Major Barclay Marlowe did not grace us with his presence, though I knew he frequented Masonic gatherings. If my other nemesis, Major Roderick Whythe, had come, as I had overheard him say he would, I did not see him.

The evening's host gestured me to a seat among the other Master Masons. I nodded to him and stepped boldly toward the chest where another man sat. Men of lesser degrees hunched together on the far side of the room, eagerly awaiting the opening ritual.

Just as I settled my bottom on the low seat, a hard hand clamped upon my shoulder.

"A word, sir," Roderick breathed in my ear.

I cast about the room with all of my senses to see if anyone had noticed this blatant breach of protocol. Outside was the place for socializing. Silence prevailed once the meeting moved indoors. Individual desires and will should have been checked at the door, along with any weapons carried.

The Grand Master of this Lodge nodded to me with a stern frown.

I returned the acknowledgment and rose quietly. Roderick and I exited the house. He kept his hand upon my shoulder, squeezing with a fierceness that belied his agitation. Hardly a Mason turned his head to follow our progress. All seemed intent upon the complex ritual about to start.

"You have not surrendered all of your weapons, Georgie Kirkwood," Roderick said with his hand still holding my shoulder like a vise.

A pair of torches marking the drive gave off a fitful light. I could see his expression without the aid of magic. He could see mine as well.

"My rapier lies with the other weapons." I kept my eyes moving to be certain his allies did not sneak up on me, like a Red Indian about to ambush.

"The dagger and the dagger-pistol? I do not see them among the weapons. Not the weapons of a gentleman," he sneered.

How much did he know? If he knew me to be a woman, he'd say so; challenge my presence on the grounds that women were forbidden the secrets of Masonic ritual.

"I am a student now, without the need to carry concealed blades."

"You will quit this place immediately," Roderick ground out. His hand dropped to his hip, where he still wore his sword. Unlike the others, he had not cached it at the door. He must be the sergeant at arms for this Lodge.

"Why?" I raised my eyebrows, feigning innocence. My heart beat too rapidly in near panic. I needed the money in the letter of credit. I needed to establish myself as a credible Mason to cash it.

"We are Grand Lodge here. We have no patience with the false rituals and mystical degrees of the Scottish Rite practitioners."

"Do you believe in anything but what you can see, taste, touch, smell, or hear? Have you no faith?" I countered with the familiar argument between the two factions of Freemasonry. According to the older tradition of the Scottish Rite, I had achieved three degrees above Master Mason, the highest rank the Grand Lodge acknowledged. Each of my advanced degrees delved into aspects of history and spirituality that challenged most traditional Christian limitations. Indeed, most of us in the advanced degrees had little patience with any organized religion. We found our own personal relationship with the Deity without the interference of priests and officials and rules.

My advanced degrees had introduced me to the other secret Lodge, the one that oversaw world politics and economics covertly. They accomplished through subterfuge what the Pendragon Society should accomplish through magic.

"We believe in God," Roderick insisted. "Our religion does not accept those who step beyond the bounds of tradition and delve into mystical balderdash."

"You attended Lodge meetings on the Ottoman border with my regiment. Most of us accept the Scottish tradition."

He reared back a moment, startled. Then he closed his eyes as if praying for patience. "I did not know the difference between our two disciplines then. If I wanted to be accepted by your comrades, I had to participate in their barbaric rituals."

I raised my eyebrows at that. Never had I heard one Mason refer to another as barbaric, despite the differences in our beliefs.

"We have rules here. Rules define civilization. You break rules every day." He hesitated.

" 'Tis the lot of a mercenary to break rules. Why else hire an army whose only loyalty is to their pay rather than their king?"

"There is no place for you or your kind here."

"What do you mean 'my kind?' " I feared he meant women. But he did not know that secret. He had no way of knowing. Did he?

I automatically reached for the sword I had left in the parlor. "You insult me when I have no arms to defend my honor," I spat at him. "Coward!"

"Here, here," Barclay Marlowe said quietly. His fair hair shone golden in the torchlight, like a nimbus or crown. "What is the meaning of this? And on sacred ground." He projected the attitude of a noble intervening in the spat of two troublesome children, or peasants.

"You have no part in this, Marlowe," Roderick said quietly. "I merely remove a rule breaker from the Lodge."

"I have heard an insult to a fellow officer. You must respond, Major."

Was that a smirk playing across Barclay's face?

"I am unarmed and reluctant to engage in a clash of arms so close to the Lodge." I would not call this sacred ground. 'Twas not a church, though some behaved as if the Lodge was more sacred than sanctified ground.

My definition of what made land holy was older and broader than either Freemasonry or Christian churches. Neither institution would recognize certain springs and standing stones as sacred.

"I offer you my weapon," Barclay said as he unsheathed his sword. Not a regulation blade. An old-fashioned broadsword. The weak light from the torches reflected redly off the deeply etched runes running the length of the steel.

I'd seen that blade before; in the hands of a highwayman who fled rather than be unmasked. I'd also seen it somewhere else, somewhere very old and magical . . . Excalibur!

How did Barclay Marlowe come by the legendary sword of King Arthur, our mutual ancestor? Excalibur belonged only to the champion who would save Britain from all foes, internal and external, mundane and magical.

Such a sword should emanate enough power to light the entire yard of this farmhouse. Such a blade should rest easily in the hands of the chosen warrior.

This sword looked heavy in Barclay's hands. And if 'twas truly Excalibur, only he could wield it.

Barclay Marlowe could not possess Excalibur and use it while acting the outlaw, even if his attack on my brother's coach was only for sport.

He played games with my mind now, as he had done on the road to London. I could not trust him.

"An apology for naming me coward is all I ask." Roderick Whythe looked pale in the fitful flare of a torch. Beads of sweat dotted his brow.

"I have seen you on the battlefield, Major Whythe. You comported yourself with honor and courage. You are no coward. I spoke in haste, in the heat of the moment." I executed a little bow. Faced with both men, I had no more desire to remain in the company of the Freemasons. Another time, another day, I would approach a commanding officer and persuade him to transfer both men to New York. Hundreds of miles from me and my work.

Another day, I would find a way to exchange my letter of credit for cash. Perhaps Thomas Jefferson. He had Masonic leanings and a sympathy for students.

A wise soldier knows when retreat is the better part of valor.

You are no longer a soldier. You are a spy. Both essential to combating the forces of darkness, my brother's voice overlaid by an older, deeper personality, whispered into the back of my head.

"I will be a soldier again. And a Mason. 'Tis what I do best."

The voices chuckled softly.

Chapter 46

Kirkenwood.

DAMMIT! Where had the chit run off to? Milton paced the
long corridors of Kirkenwood for the hundredth time. No
one had seen Emily for a day and a half. Her fencing master
seemed unconcerned, her father smiled secretly, her maid
ran from Milton rather than answer his questions. Only baby
Griffin seemed to have noticed her absence. He fussed and
reached into the shadows for someone no one else could see.

But not Neville. The ghost of Milton's son never went
near the baby.

Samuel paced three steps behind Milton. A frown marred
his square face, and deep furrows ran between his dark
brows down beside his nose. He jumped and started with
each renewal of the baby's cries.

The man was getting on Milton's nerves until he wished
he could flee this place.

Not until he found the archives.

Without Emily, Milton doubted he'd find the secret
room. None of the other girls appeared blessed with magical talent. And he was convinced that only magic would
penetrate the protections Drake had placed upon the entrance. In his day, Drake had been a formidable magician
who thought in layers. Many complex layers to his personality and his magic.

Now Drake Kirkwood was little more than a useless husk.

Milton needed help searching the manor. He needed
help he could trust.

As he passed the nursery, Griffin awoke. He cried loud

and long, deeply unhappy. The screams persisted long past the time a nanny needed to get to him.

More curious than concerned, Milton opened the door to the children's enclave. Two younger Kirkwood daughters sat quietly at a low table putting together a puzzle.

"Do your brother's cries not disturb you?" he asked them, forgetting their names.

"Griffin isn't crying. Nurse changed his nappy and feeds him now," the older of the two girls replied. She never looked up from her puzzle. "Papa says that sometimes he hears the echo of events from long ago. Perhaps that is what disturbs you, Cousin Milton." She couldn't be more than eight—possibly as much as ten and she spoke with the authority and erudition of an adult.

Perplexed, Milton marched past the girls and looked into the nursery. Sure enough, the new wet nurse sat in a rocking chair with Griffin cuddled against her, he suckled greedily at her naked breast. All the while he screwed up his face as if about to cry once more.

Ears burning with embarrassment, Milton withdrew before she noticed him.

"Which one are you?" Milton asked the eight-year-old. His query came out strained, almost as if his voice had become brittle.

"I'm Patricia, she's Hannah. Martha and Belinda are with our governess in the library," she replied, rising and bobbing a curtsy. She plunked herself down again and returned to the puzzle.

"How do you come to know so much?" Milton gentled his tone and crouched down beside her. She smelled of soap and paper and ink. He guessed that she'd recently completed a lesson—or abandoned one—and washed excess ink from her hands.

"I listen." She had outward manners but no inner sense of politeness.

He fought the urge to cuff her ears for impertinence. That would gain him nothing but ill will.

"I hear the baby crying, even though he does not open his mouth. Why is that?"

"He misses Emily. He seeks her in ways that reach beyond this realm." Never once did she lift her eyes from the puzzle.

But her five-year-old sister did. She gazed upon him with the deep and penetrating eyes, bluer than blue, Kirkwood eyes.

Milton risked a quick probe into each of the girls' minds. The little darts of magic passed right through them without encountering any sign of magic.

The baby's screams grew louder, his actual voice added to the psychic cries to his sister.

Milton fled the nursery. Once he found the archives, he could silence the child. If he found what he searched for in the archives, then he could eliminate the child and his father once and for all. No one would stand between him and total domination of Parliament, the king, and the kingdom.

He'd have Neville back to add his talent of listening and spying upon others from a distance. The two of them together were undefeatable. Separate, their talents barely approached Drake's abilities.

Ensconced in his own suite, Milton drew out his scrying bowl, a dowsing crystal, and three arcane powders. Six men who owed him their loyalties and their lives awaited his call within a day's ride. The other five of their coven were scattered too widely to be of much use, including his son Barclay. They were all becoming more trouble than they were worth, thinking too much, acting without his direction too often. But the other six . . . By tonight he would have his help.

By tomorrow, he would rule Britain in all but name. And who needed a name when one had power?

Kirkenwood, All Hallows Eve.

"Sir?" Samuel de Vere stood in the entrance to the earl's study.

Milton Marlowe had made this room his own. He'd stripped out the paintings with their gilded frames, the lavish tapestries and most of the rugs. The stark walls and massive desk suited him.

"Yes?" he replied to his bodyguard, the only man allowed to disturb him until his secretary arrived later this week.

"I may have found a trace of Lady Emily, sir."

"Where?" Good news indeed. The chit had been missing

for weeks. All of his inquiries, mundane and magical, had
met with silence and blank stares.

"If you'll come with me, sir, 'tis easier to show you."
Samuel turned on his heel without waiting to see if Milton
followed. Presumption that must be punished.

But he followed, too curious and eager to lay his hands
on the girl to insist on deference.

Samuel led him along the twisted and climbing path to the
village. As always, Milton paused before passing into the circle of standing stones. They stood brooding as they had stood
for a thousand years or more. Perhaps two thousand years.
Maybe they had been here since the beginning of time.

He didn't like them. The whorls within the grain of each
stone looked like faces, and they all disapproved of him.

He knew he should enter the circle from the east, the ritual opening to this or any circle. Knew it in his heart and
his head. In defiance of the watchful faces he stepped between two random stones on the southwest side, the side
closest to the manor.

Samuel, he noted, took the longer path and entered from
the east. He bowed slightly in respect to each of the two
stones guarding that opening.

Milton frowned. He thought he'd taught the young man
to respect only those things Milton dictated he respect.
These stones were inanimate, powerless, useless. They deserved only a passing glance at their size.

"Here, sir." Samuel knelt beside the largest stone of all,
set in the exact center of the circle. The villagers had left a
cleared space before it. They avoided it, as they avoided Milton and his men, as if they were tainted and smelled bad.

A housewife with a gaggle of children in her wake walked
past him. She carried a heavy basket. Still, she had enough
dexterity to make the ward against evil. She also scrunched
her nose in distaste.

Milton sneered at her and raised his fist. He found the
scent of burned sulfur and old blood that clung to him and
his men comforting, reassurance that Neville lingered
nearby, even when not visible.

Samuel pawed at the packed dirt and rocks at the base
of the center stone.

"What do you see?" Milton asked rather than admit that
he saw nothing unusual here.

"The villagers saw Lady Emily standing here, touching the stone, sir. Then she disappeared. They supposed she walked around the stone and out of sight. But I wonder, sir. Did she pass through the stone into one of the Other-worlds?" Samuel stood up and dusted his dirty hands upon his breeches. His queue remained neatly tied and his shirt and cuffs pristine white against his dark waistcoat and coat. Milton allowed no wasteful ornamentation among his men, and insisted upon cleanliness.

"Impossible. Lady Emily would have to perform an extensive ritual, use a number of aromatic herbs, and light a fire for such a feat," Milton scoffed at the notion.

"I was just wondering, sir. There is no sign of a ritual here, nothing recent anyway. But 'twould explain her absence." Samuel continued to scrutinize the stone and its environs with both hands and eyes.

For a moment it looked as if his hand pressing against the stone merged with it, sank deep into it, passed into one of those Otherworlds.

Milton shook his head in disbelief. Samuel's hand remained whole and on this side of reality.

"Nonsense. The girl has run off with one of her lovers, no doubt. She doesn't want to be found."

"Sir?" Samuel looked offended. "I doubt that Lady Emily would . . ."

"All women are sluts at heart, Samuel. The sooner you realize that, the better. Now let us return to the study. I have found some references to a family crypt beneath the tor. That could lead us to a more useful path than a fruitless search for a wayward girl." Milton set off for the manor and the warm fire. He did not like this talk of Otherworlds on this day, All Hallows Eve, when the barriers between them and reality thinned.

"And Lady Emily's mail, sir?"

"What mail?" Milton turned back to the man in alarm.

"Letters from the colonies, sir. I believe Lady Georgina sent them." Samuel kept his face bland, but clearly the light of curiosity and excitement burned in his eyes.

"Burn them. Come, we have a crypt to find. We'll start in the wine cellar." Neville could help. He would have an affinity with the dead in the crypt.

Chapter 47

Place unknown, time unknown.

EMILY touched something slimy and moving. She jerked her hand away and slid downward. Rough stones scraped her knees and arms and face.

She landed hard on her backside. Jolts of pain shot upward, through her back into her neck. One more discomfort added to all the rest.

"Damnit! That's the highest I've climbed yet." She slapped the packed dirt at the base of this dark well.

Demon eyes opened and closed in the darkness. Her unknown companions gibbered and giggled.

"Oh, shut up. I'm tired of being the butt of your senseless jokes." She twisted and rolled painfully until she got her knees under her again. Then she clawed along the wall until she stood, leaning and panting in the darkness. The air was foul, barely fit to breathe. She had to get out of here.

How long had she been here anyway? A day and a night at least, she thought. Her throat tasted sour with thirst. But strangely her stomach felt no hunger. If anything, it seemed overfull and churning.

Once more she gritted her teeth and set hand and foot to crevices she had discovered. Inch by inch, she moved upward.

Demons hovered near her ear, taunting her with her previous failures. She did not understand a word they said, but she knew their meaning. She swallowed her thirst and ignored them.

Right hand up. Left foot up. Left hand up. Right foot up.

She put her hand upon the slimy, disgusting mess once more and pushed it aside.

A demon flew away from the wall, scolding her loudly. The sounds of his flight and screeching disgust bounced around and around her.

She just kept climbing.

Then her stomach growled and twisted and she knew she'd been trapped in this dungeon for a lot longer than she thought.

"Papa, I'm sorry. I can't protect you from here."

Williamsburg.

Jefferson happily exchanged my letter of credit for cash, as George Kirkwood. He also gave me an introduction to a different Freemason Lodge. This one followed the Scottish Rite. If soldiers attended this Lodge, they did not wear their uniforms. I had to endure many long interviews and several longer rituals before they allowed me entry to their inner enclave. Jefferson, Henry, Randolph, and the very quiet George Washington attended regularly.

They discussed more than Masonic secrets. They planned to break away from England and depose George III's rule in the American colonies.

This was information Grenville needed to know. I could not pass it on. My oaths of secrecy as a Mason superseded any loyalty I owed to the government.

I found myself listening and agreeing with most everything said in these secret meetings.

Guilt led to many sleepless nights. Where did my loyalty belong? To my king? To my family? To these patriots who struggled for justice and a new form of government?

I wanted to go home, to ask my brother's advice, to consult the standing stones of Kirkenwood and the journals of my ancestors.

I needed to make contact with my other Lodge. They would not appreciate a letter sent openly through the mails. They could not receive communication through a scrying bowl. If only I knew one of their members in the colonies!

Emily's single letter told me I could not set foot in England again.

So I appeased my guilt by concentrating on the obvious suspects in the musket smuggling.

I gave up on my scheme to have the Majors Whythe and Marlowe transferred. I watched them, I followed them, and I learned much about the war with the Red Indians.

Roderick Whythe sought the man who smuggled arms and ammunition out of army stores for sale to the enemy. He prowled the military compounds, talking to the enlisted men, and watched the movements of all who came into contact with the stockpiled weapons.

Barclay Marlowe appeared to seek the same information in long discussions with the Indians themselves. Somehow, he had ingratiated himself into their tribal gatherings. I suspected that he had taken a native wife, but I could not prove it. My anger boiled at his betrayal of Emily. At the same time, I felt relieved that my niece would not have to endure marriage to such a cad.

Twice Barclay led patrols that surprised Indians moving eastward, heavily armed with English muskets, powder, and shot. In both skirmishes the dashing major emerged victorious. His triumphs led to more raids by the Indians upon farms in the outlying areas.

Sometimes I thought I could smell the smoke from the burned-out farms on the wind. With the smoke came the cloying scent of burning bodies as well.

I overheard talk of promoting him to colonel. At the cost of more lives on the frontier?

Other officers grumbled that Major Marlowe had cheated them out of the honor of leading punishment forays against the Indians. They also whispered that he had advance knowledge of Indian movements through his "country wife."

I wondered if the woman knew that Barclay used her information to set ambushes against her friends and relatives.

Major Whythe did not grumble or whisper. He listened as closely as I.

Between adventures, the two men met behind the Raleigh for lessons and bouts with their swords. Gradually, Whythe's skills improved from barely adequate to quite competent. Watching Marlowe at practice made me itch to challenge him. His skills had improved as much as mine had since we dueled as teenagers. Either one of us could have challenged the abilities of my master Casanova.

And then on All Hallows Eve, a very cold and wet night, shadows pressed heavier against my mind. Pumpkins and cornstalks decorated the entry and the hearth. Rich and spicy smells of ginger and cinnamon wafted out of the kitchen.

Rain lashed the shutters. The patrons huddled closer to the fire. We all drank more than usual, chasing away the chill of the night. Deep in the backs of our minds we knew that the barriers between this world and the next thinned. An ancient pulled out his pipe and began telling ghost stories. "On a dark and stormy night, much like this one," he almost whispered.

The room hushed. The murmurs of conversation fell away. The storyteller sat on the opposite side of the room from the post I had taken beside the bar. I leaned forward to listen more closely and opened all of my senses for the delicious chill of fear his words promised.

We deliver the muskets tonight. Du Carré has the gold. His allies are ready to strike deep into the western settlements.

Who had spoken? I searched the room with mundane senses and magic.

My face must have shown panic, for the barkeep, an earnest widower who had tried wooing me, placed a comforting hand upon my arm. " 'Tis only a ghost story, lass," he said quietly so as not to disturb the enthralled audience.

"I fear a chill and fever has come upon me suddenly," I said quietly, holding the back of my hand to my forehead. Rather than infect the patrons of the Raleigh, I retired to my room. Once alone, I slipped into masculine clothing and out the window. I huddled outside the taproom in the sodden night, lurking and listening.

The autumn wind ripped through my thin jacket and breeches. I longed for the layers of petticoats and chemise and kerchief that I wore under my feminine clothes.

Oblegid mewed piteously and butted her head into my leg. "Where did you come from?" I picked her up and held her tightly against my chest. Her slight warmth helped ease my discomfort. Then she burrowed beneath my coat. Her purr set me aglow, giving me the strength to fight off the chill and wet of the evening.

Then the door of the tavern burst open. Light and laughter spilled out of the smoky interior. It was the nervous laughter of men denying their superstitious fear. The ghost story must have been successful. Not many officers had come to the taproom this evening. Craftsmen and scholars made up the bulk of our patrons. Major Whythe kept his men busy and close to quarters. Major Marlowe seemingly had more free time. He and a junior lieutenant I did not know slapped each other's backs as they stumbled down the two steps to the cobbled street. Unless they had both imbibed considerable hard spirits in the last half hour, they should not be as drunk as they appeared.

Quickly, I reviewed the words I had overheard. *We deliver the muskets tonight. Du Carré has the gold.* An almost familiar cadence. Could Barclay have said them?

I could not tell for certain. But he and his lieutenant did not fit into the crowd that had filled the Raleigh this night. I kept to the shadows behind them, carefully shielding my thoughts from Barclay's magic.

My cousin proved my suspicions correct. The moment they passed beyond view of casual glances, both lost all traces of drunken wobbles in their steps. He and his companion veered down Botetourt Street. At the corner of Francis Street they turned right and lengthened their stride. I had to move at a near run to keep them within sight.

Once past the corner of Queen Street the men changed direction again, cutting across the green behind the guardhouse to the octagonal magazine. They had to circle the building to the guarded opening in the fence. Two enlisted men waited, holding muskets at the ready. They started and challenged Barclay.

He spoke a few sharp words to them. I could not discern the actual words, but the sentries saluted Barclay. Then they assumed a relaxed stance. I guessed they conspired with my cousin.

Within moments, two more enlisted men appeared with a cart. The axles were well greased and the horse's hooves muffled with rags. I heard not a creak nor a clop. Anyone else would have a hard time knowing any activity transpired around the storehouse.

The four enlisted men began loading the cart while the lieutenant held the horse's bridle. He produced lumps of sugar to keep the animal quiet. I dared not open my mind to startle the beast without alerting Barclay to my presence. If I were he, I would have my magic and my mind wide open, "listening" for outsiders.

" 'Tis a miserable night, Major. Can't this wait?" a corporal grumbled under the weight of a bag of shot. He no longer guarded his words in whispers.

"I am transferred to Boston on the morrow. It seems Miss Cummings finds herself in the family way and I am already betrothed to the daughter of an earl. My colonel believes I am more useful farther north than shackled to a careless local. We must act tonight or lose the opportunity and the gold," Barclay replied. Anxiety leaked out of his posture and his shifting feet.

Bastard!

Barclay looked up at my mental explosion of anger.

I clenched my fists and gritted my teeth in my extreme effort to clamp down upon my emotions as well as my thoughts.

What could I do to prevent this act of treachery? Who would know to come if I risked summoning them?

Only one person in this city had a close enough bond with me to understand my plight. I sent Oblegid scampering across the green and down two streets to the printing house and book bindery.

Then I fetched my horse from the mews behind William Lightfoot's house. That good squire knew only that a student at the University boarded a mount there, not having space in his student quarters for his father's gelding. I had learned enough of law and theology from listening to Thom Jefferson in the Raleigh to maintain a conversation with Lightfoot the few times I encountered him in my student guise.

I had the chestnut saddled and back within view of the magazine before Barclay's men finished loading the cart. He dumped the contents of his purse into their outstretched hands. I caught a glimpse of gold in the faint light of their lantern. "Get the others and meet us at the ambush point," Barclay whispered.

His men nodded and two of them left.

A chill wind bit through my clothing at that precise moment. Something terrible portended.

I did not like this aspect of my talent. I did not want to know that I smelled blood and death upon that wind.

Chapter 48

SCRITCH, scritch. A branch scraped against the closed shutter of Roderick's window. The sound brought him out of a deep sleep. He felt heavy, hollow, and disoriented. Somehow the innocent noise got tangled up with his dreams.

He knew his mother's ghost did not claw at the window trying to drag him into some hellish netherworld. He knew it. Still sweat chilled his naked chest and arms and his gut quivered.

Roddie, wake up! He thought he heard a feminine voice call to him. *Roddie, come to me. Help me!*

He shivered. His mother was past needing his help. She'd died ten years ago from the consumption. His father hadn't had the funds to secure her enough heat in the moldering manor, nor enough proper food, nor medicine.

Scritch, scritch. The sound came again. And again. Too rhythmic to be natural. Too consistent in volume to be the product of gusting wind and intermittent rain.

He rolled over and tried to find sleep again.

Scritch, scritch. The annoying sound came between gusts.

Angry now at the disturbance to his sleep, Roderick grabbed his knife and stalked to the window, determined to cut the branch so it could no longer reach the house. He threw open the shutters.

Meooow! A very wet and very upset calico cat shot into the room, protesting and spitting at every step.

Roderick jumped back and slammed the shutters closed again. He stared at the benighted animal with surprise.

Keeping his bare feet well away from the cat's claws, he

329

approached it. The cat seemed to relax by the glowing embers in the hearth. It plunked itself down on the colorful braided rug and began a much needed bath. Bright splotches emerged from the mud and wet fur.

"Oblegid?" he whispered.

The cat blew out a huff of air as if Roderick were too stupid to deserve an answer.

"Oblegid," he said, recognizing the cat's superior attitude. "What brings you here?" He reached a tentative finger to stroke Georgina's cat between the ears.

Oblegid presented her chin for a necessary scratch. When Roderick had obliged her, she turned her greenish-yellow gaze upon him.

Suddenly he knew that Georgina was in trouble. She needed him.

How did he know that? He did not believe in magic and Otherworldly powers.

The cat huffed again and returned to her bath, licking her paw and running it over her face. The eye that glared at him from the center of a white patch took on a peculiar glow.

Logic overrode Roderick's fear of superstition. Georgina and Oblegid shared a particular closeness. Rarely had he seen the cat separated from her mistress by more than a few feet. If the cat had come clawing at his window, she had to have a reason. Georgina needed his help.

The plank floor suddenly seemed colder, sending sharp knives of chill through the soles of his bare feet.

"Give me a moment to dress," he said to Oblegid.

The cat ceased her bath and trounced to the door. She mewed plaintively.

"Coming," he gasped hopping in a circle with one foot in his breeches.

Six mews and two stubbed toes later, he clattered down the stairs still buttoning his breeches, his sword and pistol tucked beneath one arm. Oblegid barely allowed him time to saddle his horse. Now that they moved toward her objective, she had no patience with human requirements.

Eventually, he lifted the cat onto his saddle. She perched on the pommel, claws digging into the thick saddle blanket.

"How do I find Georgina?" he asked the cat.

Oblegid stared at him as if he were indeed stupid. She meowed once, waited a moment then meowed twice.

"What is that supposed to mean?" He pulled himself atop the horse.

She repeated the sequence of meows.

"Are they directions?" What was he doing asking a cat? She meowed on a squeak once and set her nose forward.

"I'll take that as a yes. One for yes. Two for no."

She squeaked once more.

"Similarly, one for left, two for right."

Two growling meows and a fierce glare.

"Two for left, one for right."

One more squeak and she settled down with her nose pointed between the horse's ears.

The cat directed him west toward the city green and the arsenal.

Roderick's neck tingled and the hairs on his nape stood on end. He had a feeling he knew why the cat had summoned him.

Within a few moments Georgie stopped him. She sat a fine chestnut horse at the edge of the green at Market Square. Oblegid leaped effortlessly from Roderick's saddle to that of her mistress.

After a quick pet and snuggle Georgie set her cat upon the ground. "Go home," she whispered.

Oblegid arched her back and hissed in defiance.

"You heard me. Go back to Georgina!"

The cat turned her back on Georgie and sat in the mud.

"Be that way. But you may not come. Go back to Georgina."

The cat leaped to the back of Georgie's saddle in a single bound.

Georgie sighed in resignation.

Roderick almost laughed at the lengths she would go to continue the masquerade that she was not Georgina when clad as Georgie.

After biting his cheeks to regain his composure, Roderick was about to ask why they sat in the rain when Georgie held a finger up to her lips demanding quiet. Then she pointed to the little circle of light before the magazine. A one-horse cart lurched into movement, silently. He could barely discern a single man leading the vehicle. Just ahead of him, Roderick caught an impression of another silhouette atop a horse.

Questions burned for release from his throat. Georgie placed a restraining hand upon his wrist. Her touch sent his skin leaping with tingles. He wanted to reach out and tear her masculine guise from her body and then plunge into her with all of his might and his love. . . . He sighed with the inevitability of it. No matter how inappropriate, no matter how uncomfortable their relationship, he knew now that he did love her.

She squeezed his hand slightly. In acknowledgment? His heart leaped at the possibility she returned his affections.

But no, she merely pointed for him to follow the cart and its awkward load. As long as she appeared to the world as Georgie, the illegitimate half brother of an earl, she would never betray her femininity. He had to respect her disguise for her own safety and his own honor.

He resigned himself to loving her from afar. She was a woman who had no use for rules and society and propriety. He needed more from a woman than wild adventures before he bound his life to her.

But Georgina already possessed his heart.

Together they followed the men to the edge of town and beyond. Midnight came and went. The fitful rain and wind died away.

Dawn came late, beneath a leaden sky, and still they plodded forward, deep into the woods, beyond the closest farms, well into the area of large plantations. As the light grew, Roderick and Georgie had to drop well behind the two men and the cart.

Finally distance allowed him to ask, "Who?"

"Major Marlowe and a lieutenant. They meet a man named du Carré," she whispered.

"Du Carré?" Roderick had once met an itinerant trader by that name. The Frenchman stopped by the sergeant's mess whenever he came to Williamsburg to replenish supplies. Roderick thought it strange that the trader spent so much time gossiping with the soldiers. Even with a war on against the Red Indians, du Carré needed only a little information to stay away from current raiding territory.

At last they approached the clearing where Roderick and his men had dug up six crates of muskets. A clearing very close to Five Oaks plantation. Was Sir Thomas involved in the smuggling, or merely the next target for a raid?

Georgie halted Roderick and his horse with a raised hand. She dismounted silently and withdrew from the track. She and her mount seemed to fade into the mist and disappear. Alarmed, Roderick jumped free of his horse. He looked about, frantically turning his head this way and that.

Then a gentle hand reached out from behind a massive oak and tugged him. He followed, not so silently. Leaf litter squished under his feet and shrub branches rattled with his passage.

"Good thing they are making as much noise as you!" she hissed at him. "Tie your mount and stay close upon my heels. Place your feet in my footprints only."

They circled the clearing. Oblegid found them a hiding spot within a mass of ferns and low-growing shrubs that Roderick could not name.

From between branches and fronds they espied Marlowe and his lieutenant—Johnstone by name, Roderick believed. They shifted their feet and paced about nervously. The cold and damp of All Saints Day at dawn penetrated Roderick's uniform coat. He clenched his jaw rather than allow his teeth to chatter.

Major Barclay Marlowe had a reputation for laughing at danger and for grabbing the glory of successful skirmishes. He basked in a golden glow of admiration from both his superiors and his men.

So why did he betray king and country by smuggling arms to the enemy?

Was he too like his cousin Georgie, needing to break rules and defy authority just for the adventure of it?

A third man approached on horseback. Du Carré. Squarely built, wrapped in a gray greatcoat and thick muffler, the cold chapped his pale face and made his nose run.

Behind him rode ten Indian braves.

Roderick immediately reached for his pistol.

Georgie stayed his hand with an iron grip.

He tried protesting. She clamped her hand across his mouth.

Not yet.

He distinctly heard her, but did not see her mouth move. Gooseflesh arose along his back from more than just chill.

Rather than dwell on what he knew could not have happened, he listened closely to the muted conversation beside the loaded cart.

"You promised me two hundred gold guineas for the lot," Marlowe said with icy calm.

From the way he narrowed his eyes and concentrated his gaze upon the new man's throat, Roderick did not want to be on the receiving end of the man's anger.

" 'Alf upon delivery. 'T othair 'alf when my clients reach their rendezvous," the new man said in a thick French accent; thicker than when he gossiped with English soldiers.

"Du Carré," Roderick mouthed to Georgie.

Do you know him? she asked, again without moving her mouth.

Roderick nodded. "Met him once."

Georgie narrowed her eyes as if focusing exclusively on the Frenchman. Was she reading his mind?

Impossible, Roderick admonished himself.

"You have my word that these Indians are safe from my men," Marlowe replied. Again the coldness in his voice and his eyes sent warning shudders through Roderick. He did not trust his fellow major. Not one bit.

And to think he had crossed swords with the man on nearly a daily basis, exposed his throat to the man's naked blade. Drank with him and shared a meal afterward.

Major Barclay Marlowe knew nothing of honor as an officer of the king or as a Freemason.

Roderick wanted to lash out in anger.

Or vomit.

"Are these braves truly safe?" du Carré asked. He kept his hands inside the pockets of his greatcoat. Did he hide weapons there? "Three times I have brokered a sale of arms between you and my allies. Three times the braves have been ambushed en route to their next raid."

"Coincidence," Marlowe dismissed the implied accusation with a wave of his hand. The gesture brought his fingers within inches of his sword.

Georgie's eyes grew wide and she bit her lip.

Did the Frenchman know how rapidly Marlowe could unsheath his weapon and impale him?

"Draw your sword now, Major Marlowe, and my friends

will have you dead before your second breath," du Carré said coldly.

Ten braves raised war axes, ready to hack the Englishmen to pieces.

"Very well, du Carré. You win. This time." Marlowe eased his hands out to his sides, then up to his shoulders, well away from sword, dagger, and pistol.

Johnstone eased behind the cart, putting the bulk of it between himself and the Indians. Marlowe stepped back, putting two extra paces between him and the Frenchman.

"Show me the gold and you may take the cart."

Du Carré reached inside his greatcoat and slowly withdrew his hand. But he gripped a pistol, not a sack of coins.

"Now!" Marlowe shouted and dove beneath the cart.

A dozen or more musket shots blazed forth from the woods. Blood blossomed from the chests of two Indians. The rich, warm coppery smell filled Roderick's senses.

His throat closed and his stomach roiled at the senseless deaths.

He stared in horror as the remaining Indians let loose with tomahawks and hidden muskets. Their chilling war cries rose above the roar of gunfire. They kneed their horses and galloped toward the soldiers who hastened to reload their weapons.

The smell of burning gunpowder overrode the scent of blood and death.

Georgie drew her saber and dagger-pistol but remained hidden.

An Indian loomed behind a red-coated private, tomahawk raised, a sneer of contempt upon his face.

Roderick brought his pistol to bear and aimed at the Indian. He took a deep breath and squeezed the trigger carefully. He had not the time to waste a single shot. His round penetrated the oiled chest of his target. Red blood poured forth from his wound, staining the private's uniform a deeper red.

Du Carré aimed his pistol at the cart full of weapons and volatile powder.

Marlowe rolled out from beneath it just as the Frenchman's gun fired.

Roderick grabbed Georgie by the shoulders and yanked

them both away from the cart. Two heartbeats later a ball of flame erupted from the bags of powder. Two of Marlowe's men flew backward. Johnstone screamed again and again. Fire engulfed his body. He writhed.

The roar filled Roderick's ears, blessedly blocking out the lieutenant's death throes.

Above the aftermath of silence, he sensed Georgie moaning. Kneeling, she beat at flames and embers that spread from the burning cart.

He crouched over her, reloading. Just as he aimed his weapon at du Carré, Marlowe fired his own weapon. The Frenchmen went down, clutching his belly. The stench of ruptured bowel stung Roderick's nostrils.

The two remaining Indians fled. Marlowe stooped to retrieve the sack of gold coins from du Carré's still twisting body.

Roderick stood and walked into the clearing alone. He aimed his loaded pistol at Marlowe's heart.

"You won't shoot a fellow officer, Whythe."

"But I will shoot a traitor to His Majesty."

Chapter 49

"STAND down, Whythe," I said coldly to Roderick. "He's mine." Ice filled my veins along with the acrid odor of burned sulfur. This was more than the aftermath of exploding black gunpowder. This scent came straight from the depths of hell.

I had found the demon and the man who controlled it. My cousin, Barclay Marlowe.

I had no other purpose than to remove the traitorous blight of Barclay Marlowe from the face of the earth. His demon would take more work, but I could do it. I knew the demon's name.

"The infamous cousin Georgie." Barclay executed a mocking bow.

"In the flesh." I did not return the bow. The minor burns on my legs and shoulders made me stiff. I tried to ignore them.

I dared not take my eyes off his. "Draw your sword, Marlowe." I raised my saber and my dagger en garde.

The only sounds within the clearing seemed to be my harsh breathing and the crackle of a dying fire.

Where was the demon?

"I won't give a bastard the honor of a fair duel," he sneered. A second pistol appeared in his hand, as if by magic.

"And I will not allow a demon-haunted traitor to His Majesty to live," I replied. "I thought you believed in something beyond your own pleasure and power. The family taught you to value honor, justice, loyalty, and promises."

"You, of all people, should know I have no need of the

family rules. The 'family' lives in the past, depending upon the glory of our ancestors to justify their existence. Well, little bastard cousin, past glory does not buy ale and decent uniforms or custom-made blades!"

"Nor does it make whores out of innocent maids! As you did with Miss Cummings." I circled my blade, trying to find a way to disarm him before he shot me. Sometime in the earlier fray I'd shot my dagger-pistol and not reloaded.

"I did not make her a whore. She did it to herself."

He smiled in that sexy way that ten years ago would have taken me to the heights of ecstasy.

I steeled myself against his charm. Surely he used his magical talent to project such a compelling aura. In acknowledging that, I negated his power over me.

I smiled, free at last of any feeling of guilt for killing him.

"Come now, Georgie, we are alike, we two. Free spirits who disdain authority and outdated mores. Join me. I have resources you cannot imagine. This land is rich. The two of us can be richer and more powerful than all of our family together."

"At the cost of my soul given to a demon? I will not gain riches by dealing double. Stealing arms from the Crown, selling them to the enemy, and then ambushing that same enemy! Everything I am, I have earned on my own. I defy authority only when the rules make no sense. Double-dealing makes no sense. Except possibly to a demon."

Deep anger literally turned my vision red. As red as the coat Barclay wore and sullied.

Behind me, Roderick moved for a better shot at Barclay. Stupid. He made himself vulnerable.

I circled in the opposite direction. Circle. Swoop, Arc. Loop. I kept my blade moving rapidly in a complicated pattern that was no pattern at all. The polished steel made a blur as it sang through the air. Faster and faster I swept it through the moves. Each step took me a little closer to my opponent.

Barclay kept his eyes on my saber. Did he notice me shifting my grip on the dagger?

I'd seen a Barbary pirate play this game once, in Venice. Distract the enemy with false moves, then dive for the killing blow from an unexpected direction.

I only hoped that the demon had gone elsewhere with the diminishing scent of sulfur. Else it might whisper my diversion to Barclay.

Off to my left, I sensed Roderick moving closer. His clumsy pistol had not the accuracy of mine. His was loaded, mine was not.

"Nice ploy, Georgie," Barclay sneered. He kept his eyes on mine.

Before I could riposte, he swung his arm toward Roderick. His finger squeezed the trigger.

Time slowed. I saw it all clearly.

"No!"

The muzzle flashed.

Barclay jerked aside with the kickback.

Roderick fell. Blood spilled out of his shoulder.

"Roddie!"

"Good-bye, Cousin." Barclay scrambled for balance even as he ran toward his tethered horse.

I leaped and slid to my knees beside Roderick. Desperately, I tried to staunch the flow of blood from his shoulder with my hands.

Rivers of blood poured through my clenched fingers.

Barclay laughed as he galloped away, taking the last of the scent of sulfur with him.

Sharp, burning, lances shot from Roderick's shoulder to his wrist, to his heart, to his head. His legs turned to mush. He felt himself collapse. Impact with the ground hurt less than the explosion of pain in his chest and back and arms.

A warm gush down his chest. Then cold. So cold. He thought he heard his teeth chatter.

Angry words around him.

And then Georgie was there, pressing her hands against him. Something inside him eased, like a knot untying itself.

His vision became fuzzy. He closed his eyes, trying desperately to focus. His lids became too heavy to lift.

Strangely, his body was suddenly too light, seemingly drifting above himself. Only his heart remained anchored to the earth by Georgie.

"Don't you dare die on me, Major Roderick Whythe,"

she cried. "I've lost too many friends. I can't let that renegade cousin take you. I won't let him!"

A shift of his body that wasn't his body and some curses
from Georgie. She fumbled with something. A bucketful of
cold air blasted his neck. She must have unwrapped his
stock to use as a bandage. The shock anchored him back
into his body.

Then he hurt some more. More than he thought possible.
More than he thought he could live through.

How many campaigns had he survived? How many
wounds had he taken? None of them hurt as much as this
one did.

Did the betrayal behind the battle add flame to the fire
in his body?

"Goddess, I can't leave you," Georgie uttered through
gritted teeth. "You'll die if I leave you." More pressure on
his shoulder that made it hurt more. But strangely he felt a
little more spark of awareness, as if she thrust strength and
courage back into him.

He drifted for a time. Oddly content. Too tired to move.
Almost beyond caring if he breathed or not.

The ground shuddered beneath him. He shook back into
awareness. Cold sweat bathed his brow and his back and
his belly.

Hot, fetid breath played across his face followed by a
soft whicker. A horse.

Oh, God, no. She didn't intend . . .

"Roddie, you have to help me. I can't lift you alone. Roddie do you hear me."

"No," he said, shaking his head. At least he thought he
said it. He couldn't hear his words above the roaring in
his ears.

"Sorry, old man. This is going to hurt. I haven't time to
be gentle. I have to go after Marlowe before the trail goes
cold. But I have to find help for you first." She placed her
hands beneath his armpits and heaved.

Groaning and spitting curses against the onslaught of
fire in his shoulder, he had to get his feet under him just to
ease the pressure on his wound.

"Now, now, Roddie, no need to call down demons on my
head," she clucked. "Though calling me a son of a Whirling
Dervish is most creative. Have you ever seen one? I have.

Most amazing spiritual trance they induce. Makes me dizzy just thinking about it."

She was prattling. They both knew it. And he found himself listening to her rather than concentrating on how much he hurt, how much he wanted to sink back onto the ground.

And then he found his face buried in the flank of the bloody horse. The beast shied and started. Probably from the scent of blood. Even battle-trained horses did not like the reminder of death.

Georgie did or said something to the horse. It settled.

"Left hand on the pommel, Roddie." Georgie placed his hand where she wanted it. "Now left foot in the stirrup. I'll push, but you have to help. I can't lift your weight alone."

The pain assailed him anew. Little fire imps burrowed beneath his skin and started chomping away at his flesh and his sanity.

"No. Hurts." He felt himself leaning backward. If only he could lay his head back down, his stomach might settle and the fire imps would leave him in peace.

"Can't do that, Roddie." She pushed him back so that his face was against the horse's hide and his arm stretched above his head grasping the pommel.

Somehow she managed to seat him in the saddle. The maneuver took forever. He thought he blacked out once or thrice. He no longer cared. He just wanted her to leave him alone, wanted the pain to go away, wanted to die in her arms with the words "I love you," on his lips.

She was relentless. Eventually he slumped over the horse's neck. She tied his hands together around the neck. And maybe his feet, too, beneath the belly.

The agony began anew with each jolting step his mount took. Georgie kept the pace slow. But that only prolonged the pain. Before too long he lost consciousness once more.

Some unknown time later he became aware that the horse had stopped. He forced his gritty eyes half-open. Night had fallen. The scent of dew and a coming frost stabbed at his nose.

"Roddie," Georgie whispered. She was right beside him, her face pressed against his ear.

"Roddie, I have to go. I will knock on the apothecary's door to rouse him. But I have to go. I have to follow Marlowe to

Boston. I have to keep him from betraying the king again. I have to send his demon back to hell."

Roderick tried to mutter something, not sure if anything coherent emerged from his mouth. He couldn't remember what he wanted to say.

"Goddess knows, I don't want to leave you, Roddie. I love you. I know you can't hear me, but I have to say it. I love you. We can never be together, but I shall cherish the memory of the night we made love, all of my life. Good-bye my love. My only love."

Her lips brushed against his cheek, featherlight, and yet they burned a trail of longing and regret.

"Georgina," he called. But she could not hear his plea.

Chapter 50

Place unknown, time unknown.

DEMONS increased their flurry around Emily as she climbed ever higher. They pecked at her with razor-sharp beaks. They clawed at her with long talons. They screeched so loudly a deaf person could hear them.

Emily cackled with them, mocking their tortures. Then she absorbed these new torments, accepted them as part of her being, and kept climbing.

A hand appeared off to her left, beckoning to her, offering her help and a way out.

She had to ignore it. Just another trap. A ruse. If she trusted her weight and balance to that hand, it would let go and she'd fall again, all the way to the bottom of hell.

Hunger gnawed at her belly as keenly as the demons gnawed at her flesh. She longed to lick the moisture from the stones, and dared not. Like Persephone, if she consumed anything while here, she'd be doomed to hell forever.

Every ounce of her being concentrated on climbing. Today, tomorrow. Yesterday. She didn't know how long she climbed, who she was, where she was going, or why she must climb, only that she must, and that she missed her papa.

Philadelphia, December, 1764.

When I left Williamsburg to follow my cousin Barclay Marlowe north, I paused only long enough to collect my cat, extra ammunition for my pistol, and a change of clothing. The rest of my belongings I threw into a trunk. I left a note and a few coins for James Southall to send them when I notified him that I had an address. I cited the truth, a family emergency, as the reason for my hasty departure.

Major Roderick Whythe's health I entrusted to His Majesty's Army and whatever gods or goddesses looked out for him. My heart ached that I could not stay and nurse him back to health. Had he noticed the little bits of magic I had injected into him during that long slow trek back to the city?

My talent did not allow a full healing. I could only push the lead ball out of his shoulder and force some of the larger bleeders to close. Replenishing lost blood and rebuilding torn and burned muscle were beyond me.

If he had noticed, he would pass it all off as delirium. I hoped.

Over the next few weeks, I tracked my cousin with magic and cunning and close questioning of any who might have seen him. I came close to catching Barclay several times. Always he disappeared just before I caught him. He left no physical trail. He left no magical trail. I could not even catch a trace of burned sulfur.

My frustration mounted. Everything Barclay had told me was suspect. I doubted he worked as a spy for the Crown. I knew he did not love my niece.

In an unguarded moment he had said that he wished above all else to thwart his father. How did the demon figure in his convoluted plots?

Then, on the outskirts of Philadelphia, my horse threw a shoe and I could go no farther for a while.

Situated on the Delaware River, the first thing I noticed about the place was the clean cobbled streets. No open midden down the center, boot scrapers at every doorway, freshly scrubbed and swept stoops. Bustling prosperity dominated the air.

I stopped and sought information and funding from a fellow Mason. Benjamin Franklin.

A letter of introduction from Omniscient Jackson gained me an immediate interview in Mr. Franklin's front parlor. His wife Deborah served us tea and ginger biscuits with a stern frown. She lingered around her husband until he shooed her off. "Leave us to speak of boring politics," he chuckled as he swatted her ample bottom.

His graying brown hair, hanging straight below a bald pate, gave hints of a handsome and vigorous man in his youth. His vigor seemed undiminished by time.

Deborah Franklin looked over her shoulder at me with a deeper frown.

"Have I taken you away from important family matters? I do apologize for the intrusion," I blurted out, perched upon the edge of a substantial wooden chair.

All of the furnishings in the rather stark parlor were sturdy, devoid of ornamentation, and functional. The whitewashed wainscoting below pale walls reflected the meager light coming through the few panes of glass. To light the room, Franklin needed only a single oil lamp on the table at his elbow to augment the glow from the fire within a black stove set away from the wall.

"I would ask how my friend Mr. Jackson fares, but I see this letter is dated near nine months ago." Franklin peered at me over the tops of his spectacles. The humor evaporated from his voice.

"My mission took me to Williamsburg first," I explained.

"Williamsburg. Yes, hotbed of wild rhetoric but little action." The chuckle came back and his eyes twinkled. His round belly shook with the mirth he contained.

We talked for several delightful moments about the personalities who had discoursed at the Raleigh Tavern. My friend seemed as knowledgeable about Patrick Henry, Thom Jefferson, Peyton Randolph, and even the cautious planter George Washington, who spoke rarely in the House of Burgesses though everyone listened when he did speak, as did I.

Always at the fringes of our conversation lay an edge of displeasure with the government in England.

And an awareness of something more. I ran my fingers through a complicated pattern, beating a tattoo against the side of my chair.

Franklin grinned and relaxed. He drummed his fingers upon the table beside him in the proper answer to my inquiry.

We both leaned back and relaxed, comfortable with a member of the other secret Lodge we dared not mention or name.

"I have heard tales that His Majesty's Navy has found excuse to impress colonial sailors when they stop merchant ships suspected of smuggling molasses," he remarked without preamble. "Any man who shows skills among the topsails is immediately branded as a deserter from the navy even though he has never taken His Majesty's shilling."

"I thought the story I heard an isolated incident." Such stories easily grew and expanded as they circulated.

"More than isolated. Frequent if only half the tales are to be believed." Franklin peered at me so long and hard I almost squirmed. "And yet any man who shows a rudimentary knowledge of Masonic ritual is spared."

I allowed that comment to pass. Freemasonry was only an entry to the Lodge to which we both owed higher allegiance.

"Many Virginians who fought valiantly during the war, as officers, are also distressed that the Crown refuses to commission them in the army. The Crown prefers to import their own officers and men rather than depend upon colonials to defend their homes," I countered with another argument I'd heard bandied about when no army officers were present in the taproom—a common occurrence at the Raleigh. But at the other taverns in Williamsburg . . . ?

"Then, too, His Majesty expects us to pay for the army of occupation."

I opened my mouth to protest Franklin's word choice. Then I clamped it shut before any sound burst forth. I had to ask myself if I agreed with him or not.

An army of occupation? Did our superiors view the situation in that light?

Many officers and men behaved with honor and good manners, like Roderick. Just as many more treated the colonials as rightful sources of plunder without the common rights afforded to the poorest English citizen back home. My cousin Barclay was all too typical of this sort. Witness his cavalier treatment of Miss Cummings.

As the Masked Rogue, I had defended the honor of many a colonial maiden from the depredations of an . . . army of occupation.

"Mr. Franklin, as delightful as this afternoon has been, I did not come here solely to discuss politics."

"I suspected as much. My friend Omniscient Jackson

wrote to me some months ago that you might call. It seems your name has appeared on several warrants."

"I feared as much. Lord Sackville schemes most effectively to keep me in the colonies, working for him."

"Do you have objections to working for milord, Mr. Kirkwood?"

"Many. Especially since communication with my family has been . . . disrupted."

"Tampering with His Majesty's mail is most illegal. Even Lord Sackville would not stoop to those measures."

"We both know, Mr. Franklin, that where the colonies are concerned, His Majesty's mail is no longer sacrosanct. Besides, my family has . . . other means of communicating."

He raised an eyebrow at that and quirked me a smile. "I have heard rumors that Lord Sackville's ability to snoop out information and keep an eye on people far distant borders on the arcane. Now as a man of science I have to dismiss that accusation, but as a Mason and . . . a member of another brotherhood, I am intrigued."

"Rumor must be the strongest force on Earth. No matter how hard we beat it down, it never dies."

"And yet rumor often begins with a kernel of truth."

I needed to change the subject before I succumbed to Mr. Franklin's charm and told him everything.

"If I were to pen a letter to my brother and niece, could you see that it is delivered?" I asked.

" 'Twill be a few months before I plan to depart for England," he hedged.

" 'Twill be a few months before I can settle some disturbing business in Boston."

"If your private means of communication fails, what can I do?"

"A trusted courier?"

"Can you not do the same?"

"I trust very few to bypass Lord Sackville's scrutiny."

"Very wise. But you trust me."

"I trust your Masonic oath to a brother. I trust a member of the Lodge . . ." I let my words drift away. He knew who I referenced.

"Are you truly a fellow Mason, Mistress Kirkwood?" Franklin took my hand and turned it over to inspect my callused palm.

Before I could protest, he kissed my fingertips, as he would any lady's.

"Be careful, my friend. Your disguise is good. Your mannerisms near perfect. But one such as I, who appreciates beauty in all its forms, cannot help but see the feminine allure beneath the surface."

"This conversation is at an end, Mr. Franklin." I would not admit the truth of his statement.

"As you wish." He relinquished my hand with a sigh of reluctance. "Bring your letter in the morning before you depart Philadelphia. I shall do my best to deliver it. I should delight in getting to know you further."

"And I you, Mr. Franklin. Give my best to our mutual friend, Mr. Jackson."

"I shall. And I look forward to learning more about your family and their . . . other means of communication."

"Safe journey, Mr. Franklin. May the Widow's Son watch over you."

The next day when I delivered a carefully worded and magically encoded letter for Emily, Benjamin Franklin loaned me extra funds upon my letter of credit. I accepted them gratefully. The blacksmith who shod my horse had claimed the last of my coins.

Outside of Philadelphia, I picked up Barclay's trail once more. Fresh. My nose twitched with eagerness to get on with the chase. Oblegid sat at the front of my saddle, face into the wind, chirruping and chattering her teeth in anticipation of the hunt.

I spent my funds recklessly upon bribes to taciturn innkeepers and townsfolk in the taverns. Never had I met with so many men so unwilling to speak of their neighbor's affairs. They reminded me of the grim Puritans who tried to rule the thoughts and actions of much of England.

All the way up the eastern seaboard, Barclay led me. I knew he headed for Boston. Every time I tried to take a shortcut and get ahead of him—or just catch up—he took the same shortcut, or a shorter one and kept his distance.

He left an occasional trail of magic. I believe he taunted me, making sure I followed, where he led. Into a trap?

The scent of burned sulfur disappeared entirely.

At last I arrived in Boston, with a near empty purse and with little prospect of more. Within the shadows of a private mews, I changed into my one simple skirt and bodice, hid my hair beneath my mobcap and went in search of employment in the places where references and pedigrees meant nothing.

Boston abounded with public houses of all sizes and degrees of prosperity, from the single room at the front of a tumbledown house run by a destitute widow, to the many roomed, many-storied King's Arms on the Long Wharf. Luck sent me to the Green Dragon, an older brick building on Union Street.

The Green Dragon teemed with activity from noon until after midnight. They always needed extra barmaids. The girls often worked there for six months to a year before marrying one of the patrons, or returning home to some rural area with a tidy dowry saved from their wages.

Once more I passed myself off as a widow. This time I used my true name, Georgina Kirkwood. No one questioned my lineage, only my ability to work long hours and fend off men who became amorous when they drank. Before I'd fully accepted the position, a stout silversmith with big hands that wandered a little too close to my bottom found my fist planted in his face and he measured his length upon the floor.

"Hire her now," a bandy-legged man I later knew to be Samuel Adams called out to the innkeeper. "She'll keep Revere's wife from coming around every other day looking for her wayward husband." This statement met with a mighty roar from the men gathering round the fire on this bitter December evening. Candles blazed bright, making this a warm and welcome gathering place. Often warmer and brighter than the men's homes.

" 'Ey, my wife is fair worn out with childbearing. She prefers I keep company here than in her bed," the man named Revere riposted, scrubbing his jaw as he sat up. A slight inflection in his voice hinted at French origins.

This met with another roar of laughter and a call for more ale.

The landlord directed me to a house three streets over. A widow rented rooms to respectable young women seeking employment in the city. Goodwife Camden would give me a bed, feed me breakfast, and make certain I attended church on Sunday mornings and Wednesday evenings.

"I'll not need you to work Wednesdays after supper," the landlord added. "St. Andrew's Lodge meets here then. We close to the public." He elaborated no further, leaving me to surmise that St. Andrew's Lodge was Freemason. What other secret society had enough power to command a public house close one night a week just so that what happened during their meetings remained secret?

That other Lodge met more secretly and less regularly to avoid detection.

The Green Dragon was the kind of place where I could learn about conspiracies to defy royal authority. Here, I could ask about troop movements and find my elusive cousin, possibly before he betrayed the Crown and an innocent maid again.

Here, I would hear if Barclay loosed his demon upon the city.

I sent off letters to both my brother and Lord Sackville, demanding my allowance. I had little hope of hearing from either. To John Southall, I wrote a direction for my trunk. With winter closing in, I could not expect a reply from any of them for many months. Until then, I needed to earn my wages and remain in my landlady's good graces.

I could use the time to ingratiate myself into the community so that they would tell me their secrets.

That first Wednesday, I attended services with Goodwife Camden at a small church that looked little more than the front parlor of a simple home. Two old grannies claimed a broad windowsill to ease their bones. The rest of us stood in casual groups. No straight military lines here.

Many months had passed since I had attended services. Many years had passed since I had believed. My faith revolved around older beliefs, Otherworldly creatures, and a Goddess more loving than the Christian God. A Goddess who blessed my magic and gave me powers to help and defend where I could.

Yet, somehow, the simple peace of the meeting that Wednesday evening touched my heart and my mind with something I can only call grace.

I had experienced something like it in the few moments of silent companionship after Roderick and I had made love. I'd known a similar moment of bliss one day as I watched the sun set over the moors of Kirkenwood when I was twelve. One other time, during an arduous Masonic ritual, I had reached out and touched something that gave me shivers and left my heart at peace.

All of the mystical rituals of my Masonic brethren were not much more than recitation of arcane spells. Without the power of a true magician behind them, the Masons merely caught glimpses of true magic. I found the heart of magic that night.

Instead of a long sermon denouncing every meaningful action as sinful, we sat for many long moments in silent prayer. The minister trusted each of us to reach and touch God in our own way.

The concept seemed very pagan to me, despite invocations to Jesus and his mother Mary. I cared not the name given to the practice. It touched me.

At the end of the meeting, I looked around at the gathered worshipers. Almost everyone present was female. The few men tended to be young, sons or brothers rather than husbands. Clean but threadbare garments, none of it truly fashionable, dominated the room.

Then I wondered how the men of Boston tolerated this gathering.

"They are all at Lodge meetings tonight," my landlady whispered to my unspoken question. "They do not know that we worship quietly without them." She let that thought sink in. "On Sundays we attend regular services with the men."

"And the minister?" I caught a brief glimpse of the man's stocky frame disappearing through a back door.

"One of us."

A quiet smile spread through me. Like my batman Estovan, and myself at times, our pastor was a woman more comfortable in men's attire, taking a man's role in life. But she ministered to women and their needs.

I was not alone.

I took a chance.

"I journeyed to Boston not by chance, Goodwife Camden. I seek a British major who greatly wronged a woman in Williamsburg. He has used his commission to escape his responsibilities and fled to Boston, or been transferred as the men would claim."

"The man will be found if he comes anywhere near Boston."

Over the next months, none of the women of Boston heard nary a whisper about my cousin. Inquiries to General Gage brought silence. Careful listening among the members of St. Andrew's Lodge elicited no information at all.

Barclay and his demon had gone to ground.

Chapter 51

Kirkenwood, late December.

"WHO sings?" Drake asked. Wisps of melody woke him from a half sleep. A half sleep that seemed to have gone on for a long time.

"Who sings?" he called a little louder, turning his head toward the door. His bolsters shifted and made the movement very uncomfortable. He had the impression he was not supposed to watch for the comings and goings of his attendants.

No one answered. No nurse or footman appeared at his door. They never did, unless they deemed it time for food or a chamber pot. Not even one of his daughters who paraded through dutifully each evening before supper answered his call. Emily used to come. Not anymore.

They'd moved him to a small room at the end of the hall with little more than a bed, a chamber pot, and a small table to hold his bowl of gruel or a glass of medicine. No wardrobe, no chair. Just a place to park his body away from the main traffic of the house.

Still, a haunting lilt rang through the halls of Kirkenwood and through his head. A shy soprano voice. Untrained but still lovely. He could almost make out the words. Almost. Something old. Something compelling. Something . . .

"The Lady?" he asked the air.

The singing continued unabated. He needed to go to it. Needed to sing in harmony with it. Maybe then the clouds that shrouded his mind would lift and he'd know why he had slept away an entire season. The slanting light through

his window told him that autumn was long gone and winter deeply entrenched. A peat fire glowed in the small
hearth giving off fitful heat.

He shivered. He did not remember being thoroughly
warm in some time. Some long time.

Come to me, the song seemed to say. But those were not
the true words, only the true meaning. He wondered if the
singer knew the speaking of an ancient language he could
only read. Perhaps that was it.

He threw off the bedcovers and rolled to one side of the
bed only to find his left arm restrained by a leather strap
buckled to the bedpost. When did that happen? His wrist
burned with an old chafing. The redness was thick, like scar
tissue. He'd endured the strap for a long time. Many
months at least. Why hadn't he released it? He reached for
the buckle with his right hand.

A burning shock repelled his fingers at first touch.

Magic! he thought as he sucked on his fingers.

A memory broke through the fog in his mind. "For your
own good, milord," Dr. Milton Marlowe said. "We can't
have you rolling out of bed and hurting yourself now, can
we?" There seemed to be onlookers in the room at the
time of the memory. Onlookers who shook their heads in
dismay. Simpson?

"Hurt myself? I would never do that." Drake shook his
head in bewilderment. With a snap of his fingers and a dart
of magic, he stared at the buckle.

The restraint fought him. He forced his probe to penetrate the buckle's defenses. At last, reluctantly, it released
and unwound from his wrist. Absently, he rubbed at the old
chafing.

His legs did not want to move. With effort, he pushed
them to dangle over the edge of the bed. Beneath his nightshirt, they seemed too spindly to support his weight. Last
time he remembered looking at himself, his legs had been
as fat and doughy as the rest of him. Now they looked
wasted and pale. He felt around his body. His skin hung
slack where before it had been stretched tightly over his
bulk. Much of the bulk had disappeared as well. He had
many more pounds to lose before he returned to his youthful form and figure. But still, this was part of the improve-
ment Georgie had pushed upon him.

How?

He looked over his shoulder out the window again. Months had passed since he'd last noticed the season. Time enough for a limited diet to release fat from his body.

The singing grew in intensity. Calling him forth.

"I'm coming," he promised the singer.

He tested his weight upon his feet. His knees wobbled. Chill floorboards sent pins and needles through his skin. He caught himself on the edge of the bedside table. In a moment his balance returned.

Shoes. Clothing. A warm shawl. He found them in the small cupboard tucked into the eaves.

He struggled into his breeches, added braces to keep them up over his wasted frame.

The singer became more urgent, demanding.

Desperate.

No time to bother with a shirt and stock. Coat. Stockings. Shoes.

Drake opened the door to his room. He only had to use a little magic to unstick the door. Yanking it open, he thrust himself into the dark hall. The doors to all of the bedrooms on this level were closed. An aura of gloom pressed against him, almost pushing him back into his own small chamber.

This time, the lilting song penetrated the miasma of despair, showing him a lighter path to follow. It led him up to the nursery. Baby Griffin had grown. He crowed and chuckled in his cot, happy to chew upon a block of wood, painted in bright colors.

The song tugged Drake away from wondrous contemplation of his son. Down the back stairs, bypassing the kitchen, through the pantry, down to the wine cellar.

He knew where to go now. He pulled out a dusty bottle of canary wine that had probably gone to vinegar and would never entice Simpson to serve it. Removing the weight of the bottle released a spring. The entire rack swung away from the wall on well-oiled hinges.

A black tunnel opened before him. At the end, a tiny flame winked at him.

The song took on an ethereal note. It drifted away from him. He had to follow the song and the flame into the hidden archives and beyond.

How far beyond?

How deep into the Otherworlds must he go to answer the song's compulsion?

He could not resist. One step and then another into the tunnel, so like the path into death he had resisted so often when another life fled.

He released the first trap with six words and an arcane gesture. A simple spell. The next two would be harder.

Did he walk into his own death?

"Em, beloved? Is it you who sings? I'm coming to join you."

He released the second trap with effort, struggling to remember the precise order of the spell. Then he stepped forward once more. "I'm coming. At last."

"This report states that Lord Sackville is wavering in his support of the colonial Stamp Act." Peters, Dr. Milton Marlowe's secretary proffered the folded letter as if it were tainted.

Milton could not trust Simpson, nor any of the officious butler's family. So he had relegated them to the farms and brought his own men to run Kirkenwood while they waited for Drake to die or his errant daughter to return and take charge.

Until Emily married Barclay and produced a son and heir, Milton could not allow Drake to die. He needed the estates and therefore the archives within his control. A mundane great-nephew of Drake's father waited anxiously to inherit the land and the title. But he would never inherit the magic to step into Drake's shoes as Pendragon.

"Apparently a number of industries and merchants are on the verge of declaring bankruptcy from the loss of trade with the colonies," Peters continued. "They are pressuring both the Commons and the Lords to repeal the Act."

"Sackville is weak. He needs a new compulsion to keep his mind focused. Very well. I shall return to London for Yule festivities and reinforce his need to remain loyal to us." Milton sighed heavily. He'd welcome a relief from the endless boredom at Kirkenwood in winter. Drake seemed docile enough to leave in the care of trained servants, and Emily had disappeared, seemingly for good. Eloped to

Gretna Green with a totally unsuitable villain more like. Kirkenwood was safe.

He'd leave Samuel behind to be sure, though. Silent and trustworthy, his bodyguard stood by the long window, watching the grounds, watching the room, ever vigilant.

"Another matter, sir." Peters cleared his throat behind a clenched fist. He looked as if he covered a smile.

"What now? Sheep in the wrong pasture? Pigs running loose in the rose garden? I thought I gave orders that Greenwood was to handle farming matters."

"Nothing so mundane, sir." Peters was enjoying this report far too much.

Milton took a long draw on his pipe—Drake's pipe and tobacco actually, but the earl did not miss them. Normally Milton disdained the luxury of tobacco, but since taking over the management of Kirkenwood, he found the weed soothing to his nerves. He waited while the smoke invaded his lungs, lifting the heaviness from his mind. Then he released the smoke into Peter's smug face. The man thought too much of his intelligence and talents. He needed a reduction in rank, possibly some form of punishment.

"Milord Earl has gone missing, sir." Peters backed up three steps and gestured a quick ward around himself.

"What do you mean he's missing?" Dr. Milton Marlowe screamed. He kept his magic contained. Best to wait until Peters was unguarded before wasting energy on him.

Each of Milton's employees possessed a Knight's level of magical talent and training. He allowed none of them to reach Master level. Not even Barclay could match or best Milton in a magical duel within the coven.

Only Neville deserved that rank. Where was his son's ghost now? He'd taken to wandering the ruins of the castle and neglecting his father.

As he had neglected Milton's advice and joined the army, only to get himself killed.

Never mind. They'd find the archives soon. Milton had narrowed his search to the back of the house and cellars. Traces of magic enticed his senses there as they did nowhere else in the sprawling mansion.

He had nearly found the cache of arcane texts, journals, and grimoires. But each foray into the hidden recesses of Kirkenwood met with solid walls of resistance. Soon, though. He sensed a weakening in the wards. Once he had the archives in his hands, he would remove Drake and his infant son from his path to immortal legend.

He would bring his son back from the dead, whole and hale and fully talented.

"I am sorry, sir," Peters mumbled, still backing away. "But the maid—Meg, I believe—heard the earl calling in much distress. She went to him and discovered his bed empty and a suit of clothes missing."

Peters did not look sorry at all. He looked . . . smug. And superior.

"She also found this, sir." Peters held up a glass filled with a cloudy liquid. "The earl did not drink the medicine you prescribed for him."

"Impossible," Milton spat. He jumped to his feet and stalked away from the earl's study, the earl's fine whiskey, and the earl's most expensive pipe tobacco, down the hall, around the corner and down another, much narrower corridor, to the earl's bedroom.

The thought of Drake wandering around with a clear mind frightened him.

Sure enough, the door to the tiny room stood open, hanging listlessly on its hinges, as if a cannon charge had burst it open.

A chill crept up Milton's spine. Only magic could have negated his wards so explosively. Only one person in the household had enough magic to do that.

The earl himself. His daughter, perhaps, could have. But no one had seen the chit in months. He'd lost track of time in the remote fastness of Kirkenwood as the endless winter drew near and the winds howled without cease.

The chill became like the claws on demon fingers. What if Emily returned full of magic and beyond his control?

"Never," he muttered. "Never," he repeated more loudly and with more assertion. He controlled the earl and the earldom as well as the Master Magicians of the Pendragon Society—those that remained. Three elderly mages had retired and therefore renounced their powers and their right to meddle in the politics and economics of England. The remaining four had retreated to their own estates and families. That left only Drake and his sister Georgina to challenge Milton's control.

And Georgina was in the colonies. Barclay reported, when he bothered to report, that he controlled not only her person, but the contents of her reports to Sackville.

"Find the earl," Milton ordered Peters. "Send the entire staff. Search the house, the outbuildings, the cellars. Everywhere. He can't have gone far." Even as he spoke, Milton allowed his eyes to cross and unfocus until he spotted the ungrounded trace of magic trailing away from his wards.

He followed the glimmering pathway. Drake's magic had taken on a more silvery cast, stripped of the deep blue evident in his more powerful talent during his youth. The trail led Milton up the stairs to the nursery, wound around the cot of the now crying Griffin and then down the back stairs, past the kitchen into the pantries and then . . . down the steps to the wine cellar.

Underground! Halfway into the Netherworld.

Milton chuckled as he descended.

Chapter 52

THE massive bookshelves and furnishings decorating the hidden archives room paled into mist until Drake could see the bones of the Earth through them.

"Oh, dear," he sighed. The voice that led him onward came from too far away. Dared he travel that far? He'd never ventured into the Otherworlds, had no desire to explore the knowledge and power available there. And the danger.

"I do not even wish to meet a faery," he whispered.

Come! The singer demanded.

"Why?" he replied, digging his feet into the fine Oriental carpet on the stone floor. But that, too, faded into transparency. Its pale colors merely echoed the vibrancy he knew they truly contained.

Papa, I need you, the singing voice resolved into plaintive words spoken by his eldest daughter.

"Emily?"

Papa . . . She and the song faded along with reality.

"Where are you, Emily?" Vaguely he remembered that he had not seen her in a while. Not for a long, long while.

He turned in a circle, reluctant to lift his feet much or move more than a trifle. The next step could whisk solid ground out from under him and send him plunging . . . anywhere. And not necessarily into the one Otherworld that trapped Emily.

His heart began to beat double time. "Emily!"

Not Emily. He couldn't bear to lose her, too, not so soon after Em had passed.

"Emma, beloved, help me find our daughter."

A feminine face swam out of the hearth. Excalibur rested on the mantel above it. The sword appeared to be solid at least. Neither of this world nor the next, it would remain in any reality for the proper wielder.

He confronted the female spirit that hovered, bodiless between him and the sword. A magnificent woman, just past her prime, still beautiful, still proud and dignified with straight black hair that drifted about her in the celestial winds. A white streak marred the ebon tresses, running away from the left temple.

"Who are you?" Drake knew better than to back away from such a creature, though his heart was in his throat and his pulse thundered in his ears. Retreat would only drag him farther away from his own world, into the dark, demon infested depths of hell.

Cold sweat broke out on his brow.

The woman snorted in indignation.

Who are you to summon such as I? The vague outline of a body became visible beneath her face. She held something in her hand . . . something long. Possibly an echo of Excalibur from a different time.

"I . . . I am . . ." He swallowed deeply. Fear for Emily pulled the words from his throat. "I am Drake Griffin Henry Kirkwood, seventh Earl of Kirkenwood, Master Magician, and Pendragon of England." His voice became stronger with each utterance.

So they made us earls? The woman laughed, her voice rich and hearty. *Which of my get coerced such a vaunted title from the puny kings of England?* She lifted her left hand, the one that held . . . was it a staff?

"The title was first granted by James Stuart, first of that name to be king of England, and the sixth of Scotland. He gave it to Griffin Kirkwood. I forget which one. There have been too many to remember."

A Stuart on the throne of England? My, my, times have changed. The figure of the woman gathered substance. She wore a gown of ancient cut. Something in green from the Plantagenet era; possibly only the tattered remnants of her moldy shroud. Her speech was as antique as her raiment. Her staff, too, became more solid. Atop it rested an ancient Celtic cross with a huge black crystal embedded in the boss. The top piece seemed a little off-kilter,

mismatched, as if several staffs and finials had been
blended together.

*And what indiscretion did this Stuart king commit that he
found the bribe of a title beneficial?*

"I believe my ancestor bought the title. King James
found himself in need of funds separate from what the
Commons would give him. He suggested contributions to
his coffers would result in generous honors in exchange."

The spirit snorted in disgust. *I should have expected such
from a Stuart.*

"May I ask with whom I converse?" Drake tried to keep
his tone mild, though impatience and anxiety burned
alongside his fear. He hoped the spirit could not hear his
knees knocking together.

*You may address me as Raven. I, too, have been the Pen-
dragon of England and the parent of a Griffin who was des-
tined to succeed me.*

"My son will succeed me as Pendragon?"

Possibly. The future is fluid, a river with many tributaries.
She paused, her head shifting slowly through the currents
of time and place. *Why have you summoned me?*

"I . . ." Dared he admit he had not summoned her? One
must always tread carefully in the Otherworlds and with
the dead. "I seek my daughter, Emily. She is lost and needs
help coming home."

Emily, Raven mused. *I do not know Emily.* She pronounced the name strangely, Æmelie, as if spelled the old
Saxon way.

"Papa!" Emily's voice came through the fluid depths. For
half a heartbeat, Drake thought he saw his daughter's face
reflected in that of their ancestor, Raven of Kirkenwood.

Unbidden the words of an old poem in a dead language
(Sumerian? Egyptian? He could not remember which)
came to his lips.

> *"In worlds trapped between*
> *Speak out for Freedom*
> *Or forever wander*
> *'Twixt life and death's keen."*

No meter, no cadence, no rhyme in English. The meaning of the words rang loudly in his mind though the spoken

sounds themselves meant little. At least they rhymed when uttered aloud.

Before he could muse longer, power rose up in him, near lifting his body free of gravity and his chains to the Earth. His heart beat steadily and strongly for the first time in months. He saw clearly through the spirit and the mists of the Otherworlds to the solid reality of his archives and Excalibur.

He reached for the sword. It came readily to his hand.

Where? How? Raven gasped. *You dare?*

"I demand!" Drake said, emboldened by his grasp upon the ancient talisman of his office. "Release my daughter. Her destiny in this world is not yet complete. You may not keep her."

With both hands upon the ancient grip of Excalibur, he slashed through the veils of time and space.

Raven tumbled aside.

A great rift opened in the air as a silvery maw. Within the opening appeared a tiny figure.

"Take my hand, Emily. Come forth into your own world." He reached forward with his left hand, still clasping Excalibur aloft in his right.

The sword blazed with blinding, too-white light.

Raven withdrew, but did not disappear. Only her staff remained solid.

The tiny figure within the maw drifted closer. The rift began to knit closed.

"Hurry, Emily. Take my hand." Drake leaned a little into the gash.

Emily grew a little larger, a little more real.

Pressure upon Drake's back and chest told him that the opening repaired itself more quickly.

The sword, Milord Earl. Only the sword will keep it open, Raven whispered.

Drake shifted so that his right arm and Excalibur extended deep into the maw. The blade blazed brighter against the darkness of the Otherworlds. The knitted fabric of time unraveled again.

Emily closed her hand upon the blade. She cried out as if burned. But she kept her fingers clasped about its solid steel.

Slowly, but steadily, Drake pulled the sword back through the rift. Inch by painful inch, Emily grew in size and form.

Her tangled mass of blonde curls looked grimy. Her breeches and jacket were so torn and dirty they could have been Raven's tattered shroud.

As Excalibur withdrew, the opening began to close again.

"Take my hand, Emily. I have to keep the blade inside the opening until you are completely free." Drake held out his left hand once more.

A tentative flutter against his fingers. Then at last he felt the solid grasp of his daughter's hand.

He yanked both her and Excalibur free.

Together they tumbled backward onto the stone floor of the archives.

When he dared open his eyes, all evidence of the Otherworlds, the rift, and Raven had disappeared. The mists and veils retreated.

But Emily clasped the staff with the mismatched Celtic Cross and black crystal boss.

A crash against a rack of wine bottles startled Milton in his search for secret doors. He jumped back from his perusal of a particularly fine port. He could pay off much of Barclay's personal debt by the sale of this one bottle of wine.

Milton himself had never craved the luxuries Barclay deemed necessary to life. Drake, too, used to rely heavily upon indulgences to carry on his day-to-day existence.

Cautiously, Milton peered out of the alcove that housed the port. Drake and his daughter lay crumpled upon the stone floor, limbs tangled in a most unseemly and intimate manner.

He cleared his throat and averted his eyes a moment.

Drake and Emily stirred, but remained down, seemingly stunned by their fall, or in shock.

"Milord," Milton said sternly. "You should be in bed. Your heart will not support much activity."

"Balderdash, Milton. My heart has never beat stronger. Nor has my magic responded so readily to my summons." Drake squeezed his daughter's shoulders with affection and strength.

A chill of fear rooted Milton to the spot. Anxiously, he

sent out a mental summons to Samuel. And another to Peters. Then he added a request for extra footmen.

"Your daughter, however, does not look too well or very strong." Milton stepped forward and placed his fingers against the girl's neck. The great vein eluded his touch. Not that he wanted to remain in contact with her filthy person. Her hair was so grimy and matted it had lost its curl and golden luster. Her clothing was so torn and moldy, she might have just emerged from the grave.

Beneath his fingers she reared up, arching her back at an impossible angle.

"Kill them all!" she screamed. Her eyes blazed, the delicate cornflower blue of the iris turned red. She bared her teeth and brandished a staff as if it were a spear to be cast.

Milton shied away from her.

"Emily?" Drake looked at his daughter, puzzled. The earl scrambled away from her as she levitated to her feet.

"Demons infest this house! Demons claim our beloved!" Emily whirled around, sweeping the air with her staff.

"Emily, calm down." Drake reached a beseeching hand to her. "Your battle through the Otherworld is finished. You are home now. Home in the loving bosom of your family."

"Demon spawn!" Emily rounded upon Milton. She pushed the antique cross atop her staff into his face. "Kiss the cross and know your doom."

Where had the meek girl who spun romantic dreams gone?

"Peters," Milton called softly.

"Here, sir." The secretary appeared at Milton's elbow. His eyes grew wide at the sight of Emily's fierceness.

"Emily, enough," Drake roared.

Emily blinked and lowered her staff. Her eyes cleared of their supernatural color. "Who are you?" she asked meekly, still staring up at Milton. "Are you guarding the portal?"

"What portal?" Drake asked. He touched Emily's shoulders and turned her to face him. "What portal do you seek, Emily?"

"Darkness. Red lightning. Green slimy creatures. Grasping. Clawing. Blood. Pain. Fire." She swallowed heavily. "DEATH."

Then she slumped into her father's arms.

"Quickly, Dr. Marlowe. Get your bag. She needs your aid immediately." Samuel appeared out of nowhere and gently lifted Emily into his strong arms. He looked expectantly to Milton for instructions.

The girl still clutched her outlandish staff.

Peters jumped toward the stairs.

"Where are you going, Peters?" Milton asked sternly.

"To fetch your bag, sir."

"You obey my orders, Peters. No one else's."

"Don't be silly, Milton," Drake admonished. "I am master in this house."

"Not anymore, Cousin. I rule Kirkenwood. I control the Pendragon Society."

Drake's eyes narrowed in speculation.

"Peters, the draught." Milton snapped his fingers at his secretary. He had to act fast, before Drake took command of his life and his faculties once more.

"Here, sir." Peters meekly handed Milton the glass containing the cloudy liquid.

"Drink this, milord," Milton ordered. He captured Drake's gaze with his own. He wound a thread of compulsion into his cousin's mind.

Drake blinked and shook his head. "I have lain an invalid too long, Milton. I needs must retake my place in society and in the government."

"I do not think so, milord." Milton snapped his fingers once more. Two burly footmen who owed him their lives as well as their employment jumped out of the shadows and pinioned the earl's arms with beefy hands.

"Drink the draught, Drake."

"No." Drake clamped his mouth shut. He did not struggle against his confinement. Instead he faced his opponent with dignity and calm.

"Peters, force him if necessary."

"Yes, sir." The secretary signaled to a third footman.

Milton's servant grasped Drake's chin and twisted until the earl had to open his mouth or have his jaw broken. Then Peters poured the milky liquid down his throat while he pinched Drake's nose closed, forcing him to swallow.

Within moments the earl's eyes became glassy and unfocused.

"Carry him back to his room and lock the door from the outside. I shall see to a more secure confinement in a few moments. Henceforth, you are to supervise the administration of the earl's medicine. He is to drink it twice a day, even if you have to wake him to make him take it," Milton snarled. He hoped he would not have to reinforce his orders with corporal punishment within a magic circle. Such a messy affair.

The footmen lifted Drake between them and carried him up the steep stairs of the cellar.

"Samuel, take the girl. Confine her to her room."

"A draught of medicine for her as well, sir?" Peters asked. Samuel did not have the initiative or intelligence to suggest a course of action.

"A good precaution, but I do not believe she will require it. She is completely insane. Leather restraints should be sufficient."

"Sir, she will not release the staff." Peters pried at her fingers.

"Must I do everything myself?" Exasperated, Milton tugged on the staff.

Emily's hand clenched tighter.

He tried inserting his fingers between her palm and the wood.

"Sir, her flesh seems melded with the wood," Peters gasped.

"Let her keep the damn thing for now. It will keep her quiet."

"Yes, sir." Peters ducked his head, refusing to meet Milton's gaze.

"Keep them both quiet and drugged. I'm off to London in the morning. The king and the House of Lords need my attention if we are to keep the colonies subdued and paying for their keep."

"Yes, sir."

"And, Peters, there will not be a repeat of today's escape."

"No, sir."

"Hire more staff if necessary. I shall return after the New Year. No, make that spring. This place is beastly cold and windy in winter."

"Yes, sir."

"By then my son will have returned. He will wed Miss Emily then."

"Sir, she's insane! We'll have to keep her drugged and insensible," Samuel protested.

"So? She can still produce an heir."

Chapter 53

Williamsburg.

"TWO months I have languished in this bed, Colonel Barton. I need to be up and moving," Roderick said to his commanding officer.

Two months to do nothing but think of Georgie Kirkwood. Had she really said, "I love you," just before leaving him?

"I do not think you are ready for much of anything, Steady Roddie," Colonel Sir Charles Reginald Barton said. He dropped into the straight chair beside Roderick's bed. As usual, his uniform sparkled and his periwig looked freshly powdered and dressed. "You nearly died. Twice. Once from blood loss and again from fever. You are wasted and weak. The doctors do not believe you will ever recover fully."

"The doctors know nothing. They treat every wound by lopping off limbs."

"Be grateful I persuaded the sawbones to leave your legs intact," Sir Charles smiled.

"I cannot stay in my quarters a day longer, sir." Roderick tried to sit up and found himself dizzy with weakness and short of breath before he managed to inch upward. Thick bandages on his shoulder and around his chest bound him tightly and constricted his breathing. Fire lanced outward from the barely closed wound. "This place stinks of sweat, and fear, and blood," he said more quietly. The fear was his own. Fear that he might never get out of his sickbed.

Fear that he might never see Georgie again.

"Just as I thought, Steady Roddie, you are not fit to get out of bed, let alone return to your duties."

"I will be shortly, if Ian will help me out of bed and get me moving again." Roderick reached for the little bell on his bedside table, a new feature since his wounding.

"Stay, Roddie." Sir Charles stopped Roderick's reach. "I have bad news for you. You are to be pensioned off."

"What!" Roderick almost exploded out of bed. Dizziness brought black stars before his vision. Sharp, hot pain forced him back against the bolster, clutching his bandages.

Pressure against the wound helped ease some of his discomfort. Lying absolutely still made the dizziness almost controllable.

"I can't live on half a major's pay."

"I promoted you to lieutenant colonel before I signed the pension papers," Sir Charles said. His round face took on a grimace of pity.

Roderick turned his face to the wall rather than watch his friend and superior try to mask his emotions.

"That will keep me from begging in the streets but won't keep a roof over my horse and my servant," Roderick grumbled. He began listing his options. Then he realized he didn't have any.

"You could go home. The army will pay your passage."

"My brother is poorer than I am."

"I may have another solution, Whythe."

Roderick turned back to look the colonel in the eye. The man smiled with a glimmer of hope in his eyes.

"What? Make me a clerk, penning letters for you for the rest of my life?" A boring life, but at least he'd be useful and out of this bed.

"Something better. A Mr. Cummings waits to see you. He has an interesting proposition."

"Cummings? I don't know . . . does he have a daughter, pretty little brunette?"

"As a matter of fact he does." Sir Charles' grin stretched wider. "I'll fetch him for you."

With that Sir Charles nearly bolted out of Roderick's quarters.

Two heartbeats later, Roderick heard a light tap upon his door. Before he could answer, a short man in full wig, dressed in fashionable wine-colored velvet breeches and coat with a bright-pink-and-blue waistcoat entered. He carried a silver-topped walking stick and held an apple-and-cinnamon pomander to his nose.

"Lieutenant Colonel Whythe, I presume," the man said in a slow drawl typical of the locals.

"Mr. Cummings, I presume. Forgive me for not rising to greet you," Roderick replied.

"Quite understandable." Cummings gestured vaguely with his walking stick. "May I sit?" He looked askance at the stark furnishings and the absence of amenities.

"Please, make yourself comfortable. My batman will fetch tea if you like." Roderick reached for the bell once more.

"No need, my boy. I shan't stay long."

"What brings you here, sir?" No sense in beating around the bush. Sleep dragged at Roderick's eyes and sat heavily upon his chest.

"I have come with an offer." Cummings looked at the ceiling, the floor, at the shuttered window, everywhere except directly at Roderick. His pale cheeks took on the color of ripe strawberries.

Roderick waited while the man collected his thoughts and perhaps his courage.

"My daughter has found herself in some . . . difficulty."

"Major Marlowe?"

"Ah, yes. You heard." His expression fell into one of deep sadness.

"Major Marlowe explained the situation in confidence, just before he left town. I doubt he told anyone else," Roderick reassured the man.

"I have considerable assets, Lieutenant Colonel. I am a man of property and respected in Williamsburg. I have held a seat in the House of Burgesses." He puffed up his slight chest and assumed a posture of pride. "I cannot afford to have a scandal of this nature blight my name."

"I understand. I shall speak of it to no one."

"Of course." Another long moment of embarrassed silence.

"Why are you here, Mr. Cummings?" Roderick really needed some sleep. He needed to think and plan his bleak future.

"To ask you to marry my daughter, sir. And to give a

legitimate name to her child, my heir. My daughter's dowry
is one hundred acres, a house, and three slaves."

"What?" All thoughts of sleep fled Roderick's cob-
webby mind. Could he even consider marrying someone
other than Georgie?

Did he have any other choice?

Kirkenwood, spring, 1765.

Emily awoke screaming. She stabbed the empty air with
the end of her staff. The blood-dipped black claws that
haunted her dreams retreated. She wiped sweat from her
brow with her palm. Her tangled hair caught in her fingers.
She tugged at it, trying to loosen the mass.

The demon faded from her awareness. Sleep and her
nightmare drifted away as mist in sunshine.

Her breathing slowly eased and she began to make sense
of the small, stark room around her. She recognized the
shape of the moor visible outside the small window to her
left. Home. She'd managed to come home. Kirkenwood.
Papa. Safety.

Home.

How? When?

Bits of memories flashed across her mind and fled just as
rapidly.

A strange scratching noise came from the door. She
tensed and waited. The sound came again.

Her instinctive fear retreated. Whatever had chased her
in her dreams would not dare intrude upon the sanctity of
Kirkenwood.

She staggered from her bed, needing to investigate the
noise. Her nightgown tangled around her legs. She jabbed
at the carpet with her staff. Three more stumbling steps and
she found her balance. Of sorts. Without the staff to hold
her upright, her room tilted steeply to the left.

She paused a moment studying the strange perspective
of the world standing on its edge. Or was she standing
upon the edge of the world?

Did the world have edges?

She did not think so. The big globe in Papa's study was

round. Like a ball. It showed England and the other countries in pretty colors. The ocean looked blue. A deep and compelling blue. Like Papa's eyes. Kirkwood eyes. Her own eyes.

"Papa." Tears spilled down her cheeks. She missed Papa. She had not seen him in ever so long.

"Where are you, Papa?"

In the study of course. Not the public study where the servants cleaned and he received visitors. The other study. The hidden one behind the wine rack. The place where . . . She could not remember what Papa did in that study. Only that it was important work. Work she shared with him.

"I must go there."

The door latch refused her touch. She passed the staff over it murmuring a few words in ancient Welsh. She did not know the meaning of the words, only that someone had taught them to her. The simple spell should open any mundane lock.

Still the door refused to open.

"Who would dare ward my door?" She passed the staff across the entire door and spoke a stronger spell more clearly.

The scratching sound came again. Then the latch shifted and the door swung open. A large wolfhound bitch stood there, waiting, watching. A smaller version of herself paced behind her, keeping a lookout along the corridor.

"Belle?" Something stirred in Emily's mind. Belle. Her father's wolfhound, his familiar. The dogs chose the Pendragon. Why was Belle at her door with a half grown pup at her heels.

"Where have you been hiding, Belle? I have not seen you for ages, not since before . . ." A flash of memory. Falling. Falling at the foot of the standing stones. Terrible pain. Fear. Burning pain. Searing headaches. Running. Before that climbing. Always climbing away from . . . A black tunnel opening before her. Papa at the end of the tunnel. Papa surrounded by light, reaching out to her. Saving her.

The huge dog trotted into Emily's room and looked around. The pup followed her closely, nose working busily at ground level as well as in the air. Belle snorted in approval and looked steadily into Emily's eyes.

"What do I need to do, Belle?"

Belle nudged the pup over to Emily with her snout. The brindled bundle of big feet, long legs, and curious nose galumphed around the room and plunked herself at Emily's feet. She thrust her muzzle into Emily's hand and leaned heavily against her.

"Ana," Emily breathed. "Your name is Ana and you are mine."

Belle trotted back out into the hallway, nudging the door closed again with her snout.

The slight click echoed a shift within Emily's mind. The room lost its tilt. Her thinking sought straight lines instead of a downward spiral. She began to remember things. Not her time in the Otherworld. That would take more time and deeper concentration than she could devote to it now. Now she remembered strange women in maids' uniforms forcing liquid down her throat that made her limbs heavy and her thoughts disjointed. She remembered Dr. Marlowe standing over her, shaking his head and muttering things. Things about finding the archives. About needing her and Papa alive until he found the archives. Then he would gladly kill her, her father, her baby brother, and allow Kirkenwood to go to ruin.

She remembered Cousin Milton Marlowe proclaiming her insane.

Ana licked her hand solicitously.

Emily received a mental picture of Belle hiding in a cave down by the lake where she whelped her puppies and nursed them until they were big enough to hunt on their own and defend themselves against a murderer. A magical murderer who still lurked about Kirkenwood.

"Will you protect me against a magical murderer, Ana?" The young dog grinned, tongue lolling out of the side of her mouth. "Who is it, girl? Who do we have to defend ourselves against?"

Ana had no idea. She wanted a run on the moors with her dam.

"Tonight, Ana. Tonight, you and I will sneak out and go for a run. We have to be strong. We have to gain strength to fight our enemies. By day we have to hide, you in the cave, me behind a mask of insanity. He won't kill me as long as he thinks I am too addled to know what he's doing."

She thought a moment, while she petted the dog.

"I'm not insane anymore. I know who I am and where I am. But I have to pretend that I am otherwise. I can watch and listen safely if everyone thinks I have no wits."

Ana got up and sniffed the entire room.

"We need to reset the wards around the archives, Ana. The spells must be so strong and complicated neither I nor Papa can spring them. Only then will they be safe from Cousin Milton."

Chapter 54

Boston, spring, 1765.

WHEN the ice in Boston Harbor broke, the ships returned. Mail and newspapers from England became the talk of the city.

I received a letter from Richard "Omniscient" Jackson. His note stated that his private courier had delivered my letter into the hands of my niece. He had enclosed my brother's reply.

> *My Dearest Sister,*
> *We are all well. Belle has whelped and kept all of her puppies. Therefore I must presume I am to live a while longer.*
>
> *Young Griffin thrives. He grows fat and has cut new teeth. All of my girls fare well and send you their love.*
>
> *Your mission in the New World is most important. Please continue there. You have no special reason to come home.*
>
> *I regret that I am unable to send you your allowance at this time. The wool market is not up to standard and I find myself short of coin.*
>
> *The mails are now subject to mistrust on all colonial matters. I trust this courier but no one else. Do not be frightened if many long months pass before you receive another letter.*
>
> *Your loving brother,*
> *Drake*

The missive was sealed with the emblem of the Pendragon. The handwriting looked to be my brother's. But the phrasing was too simple, too terse. Did I trust the letter?

The mails might be subject to suspicion, but what about the special, but imperfect, bond Drake had worked so hard to establish? I should be able to touch his mind with a concentrated spell in a scrying bowl.

All I touched was a milky swirl of fog.

As long as Barclay and his demon remained in the colonies, so must I. I would find him eventually. He could not remain hidden forever.

Lord Sackville remained silent and his purse strings closed. I had to stay in Boston. Without money, I could not pay for passage. My letter of credit had expired.

Even though the ice broke, Boston remained in the grip of winter well into April.

I had not endured a colder or more snowy winter since I had left Kirkenwood for good. The hardy colonials bundled up, hunkered down, and drank to keep warm. The Green Dragon kept a fire blazing in the hearth and in one of the new Franklin stoves that sat away from the wall, radiating heat throughout the building. We replenished candles twice a day and made the place inviting to one and all. In the depth of a cold snap that lasted ten days even wives and children huddled inside the public house drinking hot possets rather than spend money on extra fuel at home.

Every Wednesday evening we women gathered for our meeting and the men gathered for their Lodge. I found no need to dress as a man and join the Lodge. For the first time in my life the women offered me a community I could appreciate and enjoy.

They gave me introductions by letter to many women throughout the colony. I found myself exchanging political ideas with Abigail Adams and her friends. One in particular, Mercy Otis Warren, began penning scathing political poems that we saw published in the *Massachusetts Spy*. I forwarded many of these ditties to Emily and encouraged her to correspond with my friends. I never heard if she did.

When spring came, it burst forth upon the land like a colorful explosion of fireworks. With it came a flurry of bustle and noise so characteristic of this city. Perhaps the loudest noise was the voice of Samuel Adams as he enjoined the citizenry to fight the coming Stamp Act with violence.

At first few listened to him. They had too much work at hand to mind his words. The hated Stamp Tax would not begin until November. Time enough to resist and fight after the plowing and planting, repairing winter damage to houses and docks. In the meantime couples rushed to the altar to avoid paying for a stamp upon their marriage lines. Men of substance hastened to write their wills for similar reasons. Land and cargo sales were also hastened. Men renewed or sought licenses to sell drink as well as any other legal activity early, before a stamp was required.

After the early crowding of the port, the number of ships decreased. Editorials and Mercy's poems urged all colonials to refrain from purchasing English manufactured goods. When Mrs. Hutchinson, the Chief Justice's wife, appeared in church wearing ribands and lace, she was shunned by every woman present. All across the colonies orders for manufactured goods and luxuries from England dwindled to nothing. We made do with what we had, or what we could make. Women who previously teetered on the edge of bankruptcy and starvation found new incomes from spinning and weaving cloth that no longer came from England.

And still Parliament insisted the Stamp Act must go forth. November of this year, 1765, was set for the Stamps to be delivered and required upon every document and legal transaction in the colonies.

My needlework improved by force of practice. I had to mend my clothing myself. At least my trunk arrived from Williamsburg with several changes of clothing and fresh petticoats. Mistress Camden and her neighbors spent many a morning with me, sewing and gossiping. I learned more about the doings of my neighbors through them than I thought possible. They became a valuable source of information.

I sent one last letter to Lord Sackville, informing him that without funds I could not afford to send him my reports or buy ink and paper.

I heard vague whispers about raids upon distant farms. The Indians had become particularly vicious, dismembering the bodies of their victims and scattering the pieces so far the poor souls could not be buried whole.

Colonists accused the Indians, a familiar menace. I suspected Barclay's demon. Discreet inquiries about a white man with deep blue eyes living among the Indians met with a wall of silence.

I thought to travel westward and investigate myself when the army announced a truce had been signed with Chief Pontiac. The raids ceased abruptly.

A new "Lodge" or secret society sprang up around the Green Dragon. They called themselves the "Sons of Liberty." Their membership was secret, but everyone knew that Sam Adams led them. Everyone knew that this group was funded by St. Andrew's Lodge. Everyone knew that membership in St. Andrew's Lodge became synonymous with membership in the Sons of Liberty. But no one talked about it in front of the increasing numbers of red-coated British soldiers in Boston. I certainly did not report to General Gage or any of the other officers.

Until the army revealed Barclay Marlowe's whereabouts, I gave them nothing in the way of information, though I could have earned many a coin for what I had to sell.

Roderick Whythe did not appear in Boston, though I looked for him with every passing patrol. Thom Jefferson corresponded with me. Discreet inquiries to him about Roderick revealed nothing.

Summer descended upon Boston in a miasma of heat and humidity, relieved only slightly by the ocean breeze. With the rising heat came rising tempers. Brawls broke out throughout the city; most involved British soldiers.

Sam Adams bragged how he orchestrated them with his hired bullies.

I decided the time had come to join the St. Andrew's Freemason Lodge and, by default, the Sons of Liberty. Each Wednesday night I became Georgie White, a student of law at Harvard.

In Virginia, Patrick Henry proposed a radical resolution that denounced not only the legality of the Stamp Act but Parliament's right to enforce the act. The House of Burgesses passed a modified version of the resolution. Still the language was inflammatory. Lieutenant Governor Francis Fauquier dissolved the assembly. They immediately reconvened in the Apollo Room above the Raleigh Tavern.

I wished I had been there.

Eight other colonial assemblies followed suit, passing similar resolutions. They all professed their love of the king as well as their rights as citizens of England. They acknowledged the king's, and therefore Parliament's, right to place customs duties and import and export taxes upon the colonies. Those contributions to the Exchequer were a fair share. Other than that, only the colonial assemblies of duly elected representatives had the right to impose direct taxes upon the colonies.

A new phrase was on everyone's lips. "No taxation without representation."

The phrase hinted at freedom and taking responsibility for that freedom. They did not object to taxes per se. Only over who implemented them and how. They would pay taxes to maintain their freedom. But to their own duly elected assemblies, not to a foreign Parliament.

More and more the government in London began to seem like a foreign power.

Noisy demonstrations occurred in every major city in the colonies. Citizens of Philadelphia threatened the homes of Benjamin Franklin and his chosen Stamp Agent John Hughes. Franklin had indeed traveled to London and advised caution by letter. His missives took months to arrive. In the meantime, his son William, the Royal Governor of New Jersey pleaded with his mother Deborah to retire from the family home to the safety of his palace in New Jersey. She refused. For nine days demonstrators besieged her house. In the end they retired. I do not know if they dispersed in the face of that woman's courage or because of their respect for Franklin. I like to think the former.

A mob of unemployed and dispossessed men and women gathered around Sam Adams in Boston. He controlled them with rhetoric and a few coins. A few members of St. Andrew's Lodge, legitimate members of the Sons of Liberty, added weight and authority to their numbers. I was not among them.

Yet.

Smashed windowpanes, broken shutters, and bruised pates followed in their wake. They patrolled the streets of Boston in increasing numbers. Everyone in the city held their breath and walked cautiously whenever Adams or his mob appeared on the streets.

British soldiers retreated down alleys or stood their ground with muskets loaded and ready whenever they approached.

I wondered if Barclay had loosed a different kind of demon upon the city. But I found no trace of magic and no hint of burned sulfur.

Chief Justice Thomas Hutchinson continued with plans for implementing the Stamp Act in Massachusetts.

One hot, humid, and miserable night in August, the Sons of Liberty met in the upper room of the Green Dragon. I sat in a corner quietly cursing the heat and the weight of my coat atop my shirt and the constricting breast band that concealed my sex. Shouts of indignation floated around me like so much fetid air rising from the sewage in the harbor.

I had heard it all before and rose to leave.

A strong and square hand upon my sleeve detained me. "Why do you leave?" Paul Revere asked me with that hint of a French lilt in his voice.

"I am tired of all this talk. Talk will not gain Parliament's attention. If we want freedom from Parliament, then we must act upon our demands."

"Some of us believe as do you. Stay a bit. Later, we will show Parliament that we mean business when we say we will not pay this unlawful tax." His gaze met mine. I detected a hint of steel beneath the brightness of excitement.

"How?" I asked as I sat back down, intrigued.

"You have served in the military?"

"Common knowledge that I fought as a mercenary in Austria, along the Ottoman border."

"You know of tactics and strategy?"

"Some."

"*Bon.* We have need of you."

Chapter 55

Boston, August, 1765.

AND so I found myself swept up in a rapid exodus of the airless room above the Green Dragon. Caution warred with my curiosity. I needed to know what these men planned and if a demon drove them.

I cast out my senses for traces of magic and the scent of Barclay's demon. I came up empty, free of Barclay's evil, and yet frustrated that once again I must postpone our inevitable battle.

The Sons of Liberty, with me in their midst, burst forth onto Union Street into an equally hot and humid night. Some extra sense inside me knew that a thunderstorm gathered to the northeast. The air crackled with the tension of lightning building and tempers too long confined.

No one seemed to be leading the mob as we pressed forward. Then I spotted Sam Adams near the front.

A word passed among us. "Hutchinson."

Thomas Hutchinson, Chief Justice for the Crown Colony of Massachusetts. The man responsible for the execution of the Stamp Act. And a pompous pain in the ass.

A chill of unease passed through me.

We veered right, almost due east, onto Middle Street, headed for the Cockerel Church. One block farther, where Middle Street angled left to become North Street, stood the Hutchinson mansion with its extensive gardens, stables, fences, and gates.

I had no doubt that the direction of the mob had come from Sam Adams, a lawyer who had butted heads, pride,

and philosophies with Hutchinson many times. I half expected them to unbutton, whip out their willies, and
begin a contest of size and how far and how much they
could piss.

But this conflict went beyond strong-minded men
matching wills. Did I want to be a part of it? Did I dare cast
aside my family, centuries of Pendragons guiding England
toward peace, balance, and justice?

I began to tremble with excitement. Drake and Emily
and their wolfhounds continued the Pendragon line in
England.

I could start a new one in this land.

Revere grabbed my elbow and began maneuvering me
toward the front of the no longer directionless mob.
"Sam," Revere shouted into Adams' ear. "He'll know how
to do it proper, so few of us get hurt." Then he thrust me
against Adams and retreated—or was pushed back by the
men closest to Adams who were too eager for violence.

"How do we get in?" Adams asked in his clipped precise
way. No preamble. No introductions. He had not the time
or inclination for politeness. Ever. But he got things done.

I took a deep breath. I had advocated action over rhetoric. Now I had to decided where I placed my trust. With
King George and his Parliament? With centuries of family
heritage and tradition? Or with the people of this new land
who sought ways to determine their own destiny?

No one at home seemed to want me or need me.

I had always defied a society that sought to confine me
and dictate my decisions for me. For five years I had fought
as a mercenary, a lone woman fighting side by side with
hardened warriors.

These men, the Sons of Liberty and the St. Andrew's
Lodge, defied convention to fight a different battle.

They broke rules as easily as did I.

I had worked as assassin and mage with a Lodge that
sought political balance worldwide, not just in England. I
had to look at the entire picture, not just England's self-
centered viewpoint.

My choice was clear.

My blood sang with excitement as it did just before I
rode into battle against the Turks.

Plans leaped to my mind with ease and clarity. "If

Hutchinson has guards, they will face the street, not the Clark House next door. You need men at each gate and a few nimble ones to climb over the wall from Clark's to Hutchinson's to open the gates from the inside. Only the men in front need torches to keep the attention of the guards."

I paused for breath and let those suggestions sink into Adams' mind. "The men must stick to our plan, minor damage to the house only. No threats to the people within. You need to stay out of sight or be implicated and probably arrested."

Adams nodded and grunted. As the tall chimneys of the Hutchinson estate came into view beyond the steeple of the Cockerel Church, he issued terse orders, pointing to his lieutenants in turn. "You, take five to the east gate. You take six to the back. You ten are with me at the front."

"Where do you want me?" I asked, expecting to stay by his side to whisper advice.

"You are nimble and lithe. Take two more, any two you like with you through the back of the Clark grounds and over the wall into Hutchinson's." Adams fixed his fierce gaze upon me.

I grinned at him impudently. Then I ran my hands through the dust accumulated between the cobbles. This I smudged across my face. Nighttime reconnaissance had always been my forte. It was fun.

I looked about for the most likely lads to accompany me. Three stout fellows looked at me expectantly, including Revere. I dismissed them as unlikely to get over the wall quietly.

Two wharf rats with permanently dirty faces shoved themselves forward. About my size, I guessed they had plenty of practice squeezing into and out of hidey-holes with a minimum of noise. A third youth hovered around the edges of the mob. Black of skin, I guessed him to be born of freed slaves or freed by his white father. If he belonged to someone, he'd not be running free with this mob on a hot and sultry evening. His long legs and skinny frame suited my purposes. I summoned him forward.

The four of us darted down a side street, past Paul Revere's home and silversmithy and engraving shop to Fish Street and then angled into the back of North Square. We stood in the shadow of the old North Meeting House a moment to find our best path.

The mob began crowding around the conjoined mansions of Boston's two most elite families.

Cautiously, we circled back to the junction of Middle Street and North Street.

Here, I found what I was looking for. A gardener's gate into the lush grounds of the Clark House. Set into the brick wall, its latch proved no match for my mind. I twisted it and pretended that a careless groundskeeper had left it unlocked.

We slithered through the opening, so many shadows among the natural darkness. Josiah, the colored youth and the tallest among us, cupped his hands and boosted me up to the top of the six-foot wall between the two houses. I could have jumped and scrambled up, but the young man wanted to help. I gave him the opportunity to prove himself.

I perched atop the rounded capstones a moment, surveying the cushions of shadows that indicated shrubs. The scent of roses wafted across my nose, warning me of thorns to avoid. Then the sharp smell from the silver herb garden.

When I knew the lay of the land, I reached a hand to help the next man up to my level. Once he was firmly beside me, I dropped down into a soft mulch, recently watered, surrounding an azalea. The springy greenery rustled but did not rattle. One by one, my coconspirators joined me. Josiah made it over the wall without help. I pointed them toward the different gates. They were to unlatch the portals and swing them partially open. Then they were to melt into the shadows until Sam Adams' mob invaded the grounds. I kept Josiah by my side and headed toward the front, facing the square.

The Sons of Liberty had indeed produced torches and lit them. They chanted slogans against the proposed tax. Their words became slurred, slid into obscenity, took on new meaning. The chant grew in volume. They shook their torches and pounded against the gate and the wall.

For a brief, frightening moment I thought they might break through the bricks.

As the front gate swung open, the ugly fierceness of their angry faces chilled my excitement. My stomach turned. I swallowed deeply. Violence was not new to me. I was a soldier. Yet all my battles had been fought in the open, directed by generals, backed by governments.

These men wanted blood for blood's sake. The goal of breaking a few valuables and burning official correspondence regarding the Stamp Act had disappeared under the prospect of the possibility of murdering Thomas Hutchinson and his family.

A riot would gain Parliament's attention, but in the wrong way. If Hutchinson, a royal official, or his family were hurt in any way, Parliament would not rescind the Stamp Act. They would more likely send additional troops to enforce it.

I had to find a way to control these men before things got out of hand.

What could I do? My sword and rapier along with my dagger-pistol lay hidden beneath my bed at Goodwife Camden's. I had only an ordinary dirk thrust into my belt.

A cat meowed and stropped my ankles. I jumped and nearly lost my balance, startled by Oblegid's sudden appearance. I had thought her safely tucked up in my room, sleeping away the heat.

She informed me that a hot summer night was the best time for hunting.

Josiah stroked her calico fur. He grinned. His white teeth glimmered in the torchlight.

Oblegid, help me, I implored my familiar.

Not yet, she replied. *Too soon.*

She was right, of course. If we used magic to throw a blanket of calm over the mob now, they would disperse, wondering why they had gathered in first place. We needed to make a show of determination against the Stamp Act.

I hated the idea of using magic. Cheating in battle. My skills as a soldier and leader of an army should suffice.

This is not an army, but a mob.

The time will come when we need an army.

Who said that? I did not recognize the voice in the back of my head as coming from Oblegid or my brother. Barclay? No. The thought was too logical, too calm.

I shrugged it off and returned my concentration to the mob and their mission.

The two armed soldiers who stood outside Hutchinson's

front door backed into the house, unwilling to face the mob on their own. Twenty to thirty men against two on foot were not odds I would take, even with extra arms loaded and ready.

The mob surged through the gate. They yelled obscenities and snarled.

The hair on my nape stood on end in fear of them.

The door buckled under the pressure of a dozen fists pounding upon it.

A man hurled his torch through a window opened to let any cool breeze into the house. The draperies caught fire.

I watched a man yank the draperies free and smother the flames.

More windows smashed. New fires broke out. The door crashed inward. Men surged forward.

I leaped after them, Oblegid at my heels. Josiah hung back. Mentally I urged him to stay there or return home and take his wharf rat companions with him. I could not see Adams in the crowd. If he were caught in this mess, Hutchinson would see that he rotted in gaol. Or hanged.

Inside, the mob began random destruction of furnishings. They threw fragile French chairs against the walls where they splintered. A treasure trove of books fairly flew off their shelves and into hands that tore off the covers and ripped the pages. Fine porcelains crashed into the brick hearth. Knives slashed at brocaded walls and delicate upholstery.

Too many torches came dangerously close to starting fires.

Thomas Hutchinson, his wife, and young daughters huddled in a corner of the parlor. The two armed soldiers stood between them and the mob, their weapons aimed into the heart of the crowd of invaders.

> *"By the Earth that is my bones,*
> *By the Air that I breathe,*
> *By the Water in my blood,*
> *By the Fire of my spirit,*
> *I bless the powers of life.*
> *I seek balance among the elements.*
> *I seek balance in these men."*

I chanted the simple spell over and over. Oblegid wound the symbol of infinity around my ankles. She added her meows to punctuate my pleas. I stood in the doorway, a symbolic portal between this world and the next, between life and death, between violence and peace. With my feet braced wide and my arms extended, I pulled violence from the air and grounded it.

With a unified snarl the mob backed away from the royal Chief Justice and found his study. A man who liked neatness and order, Hutchinson had filed away all his correspondence rather than leave it lying upon his desk. The curse of a neat and orderly mind, the men had no trouble finding what they sought in logical drawers and cupboards. They hauled stacks of parchments, official seals, and wax into the front garden.

I repeated my chant of balance and peace again and again.

The Sons of Liberty contented themselves with burning the papers and melting the wax. The seals fell victim to the flames as well.

One more plea for balance.

Adams called them to order and they dispersed, leaving Hutchinson and his family frightened but unharmed.

"Bless you, young man, whoever you are," Mistress Hutchinson called to me as her husband ushered her upstairs.

"Hush. Those pagan spells are as dangerous as the heathen mob," Thomas Hutchinson hissed at his wife. "We'll not speak of this man again. Nor what he did. If he did anything. 'Twas probably all for show."

I nodded and backed away, letting the shadows hide my identity. I sincerely hoped Mistress Hutchinson did not recognize me as the woman who stood behind her and to the left on Wednesday nights at meeting. And if she did, would she betray me?

Chapter 56

Whythe plantation, Virginia, August, 1765.

RODERICK sat upon the knoll overlooking his white clapboard house in lonely silence. In the distance his slaves sang their mournful hymns. Ian had taken off for town to visit his lady love. Sunday afternoon Roderick had no duties to command his attention or his energy.

He had only his sleeping daughter in his lap and a tombstone at his side.

"I miss you, Jane," he said. "I know we barely knew each other. But I miss your laughter that lit the house. I miss talking to you."

He let a long period of silence engulf him before he spoke again. "Zaneta looks to be cutting a tooth. Ian rubbed some whiskey on her gums so she would sleep. Our daughter is growing fast. She discovered her hand yesterday. She holds it in front of her face all the while she's awake and just stares at it. Such awe on her face."

The baby in question burbled and opened her eyes. She smiled up at Roderick and showed him the wonder of her fist. Roderick grabbed his daughter's hand in two fingers and caressed it. He shared meaningless baby talk with her for a few moments until a smile replaced his gloom.

"Ah, there you are," John Cummings said as he panted up the hill. "A pretty view. Can't see why else you'd traipse all the way up here." He looked around at the fertile fields of tobacco, corn, and beans.

Today he wore blue satin with a yellow-and-pink-brocade waistcoat. In the past nine months Roderick did not think he had seen his father-in-law in the same suit twice.

"I bring Zaneta up here whenever I can. I think she should get to know her mother a bit." Roderick looked at Jane's tombstone and sighed.

Cummings glanced briefly at his daughter's resting place, then quickly back to the fields.

"The tobacco is near to harvesting," Roderick said. He never knew what else to talk about to the man other than the plantation and the weather.

"I expect you'll be moving on then, as soon as you deliver the leaves to the broker." Cummings sat down on the other side of Jane's tombstone from Roderick. He kept his eyes focused on the fields rather than look at his granddaughter.

"I intend to stay and work my daughter's land," Roderick replied. He looked at Cummings sharply.

"She's not . . ." Cummings bit off his comment. "No need for you to stay. You fulfilled your obligation to me. You married my daughter and gave the babe a legitimate name. I'll take the plantation off your hands and raise the child. As I did her mother."

"I have an obligation to my daughter. I'm staying."

"Look, we both know the babe was sired by someone else. You barely knew Jane. You certainly couldn't have loved her, soiled goods and all. You've recovered well enough from your wounds. You can take off, return to England. Do what you want." Cummings gestured broadly in his affable guise. Behind his bright voice lay acute cunning. He'd amassed several fortunes by jumping upon every opportunity to make and keep his money.

"The land reverted from Jane to my daughter, according to the marriage contract. I intend to stay and work it." Roderick placed Zaneta upon his shoulder, gently rubbing her back.

"The land is mine. I bought it, cleared it, got it working. I want it back."

"Then take me to court. The land belongs to my daughter."

They stared at each other a long moment.

"No need to go to court. How much do you want for me to take the land off your hands?"

"I want nothing from you. Zaneta and I belong here. This is our home."

"I will take you to court . . . you're an unfit father."

"Oh? And you would make a better one? You don't even know your granddaughter's name."

"You are nothing, just a common soldier."

"I am the son of a baronet. And I carry the rank of lieutenant colonel, retired. I may be an officer and a gentleman, but I am willing to tell the whole truth of how I came to marry Jane. You will never get elected to the House of Burgesses again. You will never be appointed agent for Virginia in London. You will become the laughingstock of Williamsburg. I will keep the plantation in my daughter's name."

"Stubborn fool. You'll get no more help from me. Try running this mere one hundred acres on your own. You'll be bankrupt in a year." Cummings stalked back down the hill to his light carriage parked at the front of the house.

"Stubborn fool I may be, but I'm your father, Zaneta, and I intend to do my best for you, no matter what it takes."

As long as he had Zaneta, he need not think too long or too hard upon Georgie Kirkwood and her parting words to him.

"I love you."

Kirkenwood, summer, 1765.

> *"Ring around the rosie*
> *Pocket full of posie*
> *Ashes*
> *Ashes*
> *We all fall down!"*

Emily spun in a circle as she sang until she grew dizzy and fell down.

The tall, silent bodyguard outside Milton Marlowe's suite—the *Master* suite of Kirkenwood Manor—raised his eyebrows and quirked a smile at her performance.

She idly traced the roses woven into the carpet beneath her, continuing her nursery rhyme.

Damnation! That bodyguard was everywhere, watching her. Always watching her. How could she sneak past him to the main staircase and then outside to spend time with Ana, her wolfhound, with him always watching her?

She couldn't use the back stairs. Peters, Milton's secretary, and one of the nursery maids kissed and fondled there.

She gathered her knees beneath her and raised her arms as if touching hands with some invisible playmate opposite her.

> *"London Bridge is falling down*
> *Falling down, falling down*
> *London Bridge is falling down . . ."*

"Time for you to go back to bed, Lady Emily." The bodyguard bent down and lifted her effortlessly into his arms.

Emily forced herself to lie limply, though she gnashed her teeth in frustration.

> *"Sing a song of six pence*
> *Pocket full of rye."*

"No need to get upset, Lady Emily, I have something that will soothe you."

Emily tensed. She would not take Milton's medicine. She would not become listless and malleable like her father.

"Not the medicine." The bodyguard chuckled.

Had he read her mind? He must have. Milton employed only magicians. Evil, blood magicians. Emily had watched Milton draw blood from this man for a scrying spell. They all smelled of old blood and mold and decay.

"My name is Samuel, by the by," the bodyguard said as he laid Emily upon her narrow bed. Then he closed the door. He made several arcane gestures around the frame. "I can't lie to Dr. Marlowe. He'll know if I do. So I have to burn these letters." He pulled a fat packet from inside his black coat. "But first I thought you might want me to read them to you."

Emily couldn't help herself. She had to stare at the man.

"Ah, I see there is some awareness in your eyes. I thought as much." He chuckled again as he drew a straight chair close to her bed and adjusted the candle to shine upon the letters. "Let's see if we can reach a little deeper inside you."

Then softly he began reading a letter from Aunt Georgie explaining that she had to move from Williamsburg to Boston, that she worked in a tavern and listened closely to talk of rebellion. The next letter contained clippings from a colonial newspaper with some interesting poetry about loyalty and a second poem full of images about breaking chains of servitude to a foreign master. The letter also gave her the addresses of two women who might interest Emily, Abigail Adams and the author of the poetry, Mercy Otis Warren.

Samuel's voice drifted off. "That's enough for tonight, Lady Emily. I'm going into the study to burn these two, then come back tomorrow night and read some more. I don't think I'll hear a thing while I'm in there. A whole army could go up and down those stairs and I'd not know it."

At the door he repeated his gestures, reversing the wards. "Just be careful when you come back in. Peters will be staying in the maids' chamber close to the back stairs. He's a light sleeper."

Emily didn't stop to question what had just happened. She darted into the corridor and down the stairs to the French windows in the parlor. In moments she and Ana ran the length of the lake and into the woods seeking out herbs by smell and calling faeries to dance with them in the moonlight.

Boston.

Boston seethed with tension through the rest of that long hot summer of '65. Hutchinson made no arrests. His wife made no indication that she recognized me.

Both my brother and Lord Sackville remained silent.

I threw myself wholeheartedly into the St. Andrew's Lodge and my new loyalty. I belonged in the New World. My responsibilities to England and the family ceased.

I just wished I could find Barclay and get rid of his demon. Then my conscience would rest easy.

At Sam Adams' instigation, the Massachusetts Assembly called for a gathering of representatives from all of the colonies to meet in New York to take a stand on the taxation issue. Eight of the colonies sent representatives. They adopted a resolution very close to the one Virginia had proposed. Virginia, of course, could not send representatives to the congress. Their assembly had been officially suspended. Thom Jefferson, though, sent me by private courier a thick packet of letters from a number of prominent Virginians to pass on to Sam Adams.

The unity demonstrated by the Stamp Act Congress sent thrills of excitement up and down the coast. News traveled faster than post horses and the Royal Mail. Stamp Act riots in every major city and town began to resemble armed revolt.

I had to pause and think about that as, I was sure, did many others, leaders and followers alike. If we revolted against the king and Parliament, who would rule us?

Could we elect our own national Parliament and leader, as Englishmen had during the years of Oliver Cromwell's republic? We'd have to do a better job than Cromwell, for upon his death Englishmen had crawled back to Charles Stuart begging him to be our king.

King George III behaved as a king should. Prime Minister Grenville, the author of the Stamp Act, had failed in his leadership. The king replaced him with Lord Rockingham, a man who adopted a policy of wait and see.

November crept closer. The weather cooled, but tempers did not. The stamps arrived. Bands of the Sons of Liberty refused to allow them to be offloaded. After November 1, 1765, colonial agents argued that the stamps could not be delivered without an official stamp. None were available. In some ports the stamps were burned.

I served beer and food at the Green Dragon and watched and waited, much like our prime minister. Beer and ale being domestic products required no stamps for their sale and consumption. Other trade ground to a slow halt.

We made do, bartering for services, entering into common law marriages, delaying lawsuits and land exchanges, even criminal activity slowed because the courts could not charge, try, or sentence without stamps.

Debate raged in Parliament. Once more William Pitt, the

senior statesman of England, stepped forth. He transformed the issue of the Stamp Act from a matter of revenue gathering to the constitutional rights of the colonists. Our representatives, including Benjamin Franklin, spoke before the House of Commons. By law, his testimony could not be published. A transcript of it leaked to the public. His simple and logical statements, his unassuming dress, his wit, and his wisdom impressed many in and out of Parliament.

On March 18, 1766, King George gave his assent to the repeal of the Stamp Act. We had won!

But the king also accepted the Declaratory Act which reaffirmed Parliament's right to tax the colonies in any way they deemed necessary.

Business resumed. Life continued on a carefully balanced even keel. For a time.

Chapter 57

London, March 19, 1766.

"PETERS, make an appointment for me with William Pitt, Lord Chatham," Dr. Milton Marlowe said to his almost invisible secretary. He ground his teeth together as he paced before the hearth in a private lounge at his club. He cared not if his companion, Richard "Omniscient" Jackson, listened or not, gave advice or not. 'Twas more important to be seen with Pitt's private secretary than to actually converse with him.

"Chatham had no right to subvert my influence," Milton complained. The former prime minister had resisted magical influence time and again. He simply would not succumb to persuasion or coercion or compulsion.

"Pitt has always been an independent thinker. He sets policy, he does not follow others. Give it over, Dr. Marlowe," Jackson said. "The Stamp Act is dead and cannot be revived." He sat before a gaming table to one side of the hearth playing endless games of patience. A painted Chinese screen protected him from the blazing fire.

"The colonists must be punished!" Milton rounded upon the agent for Massachusetts and Connecticut, as well as Chatham's secretary, who was possibly the most influential man outside the cabinet these days.

"Colonial defiance of Parliament, unified and armed, certainly does not bode well for the empire . . ." Jackson did not look up from his fascination with the cards. "And yet that independent spirit of the colonists is why they were able to tame the wilderness, subdue the natives, and prosper. Their prosperity becomes England's prosperity."

"I do not care about prosperity. All Englishmen need to live more simply for the good of their souls. The colonists teeter on the edge of treason, they must be punished in order to bring them into line." Anger burned within Milton's gut.

As you have brought Drake and his daughter in line? Neville taunted him.

Neville's ghost had become less substantial since returning from Kirkenwood. Milton checked the shadows on the opposite side of the hearth from Peters to make certain Neville remained at least partially in this realm.

Colonists had turned their backs upon Neville and allowed him to be slaughtered. They were all responsible, all must pay for the loss of a beloved son.

Drake lies semiconscious in drugged fog hundreds of miles from here, Neville reminded him. *He does not obey you, so you resorted to drugs to control him. Him and his daughter.*

Sometimes Neville's voice sounded different, more mature, of a deeper register and more lilting cadence. As if the voice of another magician controlled him.

Nonsense. Drake was the only magician with enough talent and skill to do that. *Drake cannot interfere with our plans.*

Are you certain? That voice was different, many voices in one with a husky feminine voice dominating.

Who was that?

Do you truly wish to restore Neville to life, or do you become obsessed with punishing the colonies for taking his life?

Milton lashed out with a questing probe. The little bolt of magic dissipated without finding any target.

Neville laughed at him.

Jackson shivered and adjusted the screen to allow more heat to warm him.

"The colonists have shown that severe measures only provoke them to more severe rebellion." Jackson gathered his deck of cards and began shuffling them. "I agree with Lord Chatham. We need to work with them, not against them." His motions seemed idle, automatic. He did not lay the cards out again for another hand of patience.

"Are you a gambling man, Jackson?" Milton studied the man's hands, his fingers were long, elegant, and graceful. He manipulated the cards with considerable skill.

"Upon occasion." Jackson stilled his shuffling of the cards.

"Are you willing to gamble with England's future? Are you willing to bet that the French and Spanish do not see our capitulation on the Stamp Act as a weakness?"

"Neither the French nor the Spanish are in a position to take advantage of any perceived weakness."

"Are you certain?"

"I must think on this."

Milton pulled a lyre-back chair over to the card table with his foot, then swept aside the tails of his coat and sat across from the man he decided to woo into his sphere of influence.

"Deal, Mr. Jackson."

"What game?" Jackson met his gaze and held it steadily. He did not have the fixed stare of a man under magical influence.

"No game. Simple chance. One card each facedown." Milton kept his smile to himself. The cards obeyed him no matter what game he chose.

Jackson drew one card off the top and placed it facedown in front of Milton. His movements were slow and deliberate. Then he drew and placed a second card in front of himself.

"The stakes, Dr. Milton?"

Jackson's eyes remained clear rather than the fixed stare of a man under magical influence.

Your soul!

"Your support for my next tax plan for the colonies."

"I must represent my constituents and my clients honestly. Many of the people who elected me to Parliament lost a great deal of money when the colonists boycotted English goods. An effective political tool when organized and enforced. I also represent the interests of two colonies. I cannot betray any of them."

"Keeping England strong and out of war with France and Spain is in the best interests of all of your clients and constituents. We cannot afford another war." Milton allowed his voice to fall into a gentle chant, weaving subtle magic into each syllable.

Jackson's features relaxed, his eyes became glassy. "We must keep England strong," he mumbled.

Milton smiled, his influence snaring another powerful man into his nets.

"If I have the high card, you will support me unconditionally. If you have the high card, then we never met, and I never asked anything of you."

Jackson turned over a queen of clubs.

Milton turned over a seven of diamonds.

"You have the high card. You win," Jackson said again, still slurring his words. He had not even looked at the cards.

"I always win, Jackson."

Not this time! The air crackled and flashed. Tiny bolts of blue-and-yellow lightning sizzled between Milton and his quarry.

The energy shot into Milton's eyes, triggering a blinding headache.

Jackson blinked and shook his head. He looked at his card with clear eyes and mind. "My queen tops your seven, Milton. Sorry, old man. I cannot support your tax plans." He pushed back his chair and rose from the table. He adjusted his coat cuffs over the lace of his shirtsleeve. Then he turned on his heel and departed. His firm closing of the door reverberated in Milton's head like the tolling of a great bronze bell.

Milton pressed his hands against his temples, trying to contain the pain.

"Who did this?" he asked the air. Each word sent new waves of blinding light into his closed eyes. "Who has the power? Who would dare?"

Maniacal laughter swirled around him along with the odor of burned sulfur.

He could not think through the pain. Nausea besieged his stomach. Blindly he stumbled to the windows and stepped through onto a small balcony. Cold wind and rain blasted him from the north. He lifted his face, letting the chill air and water cleanse him of the backlashed magic.

Rain soaked his coat and breeches. Water dripped from his eyelashes and nose. He began to shiver.

And still the pain persisted.

Peters appeared at his elbow. "May I assist you, sir?"

Milton waved him away with a snarl. He scuttled away like a beetle.

"Where are you?" he whispered.

I am the wind.

"You are a magician. Therefore, you are human."

Am I?

"I will find you."

More high-pitched laughter that bordered on hysteria.

As the voice became less logical, his own mind began to clear. The pain receded like the tide.

"If you are this wind, then you come from the north."

The laughter sounded less certain. It circled around him, trying to confuse him. But it sounded loudest, most certain when it came from the north.

"Peters," he called into the salon, "we leave at dawn for Kirkenwood."

"Sir?" his secretary appeared from a side door. "The roads are still mired from the winter storms."

"Then we abandon the coach and ride. We return to Kirkenwood at dawn. Something has gone amiss."

"I have had no reports, sir."

"All of you are incompetent. I tell you something is amiss. I shall correct it."

But when he arrived at Kirkenwood, nothing had changed. Drake was still drugged to insensibility, the younger daughters still recited their lessons, and Emily was still an unwashed lunatic who wandered the halls reciting nursery rhymes.

Emily stared directly at him. For half a moment her eyes cleared of madness. Then she looked away and recited her latest poem.

> *"Hector Protector was dressed all in green;*
> *Hector Protector was sent to the queen.*
> *The queen did not like him,*
> *No more did the king;*
> *So Hector Protector was sent back again."*

What, in all the nine hells, did that mean?

Samuel just smiled at his questions and said he did not know.

Chapter 58

Williamsburg, October 1, 1769.

RODERICK walked into Colonel Sir Charles Reginald Barton's office near the Masonic Lodge on Queen Street in Williamsburg. If he did not have a few pounds to collect every quarter day, he did not know how he would manage to pay his taxes and provide for little Zaneta. Her curious mind gobbled up information as rapidly as he could provide it. His few books of sermons bored her. She needed a better education, a governess, something he could not afford. His meager one hundred acres just barely fed them and their few slaves. The cash crop of tobacco had produced smaller yields these last two years than ever before.

"Colonel Barton just stepped out, sir," the aide-de-camp said upon Roderick's inquiry. "I believe you can find him down at the King's Arms." The lieutenant proffered a small bag of coins and returned to the reports he penned.

Roderick accepted his pension and backed out of the military headquarters. Should he take the time to converse with his commanding officer?

Zaneta was safe with her nanny, one of the three slaves who were part of Jane's dowry. He needn't worry about her. But he did. No telling what kind of trouble her mischievous energy would conjure.

Still he wandered down Duke of Gloucester Street drinking in the familiar sights of the city. By the time he reached the loyalist tavern—as opposed to the Raleigh where the local rabble-rousers met—he hungered enough to warrant the expense of a few pence for a pastie and a beer.

Inside the bright and cheerful tavern, he found his colonel ensconced with three other officers at a table near the roaring fire. A mixture of wealthy planters and government officials sat at a scattering of tables nearby.

"Well met, my friend," Colonel Barton rose to greet Roderick with a handshake and an offer of beer and a pipe.

Roderick accepted both gratefully, including the pastie Barton added to the order.

The conversation continued on general topics of weather and the price of tobacco for several minutes.

Then five men at a nearby table raised their voices in argument.

"I tell you there are witches lurking about this city," one of the young assistant priests from the church said. He slurred his words a little as if he'd had one pint too many.

"Not just in the city, my friend," John Cummings added. Roderick's father-in-law waved his tankard around as if he, too, had drunk too much. But his eyes remained clear and he sloshed not a drop of his beer.

Roderick hunkered down, not willing to be noticed by Zaneta's grandfather.

"Witches are corrupting children on the outward plantations, teaching them in secret, plotting our destruction," Cummings continued.

"Like as not Jefferson and Randolph and them other Scottish Rite Freemasons are harboring them. All that mystical nonsense. Everyone knows they's but three degrees that's legal in Masonry," another man Roderick did not know continued.

"We can't allow the children to grow into their powers," Cummings insisted. "It's the children we have to worry about."

"And the ones that teach them," the priest added. "We have to stop them, one and all."

Colonel Barton groaned. "It looks as if we will have to go on a witch hunt for them or watch them burn the entire countryside in their crusade."

"How . . . how long has this talk been going on?" Roderick stammered. His mouth went dry and he lost his appetite.

"A month or more," Barton replied. "Cummings has this bee in his bonnet. He won't let it rest. Now that the harvest is in and All Hallows Eve approaches, he's gathering followers, men who didn't have time to listen to him before."

"Thank you for your hospitality, sir. The day grows late and the sun sets early now. I'd best be on my way." Roderick excused himself and half ran back to headquarters and his horse. He had to get back to Zaneta. Now. He had to make sure she was safe, no matter what. Nothing else mattered to him but his daughter's safety.

Boston, autumn, 1769.

A fierce knock came upon Goodwife Camden's front door. I looked up from the latest pamphlet that I composed for distribution at the Green Dragon—now Freemason Hall, having been purchased by the St. Andrew's Lodge—but no one called it that.

The knocking persisted. Only one person would dare come calling so early on a Friday morning, when everyone in Boston knew that my landlady shopped at the fish market.

Sam Adams come for the pamphlet he demanded I compose. I had not finished it. His Majesty's Army had occupied Boston Common last year under protest from the city. They were still there even though the number of troops overall in Boston had been reduced.

I grew tired of berating General Gage in my pamphlets for his occupation of the city common. Today I wrote protests against the Crown funding our governor, lieutenant governor, and chief justice. These officials no longer held loyalty to the colonies they governed because they owed us nothing. Nor had we the leverage to withhold salaries from incompetent or prejudiced men who worked against our best interests in the name of our duly anointed king.

Tomorrow I planned to write an inflammatory piece about the unfairness of His Majesty moving the Admiralty Court to Halifax, far away from the population centers. More and more petty offenses came under their jurisdiction. Once remanded to the Admiralty we had no recourse to trial by jury or choice of defense lawyer.

Yesterday I had written against the taxes and other

restrictions proposed by Chancellor of the Exchequer, Charles Townsend, before his death.

Soon I would rail against Parliament for invoking a law that dated back to the time of Henry VIII: any colonial accused of treason had to be transported back to London for trial. We no longer had the right of trial by a jury of our peers for serious crimes.

I dotted the last *i*, crossed the last *t*, and fixed the last period of the sentence. Then I set down my reading spectacles and made my slow way from the parlor to the front entrance.

Grudgingly, I opened the door to face a clenched fist ready to pound upon the wooden panels once more. I stood staring at the tall muscular man in a plain suit of brown gabardine, finely cut and tailored, but not of the best quality.

Not Samuel Adams. That firebrand cut not so fine a figure in his stained and patched blue coat and buff breeches. No one had seen the bandy-legged rabble-rouser in any other clothing for years.

"Roderick Whythe, you live," I said on a long exhalation and forgot to breathe in again.

"Obviously." He clenched his jaw as if he begrudged even that one word.

I held his gaze, begging him with my eyes to forgive me for abandoning him.

He did not look away, but his expression remained stern.

"Did you—or your brother—find your Marlowe?"

I breathed a little easier. He did not know that I masqueraded as a man.

"No. We lost his trail outside Providence. The army here will tell me nothing of his whereabouts. My contacts in the city have not seen him." Now I hung my head. I should have pursued Barclay Marlowe more diligently. The home and community I found in Boston made me reluctant to leave. I had a new mission and as long as Barclay kept his pet demon under control I found fewer and fewer reasons to seek him.

I squared my shoulders and fixed my gaze upon Roderick once more. Boston was my home now, the first true home I had known since leaving Kirkenwood. I had friends, a position in society, and nearly enough money saved to open my own coffeehouse in a good location.

"And your brother?" he asked with one eyebrow quirked. I could not read his expression, but I sensed disapproval. "Here and there. I do not keep track of him."

A whisper of movement behind Roderick caught my attention. A little girl of about four or five years peeked out from behind his legs.

His hand automatically caressed her blonde curls. A gesture of familiar affection.

My heart skipped a beat.

These two belonged together. I could think of only one relationship between them.

Roderick had married and sired a child since last I'd seen him.

I wanted to faint, or vomit. Instead I invited him and his daughter into the parlor.

Roderick drank in the sight of Georgina. Maturity had only given her more beauty. She wore her simple gown with more ease than he'd ever seen her do in feminine clothes. He detected no trace of the stiffness of a corset beneath her layers of clothing. That secret knowledge warmed his face and sent lances of desire through his blood.

He bit the inside of his cheek to keep from grabbing her right there in the hall and kissing her breathless.

"Please sit. May I offer you tea or some biscuits?" Georgina asked.

Roderick could not read her expression, or intonation. From all appearances she played the role of a simple spinster entertaining morning callers as easily as she did the flamboyant Masked Rogue or mercenary major—better than she did the role of dowager princess or governess to a plantation family.

He took a seat. "My daughter, Zaneta," he said plunking the little girl into his lap.

"Good morning, Zaneta." Georgina held out her hand as if greeting an adult of equal status.

Zaneta responded by putting her own tiny hand within Georgina's.

They remained linked together for a brief moment, only a tiny bit longer than politeness required.

Roderick nodded approval.

"Daughter?" Georgina lifted her eyebrows and glared at him.

"My daughter," Roderick repeated firmly. "I heard you remained in Boston rather than returning to England."

"England is no longer my home. I belong here. What brings you to Boston?"

"A long story."

"Perhaps best told over a cup of coffee. May I take your coat, Zaneta? Perhaps you would like to help me in the kitchen." Georgina rose and offered her hand to the little girl.

Alarmed, Roderick clutched Zaneta a little too fiercely, keeping her in his lap.

"May I please, Papa?" Zaneta turned her big blue eyes up to him.

His heart melted, as it did every time she looked at him with such love.

"Mind your manners, love," he whispered as he kissed her temple and released her. She jumped down, shed her coat, and dropped it on the floor. Then she took Georgina's proffered hand and skipped to the kitchen with none of her usual shyness.

Biting his lip, Roderick shed his own greatcoat, draping it neatly across the arm of the settee, added Zaneta's to his own, and followed them. He did not like his daughter beyond his sight around strangers.

Georgina was not a stranger.

He still did not trust her, or his daughter. The thought of the trouble the two of them together could dream up chilled him to the bone.

Zaneta carefully placed a dozen ginger biscuits upon a cracked china plate while Georgina poured hot water into a matching pot, to warm it before filling it with the fragrant brew coming from the hearth. The delicate pink flowers gracing the gleaming white porcelain seemed out of place in the homely kitchen. He noticed that plain pewter plates and cutlery were spread upon the table for their use. The fine porcelain was for guests.

"May I take the coffeepot off the fire, Mistress Georgina?" Zaneta asked politely.

"Not yet, sweeting. When it boils, we'll ask your father to

lift it." Georgina lifted her face and flashed Roderick a brilliant smile. "Iron makes the kettle frightfully heavy."

"When did you ever defer hard work to a mere man?" he asked quietly.

"When Zaneta and I decided you need to be part of our conversation."

He wished he could read her eyes. She was trying to tell him something. What?

"If we do not need to rely on formality, shall we sit comfortably here?" He gestured to include the long room that was easily as large as the two front rooms. A steep set of steps along the interior wall must lead to the loft rooms, probably to Georgina's bedroom. Her chamber would be warm and cozy from the central chimney even if she did not have her own hearth.

He would not think about her and a bed in the same sentence.

"What brings you to Boston?" Georgina sat upon a long bench set at the central worktable.

Zaneta took a place on a high stool opposite her. Uncharacteristically, his daughter studied their hostess rather than hide behind her father.

This was what he wanted. Wasn't it? Then why did jealousy burn in his gut like etching acid upon copper?

"Your eyes are amber, like your hair, but there is a deep blue ring on the outer edge. That's the same color blue as my eyes," Zaneta said. She placed her elbow upon the table and her chin in her hand while she continued her scrutiny.

" 'Tis a trait that runs through my family, even to the most distant cousins," Georgina replied with equal frankness. "May I ask where is your mother?"

"In heaven with the angels," Zaneta replied with no trace of remorse. "She died when I was born. I never knew her. Did you know my mother? Was she a cousin of yours?"

"If there is a relationship between you, it comes from elsewhere," Roderick muttered.

Georgina transferred her attention to Roderick as he drew the spider arm out of the hearth with a hook and wrapped a towel around the coffeepot's handle before lifting it free.

"Who?" she asked soundlessly.

He saw the word in her mouth. His blood roared in his ears as he had to admit the truth.

"Zaneta's mother, my wife, was Miss Jane Cummings." Let Georgina do the math and draw her own conclusions.

He could almost see her mind spin as she sought a memory of the name and where she had heard it before. Her eyes went wide as she made the connection.

"Oh." She turned back to Zaneta with a composed face.

Roderick hid his own disconcertment by pouring the bubbling coffee into the warmed china pot.

"I do not believe I ever met your mother, Zaneta. But I heard her name mentioned several times when I lived in Williamsburg."

"Grandpapa is quite angry with Papa and me. We sold our plantation. He thinks the plantation should be his, but it belonged to Papa and me. Ever since my mama died, it was ours and we did not want it anymore."

The less said on the subject of his father-in-law, the better, Roderick mused.

"I am not cut out to be a farmer." Roderick grinned with a little chagrin. Or protect his daughter from Cummings' witch hunt. The man was willing to watch his own granddaughter burn at the stake just to regain the plantation.

"You resigned your commission in the army," Georgina said flatly.

"My . . . er . . . battle wounds were significant enough that my colonel gave me a promotion and then pensioned me off. He did not believe I would recover enough to be of service to His Majesty."

"Does the wound trouble you still?"

"Upon occasion."

"Papa says his wound aches just before a storm. He can predict a change in the wind even before I can," Zaneta informed them. "But I know when someone is coming before we can see them on the road." She smiled smugly.

"And can you tell other things before they happen?" Georgina asked cautiously. She nibbled on one of the ginger biscuits, giving it her overt attention.

But Roderick knew she studied his daughter from beneath lowered eyes.

"I am not supposed to tell." Zaneta lowered her eyes to her clenched fists in her lap. Then with a measure of defiance she reached for a biscuit and took a big bite. She fixed Georgina with her gaze.

Where did this boldness come from? Zaneta never spoke to anyone but her father.

"And well you should not tell. Most people do not understand special gifts and fear them. They will fear you," Georgina said.

"Do you have special gifts, Mistress Kirkwood?" Zaneta's eyes opened wide and a smile began to tug at the corners of her mouth.

"Perhaps I should have brought you to visit Mistress Kirkwood sooner. You seem to have found a kindred spirit," Roderick teased his daughter. He played at tickling her.

She giggled and tried tickling him back.

"Kindred, indeed." Georgina sat for a moment in silent contemplation of her coffee. Then her posture shifted and she smiled at him, a bit falsely. Without asking, she poured a little milk and sugar into a pewter cup for him then filled it with hot coffee.

He wondered if she preferred coffee to tea or disdained tea as an English drink. In Williamsburg, he could tell a man's politics by his choice of drink.

"Have you found lodgings in Boston?" she asked.

"I purchased the Crown and Anchor public house down on Clark's Wharf. We will live above it." He sipped at the coffee, surprised at the fine quality in this simple household. "My old batman Ian is there now, making some minor repairs."

"Long Wharf is a better location, but Clark's is adequate," Georgina pronounced with some authority. "When did you arrive? I had not heard of the change in ownership, though John Porter has spoken often of wishing to sell. I had thought to buy the place myself."

Was that deep disappointment in her voice?

"We arrived two days ago. Tonight I open for business on my own. I could use a good barmaid." He looked at her hopefully.

"Before I agree to anything, Roddie, I must know why you brought Zaneta to me."

"You were the only person I could think of."

"Why?" She speared him with a gaze that would brook no lies and no misdirection.

"The world does not always operate according to the rules when you are around."

"Such as?"

"Your cat. Your disguises. Your talent with a blade. I do not know how or why you do what you do, but you seem to live in a different orbit than the rest of us."

"Drink your coffee, Roddie. Then go sweep the floor of your tavern, or wash your tankards, or count your kegs and casks. I shall bring Zaneta to you in a few hours. Then we will talk."

"Georgina . . ."

"After I have discussed some things with your daughter."

"Georgina . . ."

"Go."

Chapter 59

I DRANK a dish of coffee, and then poured another from cup to saucer before speaking to Zaneta. Her big blue eyes—Barclay Marlowe's eyes—followed my every move. From one breath to the next she moved from chatterbox, perfectly at ease in my company, to wary kitten hiding from a hawk.

As if called, Oblegid, now a fat and lazy mature cat, sauntered over and inspected every inch of Zaneta's hem with nose and tongue. Satisfied that she carried no menace, my familiar leaped into the little girl's lap and purred.

"Oh!" she cried and buried her face in soft fur.

"Have you ever had a cat before, Zaneta?"

"Papa let me play with the barn kitties."

"But none of them have become special pets."

She shook her head, soft blonde curls wiggling vigorously. Her hair would be impossible to contain into a proper coif, much like mine at her age. I reached my hand across the table and wiggled my fingers.

Tentatively, Zaneta inched her own hand into mine.

I did not clasp her fingers, I just let our two palms touch.

"Zaneta, I mean it when I tell you that you must speak to no one else about our special gifts," I reminded her sternly. "People who do not have these gifts are jealous, or frightened. They will hurt us sorely if they find out."

"Yes, ma'am," she said; hints of a soft Virginia drawl crept into her speech. I'd noticed a similar accent in her father. Five years of living the slower-paced life in the southern colonies would do that.

"The only exception is you must talk to me. I can help you control your talent. I can help you explore the limits of

411

it, maybe even expand your talents as you grow older." As
Drake had helped and trained me.

"Can you talk to your kittie?" she asked eagerly.

"Sometimes, when Oblegid has something important to say
to me."

"I talk to the barn kitties and Papa's dogs all the time.
But horsies are the best. They have the most interesting
things to say. Pigs and sheep are dumb, though. They only
talk about what they are eating and can't remember that
they've just told you that patch of grass is sour so they say
it over and over and over and over . . ."

"Yes, I know." I cut her off and we both giggled. "What
else can you do, Zaneta?"

She sat silently staring at her hands once more.

"I have to know, Zaneta, if I am to help you."

More silence.

"Does your papa know that you can do something else?"

She nodded her head and still would not meet my gaze.

" 'Tis this new trick that prompted him to bring you to me."

She nodded again. Shyly she lifted her lashes a tad. Just
enough for me to see again that flash of brilliant blue.
Kirkwood eyes. She could be capable of anything.

I drew a deep breath and centered myself. I had not
worked much magic these last five years. Not since the
night the Sons of Liberty invaded the Hutchinson mansion. I had not needed to. Nor had I thought much about
my family, the Pendragon Society, the enemies who threatened both.

Barclay Marlowe and his demon were the only enemies
I considered worth working magic.

"Show me, Zaneta," I said quietly. I added a tiny probe
of compulsion and sent it into her barely raised eyes.

She giggled again and lifted her hand. With one finger
she pointed to the coffeepot. Slowly it rose and tilted. A
stream of rich brown liquid streamed from the spout into
my cup.

She lowered her hand. The pot remained in the air, still
pouring. The cup overflowed, into the saucer, onto the
table. Had there been more liquid, it might have flooded
the kitchen.

Zaneta's eyes opened wide in panic. She gestured again.
The pot did not respond to her command.

I grabbed the handle and set the precious porcelain upon the table

Zaneta sagged in exhaustion. Her eyes closed and she lowered her head to the table.

And faded from my view.

I had never heard of anyone who could do that.

Suddenly I knew why I could not find Barclay Marlowe, how he seemed to appear and disappear from rooms without using the door. I'd thought he merely made use of my distraction and a quiet tread. He had the talent to disappear at will. Zaneta had inherited it from him.

I sensed that she slept now, literally unable to stay awake longer. Her pewter plate with a half-eaten ginger biscuit still upon it rose up and circled where the little girl's head should be. The milk pitcher and sugar bowl joined it. They swirled faster and faster, gathering pots and knives and ladles and fresh apples from their bowl into their maelstrom.

The spiral of kitchen utensils tightened, coming closer and closer to my head, and Zaneta's.

I heard Goodwife Camden at the stoop, juggling packages as she opened the door.

I had to stop this before she entered the room.

"Enough!" I clapped my hands three times and willed each utensil back into place. Then I felt for Zaneta's shoulder and shook her awake. She came into view, lifted her head drowsily. A quick look around to be sure that everything was in its place, then she slept again.

"Good morning, Miss Kirkwood. Did you finish writing your pamphlet?" Goodwife Camden asked.

An apple dropped into my lap as everything else settled where it belonged. Except the half eaten biscuit. It crumbled into Zaneta's hair.

Roderick drew a tankard full of ale for his first customer. The garrulous old man thanked him and plunked a few pence upon the bar.

"Thank ye," Roderick said, whisking the coins into his apron pocket.

The old man nodded and eyed him over the rim of the tankard as he quaffed half the brew. "Fair to middlin'," he grunted in his clipped accent peculiar to the locals. Then he ambled off to a freshly polished table.

Another old man with tobacco stains on his grizzled chin replaced him at the bar. "A pint, if you please, Goodman." This one watched carefully to make sure Roderick had just the right amount of head in the tankard. The customer offered a few comments about shifting the angle to get a better draw. Then he, too, pronounced the brew acceptable and joined his companion at the table.

They sat reading a broadsheet they'd brought with them.

No one else entered his establishment. Early days yet. John Porter had only closed the place three days ago. Word of reopening under new ownership might not have spread through the city yet. Though he had seen notice of his taking over Porter's pub license posted outside the Customs House.

"Fixed the cellar door," Ian McTavis said from the back doorway. "I'll start the soup for supper." He wandered into the kitchen.

Roderick inspected his array of pewter tankards, the length of the multitude of candles he'd lit against the darkening autumn day. Something was missing.

Zaneta.

He'd not been separated from her for more than a few hours since her birth. Most nights she shared his room, unwilling to entice nightmares by sleeping alone. He'd not pushed her away. The tiny bundle of energy and mischief had stolen his heart the first time she fixed her impossibly blue eyes upon him. He frequently forgot that he had not sired her, indeed had never lain with her mother. After the hasty marriage ceremony he'd felt honor bound to spare Jane Cummings the expected intimacies until after she'd given birth.

Jane had lived less than six months more, surviving her labor by less than a day.

What was keeping Georgina so long? He'd left Zaneta with her hours ago.

Worry ate at his gut. No telling the trouble Zaneta—and Georgina—might get into. If Virginians did not tolerate witches among them, then Bostonians, with their stern religion and outlook upon life, were less likely to. Less than a century before, numerous witches had been hanged . . . No. He would not think on that. He had to trust Georgina.

Though she still did not trust him enough to admit that she and her "half brother" were one and the same person.

He swallowed his resentment and returned his attention to his customers. They continued to argue about the new taxes proposed by Parliament and the increased number of troops housed in the city.

The door latch rattled.

Roderick looked up and pasted a welcoming smile upon his face. He needed more customers to keep the candles burning and the ale flowing.

Zaneta burst into the room and ran to him.

"Papa!"

Roderick's smile became genuine. He hugged his daughter tightly.

"Got a young 'un," the grizzled man at the table frowned. "Public house ain't no place for little folk. Less'n you got yourself a wife to go with the tyke."

"I'm widowed," Roderick explained. His eyes strayed from his customer to the doorway. Where was Georgina? Had she turned Zaneta loose to find her own way home?

The latch rattled again.

"You may put it there," Georgina directed.

Two youths lumbered into the room lugging a copper-and-brass contraption between them. They set the thing to the left of the door, right where customers would trip over it.

"Hey!" he called after them as they sidled out the door.

Georgina replaced the lanky young men in the doorway. She clutched a bulky package to her breast. Her calico cat draped over her arms along with the package.

"I have a partnership proposition for you, Roderick Whythe," she announced without preamble.

Roderick raised his eyebrows, not knowing what to say.

"Say yes, Papa," Zaneta whispered. "Please say yes. I like Georgie ever so much."

"Who gave you leave to be so familiar with Mistress Kirkwood?" Roderick looked down at his daughter sternly.

"She did," Zaneta said quietly. "We're great friends now, Papa." She looked suspiciously at the two customers and reached her arms up.

Roderick obliged her by lifting her into his arms. He felt so much safer with her close.

"What do you propose, Mistress Kirkwood?"

She looked away from him, suddenly shy. He expected such behavior from Zaneta, never from Georgina. The cat jumped down and began inspecting the place with nose and whiskers and tongue.

"A partnership, Goodman Whythe." Georgina seemed to have collected herself and her resolve as she faced him squarely. Her face held the firm expression she adopted when facing an opponent at the other end of her sword.

"I have no need of a partner in the business."

"Best barmaid in Boston," the clean-shaven customer called out. "She keeps order and keeps the men coming back for more ale, more conversation, and more hopes." He laughed uproariously at the last.

Roderick frowned at the implications that other men lusted after Georgina.

When had he begun to think of her as his? Georgina belonged to no one but herself. She certainly obeyed no one but herself.

"This machine is a coffee roaster. I have five pounds of roasted beans here, ready for grinding and the contacts to purchase more. I offer them to you for a stake in this public house. I'll make the coffee and serve the ale. Keep order, too. But I can't cook."

"Ian cooks. Your offer is not good enough," Roderick found himself saying.

What was he thinking? He'd come here for her help with his daughter.

"What more can I offer? I'll help with Zaneta. That goes without saying."

Zaneta turned her head from Roderick's shoulder and looked at Georgina. A big smile spread across her face and her eyes sparkled. "Go ahead and say it, Papa. Say what you are thinking," she said just loud enough for him to hear.

"Reading my mind again?" he whispered.

She nodded with a mischievous grin.

"Very well." He took a deep breath for courage and faced Georgina. "I do not need a partner in the business, Mistress Kirkwood. I need a wife, and a mother for Zaneta. I'll take you and your coffee roaster on those terms and none other."

He had not planned to propose. Had only daydreamed of the two of them together. The practicality of living with a woman with no respect for the rules of society frightened him no measure.

"Very well, then." Georgina nodded her head. "I accept your terms. We will post the bans at the Cockrel Church this Sunday."

Why did he feel as if he faced his doom?

Chapter 60

Kirkenwood, Yule Eve, 1769.

EMILY snuffed a candle upon the mantel of the drawing room by the simple expedient of willing it to die. Garlands and wreaths of evergreen graced the room in preparation for the usual family festivities. The fifth such joyless celebration since Cousin Milton Marlowe had taken charge of the estate and the family.

Belinda, Patricia, and Martha, her three middle sisters clattered down the staircase, pigtails held up in loops of ribbon to match their newest gowns. Patricia now wore Emily's castoffs. Belinda, at eighteen, had her own wardrobe. She had just survived her first limited season in London, all Cousin Milton would pay for—a season denied Emily because of her feigned madness and extended engagement to Barclay Marlowe.

Where were all the pretty romantic dreams she had woven around her coming marriage?

What good the increase in her control of magic when she was reduced to parlor tricks simply to annoy Milton?

She had wasted five years, always looking for one more spell, one more talent, one more layer of protection upon the archives. She could think of nothing more that she had to do. Her life was easier when she did not contemplate the responsibility of assuming control of the household, of battling Milton, of retaking the reins of the Pendragon Society.

The time had come to take action against her cousin. She could no longer make excuses to delay.

The colonial women, Abigail Adams and Mercy Otis

Warren, who corresponded with her might feign meekness in public. In private, they fought as fiercely for what they believed in as any man. As fiercely as Aunt Georgie had fought the Turks.

How could Emily hope to match them?

Belinda and Martha pushed past Emily to take their places beside the hearth.

"Emily." Patricia stopped dead in her tracks. "Join us. Please." She took her oldest sister's arm and led her into the large room that had taken on a semblance of coziness thanks to the extra candles, fragrant greens, and bright red ribbons scavenged from the treasure troves of all five sisters.

"Cook has promised us plum pudding tonight. She baked tokens and surprises into it. I hope you find a nice surprise in your portion, Emily." Patricia alone of all the household spoke to Emily as if she had not truly lost her wits.

And Samuel. But he was not officially part of the household.

Emily smiled at her sister, banishing the glaze of madness from her gaze and expression.

"Where is Griffin?" Emily asked. Possibly the first coherent sentence she had uttered to any but Ana, her dog, in five years.

As if summoned by her thoughts, the immense wolfhound pranced down the hallway from the kitchen wing. She sported a bright red collar and long leash. At the other end of the lead, Griffin stumbled at a breakneck pace. His head barely reached the dog's shoulder. He clutched the worn leather tightly. Ana grinned, mouth open, tongue lolling. She paused halfway down the hallway to allow Griffin to catch up with her.

"I found him! The doggy is mine. I found him. He's my Yule gift. Uncle Milton is giving him to me," the little boy proclaimed. Behind him, his next older sister Hannah strode with all the dignity of a girl just reaching toward womanhood.

"The dog is a female. And she can't be one of ours. You found her running loose near the lake. Therefore she must be a mongrel and not suitable for one of the family," Hannah proclaimed as if she were the ultimate authority on canine pedigrees.

Ana pulled Griffin to Emily's side where she sat politely and butted her head beneath her hand.

Emily scratched her ears and jowls with loving affection. "Ana, what are you doing in the house?" Emily asked her dog.

Ana replied with a flick of her tongue across Emily's face. *Cave cold and lonely*.

Ana had recently weaned her latest litter of pups. Probably her last at the great age of five. Large dogs did not live long. One of those pups, a female, had already claimed Emily as a familiar. She had secreted the next Ana in the cave with her dam.

But if the cave was cold and lonely, where had little Ana gotten herself to?

Ana showed Emily an image of the pup wandering around the castle ruins upon the tor, hunting her next meal.

"Ah." Emily replied, pleased that her familiars were so independent and hardy. "But you must go back . . ."

Why?

Emily smiled to herself. Then she faced her assembled sisters and little brother who stared at the phenomenon of a wild, and therefore ferocious, wolfhound behaving like a pet.

"Girls, this is Ana. She has been my familiar for a number of years. I have had to keep her hidden because I did not know how to keep her safe from . . . whoever murdered Belle's first litter."

"But I want her to be my dog," Griffin pouted. "I found her!"

"We shall find you a pup among the kennels as a pet, Griffin." At least Milton had maintained the breeding kennels. Sale of the wolfhounds provided a good percentage of the family income.

"But Uncle Milton will not allow any animals in the house," Belinda said. She eyed the dog enviously. "Only Belle, and she stays with Papa all the time."

"The time has come for a change," Emily announced.

"Then you are not insane and to be locked away anymore?" Patricia asked. She squinted her nearsighted eyes at Emily. She would not wear her spectacles. Defiance of "Uncle" Milton, or vanity?

Emily wished she had spent more time with her sisters, allowed them to be privy to her deception. She realized she hardly knew them at all.

Samuel had told her much of their doings, but he could not know them as a sister should.

"I am no longer insane. Nor have I been for several years."

"But . . ." Belinda protested.

"A ruse only. To protect myself."

"But Uncle Milton . . ."

"Is a dangerous man. Or have you forgotten that he is a Master Magician? Have you forgotten that with Papa and me out of the way he controls the estates and fortune of this family as well as the Pendragon Society?"

"Stuff and nonsense," Belinda snorted. "There is no such thing as magic."

"Is there not?" Emily waved her hand. Every remaining candle flame and lantern glow in the drawing room and hallway died.

"A draft," Belinda said. She clutched her arms as if chilled.

"A draft? Can a draft do this?" She snapped her fingers. All of the lights flared into life. The fire in the hearth shot higher, brighter, and warmer.

"Wow!" Griffin stood with his mouth open, his envy over possession of the dog forgotten. "Can you teach me to do that?"

"Possibly." Emily smoothed her skirts and perched upon the wing chair as if on a throne. "We need to talk," she said to her sisters.

"But Uncle Milton . . ." Belinda protested.

Emily silenced her with a pointed finger. "This is about us, not our cousin. This is about preserving our heritage, indeed, possibly preserving all of England."

Belinda narrowed her eyes. "I will not go against Uncle Milton. He has taken care of us all for five years. He nursed you personally while you were insane. I will fetch him now and tell him that you plot against him. That you betray him." She turned and flounced out of the drawing room.

Boston.

Aunt Georgie, help us! Griffin screamed into my mind.

Startled, I looked up from sweeping the tavern floor.

Never before had anyone jumped into my mind so completely. He must be desperate. I had no doubt who had called, though we'd had no contact until now. His cry sounded almost as if he were in the room. I looked around, but encountered only the sight of mundane walls and floors and tables and such.

Outside the shuttered windows a snowstorm howled in competition with Griffin's cry for aid.

"What?" Roderick looked at me with concern. "What is Zaneta up to now?"

I had only told him some of his daughter's—our daughter's—talents and given him a sketchy history of my family and their role in advising monarchs in the past by way of explanation. He had no idea of the extent or magnitude of the magic either Zaneta or I possessed.

She was at the Cockerel Church with the other children of the congregation preparing for the pageant portion of Christmas Eve services.

"Not Zaneta," I said. Why did I have trouble breathing?

"Who?" Roderick abandoned washing the pewter tankards left over from last night to put his arm around my waist. Gently he kissed my temple.

For once, I leaned into him for strength, grateful for his support while my knees wobbled with concern for Griffin and a continued heaviness in my chest. Seven weeks of marriage to Roderick and I still was not used to the frequent caresses. No man in my life—not even Casanova—had indulged in the overt displays of affection outside the bedroom. I was not certain I approved of the distraction from my mundane—and now magical—tasks.

Something terrible was happening at Kirkenwood. I had no idea how to explain how I knew that to my husband.

"Back home." I staggered to the nearest chair. I needed to concentrate, to pull a vision through Griffin's eyes into my own. For five years I had separated myself from my past, from all emotional ties to my home and family.

Now, all of my longing for Kirkenwood, Drake, Emily, and Griffin slammed into my midsection with the force of a cannonball.

"Talk to me, Georgina. I cannot help you if I do not understand." He knelt beside me and squeezed my shoulders.

Aunt Georgie, what do we do? Griffin sounded desperate.

"I need quiet!" I nearly screamed at Roderick and pushed away from him. I know my husband merely meant to comfort and soothe me.

I wanted neither. I needed to be alone.

I turned and bolted up the stairs to our chambers.

"Breeding, is she?" a customer commented, just entering the tavern. "Never mind her moods. Seen it seven times with my woman. They be hell to live with the first three months."

I dismissed the comment. Let the men think what they wanted, for now. So long as they left me alone to deal with Griffin and his crisis.

Kirkenwood.

Emily bit her lip as she ran fifteen plots through her head. When Milton Marlowe walked through that door, he'd have an arsenal of spells at his fingertips. She had to have three for every one of his. He was older, more experienced, possibly more powerful.

Belinda stopped short at the door. Griffin darted between her and the exit faster than Emily could see. The little boy grinned from ear to ear.

Belinda roughly thrust him aside. Griffin stumbled down the two steps to the main room. He came up hard against a lyre-back chair and folded game table. He and the furniture skidded a few inches across the parquet floor. His grin remained intact.

Belinda rattled the latch. The door did not budge. She pushed with both hands. Nothing happened. She leaned her shoulder into the door and pushed again.

Griffin laughed.

Emily's face broke into a wide smile. Her mouth turned up so far her cheeks hurt. Why had she not thought of her brother's simple ploy?

"Aunt Georgie says that Uncle Milton thinks in terms of power. We have to think in terms of guile. Why does she call him 'cousin' instead of 'uncle'?" Griffin said. He'd managed to straighten himself, but his hose sagged and the buckle at his right knee looked bent.

"Uncle Milton!" Belinda screamed pushing and pulling at the latch. The door rattled.

"Silence," Emily shouted at both the door and her sister.

Belinda grabbed her throat in panic. She continued to open and close her mouth, like a landed fish gasping for water.

"What was that about Aunt Georgie?" Emily walked slowly toward Griffin. Dimly she was aware that Patricia, Martha, and Hannah huddled together, sobbing, on the other side of the long room. She needed them cooperative and trusting of her. She had to proceed slowly, calmly. Most of all, she needed to keep from frightening them while reminding them that magic must be used for the good of the family and the good of England.

She had to remain calm and in control, no matter how much she wanted revenge upon Milton Marlowe. Messy, violent revenge. Total annihilation of the man and every one of his minions.

Five years gone from her life. Five years, her youth, her season in London, her marriage to Barclay, all gone. All her pretty dreams. Her faith in the goodness of all people. Her ability to trust. Never to be recovered. Never.

"What is this about Aunt Georgie?" she asked Griffin. Her voice came out strained, but she refrained from shouting. With effort.

"Aunt Georgie says you must dis . . . disp . . ." He paused and cocked his head as if listening. "Separate. Take them out one by one."

"How? How are you speaking to Aunt Georgie?" Hope coursed through her veins in wild exultation.

"She's just there." Griffin shrugged. He pointed to the back of his head, near the nape. "She's always been a part of me."

He sounded so matter-of-fact, so accepting of this miracle, Emily almost did not believe him. But Aunt Georgie was a formidable magician in her own right, probably a Master Magician in the Pendragon Society.

"We need the Pendragon Society, Griffin. Ask her how I find them." Emily breathed a little easier.

"She says that our papa has to call them. They will not listen or receive a summons from anyone else." Griffin recited the words as if they were a lesson. "Aunt Budgie might come on her own but not the others."

"Papa." Emily sank to the floor in defeat. "Papa has been drugged unconscious for nearly five years."

"Belinda?" Milton Marlowe called from the other side of the door. "What ails you?" The latch rattled. "Open the door, Belinda."

"I can't, Uncle Milton," Belinda sobbed inaudibly. "I can't. They are holding me prisoner with magic." She hiccuped through her tears.

The latch turned and the door opened.

Chapter 61

DR. Milton Marlowe hesitated before he pushed open the door to the drawing room. Something in Belinda's barely heard voice sent the fine hairs along his spine standing on end. At least he thought Belinda called to him. Hard to tell the older girls apart.

Three quick breaths centered him.

Strengthen your wards, Neville reminded him. Needlessly.

"I always have solid wards, Son. None of our men in the coven have been able to penetrate my protections. Nor have the Master Magicians in the Pendragon Society found chinks in my personal armor."

Of course not. Those old biddies are more concerned with improving the crop of sheep wool and reducing spring floods than in true power. Neville drifted around Milton. Ghostly blood dripped from his gaping wounds and severed limbs but never reached the floor.

"I am always prepared for the worst—a concentrated attack by the Pendragons," Milton reminded his son as he pushed the door inward.

A tongue of flame shot across the doorway. He waited until it passed to step forward. Green flames blazed from his fingertips.

"Look before you aim next time!" a female voice he should recognize taunted him on a laugh. The fireplace poker, thrown by mundane force since no magic trace trailed after it, followed the words.

He ducked the tool and dove to his right. The poker passed through Neville's form.

Milton thought darkness. A dozen candles snuffed out.

426

The premature sunset at this northern latitude sucked even more light from the room.

He pulled energy from every hidden crevice in his body and forced it into his eyes. He spotted the immature and mundane auras of Hannah and Martha with no problem. They glowed white beside the dying embers of the fire in the hearth. Patricia had moved away from them. Traces of her more developed yellow life force showed as partial footprints where she had stepped on tiptoe in her withdrawal. The larger outline of her body could not hide behind the draperies from his magical sight.

That left Belinda, the dim pink froth of energy directly before him. So who had attacked him with magical fire?

A tiny giggle to his left. No discernible aura. Only a magician of high power and long training could do that.

He drew energy from his wards and launched a swath of fiery snakes in the direction of the mirthful one.

The magic backlashed into his eyes. Blinding pain lanced from one temple to the other, then down his jaw and around to his neck. Which Master Magician had the strength and experience to erect such formidable shielding?

Another lash of fire came from the other direction.

Two of them! Which two would dare?

An image of Georgina Kirkwood flashed before his memory. He'd never fully explored her talent. Never learned her limitations—or her true strength.

But if she had left the colonies and returned, he'd have heard about it. Surely Barclay would have sent him the information through a fire-and-water communication.

Barclay, bah! The boy had disappeared into the wilderness just as his older brother had. But unlike his more honorable and more talented brother, Barclay had not the decency to die. His life force plagued Milton's scrying spells every night without giving any direct information of his location or condition.

"Fire," a feminine voice shouted from in front of him.

Not Belinda. Her fuzzy pink form shrank to a sobbing knot on the floor.

Every candle in the room blazed forth with new flame.

Milton blinked in the sudden brilliance. He swept his hand across the air in front of him, willing the candles to extinguish once more.

"Not so fast, Cousin," the same feminine voice sneered.

All the children called him "uncle" now. That left only . . .
Emily.

His heart leaped in panic. She sounded sane at the moment. Who knew what deviousness her madness had cooked
up in the last five years.

The room dimmed. All the light seemed to collect in one
point.

Milton's vision cleared. Then he saw his nemesis. Emily,
properly clothed and groomed, eyes clear of insanity and
full of anger, stared right through him. She seemed to penetrate his deepest desires and most carefully hidden
thoughts. Half the light in the room gathered into a single
ball of fire in her outstretched hand.

Quickly, he clamped down on any stray musings. He channeled every bit of his magic into his wards. Neville faded
from his sight but left behind the hint of burned sulfur.

"Peters!" Milton called for aid.

"S . . . sir?" His secretary cowered just the other side of
the door.

"Call Water," Milton ordered. "Water is your element.
Douse her Fire."

"Sir, I cannot," Peters stammered.

"What?" Panic bounced in Milton's gut. How could he
counter Emily without dropping his wards?

"Sir, my powers are chained."

"Chained? Impossible. Only . . ." Milton spared a glance
over his shoulder, still keeping half an eye on Emily and her
deadly ball of Fire. The rest of the room had grown dark
again. Her weapon blazed brighter and brighter, she seemed
to gather even more fire from the distant moon and stars.

The Wind, sister to Fire, howled louder, circling the
house, seeking entrance.

Milton controlled no single element, only bits and pieces
of all four. His strength was in telepathy and sight beyond
sight. Could he muster enough Water and Earth to protect
himself from Fire augmented by Air?

"Who chains you?" Milton gulped. In thinking of a defense, he felt the resource drain away from him. A second
magician was in the room, somewhere. Possibly the most
powerful magician he had ever encountered.

Who?

Drake? Possibly. If Emily had freed herself from her blanket of insanity, could Drake have freed himself from the drugs Milton poured into him?

Peters did not answer his question.

"Who chains you, Peters?" Milton said a little louder.

"The dog, sir."

"Belle? Belle cannot chain your magic." Incompetent bungler.

"Perhaps not. But she can break my leg in two if she closes her jaw any . . . further." Peters' voice broke in fear.

"Then throw elemental Water into her face." Disgusted, Milton marshaled his powers.

"If I do that, sir, the boy will decapitate me with a rather wicked-looking knife."

"The boy?" Milton gulped. Had Griffin attracted a familiar? If so . . . then . . . Milton directed all of his pent up magic at the fireball in Emily's hand.

Flames scattered and lighted in the drapes, upon the furniture, in the carpet. Little fires grew, blended became larger fires. Dozens of them. Too many for Emily and her sisters to stamp out.

"Now, Peters." Milton directed one last bolt of magic at the dog.

She yelped.

Peters loosed something magical.

The boy screamed.

The sound of pounding feet echoed.

Milton fled the room. Time to regroup, take stock, and discern what the children planned. Why had they attacked him now? He'd been like a father to them for five years. A stern father certainly, they needed guidance and discipline.

"This way, sir," Peters took his arm and led him to the stables. "We have to retreat. Emily . . ." he gulped.

"Yes, Emily."

Together they threw saddles upon the finest of the mounts and rode out into the teeth of the storm.

"I will return," he vowed. "I will have control of them."

We must talk to the demon, Neville said, floating beside him. *We can only fight the demon Emily with a demon of our own.*

Emily stomped diligently at the flames that ate at the carpet. For every ember she smothered three more sprang up.

Patricia screamed and tangled in the blazing draperies. The scent of burning flesh mingled with burned fabric and candle wax.

Hannah and Martha beat at the flames that scorched their sister with cushions from the settee.

"Elemental Fire," Emily cried. So much magic had flitted about the room tonight, she had forgotten that the element had been loosed. It had to feed. Only more magic could quench it.

Gathering the last of her reserves, she recited a few lines in ancient Welsh.

The Fire at her feet retired.

Patricia's hiding place became an inferno.

Griffin stumbled into the room with Ana. He carried a basin of water. It was too heavy for his small hands. He stumbled. Water splashed upon the greens gracing a side table.

Emily shouted the Welsh spell at the blazing draperies.

Reluctantly the Fire retreated. Then it surged forward again, not satisfied.

Patricia's screams became whimpers. Her pain and fear radiated out from a ravaged body hotter than the Fire.

The stench of raw and burning flesh nearly gagged Emily.

Truly frightened now, Emily called out the words that should placate the element of Fire. She repeated the words in English, in Latin, and in French.

At last the heavy velvet curtains resolved to ash and fell away from their victim.

Hannah and Martha drew away, hands covering their mouths, eyes wide in horror.

Patricia lay in a sobbing heap, her fine red gown now black and melted into her skin.

"Aunt Georgie, says that Papa is the only one who can help her," Griffin whispered.

Emily barely heard him.

Ana crept forward. She tried to lick Patricia's face. She jerked back before she actually touched Emily's sister.

"Belinda, get Papa!" Emily ordered. She had to fight to hold back the bile that nearly choked her. "Martha, get the servants. Get water. Bring anyone who can help."

"Papa is too ill . . ." Belinda protested. She edged toward the doorway and away from the frightful scene.

"Papa is drugged. Drugged by your beloved 'Uncle' Milton so that he cannot run the earldom. Drugged so that he cannot use his healing magic to help your sister," Emily screamed.

"I can wake him," Griffin said with more confidence.

"Go with Belinda, Griffin. Bring Papa, even if you have to levitate him."

"Aunt Georgie says that magic always has a cost." Griffin cried openly now. Tears streamed down his cheeks. His nose ran. He wiped his face with the back of his hand. "She says that we . . . we have to be willing to pay the cost of magic every time we use it."

"Is killing Patricia worth getting rid of Uncle Milton?" Belinda pointed an accusing finger at Emily. "Her pain, this horror and ruin is the cost of satisfying your twisted mind and its power games," she sneered.

"I only want what is best for the family," Emily whispered. Her belly felt empty and her mind too heavy.

"Is the death of your sister the 'best' for the family?"

Chapter 62

Boston.

THE images at Kirkenwood in my scrying bowl faded. Heavy exhaustion dragged at my bones. I had to lay my head down beside my basin before I fell face first into the water and drowned.

In the tiny apartment above the tavern, we had only two rooms, one for Zaneta, and one for Roderick and me. Ian had a house in town with his new wife.

The bed, covered in a faded patchwork quilt, dominated the room. I knelt before the washbasin on its stand in the corner. The plain white crockery served as my magical tool for observing events at home in Kirkenwood.

"Georgina?" Roderick's hand touched my shoulder gently. "Georgina, what ails ye?"

I felt him kneel beside me. He hesitated to take me into his arms. I could not look at my husband. I could not trust myself not to blurt out the entire episode to him.

He was mundane, totally lacking in talent. He would never understand, despite his observations of Zaneta's talents, never truly believe that I used my talents for good rather than evil. Too many people still feared and hunted witches.

I realized with a chill that I did not trust my husband with this knowledge, though I trusted him with my life on the field of battle.

"A headache," I mumbled in answer to his questions. A true enough statement.

"I wondered . . . are you . . ."

"No, I do not carry your child." The wound from the Turkish scimitar had seen to that. Drake had not healed my womb. "I cannot bear children. We must content ourselves with Zaneta."

Zaneta!

"Where is Zaneta?" I lifted my head and looked about despite the throbbing between my temples and behind my eyes.

"I sent her to her room with a list of sums to practice."

I crumpled onto the floor with relief that she had not shared the horrific events at Kirkenwood. We still explored the extent of her talents. I was never sure if she exhibited her own growth or my talent for strengthening another pushed her beyond her own levels.

He withdrew his hand from me. I felt him put emotional barriers between us.

"What are you teaching my daughter?" he asked. His voice broke with hesitation.

"I teach our daughter to read and write and cipher. I teach her to control the wildness in her spirit that manifests in strange knowledge." I gave the careful answer I had prepared weeks ago, before I accepted his abrupt proposal. I did not tell him, or anyone, that I also trained Zaneta to be a Master Magician of the Pendragon Society. Here or in England mattered not.

Where had the Society been during the crisis at Kirkenwood? Where had they been for the past five years while Dr. Milton Marlowe usurped Drake's authority, his position, his family?

If Barclay Marlowe wished to thwart his father, where were he and his demon now?

The same place I had been, pursuing my own interests; duped by Milton into believing all was well at home.

Guilt dragged me further into the depths of exhaustion and mistrust.

I needed to go home. The journey would take a minimum of a month from Boston Harbor to London. Then close to another month north to Kirkenwood along muddied roads, streams in spate and winter storms.

Could I abandon Zaneta and my husband? Did I want to?

Perhaps I could serve the children better from here, maintaining contact through Griffin and the scrying bowl.

Roderick rose from his kneeling position. "Come down when you are no longer ill."

He withdrew.

"Roderick," I called after him. All I heard was the clump of his shoes upon the stairs. "Roddie, don't desert me now," I whispered. "I need you. I wish you would hold me close and chase away the demons in my mind as you did once before."

For the first time in my life, I did not want to face my tasks alone.

For the first time since our marriage, Roderick did not enfold me in his arms as we slept that night. When I reached a tentative hand to touch his chest, he rolled over and turned his back on me.

Kirkenwood.

Emily approached her father's room with caution. Milton had moved the earl to a small guest room at the end of the hall with only one entrance. The single barred window in the room looked out over a sheer drop of three stories onto a flagstone terrace. If Papa could pry apart the bands of steel, jumping from there would most certainly kill or maim him. Emily doubted her father had enough strength of body or of will to do more than walk about the room with the aid of a strong footman and a cane.

Not all of Milton's servants and minions—all of them men except for the two maids who assisted Emily and her sisters—had fled into the cold dark night. Some cowered in their rooms. Some went about their business of maintaining the house and family, loyal to the holder of the purse strings rather than one individual.

What about the minor magicians who sat with Papa day and night?

What about Samuel? Was he truly a friend to her or just seeking to break down her defenses in order to betray her?

Emily waved her staff over the door. She heard the latch click open. The sound seemed to reverberate up and down the hallway. Surely the minion inside heard it.

One breath, then two more. Emily heard the minion

moving around the room, but he did not investigate the door. She waited through another three deep breaths. Magic coursed through her system like tiny bolts of lightning. She pushed the door open with her foot, keeping her staff ready to defend herself.

Darkness greeted her. Darkness and silence. She could not even hear her father's raspy breathing.

Had the minion killed him? Without Papa, she had not a prayer of saving Patricia.

She chanced a single step past the doorway. To her right, a dim glow peeped from a single shielded oil lamp on the bedside table.

"He panics if there is no light," a soft masculine voice whispered from Emily's left.

She breathed again, willing her eyes to adjust to the limited light. Gradually, the room's shadows began to take shape and form.

The minion sat in a chair pressed against the wall. He held a blunderbuss across his lap, its bell-shaped muzzle pointed toward her.

"I thank you for your care of my father," Emily replied in an equally hushed tone, as if she feared waking the man who tossed restlessly on the bed.

"I rather enjoyed the old gentleman during his few lucid moments. He has taught me much."

"Will you help me help him now?" Emily advanced one cautious step further into the room.

"Now that depends upon what you intend to do to him." The man brought his weapon to bear upon her.

"I intend to rouse him from the drugs imposed upon him."

"That may be difficult to do." She recognized Samuel's voice now. She wanted to trust him.

Dared she?

"Difficult but necessary. My sister," Emily choked at the thought of Patricia's burned face and hands. "My sister has need of his healing talent. He is the only one."

"Interesting." Samuel stood, keeping his blunderbuss aimed at Emily's breast. "Can the earl teach me to work a healing spell?"

Emily shrugged. The movement allowed her to move her staff forward a little. Her only hope of deflecting a blast from the gun depended upon a quick movement of her magical tool. She'd become so attached to the staff, she did not think she could work any magic without it.

"Healing is a talent you are born with, or not. If you have it, you need some training to control it. But you would know if you have it. You see a wounded or ill person—or an animal—and you cannot help but lay your hands upon them." She made up the last bit, guessing that was how the magic worked from what she'd seen of her father before his illness.

"Then I do not believe I have the talent. But can he train me to use what talents I do have?" Samuel looked at the man upon the bed with hope and . . . and wistfulness. She'd seen that look before, when he finished reading a letter to her from the colonies, or when he carried off a missive she left under her pillow.

"My cousin did not train you?" Emily moved her staff a little more while his attention rested elsewhere.

"Dr. Milton Marlowe allows his recruits to develop only a little of one talent, the one he needs at the moment. None of us dare learn more, lest we rival his power and challenge his authority."

Emily snorted in disdain. "The sign of a man who has no confidence in his own powers."

"But . . ." Samuel looked back at her. Then he smiled.

She wished she could see more of his expression in the dim room. Without looking into his eyes, she could not read his true intentions.

"This conversation is not helping my sister. She writhes in agony!" Emily moved her staff back and forth as if agitated. A tingling on her skin told her that she built protective wards around her.

"What will be my reward for helping you rouse your father?" The man narrowed his eyes and resettled the blunderbuss so that it aimed toward Drake Kirkenwood instead of Emily.

Emily gulped and fought panic.

"Training. My father and I will help you develop as much talent as you have. Possibly admit you to the Pendragon Society." Her words came out too rapidly. She betrayed her panic.

The man laughed. "Even I know that only members of

your family are admitted to that arcane society. I'd have better luck joining the Freemasons."

"Sometimes a spouse . . ." Emily let that half promise dangle.

"Offering yourself, Lady Emily?" Samuel stepped forward until he was close enough that she could see his leer.

"I also have four sisters. One of whom is in dire need."

"Very well. We deal with your father and sister. And then we discuss the future."

Emily let go of the breath and the fear she had been holding deep inside herself.

"I've removed the magic from Milton's potions," Emily offered.

"And the earl is becoming resistant to the drugs. Can you reach into his mind?"

"I can only try."

"I have tried and he has formidable barriers. He must know that Milton tried many times to pry secrets from him through coercive magic."

"I have touched his mind before, when he trained me. Perhaps the familiarity will allow me to break through his barriers. Samuel, please prevent interruptions."

Emily placed her staff upon the floor and kept one foot upon it. The Celtic cross finial would keep it from rolling. Gently she placed both hands upon Drake's temples. He thrashed beneath her, trying to throw her off balance. She pressed harder with her fingertips, while pushing her foot against the staff.

Samuel crept up behind her. She felt the warmth of his body and smelled his masculine scent overlaid with wet wool, cold wind, and pine. He'd been out of doors recently. An alarm bell chimed deep within her mind. She ignored it. She would deal with that later.

"A hand upon my shoulder," she whispered as she pushed her concentration deeper into her hands. Energy tingled beneath his palm as he placed it where she requested, hesitantly at first. Ladies did not allow such a familiar touch from a stranger.

"Open to me, Papa," she said loudly. "Let me help you."

Clouds of fatigue and confusion pressed against Emily's mind. She wanted nothing more than to forget . . . forget . . .

She visualized a bright arrow of blue fire and launched it against the clouds. In her mind, she saw the drug-induced fog ignite and shred as mist in noon sunshine. Images of shadows and snuffed candles replaced the fog.

A new arrow, this one flaming red, sped from her mind to the candles. One by one they ignited, banishing small circles of shadow. Large patches of darkness remained between the candles.

Beneath her hands her father stirred, then stilled as he absorbed her awareness. Then his hands shot upward and grasped her head at the temples, in the same grip she maintained upon him.

"Give," he croaked in a voice little used to exercise.

"Take," she replied, feeding him the most pressing information: her challenge to Milton's authority, the battle with magic, the ensuing fire, Patricia.

"No." Papa tried to pull away. His hands remained melded to her face.

Emily firmed her grip. Samuel did the same upon her shoulder.

"Yes. You must awaken. You must help my sister. Your daughter," Emily commanded.

"My baby. Patsy." He sobbed.

"Help me get him up," Emily said softly to Samuel.

"May I remove my hand from your shoulder?" Each word came out hesitantly, as if he tired—or explored new worlds.

"Um . . . ?" Could she continue without the subtle strength he fed her? She had to. "Yes. Move to the other side of the bed. Get your hands beneath him and help me lift."

Together, they managed to force the earl to sit. Samuel had to move around behind the wasted man and prop him upright with his body.

"My baby, Patsy," Drake continued to sob. Tears streamed down his face.

Emily tried another probe to break through some of the remaining drugging clouds.

"You have to help Patsy," Emily reminded her father. "You are the only one."

"Emma," he reached out a hand to his long dead wife. Did he remember they had buried her over five years ago?

"Mama can't help you, Papa. She has no magic to heal

Patsy. You have to do it. I will help you. And so will your son Griffin."

"Griffin. Such a sweet baby."

"Baby no longer." Emily swung her father's legs over the side of the big bed.

Samuel pushed until Papa teetered upon the edge. Then he scooted around to his side.

Together they dragged Papa upright, uncaring of his nightshirt ruched up around his hips. One step at a time they maneuvered him toward the door.

"Dressing gown," Samuel reminded Emily. "I can hold him upright if you can find it.

Emily grabbed the garment from a hook on the end of the wardrobe and flung it about her father's shoulders. Then they continued down to the drawing room. By the time they got there, Papa was moving his legs on his own, but still too wobbly to walk without help.

He collapsed at Patricia's side. His middle daughter had fallen into unconsciousness. She still whimpered and tossed, less violently than before. Her breathing was shallow and too rapid. He held his hands above the burns upon her face. Emily sensed his actions were automatic, with no conscious effort to push healing magic into the burns.

Nothing happened. He sank back onto his heels, looking utterly defeated and exhausted.

Belle crept into the room, somehow loosed from her banishment to the stables; Ana at her heels. Emily's familiar must have had something to do with opening latches and gates for her ancient dam. The dogs licked Papa's face.

He gathered them close to his chest.

"Let us help you, Papa," Emily whispered, dropping onto her knees beside him. Her beautiful holiday gown spread out around her in a puddle of sooty satin. A torn piece of lace from her sleeve dangled uselessly. She ripped it off and cast it aside. She draped her arms around her father and the dogs, willing them all to do something.

After a few moments Papa placed one hand over Patricia's face, keeping the other tangled in Belle's ruff.

Tiny bolts of blue lightning crackled from his fingertips. The hideous black skin moistened, peeled, shed, revealing new pink, and very tender flesh beneath.

Papa slumped.

"Thank God someone in this family has the sense to do something," Belinda fanned herself as she perched upon her chair. "Perhaps now we can call Uncle Milton back and return to normal."

"Shut up!" Griffin screamed. "I hate Uncle Milton. I hate him, hate him, hate him." He threw a fistful of air at his older sister.

She gasped and swallowed. Her mouth opened and closed. No sound emerged. She clasped her throat in panic.

Griffin grinned in satisfaction. Then he crawled over to Patricia and his father. "Can I help?" he asked.

"Hold your hand atop Papa's," Emily instructed. He did so with all the confidence of a five-year-old intent upon conquering the world. Then she placed her own hand atop his and moved all three of them from Papa's face to Patricia's left arm, the one that had been trapped in the folds of draperies and burned the worst.

"Breathe deeply, on my count," she commanded. All three of them inhaled and exhaled together. Magic rose in her.

The dogs grinned and nuzzled wet noses against Patricia's neck. Again the blue lightning sizzled. This time, Emily felt the burst of energy all the way up her arm, through her shoulder and neck and into her eyes.

Again the burned flesh sloughed off.

"Did I do that?" Griffin gasped in wonder.

"You helped, little brother."

They repeated the process upon Patricia's torso. Then they moved on to her legs.

"Can't. Too tired." Papa tried to withdraw.

Emily forced his hand back into position.

"Once more, Papa. Breathe deeply. We have to do this. Then you can sleep. Then you can take Belle back upstairs."

He leaned heavily against his dog as he pushed magic once more into his injured daughter.

The lightning that dribbled from his fingertips was pale and weak. It made no sound and affected the burns very little.

"Again, Papa," Emily insisted.

He tried. She felt him try. She felt him strain, and understood his agony of defeat.

At last she allowed him to withdraw, all three of them pitifully exhausted.

But Patricia was awake. She hurt, but she would live with only her legs wasted and scarred. She would live.

They all would.

And they were free of Dr. Milton Marlowe.

"I'll put your father to bed, Miss Kirkwood," Samuel offered.

For good or ill the man had become a part of the family.

Emily decided to trust him, a little.

Chapter 63

Boston, March 4, 1770.

"I MARRIED a witch," Roderick muttered to himself as he washed an endless batch of pewter and wooden tankards at the scullery behind the public room of the Crown and Anchor. Even on a Monday afternoon, he had tankards and coffee cups to wash. All of Boston seemed to have come through his public house today. Several fights had broken out between civilians and redcoats over the last three days. Ian had broken them up. The extra barmaids had refused to work today.

The populace had much to discuss.

Roderick had more important things on his mind.

"Georgina peered into a bowl of water speaking in tongues. I saw the lightning flash from her eyes and moving images appeared on the surface. The water was not even clean."

He shuddered at the memory that haunted him night and day. Two months he had lived with the knowledge that Georgina consorted with the devil.

At least that was what the church taught.

In the mood Boston was in, the people needed someone to burn. If not a man of the British Army, then a witch would do.

Grimly, he closed his eyes and accepted the fact that he must say nothing. "You could have trusted me with the truth, Georgina. I would not have betrayed you. I would not even consider it, if you had just trusted me."

At least Georgina had given up her unnatural habits,

dressing as a man and wielding weapons with less effort than he did. She attended church meetings Wednesday evenings with other women rather than Masonic Lodge meetings disguised as a man.

"Married her, I did. Married to her, I must remain," he sighed. Tonight he would hold her close again and try to forget her witchcraft, and that he knew she had masqueraded as her own brother. He'd try again to make her believe she could trust him with the truth, with everything in her life.

The long case clock in the corner bonged four of the hour. Monday afternoon, a slow time at the public house. His chapter of the Grand Lodge convened informally at the Crown and Anchor on Mondays to drink coffee, leaving some of the members to maintain affiliation with St. Andrew's Lodge of the Scottish Rite at the Green Dragon. He must go up and fetch his white lambskin apron and other regalia. Informal or not, this chapter of the Grand Lodge insisted upon full trappings to remind all participants that once a Mason, always a Mason.

He heard Georgina's light step upon the stair. She must be leaving for a quilting circle at Mistress Camden's home, taking Zaneta with her.

He turned to wish her good evening.

She had already disappeared through the door. He caught a glimpse of breeches and stockings and shoes. Then a flick of movement. The tip of her saber scabbard trailed behind.

His heart chilled. What the hell was she up to now?

"You cannot trust me, Georgina, with your secrets. You cannot trust any man. We should never have married."

The Sons of Liberty barely noticed my presence at the Green Dragon. Their numbers had grown far beyond the members of the Masonic Lodge and they met at any time, not just Wednesday night Lodge meetings. Every man who had lost his employment or home or fortune in the last few years and blamed the Townsend Acts for their loss, found sympathy in the gathering. They blamed Parliament and the army rather than their own embargo against English imports. Wealthier members like Paul Revere dispensed a few coins to the men. Sam Adams gave money when he had some. Mostly, he contributed fiery speeches that inflamed the general mood.

Not a few of the fistfights between civilians and redcoats had begun after one of Sam Adams' speeches.

The members greeted me with hearty welcome. I convinced them that I had finished my law studies and returned home. Now I had come back to be a part of their movement.

I listened with only half an ear to the latest outrages from the Townsend Acts. I needed to find myself among the familiar. I'd found little comfort and familiarity of late from my husband.

I had tried to be a good wife and mother and failed miserably. I did not know how to break down the emotional barriers between Roderick and myself.

I had too many secrets. I dared not trust him with my magic, with my masquerade, or my politics. He still drew a pension from the army and met with the paymaster and officers regularly.

I was too comfortable living as a man, with a man's freedom.

The simmering violence in the room irritated and alarmed me. Pressure in the air against my chest and temples robbed me of my ability to think rationally. I wanted to lash out at anyone, just to relieve that pressure.

A jolt from my own magic shocked me into awareness of my surrounding. The wards every magician developed against assault, mundane and magical, kept the pressure at bay.

Magic?

Who among the brethren would dare work magic on fellow Masons, especially during a meeting?

One hasty glance around the room and I let my gaze land where it would. Barclay Marlowe sat beneath one of the high windows, grinning smugly to himself.

Roderick listened with only half his attention as one Master Mason after another droned on and on about the injustice of the Townsend Acts. He'd heard it all before, on a daily basis. His mind tumbled about Georgina and where she had gone, armed and dressed as a man.

Zaneta was safely tucked into bed at Mistress Camden's home. He'd checked on that before admitting the first Mason to his taproom.

"What are we going to do about this?" he found himself asking. About the Townsend Acts or his errant wife?

"Master Publican," the Grand Master addressed him in superior tones. "Learned debate is the core of civilized society."

"But to what purpose? Will this debate touch the heart of Parliament and force them to repeal the taxes we find so offensive to our dignity as Englishmen?"

"It is our hope that our members will correspond with other Masonic Lodges back home and those brethren will address their MPs."

"Should we not have our own MPs to carry our arguments directly into the Commons and Lords?" He found removal of the Admiralty Court to Halifax most offensive. For serious crimes, colonists no longer had the option of trial by a jury of their peers. The prisoner must be transported to Halifax, or to England, for trial and certain conviction there.

"We have our colonial agents in London." The Grand Master dismissed Roderick's argument with a wave of his hand.

"Lord Hillsboro, the Minister for the Southern Department and therefore all of the colonies, has declared that only royal governors or the Crown can appoint a colonial agent. We have no one with our best interests at heart to plead our case!" Anger at Parliament, at life, at his wife propelled him to stand and raise his fist.

"I am certain, sir, that Parliament . . ."

"Has a stick up its ass!" Roderick stalked to the door, grabbed his greatcoat from the rack, and burst out into the wind and snow and ice. "As do you, Milord Grand Master," he added once safely away from his tavern.

He could not do anything about the punishing taxes as an individual, but he could go find his wife. He had a good idea where she might be lurking. Ian could watch the tavern better than he could at this point.

Quickly I reined in all traces of my magic lest Barclay Marlowe sense my presence. Keeping my head down and my tricorn low, I wended my way around the meeting room above the Green Dragon. Waves and waves of a compulsion to violence bounced off me.

I sensed that most of the men in the room absorbed that compulsion. Wild and insane emotions swirled in the eyes of each man I passed.

Fear lodged in my throat and refused to go away.

The closer I came to Barclay Marlowe the stronger became the unchecked emotions around me. I had to get closer yet to figure out what game he played and if his demon aided him.

From the smile on his face I knew 'twas all a game to him. Nothing mattered to him but his own pleasure—not honor or decency or laws. Not even love. His father had taught him that he was unlovable and therefore incapable of giving love.

Milton loved only himself and possibly his eldest son Neville. The one who betrayed him by dying and who haunted him as a ghost. Barclay betrayed him by living.

Logic had no part in the magic my cousin spilled into my friends with reckless abandon. 'Twas the magic of Chaos. Would I be able to see Tryblith, the Demon of Chaos, if he were present?

Could I defeat him on my own?

I shuddered in fear of a battle I knew must come.

By the time I reached his side, Barclay showed signs of fatigue. Good. If I could but touch him, on the shoulder or the neck, I'd know his plans and goals in less than a heartbeat.

An image of my nephew's face superimposed upon my brother's crashed into my mind. *You are a catalyst. That is your talent. Whatever magic you touch becomes greater than itself. Greater than the magician controlling it. Take care that the magic does not grow into an entity whole unto itself, without restraint, unthinking, uncontrollable.*

He might have stood beside me with this reminder, though I knew him to be three thousand miles away.

A hair's breadth from touching Barclay, I jerked my hand back to my side and stepped away from him.

I was too late. As one, the assembly of the Sons of Liberty rose and marched out of the room. They filed down the stairs and out into the street. Barclay followed, directing the mob with hand motions. Even hard-headed Sam Adams and Paul Revere marched to the drumbeat Barclay heard in his head. I caught echoes of it. But I had to keep reinforcing my wards to keep from following it myself. A shimmer in the air dancing around and around the mob told me that some Otherworldly creature aided my cousin.

In the interest of discovering Barclay's plots, and hopefully foiling them, I trailed behind the group. Barclay's compulsion had nothing to do with my steps. Absolutely nothing.

Or so I told myself over and over.

Left on Union Street, past Dock Square. The Customs House came into view. A crowd had already gathered. They shouted insults at the lone sentry who stood his ground, musket loaded and primed, bayonet at the ready.

"Come any closer and Oiy'll run you through," the panicky soldier shouted at the milling mob.

"Drop your musket," Sam Adams replied. He gathered up a fistful of dirty snow, wadded it into a ball, and flung it in the general direction of the poor soldier. That snowball landed wide, harmlessly hitting the bricks of the Customs House some six feet to the soldier's left.

Other members of the crowd repeated Adams' actions. Some with more accuracy; some of the balls, primarily the ones thrown by Barclay Marlowe, contained chunks of ice and rock.

I tried repeating the calming spell that had worked so successfully at the home of Thomas Hutchinson. I could not drop my wards long enough to allow my magic to spread. Barclay's compulsion to anger and violence, augmented by the demon still beat at me.

All the bells in Boston began to peal a warning. Moments later I heard the measured tread of a full guard jog trotting up King Street from the Long Wharf. Six privates and a corporal followed by Captain Thomas Preston marched through the mob in an orderly fashion, keeping order with fixed bayonets.

The poor sentry breathed an audible sigh of relief. I did, too, nearly gasping in an effort to bring more air into my body.

Surely Preston would gather up the sentry and return him safely to barracks.

"Form up, straight line. Prevent civilian entry," Captain Preston ordered in his resonant voice that carried above the noise of the mob.

I stood there gaping as I watched the men obey the stupid order. Did Preston want a confrontation? This demon-inflamed mob would not disperse under the threat of a few muskets.

In the background Barclay Marlowe grinned. Somewhere, somehow, he had shed his homespun brown suit and now wore the trim red-coated uniform of a lieutenant colonel.

Chapter 64

Kirkwood House, Chelsea, England.

MILTON drew a deep breath. He had only Peters and Neville to assist in this spell. And Neville had lost all of his powers when he died. But he had retained knowledge. Before dying, Neville had studied every bit of demonology he could lay his hands upon. He had gathered arcane texts on the Continent. With Neville's aid, Milton had experimented with new spells and combinations of herbs and minerals. If anyone could raise a demon and then control it, 'twas Neville Marlowe.

Fitting that we do this at the heart of the Pendragon Society, Neville chuckled. He floated around the perimeter of the subterranean meeting chamber, inspecting the pentagram permanently etched into the stone floor.

Peters lit the torches he had placed in a ring around the pentagram. He nervously checked the entrance tunnel time and again.

Neville stationed himself in Peters' path. The secretary licked his lips and stepped around the ghost. He made a warding gesture behind his back.

Neville blew chill air onto the man's neck as he passed. He laughed when Peters jumped and nearly dropped the taper he used to light the torches.

Milton frowned at the two of them. "Get on with it," he ordered. He continued to dribble charcoal mixed with a long list of ingredients to contain the demon along the lines of the pentagram. At each step he murmured warding spells.

"Are you certain we can contain the beast?" he asked Neville.

Of course I'm certain. As long as we name it in our summons, we have the power to order it to behave.

Milton humphed, uncertain he trusted his son's cavalier dismissal of concern for this dangerous spell.

At last Peters finished tracing the sigil with the charcoal mixture. Milton beckoned both Peters and Neville to his side. Peters obeyed immediately, being careful not to touch Neville in any way. The ghost drifted casually around the perimeter before assuming a place at Milton's other side. As he passed Peters, he feigned dropping his severed leg. Peters automatically reached out to catch the grisly thing. When he realized what he had done, he shoved the ghostly limb back at Neville with a shudder and grimace.

"Enough," Milton snarled. He glared at his son.

Neville shrugged, nearly dropping both the arm and the leg he was doomed to carry.

Cautiously, Milton began the chant to raise the demon.

Remember to name him, Neville whispered.

"I name thee Tryblith, Demon of Chaos. Answer my summons. Appear at my command!" Milton intoned with a final burst of magic.

The torches dimmed and guttered.

Darkness descended upon the cavern.

Only a red glow at the center of the pentagram cast the scene in a ghastly light.

A black mass began to rise in the center of the glow. Blood-red eyes opened, blinked, and fixed upon Milton.

You have named me. I am yours to command, a deep voice rose from the depths of the Underworld.

"Tryblith, Demon of Chaos, I have need of a grimoire that contains a spell to return my dead son to me," Milton said, careful to keep his voice neutral, devoid of any inflection that the demon might misinterpret and use to seize control.

I know of this grimoire.

"Are you able to fetch it for me?"

What will you grant me in return for this service?

"What you desire most."

Freedom.

"When I have the grimoire."

Now.

"When I have the grimoire. Not before."

*Another commands me. His power is greater than yours.
I must obey.* The beast sank back into darkness.

No! Neville dove into the center of the pentagram. He
reached a ghostly arm to capture the demon.

With a great sucking noise, Milton's son disappeared
along with the demon into the abyss.

Boston.

"You may not kill Barclay Marlowe!" Roderick shouted
into Georgina's ear as he pinned her arms to her sides
from behind.

She squirmed and twisted and almost escaped him. He
leaned back and lifted her off the ground, still pinioning
her arms.

Deprived of leverage, Georgina relaxed, almost to the
point of sliding through his grip. He'd forgotten that she
had defended herself in frequent brawls as well as on the
field of battle during her years as a mercenary.

"He is an officer in His Majesty's Army. Killing him will
mean a death sentence for you," he reminded her.

"My cousin uses magic and a demon to manipulate this
riot," she said. Anger still colored her voice.

"There will be other times, and other places."

"Must we sit by and watch this . . ."

Richard Palmes, a neighboring merchant, highly respected in the community, pushed to the head of the
crowd. Short and portly, he managed to hold his arms out
and keep a few of the mob from pressing any further toward the line of soldiers. To their credit none of the privates quaked in their boots.

"Preston," Palmes called out to the officer in charge in a
broad accent that demanded attention. "Hold your fire. For
the love of God, do not fire upon my fellow citizens. We are
all Englishmen, loyal and true."

The words meant to calm both sides fell flat, as if he'd
whispered them in private.

Marlowe's grin spread so wide his face just might split.

"The course of this day's actions falls to you and your fellow citizens, Merchant Palmes," Preston acknowledged.

Only a few feet separated Palmes' round belly from the forest of bayonets. The men pressed him close.

Still smiling, Marlowe caught up a piece of ice, nicely pointed, like a miniature bayonet, and hurled it toward the line of soldiers. A private ducked the missile and in doing so, slipped upon the icy cobbles.

Just then a musket fired.

Roderick dropped Georgina and pulled her into a low crouch. He searched the crowd for signs of the next attack.

The rest of the soldiers loosed a volley point blank into the crowd.

Screams.

Blood staining the snow.

Bodies falling.

Shock stilled the mob for only a heartbeat. Then they scattered, not for shelter, but to summon the rest of the city.

"They'll tear the soldiers limb from limb," Georgina whimpered.

"Come," Roderick ordered. He grabbed Georgina by the scruff of her neck and dragged her into the fray. "Get the soldiers into the Customs House." He grabbed Palmes and three others along the way, all respectable, sensible fellows.

Behind him, he heard the sound of breaking windows, smelled smoke and . . . and tar. Someone in the mob had prepared for this disaster and planned ahead to tar and feather the hapless soldiers.

He knew the garrison and the commanders. They would retaliate heavily. The people of Boston were in no mood to tolerate any action or reaction by the army. Open and armed rebellion would certainly follow.

Were the colonies ready for this?

Roderick did not think so.

He shouldered men aside in his desperate dash to protect the soldiers who reloaded in rapid and disciplined fashion.

Another round of musket fire pierced the air before he gained five steps.

More screams. More blood.

The acrid odor of burned sulfur filled the air.

More men screamed.

"My God, the demon is killing them!" Georgina's face went white. She tried to run again.

Roderick tackled her about the knees. They both fell to the ground. Georgina's body went limp beneath him.

"Don't die, Mama," Zaneta pleaded with me from a great distance.

I shut her out, not wanting the little girl to be witness to the horrible events of this day, even if only through her mental contact with me.

"Get up, Georgie. Get up or be trampled," Roderick insisted, lifting me beneath the shoulder.

Three colonists lay dead, and a fourth mortally wounded.

How many had the soldiers killed? How many more had the demon felled?

"I have to stop this," I muttered, trying desperately to regain my balance and separate myself from Roderick's fierce grip.

"If I'd challenged the demon at the Green Dragon . . ." Goddess, what more fitting place to take down a demon than at the Green Dragon!

"You can't change what is done. You have to get up and help me, before more men die needlessly." Roderick dragged me in his wake.

I stumbled along, fighting his grip upon my collar as much as the icy surface beneath my feet and the need to throw a slew of spells after the demon.

"Let go. I can walk on my own," I insisted.

Roderick loosed his hold. I staggered upright and held my balance. I breathed deeply and let my anger fade. I turned my attention to getting the soldiers to safety. 'Twasn't their fault they'd been impressed by the government into the thankless life of a recruit. 'Twasn't their fault Preston had not removed them all to safety when he had the chance.

'Twas Barclay Marlowe's fault.

Had Tryblith driven him to betray his fellows?

Had Tryblith propelled him to create Chaos?

A push from behind nearly sent me sprawling. Roderick caught me, set me on my feet, and plowed on.

Like the good officer he had been, he barked orders, demanded attention and obedience. Within moments, he and I and a few other sensible citizens, the ones who had been here before the demon and were still immune to the Chaos, had ushered the soldiers into the Customs House and relative safety.

I breathed deeply, not realizing how short of breath the efforts of the day had made me. Roderick bent over, hands upon his knees, and coughed. He, too, was winded. He did not like to admit that the old wound from Barclay's casual shot had cost him much in health and stamina.

I wanted to put my arm around his shoulders. Then I remembered how coldly he had treated me these last two months. I still wore my masculine guise. He did not know me as his wife in this form, I preferred to keep him ignorant.

He'd not welcome attention from me as either his wife or her bastard half brother.

Our compatriots milled around the entry of the government building. A quick look out the window showed the mob dispersing, running about the town in disorganized groups shouting threats and throwing stones.

I caught no sight of Barclay Marlowe, nor did I sense the presence of his demon. His dastardly deed accomplished, he had withdrawn like a coward.

Would a meager three deaths satisfy the appetite of Tryblith?

Preston gathered his wits and his men and prepared them to march out the back way in orderly fashion. The merchants elected to follow them, gaining what little protection they could from the reloaded and primed weapons.

Not knowing what else to do, I set my feet to join them.

Roderick held me back with a punishing grip upon my arm. I'd have bruises in the morning and the devil's own time explaining them.

"You could have told me, Georgina. You could have trusted me," he hissed in my ear.

My heart skipped a beat. I forgot to breathe.

"How can I trust you if you cannot share with me what you truly are. How you truly live."

"I . . . I . . ." I had no words, no argument. "Would you

have allowed me the freedom to be who I truly am if you knew?" I snarled at him instead.

"And what are you, Georgina?"

I clamped my mouth shut. Too long had I kept secrets to blurt them out now.

"See? You do not know yourself. How can you accept the responsibility to be free if you do not know what you need freedom from?"

"I know that I need to be free of the tyranny of a husband who owns me." My voice sounded lame. I was allowing my old habits of reticence to dictate this argument.

"When have I ever owned you?" He looked tired and bewildered. "I thought we were partners."

He had treated me honorably. I could not deny that. But would he allow me to continue my life as a Mason, a swordsman, as a person with thoughts and ambitions and opinions of my own?

"How long have you known?" I had to think. I had to make up my mind right here and now what I truly wanted in my future. To go on living the precarious life of a mercenary and spy? Or to help this decent man run a coffeehouse and raise his daughter, a budding magician who desperately needed my training. And my love.

What did he need?

"I figured it out in Virginia," he said. He did not look at me.

I was on my own with this decision.

"Did you . . . did you hear me when I left you at the edge of Williamsburg?"

He nodded silently.

"Did you mean it?" he asked after too many long moments.

"Yes," I whispered, not knowing if I wanted him to hear me.

He swallowed. I watched his Adam's apple bob.

"And the rest? You brought Zaneta to me for a reason."

He shrugged. "A guess. Too many unexplained things about the way you know things, the way you manipulate crowds."

If he knew what I was and had still married me, there was hope for us both.

"I was a mercenary soldier. I am your wife. And . . ."

Hope glimmered in his eyes.

The last confession stuck in my throat.

"And what, Georgie?"

"I am a Master Magician initiated into the Pendragon Society." I exhaled long and deep, shedding the weight of years of silence. That other Lodge must remain my secret upon pain of death.

"I am not familiar . . ."

"Oblegid is my familiar." The fat and lazy cat spent more time asleep before the fire than aiding me or catching mice. A poor substitute for a wolfhound. But Emily had inherited a wolfhound. My brother's family was a problem I could not address at this time and place. Roderick and his daughter were my problem, my dilemma, my life.

"I had gathered that Oblegid was more than just a cat when she fetched me that last night in Williamsburg. What makes you a Master Magician and not a witch?"

"Do we have to discuss this here?" I asked. I searched the hall for signs of eavesdroppers. Thankfully the soldiers and merchants had left. But this was a public building and these were subjects not for public consumption.

"Make your way home any way you can. I will collect Zaneta and join you there."

"I am better equipped to defend our daughter should the mob spread and lose total control."

"I know that. I would rather have you home and dressed as Zaneta's mother when I bring her. Time enough for her to learn the whole truth later. We should not overwhelm her with too much at once. May I borrow your sword, Georgie?"

"Since you asked politely and you do have our daughter's best interests at heart, you may." I unbuckled the scabbard. "You have not forgotten how to use this?" I asked as I handed it to him.

"Not bloody likely. I spent more time in the army than you did."

I grinned at him. "Ah, but I had better training." The breach between us was mending. We still needed time and honesty.

"Then you will have to give me lessons. I fear this is not the only fray Boston will have to fight."

"I fear so, too." I sobered immediately.

"Are we fighting together, Roddie?"

"Yes." He held my gaze.

"What are we fighting for, Roddie?"

"Freedom." He grinned at me.

"Honor, justice, rule by law, and promises mean something." I repeated the litany of King Arthur as handed down to the Pendragon Society and all English citizens.

Chapter 65

Boston, spring, 1770.

FATE must have laughed hilariously at the irony of the Boston Massacre. Parliament rescinded the Townsend Acts on the very day the mob forced a squad of soldiers to fire upon them. All of the taxes we found so hateful fell away.

All except the tax on tea. That would remain a bone of contention between England and her colonies.

Paul Revere created an etching of the massacre that circulated throughout the colonies and England. We'd not soon forget our dead.

The city of Boston gradually calmed enough to allow Captain Preston and his guard of privates and a corporal to come to trial for killing civilians. John Adams, cousin to the volatile Samuel Adams, took on the onerous chore of defending the soldiers. Though he supported the aims of the Sons of Liberty, he held that all men, even the enemy, deserved a fair trial with a defense lawyer. To deny this to the soldiers involved in the Boston Massacre was to deny ourselves the same rights.

Most Bostonians found the tight-lipped lawyer pompous and annoying. I found him shy, extremely intelligent, and quite charming. His beloved wife Abigail kept mostly to their farm in Braintree. Each time she ventured into the city, we were newly astounded at her beauty, her wit, and her intelligence keen enough to rival John's. In her absence, John's standoffish behavior allowed us to believe that she must be plain and shrewish, incapable of attracting a more pleasant man.

The two were made for each other, as I came to believe

that Roderick and I belonged together. Almost as if our union had been determined in another lifetime.

John Adams managed to win an acquittal from the jury. Governor Hutchinson exhibited the extreme good sense, for once, in posting all of the defendants to duties that confined them to Castle Island in the middle of Boston Harbor and not in the city itself.

Barclay Marlowe joined them. He appeared in the city upon occasion, always safely in his uniform and with a squad of armed soldiers in his wake. If he knew of the Crown and Anchor and who owned the coffeehouse, he made no indication in public.

I detected no evidence of the demon at his side when he prowled the city.

His shadow never darkened our door. I warded it to ensure that he could not enter even in disguise or magically cloaked. This measure also kept Zaneta from sneaking out without me knowing.

In private, I found plenty of evidence that Barclay guarded against me. Magical wards appeared at every military post and cache of arms. They irritated my senses, like nettles on the skin. Others felt it, too. Mundane others.

Citizens threw insults at any soldier who dared walk alone in the city. Pamphlets circulated with more virulent rhetoric.

My cousin made a show of burning piles of pamphlets upon a bonfire before the Customs House. The locals only printed more.

I wrote three a week for Sam Adams and the Sons of Liberty.

The city simmered on the edge of rebellion.

I had no doubt that Lieutenant Colonel Barclay Marlowe manipulated all the parties involved. The question remained: Why? How did this thwart his father?

I decided to go demon hunting.

To find a demon, I needed more than just a scrying bowl. I needed a bigger space than the tiny chamber above the Crown and Anchor. Truth be told, I wanted Emily's help. The strength of a wolfhound and the entire Inner Circle would help as well.

I had none of those things and I would not endanger Zaneta by tapping her powers.

"So, where are you going to do it?" Roderick asked as I closed and grounded my communication with Emily through the scrying bowl.

"How long have you been standing there?" I asked, rather than answer his question. My habit of reticence was hard to break.

"Long enough to hear your side of the conversation with your niece. You asked detailed questions about a book of demonology."

I nodded.

"You are going to hunt this thing."

"Aye." Emily and Drake had agreed that I had acted correctly in staying in Boston. As long as Barclay and the demon were loose, someone from the Pendragon Society needed to monitor and possibly counter them.

"Alone?"

"There is no one else to help me."

"I am going with you."

"Roddie, you can't help me. You have no talent."

"I can watch your back and wield a sword and pistol."

"Yes, you can." I smiled warmly. "And you have strength you can loan me."

And so we left the tavern in Ian's capable hands, sent Zaneta to Mistress Camden, and hired horses to take us out of Boston.

We rode half a day west and north to a pond, hidden from view from the road by half a mile of woods. The dark water sank to unknown depths. It could have been only three feet. Or it could reach into the center of the earth. Or it could cross into the Netherworld. The mystery of it connected me to the demon.

"I don't like this place," Roderick said upon a shiver.

Spring had not yet reached into these hidden depths of the forest. Patches of dirty snow littered the ground in sheltered places. Snowdrops and fresh greens did not yet poke their heads through the leaf litter.

The sky darkened and the wind came up. The building pressure of a thunderstorm made my ears ring and the hairs along my spine stand up.

I turned a slow circle looking up through the bare branches—like skeletal arms reaching across the canopy to strangle each other.

Then I found what I sought; a clump of mistletoe in the crown of an aged oak.

Slowly I paced a circle around the tree, making certain that Roderick stood within its protection. Then with a lump of charcoal, I drew a pentagram upon the trunk at the east. Amber fire followed my tracings. Roderick started mumbling prayers with his eyes closed.

I repeated the sigil at west, north, and south, invoking the element associated with each direction.

"Boost me up?" I asked Roderick. I grasped a section of the trunk between sigils.

He placed his cupped hands for my foot. I stepped into them and bounced. He pushed up. The lowest branch came within my grasp. I scrambled up.

"Watch my back," I called as I climbed.

He hoisted himself up behind me.

"I meant down there." I pointed to the lake edge where wind rippled the water. It lapped higher and higher as if reaching to consume whatever stood on the verge.

"I'm not leaving you alone up here where I can't reach you if something goes wrong." He set his chin.

"Scared?" I challenged, trying to lighten our mood.

"Yes."

"Good." I sobered. "If we are scared, we'll be more watchful."

"Like just before a battle."

"Yes." I let that sink in as I shimmied out on a sturdy branch that spread over the water. "Promise me, if anything goes wrong, you will take me back to my brother. He has the healing touch. He's the only one who can cure a demon-inflicted wound."

"I promise." He kissed me quickly.

Then I scooted out of his reach.

Lying flat upon the branch, I waited for a moment of stillness. Several long minutes passed before the wind gave any relief to the disturbed water surface. The second I could see a clear patch, I dropped a pebble from the lake edge into the pool.

I spoke aloud in ancient Welsh an invocation calling and naming the demon Tryblith as the pebble fell into the murky depths.

Ripples spread out from the point of contact. Lightning flashed. Thunder roared. Rain poured down. The wind howled. The ripples became waves. The water churned as if something huge and primeval roused from the deepest lake bottom.

The water's surface turned black. I had opened a door into the Netherworld.

Two red eyes rose to the surface of the pond.

You called me. Now release me. His form became visible: a great dragon maw, potbelly, engorged genitals, and black claws that dripped venomous ichor.

I gulped and shivered in terror. I had not consciously called the demon. I wanted only to spy upon it and its current master.

"Where is your master?" I asked, hoping I had banished the quaver of fear from my voice.

I call no one master. I master those who call me.

"I will not release you. I banish you to your lair behind the seal of the Pendragon!" I shouted.

The demon laughed as it sank back to the bottom of the lake.

But I had caught a glimpse of Barclay behind the demon, tethered, heart to heart by a black whip of magic. A second whip, thinner, frayed, and incomplete snaked out to encircle Milton's neck.

"Tryblith was right," Roderick said quietly. "Those who call the demon become ensnared by it. He becomes the master and they the servant."

"You saw?"

"I saw. And I fear. Is it truly gone?"

"From here, for now. We have to leave quickly. I have to erase the pentagrams and the circle so that he cannot use them to come back."

"At least we did not have to take you back to your brother for healing."

"This time." I grabbed him in a fierce hug the moment we reached the ground. I had to touch someone real, someone who loved me and would protect me.

Chapter 66

Kirkenwood, summer, 1770.

"WHY did you wait so long to act?" Samuel de Vere asked Emily quietly. He sat beside Papa's chair by the hearth, reading the latest newspapers from London. He had the habit of pulling questions out of the air just as Emily thought of the same subject. Yet he claimed no talent for mind reading.

Emily scrutinized Papa as he dozed in the big wingchair with his feet propped upon a footstool. Every time she thought of the years she had wasted, she wondered if her beloved father would recover from the drugs and spells poured into him by Dr. Milton Marlowe.

"Fear. Habit. I concentrated so hard on keeping Milton out of the archives, it never occurred to me that the best way to do that was to evict him from the house." She shrugged rather than confess her deep guilt.

Then she reached for Ana beside her chair, her newspapers forgotten in her lap.

"I understand." Samuel nodded. "I watched and waited for an opportunity to break away from Dr. Marlowe, never considering that I could just walk away."

"Could you truly just walk away? Would he not follow?"

"I don't know. He threatened dire consequences. I don't know if he had the courage to follow through."

"I know."

Several long moments passed in amiable silence.

Papa roused. "I need to walk, Samuel. Will you help me up?"

Samuel grasped Papa's elbow and lifted him upright before Emily could put aside her papers to help.

"Perhaps the time has come to move to London," Samuel suggested as he guided Papa about the room. "We need to be close to hand when Dr. Marlowe makes his next move."

"Mr. de Vere, we are vulnerable. We are only safe here, at Kirkenwood," Emily protested. Inside she quaked at the thought of leaving the secure walls of the remote estate.

"All magicians are vulnerable at all times. If Dr. Marlowe decides to launch an attack, he can strike you anywhere. We must take the initiative," Samuel countered her argument.

Papa nodded agreement. He had gained a great deal of strength since Christmas. Not enough to walk without assistance, and he still needed help dressing. But he read arcane texts and worked scrying spells to keep track of Dr. Marlowe and the other members of the Pendragon Inner Circle. Once a week he tried healing spells upon Patricia's wasted legs. Sometimes she regained a little flesh and strength. Mostly the magic accomplished little or nothing.

The entire household acted as a house in mourning, moving quietly, speaking in whispers.

Emily's hand automatically went to Little Ana's ears.

The big dog lifted her massive head and licked Emily's hand. Her dam, the first Ana, had passed the mantle of responsibility to her pup. Now the pup was well grown, full of energy and ready for adventure. Not even she could give Emily an excuse to delay.

"Papa is not strong enough to travel."

"I gain strength by the day, Emily," Papa replied. To prove himself, he shook off Samuel's supporting hand and walked—albeit slowly—the length of the small salon that overlooked the lake.

Samuel followed close upon the heels of the earl. As Papa turned to come back toward the settee where Emily sat, he stumbled. Samuel caught him and set him back upon his feet. He'd had a lot of practice doing just that.

"We must travel by slow coach," Papa said, as he sat heavily in his wing chair beside the hearth. His hands shook and he drew a robe over his lap. "Samuel, please compose the letters to prepare the house in Chelsea and to arrange accommodations each night. Ten miles a day should be about the proper distance to begin."

"I will see to it, milord." Samuel bowed and retreated to the writing desk in the corner.

"Ten miles a day will take us nigh on six weeks to reach London. The trip will kill you, Papa. Then what will we do? England will be without a Pendragon."

"England has been virtually without a Pendragon for five years. If I die, then you will be Pendragon. The dogs have chosen." He dropped his hand over the side of the chair seeking his aged Belle. She wasn't there.

The big dog had passed on Christmas morning. The exertions of healing Patricia, even if only partially, had proved too much for her.

"Papa, I am not a Master Magician. I have not been admitted to the Inner Circle . . ."

"The Pendragon Society has abandoned us. They have never chosen the Pendragon. The dogs do," Papa replied with more strength and conviction than Emily had seen from him since before Dr. Milton Marlowe took over the family.

"I believe I have packing to supervise. Including an artifact in the archives." Emily leaned heavily upon her everpresent staff to rise from the low settee. She would miss this room and its view of the lake. She would miss knowing that the Lady slumbered so close by. The Lady had given her the sword Excalibur for a reason. Emily had attached herself to the staff for a reason.

Was she ready? Would she ever be ready?

She needed help. Samuel was good. But he was not a member of the family, did not have the sense of antiquity and balance in his magic that the Kirkwoods did.

Only the Inner Circle of the Pendragon Society had the strength of magic to combat one of their own. "I'll summon them to meet us in London at the end of September, the beginning of the season and the opening of Parliament," she whispered to herself. Somehow she had to make the unknown members listen to her summons.

They were not entirely unknown to her. After all, to be a member of the Society one had to carry the blood of the Pendragons. She knew all of the family, either personally or through the extensive family tree in the archives. Among the senior members of the family, she should be able to deduce who had enough magic to help lead the Society and guide the Pendragon.

A deep breath for reassurance and she left to delve into the archives for the sword and several grimoires she thought might help her in this decisive journey.

White Hart Club, London, England, October 31, 1770.

Dr. Milton Marlowe spread a deck of cards before him in an arcane game of patience. Only he knew the rules to this particular game. He made them up as the cards revealed themselves.

"The Queen of Hearts," he mumbled. "The Lovers in another deck. I see that Samuel has followed orders well. But he has taken too long. I need a Kirkwood heir in my control now."

He turned over another card. "The Ace of Spades. Death. Certainly Drake Kirkwood cannot live much longer." And then Samuel would deliver the malleable Griffin into Milton's hands. He'd given up waiting for Barclay to come to his senses and return from the colonies and marry Emily, the bitch.

The third card flipped over, almost of its own accord. The Joker. The Fool. The Trickster. No matter which name he gave the card, it spelled trouble. He buried the card in the middle of the deck, where it belonged, unseen and powerless.

He thought he'd removed the wild cards from the deck before beginning this game.

He turned the top card. The Joker again. Another card. Another Joker.

His eyes grew wide and his breath short.

Who is the Trickster?

Tonight. Midnight. Come.

A mental summons wafted through the air. Or did it come from the cards? It carried the harmonic vibration peculiar to the Inner Circle of the Pendragon Society. Someone convened a meeting. Tonight, at midnight.

"Very well, Drake Kirkwood. I shall come tonight, and end this farce once and for all. But I shall turn up where and when you least expect me. I shall lay the traps, not you."

"Excuse me, Dr. Marlowe." A liveried footman proffered a silver salver with an envelope upon it.

Milton examined the heavy red seal upon the vellum before picking up the envelope. The royal lion rampant stood out prominently at the center of the wax.

His hands shook with anxiety as he broke open the seal.

"The courier awaits a reply, Dr. Marlowe," the footman reminded him.

Of course a personal summons by the king required an immediate response. "Pen?" Milton held out his hand to the footman.

"Upon the desk, sir."

Scowling that the underling had not fetched it for him, Milton retreated to the nearest writing desk. Quickly he penned an acceptance of the invitation to attend His Majesty this very afternoon. Long shadows already crept through the long windows of the salon.

"Summon my carriage," he ordered the footman as he handed him the reply.

"Sir, will you require a change of clothing as well?" the footman reminded him that he wore a gabardine suit and matching waistcoat. Totally unsuitable for a summons to court.

"Of course. Fetch them from my secretary immediately." Milton dismissed the man.

He twisted his signet ring anxiously. How could he drive to Richmond Palace, attend the king, and return to Chelsea by midnight?

He could not. Confrontation with the Pendragon Society and Drake Kirkwood would have to wait.

Drake Kirkwood would have more time to regain strength and solidify his power over the Society. But All Hallows Eve would pass. Drake would not have easy access to help from the Otherworlds at a later date.

Milton smiled. If he managed to summon assistance from the Otherworld after sunset and before midnight and set it to wreak havoc among the Society tonight . . .

Richmond Palace.

"The king summoned me personally. Why have you kept me waiting?" Dr. Milton Marlowe demanded of the slight figure who stood in the doorway. Milton anxiously paced

the tiny antechamber he'd been shown to upon arrival at
Richmond Palace over an hour ago.

"His Majesty is otherwise occupied," Lord George
Sackville said. His tone was grave, but a tiny smirk drew
one corner of his mouth upward. "I will relay your words
to the king. When I have the opportunity."

Milton clenched his fists to keep from blasting the toady
with a magical noose and choking the truth and then the
life out of the man. A powerful speaker in the House, his
presence would be missed but not mourned. No one liked
the former Treasurer of Ireland.

But Milton had found him useful in the past.

"The note summoning me here was penned and dated
by His Majesty. I will speak to none other." Milton dismissed Sackville. The man had ruined his own military career back in '59. Why was he continuing to plague the
government? He should be bowing to Milton for the help
he'd given the lord.

Milton continued to pace his circle, intent upon his primary mission. In his mind, he pictured the pentagram he
had drawn with his finger and his own urine in the carpet.
Time moved forward. He needed to complete this ritual
before midnight. He'd already wasted hours on this bogus
summons.

One did not have to be present in the Pendragon temple
to confront them. To battle them. To bring them to the
brink of ruin.

Lord Sackville shifted his weight from foot to foot and
fidgeted with the gold braid upon his cuffs.

"Unless the summons from His Majesty was a master-
work of forgery," Milton stopped just before he finished his
circle. Best to leave an opening.

Sackville smiled that half smirk of his that irritated
friend and foe alike.

Everyone knew that Sackville had his own agenda for
accumulating power. Intriguing possibility that he added
forgery to his skills.

But possible allies did not move the spell apace. Milton
took the final two steps to complete his ritual circle.

Power rose in a solid cone. He needed one more ingre-
dient to bring his plans to fruition to ruin the Pendragon
Society once and for all.

Lord George Sackville looked a likely provider. The blood of a traitor was more powerful than that of a Master Magician for this spell.

Sackville held Milton's gaze in silence. The cone of power within the circle began to vibrate with impatience. Milton sensed two eyes from the Netherworld staring at him from within the murky depths he had drawn forth. He had to act soon or lose his opportunity.

Twice before he had summoned this demon and lost it. He dared not do so again. If he failed again tonight, Tryblith would respond no more to the spells cast by Milton Marlowe.

"Your bogus summons has disrupted very important work, milord." Milton advanced upon Sackville, fingering a stiletto he kept hidden in his sleeve.

"I know that you work to control Chaos. The Chaos centered in the American colonies. I offer you the opportunity, once and for all to avenge yourself upon the people who murdered your oldest son so ignominiously and corrupted your second son into their ways." Sackville did not flinch at the sight of the knife.

Too late. Within the cone, the large being with the piercing eyes drifted back into its own world. The cone cracked and began to dissolve.

Milton's power crumbled with it.

A dozen other minor entities scampered out of the circle that should have contained them.

Chapter 67

Kirkwood House, Chelsea, England.

ANA scratched and whined at the long windows of the library at Kirkwood House, eager to be out and about the night's adventure.

Emily paced the room, equally impatient. She wore the blue robe of an initiate. The whisper-weight wool brushed softly against her naked skin as she paced before the French doors. She carried her staff with the Celtic cross finial as usual. Indeed, she felt more naked without the staff than she did without clothes. Excalibur, she had strapped to her back in its plain leather sheath.

She wondered how she could manipulate both tools. The sword weighed heavily upon her shoulders and in her hand. She would rather leave it behind than the staff but sensed that she would need both tonight.

The summons must come soon. An hour had passed since Papa had disappeared into the garden wall. Seven other senior relatives had arrived an hour before that.

What was he waiting for?

Papa had assured her that the Pendragon Society had no business tonight other than to initiate her as a Master Magician of the Inner Circle and expel Dr. Milton Marlowe from access to the Society at any level.

With one hand upon Ana's ruff, she cast her senses outward, listening, feeling, for some inkling of the cause of the delay. One by one, she felt the heartbeats of every member of her family within the house. She removed each from her awareness as she identified them. Then she moved on to the servants.

Thankfully the Simpsons had returned to the household within hours of her dismissal of Dr. Milton Marlowe. She trusted the butler, housekeeper, maid, and footman more than she did the Inner Circle who remained unknown and alien to Emily. The longtime servants made a formidable barrier between the family and the outside world. Other faithful retainers stood guard at the exterior gates as well as the interior portals.

Then she found Samuel de Vere's heartbeat among the household and smiled. Warmth infused her being. He stood guard in the nursery to keep precocious Griffin from "investigating" tonight's proceedings. She wished he could join her in this initiation. But he was not family. Yet.

He had proved himself reliable and trustworthy many times these past few months.

But Emily no longer trusted easily. Milton Marlowe had taught her that.

A curious hollow space remained where her senses could not penetrate. The inner sanctum of the Pendragon Society was shielded against magical and mundane interlopers. She'd discovered that when she stepped up to Knighthood level in the Society.

This emptiness tasted different. She caught a whiff of sulfur and another scent, more acid, like . . . like rancid urine.

Richmond Palace.

Milton whirled to face the eyes that blinked at him in disappointment.

Freedom, a guttural voice whispered from the cracked cone of power. *You promised me freedom.* The entity sank lower, back toward the Netherworld that had spawned it.

"Wait!" Milton shouted.

"Dr. Marlowe?" Sackville replied.

"Not you, you twit. That." He pointed desperately at the shimmering light within the circle. As he pointed he drew the stiletto blade across his palm, flinching at the sharp pain that followed.

He'd never liked this part of magic and usually took the

donation of blood from one of his underlings. Samuel de Vere seemed to have an abundance of it.

The blood welled up along the knife cut and dripped off his palm into the cone of power. It sank slowly toward the carpet.

A mouth appeared before the red eyes. Then a fat, black tongue darted out from the maw of sharp teeth and caught the blood. The tongue disappeared into the mouth and the being closed its eyes in ecstasy.

More.

"What is happening, Dr. Marlowe?" Sackville demanded. He tapped his foot impatiently.

"A moment, milord." Milton squeezed a few more drops of blood into the demon's waiting mouth.

More. Its voice grew stronger, almost audible.

"Dr. Marlowe, I see only you, mutilating yourself, much as I would expect the Red Indians who murdered your son to do."

"You would see only that," Milton ground out. His knees began to wobble and his head nearly disconnected from his neck.

Then he noticed how wide the crack in the dome had grown. His heart leaped to his throat. What if the demon escaped?

He needed to control the beast not loose it.

"I need allies, Dr. Marlowe. Allies with similar goals to my own, not madmen."

More, the demon demanded.

Milton saw the vague outline of a bulbous body and dragon maw beneath the beady eyes that wanted to rip away his defenses and read his soul.

He could not allow that. He had to control the demon, at the same time he needed Sackville's goodwill.

"Milord, we seek the same thing. A destruction of the Red Indians and total control over the colonists and their trade." Milton's words came out hesitantly. Not at all the impression he wished to make upon this powerful lord.

"And how does bleeding all over the carpet, and . . . and. . . . Is that urine I smell?" The lord wrinkled his nose in distaste as he fished for the lace-edged handkerchief tucked into his sleeve.

"You seek power in the political realm, milord." Milton

dropped to his knees in an effort to remain conscious. More and more of his blood flowed from his hand to feed the demon. Power and magic drained from him at a more rapid rate. He needed to staunch the wound before the demon escaped.

"I seek power from a different realm altogether. If we are to rid the world of the menace of the Red Indians, then we must first rid the world of Britain's Pendragon." The words exhausted Milton. He panted heavily as he sought his own handkerchief in his pocket.

Sackville came to his rescue, wrapping his own clean linen tightly around Milton's palm. At least the man had good hygiene and did not have dirt encrusting his collar or his skin pores.

The demon growled. *More blood. I need more blood to live. My dieflyn must have blood to combat our mutual foes.*

Milton pulled his bandaged hand away from the cone of power. He had not realized that he'd held it in contact with the magic. Once removed, strength returned to his limbs and his mind instantly.

"Tell me more, Dr. Marlowe. I believe you and I can assist each other. But I must know everything you do and why." Sackville kept looking at the circle of power, dimmer now that the demon's feeding frenzy had abated. The crack repaired itself.

"What I am about to say may be hard for you to believe, milord."

"If you can help me gain more power, a ministry, a cabinet position, or possibly to become prime minister, then I will use whatever form of power you have to offer, Dr. Marlowe. More than position in government, I wish control of the army that treated me so ill in their courts martial ten years ago. I have heard His Majesty curse his Pendragon for interfering with his government. I would know more."

"Help me destroy Drake Kirkwood and I shall tell you."

Kirkwood House, Chelsea, England.

Dozens of tiny shadows ran across the garden in front of the entrance to the subterranean chamber.

Alarm lent speed to Emily's bare feet. She ran across the back garden heedless of the wet and cold. Ana raced ahead of her and skidded to a stop at the garden wall. She yipped and jumped, biting at the air.

Senses still extended, Emily sought the "nothingness" in the wall. All she found was dressed stone and mortar. The door remained hidden.

"Bloody hell," she seethed and aimed the top of the black crystal boss of her staff at the section she knew must contain an opening.

Lightning flashed. The crystal caught the energy and crackled. Red-and-yellow sparks flew from the cross into the wall, snaked through the mortar, and set it aflame.

Emily shielded her eyes from the fire. Ana sought cover behind a stone bench.

The wall groaned.

Emily dropped to the ground, covering her neck and head with her hands and the ubiquitous staff. Ana crawled on her belly to Emily's side. She placed her great head across the back of her mistress' neck and growled at the wall in defiance.

The reek of sulfur and body waste intensified. The wall exploded.

Emily felt a moan from the wall. The earth sagged beneath her. When she looked again, the illusion had melted away. A gaping hole opened within the wall. Eight stones lay strewn where lightning had flung them. Three at her feet, three atop the wall, one behind her amid the roses and the last stood upright beside the sundial, tilting the edifice at a thirty-degree angle.

Cautiously, she and Ana crawled into the opening.

Chapter 68

Kirkwood House, Chelsea, England.

EMILY brought a tiny flamelet to her fingertip. Still crouched at the entrance to the temple, she surveyed her path and the damage she had caused. The stonework was repairable. Was the cloaking illusion that kept the passageway hidden from mundane invasion equally fixable?

Most of the members of the Inner Circle were in their sixties, Papa the youngest and strongest among them. She shuddered at the thought of the devastation time and Milton Marlowe had wreaked among them.

She suddenly felt very alone and vulnerable. She wrapped an arm around Ana, wishing the dog could talk her into feeling brave.

If only Aunt Georgie had returned from the colonies, Emily might not have to face the coming terrors alone.

An entity, barely one foot high, with more mouth and teeth than body flitted past her field of vision. Ana snapped her jaws at the thing and missed.

"A *dieflyn,* Ana. We'll not catch them easily." Was it a harbinger of a larger demon to come? The sulfur and rancid waste she had smelled earlier could only have come from something larger.

She cleaved the imp in two from top to bottom in a single swipe with the cross atop her staff. The halves of the being lay limp and quiet. Black ichor oozed away from the parts. The stench of something rotten rose up in an inky miasma.

Emily gagged. Her knees grew weak. She dropped back onto all fours, heaving the remnants of her dinner. Ana stood guard over her, pressing her tremendous weight into Emily's side.

The two pools of ichor slid across the floor and through her vomit. Then the thick puddles suddenly grew and streamed back into the two halves of the imp. Stinking smoke hovered above the traveling gore.

Suddenly the remnants of the Underworldly being became two new imps. Where there had been one dead demonet, two now grinned at her and snapped their voracious jaws. Foul sulfur stung Emily's nose. Her eyes watered and her vision blurred.

With a gasp that bordered on a scream, Emily jumped back, staff at the ready.

A third *dieflyn* jumped clear of the wall. Emily swung at it and missed. It scampered down the passageway. The first two snapped at empty air once more and followed their companion.

Emily dragged herself to her feet, resting her weight upon Ana's shoulder. Excalibur weighed her down, making each movement slow and ponderous. The length of the blade seemed to burn through its scabbard, her woolen robe, and undergarments, branding her back. She gulped back the growing discomfort and hastened down the sloping passageway toward the ritual chamber.

Six more *dieflyn* passed her on the seemingly endless journey. The third one took a bite out of her calf. Fiery pain lanced up to her groin and then into her head. Warm blood gushed from the wound. Her steps grew weak. Her head grew light.

She had done this before. Memories of her time in the Underworld five years ago washed through her, filling her with terror and robbing her of the will to proceed.

Ana caught a *dieflyn* by the neck and flung it into the wall as she would a rat. It smashed against the bones of the earth with a bone-grinding crunch and flopped uselessly to the ground.

Emily drew a deep breath and banished the memories that had driven her insane. She had to go on. She had to protect Papa and the other Pendragons.

Two more of the demonets paused to lap the drops of blood that spilled onto the stone floor. Suddenly they grew to twice their size. Emboldened, they began to lap at the open wound on Emily's calf as she limped onward. They grew again. Ana worried at them, but they snapped their jaws and yanked away great mouthfuls of her fur. The dog danced away and attacked again from a different angle.

More imps poured out of the wall than Emily or Ana could attack at once.

Emily fought back the urge to slay each of the Otherwordly beasts as they passed. How did she fight enemies that resurrected themselves in double their numbers? Instead, she batted them away with the flat side of the cross. Hopefully, she pushed them backward, delaying their progress toward the others. She lost track of direction and stumbled.

Ana led her downward. She had to follow the slope downward.

No time to think. She had to get to the others. This menace required the combined magic of the Inner Circle.

At last the passageway opened into a large cavern. The blue-robed Master Magicians of the Inner Circle had arrayed themselves in two wings spreading outward from the central dais where Papa blasted *dieflyn* after *dieflyn* with bolts of magical fire. He succeeded only in pushing the onslaught away. They did not die. They did not diminish in size.

Still the numbers of the enemy increased, pouring from the walls as if a dam had burst.

Great-Aunt Budgie held an imp by the leg and swung it in a great circle over her head. Then she loosed it into the mass that worried her feet. The *dieflyn* bowled backward like a game of ninepins. They gnashed and growled at each other, tasting blood and growing larger.

A great-uncle, with a head full of white hair and a face full of wrinkles, kicked at the beasts from the Netherworld. He plucked one off his foot and held it before his face. The imp squirmed and snapped its jaws. The uncle blew fire like a dragon of old. The imp's head shriveled and died even as the body continued to jerk and twitch.

A swarm of *dieflyn* surged toward Emily the moment she stepped into the room. She kept them at bay with her staff. The black crystal at the center of the Celtic cross glowed with red depths.

Excalibur burned at Emily's back, begging to be put to

use. She dared not drop her staff long enough to draw the sword.

"To me!" Papa called to one and all. "Gather to me."

Emily and Ana fought their way forward.

The numbers of the imps increased with each step. They snapped at heels and tail as they shied away from the top of her staff that now pulsed with energy.

She swept the staff in large circles, pacing a serpentine pattern that René du Pec, the fencing master, had taught her. She kept moving forward and sideways at the same time, never exposing her back to any one direction for more than a heartbeat.

Ana caught three more demonets and broke their necks. They continued to live but could not move.

Black elemental Fire trickled from the pulsing black crystal. The imps danced away from the killing flames. But for each one that fled, three more replaced it as she moved through the constantly changing pattern.

Finally Emily and Ana reached the dais. Eight Master Magicians crowded the space. An elderly couple, as gray of face as their hair, held up their clasped hands in defiance of the onslaught. Weak yellow flames shot from their free hands, one line of fire for each extended finger. Their breaths came short and shallow. Their magic dwindled even as Emily watched.

They'd not last long.

Ana dashed to stand before the elderly couple, propping them upright with her bulk.

Suddenly the hot weight on Emily's back evaporated. She whirled around, staff at the ready to face this new menace.

Papa held Excalibur aloft. Bright red runes running the length of the blade caught the light from the torches in sconces around the dais.

Emily almost saw the meaning of the pictographs.

Papa shouted words in a language long dead before the ancients of Britain were born. Somehow the arcane words matched the runes.

The sword drew all the light in the chamber into itself. The energy built and glowed.

"Cover your eyes," Papa panted in English.

The Master Magicians obeyed in an instant.

Emily was slower. She watched Excalibur pulse, much as the black crystal had.

Just as she closed her eyes, the sword exploded into a million points of fire. Like Chinese fireworks on Guy Fawkes Day, the points of light cascaded down in myriad colors.

Each flamelet landed upon an imp.

The demons writhed and screamed and died by the hundreds.

One by one, the elderly members of the Inner Circle dropped to their knees and lowered their heads in exhaustion until only Emily, Ana, and Papa remained standing. Then Papa dropped Excalibur.

Richmond Palace.

"Not now," Milton gasped at Lord Sackville's plea. "I can tell you nothing at the moment." The demon pulled more and more strength from him. His face grew too cold below the skin and too hot on the surface. His vision narrowed to a single darkening tunnel focusing solely upon the ritual circle. Tryblith, the Demon of Chaos, filled the pentagram within the circle. Soon it must burst the bounds of his spell.

"Dr. Marlowe, what ails you?" Sackville grasped Milton's elbow and held him upright by will alone.

Milton leaned his entire weight upon the slighter man.

They kill my dieflyn! the demon protested.

Milton felt the fiery blows against the Netherworld minions. In his mind's eye he caught reflections of the battle in the subterranean chamber of the Inner Circle. He felt the mighty sword burst free of its scabbard. His skin burned from the million points of elemental Fire the weapon showered upon the imps.

His knees turned to water.

Bit by bit the demon diminished in size and clarity within the circle. Eventually it closed its eyes and sank back beneath the barriers of time and space.

The long case clock in the corridor struck midnight. The barriers between the worlds firmed. Milton would not coax the demon forth again. Three times he'd tried. Three times he'd failed to acquire the grimoire.

He'd used his last chance.

Milton sighed in weary disappointment. The weight of Tryblith's presence evaporated from his shoulders.

"Do you battle the Pendragon through some silent magic?" Sackville asked as he pushed Milton into the welcoming softness of an armchair.

"They have fought me to a stalemate," he whispered. "I have no strength left to draw upon. They are too exhausted to come after me."

"This can be a good thing," Sackville said eagerly. "If the Pendragons cannot draw enough strength to fight against us, then I can wield enough political power to hold them in check."

"Does the king listen to you, then?" Milton asked. Hope dawned in his aching chest. He'd not get the grimoire this time, but he might use this man to punish the colonists for their betrayal of his son.

"I can make His Majesty listen to me. Together we can force him to keep the colonies under control. He has no reason to listen to the Pendragon with you and me at his side."

"That is all I can ask, for now. Until I regain enough strength to launch the next campaign. For the crime of inaction while the Indians tortured and mutilated my son, I will see the colonies crushed, their spirit broken."

"When will you be ready?"

"Before Drake Kirkwood and his daughter can think to act. Before the colonies break free of His Majesty's control."

"I know the weapon we must use," Sackville mused. He began to pace a random pattern that avoided the ritual circle. Every other step he glanced at the spot where the demon had been. "You wish to crush the colonies. I will lead the army that destroys them. But I need time to put everything into place."

"What is your weapon of choice, milord?"

"Tea."

Chapter 69

Boston.

A FLASH of pain through my temples near blinded me. My awareness of the busy taproom at the Crown and Anchor faded to a dull roar. Nothing existed but the band of pressure inside my head.

"Griffin, you must learn to be more gentle in your summons," I whispered. Hastily, I resumed my chore of passing out frothing tankards of ale to my customers.

Roderick touched my shoulder with a gentle hand. "Upstairs with you, Georgie," he whispered as he took the tray from my limp and shaking hands. He'd learned to tell when something was amiss with my arcane talents.

Zaneta must have heard echoes of Griffin's imperious summons, or something strange in my dragging steps upon the stairs. She met me on the landing, hands upon hips and a frown upon her face. One look into my eyes and she grabbed my hand. Gratefully, I allowed her to lead me to my basin in my bedchamber.

I felt as if Griffin continued to beat at my mind with his fists. My vision dimmed to just a few square inches around my feet.

Zaneta filled the basin with fresh water and held my hand as she dropped an agate into it.

The ripples fanned outward. My stomach sloshed with seasickness.

"Concentrate, Mama," Zaneta commanded. "You need to see this." She yanked on my arm to drag my attention away from my body and into the scrying bowl.

The battle of the *dieflyn* unfolded before my eyes. I gasped in horror as the little demons chomped upon Emily's leg. I shared her pain and fear. Trembling, I forced myself to cling to the edges of the washstand and stare at the disaster. Weak and near vomiting, I murmured protection spells for myself and my daughter. I could not allow those miniature demons to find their way through the scrying spell into my bedchamber.

Where had the beasts come from?

The demon Tryblith laughed without humor in the back of my mind.

Had Barclay set the Netherworld imps upon my family at the behest of the Demon?

Milton, Tryblith chuckled. *I fight his battle for him.*

I nearly gagged.

And then wonder of wonders, my brother Drake drew Excalibur, the true blade of Arthur, not the cheap and rusting imitation that Barclay carried. The great sword blazed a path of light through the growing darkness from the Netherworld.

When it was all done, I collapsed with the same exhaustion my fellow Pendragons suffered.

"Is this why you train me so diligently?" Zaneta asked, old beyond her tender years. She, too, trembled in fear.

"Aye, sweeting." I gathered her into a fierce hug, filled with remorse that she had to witness the terrible battle, grateful that she had not left me alone with the scene. "We must hone our talents daily to remain strong against the forces of evil." My stomach settled as the images faded. Every muscle in my body ached as if I had fought the battle myself.

"What do we do now, Mama? They need our help," Zaneta gulped back tears.

"I'm not sure, Zaneta. We have our own demons to battle here." Like Barclay Marlowe and the growing discontent against Parliament and the king.

Over the next few weeks I communicated often with Griffin and Emily. The Pendragon Society was rendered nearly useless in the aftermath of the battle. Our elderly aunts and uncles, my brother, all walked about with glazed eyes and little concentration. Their magic had drained away, possibly never to return. Drake barely managed enough power to heal the gaping wound in Emily's calf.

Dr. Milton Marlowe had beaten us badly. But I think we had drained him as well. He did not follow up with a new attack when we were all at our weakest.

Emily and I alone, with the aid of Samuel de Vere—who I did not trust at all—remained to guard Britain from magical attack. Emily held Griffin close at her side, guarding him jealously from our enemies. I kept Zaneta with me for similar reasons and for the strength she loaned me in my spells.

Barclay Marlowe strutted around Boston with a smug grin on his face.

Roderick shook his head and left Zaneta and me alone whenever we delved into magic.

The next year my niece Belinda married well. At my suggestion, Emily warded her mind so that she had no memory of the Pendragon Society or the magic that flew about the house on a regular basis.

The time came for Griffin to go off to school. Both his sister and I gave him strict instructions never, ever, under any circumstances to use the magic that came to his fingertips so easily. I kept a wary eye on him through the scrying bowl and the unique link he had forged by summoning me twice during crises. That alone, I believe, kept him from throwing fireballs at bullies. If he kept those boys in line through magic, he developed a subtlety that augured well for his future.

And then in 1772 the East India Tea Company went bankrupt with eighteen million pounds of tea worth over £2 million in a warehouse in London. The American colonists had not bought tea in normal quantities since the rescinding of all the Townsend Acts except the tax on tea. The East India Company paid an import duty on tea when it offloaded the cargo in England. A second duty—the Townsend Tax—came due when the tea arrived in the colonies, and, of course the tea could not be shipped directly from India to the colonies to avoid one of the taxes. Tea became too expensive for any but the very wealthy or special occasions. Then, too, we in the colonies did not buy tea as a matter of principle.

The Crown and Anchor flourished because we offered coffee—an equally expensive alternative to tea but less onerous in taxes.

And so the surplus tea kept piling up in the warehouse. The East India Company could not sell its biggest asset to offset its debts.

Smuggling became an honorable profession in the colonies. I refrained from adding my talents and expertise to those who sought ways around the customs agents. I wanted to join them. I longed for the action, and the possibility of using my skills as a soldier and master swordsman.

For my husband and our daughter I stayed at home.

King George lost confidence in his government and once more changed prime ministers. Lord North seemed a reasonable man, especially when he wrote to me directly. The letter arrived by special courier. He awaited me when I returned from the market early in the morning. I had Zaneta with me, or she would have summoned me home with a mental prod as sharp as any of my weapons.

Dressed in ordinary brown gabardine, with a beaver tricorn rubbed smooth by time and fingers that worried the nap, a nervous habit of long standing, I guessed, the courier paced restlessly about the common room of the Crown and Anchor. Roderick watched him suspiciously under the cover of rearranging the lines of pewter and wooden tankards behind the bar. The stranger's eyes darted hither and thither in near alarm. His shoulders sagged a little and he twitched.

He projected an aura of meekness. I expected him to fade into the woodwork, a skinny ghost of a man not worth noticing.

But I did.

"S . . . sir W . . . William Tr . . . Trevalyn, milady," the courier stuttered. Then he bowed neatly as an afterthought.

I curtsied. His title was above mine, after all. I dug my elbow into Zaneta's side. She eyed the man suspiciously before reluctantly bobbing something that resembled a respectful greeting.

Had I been as insolent at her age, barely eight? Probably.

"Sir William, how may I serve you?" I asked, doffing my plain cap and shawl. Roderick took them from me, hovering all too close. He dropped a proprietary kiss upon my cheek. And then he pressed my dagger-pistol against my leg, hidden by the folds of my skirt. My hand rested comfortably around the grip before he stepped away.

Beside me, Zaneta clenched her fists and stared at the heavy club we kept near the bar to use for breaking up the infrequent brawl when the drink flowed too freely and tempers overcame good sense.

I clenched her shoulder fiercely with my free hand. She heeded my silent warning a little. Her body remained tense and prepared to throw the club at Trevalyn's head with her mind if need be.

"I . . . I h . . . have missives for y . . . you, milady." Sir William patted a small bulge inside his coat. With my senses extended to take forewarning of an attack, I heard it crackle. If he carried a hidden blade or pistol, it rested elsewhere on his body.

He looked askance at my husband and daughter.

"I have no secrets from my family, Sir William. What you have to say to me can be said to them as well." I lifted my chin and held his gaze, as strongly as any man would do.

"A . . . as y . . . you wish, milady." He handed over a single parchment folded small and sealed with a small blob of green wax. I could not make out the signet impressed there in the dim light of the tavern. We did not waste money on expensive candles until we opened to the public, closer to noon.

So I broke open the seal and unfolded the parchment, careful not to tear the thin sheet. The crabbed writing ran together before my eyes as if bespelled. I squinted at it, unwilling to admit that in the last year my eyesight had begun to fail at close quarters. Only in private did I resort to spectacles.

"Lord North wishes you to resume the work you performed for Lord Grenville, some years ago," Roderick summarized the long letter in a few short words.

"Why?" I did not relax my stance or my gaze upon Sir William.

"I . . . if I may, milady?" Sir William interrupted. "The prime minister entrusted me with certain details in case you proved reluctant." His stammer disappeared and he assumed an air of confidence. Dangerous confidence.

He also appeared taller and stronger than before. Now he would stand out in any crowd.

"What details?" I shifted my grip on the dagger-pistol, finding better balance.

"His Lordship's agents have detected some . . . interference, or perhaps manipulation of the East India Tea Company. They are not as mismanaged as they appear."

"Why should this bit of information intrigue me?"

"The persons involved are distantly related to you."

The fine hairs along my spine stood on end.

"Every poor decision made by the Company occurs soon after the members of the board of directors have been visited by men who owe loyalty to one man and one man only."

"Dr. Milton Marlowe, perchance?" Roderick asked. I had hesitated to name the man.

Sir William nodded. His expression became tight and he clenched his jaw. "Lord George Sackville is seen often in Dr. Marlowe's company. They have both prospered much of late, even though they have invested heavily in the East India Company."

"You do not like or trust my cousin any better than I do," I said quietly.

"I am also to inform you that Dr. Marlowe has become a close associate of one Honorable Belinda Kirkwood Grissom. Your niece, I believe. Her husband, Sir Henry Grissom, is a distant cousin of Lord Sackville's."

A chill brought goose bumps to my arms.

"How much do you and Lord North know about my family?"

"As much or more than His Majesty."

A great deal, in other words.

I shifted my feet to en garde. My skirts I bunched into my left fist to keep from tripping on them as I prepared to lunge.

"We have also . . . ah . . . relieved Lord George Sackville of certain correspondence."

Zaneta sidled out of my way, fully aware of how much room I needed to take this man down, should the need arise.

"Lord North has authorized me to assure you that he holds you blameless in the matter of the death of the King of Poland."

I breathed a little deeper but not much easier.

Sir William had also assumed a stance that would allow him to defend himself.

Pieces of an almost forgotten puzzle began to fall into

place. Cousin Milton Marlowe wanted me out of England so that I would not interfere with his bid for power—or was it his quest for a particular grimoire in the family archives? Lord George Sackville had provided the blackmail material to force me to come to the colonies. The two worked together, one in the mundane political forum, one on the magical plane.

I wondered if these two men manipulated King George in his insistence upon forcing the colonies to pay unprecedented taxes and adhere to trade restrictions no true Englishman would accept.

"What do I gain if I do as Lord North bids?" I asked of both Roderick and Sir William.

"The letter promises a stipend," Roderick said, frowning at the parchment. "Coin we could well use." Often payment for the food and drink we served at the Crown and Anchor came in the form of bartered goods and services. Often enough, in the form of signed notes.

"What else?" I shifted my attention back to Sir William.

"The gratitude of the Crown and prime minister," he said flatly.

I snorted at that.

"Full pardon for the affair of the Polish king's death."

"Better," I replied.

"Restoration of the Pendragon as adviser to the Crown and prime minister."

"Interesting, but useless to me."

"But not to your niece. Lord North understands that your brother's wolfhound has died. His daughter, the Honorable Emily Kirkwood has inherited a bitch wolfhound from him. He does not know the significance of this, only that the dogs are significant within the family."

"Very significant." My link to my familiar had faded over the years. Cats just did not have the long-term loyalty bred into them that dogs did. If Emily now walked with a female wolfhound at her side, then she must succeed her father as the Pendragon.

"Lord North might listen to my niece. I doubt the king will, and 'tis George who has the final say in political matters. He has made that clear many times since his ascension. Dr. Marlowe and Lord Sackville hold more sway with His Majesty."

"That we cannot help. But if you work for us at this end, perhaps we can adjust the balance of power among the king's advisers." His hand worked in an arcane symbol.

I blanched. I'd not seen anyone use that gesture since . . . since the day I received orders from a secret Lodge with ties to every court in Europe and many places beyond to assassinate the King of Poland.

I knew this Lodge, trusted that they knew the consequences of this order better than I did.

"Before I answer yea or nay, I would know why Lord Grenville ceased communications and aid nigh on ten years ago. I consider myself dismissed from public service."

"I cannot answer for Lord Grenville unless he, too, fell under the influence of Lord Sackville and Dr. Marlowe. They abandoned you. Lord North is a different man altogether and so far immune to our enemies. He seeks your advice about your observations as well as whatever your niece can give in aid."

He'd do well to let Emily place wards around his person and his dwellings if he truly wished that. But that was something I would have to communicate to her in private, via the scrying bowl.

"I will settle for nothing less than the total downfall of Dr. Marlowe and his coven of helpers. Sackville I leave to you."

"So be it."

"Let us pray that King George and his colonies can find compromises before armed rebellion breaks out," Sir William said on a sigh. He flashed a signal again. The secret Lodge had not decided if armed rebellion here aided their long-range policies.

"Is armed rebellion what we truly need?" Roderick whispered to me.

Chapter 70

LORD North sought compromise and wished to keep the issue of tea taxes and smuggling quiet until he could persuade Parliament and His Majesty otherwise.

However, on June 9, 1772, Navy Lieutenant William Dudington ran the *Gaspée,* a small patrol vessel in pursuit of smugglers, aground near Providence, Rhode Island. The locals, augmented by some of Sam Adams' rabble rousers, rowed out to the boat. They shot and wounded Dudington. His crew surrendered despite his harangue and threats to hang them one and all for disobeying orders. The patriots burned the ship to the waterline.

The smugglers disappeared into the night along with their cargo.

My report to Lord North on the matter mentioned few specifics, only the extent the colonials would go to in order to avoid paying the extra duty on tea. He had no need to know that I had advised the attackers on their strategy and drilled them in the use and rapid reloading of their firearms.

My report to the Lodge was much more extensive and inclusive.

Colonel Barclay Marlowe headed the party that investigated the *Gaspée* incident. The entire colony of Rhode Island remembered nothing of that night. I made certain that key witnesses truly did not remember with a spell similar to the one Emily performed on Belinda. The Sons of Liberty suddenly increased in numbers with an influx of men from Rhode Island. Two men took shelter in our storeroom. Others blended into the masses of laborers in Boston. Zaneta gleefully put together a spell so that our regular

489

customers remembered our refugees working at the Crown and Anchor for over a year.

Like Barclay Marlowe—I could never think of him as her father or sire, though I knew well their blood kinship—she found manipulating minds as easy as the remote throwing of obstacles about the room when in a temper.

Barclay followed our men but never found proof of their identities. Every time he used magic to pry information out of the minds of the people, I intervened with spells of my own.

We worked against each other in a stalemate as profound as the one that existed between his father and the Pendragon Society.

By this time, he had to know of my presence in Boston. We passed each other nearly every day in the streets. Yet he never acknowledged me.

Sam Adams established a Committee of Correspondence to keep the other colonies informed of matters in Boston. My old friend, Paul Revere, often rode the rapid route between Boston, Providence, and New York. Upon occasion, Roderick and I relieved him of his duties. Virginia and the other colonies soon followed with a similar group of letter writers.

In March of 1773, the East India Tea Company requested permission from Parliament to ship its eighteen-million-pound surplus of tea to the colonies duty-free. But they never specified free of which duty, the English import tax or the three-penny Townsend colony tax.

King George gladly rescinded the import tax for this one shipment. He refused to consider ever dropping the Townsend Tax. The tax had remained in effect to raise money to pay the salaries of royal governors and judges. The colonists were no longer allowed to control these officers by paying them directly. In His Majesty's view, the colonies also needed to be taught to obey his laws without question.

The basic right of all Englishmen to speak to the king via our elected members of Parliament was denied to us. Our basic rights as Englishmen to a speedy trial by a jury of our peers was denied to us. Our right to control the salaries of judges and governors was denied to us.

Lord North failed to moderate King George's stance

upon colonial politics. His Majesty refused so much as an interview with Emily or her father.

Dr. Milton Marlowe and Lord George Sackville remained a staunch barrier between the Pendragons and their king.

I severed my connection with Lord North. He had failed to uphold his end of the bargain. Even my pardon regarding the death of the King of Poland never arrived.

On Sunday morning, November 28, 1773, the East India merchant vessel *Dartmouth* sailed into Boston Harbor carrying one hundred fourteen chests of tea. The captain registered the cargo with the customs officer of the port. He had twenty days to make payment of the duty on the tea. To do that, he had to sell it.

Barclay Marlowe may have been the only person in Boston who wanted that tea to be unloaded. His reasons remained his own and the demon's. Tryblith wanted Chaos. He manipulated Barclay into creating it.

Trouble and Chaos he found aplenty twenty days later.

Boston, December 16, 1773.

"Georgina," Roderick grabbed me about the waist. "Do not go out there this day."

I kept my back to my husband as from our bedroom window I watched the milling crowds gathering in Boston. Men and women, highborn and low, wandered the streets. Hundreds of them, perhaps thousands. They spoke quietly among themselves, their restless movements betraying the anger that drove them out-of-doors on this bitterly cold day.

"I have to know what happens. I have to keep Barclay and his demon from inflaming disagreements into a riot," I insisted.

"Georgina . . ."

"I can defend myself."

"In a duel, yes. On the battlefield, yes. Against an angry mob of thousands? No one can. Please, Georgina, watch from here." He held me tightly, burying his face in my neck.

I pressed the length of my body against him, cherishing

his warmth, and his love. Not for the first time I wished I could have given him children of his own blood.

"Is it not enough that a mob of five thousand forced the *Dartmouth* to tie up at Griffin's Wharf where we could post our own guard to keep the tea aboard?" Roderick asked, still holding me against him.

"It will not be enough until Governor Hutchinson allows the ship to debark with its cargo intact and without paying the tax." I stiffened a little, wondering how I could break his embrace without destroying the trust we had rebuilt between us.

"I can watch from inside Faneuil Hall," I suggested. "I know a place . . ."

"Watch from here, or from the steeple of the North Church. No closer, please."

"Roderick, you know I cannot. I have to go to the Green Dragon. I have to insert myself into the midst of the Sons of Liberty. I have to be a part of this, as much for the right of the thing as to keep Barclay at bay."

"Tomorrow is the deadline. The tax must be paid or the cargo seized and sold. If there is aught to report 'twill be tomorrow." His hands eased upon my waist.

" 'Twill be tonight." My words chilled us both.

"Then we lock the tavern, entrust Zaneta to Mistress Camden and we both will observe. I will watch your back."

"If we die this night, we die together," I murmured. I trusted Emily to collect Zaneta and train her properly.

"So be it. I want it no other way." He kissed me soundly.

The Green Dragon (Freemason Hall), Boston, Massachusetts.

"Let's torch the ship!" one of Sam Adams' wharf rats screamed to the assembly in the upper hall of the Green Dragon.

Roderick cringed. How many riots had been spawned in this very room in the last few years? How many demonstrations? He could no longer count the number of pamphlets he and Georgie had written and brought here for distribution.

He glanced at his wife beside him. Excitement lit her eyes and she bit her lower lip in anticipation. He'd seen the same eagerness on her face just before she charged the Turks on the Ottoman border so many years ago. Not a violent person by nature, but she came alive at moments like this. The only other time he saw her thus was when she trembled beneath him in bed and her skin was so hot the lightest touch sent visible waves of pleasure rippling up and down her spine.

He gulped back his trepidation. From the time of that first battle where they'd fought side by side, he'd known that Georgie Kirkwood would die by the sword.

Tonight?

He prayed not.

"If'n we burn the ship, she can't off-load that damnable tea," Sam Adams mused. He spoke quietly from his position behind the writing table on the dais at the head of the room. His rumpled suit with ale and ink stains on his cuffs and shirtfront, his scuffed shoes with tarnished buckles, and darned stockings made him look as if he had sprung from the same vile nest as the men he ordered about. Sam Adams never cast a stone or threw a punch, never called an insult to a British soldier, never posted a single pamphlet. But he directed every one of those actions that occurred in Boston.

Was he also manipulated by the demon that only Barclay and Georgie could see?

"We do not need to destroy the ship," the moderate lawyer John Adams spoke quietly from his seat beside his cousin Sam. "We need only destroy the tea."

"Follow his lead, Georgie," Roderick whispered.

She looked little more than a boy, slim-hipped and narrow-shouldered in her "Masonic" suit. She'd taken to roughing her face and darkening her hair with soot as part of her disguise. He'd know her anywhere. If the other men recognized her, they respected her sword enough to say nothing.

"What do you want me to do?" She turned to him, her eyes clearing of the glaze of excitement.

"Prevent these men from starting a war this night. If a revolution begins, tonight is not yet time," Roderick whispered.

Very few ever spoke of revolution. The thought of actually separating from England's protection, from denying an anointed monarch His authority over them, made most men quake in their boots. But more and more the idea seemed inevitable, especially to learned men like John Adams, his volatile cousin Sam, to Thom Jefferson in Virginia, and Ben Franklin of Pennsylvania.

"The cargo is our focus, not the ship or the sailors," she said firmly, loud enough for John Adams to hear.

"Nor the soldiers guarding the ship," Roderick reminded them.

"We could turn Boston Harbor into one giant teapot!" Georgie proclaimed to the room in a voice that carried to every corner, though she spoke barely above a whisper. 'Twas a voice she'd developed to quell a tavern's patrons before a brawl.

The Crown and Anchor had had no fines for unruly behavior in three years because of Georgie's voice.

"Who said that?" The questions went around the room.

"Let the tea brew in the harbor waters," John Adams mused and relaxed a little bit. Sitting beside his volatile cousin had to be unnerving.

"We'll offload the cargo into the sea," chuckled a grizzled rabble-rouser near the front of the room. His laughter echoed around the room.

"No true violence. We destroy only the tea," Paul Revere added from beside Georgie. He grinned at her with a knowing twinkle in his eyes.

Did he know the truth behind Georgie's disguise? If he did, Roderick trusted his discretion. He'd been chosen to ride circuit for the Committees for Correspondence for more than just his horsemanship and incredible stamina.

"Disguises," Sam Adams finally added something useful to the planning. "We must all be disguised as Red Indians so that no one can be identified."

Mumbles and grumbles spread outward from the knot of men who depended upon the few coins Sam Adams gave them to create turmoil. Too many of them liked bashing heads and brawling in the streets.

" 'Twill be a fine show to watch," Revere muttered. "Don't think I want the world to know I was among that rabble." He grinned widely, showing off a gold tooth. He'd made a tidy fortune crafting replacement teeth for the wealthy of Boston, as well as other metalwork and etchings.

"Who can identify anyone behind those disguises?" Georgie returned. The light was back in her eyes.

"No, Georgie," Roderick whispered, grabbing her elbow. "This is not something you can fight your way free of if aught goes wrong."

"I have come this far . . ." she rounded upon Roderick, anger replacing the excitement in her countenance.

Then her face went blank. She stood absolutely still for several heartbeats. Then she whipped her head around, staring wildly about the room.

"Barclay is here," she whispered through her teeth. "I can't see him, but I can feel him, and I smell his demon."

"If you can't find him, then he does not wish to be found. That bodes ill for us all."

"Worse. Zaneta is here as well. Hiding from us. Hiding from him."

Chapter 71

I'D learned the trick of finding Zaneta through long hours of hunting her during her training. The trick was not to look for her where she was but to look where she was not.

So I turned my back to the room and darted glances from the sides. With each glance, I took one step closer to the wall. I braced my hands against the dark wainscoting and pressed my face into the white clapboard paneling above it. No one stood between me and the wall. A few square feet of space eliminated from my search area.

Roderick shifted to cover my back. I felt Revere move up beside him. The two men muttered something I did not bother to overhear. I had to find Zaneta first and remove her from danger.

A flash of movement away from my left side. I reached out and caught the collar of Zaneta's sprigged gown. She struggled only briefly. But instead of her bright giggle at the end of our usual training game, she scowled at me, hands on hips and head cocked to one side, pure imitation of Roderick in a temper.

"Why are you here?" I demanded, crouching to her level behind the protective backs of my husband and Paul Revere.

"He called me," she spat out at me.

"Who?" Though I knew. My heart clenched in despair.

"My true father." Her lip trembled a bit beneath her anger.

Roderick started at that. I felt him blanch.

"There stands your true father." I pointed at Roderick. "Any man who tells you different lies. He lies to hurt your father and me. He lies to make you do things that you

know are wrong." I put as much compulsion into my words
as I dared. Too much and she'd throw the magic back into
my face threefold.

"W . . . why would he do such a thing?" Zaneta wrinkled
her nose and stuck out her lower lip to keep from crying.

"Because he wants to cause trouble. Now show me
where he hides."

"H . . . he has to be my da, otherwise he couldn't hide like
I do. Only us with magic can hide."

"Magic tricks do not make him your father." Anger
burned in my gut. Barclay had wanted no part of his
daughter or her true mother when they represented responsibility and honoring promises. Now that Zaneta was
old enough to be his tool, he sought to steal her from us.

I'd never allow that.

And Barclay must know that.

So why?

Tryblith.

To keep me from interfering tonight.

Keeping my hand tightly tangled in Zaneta's collar, I
rose to my feet. She had dropped the spell that made one
look anywhere but at her. Every man in the room could see
her if they bothered to look beyond their own gleeful donning of blankets, feathers, and war paint.

"You two must keep tonight's actions from becoming violent," I whispered to Roderick and Revere. "I will do my
part from a distance."

"Georgie, no." Roderick clasped my arm tightly.

"Roddie, I must." We stared at each other for a long lov-
ing moment. I no longer cared if my fellow Masons and the
Sons of Liberty knew me for a woman or a magician. For
Zaneta's sake, I had to stop Barclay tonight. I had to send
Tryblith scuttling back to the Netherworld.

I prayed I had enough magic to do both.

At long last, Roderick dropped my arm. "We will do
what we can. Though 'twould be easier with you."

"Go with her," Revere insisted. "Yon Johnny Adams and
I will keep them in line. You need to be about your family's
work this night."

How he knew what he knew, I never asked. I only
thanked any and all Gods that might listen for his solid
presence.

"Show me the man who tells you lies," I said to Zaneta, capturing her gaze with my own and never releasing my grip on her.

"You can't have her," I said to a seemingly blank corner of the upstairs room of the Green Dragon.

Slowly the outline of a man emerged, as if he stepped out of the white wall above the wainscoting. A disturbing shimmer in the air to his left showed me the demon.

Barclay flashed his charming grin at me.

For the first time in my life I remained immune to his heart-stopping beauty. The clean lines of his face and the silky texture of his blond hair—nearly the same color as his golden velvet suit—clubbed back with a green ribbon to match his waistcoat did not touch my soul.

"Mama, he can do my trick," Zaneta said on a gasp. I felt her reach for the man who had sired her. His deep blue eyes, Kirkwood eyes, matched hers in color and intensity. The eyes alone identified whose seed had given the child life.

They did not say anything about who had raised her, nursed her through childhood illnesses and traumas, taught her the wonders of a sunrise and given her her first taste of molasses. My heart wrenched in agony for Roderick, Zaneta's true father.

"You have no claim on this child," I reiterated.

Behind me, I heard the Sons of Liberty clattering down the stairs, half drunk on excitement and rum. They paid us no attention. I knew that Revere and John Adams would take the rear guard to make certain the room cleared for this very private confrontation.

"Oh, but I do claim this little girl as my own. Her magic makes her mine." Barclay continued grinning. A false grin that showed his teeth but not his soul.

"Her magic makes her mine. Her rearing makes her Roderick's," I snarled back at him. I fingered the dagger-pistol at my hip, wishing I'd brought my saber with me.

Barclay wore his military issue saber belted about his slim waist even though he did not wear his uniform.

"Colonel Marlowe," Roderick said through labored breaths. "I request that you return to your unit. You have witnessed the formation of a plan tonight. Surely you wish to communicate those plans to your fellow officers so you may put a stop to this act of rebellion."

"What I wish is of no import to you, barkeep." He sneered the last word.

Roderick stiffened at the insult. " 'Twas you who rendered me unfit for military duty, Colonel. You have no right to disdain my honest trade."

"I disdain everything about you, barkeep, even the useless honor that drove you to accept the burden of a wife and child you do not love." Barclay smiled again, baiting my husband to violence. I'd seen him do the same to his father, to servants, and to tradesmen, just to satisfy his own need to bully.

"Why now?" I shouldered my way between my husband and my enemy. "Why have you waited all these years to make your move?"

"Because, dear cousin, my father is nearly ready to make his move against the Pendragon Society. And I intend to snatch away his triumph at the last moment, when he can taste victory but never have it. He will never get his hands upon Resmiranda Griffin's grimoire. I intend to crush him with failure as he has crushed me all of my life. For that, I need my daughter and her talents."

"Too late. Too late by many years." I shook my head. I needed all of my concentration upon him and Zaneta to keep from thinking about Milton Marlowe and what he planned for my brother and his daughter.

The shimmer was all that showed of Tryblith prodding Barclay.

He seemed not to notice. But he opened his mouth to counter my argument.

"Is this what you wanted, Mama?" Zaneta held up my saber, still within its worn leather scabbard. "I snatched it from your hiding place beneath your mattress, just as you taught me to snatch the club from behind the bar when you and Papa must stop a brawl." She chirped in her innocent voice. But from the cloud in her eyes and her quivering chin, I guessed she must understand somewhat of our conversation.

Barclay snapped his mouth shut. Tryblith continued to poke him.

"Thank you, Zaneta." I took hold of my weapon at the grip, unsheathing it as I moved.

Before Barclay could draw his own weapon, I'd touched him beneath the chin with the tip of the saber.

"You will not take our daughter away from us. Now or ever." I kept my gaze upon his eyes, waiting for the tiny telltale flicker that told me he drew his own weapon. In these close quarters he could not do much until I backed away.

"Take Zaneta to safety, Roderick."

"Georgie . . ."

"Now! I will not have our daughter witness the death of this man." Or my own death.

My only regret was that I had not time to warn Emily of her coming battle.

"Georgie, he'll cheat," Roderick called to me. He picked up Zaneta, dragging her clinging fists away from my belt.

"I know he'll cheat." I flashed Roderick a grin. My blood began to sing in my limbs and new clarity came to my vision. "I taught him how when I was fifteen."

Almost before I'd finished speaking, Barclay drew his dagger and pressed it against my chin, pinioning me with his longer reach as I held him with my sword.

I retaliated with a swift step backward, sweeping my dagger-pistol free.

Roderick clattered down the stairs.

"Mama!" Zaneta cried in near panic.

I ignored them, kicking over two chairs behind me to clear a path to the broad center aisle. Thankfully, the Sons of Liberty did not place much stock in sitting, preferring to roam about shouting at each other.

Barclay attacked low, to the septième. I parried and riposted underhanded toward his belly. He retreated. I countered with a lunge and circle of my blade directly to the middle a lá sixieme. He evaded my envelopment and pushed my saber upward.

I recovered, stalking him widdershins, trying to enclose him and the demon in a ritual circle.

"Nice try, Georgina," Barclay laughed. "But I mastered the circle long ago and trapped the Demon of Chaos as my partner."

"Chaos? Is that all you seek?" I drew the magic back within me, not allowing it to ground. I might need it later.

"Chaos is but a means to an end." He swept my blade aside in a tight movement that left his side vulnerable. I darted in close to take advantage. But he was ready with a sidestep and a swinging blow that nicked my left arm.

I heard cloth tear and felt warm blood trickle down my arm before the wound began to burn. My fingers still flexed around the grip of my dagger. The wound was not deep.

"Give up, Georgie. I have the advantage in reach, in stamina, and in guile."

"Do you?" I raised the dagger-pistol and took aim.

He had the grace to blanch.

I pulled the trigger.

Gunpowder exploded. Acrid smoke filled my nose. The pistol bucked. I held it steady.

As steady as Barclay held the bullet suspended in midair between us.

He raised an eyebrow at me and lunged.

I jerked my hips back and away from his strike. His blade whistled past my midriff a scant hair's breadth away from my shirt. One of the brass buttons from my coat clattered to the floor.

"A true seamstress would have sewed that button on properly so that I could not remove it so easily. You never were much of a seamstress, Georgie. But you have always been one hell of a woman."

I did not bother to reply. While he gloated, I lunged. The golden velvet covering his thigh sprouted a red blossom of blood.

He gasped and dropped his dagger to clutch at the wound. Before I could shift my grip and deliver a killing blow he rounded upon me. Anger twisted his handsome face into a gargoyle's parody of beauty. He caught my blade.

We exchanged a rapid series of blows that defied definition or rules. We exchanged cuts.

The front of my shirt was in ribbons. His stylish and expensive coat was stained and slashed beyond redemption.

We both bled. We both panted.

And then a glint in his eyes belied his next move. A feint to the right. A ball of fire appeared in his left hand.

I saw it coming and dropped to my knees, driving my

sword upward and to my right in a low lunge that cut beneath his reach, directly into the gut of the demon.

Tryblith lashed out with his claws. Long cuts slashed from my right shoulder to my left hip.

The demon collapsed.

Barclay dashed to the demon's side, dropping his witchfire. Unspent, ungrounded, the blazing spell sought fuel to sustain itself.

Tryblith reached out and enclosed Barclay in both of its huge arms. The blackness of the Netherworld engulfed them.

Or was that merely my vision fading into death?

I needed to say good-bye to Roddie and Zaneta.

Chapter 72

RODERICK hesitated at the bottom of the stairs. He smelled smoke coming from the meeting room above the tavern. Should he return there to help Georgie or continue home with his daughter?

At the same moment he spotted a squad of six red-coated soldiers led by a lieutenant entering the Green Dragon. He marked them as seasoned professionals by the way they carried their muskets and marched in tune while keeping wary eyes on all that surrounded them.

"Barkeep, we need to know the whereabouts of Colonel Barclay Marlowe," the lieutenant snapped at the only man remaining inside the tavern.

Roderick, still shadowed in the stairwell, pressed a finger to his lips in signal to Zaneta for absolute quiet.

She nodded and pressed her face into his shoulder. Her little body trembled in fear. He wished with all his heart he could spare her this. But he had to save Georgie.

"Do your trick," he whispered against his daughter's ear. "Disappear and hide in a corner where no one will trip over you." He set her down beside the first stair.

Zaneta nodded. Her chin trembled and her big blue eyes moistened. She squeezed his hand and . . . faded into the woodwork.

"Don't rightly know a Colonel Marlowe," the barkeep drawled. "He be related to the Marlowes what's got steading ten miles west of Lexington?"

"Colonel Marlowe is descended from a long line of no-bility, born and bred in England," the lieutenant sneered as if colonials were an inferior breed, akin to black slaves and

Red Indians. "We have orders to arrest certain insurrectionists he has discovered habituating this tavern."

Roderick backed up the stairs as quietly as he could. The barkeep would keep the soldiers occupied for a few moments only. Soon the lieutenant would become suspicious and order his men to search the inn. Thank God the smoke had dissipated. The need to extinguish a fire would draw them upward faster.

"Georgie!" Roderick ran to his prostrate wife where she slumped on the floor. Marlowe lay propped against the wall, eyes closed. He breathed shallowly. Blood covered them both.

"Georgie." He shifted her body so that he could cradle her head in his lap. Her eyes remained closed, her breathing so weak he almost missed the faint trace of it.

But she breathed. Her hands were icy cold and her face too white. But she breathed.

"Georgie, wake up. We have to leave. Now."

She moaned slightly.

Then he noticed the black gash across her torso from shoulder to hip.

He drew in a long shuddering breath.

"Awake, my love." He kissed her brow and gently stroked her temples.

Georgie's eyes flew open.

"What?" She tried to scramble to her knees. He held her in place a few heartbeats longer until she caught her bearings.

"Georgie, soldiers are downstairs. They'll arrest us if they find us."

"Barclay?" She twisted to stare at her cousin.

"Sorely hurt, maybe dying."

"I killed him. But I was certain the demon took him."

"He's right over there. If he dies, they'll hang you, Georgie."

"The demon will kill me first."

"I have to get you to your brother. By the first ship to leave Boston."

"Zaneta?"

"Hiding."

"Get her."

"I'll send her to fetch Ian. But I have to get you out of here first."

He crept to the head of the stairs.

"Some witch who wields a blade as if it were an extension of her arm. An unnatural woman. She'll hang or burn afore morning," the lieutenant said. His voice moved closer to the stairwell as he spoke. Then they heard his step upon the stair.

"Is there another way out of here?" Roderick whispered in Georgie's ear.

"This way?" Zaneta appeared beside the window at the far end of the room.

"I thought I told you to hide." Fear clutched at Roderick's middle. He'd lose both of them tonight if he was not careful

"This way, Papa. The roof over the stable is right here. The toolshed is right beside it. Short drops to the ground. We can all make it if we hurry."

"She's right. 'Tis the only way." Georgie began crawling toward the window.

Roderick hastened to open the sash, then he hoisted Georgie to his shoulder. She seemed to weigh so little, as if half her body had already passed into the Netherworld with the demon.

Zaneta scrambled out the window and balanced easily upon the roof, as if she had done this a dozen times at home. His heart stuttered at the thought of how much trouble she could get into on her own.

Then he shifted Georgie to sit upon the sill. She grabbed the window frame for balance. Gritting her teeth she swung her legs to the outside. Zaneta helped hold her upright.

"How much does it hurt?" Roderick asked.

"I can manage. It won't kill me yet. But I won't be well." She slid to her knees outside, making room for Roderick to climb through and close the shutters.

Just in time. The heavy tread of many boots sounded upon the floor of the meeting room. Then their shouts of dismay and alarm as they discovered their colonel's body.

Roderick wasted no time on stealth, counting upon confusion above to cover the sounds of their retreat down the roof to the shed and thence to the frozen yard behind the tavern.

Roderick landed heavily upon the ground first. He

turned and reached upward to catch Zaneta where she dangled from Georgie's grip. The moment he held his daughter fast, Georgie dropped to the ground, landing in a weak crouch.

"I left my saber up there." She pointed to the meeting room. Pain made her face white and unearthly in the dim light spilling from the buildings around them. "They'll trace it to me."

"We have to leave Boston tonight. They are hunting you." Roderick gulped. He'd grown to love this city and his business. He felt at home here. He had not had a true home since he was sent away to school at the age of eight. He had not had a real family from that time until Zaneta came into his life. Zaneta and Georgina. His wife made Boston as much a home as his daughter.

"As long as we are together, we will be safe," he affirmed.

"No. I have to leave Boston alone. You heard them. Barclay branded me a witch before he set about tonight's business. If you leave with me, you condemn both youself and our daughter. That warrant will follow me everywhere in the British Empire."

"Georgie," he gulped back his pain. "I don't care about the warrant. You are ill. You can't make it back to your brother for healing alone. We are in this together. For better or for worse." He pulled her close. "Now let's get out of here. We need clothes and money. Ian can manage the tavern. He can have the damn place."

Zaneta began to cry. Quietly. Her body shuddered in his arms as she swallowed her sobs.

"I can disguise myself easier than an entire family. I hate to leave you, Roddie, Zaneta. But for both your sakes, I have to go. Now." She stood on tiptoe and kissed his cheek. With one hand she caressed Zaneta's fair hair.

"We go as a family or not at all." Roderick wrapped one arm around her waist and began walking.

"Zaneta, fetch your Mama's saber and send it home. Then run and fetch Ian. Have him meet us near the back door." He set his daughter down, kissed her crown, and pushed her gently ahead of him.

"Alone? You want me to go out alone?" Zaneta looked ready to cry again.

"Time to grow up a bit, little one. I have to help Mama. I'm going to have to help her a lot in the months to come."

His little girl ran off into the night.

Roderick lifted his wife into his arms and began the long slow walk back to the Crown and Anchor.

Chapter 73

"THIS time is the last time I run away," I whispered to Roddie as he set me down in the shadows of our tiny garden behind the Crown and Anchor.

Fire burned across my chest with every breath. The rest of me was growing cold and numb. Every movement sent the demon's poison deeper into my body. I needed to wash my wounds and wrap up in a blanket beside the fire. A nice hot toddy would help.

Three soldiers milled around each door of the tavern. They stamped their feet and blew on their hands to keep warm on this clear and frosty night.

They stood between me and warmth.

A few soldiers could not keep me out of my own home. I was a Kirkwood by birth and a descendant of Merlin. I suggested a tickle in the back of three throats. The trio doubled over coughing. They dropped their weapons and rolled on the ground. Roderick and I slipped past them through the back door.

Zaneta and Ian were already there. "Mama, I figured out how to make him disappear, too!" she whispered excitedly.

"I packed a small trunk for each of you, sir," Ian said, still behaving as a servant though we'd made him a partner in the business a year ago.

"Shall I send the soldiers after the Sons of Liberty, Mama?" Zaneta asked. She nearly bounced at the prospect of using her magic openly.

I had to let her do it. I had used up the last of my strength.

I slid to the floor and rested my forehead against the chill floorboards.

When next I became aware of reality, I was warmer and lay flat upon the hearth before a crackling fire. The demon slash still burned sharply. The flesh on either side of the wound felt as if Tryblith had left ice crystals in my skin. Bandages bound my various wounds. Roderick tucked a blanket around me.

"Are you awake enough to drink a cup of coffee?" he asked quietly.

"If you help me sit," I replied, struggling to find the strength and balance to move.

He slid his arm beneath my shoulders and lifted me. Then he placed a mug of steaming coffee—heavily laced with cream, sugar, and brandy—into my hands. I held it a long moment letting its heat infuse my hands. Then I pressed it against my chest, trying to warm the area around the wound.

"I've dressed your wounds. On the worst of them I used the ointment I found in the false bottom of your big trunk," he said.

"I guess the compartment is no longer a secret," I mused. "Was it the blue ointment or the yellow?" I hiked the blanket back up over my naked shoulder. The fire was warm, but the room still chilled. I didn't know if I would ever be warm again.

"The yellow ointment. It looked more natural than the blue."

"Good thinking." I almost chuckled. His love and care for me did more to alleviate the pain and weakness than the magical healing properties in the ointment. "The blue stuff leaves a silver trail behind so that I can track whoever is wearing it. It also stinks to high heaven."

My husband half smiled. "I selected a warm traveling gown and underthings for you. But I need your help to get you properly dressed."

"The sentries outside?"

"Gone. Zaneta made them believe they had orders to observe the activities down at Griffin's Wharf. We are alone. Ian has gone to find us a ship departing with the dawn tide. He took Zaneta and our trunks with him."

"My weapons?"

"Right here." He patted them where they rested upon a nearby settle, along with our long cloaks and a fat purse.

"We have to go." I breathed heavily, dreading the prospect of moving from my nice warm cocoon beneath the blanket.

The streets of Boston were deserted that night. Roddie had to near carry me. I hated the weakness in my legs and the heaviness in my head. My eyes kept wanting to close in sleep. A sleep from which I might not wake.

Our path took us past Faneuil Hall, the meeting house where thousands of locals held the city government hostage. They jeered and chanted. They threw stones at anyone in uniform. They demanded that the three ships full of tea leave the port without paying the three-penny duty.

If anyone followed us, they lost our trail in that crowd.

Ian and Zaneta awaited us near Long Wharf. A number of ships docked there, many of them carried passengers.

"General Gage will look here first for a fugitive who has injured or murdered one of his colonels," I protested. But I could walk no farther.

"General Gage and his men are otherwise occupied tonight," Roderick replied.

I stared at the Long Wharf, over one hundred yards from here to our ship. My body began slipping through Roderick's grasp even though my mind was already aboard and sailing toward England and Drake.

"I've got ye, missus," Ian said as he caught me and lifted me into his arms. He carried me aboard the *Persimmon* and settled me on a low bunk in a tiny cabin. Another bed was stacked upon mine and a third butted up against the opposite bulkhead. Our trunks littered the floor.

Within moments, I felt the ship creak and sway. We slipped into Boston Harbor under cover of darkness. I wondered how many coins Roderick had to pass to the captain for this quick departure.

"Look, Mama. Look at the Indians." Zaneta jumped up and down upon one of the trunks beneath the porthole.

I dragged myself over to the round window. Torchlight silhouetted two dozen "Indians" on the decks of the *Dartmouth* and her sister ships. The Sons of Liberty whooped war cries as they hacked open chest after chest of tea. Others of their comrades dumped the broken crates into the murky water of the harbor.

The flickering light lent an unearthly quality to the scene. My head was light and my vision far too sensitive to separate the reality of the scene from ghosts of the past. If I had not spotted the solid figure of Paul Revere and his bandy-legged companion John Adams guarding the soldiers who were supposed to guard the ships, I might have believed I had stumbled through time to a true massacre by Indians upon settlers.

"We're bound for a rough crossing, Georgina," Roderick grumbled as he ducked into the cabin. He rubbed his hands together and blew on them. "The captain says that like as not we'll lift a New Year's toast on the Newfoundland Banks. But we should have you home by the end of February."

My gut wrenched. We'd spend Yule at sea. Had Roddie found the cap and mittens I had knitted for our daughter's present? Did he even look for the new silver buckles for his shoes I had commissioned Paul Revere to make for him?

Would I live to celebrate with them?

"We'll be together and that's all that matters," I whispered.

Storms tossed the *Persimmon* about like a cork. The winds drove us south, farther and farther off course for Plymouth, or Bristol, or any other home port.

For the first time in my life, I suffered seasickness so violently I could not rise from my bunk. I grew weaker. Fever racked my body.

I knew the air grew warmer, but my wound still felt frozen. I dreamed strange visions of Tryblith rending each and every member of my family limb from limb.

I woke screaming most every night.

Zaneta cried with fear. Roddie's eyes grew dark and heavy with sleeplessness. He sat up cradling my head in his lap, smoothing my hair, and washing my face with cool water.

By the end of January, when we finally limped into port in the Bahamas, my dowdy gown hung on my wasted frame and my hair had grown dank, lacking any trace of its former luster.

But I managed to walk off the gangplank, leaning heavily upon Roderick's arm. We found an inn and my husband went in search of another ship. The *Persimmon* needed at least a month in dry dock to repair storm damage.

Roderick reported back that the islands bustled with trade from all over the world. Nearly every cargo passed through this part of the world. Since the colonies had ceased importing goods from England, the triangular trade route from Portsmouth to the Caribbean to American ports had fallen sharply. No ships were bound for England or back to Boston in February of 1774.

English merchants must be petitioning Parliament for relief. So why did Parliament turn a deaf ear to the pleas of their colonists as well as the merchants?

Because Dr. Milton Marlowe and his demons controlled the government, not the citizens, and probably not even the king.

We finally booked passage in mid-February for Spain, hoping a layover in the Canaries would provide us with better transportation.

The Spanish ship was wide-bellied and slow, filthy, and crewed by miscreants who could not qualify for a better ship. With the winds and currents running in her favor, we managed to make port in Tenerife near the end of April. I could barely lift my head from the bolsters and ate almost nothing.

Tenerife, Canary Islands, April 27, 1774.

Roderick wandered into yet another dockside pub near the port of Tenerife. His sober brown gabardine suit and neatly restrained queue nearly screamed rustic Englishman. Every man here wore bright colors, many in garish combinations; their breeches were fuller, they wore neckerchiefs instead of stocks, and their shirts bloused open nearly to their navels. None of them restrained their hair and many wore gold earrings.

Conversation ceased abruptly the moment his shadow darkened the door.

He did not belong here among these wild sailors.

He had no choice. He had to find a ship that would take him and his family to England. They'd wasted nearly two weeks in a filthy inn while he searched for any captain willing to make the journey.

Georgina wasted away by the day. She ate very little but drank copious amounts of water and ale. Her skin was whiter than her bleached linen shift. She spent nearly all of the daylight hours peering into a basin of water. What she saw she did not tell him.

"I need passage to England," Roderick called into the silent pub in a rough approximation of Portuguese.

The sailors turned from their scrutiny of Roderick back to their drinks, their conversation, and their rowdy songs in a mixture of languages.

Roderick's heart sank. He turned slowly to retrace his steps to the inn and Georgie. He didn't know if he could bear to watch her fade away to nothing, all for lack of a ship.

"Hey, English," a rough voice, heavily accented called out in Roderick's native language.

Roderick stopped his retreat. He looked over his shoulder. A sailor, who looked no different from any of the others, sitting at a table in the center of the room, beckoned Roderick to sit beside him.

Cautiously, Roderick made his way to the table.

"Do you have a ship that will take me and my family to England?" he asked, still standing.

"Sit and share a drink with me," the sailor shoved a stool out from beneath the table with his foot.

"Do you have a ship?" Roderick remained standing. He resisted pounding his fist upon the table.

The sailor smiled showing two broken and badly stained teeth. He looked familiar. Where had Roderick seen him before?

Roderick could not dredge up a memory of the man. Still, the face and grin haunted him.

"I am first mate aboard *El Tigre Nigre,* the *Black Tiger.* I might persuade the captain to take you to England."

"Might? I need more reassurance than that. My wife is ill." The sailor reared back.

"She's not contagious. A wasting disease. I have to take her home to England, soon."

"Tell me about your wife, Captain Whythe." The sailor nudged the stool out another inch.

"How do you know me? And it's Colonel Whythe. Retired." He sat abruptly.

"Last time I saw you was on the Austro-Ottoman border. You were recruiting light cavalry."

Roderick sifted through his memories of those weeks on the backside of nowhere, the place where he had first met Georgie, Georgina.

"Estovan?"

"Sí. I was Major Kirkwood's batman. Tell me, is Georgie your wife?"

"How? Of course, you must have known."

"Like is attracted to like," Estovan said from behind her mug. She took a deep swallow. "But Major Kirkwood likes the men. I prefer women."

"Of course," Roderick replied flatly. "Georgina is very ill. I need to take her home. Her brother has . . . has a special treatment that might help her. But we are running out of time."

"We sail on the evening tide." Estovan stood up, took the last swig of ale and banged her mug onto the table.

"Your captain will agree? I have a little money. We can get more from Georgina's brother in England."

"Keep your money. I've been looking for an excuse to kill the captain and take over the crew."

Roderick gulped. "You are not regular merchants then."

"Pirates. Fetch your wife and luggage. Be aboard the *Black Tiger* before sunset."

Chapter 74

Portsmouth, May 1774.

MY reunion with Estovan was brief and tense. We no longer had common interests or motivations. And I was too weak to carry on a conversation for long.

I could not allow her to kill her captain. So we set him adrift in a small boat just outside the harbor. The journey to England was fast, only a little over a week with a good southerly wind all the way.

I wanted Estovan to sail around to Tilbury. From thence we could take a barge up the Thames to London. She refused to spend so long in British waters and dumped us unceremoniously at Portsmouth.

Our passage had been free. We could not readily complain.

The moment my feet touched British soil, a tense thrumming in my feet sent heat and strength through my body. Not much, but enough to get me to the first posting inn.

My back ached, my belly growled, and my eyes barely focused. I longed for nothing more than to find a bit of privacy and scry for Emily and Drake. I prayed they were at the Chelsea house and could meet us halfway between here and London. I was not certain I could ride as far north as Kirkenwood.

"Georgie Kirkwood, as I live and breathe!" Two thick arms enfolded me in a hug that would choke a bear the moment I set foot in the common room.

I peeked up from the massive chest where I nearly smothered in damp green wool.

"Prince Heinrich der Reusse?" I squeaked.

He nodded and swallowed deeply. Moisture gathered in his eyes. "We thought you dead twice over, Georgie. 'Tis right glad I am to find you alive if not exactly hale. You're as thin as a matchstick." He thumped my back then held me at arm's length, peering at me. "Pale and sad, too. Come, eat and drink. Then we must talk."

"My wife is ill and needs her rest." Roderick set a hand upon der Reusse's arm. "But I will certainly join you for a meal, my friend."

"I think this calls for a private room. Zaneta and I will join you," I replied, laying my own hand atop Roderick's on der Reusse's arm.

I ate sparingly of the good mutton pie and a tankard of ale. Then another tankard. My throat was still parched. I could never get enough liquid.

Heinrich watched me carefully through the entire process.

"What brings you to England?" I asked when I had finished my few bites and the others kept eating.

"Finish eating. Then we talk." He handed me another portion of the pie.

I pushed it aside in favor of more ale. "I have eaten my fill, Heinrich. Talk."

Roderick reached over to feel my forehead. I knew the fever still ate at me. But I determined to remain in this good company as long as possible.

"So 'twas this randy Englishman who captured your heart," Heinrich said with enthusiasm, completely avoiding the issue of my question.

"Aye. So why are you here?"

"I have retired. Our company is dispersed. His Majesty hired most of the men into other regiments. Now I must make my way home to the wife and the princedom." He heaved a tremendous sigh of boredom.

"We seek Georgina's family. She needs to be home to get well," Roderick said quietly.

Heinrich knew somewhat of my talent but not the extent of my family's history or the magnitude of my own power. He might believe my tale of a battle with a demon. Then again he might not.

"A curious wasting disease that can only be cured by a

trip home. I surmise that your brother, Drake of the dragon heritage, is a big part of your healing?"

Roderick and I stared at him, openmouthed.

"What do you need of me?" he asked as if dealing with magic and demons was an everyday occurrence.

"Can you spare a few weeks to see us safely home?" I asked.

"My only contract is with my wife in the Sovereign States of Reusse."

"Surely you must miss . . ." Roderick protested.

"The roof of the castle is fixed well enough to last another twenty years. The last of my daughters has married well. My son has married and is soon to make me a grandfather. And my wife threatened to divorce me for a younger man if I did not come home." He laughed long and loud. "I'm inclined to call her bluff."

"She'll argue and rail, but she will never replace you, Heinrich. No other man would give her the freedom to rule your princedom in your stead," I reminded him.

"Seriously, Georgie, what can I do? 'Tis more than healing that has brought you home."

"There will be a battle within the family, for power and authority," Roderick said quietly.

"Does this battle involve powers that you and I, Roderick, cannot fully appreciate?"

"He means magic, Papa," Zaneta said, her first words since tucking into her meal.

"Do I?" Heinrich responded.

We met his question with silence. Zaneta wanted to inform him. I squeezed her knee sharply to keep her quiet.

"Your silence tells me more than words. In the Sovereign States of Reusse, we have an old saying: 'Slay not the old crone for a witch. Look closer to home for the young knave who holds the balance of light and dark.' Are you the knave?"

"No."

"Is your niece?"

"Possibly."

"Your brother."

I took another drink.

"We ride at dawn." His chair came crashing back onto all four legs and he slapped the table. "To bed, my young friend."

"No longer so young," I muttered. My newfound energy

drained out of me. For the first time since my fight with the demon I cried. I cried for my lost vigor. I cried that I failed my family. I cried that I might die and never know Roddie's love again.

London, May 1774

"You failed, Father."

Milton stopped short as he entered his private study in the home Drake Kirkwood's money had bought for him before Emily managed to usurp his control of Kirkenwood.

Two ghosts awaited him before the hearth. Neville stood, holding his severed limbs as always. Another lounged in Milton's favorite chair with one leg dangling over the arm. Barclay seemed more substantial, but just as covered with wounds. At least he had all of his limbs intact.

"W . . . who spoke?" he asked hesitantly.

"We both did." Barclay and Neville spoke together.

Milton forced himself to take a closer look. Barclay wore a new golden velvet suit, emerald-green waistcoat and a shirt that dripped lace. His left arm hung limply within a sling. His skin was so pale as to be nearly translucent. His eyes looked like sunken hollows into the depths of hell.

"Barclay, are you alive or dead?." Air seemed to whoosh out of Milton. Suddenly deflated he groped for a chair and dropped into it.

"Alive. Barely. Georgina Kirkwood, the bitch, ran me through with her cursed blade," Barclay pouted. "She cheated."

"And did you not cheat as well? I thought I taught you that winning is more important than the means. Damme, Barclay, I need that woman dead!"

"No concern for my health, dear father?" Barclay sneered. "No care that I spent months in bed from loss of blood and fever and only now had enough strength to return home? Well, believe me, the only reason I return to you and agree to ally myself with you is because together we have a better chance of killing Georgie Kirkwood. I want her dead more than you do."

Concern yourself with the witch's presence in England, not in casting blame, Neville's ghost reprimanded them both.

"Always the sensible one," Milton muttered. "You would have carried this fight to a conclusion years ago."

Georgina Kirkwood allies herself with the enemy, Neville said. *She seeks her family and allies as we speak.*

"The family is at Kirkenwood. Georgina is powerless so far north. I must stay in London to control Parliament. The port of Boston closes and will be blockaded in a few days. Reparations and sanctions have been levied. Westward expansion has been halted. Soon all of the colonies will be on their knees; helpless, docile, and punished for the death of my son."

"At Kirkenwood, Georgina will bind her power to Emily's. She is a catalyst, she enhances another's powers. Together, they can block all of your plans," Barclay reminded him.

At Kirkenwood, Georgina has access to the grimoire with the spell that will reattach my limbs. She will control the spell that will free me from the chains of death, Neville added.

"Georgina has no reason to destroy the grimoire."

Barclay blanched even more.

"Damme, did you tell her about it?" Milton screamed.

Of course he did. He tells Georgina everything. He has since they were children and she first wrapped a love spell around him.

"We leave for Kirkenwood the first of the week. I need to complete some matters here," Milton decided. "I will take down Drake Kirkwood and have the grimoire. Barclay, you will fetch it from the archives with magic."

"I have to know where the archives are, and what the book looks like to do that."

"Seduce Emily. It is the one thing you are good at."

Portsmouth, England.

"Cousin Griffin says they are settling into Kirkenwood," Zaneta announced the next morning. "Is that far?"

"Too far," I sighed, barely audible. Hope for my life drained out of me. I could not travel all the way to Kirkenwood. The fire and ice of my wound now engulfed nearly all of my body. My entire being consisted of pain and weakness.

And tears. A new spate trickled from my eyes.

Roddie was there with a cool cloth to wipe them away and refresh my face.

"Is there anyone else?" Roderick asked. "Surely another member of the Pendragon Society can help you." He nearly choked on his own grief.

Heinrich stood behind him, his face set in a commander's worried assessment of a difficult situation.

I thought carefully, running the roster of family members in the Inner Circle through my head time and again. Each time I lingered on a spark of humor in twinkling eyes.

"Great-Aunt Budgie," I whispered.

"Budgie? What kind of name is that?" Heinrich blustered and raised his fist as if needing to pound it into something.

"Where does she live?" Roderick asked. He lost a little of the grimness about his eyes.

A tiny ember of hope came to life in my heart.

"Isle of Wight. Ryde," I breathed.

"I will commandeer the first boat I can find to take me there. I will have her back by sunset," Heinrich slammed his tricorn upon his head.

"Her name is Lady Bridget Kirkwood Sanderson. Widow of Lord Byron Sanderson," I added. "Her home is a creaking monstrosity that looks like it grew out of the ground, each room added by a later generation and style." I almost laughed at my childhood memories of exploring Sanderson Manor.

Heinrich did not return until noon the next day. I knew Aunt Budgie could not be rushed, unless she wanted to be.

Looking more like a crone than the last time I had seen her, my great-aunt and friend bustled into our private sitting room at the inn carrying a satchel marked with blue crescent moons and bright yellow suns.

"Don't bring in all of those trunks now," she called to her two footmen. "We are traveling north in the morning. I need only the small casket for today and tonight." She almost paused for breath. "You, there, landlord, I need a large soup kettle, scrubbed clean with sand and then filled with boiling water. And what are you doing standing there like a meek suitor, Prince Heinrich? I told you I will need several strong leather straps and a jaw block. Get off to the stable and find them. You must be Steady Roddie. Hasten off to the apothecary. I need everything on this list. Mind you, they must be fresh, harvested this morning. Ah, Zaneta, you'll be wanting to help too. I need you to go to your scrying bowl and warn my worthless nephew Drake that he needs to prepare to work with me through the water."

"Hello, Aunt Budgie," I said.

"What are you doing out of bed, girl? Off with those clothes, I need to strip off the bandages and get a good look at that wound." Despite the differences in our heights and ages she proved stronger than I as she hoisted me up by the elbows and pushed me to my bed.

Within the hour, all was settled according to Aunt Budgie. She had me strapped to the bedposts with Roddie soothing my limbs with a fragrant lotion. Zaneta with her scrying bowl on a low table waited beside her. Aunt Budgie continued mixing a foul-smelling paste in her mortar and pestle made from the skull and thighbone of a goat.

A light blanket covered me from the waist down. I wore my shift. Budgie had removed all of my bandages.

Zaneta dropped an agate into the bowl of water. She spoke aloud her desire to contact Drake Kirkwood, Pendragon of England.

You must use Georgina's power as a catalyst to help us, Drake's voice drifted out of the water.

"My dear nephew, that is unprecedented. The patient is never part of the healing."

You must use her talent, I am too weak, and the healing must pass through this uncertain link to you. 'Tis the only way to save her.

"Georgina has very little strength. To involve her in this spell will surely kill her."

"I would rather die in trying than exist as a mere shadow, half in this world and half in the Netherworld with a demon in my gut. Do it, Aunt Budgie. Do what

you must." I breathed heavily, noisily, just from that little exertion.

"Are you certain, my love?" Roderick asked me. He held
my hand tightly.

"I love you, Roddie. I love you, Zaneta. Now, Budgie, do
what you must."

"If you insist. Ready, my girl?" Budgie looked at me with
heavy eyes that belied the brightness of her voice. "This
first part is going to hurt. I have to draw the poison out."

I gritted my teeth and nodded. Then I focused my eyes
on Roddie. If I died in the next moment, his beloved face
would be the last thing I saw.

Without a word, Budgie ripped open my shift, all the
way to my waist. Then she spoke a spell in Greek. She
spread her green potion the length and breadth of the still
gaping slash across my chest.

Flames and ice burned all the way through to my spine.
All of my blood and vital fluids rushed to the wound site
to join the party of ripping me in two. I may have screamed.
I could not hear it over the roar of thunder in my head.

Mercifully, I passed out, or into the Netherworld, I never
knew which. My vision was haunted by nightmares of Tryblith and his *dieflyn* dancing about my innards with teeth
and claws bared.

Then, suddenly, I was free. Free of pain. Free of weakness. Free of my body.

I looked down upon my family from the ceiling. Curious,
I sensed none of the magic I could plainly see coursing
through my body. I sensed none of the emotions evident in
the tears of my daughter and my husband.

A black mass, roiling with red lightning and amber
sparks lifted free of my body. It came in a single lump. A
faint trail of amber led back from it to my heart. I willed
myself closer to examine the demon's poison so heavily
laced with my own essence.

"Don't die, Mama. Please don't die!" Zaneta wailed.

Tears streaked Roderick's face and he bowed his head.

Budgie's chin quivered.

Their grief rose up to swell my heart near to bursting.
Sobbing silently, I sank slowly back into my body. At the
last moment I thought to draw the amber essence out of

the mass of black poison. A thimbleful of the blackness came with it.

Then I opened my eyes and shared tears of relief with them all.

Chapter 75

Kirkenwood, June 20, 1774.

"I HAVE not been a very effective Pendragon, Patricia," Drake Kirkwood admitted to his middle daughter. He sat with her every morning before going down to break his fast.

"Nonsense, Papa. The spell you contrived to keep calm, compassion, and compromise open in Parliament was brilliant." Patricia made a note in the heavy tome she kept open on her lap on the chaise lounge of her room. The woolen blanket over her lower body barely disguised her wasted and twisted legs.

"But when I had my first heart attack, the spell unraveled without grounding. The backlash . . ."

"Is one of the problems of life," Patricia finished for him.

Where did she get her cheery nature and optimism? Her life was as wasted as her legs.

The sun rose a fraction, enough to peek through the tall trees outside the window. The clear light lent a translucent quality to Patricia's skin. Truly the loveliest of his five daughters, and never to know the triumph of a successful debut, of finding a husband to love, of bearing him children.

"Not every woman finds fulfillment in the role of wife and mother, Papa," Patricia said without preamble. "Look at Aunt Georgie. I do believe she was quite happy as a mercenary and as a barmaid. She found love, but late in life, to a man of her own ilk."

"Did you read my mind, Patricia?" Drake asked. In the past few years, since her injury, Patsy had exhibited some amazing insights, almost as if the pain she endured had opened the channels of dormant magic deep within her.

"Hardly, Papa. We discuss this nearly every morning. You forget." She made some more notes in the margins of her book.

"What do you study today?" He lifted the spine enough to look at the lettering.

"Resmiranda Griffin's journals. Emily's dogs are named for her. Her family called her Ana. She cloaked the most amazing spells in ordinary receipts. The ingredients listed here for lamb stew seem quite ordinary until you put them together. I do believe . . ." Her voice trailed off as she studied the ancient script more closely.

Drake reached automatically to ruffle Belle's ears. His familiar had passed on years ago. Emily had the only familiar now. He felt empty. As empty as he always did when he realized that with the passing of Belle, he had to acknowledge the passing of the responsibilities of the Pendragon and his own eventual demise. Without the authority of his title, he was half dead already with nothing to cling to. He'd been the Pendragon so long he had nothing else to claim as his own.

Soon, he thought. He'd join Emma in death soon.

"You have your children, Papa. We are testimony to your good character," Patsy said quietly.

Then she lifted her head abruptly. "Someone comes. Three riders. Two coaches. They come fast, but wearily."

"How . . ."

"I listen. Go, Papa. You need to eat; your skin is quite green and clammy. The visitors will join you shortly." With that, she buried her nose in the book and refused to look up again.

Emily and Samuel already sat at the head of the table with plates mounded high with food. The morning room faced east and caught the same bright light as Patricia's chamber. As usual, Samuel had dressed neatly, precisely as a gentleman should despite his lowly birth—second son of a second son of a minor baronet. He ran the estate admirably.

Emily, on the other hand, always looked disheveled. Her cap sat askew upon her tousled curls and soil marred the hem of her sturdy gown. Ana, the third familiar of that name lounged at her feet, drool hanging from her mouth in long ropes.

The staff, topped by the Celtic cross and black crystal, rested lightly in Emily's left hand as she shoveled food into her mouth with her right.

Drake wondered why Emily had never married Samuel. They seemed fond of one another and they worked well together. Drake trusted the man, had worked magic with him.

But Emily still walked warily around Samuel. She did not trust easily, even now, years after her experiences in the Netherworld.

"Where are Martha and Hannah?" he asked the room in general. He placed a single egg and rasher of bacon upon his plate along with three of the first of the wild strawberries.

"They stayed in London with Belinda. They will be home before the end of June. I told you that yesterday," Emily replied around a mouthful of food. "You need to eat more, Papa." She thrust the toast rack toward him.

"And Griffin?"

"Here, Papa." Drake's ten-year-old heir ran down the corridor until he rounded the corner into the morning room. Then he slid upon the smooth wooden floors in an arcing line that brought him to a halt before the buffet.

"Decorum, young master," Samuel said quietly.

"Sorry," Griffin stuffed half a rasher of bacon into his mouth at the same moment as his reply.

"If you married Emily, your words would carry more authority," Drake said quietly. No one seemed to hear him. Perhaps he'd said the same thing yesterday and the day before and the day before. He did not remember.

If Belle still lived, she'd help him keep the fog of forgetfulness at bay.

And yet he still recalled in precise detail every spell he had ever cast, every meeting of the Pendragon Society . . . and the precise order of the ingredients for Resmiranda Griffin's lamb stew. The addition of vinegar and cumin would make a very sour-tasting meal. But those two ingredients plus a little thistle and catnip did something else entirely.

The clatter of horses upon the drive sent his thoughts skittering away like dust bunnies before a broom.

The family stilled. Waiting. Few called upon the Kirk-wood family these days. Fewer still timed the long journey for an arrival this early.

Heavy boots and spurs clanked upon the parquet in the entry. Other, more metallic sounds followed.

"Armed men," Drake said quietly. His hands and feet grew cold. Heat flushed his face. He needed to think, needed to act.

Emily rose and whirled in one movement, bringing her staff to bear. The embers of a fireball glimmered on the fingertips of her raised right hand. Samuel stood at her left shoulder. He traced an ancient sigil of warding in the air. Yellow fire trailed away from his gestures, defining the protection.

"Drake!" a husky feminine voice called from the doorway.

Drake looked up to find his sister smiling at him beneath several layers of travel grime and a battered tricorn that barely held a discernible shape. She wore men's clothing and carried numerous blades and firearms about her person.

She looked as if she'd been to hell and back: much too thin, a gray cast to her skin, and eyes sunken in their sock-ets. But then, she had journeyed to the Netherworld and back just a few weeks ago.

"Georgie," Drake sighed. He opened his arms to her. She swept off her hat and stumbled to kneel beside his chair and wrap her arms about him. He rested his cheek atop her lank hair. "How are you?"

"Tired. I'm not truly healed, just relieved of the pain and most of the weakness."

"We did not get out all of the poison." Drake's heart felt as if a heavy stone pressed against it. "We'll try again tonight."

"If we have time."

"Stand aside, whelp," something growled.

Drake opened his eyes to find a bear of a man in equally disreputable habiliment facing Samuel and Emily with a drawn saber.

"Your husband?" he asked.

"No," Georgie replied faintly. Stiffly, she resumed her feet and faced the family. "May I present His Highness, Prince Heinrich der Reusse, an old and dear and trusted friend. My husband is helping Aunt Budgie and our daughter out of the traveling coach."

"Prince?" Emily snorted. "He dresses no better than a common . . ."

"Mercenary," Georgie finished the sentence for her niece. Her gaze raked Emily with disdain. "Change the gown for a uniform and you might fit the same description."

Emily and Georgie walked around each other like bitches sniffing and guarding territory. Ana, the only true bitch in the room observed them with an openmouthed grin.

"Down, girls," Budgie ordered as if training a new brace of pups. "You can stake out territory after we confront Cousin Milton and his sons."

The man behind her, carrying a small girl child, laughed with her. He must be the husband.

Mostly polite introductions followed.

Griffin wandered about, touching each of the weapons bristling from his aunt, her husband, and their friend. He kept looking at his fingertips after each touch, questioning the sensations he evoked.

"You sorely wounded Cousin Barclay with that sword," he announced to the room.

No one seemed to hear.

"We have to hurry and make preparations," Georgie broke the false politeness. Roderick and Zaneta stayed close to her side, always within touching distance as if they feared she'd slip away from them into the land of demons.

"Prepare for what?" Emily challenged her. She had not eased the position of her staff or her wary stance. "You need a bath before you do anything."

"Aye and a meal." Georgie looked longingly at the cooling eggs and greasy bacon on the sideboard. "Dr. Milton Marlowe rides at our heels. A day behind us at most. Twelve men accompany him and his two—the ghost of Neville and someone who resembles Barclay but is not wholly in this world. The demon still tempts him into the Otherworld."

"They come seeking form and substance, or freedom from the forces that chain them between life and death," Drake said.

Suddenly Drake's thoughts assumed an orderly pattern. His heart beat an odd tattoo then calmed.

I will die tomorrow.

I will guide those hapless beings into their next reality and not be able to come back.

Not want to come back, he corrected himself.

The Stone Circle of Kirkenwood, near midnight the next night.

"Get these villagers out of here," Heinrich der Reusse bellowed.

Emily watched a dozen farm folk clutch each other and run downhill toward the manor and the lake. They looked furtively over their shoulders as they melted into the shadows of the forest. During the centuries of border warfare with Scotland, escape and stealth had been bred into every one of them. Perhaps the ancestral memory remained.

She drew Excalibur from the scabbard strapped to her back. Clumsily, she hacked at a tuft of grass with the keen edge.

"If you cannot wield that great bloody sword with both hands, then don't bother!" der Reusse hollered at her.

She looked up, startled.

"Screaming useless, that thing is," der Reusse continued to bluster. "Needing two hands; no maneuverability. It belongs in a museum." He glowered at Emily and reached for the blade.

Bright blue light snaked from the sword to his hand and back again. He jerked away, sucking on his hand. A stream of Germanic curses belched forth around his injury.

"If you cannot speak coherently, then confine yourself to doing something useful, like building a signal fire on yon hill," Emily spat back at him.

"Ah, a warrior lass after my own heart," der Reusse smiled.

Emily's dislike of him melted a little.

"Since I've lost Georgie to another, perhaps you will take her place at my side." He reached a rough hand to caress her hair.

"You, sir, are married. And a foreigner. And obligated to a great pile of stone you call a castle, just as I am obligated to this grand circle of stones." Emily looked out at the ancient monument wistfully. Would the circle with the faces of her ancestors etched in the granite whorls still stand at dawn?

"A bloody bad time to launch an attack. The man should wait for daylight and come at us from the east with the sun half blinding us, and a long night of watching that drains our strength and adds weight to our weapons."

"The man has a ghost and a demon pawn directing him," Aunt Georgie said. "They dictate the time of their greatest strength. Between midnight and dawn 'twixt one day and the next, 'tween life and death." She added some twigs to a warding fire beside the westernmost stone.

"Piss on that, Heinrich," she directed.

"Bloody hell, woman, I will not," he blustered. His face grew bright red.

"You bloody well will. 'Tis either that or bleed on it. I need the bodily fluid of a defender to complete the spell. Now do it, or go fight your own battles with your wife and neighbors in your benighted sovereign states." Georgie stood with hands on hips, feet apart, and a stubborn lift to her chin.

Emily chuckled and moved on to the next ward. She added her own spells to Georgie's and her father's. Three layers of magic to hold off the enemy. The battle plan devised by der Reusse and Roderick, the professional soldiers, was to limit Milton's access to the circle, make his magicians file in one by one. With luck, they could cut them off, one by one, reducing the odds.

Thirteen strong magicians against herself, Samuel, and Georgie, with limited help from Papa, Griffin, and Ana. Aunt Budgie and Zaneta were unknown powers in this. Der Reusse and Roderick would protect them from physical attack.

Milton would not limit himself to magic. Undoubtedly, he had dozens of mundane retainers to back him up.

But the stone circle was home ground to the Kirkwoods. The stones held the spirits of their ancestors.

Each of the defenders, or paired magicians, had one of five warding fires to man. Every one of them had walked an invisible pentagram within the circle of standing stones.

The stage was set.

"Does anyone know if the stones will dampen an enemy's magic?" Emily called out to the family.

"Oh, dear, I don't know." Aunt Budgie held her hands to her pudgy cheeks in dismay. "I don't think the circle has been assaulted by magic since . . . oh, since Elizabeth's time. Tryblith was part of that attack, too. But he didn't get very far. Griffin was Pendragon then and he beat them back."

"But a magic-sped arrow penetrated the castle and killed the laird's wife," Emily finished the story. Still no answer to her question.

One last look around showed all in place. Papa and Griffin sheltered behind the center stone that dominated the village and towered over all its fellows. Georgie and Samuel set themselves on either side of the entrance between the two easternmost stones. Budgie and Zaneta took up a post on the north side of the circle where three stones had fallen and left a large gap. Der Reusse and Roderick roamed among the cottages. Ana trotted beside them. Every fifth step the dog lifted her muzzle to sniff the air. Emily placed herself before the center stone, staff in hand.

"Here, Papa." She unbuckled Excalibur's scabbard that weighed nearly as much as the sword itself. "The sword needs two hands and the staff needs two hands. I'm more comfortable with the staff."

"But I have not the strength . . ."

"Then find it," she snapped.

"I'll help you, Papa," Griffin whispered. He reached his young hands to cradle the scabbard. "We'll give each other strength."

Only one thing remained to do. Emily unwrapped the great tome of Resmiranda Griffin's journals and grimoire and placed the book on the ground before her. An enticement to lure the enemy in.

She just wished she knew what was so important about that book that Milton had plotted and schemed for over ten years, fought the Pendragon Society to a stalemate, and now risked all-out war that would unleash more magic than Britain had seen in centuries. The risk of any of that battle magic escaping ungrounded made her shudder.

Ana trumpeted a warning. Her howl echoed around the stone circle, picked up volume and filled the entire valley.

"Here they come," Georgie said. "Right on time, the stroke of midnight on the dark of the moon."

"We have the advantage. 'Tis the Summer Solstice, the shortest night of the year," Budgie reminded them all.

Chapter 76

MILTON stood on a slight mound across from the eastern entrance to the stone circle. I stared at him, magic enhancing my vision. I found no chinks in the personal armor he had enveloped around his person. Only the ghost and insubstantial Barclay at his sides seemed capable of piercing the cloud of magic.

The demon hovered behind and above the trio.

I watched my cousin test the wards from a distance. Then he sent three magicians, wearing unadorned black suits, red sashes, and matching stockings in each direction around the circle. They paused at the fresh marks in the turf I'd made with a hoe at the bottom of the ditch. I had not had the energy to spare to infuse it with true magic. Cautiously, they tested and prodded first the circle and then the wards. Within moments, they discovered the absence of magic in the ditch. They surged forward.

They made it as far as the outer surface of two stones. The rest of the wards held.

For now.

Three more magicians, these wearing blue sashes and stockings with their sober suits, approached the entry to the circle. Two stones stood side by side with barely enough space between them to admit two men standing shoulder to shoulder. They stopped abruptly at the outer edge. The man on the left took out a small willow wand and touched it to the space between the stones. Blue magic crackled and sizzled. A puff of pungent smoke that smelled of sour urine and old blood rose from the tip of the wand. Budgie had set that ward well.

Two more magicians wearing yellow sashes pushed the three aside. They joined hands and chanted. The slice of bright color across their chests glowed as they concentrated their magic. Brighter and brighter.

A loud, discordant hum set the stones to vibrating. Ana added her howl, trying to force the magic into harmony. I had to cover my ears. But I needed to watch, my gaze riveted on the sun-bright bubble that now surrounded the two senior magicians.

Louder and louder the magic rang. I moaned. Ana howled. The stones groaned.

"No!" I screamed. I could no longer wait and defend. I had to take the attack to the enemy before they destroyed the stones, the circle, the spirit of my ancestors that defined the Pendragons.

A crack danced upward along the inward face of the left-hand stone. The right hand monolith quivered and swayed.

> *"Fire, Fire, burn no brighter,*
> *Air, Air, hum no louder,*
> *Earth lay quiet,*
> *Water become the binder."*

I shouted the simple spell three times, in English, in Italian (my Latin deserted me), and in ancient Welsh. I spun a circle deasil with each recitation. Upon the last I drew my pistol and shot one of the magicians.

He slumped to the ground.

The buzz of ten thousand bees assailed my ears. My wards crumbled around me, broken by my own pistol shot.

The second magician jumped backward with a gasp.

My boot knife found that man's throat.

The night became deathly quiet.

Milton strolled through the archway of the entry stones. The scent of burning sulfur accompanied him, along with his sons. The demon became fully visible once inside the circle. He reared up and pierced me with his gaze.

My blood burned in response. A bit of demon poison still responded to his lure.

Roderick drew his own pistol and saber. He edged so that he stood with his back pressed against Georgie's. He did not understand the magic, but he smelled the sulfur and the stale urine. He'd take down these enemies the only way he knew how.

Darkness obliterated the stars. He whirled to confront this new menace.

The demon loomed above them. His teeth dripped black poison.

Instinctively, he aimed and pulled the trigger.

Tryblith roared and lashed the air with his claws.

Barclay Marlowe jerked and clutched his throat as if strangling.

Milton pointed his fingers at Roderick. He ducked, pulling Georgie down with him. Ten streams of black flames sped over the tops of their heads.

Ana leaped onto the chest of one of the blue magicians the moment the wards failed. Emily allowed her familiar's triumph at ripping out the man's throat and tasting hot blood to fill her with purpose. She swept her staff in a great circle, making certain she kept the book within the arc. If she thought too long on horrible pain and death ... A quick assessment showed der Reusse deflecting fireballs from two opponents with the flat of his blade. He sweated and cursed but seemed to be holding his own.

Georgie spun in a circle on her knees, reciting some arcane words. As she completed the ring, she pointed to a downed stone. It erupted in a shower of shards. Three large fragments felled a red magician. A long spike of granite pierced his heart.

The demon pulled a spear of granite out of the air and stared at it as if wondering what to do with it.

Roderick engaged Barclay with his sword.

She could not find Samuel anywhere in the fray.

Emily gulped. Which of her ancestors had inhabited that stone? She hoped they rested in peace after this battle.

Strangely, she felt no emotion about Barclay at all.

The ground heaved as Georgie pointed again. The great stone split once more. A rolling boulder toppled another magician and trapped his legs. He screamed again and again.

Half of Milton's minions were out of the action and her cousin marched forward toward the book, eyes focused only upon the prize. Smoke and death and swirling magic did nothing to deter him.

A man-shaped ripple in the darkness showed Emily where the ghost of Neville followed his father, tied to him in some way she did not understand. Neville paused and then jerked forward, dragged by his father's single-minded march toward the book.

Emily repeated her sweep with the staff; this time she invoked all four elements. She could not count upon her father or Griffin to help. And Samuel . . . had disappeared. She expected no less. The man had turned traitor once, why not again?

She'd not married him for just that reason.

Budgie and Zaneta seemed engulfed in smoke.

Milton halted at the edge of her circle. He smiled at her knowingly, finally lifting his gaze from the book. "Too easy, child," he said and began to chant, moving his hands in incomprehensible gestures.

Emily threw a fireball at him. It bounced off the inside of her own circle back into her eyes.

Panting for breath, I quickly grounded my spell, letting the magic rest at its origins, deep within the earth. I drew my saber and rapier. A long sword fight would take less of my waning strength than another spell.

"Out of luck and out of time, Georgie, my love," Barclay's voice caressed my ears. He stood behind me, alive if not well.

Roderick engaged one of the blue magicians. Blue threw spells. My Roddie dodged them and pressed the magician toward the outside of the stone circle with his saber. The blade fairly sang through the air in a blur of motion. I had taught him that particular motion.

"I defeated you once. I can do it again, Barclay," I snarled, whirling my body and my blades.

I sliced right through where Barclay had stood an eye blink ago.

"Tsk, tsk, my dear. My pet demon has given me powers you can only dream of. I'll kill you this time since you forsook me in life."

His cold, cold hands encircled my throat, cutting off the magic I summoned.

I grabbed what little air I could into my lungs. Then I drove both my arms upward, between his. His grip broke. I spun and came up behind him with my dagger against his throat and his arms pinioned by a coil of magic.

"Tryblith!" I called. "Tryblith, Demon of Chaos, I command you to stand in the center of the circle."

You have no power over me, Tryblith replied. His roar inside my head nearly deafened my mind and my magic.

"I command you by the power of your blood inside my body. I command you by the bonds of the Netherworld that we three share."

Chapter 77

DRAKE watched Emily's backlashing spell blind her.

He sensed Georgie maneuvering the demon into the invisible pentagram. Budgie and Zaneta were already in place, anchoring one of the five points of the giant sigil.

He had to move now, to protect Emily and get her into position.

Then, miraculously, the black crystal in the boss of the Celtic cross of her staff caught the piercingly bright magic, absorbed it, and then shot it back toward Milton.

The ghost of Neville stepped between his father and the light. It drove him backward.

Milton caught the mutilated form. It gained substance from the focused light. His limbs reattached themselves. He ceased to bleed. A pulse visibly pounded through the great vein in his neck.

"I'm alive," he whispered.

The vibrating light from the staff almost passed through him. He had not fully returned to the mortal plane.

"If I'd known it was that easy, I'd have stolen the staff from you years ago, Emily," Milton sneered. "Now step out of the way and give me the book."

"Never." Emily lashed out with her staff. It caught Neville in the middle. He grasped the cross with both hands and then jerked them away, screaming in pain.

Emily smiled and recited a spell in ancient Welsh.

Milton reached around and almost through Neville to clasp the cross atop her staff.

"Mundane symbols of power do not affect mortals!" He tried to jerk the staff out of her grasp.

Emily held on, still chanting words, this time in Anglo-Saxon.

"The sword, Griffin," Drake demanded. "I have to use the sword." With both hands upon the grip he pulled the heavy blade free of its scabbard. The weight dragged at his shoulders. Lances of pain shot through his arm muscles down to his fingers. He could not lift the thing. But he had to.

For Emily. For Georgie. For the future, he had to lift the sword of Arthur and smite his enemies.

Mere mortals had not the right to bring the dead back to life. Mere mortals had not the right to tamper with the balances decreed by the gods of the ancients.

"Let me help." Griffin reached to add his small hands to his father's upon the grip.

"Nay, boy. Keep your touch on my wrists and arms. The sword was given to Emily and me. Only we two can wield it with immunity in this lifetime."

Obediently, Griffin did as he was told.

Drake paused only long enough to raise his eyebrows in question. The boy never obeyed. He always pushed for more responsibility, more authority, more privilege than he could handle.

"Think well on what you see this night, Griffin," Drake whispered. "I hope you never see its like again."

"There is so much magic flying, how can it all ground? How can I absorb the backlash?" Griffin asked in wonder.

"Do not even try. Just hand me the spell bag and then lend your strength to mine." Drake looked proudly down at his son. "You will make a fine earl, Griffin, and a better Pendragon. Follow well in your sister's footsteps."

Griffin held his father's elbow with one hand while he reached for the ingredients within the spell bag.

"In the precise order we rehearsed," Drake warned.

"Onion, bitter root to ground you," the boy said, handing Drake the onion.

Drake rubbed it along the blade.

"Vinegar, sour to pickle you."

Drake poured the vial of vinegar along the same path as the onion.

Rue and mandrake, elderwood, sandalwood, mistletoe, and finally salt wrapped in a silk bag. Griffin slipped the handle of the bag over the blade so that the ingredients dangled from the hilt.

Closing his eyes for strength and balance, Drake lifted the blade level with his shoulders and paced forward. One painful step after another he trod forward until he stood beside the book.

> *"Unholy Spirits loosed upon the earth*
> *Find the ground to hold you*
> *Return to your maker*
> *For cleansing*
> *For healing*
> *For peace."*

Blue fire danced along the blade of Excalibur.

Drake dropped to his knees, no longer able to stand. But he and Griffin kept the blade level.

"No!" Milton reared back in panic. He placed his arms in front of his son's ghost. "You may not pervert the spell thus. I will not allow this."

Magic spurted from the tip of Excalibur. It formed sigils in the air spelling out the nature of the incantation.

" 'Tis you who perverts this spell, Cousin. 'Tis you who perverts England in your mad quest for vengeance. 'Tis you I take to your death." With one last mighty effort Drake lurched to his feet. He staggered under the weight of the sword and of his magic. Three long strides.

The first one brought the tip of the blade to Milton's chest. The second drove the blade through the mortal man. The third pierced the shade of Neville.

Samuel rose up from his hiding place behind a standing stone. The blood of three dead magicians smeared his face and hands. He reached into his own spell bag and threw a handful of ingredients into Milton's face.

"Find your maker and never rise to haunt this place or these people. Die and ne'er darken the face of this earth again."

Neville faded away slowly, a smile of gratitude on his face.

Milton slipped a stiletto out of his sleeve and slit Drake's throat as his own heart ceased to beat.

"Samuel, Emily, take your places. We have to ground the demon!" I ordered. My voice sounded weak. "Griffin, take your father's place. Zaneta, into my place."

No time to grieve. No time to think.

We had to work fast. I couldn't hold Barclay long. His body tensed and I knew he planned something. Something dangerous to me and mine.

I pushed Barclay toward the center of the pentagram centered on the altar stone.

"Emily, close the sigil," I gasped.

"Done," she replied after only a few heartbeats.

"Emily, my love, you can't do this to me," Barclay pleaded. "We are betrothed. You love me!"

Emily snarled something incomprehensible.

I nicked Barclay's throat with the blade.

He shut up.

"Begin," I panted.

Roderick and Heinrich paced a circle outside the pentagram. They had no talent, but they could follow the lines I'd drawn earlier.

All five magicians, Budgie, Zaneta, Samuel, Emily, and Griffin chanted the binding spell.

> *"Darkness to Darkness*
> *Like to Like*
> *Retreat behind the seal,*
> *Stronger than a river's dike.*
> *The door of bronze and iron,*
> *Marked and held in time*
> *by the dragon gold.*
> *Retreat and find your kin,*
> *Where once you dwelled within."*

I added my voice, shouting the spell in Latin, Greek, Welsh, German, and finally in English, in unison with my chorus of Pendragons.

The stones screeched, rending the air. A black-and-silver rift tore open in the ground beneath Tryblith's feet.

Noooooo! Tryblith screamed. Not the door. Don't put me behind the door again. You promised me Freedom.

"You have never taken responsibility for how you use freedom. I hereby revoke it forever!" I ordered.

The demon's protests faded away as the Netherworld sucked him down through the rapidly closing tear in the land and reality.

"Tryblith, no. You can't leave me alone." Barclay tore free of my weakening grip. "I am nothing without your power."

I clasped the back of his belt, trying desperately to keep his body and soul alive.

He dove into the rift, dragging me with him.

Chapter 78

The Stone Circle of Kirkenwood.

EMILY let the staff drop from her numb fingers.

Dead.

All dead.

Nine alien magicians sprawled upon the ground. Four had fled. Milton and Barclay were also dead.

Griffin heaved and sobbed. He beat his fists against their father's back, desperate to bring the man back to life.

Roderick cradled Georgie's inert body. He rocked silently. Zaneta stood mutely beside him. Tears streamed down her face. Der Reusse knelt beside the little girl and hugged her tightly.

Their raw grief broke through Emily's leaden fatigue.

Wordless in her own emotions, Emily gathered her brother into her arms. She rocked him and herself.

She had no time, no emotion to spare for the others.

Samuel moved around, checking the dead for signs of life, straightening limbs, grounding the stray magic that still careened around the inside of the stone circle in great balls of witchfire.

"Bring him back," Griffin demanded between sobs. "We can do it. We have the spell."

"No, Griffy. No, we don't. The spell puts a soul to rest. It does not bring it back to life. We have not the right to do that. Only God can do that."

"It's not fair. He didn't have to die," Griffin continued his demands upon the universe.

"Life is not fair, Griffin. But it is up to those of us who

are gifted with magic to make life a little easier for those who become victims of the unfairness. We just did that."

"But ... but ..." he blubbered on a new round of tears.

Emily had to wait a moment before she could speak. "I know. I know."

Samuel grounded the last ball of magic. The torches guttered and ward fires dimmed to embers.

To the east, the faintest glow of dawn peeked over the crest of the hills.

"I need to seek out the villagers, Emily, make funeral arrangements, get help to clean up this mess," Samuel dropped to his knees beside her. Her wrapped one arm around her shoulders. "You shiver with cold. I need to fetch your cloak."

His warmth penetrated her miasma of grief. She leaned her head upon his strong shoulders, as she should have done many years ago. He'd proved himself loyal. She should have trusted him.

A new hole opened inside her.

"Forgive me, Sam."

"I did years ago, Em. Life has been unkind to you and your clan. You do not trust easily. That is good. I'm glad you finally find me worthy."

"Can we marry, Sam?"

"Yes." He heaved a sigh of relief. "Soon. When we have buried our dead and mourned them properly. We need food now, for those of us who live. And warmth. Baths and sleep."

"T ... take Griffin with you." She pried the boy out of her lap and into his arms. "He needs something to do."

Samuel stood, bringing the boy with him. Griffin dashed the newest spate of tears from his face with the back of a grubby hand.

They were all grubby, with soot, and sweat, and the stink of rotten flesh, and magic.

"He's the earl now," Emily said quietly. "See that the village and the servants acknowledge that." Then she turned her attention to Georgie.

The big mercenary prince crossed himself as he straightened Georgie's twisted limbs with his left hand. His right arm dangled uselessly.

Dislocated shoulder, Emily registered. She and Samuel could set it right, but healing the muscles ... None of them had Papa's healing talent and now Papa was gone. For good this time.

"You should not have left me so soon, Georgie," Roderick moaned. "You should not have died a second time on me. I do not know if I can bear the grief." His voice broke. He gulped and lifted his face to the lightening sky. After a few moments he dropped his face to Georgie's still form. "I'd give my life to bring you back, Georgie. I love you that much. I have loved you since that first time we made love on board that stinking ship. I loved you with the light of battle in your eyes. I loved you when you beat the entire regiment at cards. I love you even now when you have deserted me."

He reached to close her staring eyes.

The lids sprang open the moment he released his touch.

"What?" Emily gasped. She knelt beside her aunt. "She has a pulse. She breathes."

"But I saw her shade follow Barclay and the demon into hell."

"Only her shade followed, the part that was still tied to the demon from her wound. Some small piece of her still burns inside her body, waiting," Budgie said around a gulp of sobs.

"Help me get her up." Emily grabbed Georgie's arms and pulled her up to a sitting position. Her body slumped forward, unable to support itself.

"She continues to stare blindly," der Reusse said, puzzled.

Emily thumped Georgie's back, trying to force some reaction. "I heard Barclay say something as he crashed through the ground."

"He said 'I'll drag her into the Underworld with me.' " Budgie looked up, her eyes hooded with weariness.

"Then her spirit is gone. Her body will die soon," Emily said quietly. Fear made her draw away, as if her aunt's body was tainted. Indeed, it was. It would poison Emily's soul if she touched her again.

"If her soul wanders the Underworld unguided, then you have to go in after her. You have to bring her back!" Roderick shook Emily until her teeth rattled.

"I cannot go back there."

"You have to. For your own sake, as well as hers," Samuel said. "Her soul is doomed for all eternity if you leave her. You have to either bring her back or show her the way to the other side."

He gathered Emily close into his arms once more.

"You are the only one strong enough, mature enough, skilled enough to do it, Emily."

"You are the Pendragon now, Emily," Budgie added.

"I . . . the last time I trekked through the underworld, I was lost for months. I came back insane. If I go back there, I am the one who will be lost forever."

"Can you condemn another soul to that?" der Reusse asked.

"I have responsibilities here, in this world. I cannot risk it."

Ana nudged her muzzle beneath Emily's hand. When she lifted it to scratch her familiar's ears, the dog pushed her big body between Emily and Georgie.

I am here, I will help.

"Georgie is a wife and mother. She has responsibilities here, too. She is the Pendragon's representative in the New World. She needs to go back there, to manage the chaos, to keep evil from taking the upper hand," Roderick reminded Emily.

"You are the only one who can do this, Emily," Budgie insisted. "You have to do it soon. She will not last long without her spirit."

We will go in together. Come back together, Ana added.

Chapter 79

The Archives, Kirkenwood Manor.

EMILY sat alone upon the floor of the archives. A rich Persian rug in reds and yellows with hints of green and blue cushioned her. Her Aunt Georgina lay upon the floor beside her, eyes still wide and staring blindly into the unknown.

The great sword Excalibur lay naked upon her chest, the pommel beneath her chin and the tip of the blade between her knees. Her hands folded across the sword in imitation of the ancient grave effigies in the crypt.

Emily could barely stand to touch her staff after the battle. It had been a part of her so long, she felt empty without it in her hand. And yet, she had channeled so much lethal magic through it, she hated the reminder of all that had happened, all she had lost, last night.

She had to touch it one more time. She laid it across Excalibur on a level with Georgie's heart.

"I wrote the letters you would have commanded me, Aunt Georgie. Roderick dictated many of them," Emily said quietly. "I wrote to every member of Parliament and every sitting lord I could think of. Dozens of letters, begging them to reconsider the blockade of Boston Harbor. I informed them of all the reasons the tea tax must be repealed, and why the colonials must be considered as Englishmen with all of the rights and privileges of citizenship. I sent copies to Benjamin Franklin by private courier so that Lord Sackville could not get his hands upon the letters going through the Royal Mail. I included the correspondence between Governor Hutchinson and several lords in the packet to Franklin. He'll make certain the right people read it and know how devious and malicious the man is."

Emily surveyed the room while she thought of something else to say; some other reason to delay. Ana snoozed by the fire with one eye upon her mistress, waiting, reproachful that Emily took so long.

The ritual circle was drawn in chalk upon the floor around the rug. She'd marked a pentagram in soot within the circle, mindful to keep the pattern along special black lines woven into the carpet. She had set the wards and burned a special incense with all of the necessary ingredients.

Yet, still, she waited.

"Patricia wrote some of the letters, actually. She is much better at it than I. Der Reusse helped with the wording. He is a prince, after all, even if he does come from some barbaric country around the Germanies. He's been very good to help us recover. He wanted to be here today. But I could not allow that. He is so mundane it is almost painful to look at his aura."

Was that a flicker of a smile from Aunt Georgie? Perhaps she could find her own way back from the Underworld.

Ana snorted and heaved herself to her feet. The dog plunked herself down alongside Emily and prodded her with an imperious nose.

"I guess we have to do this, Ana."

Now.

"I'm coming with you," Roderick announced from the door.

"How did you get in here?"

"Aunt Budgie led me through your magical traps. She's quite determined we do this properly."

"It breaks all the rules to include a mundane in spells of this magnitude."

"I am not just any mundane. I am Georgie's husband. She will respond to me even if she rejects you."

"This is a dangerous journey. Both of us may never return and if we do, we are likely to be insane." Emily shivered in memory of the time she had spent trapped in her own mind.

"I am prepared to take the risk. For Georgie. She is my life."

"What about your daughter?"

"Budgie and Patricia will care for and train both Zaneta and Griffin. She will be with her own kind and learn what it is to be a Pendragon and a Kirkwood."

"If I must do this, then so must you." Emily took three deep breaths in preparation. Reluctantly, she grasped the staff just below the Celtic cross. She kept her other hand on Ana.

Roderick mimicked her motions. He must have learned something of magic ritual during his years living with Georgie and Zaneta.

On the third breath she closed her eyes and reached out with her extended senses. Darkness enfolded her. Unearthly quiet. A chilling cold.

She looked down at herself. Her body appeared wasted, transparent. The room with its comfortable furnishings and stacks of books and sheaves of parchment faded into insubstantial echoes of reality.

Roderick and Ana stood beside her, equally translucent, equally apprehensive and determined to plow forward.

The memories of the time she had passed this way before, all neatly stashed away in the back of her mind where she could not easily reach them, came rushing back to her. She had been here before. She wanted to run back to reality.

Ana's spirit shifted closer, warm, reassuring, more solid than anything else in this reality. Emily took another deep breath and extended the three of them once more.

Something beckoned to her off to the left. She looked more closely with her inner self.

A twisted and broken path made up of glowing amber shards wound away from her. She recognized the trail as bits and pieces of Aunt Georgie's broken life spirit. One by one, Roderick began picking them up. He held them close to his heart, kissed the largest pieces. They began blending back together, forming a whole.

Back in the real world Emily sensed Georgie stirring.

Something dark flashed across the path, momentarily obscuring the way.

Emily took a mental step backward. The thing dashed around her. It slashed at her legs with sharp teeth that dripped green ichor.

A *dieflyn.* One of the imps she had killed in a previous

battle. It ignored Roderick. A second dark being joined it, worrying at Ana. Then a third demon rose up through the semisolid ground; bigger, with a bulbous body, engorged genitalia, and a dragon's maw for a head.

Freedom, it demanded. *Always your kin promise freedom to me and mine and then renege. You will not escape this place without me.*

Emily shied away from the demon, weaving an arcane sigil of warding with her staff. "I name you Tryblith, Demon of Chaos, and command you to withdraw!" she shouted aloud.

Tryblith gibbered in fear as it retreated beyond the sweep of her staff. It dogged her steps as she proceeded.

But she had called its name and it had to obey her.

Other things reached for her, clawed at her, tried to invade her mind with tricks and suggestions.

She fought to keep them away. She had been here before. She had succumbed to them before. If not for her father's love and magic, they would have dragged her down and kept her here forever—lost, alone, helpless.

Roderick turned in circles, kicking at demons. He made to draw his sword. Excalibur came into his hands. The blade glowed red with runes of power rippling up and down the blade. Things ran from him. He slashed at those that did not move fast enough. They flamed and shriveled to ash.

Tryblith reached to take the blade from him. His talons singed and still he clung to the blade. Roderick drove the blade into the demon. He backed off but did not go away.

Emily almost gave up. Too many memories, too many hurts blinded her.

We are with you, Ana reminded her.

"Who is 'we'?" Emily asked her familiar.

All of us. All of the wolfhounds of Kirkenwood who have passed on before. All of you and yours who have passed on before. We walk beside you. We guide your steps.

"And I thank you." Emily looked back along the way she had come. Every step she had taken on this treacherous path glowed bright and certain. She had a trail to follow back home.

She moved forward with more confidence.

Ahead of her a tiny light flickered, wavered, winked out. She gasped.

"Georgie?" Roderick asked.

The gloom swallowed his words.

Rekindle the amber ember! The voices with her familiar ordered. *Rekindle her life, now, before she wanders too far away.*

Emily blew a gentle breath in the direction of the tiny light. It glowed and burst into life once more; still faint, still weak, but still there.

She hastened toward it. It darted away to the left. Emily reached with her staff to capture it. The light eluded her. It slipped away like an eel.

Dimmer now, the ember of life paused as if seeking something.

Another light, this one dark red, blinked at them from the near distance. It prowled around Emily and the tiny light in a circle. The dark red pulsed. The little light tried to go to it.

Emily drew a new circle with her staff. The little light halted just inside the perimeter.

"Blow on it, Roderick," she commanded.

He hesitated.

"She will respond to you when she does not recognize me," she repeated his argument back to him.

The dark red light reached out a ghostly white hand, offering it to the little light. Demanding she take it and leave with him.

So like the hand that had reached for her in the black well of hell.

Roderick took a deep breath and gently let it out, feeding the flame with the fuel of love.

The light hesitated. It looked at the hand reaching toward her. Then it looked back at Roderick and Emily, pleading with her for sanctuary from what the hand offered.

Emily pounced upon it like a cat stalking a mouse. The life light slipped through her grasp and circled around behind her. Desperation and confusion radiated out from the light.

Ana dropped a metaphysical paw upon it. It jumped onto her nose. Ana peered at it crosswise, then flipped her head upward.

The light sprang away toward the perimeter of the circle and the waiting hand.

Roderick caught the little fluff of light and closed it lovingly into his palm with the shards of spirit he had collected along the way. The light snuggled in and began mending itself.

"Let's go home, Georgie, my love," Roderick whispered and kissed the spirit of his wife.

Epilogue

FOR days I lay too weak even to feed myself. I slept more than I wakened. Roderick moved me from bed to chaise and back to bed. He bathed me, fed me, shifted me. Emily, Griffin, Budgie, and Zaneta came to me every day.

At first, I had not enough strength to do aught but acknowledge their presence with a nod. Listening to their recitation of events proved more than I could manage. Yet I must have heard them, for I knew that Parliament did not rescind the order of blockade upon Boston. I knew that the tea tax, so hated by my fellow colonists, remained in place. I knew that Emily married Samuel in a quiet ceremony in the family chapel. I knew that they took Griffin to London to have him installed as the new earl.

I knew that Zaneta thrived under Aunt Budgie's care and tutelage.

And I knew that they buried my brother with honor among our ancestors.

Heinrich der Reusse came and went, uncomfortable with the sickroom regime and atmosphere, but devoted.

"I am raising a new regiment of mercenaries. I think we will be needed by your friends, the Sons of Liberty, ere long," he chortled.

He kissed my hand, holding it more gently than he would a wounded bird.

"Against the rules," I whispered. "You fought for George III last I heard."

"Sometimes you have to break the rules to do what is right," he whispered back to me conspiratorially.

Gradually I gained enough strength to sit up, to take an interest in living.

Kirkenwood and its people had endured mundane and magical battles many times over the centuries. Life continued. They went about their business as usual.

Roderick and I settled in, waiting for my body to finish mending. Miraculously, when Roderick put my spirit back together in the Underworld, he made my body whole and uninjured as well.

At the end of October I dragged him out of the library and up onto the windy tor. I faced west, the direction of home.

The wind at my back seemed to push me there.

"I'm pregnant."

For a moment I did not think he heard me over the gusts that blasted the hilltop.

"Are you certain?"

When I looked at him, his eyes were wide, staring at me in happy amazement.

"Quite certain. I want our baby born in the New World. In our home."

"So be it."

We sailed within the week with one of Ana's latest pups. I did not know if my little Newynog was a familiar or not, but she was a friend to replace the fat and aging Oblegid.

North Shore Charles River, Boston, April 18, 1775.

Roderick pulled on the muffled oars of the little skiff he'd borrowed from a friend. At the stern, Paul Revere kept looking over his shoulder toward the darkened town of Boston.

Moonlight guided them to the north shore of the Charles River.

"No signal yet," Roderick whispered, cautious of how sound carried over the water.

"He's late," Revere complained.

"No, he's not. You are just anxious."

The boat scraped bottom. Roderick jumped out and hauled the craft up onto the bank. Nearby, a horse whickered a greeting.

Georgie quieted the beast.

"The stableboy sleeps." She jerked her head toward the complex of barns where many people in the crowded city kept their mounts. "He dreams that all of the horses remain in their stalls—all night," she said quietly.

Newynog sniffed around Georgie's feet, anxious and wary of the night and the dangers it hid.

"I wish you had stayed home." Roderick scowled in disapproval at her swollen belly.

"Your son will not be born tonight," she returned with a smile. "Newynog has done her job well and protected me, as a familiar should."

"At least you agreed to let Paul ride tonight instead of yourself," Roderick sighed.

"I could do it better, but getting on and off the bloody horse would be a bit awkward." She grinned and rubbed her belly in a circular motion.

"Don't argue with her," Revere growled. "Women in that state are never rational. Believe me, I've lived through this seven times." He took the horse's reins from Georgie.

"Are we doing the right thing?" Roderick asked Georgie.

"Yes. We have to. The time has come," Georgie reassured him. "General Gage sends his troops to confiscate our stash of arms and powder."

"Aye. The time has come to break every rule of government ever written," Revere added with conviction.

"You sound like my wife," Roderick grumbled. But he could not help the smile that crept over his face.

"Who do you think taught me that sometimes you have to break the rules to do what is right?"

"Look!" Georgie said. Excitement made her voice sharp with command.

"Two lights in the tower of the Old North Church," Revere breathed.

"One if by land, two if by sea," Georgie affirmed.

"The redcoats come by sea. Off with you now." Roderick cupped his hands to help his friend mount the big horse with the barrel chest, Georgie's horse. It would run forever without a break.

"Get you back home, my friends. I'll see this through. Tomorrow we'll see a new future."

"Our son will be born free," Roderick said.

"I promise to teach him what the rules are before I show him how to break them," Georgie said.

Afterword

PAUL REVERE'S RIDE
by Henry Wadsworth Longfellow

Listen my children and you shall hear
Of the midnight ride of Paul Revere,
On the eighteenth of April, in Seventy-five;
Hardly a man is now alive
Who remembers that famous day and year.

He said to his friend, "If the British march
By land or sea from the town tonight,
Hang a lantern aloft in the belfry arch
Of the North Church tower as a signal light,—
One if by land, and two if by sea;
And I on the opposite shore will be,
Ready to ride and spread the alarm
Through every Middlesex village and farm,
For the country folk to be up and to arm."

Then he said, "Good Night!" and with muffled oar
Silently rowed to the Charlestown shore,
Just as the moon rose over the bay,
Where swinging wide at her moorings lay
The *Somerset,* British man-of-war;
A phantom ship, with each mast and spar
Across the moon like a prison bar,
And a huge black hulk, that was magnified
By its own reflection in the tide.

* * *

Meanwhile, his friend, through alley and street,
Wanders and watches, with eager ears,
Till in the silence around him he hears
The muster of men at the barrack door,
The sound of arms, and the tramp of feet,
And the measured tread of the grenadiers,
Marching down to their boats on the shore.

Then he climbed the tower of the Old North Church,
By the wooden stairs, with stealthy tread,
To the belfry chamber overhead,
And startled the pigeons from their perch
On the somber rafters, that round him made
Masses and moving shapes of shade—
By the trembling ladder, steep and tall,
To the highest window in the wall,
Where he paused to listen and look down
A moment on the roofs of the town,
And the moonlight flowing over all.

Beneath, in the churchyard, lay the dead,
In their night encampment on the hill,
Wrapped in silence so deep and still
That he could hear, like a sentinel's tread,
The watchful night-wind, as it went
Creeping along from tent to tent,
And seeming to whisper, "All is well!"
A moment only he feels the spell
Of the place and the hour, and the secret dread
Of the lonely belfry and the dead;
For suddenly all his thoughts are bent
On a shadowy something far away,
Where the river widens to meet the bay,—
A line of black that bends and floats
On the rising tide, like a bridge of boats.

Meanwhile, impatient to mount and ride,
Booted and spurred, with a heavy stride
On the opposite shore walked Paul Revere.
Now he patted his horse's side,
Now he gazed at the landscape far and near,
Then, impetuous, stamped the earth,

And turned and tightened his saddle girth;
But mostly he watched with eager search
The belfry tower of the Old North Church
As it rose above the graves on the hill,
Lonely and spectral and somber and still.
And lo! As he looks, on the belfry's height
A glimmer, and then a gleam of light!
He springs to the saddle, the bridle he turns,
But lingers and gazes, till full on his sight
A second lamp in the belfry burns.

A hurry of hoofs in a village street,
A shape in the moonlight, a bulk in the dark,
And beneath, from the pebbles, in passing, a spark
Struck out by a steed flying fearless and fleet;
That was all! And yet, through the gloom and the light,
The fate of a nation was riding that night;
And the spark struck out by that steed, in his flight,
Kindled the land into flame with its heat.
He has left the village and mounted the steep,
And beneath him, tranquil and broad and deep,
Is the Mystic, meeting the ocean tides;
And under the alders that skirt its edge,
Now soft on the sand, now loud on the ledge,
Is heard the tramp of his steed as he rides.

It was twelve by the village clock,
When he crossed the bridge into Medford town.
He heard the crowing of the cock,
And the barking of the farmer's dog,
And felt the damp of the river fog.
That rises after the sun goes down.

It was one by the village clock,
When he galloped into Lexington.
He saw the gilded weathercock
Swim in the moonlight as he passed,
And the meeting-house windows, black and bare,
Gaze at him with a spectral glare,
As if they already stood aghast
At the bloody work they would look upon.

*   *   *

It was two by the village clock,
When he came to the bridge in Concord town.
He heard the bleating of the flock,
And the twitter of birds among the trees,
And felt the breath of the morning breeze
Blowing over the meadow brown.
And one was safe and asleep in his bed
Who at the bridge would be first to fall,
Who that day would be lying dead,
Pierced by a British musket ball.

You know the rest. In the books you have read,
How the British Regulars fired and fled,—
How the farmers gave them ball for ball,
From behind each fence and farmyard wall,
Chasing the redcoats down the lane,
Then crossing the fields to emerge again
Under the trees at the turn of the road,
And only pausing to fire and load.

So through the night rode Paul Revere;
And so through the night went his cry of alarm
To every Middlesex village and farm—
A cry of defiance, and not of fear,
A voice in the darkness, a knock at the door,
And a word that shall echo forevermore!
For, borne on the night-wind of the Past,
Through all our history, to the last,
In the hour of darkness and peril and need,
The people will waken and listen to hear
The hurrying hoof-beats of that steed,
And the midnight message of Paul Revere.

Cast of Characters
*denotes historical figure

Georgie Kirkwood (Georgina Marie Deirdre Henrietta) b. 1739. Alias Georgina Mondo, Princpessa del Porto Ricinum.

Drake Kirkwood: 1722–1774. Seventh Earl of Kirkenwood. Older brother of Georgie. Current Pendragon.

Countess Emma Kirkwood: 1720–1764. Drake's wife.

The Honorable Emily Kirkwood: 1750–? Their eldest daughter.

Dr. Milton Marlowe: 1713–1774. Second cousin to Georgie and Drake. A medical doctor with the king's ear.

Barclay Marlowe: 1737–? Milton's son. Officer in His Majesty's Army.

Neville Marlowe: 1734–1759. Milton's older son, killed in western New York during the French and Indian War.

Jenkins: Coachman to Dr. Milton Marlowe.

Great-Aunt Bridget Kirkwood (Budgie), Lady Sanderson: 1715–1776.

Simpson: 1720–? Butler to Kirkwood family. Longtime retainer. His father was butler before him and Cook is his wife.

*Giovanni Giacomo Casanova, Chevalier de Seingalt: 1725–1798. Venetian adventurer and sword master.

Belinda b. 1752, Patricia b.1754, Martha b.1756, Hannah b. 1758 Kirkwood: Emily's sisters.

Griffin Kirkwood b. 1763: Emily's brother.

Daisy: Lady's maid to Emily and Georgie, probably Simpson's daughter.

*Heinrich der Reusse: 1722–? Colonel of Georgie's mercenary regiment.

Roderick Whythe: b. 1730. Major in His Majesty's British Army.

Estovan: b. 1744. Georgie's batman. Spanish

Ian McTavis: b. 1728. Roddie's batman, old family retainer.

Samuel de Vere: 1738–? Milton Marlowe's silent bodyguard.

*John Stuart, Earl of Bute: 1713–1792. Scottish Peer, friend of Princess Augusta, George III's mother. Tutor to the teenaged George. Prime Minister 1762–63. Not well liked by other Parliamentarians.

*George III, King of England: June 4, 1738–January 29, 1820. Ascended to the throne 1761.

*Lord George Sackville, later Lord Germain: 1716–1785. Lord Treasurer of Ireland, vehemently opposed to granting colonies any rights at all.

*George Grenville: 1712–1770. Prime Minister 1763–65. An accountant at heart.

Josiah: Drake's coachman.

*General Sir Thomas Gage: 1721–1787. Commander of British Troops in the American colonies, relieves Amherst during Pontiac's War.

*General Jeffery Amherst: 1717–1797. Commander of British Troops in the American colonies at the end of the French and Indian War.

*Richard "Omniscient" Jackson: Bachelor politician, friend of Ben Franklin, MP, Parliamentary agent for Massachusetts, Connecticut, Pennsylvania and private secretary to Prime Minister Lord Grenville. School chum of Roddie.

Malachi: 1704?–1765. Negro coach driver owned by Sir Thomas Mercat.

Zebadiah: 1752–? Negro coach boy also owned by Sir Thomas Mercat.

Dulcie: 1749–? Mulatto house servant owned by Sir Thomas Mercat—probably his daughter.

James: 1720–? Slave butler at Five Oaks. Very deep voice.

Sir Thomas Mercat: 1726–? Plantation owner of Five Oaks, intimate of royal governor of Virginia.

Maria, Rebecca, and Penelope Mercat: Sir Thomas' daughters, ages ten, eight, and six.

Rachel: 1734–? Sir Thomas' slave mistress.

Melissa Lady Mercat: 1735–? Sir Thomas' wife.

Rose: b. 1754. House slave.

Annie: b. 1740. Slave nanny to Maria, Rebecca, and Penelope Mercat.

*Colonel Francis Fauquier: Royal Governor of Virginia 1758–1768.

Private Jones: 1747–? Army youth on patrol with Roderick.

Private Martins: 1744–? On patrol with Roderick.

*Joseph Royle: d. 1766. Bookbinder and third printer of the *Virginia Gazette* in Williamsburg. Also owner of the only paper mill in Virginia. Sold paper to Benjamin Franklin.

René du Pec: 1730–? French sword master hired to teach Emily.

Sergeant Rodger Axely: British Army.

Lieutenant Richards: British Army

*James Southall: Proprietor of the Raleigh Tavern in Williamsburg.

William Lightfoot: Citizen of Wiliamsburg who rents a horse stall to Georgie.

Du Carré: d. 1764. French arms merchant working with the Indians.

Lieutenant Johnstone: d. 1764. Subordinate to Barclay Marlowe.

Peters: Milton's personal servant.

*Patrick Henry: 1736–1799.

*Thomas Jefferson: 1743–1826.

*Peyton Randolph: 1721–1775.

*George Washington: 1732–1799.

*Benjamin Franklin: 1706–1790.

*Deborah Franklin: d. 1775. His wife.

*William Franklin: 1731–1831. Benjamin Franklin's illegitimate son raised by Deborah as her own, royal governor of New Jersey. A loyal Tory throughout the Revolutionary War.

*Samuel Adams: 1722–1803.

*Paul Revere: 1735–1818.

*John Adams: 1735–1826.

*Abigail Adams: 1744–1818.

*Mercy Otis Warren: Poet and playwright of the American Revolution.

Mistress Camden: 1729–? Landlady to Georgie in Boston.

Josiah: Negro boy in Boston.

Miss Jane Cummings: 1745–1765. Planter's daughter courted by Barclay Marlowe. Marries Roderick Whythe to give her child a name.

John Cummings: 1715–? Her father.

Zaneta Whythe: b. 1765. Her daughter.

Colonel Sir Charles Reginald Barton: 1725–? Roderick's commanding officer in Virginia.

*Captain Thomas Preston: British officer involved in the Boston Massacre.

*Richard Palmes: Boston merchant who tried to stop the Boston Massacre.

Tryblith: Demon of Chaos.

Sir William Trevalyn: 1738–? Spymaster for Lord North.

Irene Radford

"A mesmerizing storyteller." —*Romantic Times*

THE DRAGON NIMBUS

THE GLASS DRAGON
0-88677-634-1

THE PERFECT PRINCESS
0-88677-678-3

THE LONELIEST MAGICIAN
0-88677-709-7

THE WIZARD'S TREASURE
0-88677-913-8

THE DRAGON NIMBUS HISTORY

THE DRAGON'S TOUCHSTONE
0-88677-744-5

THE LAST BATTLEMAGE
0-88677-774-7

THE RENEGADE DRAGON
0-88677-855-7

THE STAR GODS

THE HIDDEN DRAGON
0-7564-0051-1

To Order Call: 1-800-788-6262

GARDENING IN SMALL SPACES